I0634193

"But what use is a soldier if it cannot resist the simplest of tools?"

The machine swings, opening long slices across abdominals, shoulders, and back. The face is slashed, left arm hacked away, right leg amputated above the knee. And then the machine punch-stabs through the back, blade tip erupting through the chest right where the heart would be. It retracts the blade slowly, serrated edges hissing through muscles maintained and tuned as carefully as any piece in her kit over a lifetime.

The chassis surges at Shao-Lo, whipping the blade at her. She steps in and blocks automatically, shattering the blade against hard angles of her arm; and the tip whizzes *across the room.*

Shao-Lo leans forward and spreads her shoulders, primed for a deadly contest. To her disappointment, the combat chassis steps back and lowers its raised arm.

"Again, we see unacceptable vulnerability. A laughably simple piece of metal was sufficient to ruin this...*being.* Whatever skills a flesh-based soldier learns are lost, irretrievably, in death. There is no auto archive, no backup, and you must start all over again from the beginning."

The chassis steps over to the last frame, grips the femur, and powers it from the reinforced hip socket. Letting the lower leg and foot swing freely by cable and ribbon attachments, the chassis grips the long bone in both segmented hands, lifts it overhead, then slams it down onto a raised knee with a thunderous CRACK. Off-white splinters explode, clattering against walls, ceiling, and floor.

Making show of still-pink marrow inside, Honniker adds with mocking tone, "This is your body, which I have broken for you."

PLASMA RAIN

PLASMA RAIN

F. ALLEN FARNHAM

CADRE ONE PUBLISHING
PFLUGERVILLE, TX
2019

CADRE ONE PUBLISHING, LLC.
(WWW.CADREONEPUBLISHING.COM)

COPYRIGHT © 2019 BY F. ALLEN FARNHAM
ALL RIGHTS RESERVED.

LIBRARY OF CONGRESS CONTROL NUMBER: 2019910953

SOFTCOVER ISBN: 978-0-9827116-6-8

This book may not be reproduced or transmitted in part or in whole by any means mechanical or electronic without the express written consent of the copyright owner.

Names, characters, and events in this work of fiction are exactly that: *fiction*. Resemblance to any persons (dead or living) or events is purely coincidental.

This book was produced *entirely* in the United States of America.

Author Bio Photo by Kenny Thomas
Cover art, *Maiella and Argo*, by Marek Okon www.okonart.com
Book/Cover design and layout by Cadre One Publishing, LLC

Musical inspiration for dance sequence taken from Dead Can Dance, *Yulunga*, *Sanvean*, *The Host of Seraphim*, and *Cantara*.

Guitar and other dance elements inspired by Spanish Flamenco.

CONTENTS

PART ELEVEN

Dedicated To

Mike L, Bridgette B, Amanda B, Rick B, and Sarah B

Would not have made it without you

"I did not know then how much was ended. When I look back now from this high hill of my old age, I can still see the butchered women and children lying heaped and scattered all along the crooked gulch as plain as when I saw them with eyes still young. And I can see that something else died there in the bloody mud, and was buried in the blizzard. A people's dream died there. It was a beautiful dream."

-Black Elk, speaking of the Wounded Knee Massacre

"I have tried to save you from suffering and sorrow. Resistance means all of that. We are few. They are many. You can see all we have at a glance. They have food and ammunition in abundance. We must suffer great hardship and loss."

-Hinmatóowyalahtqit (Chief Joseph) Wal-lam-wat-kain Nez Perce

CADRE ONE

PART NINE

PART NINE

In Somnum Veritas

Wind rushes through arboreal canopy overhead. Shafts of warm, golden light spill through to a soft floor of broad leaves, vines, and grasses. Insects buzz about in random spirals. Birds chirp and tweet territorial warnings. Nearby, a stream of clear water tumbles over round gray stones.

Tranquil.

Thompson stands in place, inhaling rich forest air, noting layered scents of damp earth, pine pitch, pollen, and the musky hint of a large animal just out of sight. Spongy moss beneath his lace-up boots reminds him of plush carpets aboard Shondre's limousine, yet no factory has produced this landscape. It expands around him, wild and alive—uncontained by wall, hull, or breathing apparatus.

The way it's meant to be.

Over his shoulder he spies two ancient trees, standing side by side. Both are knotted and stunted, every gnarled branch lined with curled yellowing leaves. They hunch beneath taller trees like decrepit old men without obvious reason. Curious, the Gun steps toward them.

A ray of sunlight sneaks through wind-swayed canopy above. For an instant it glints off a gossamer shroud that binds each tree like a translucent straitjacket. Suspended between is a broad net of the same gossamer threads. Wind abates, the gap closes, and the beam of light is blocked, leaving the fine threads invisible once more. Intrigued, Thompson steps closer.

At his approach, a bulbous black spider slips down an anchor thread and climbs the spiral rungs to the center of the net. Its spherical body is as large as the Gun's hand with a thick matte black carapace, and it taps the strands with an articulated foreleg.

Thompson leans in, fascinated by such mechanical intricacy. The spider raises its forelegs, as if in greeting, and he offers his bare hand to it.

The prickly creature reaches out with a leg, taps his fingertip, then crawls out onto his palm. Thompson's brow scrunches in surprise at its lightness, and he studies the joints of its dark carapace as it swings around to the underside of his hand. It clings there, as if shy. Afraid it might fall, the Gun turns his hand over. The spider scuttles around to the underside again.

Slowly, he turns his hand over, and this time, the creature huddles against his palm. It stares with an array of unblinking eyes and reaches toward him, stroking the softer flesh of his wrist. Entranced, Thompson gazes into an abyss of soulless eyes, falling into them by degrees. The spider creeps forward, spreads a bright red maw, and dives into his wrist with curved fangs.

Thompson flings the creature to the ground and stomps it flat. Blood-red gore spurts from under his heel in a fan that wilts the moss. Spindly black legs twitch then curl around his instep.

The Gun clamps a hand around his forearm to halt the searing jet of venom racing up it, and he lifts his foot to view what remains. The arachnid is collapsed and folded, softer parts jettisoned through a split in semi-rigid exoskeleton. Still fascinated, Thompson kneels down for a closer inspection, finding no markings in the dull black exterior. When he flips it over, however, he finds a mark in lighter gray across the abdomen: Cadre insignia, wings outstretched.

Sweat beads on his brow. His eyes defocus. Panting, he slumps to the moss and flops onto his back. Numbness advances from extremities inward, paralyzing and sudden. In shock, he gawks at forest canopy above, unable to comprehend the swiftness of his physical collapse.

Between wind-swayed branches the sky blazes in hues of orange, yellow, and red. His first thought is of a mountaintop sunset during the Forestall rotation, but this is too high in the sky, nearly overhead. Foliage parts in a gust and the Gun spies a colossal fireball streaking in from space. It swells larger, tumbling, jettisoning city-sized chunks of burning rock, looming larger even as it throws off more and more debris. Confusion...wonder at its enormity, at its perplexing slowness. Gusting wind becomes a gale, whipping leaves and branches from sturdy trunks until the entire sky is revealed through denuded trees. A shock front expands around the fireball, sweeping clouds away in all directions. Searing heat stings his eyes, drying them, and he narrows them to slits. Stripped limbs above ignite. His face scorches then peels in layers. Threads of his uniform fray and melt.

The fireball barrels nearer with a roar like the tearing of continents. Pressure drives him down into spongy ground. His chest compresses. Ribs snap. Eyes and eardrums burst, gaping mouth fills with blood and bile, every burning nerve screaming agony into his skull...

Thompson jerks awake and head butts hard crates stacked beside him. He scrambles to bare feet in sweaty alarm, feeling around himself in darkness. Metal floor beneath him is cold. A soft bedroll is heaped nearby. And over the banging of his heart he hears his own panicked breaths reflected from close walls.

Dim red lamps flick on from recesses in the ceiling, and the Gun freezes. Around him is a simple storeroom, with unadorned metal walls. Stacked crates are marked with Cadre insignia, but he cannot fathom where he is or why he is here. All he is sure of is that this cannot be Cadre One.

An intercom speaker in the wall asks with Maiella's voice, "*You all right?*"

Thompson blinks at his surroundings until delinquent realization dawns. *This is Shondre's limousine... We're on course to Cadre One... Wait, why...? Ah, yeah, gonna try to convince O'Kai to halt his assault.*

He rubs his damp face.

Change O'Kai's mind? Yeah, right. We're either stupid or insane...

"*Hey,*" the intercom demands, "*you okay or what?*"

"Yeah, yeah, Maiella, I'm good."

Silence. Then, "*The dream again?*"

Thompson looks down at his wrist, expecting it to be black with necrotic tissue. To his relief it is not, and he exhales a held breath.

"Something I'm working through."

"*Well, it's been a month. Every time I try to sleep beside you, you kick me to pieces. You CAN talk to the Counselor about it, you know. Or me.*"

Thompson glances at his arm and flexes his hand, unsure why it aches so much. "Maybe I should."

"*Mean it?*"

Thompson glares at the intercom speaker then grunts. "Yes, I'll talk to the Counselor about it."

"*Thank you. Seriously. Anyway, you need some more rack time or are you good? 'Cause Shondre has some things she wants to share with everyone.*"

"Now?"

"*Well, now-ish. We're close to Cadre One and she says we gotta chat before we get there. Was gonna wait for the end of your interval, b-u-u-u-u-u-t since you're awake... Up for it?*"

"Be right there."

"*Roger that. I'll let 'em know. Out.*"

Thompson snatches up his folded uniform, rises from the floor, and staggers, his brain not quite ready to give up on getting a full four-hour sleep interval. He reaches to either side of the cabin door, steadies himself, and punches the panel. The door opens, allowing more red light from the corridor. As he dresses, he thinks, *It's always the same dream... Two gnarled trees...tangled in webs...getting smothered by them... And the spider, with the Cadre emblem...it bites me every time... What does it mean?*

He shuffles toward the shared bathroom at the back of the limousine.

And that asteroid streaking in... It looks exactly like Cadre One... How could it be at Earth? We couldn't haul that much mass across eight point six light years... Bizarre...

The bathroom door slips aside at his touch. Overhead lamps illuminate a tiny room dominated by a stainless steel convenience. Mirror and washbasin occupy the wall on the left. Wrinkled white towels hang from bars on the right.

Thompson steps up and relieves himself without bothering to close the door.

Am I too dull to grasp the message? Or is it just noise of a distracted mind?

He steps on a pedal near the basin, and the bowl's contents whisk away with a whoosh of suction. In glum automation, he turns toward the mirror and reaches into the washbasin. A thin stream of water arcs into his hands.

The latter, more likely.

He bangs some powdered soap from the dispenser, works up a lather, and scrubs his face, feeling anti-septic sting through his eyelids. Blindly, he snatches a towel from a rack beside him and drags it over his head, face, arms, and legs. Sticking his tongue out, he groans at a pale white coating and decides a gargle of enzymatic wash is in order. He swishes and spits a foamy mess into the basin, then plucks a razor from the cabinet and drags it across cheeks, chin, jaw, and throat. Graying beard gone, the scarred man in the mirror appears years younger.

Better, but still...

His hand slides into his pants pocket and finds a mashed bar of steroid-enriched amino-protein—the one Chusan gave him on the bridge of the *Europa*. Carrying it so long has made it nearly flat, yet the durable plasticine wrapper is unbroken. He pulls the bar from his pocket.

Feels like I lost thirty IQ points since giving up Cadre rations. And the depression... Bayonet in hand, poised for the cut... I almost did it.

He turns the protein bar over in his hands.

This might be all I need to get right again. After a lifetime on inhibitors and stims, does it even make sense to be off them? Why am I struggling when it could be this easy?

He glances down the short corridor where the others are waiting.

Maiella made a clean break, and she hasn't looked back. Doing better than ever. Begged me to give it time. She'd be disappointed if I backslid...

He shoves the bar back into his pocket.

Stick it out. Be stronger. Work harder.

With a sharp sniff, he scrutinizes his reflection. The man in the mirror is tall, spine straight, broad with muscle in the shoulders, narrow at the waist. He closes the fasteners of a charcoal uniform jacket once heavy with decoration. Now collar and breast are bare with only pinholes to remind him of awards earned in honorable service.

Let's see what Shondre has to say.

Thompson turns about and walks the short corridor, emerging into the main living area aboard the converted limousine. What was an elegant space of plush carpets, soothing artwork, soft couches, and refreshment taps has been stripped to the subframe and outfitted with barest of Cadre essentials. A food and water machine recesses in the forward wall. Canned lighting shines down in diffuse red hue. And for every passenger a metal recliner is suspended from the ceiling, which—despite a sterile, clinical appearance—is custom-fit and surprisingly comfortable.

Sharon Jones, having briefly succeeded Keller as *Europa's* captain and now representing all colonists for the peace mission, relaxes in her recliner. Her full attention is held by a slate in her hand, streaming video. A bowl of circular crisps nestles in her lap, from which she pulls occasionally, never taking eyes off the contrived drama on screen.

Colonel Munro, senior most of Cadre MedTechs, is a colossal man of broad shoulders and stout build. He fills his large recliner, chin lowered, eyes closed, large arm and dwarfed arm crossed.

The Counselor leans back in his recliner, contemplative, hands on the armrests. As always his black hair is at odds with itself, and his familiar white lab coat and brown trousers are worn so thin at the joints the threads have gone shiny.

Shondre stands lost in thought beside her recliner, gripping its ceiling support rail with one clawed hand and gripping her long chin with the other. Her saffron yellow eyes stare through the floor; her whiptail switches side to side randomly as if taking opposite parts in an unspoken internal debate.

A clatter of harness buckles heralds Maiella's departure from the flight deck. The Geek arrives wearing her Human Digital Interface over golden cranial terminals. Goggles cover her warm brown eyes, streaming ship dashboards in the periphery of her view. A snug black T-shirt and olive drab cargo pants hug feminine curves that accentuate square shoulders, toned arms, and strong legs.

"Oi, Gun, you're here," Maiella calls out. Turning to Shondre, she adds, "That's everyone. So let's hear it. What's up?"

Sharon perks up from her tablet screen. Seeing everyone gathered, she pauses the video and powers the slate down.

Shondre lifts her gaze from the floor, licks her lips, nearly speaks, then grimaces at the Counselor.

"No problem," the Counselor says, clapping his hands together. "With your permission I'll translate."

"Don't be ridiculous," Sharon says, "*of course* you're translating. I don't care if we're discussing what's for dinner, we need to be absolutely clear on everything from here on."

The Counselor nods modestly then extends a hand toward the azure-skinned being with saffron eyes. "Madame Shondre, are you ready?"

Shondre blinks and holds up a hand. "Furssst, thisss hwon hwill try hyoo-mann hwords, Konn-Zill-Urr."

The Counselor bows in deference. Shondre smiles and composes herself, fingers interlaced.

"Hwee soon uh-ryf at how-sss of Oh-Kai. Hwee tock of plan hwith Oh-Kai, yesss. Iss good plan. Hwee mussst ahl-so tock hwatt too doo iff Eh-lee-toh at Kad-Ra Hwon. Bee-koss that iss furssst kon-takt. If hwee not noh hwatt too sssay," Shondre warns, pointing at herself, "Eh-lee-toh tayk thisss hwon by forsss, kill ressst." Shondre meets eyes with each of her comrades again, adding, "Hwee musst bee shurr hwat too sssay, *na-ow*."

A grim silence falls over the group as each person contemplates Shondre's straight talk.

"My God," Sharon says, staring at nothing, "I never considered we might run into Eleto at Cadre One."

"It's a strong possibility," Munro admits. "We know they sent a probe and imaged the complex. Maybe they're waiting nearby to see who shows up?"

"Or maybe they've already appeared in force, and they're in a standoff," Maiella states. "Our arrival could unbalance it."

Thompson frowns with half his face. "And if they're already shooting it out? O'Kai would go all-out in defense. Nothing held back. We may not be able to get anywhere *near* Cadre One without taking hits."

Munro juts his lower lip and nods.

Sharon bites a thumbnail, glancing back and forth between Munro and

Thompson. "Suggestions are welcome," she urges them.

"We could observe from a safe distance," Thompson says. "If they're in a shooting war, we won't have to be close to know it."

"I'll make course changes," Maiella declares. Her goggles strobe with code. "Okay, done."

Sharon stops biting her thumbnail. "All right, Thompson, let's say there is a shooting war. Then what?"

Thompson thinks carefully, looks at Shondre, and answers, "We have something we've never had before: people on *both* sides who want to end this. Doesn't matter what the situation is, we tell our people precisely what we intend and we convince them to let us try."

"Doesn't matter?" Sharon rolls her eyes, incredulous. "It *bloody well does* matter if Honniker and his evil little minions are involved!"

"Honniker's a coward," Maiella volunteers. "He won't crawl out of his lair and risk being discovered unless forced. He'll stay put, safe and snug..." She halts mid-sentence and stiffens. "Unless Shao-Lo convinces him otherwise."

"That's right," Thompson adds. "Shao-Lo's there now, trying to commandeer his troops and Mikato's war machines. I don't know what she could offer that could lure him out, though."

"There's only a couple things Honniker really wants," Maiella counters. "Breeding drones for fetal tissue and getting Shao-Lo back on his table. She delivered *both*."

Sharon's eyes bulge and she swivels in her seat. "Shao-Lo went back to Cadre Two? *Willingly?*"

Maiella lifts her eyebrows, crosses her arms, and looks at the floor. "Yeah. She went solo, too. No backup."

"Well that's just *goddamn FANTASTIC*," Sharon blurts, arms thrown up. "Why in eighty hells would Shao-Lo go *back*? Did she *so* enjoy the service at *Chateau de Psychopath* she had to have another stay?"

Maiella shrugs and says, "Ordered back by O'Kai. You saw what it was, Sharon. Hidden location... Plenty of living space with pristine mechanicals... Advanced defenses... Makes it an appealing place of retreat if Cadre One falls. Sound about right, Munro?"

Munro scowls. "I will not discuss Cadre strategy or tactics while the enemy is present."

Shondre blinks as if punched. "Enn-uh-mee?" She lays a taloned hand over her chest. "This hwon nott enn-uh-mee!"

"Oh, *for fook's sake*," Sharon fumes. "Honestly, Munro, you can't be *that* deaf to what's going on. Having Honniker in the mix could undermine everything. Anything you know could be a huge assist."

Munro's features petrify with stoicism.

Sharon leans forward in her seat, hands perched on the arms as if she is going to launch. "Maiella and I were there at Cadre Two, Munro. Honniker'd just as soon play jump rope with your guts as talk with you. So if you think he'll honor some *deal* you and O'Kai twisted up..."

From behind the wall of his crossed arms, Munro counters, "Colonel Shao-Lo was *also* at Cadre Two, Captain. She knows what she is doing."

"Ha! If Shao-Lo thinks Honniker can be reasonable, she's as mad as he is."

Munro is a statue, unmoving, eyes half open and glaring.

Shondre looks frantically around the group, pleading, "Pleeez! *Pleeez*, do not fy-t! Hwee mussst bee too-geh-thur! Nott in-ssull-ting of frends!"

Sharon slumps back in her recliner, frustrated by Munro's obstinacy. Her fiery eyes turn on Thompson. "Have anything to add, other than your strong silence?"

Thompson takes a deep breath. He turns his face toward Munro then says, "Colonel, do you believe there could be a future without fighting?"

Munro glances at the Gun suspiciously. "I have no patience for rhetoric. The Colonists use it enough, I'll not hear it from you."

"I am using none. I'm asking you, directly, not as an officer. Do you, *yourself*, believe there can be a future without war between Eleto and Human?"

The colonel's stony edifice cracks and he admits, "There is a small statistical probability it could happen, yes. That is the only reason I'm here, which should be abundantly obvious. However, it is a *small* probability, and we must have a contingency plan in place."

"I agree completely," Thompson states.

Munro waits for a follow up question from the Gun. When it does not come, he prods, "Are you going somewhere with this?"

"Aye. To a world where we can breed out our genetic diseases. A world where Operators no longer range the Black. A planet with *atmosphere*, *oceans*, and *continents* where we can *build* things. A place where we raise crops and healthy children. I've seen the embryos in stasis aboard the *Europa* and the seeds of living nutrient assemblers. All we need is credible assurance of safety or at least non-aggression."

"*Living nutrient assemblers*...?" Sharon's face scrunches in bewildered amusement. "Do you mean *plants*, Thompson?"

The Gun nods at Sharon then turns back toward the stoic MedTech. "I've seen Earth with my own eyes, Colonel. A living, breathing world where we can thrive...it could be ours."

"I have fully inventoried the *Europa*," Munro explains, "and I am fully aware of her cargo. And I have reviewed your logs from the Forestall rotation. Flora and fauna, organically recurring, self-replenishing... Such an environment is desirable."

"*Desirable*?" Sharon sighs in disbelief. "Is that all?"

Thompson holds up a hand to Sharon, and maintains a serious gaze at Munro.

After an awkward silence, the big MedTech admits, "There's appeal in what you describe, yes."

Thompson nods. "Okay. Then what would you say to a man who was determined to destroy *all* chance, *all* hope of attaining that world?"

Munro rubs his chin shrewdly. "You're implying General O'Kai would be the destroyer of this future, yes?"

"Not if we can convince him otherwise. Not if we can make our efforts of peace with the Eleto first...*before* he commits to a suicidal plan."

"*Suicidal plan*?" Munro unfolds his arms and leans on one knee. "You were a Major in the Corps once and highly decorated, as I recall, but you have *never* been on the Leadership Council. Nor have you ever carried the burden of responsibility that comes with being General of the Cadre. You speak of O'Kai as though he is *so* unreasonable, *so* shortsighted that he could doom us all. You judge his actions as if you had ANY idea of his motivations, what he has *endured*, what he has SACRIFICED to keep us strong and alive. He has proven himself to me and everyone else in the Cadre a *thousand* times over. What's more, he does not suffer the *breakdowns* that leave you muttering like some *brain injured drone*!"

Sharon purses her lips. Shondre looks at the floor. Even Maiella is stunned to silence.

Thompson lays his arms across his knees, pressing his fingertips together and gazing into them. "Your assessment of me, Colonel, does not change the fact that O'Kai has put us on a course that could annihilate our kind, entirely." He looks up at the huge MedTech, grim and determined. "My limitations have NOTHING to do with the question at hand. What I am asking you right here, *right now*, is this: if given the chance, *will you ask your General to cease fire and let us try talks*?"

"*Yes*," Munro says, leaning aggressively toward Thompson. "I *will*."

Sharon, Shondre, and Maiella all let out held breaths.

Munro looks around at the others, adding, "*AND* I will obey O'Kai's orders, no matter where they lead us." Swiveling his recliner directly toward Sharon, he continues, "That includes his directive that I follow *your* orders, Captain, as though they come from the general, himself..." Sharon opens her mouth to speak when Munro raises a finger on his large hand and finishes, "...so long as those orders *do not contravene previous orders or the Cadre code*. I will *never* discuss Cadre tactics with you, nor will I ever discuss anything that is considered privileged or secret. Can you accept that, Captain?"

Sharon nods quickly, answering, "I can. And I will. I apologize for having a go at you, Munro. To be frank, that whole Honniker angle scares the *bu-Jeezus* out of me. I shouldn't have taken it out on you."

"I accept your apology," Munro says calmly. He extends his great mitt in reconciliation. Sharon takes it unsurely, watching her hand disappear in his enormous grip, but they shake, friends once more.

Shondre reaches out to both of them, laying a warm hand on each of their wrists before they pull apart. "Glad forr thisss," she says. Taking her hands away, she looks to the Counselor and asks, "Lay-turr, pleez tell this hwon uh-bowt Kad-Ra Too and Hah-Nih-Kurr?"

The Counselor answers with an assuring nod.

Maiella returns to her recliner, purposely detouring in front of Thompson and whispering, "You okay?"

Thompson nods. "Yeah, yeah. It's nothing." He waits for the Geek to sit then addresses Shondre directly. "All right. Let's say we encounter an Eleto vessel. Maybe a warship. What happens?"

Shondre's face contorts as she wrestles with a concept she cannot yet fit into human words. The Counselor, sensing her need, leans forward in his seat. Shondre nods hurriedly to him with eyes closed and says, "Pleez help thiss hwon ssspeek."

"Of course, Madame," the Counselor says, "I'm ready."

The Eleto's eyes turn directly to Thompson, and her voice sings through a long stream of connected syllables and gestures.

The Counselor relays, a breath behind her, "All of the People are now suspicious. They might recognize this vessel as belonging to their Sovereign, but changes made are drastic. They will assume it has become another warship of the Cadre. If we approach, attack is presumed and we will be destroyed."

"Okay," Thompson says, "we can stand off—"

Shondre raises a slender hand to interrupt him.

"This one must first explain how precarious the situation has become," the Counselor interprets. "This one wishes to be delicate and not offend, but she also must be plain so you fully understand." Shondre places her hands together in a moment of preparation.

"We're listening," Sharon offers.

Shondre looks up, bunches her mouth on one side, then speaks gravely.

The Counselor translates, "Genocide of Human-kind is a heavy sin around the People's necks and will forever hang...unless we earn forgiveness. This one will never waver from that truth. Reconciliation of our two nations is her greatest mission.

"Many believed the People must atone for the tremendous evil of genocide, and that disappearances of ships in space are fair punishment for crimes of our ancestors. They believed we must reach out and absorb human anger with our lives, if necessary, so that we may, at last, know tranquility. This idea was once majority opinion, but that is no longer the case."

Sharon's brow bunches together. "Are you saying, your people *don't* think the genocide is a crime anymore?"

"She is saying there is new debate on that matter," the Counselor explains, and he turns toward Shondre, waiting.

Shondre clasps her fingers together in her lap, looks down at her hands, then speaks.

"In the beginning," the Counselor translates, watching Shondre closely for body language and inflection, "ships and crews disappeared infrequently. Perhaps two or three in a generation. This was within statistical probability of risk, and was not understood for what it was. With passing of time, disappearances increased in frequency and in scale. All realized something was *making* ships and crews vanish. This became a great terror in the chest, because we could not discover *why* or *what* was making them happen.

"No one now lives who remembers a time before the disappearances. Yet *all* are impatient to find answers, to find the cause, and to find an *end*, no matter what. Few speak of the genocide in negative terms, instead claiming it was *right action* and that the terror would be worse now if our ancestors had *not* burned humans so extensively.

"This one feels that idea is repugnant...that it is a sickness in the soul of our People. But without cure, the sickness spreads."

Shondre pauses, looking at Thompson and choosing her words carefully.

"This one called a summit at the human world. This one knew she had to bring those who opposed reconciliation to the home of Humanity so they would witness the craters we made of great cities. They must look upon the shattered spans, the ruins of a civilization. The People had to *experience* the full extent of our crime so they would understand: we had allowed fear and prejudice to carry us into madness. No longer would this one tolerate further call to complete the genocide until my opponents had gazed upon a world we had utterly crushed."

Shondre turns her half-lidded saffron eyes toward everyone in the circle.

"Our talks lasted for days. We toured the wrecked spans, the irradiated bones of towers. We unearthed works of beauty that we had never paused to look for before... This one had the People's attention, at last. Tide of opinion turned back toward reason..."

Shondre's head droops, her voice losing all enthusiasm.

"Your arrival, Thompson, could not have been more poorly timed."

MELTING STONE

A pall hangs over the room, but it is nothing compared to the cloud forming in Thompson's mind. He falls back into his recliner and stares into the red glow of a recessed ceiling light, reliving the violent path he hacked and blasted throughout the Forestall rotation. Previously he imagined it was his team's cunning that permitted them to endure and escape Eleto might. Shondre's revelation makes it far more likely that he, Argo, and Beckert survived because the enemy was practicing phenomenal restraint.

Shondre assembled her people there for talks in our defense...? And I showed up, killing everything I saw... How can I fault O'Kai when I may have already ruined everything?

Munro shifts in his recliner to ask, "Are we losing you again, Thompson?"

"BACK OFF, MUNRO," Maiella barks, already on the edge of her seat, face flushing red. "You and O'Kai are the ones who SENT HIM! And if you hadn't rated me as *damaged*, I'd have been right there with him on your fucked up fire mission!"

"Colonel," Sharon says, laying a hand on Maiella's arm to keep her in her seat, "Shondre just told us she was arguing for peace between our peoples...and then Argo, Beckert, and Thompson arrived, *blasting*. Do you understand what that means?"

"Yes, I understand it harms our cause," Munro answers.

Sharon looks away, muttering, "A *master* of understatement..."

"Please, Shondre," the Counselor interjects with a subtle glance at Munro, Sharon, and Maiella, "you were saying before you were interrupted?"

Shondre bows her head to the Counselor's courtesy and takes a deep breath. She looks into her open hands points at herself, and continues.

The Counselor faithfully translates, "This one was aboard her ship, preparing speech to the people. Reports came up from the planet..." Shondre pauses, haunted by recollection. "...wild humanoid machines...they *had* to be machines, because no living beings could possibly be so cold and methodical... Tremendous firepower they carried...able to disappear at will... could walk through stone or water and emerge far away...no need for breath, immune to radiation... The reports were incredible. Difficult to believe. Then, the breach of an undersea dome..."

She purses her lips with pained expression and continues.

"An entire community, drowned in moments..." the Counselor says for her. "A horrible taking of life...

"This one saw telecast of hostages aboard a shuttle...how one heavy with child was pulled from the group. Her Other Self intervened, and was taken in her place...then he was marched down the ramp and shoved from it... A fall so long there was ample time to contemplate his death..."

She flips a hand at the wrist as if dealing a card to the air.

"No hesitation... No feeling... A quick shove, like tossing garbage onto a heap. But no one aboard that shuttle fared any better."

Shondre bites her lip, suppressing angry tears, and smacks a fist into her open palm.

"It was *deliberately* crashed into a crowded landing bay on my ship..." the Counselor interprets. "Our computer networks were invaded, and the ship dived from orbit. It was not built for atmospheric entry. We were burning up...

"This one's bodyguards rushed her to evacuate. Along the way to her limousine, this one received reports of cruel, sadistic acts that scarred her deeper than wounds of flesh and bone...until she was face to face with something terrifying and vicious...a blood-drenched nightmare... She expected to be another victim of its rampage. Yet...in its gray eyes, there was vulnerability this one did not expect... It was in immense pain and did not revel in its actions... This one had an impression as if its will was submerged in service of someone or some*thing* else...something even more terrifying... the impression is difficult to explain for it was only that. A fleeting moment.

"This one was dragged away from her subjects by force, taken to a place of bitterness and isolation where she could not serve them...and in that lonely cell, this one grappled with remembered horrors that screamed behind her eyes. All the legends were true. *Ravenous, Angry Ghosts* were real."

Shondre sits upright, thumps her chest.

"It took much time for this one to see past the walls of what she believed was a cage. At last she saw the *real* master that drove these monsters to acts that seemed so wanton, so savage. That master is the looming threat of extinction."

Shondre pats a flat hand on her chest, and the Counselor mimics the gesture as he translates.

"This one also knows that this new aggressive breed is OUR CREATION. We *made* this terror by denying Humans' right to exist, by burning their cities with stellar fire, by seeding their homeworld with plagues...

"We left the only survivors huddled in cold, sterile reaches of space. Space is harsh in the extreme, it is well known, and it does not forgive half-measures. There is survival or there is death and nothing in between.

"This one cannot ignore fact: Cadre Operators are aggressive and violent because they *must* be."

Shondre looks directly at Munro.

"We left you no alternative."

Shondre looks into the faces around her.

"This one will never be swayed from what she knows is correct: we, *the Eleto*, must provide a better alternative. But too many are ruled by their fear. Mercy does not live in the arches of the chest, and their hatred burns as bright as your blue sun at Cadre One."

Shondre places her hands together and she looks down upon them in silence.

Sharon swallows hard. Her voice is dry. "How do we fix this? What can we do?"

Shondre lifts her head and speaks sincerely.

"The People expect *total* disarmament," the Counselor interprets. "Return all stolen ships. Zero aggression, and accept Overseers to ensure no future expansion or militarization."

Sharon asks, incredulous, "To live in a managed camp, what, like prisoners of war? Armed guards patrolling the gates... Even *I* couldn't accept that."

Shondre nods in understanding and speaks softly.

"It is what the People will demand," the Counselor translates. "Or at least a strong show of good faith."

Thompson shrugs. "Such as?"

Shondre answers plainly, head level, then turns her hands up in questioning shrug.

"Give the People something they do not already have, to foster trust. The location of Cadre Two, perhaps?"

"We can't," Maiella says. "Shao-Lo's there now, and if the Eleto show up, Honniker'll take it as a betrayal on her part. No telling what would happen to her."

"Not to mention if Mikato and Honniker are flushed out," Thompson adds. "For the same reasons we keep O'Kai's fleet secret, we can't talk about Cadre Two."

"If we're talking about a good faith gesture," Sharon says, "it's hard to ignore that the six of us are arriving unarmed, and we're bringing Shondre back home. We can certainly turn the ship over upon arrival, though, as Munro has said, it may be fully used up by then."

Shondre nods and speaks, gesturing toward herself.

"This one has been away for a long time," the Counselor translates. "Her responsibilities are such that her role cannot remain unfilled. Yet she may have influence still. This one will speak to any Eleto vessel we encounter so the people know this one has not been harmed. She can also request escort and protection for a delegation of ambassadors who seek armistice and open dialogue."

Thompson's eyes narrow in skepticism. "Will it be enough?"

Shondre thinks then looks up.

"It will have to be," the Counselor relays. "This one must make them see that although our delegation is small in size, it is great in importance. We *cannot* allow ourselves to fail."

"Lots of folks will be happy to see you again, Shondre," Sharon offers.

The delicate Eleto smiles broadly and replies.

"Yes, and to see them, this one will rejoice! In that spirit we should begin. Joy of reunion and hope for a future without fear and killing. The People must know there was no kidnapping, no ransom. It was this one's fate to go with Thompson, so that she might see and learn and *understand*...so that, once again, we can *all* become the People we are meant to be."

"What if..." Sharon begins, but pauses. Her expression blanks to a mask. "What if they execute us on sight?"

Shondre shakes her head and points at her chest.

"Any who wish you harm must first get through this one, because she will shield you with her life. Even so, it will not come to that. There is fear and terror of Human kind, but curiosity will prove greater. Given a chance to see you, to look, stare and gawk...this one believes the People could not resist. And no matter what side of the debate is carried in the arches of the chest, *all* the People want attacks to end. Harming this delegation defeats both."

"I don't like it," Munro says. "There's no solution, no certainty. We have to wait for them to decide what to do with us? Too many unknowns."

"I agree," Thompson says, "so what's Plan B?"

"I don't see any Plan B," Maiella says, "but this isn't a bad way to go. Provided Ralla and Chusan aren't already in there tearing it up..."

"Nothing of value is ever achieved without risk," Sharon states. "Didn't I read that in one of your books, Counselor?"

The Counselor arches an eyebrow in surprise. "That's a paraphrase of Machiavelli, but yes, that's one in my library. An interesting choice, considering what we've embarked upon. Care to share why you picked that one?"

Sharon frets. "Every time I think I've got a grip on the big picture, perspective shifts and I see entire angles I haven't considered. Trying to get wise to as many points of view as I can, both good and bad, so I'll recognize one from the other."

Munro juts a lip in contemplation and nods in agreement.

Thompson shifts in his recliner. "Can I ask you something, Counselor?"

"Of course."

"If this goes wrong, and the plan doesn't work...whose side will you be on?"

The Counselor looks the Gun directly in the eye to be sure there is no mistake. "I will be on the side of *right*, Thompson, *not* might."

"Thank you for your sincerity," Sharon says distantly.

"It's freely given, anytime."

Shondre claps her hands and rubs them together.

"Now, we plan what will be said," the Counselor interprets. "Our words must thaw coldest enmity and melt stony indifference to compassion. There is no room for hesitation. We must commit ourselves fully. Agreed?"

Maiella, Thompson, Sharon, and Munro look each other in the eye and reply as one, "*Agreed.*"

PHYSICS

Maiella parks herself in the limousine's pilot's seat and leans on the armrest. Her goggles flash with occasional updates on ship systems, but her mind is elsewhere. Every kilometer closer to Cadre One brings her that much nearer to a difficult confrontation. O'Kai might refuse their proposal, possibly order Munro to commandeer the vessel. The Eleto might be there right now, shooting it out. Or maybe they have already finished Cadre One off, and lie in wait with crackling nets of anti-energy. Frustrated and anxious, she grips the ship's stick for its reassuring feel of control.

Needing distraction, the Geek sifts EM bands for signs of life: radio broadcasts, Infrared blooms, unusual emissions, any hint of what may await them at Cadre One. Channels fizz and pop with cosmic background radiation. Neutron stars pulse away like galactic beacons. Infrared glow from the galactic center is broad and bright to starboard, just where it should be. Distant X-Ray sources hint at hypermassive objects nestled deep inside discs of accelerated matter. Then her goggles glitch, and she blinks as if struck. Console lights around her shift to amber. One by one, they reset to soothing green as ship systems stabilize.

Whoa... Did we just fly through a Gamma Ray Burst? Can't even calculate the odds on—

A second glitch trips every circuit breaker overhead, and the ship is jolted from warp space. The console goes dark, interior lighting goes dark, even her HDI blacks out. Gravity assist fails, and she floats up against her harnesses. Gasps and shouts filter forward from the living area.

Brain buzzing, eyes bulging, she pulls her lanyard from the console and attempts a reboot of her HDI. Goggles illuminate, scroll commands, halt with the words, UNRECOVERABLE ERROR, and go dark.

On the verge of panic, she restarts her HDI, silently begging, *No, no, NO, PLEASE, NOT AGAIN!*

Her goggles illuminate, scroll startup codes, confirm system components are within normal parameters, and restart. She gives them a full and thorough diagnostic. Once complete, and all synaptic bridges show full throughput, she leans back with an immense sigh.

I could NOT handle being damaged again...

The Geek cycles breakers on overhead panels in sequence, watching for the diode to switch from red to green before moving to the next. With the last breaker closed, a shudder begins deep within the ship and settles into a more regular thrum. Interior illumination fades up to normal and gravity assist gently reasserts itself. Triggering the intercom, voice calm, she announces, "Stand by, everyone, no cause for alarm. Just a minor glitch. Keep your seats, I'll have it smoothed out in a moment. Thompson to the flight deck, please."

A hand lands on her shoulder, telling her he is already there. "SitRep," the Gun states.

Maiella pulls up a holowindow, displaying all of the ship's vital indicators. "Encountered double GRB, origin undetermined."

"You can't tell direction?"

"We were FTL when it hit. It'd look like it came from ahead, no matter where it originated."

"On screen, frequency and intensity."

"Aye."

A simple graph of the EM band stretches across the window, showing signal strength for each frequency. Maiella rolls the time clock back two minutes and plays it back. The band dances with cosmic background noise and occasional random pops until a sharp spike appears at the far right. She freezes playback.

"Just over a minute ago we got hit with a sizable burst, but the ship handled it." She rolls the video forward. "Then, we got *that*." Maiella freezes the graph again where a second spike rises ten times higher. Thompson boggles at the scale.

"*Two* GRBs?" He scratches at his recently shaved cheeks. "Can't even comprehend the odds on that..."

"That's what I said."

Thompson mulls the data on screen. "If we were FTL, they'd seem a lot closer together than they really were. What's the *actual* interval?"

"Hard to say for sure, without knowing origin."

"Best guess."

Maiella shrugs. "Maybe fifteen to thirty minutes, real time."

"Half an hour?" Thompson looks directly at her. "Stars don't *bounce* when they collide... So these are separate events?"

Maiella hedges, "Maybe a trinary system collapsed, and the larger companion fell in later—"

"Even if it *was* a trinary, which I doubt, where's the afterglow? Source should be *blazing* with X-Rays." The Gun rubs his chin in thought, and then he points to the graph. "No, this wasn't a natural event. That's an H-bar blast."

"*Anti-matter*?"

"Affirmative. How far are we from Cadre One?"

"About a day..." Maiella's jaw drops. Her ears slide back. "*Shit*."

"*Yeah*. Maybe the Eleto torched Cadre One. Or maybe the MedTechs cooked something up?"

Maiella's eyes light up. "I know who to ask." She triggers her intercom and announces, "Colonel Munro to the flight deck, please."

Munro excuses himself from a conversation in the passenger cabin. Long-handled wrenches of his toolbelt clatter as he rises from his recliner, then heavy footfalls mark his progress up the corridor.

At the base of the short stairway up to the flight deck, the big man asks, "How can I help?"

Maiella glances at him and asks, "Everyone all right back there?"

"Yes, all have been attended," Munro relates. "No injuries, just some minor bumps. What happened? Is the ship damaged?"

"GRB knocked us off-line," Maiella replies. "I've got everything back up and running, but we'd like your eyes on something."

"Of course."

Thompson steps to the side, giving Munro a clear view to the holowindow. Playing on screen is a continuous loop of the first gamma ray burst, followed by the second. The instant Munro sees them, his eyes flick to estimated energy on the Y-axis. Breath leaves him in a huff and he slumps against the wall.

"Option Zulu..." the big man utters. "It's done."

Thompson and Maiella look at each other, brows wrinkled. Turning back to Munro, Thompson asks, "*Sir*?"

"Option Zulu," Munro explains, "was our guarantee the enemy would not capture Cadre One. It means the enemy arrived in overwhelming force and our home could not be defended."

"So, Cadre One..." Maiella struggles to say, "It's..."

"Gone." Munro pushes off the wall with his shoulder, tugs at each cuff of his uniform, and regains his austere demeanor. "Now then, is the vessel damaged or not?"

"How are you sure?" Thompson asks. "Could the Eleto have—?"

"I think I should know my own design," Munro interrupts. "We bred sufficient anti-hydrogen for Cadre One's disintegration plus a second device of approximate one-tenth yield. What I see on screen matches those ratios, which is sufficient proof to me that Option Zulu has been executed. I'm surprised an Operator of your experience failed to recognize an obvious anti-matter signature. That you required someone else to explain it to you is doubly disappointing. How you outlived Operators with greater acuity leaves me at a loss."

Thompson looks back at the colonel, straight faced. "And yet, here I am."

Munro frowns. "If you have no further need, I'll be discussing our next steps with the others. Maiella, alert me *at once* if you discover damage to the vessel."

"Roger that," the Geek says flatly. She watches Munro stride back toward the living area, listening for him to rejoin the conversation. Then she says to Thompson, "I'm *really fucking tired* of him talking to you that way. Why do you put up with it? Fight back!"

Thompson smiles. "He's getting used to lecturing me. And it's becoming a good source of information."

"Wait, *what now*?"

Thompson arches an eyebrow. "You think he'd've told us anything if we straight out asked him? Probably give us another speech about '*tactics and strategy*'."

Maiella shakes her head. "So that stunt you pulled the other day.... when you walked into the cabin all disoriented, in your skivvies... That was *planned*?"

The tall Gun stoops under the low ceiling and parks himself in the co-pilot seat. With a knowing smirk, he says, "Obviously."

"Liar."

He winks at her then stares through the clear plexi-steel at a distant field of stars. A brilliant blue-white dot captures his full attention, and the smile straightens. "It's starting to sink in. Every time I left on rotation, I never knew if I'd ever see Cadre One again. Now... I *know* I won't."

Maiella purses her lips, jaw clenched. She reaches a hand over to him, and he takes it. Together, they stare through the windscreen at immenseness of space.

"All right, Geek, where do we go from here? Do we look for survivors at Cadre One?"

Maiella shrugs. "Don't see the point. I mean, if O'Kai blew it all up there's nothing, and no one, left."

Thompson nods. "And we can be sure Eleto warships are waiting, in case any of us decide to check up on the place."

"Roger, that," Maiella says. She thinks back on all the joyous homecomings following successful rotation and how there will never be another. Then she imagines herself at Cadre One right before its end, patrolling the vacant halls as O'Kai surely did. Alone in humanity's last fixed refuge, his people gone, enemy encroaching...knowing that Cadre One had survived for over a thousand years, but was lost on his watch.

Troubled, Maiella asks, "Think he stayed behind to do it?"

Thompson mulls the idea, stares quietly through the windscreen, then answers, "Yeah. And it's one of the most depressing thoughts I've ever had." He lets go of Maiella and balls his hand into a fist, sad expression furrowing to lowered brow and gritted teeth.

"Sometimes, it's all *too much*," Thompson blurts. "First, Keller and his teams slaughter Eleto at New Dresden. Then, the Eleto burn us from our own planet and build homes on our ashes. Then, O'Kai sends me to Earth. I shoot the hell out of the place and get 'em all so stirred up they come and wipe out Cadre One... Everything's happening again, over and over, because we're so *stupid* we don't learn! How much do we have to lose before we finally get it? And, the worst part..." he adds, eyes wild, "I've been *at the center of it the entire time*! I can't believe I've been this blind my whole life. Maybe if you were there, on Earth... Maybe you would have kept me from doing those things... Might have been—"

"*No*." Maiella lays a hand on his wrist and gives it a squeeze so he will look at her. "It *wouldn't* have been any better if I was there. I'd have backed every play you made. Wouldn't have hesitated the way Beckert did, wouldn't have shown any restraint. It would have been worse."

"How could it be worse?"

Maiella nods. "I thought a lot about this. If I *were* with you...you, me, and Argo would've had no reason to return. We'd've carried out our sentence to the letter, fighting 'til we died. And no offense to Beckert, I'm pretty confident I'd have tripled his kill count, at least. But the only reason you and Argo stopped was to get Beckert home alive. He was too wounded to make it on his own. You had to carry him. That brought you and Argo back to me, and nothing else matters. *Nothing*." Maiella looks out through the plexi-steel windscreen. "But if you *hadn't* tried to get Beckert home, you couldn't have brought Shondre to us. What we're doing now wouldn't be happening. You, Argo, and me...we'd be dead on Earth. The Eleto still would have found

F. ALLEN FARNHAM

Cadre One. And the *Europa* would be on the run until she gave out or was discovered. There'd be no future. None. It's fucked up, but...if you'd taken me instead of Beckert...we'd probably all be dead."

Thompson gives Maiella a begrudging look. "Well I'm sick of being the triggerman. Sick of being wrong for so long."

"Yeah. But remember, O'Kai gave you *direct* orders on the Forestall rotation," Maiella counters. "He sent you and Argo, knowing what you could do, what you *would* do. The will to inflict injury and destruction was O'Kai's, *not* yours, okay? Took me a while to realize this...because I pulled the trigger on the *Europa*, and I'll always have guilt for that... But intentions *do* matter. I've talked with Shondre and the Counselor a lot about it. They helped me understand there *is* a difference between fighting hard for survival and killing out of spite or vengeance."

"Not to the ones you've killed."

Maiella's eyebrows lift. "Maybe so. But if we're going to prove we aren't some insane, violent species—if we're going to convince the Eleto we *can* co-exist in peace—we have to show we had *reasons* for what we've done, reasons they can understand."

"I don't care about *reasons*, Maiella. I just want it to *stop*. The fighting, the killing, the destruction... If we hold to this path we go extinct, and everything we've done, everything our ancestors have done for a thousand years to keep us alive, will be *wasted*. So much effort... The risk, comrades lost... Liquefying the dead for nourishment... For what? To stretch out a meaningless existence a few more generations just so it could end in a burst of Gamma Rays?"

Maiella looks ahead, letting Thompson's anger fade. "Our MedTechs are aboard the *Europa* now. They haven't been lost. Cadre One was a *place*, Thompson. An important one, but it's just a *place*."

Thompson turns toward her, face scrunched.

"There's a better one, I hear," Maiella continues. "Someone told me about this place with sky, mountains, and oceans...remember? Maybe this is the shove off we needed. We can't go back to Cadre One. That means we have to go forward. There's nowhere to retreat, so we can't fall back on old habits. We stay at the bargaining table." She pauses to make sure her words sink in. "Just remember, if we succeed it's because *you're* the one who found Shondre and got us on the right path."

Thompson circles a raised finger in the air as if lassoing the entire ship. "It'll take all of us, Maiella. No way this happens without everyone pulling in the same direction."

"Fair enough." Maiella turns pensive and stares through the augmented

23

overlay in her goggles. "This is terrible to say, but...it'll be easier with O'Kai out of the way."

Thompson glares at her in surprise. Considering her point, he looks forward again. "I don't know about that. Munro was right, I haven't the first idea what it means to be General of the Cadre. In the Corps, my orders came from Zaius and Enyo. Spoke with General Dryden only a few times. I've had way more face time with O'Kai, which is odd, all things considered." He shakes his head. "Nothing works the way it used to."

Maiella scoffs. "Physics."

"Hmm?"

"*Physics* works exactly the way it has, and will *continue* to work exactly the same way for as long as the universe lasts. Don't paint everything with such a dismal outlook."

Thompson shows his hands. "Okay, okay. So, back on topic... O'Kai is either MIA or KIA. Cadre One is destroyed, with a probable Eleto military presence waiting in ambush. Can't go there, and there's no point, anyway. We still don't know where the Cadre fleet will rendezvous, so we have no heading. And we can't go to Earth and start a dialog without knowing for sure the Cadre fleet won't rush in shooting halfway through. Suggestions?"

"I say we chase down one of the freighters. Loaded up or not, they're way slower than the rest of the fleet," she pats her arm rests, "and a *hell* of a lot slower than this thing."

"Being slow, they'll take the straightest course toward Earth," Thompson reasons. "Really think you can get us within ten light minutes?"

Maiella grins. "Yep."

"All right, Geek. Start your calculations—"

"Done."

Thompson glances at her, eyes narrowed in either surprise, dismay at her presumption, or both. "Don't execute until I have agreement from everyone else aboard. Everything has to be done by committee now."

Maiella blanches. "If blending colonists and Cadre means we have to live with byoo-ruh-crats, I might try living with the Eleto."

Thompson smirks as he rises from the co-pilot seat. "We only need the six of us aboard to agree. That's a big improvement from twelve hundred on the *Europa*."

"Democracy is overrated," Maiella says, her goggles already streaming course adjustments to the console. "Cast my vote however you need it."

"No, you keep it. Even if we end up voting the same, it'll mean more that you're the one deciding." Thompson ducks under the ceiling and heads for the stairs when Maiella catches him by the arm.

"On second thought, whichever way Munro votes, I'll go the opposite. Since I can't kick him in the balls for being a pompous ass, watching him ping off of his conditioning caps will be a nice substitute."

"Only use your powers for *good*, Geek."

"Eh, you're no fun."

"No?" Thompson circles back, leans over and kisses her on the lips.

The Geek's goggles cease their flashing with lines of stalled code.

Mmmm, Electric...

Thompson pulls back, tilts his head, and winks.

Maiella arches an eyebrow. "You're playing with fire, Gun."

"Fire... Just one of a thousand things I love about you."

"Talk like that's gonna get you naked."

"You know where to find me."

Thompson hops down the short stairway and strolls back to the living area with a bit of swagger. Maiella turns in her seat and looks over her shoulder, watching him leave. Under her breath, still grinning, she says, "Oh, yeah. We are gonna *break* it tonight."

REINTRODUCTION

The entrance to Cadre Two's Medlab was once titanium white and spotless. That was centuries ago, before the facility's sudden change of management. Now, the portal is stained brown with old blood, overlapping spatters smeared from countless passes in and out of the wall jambs. It would be a simple matter to clean them, as the white enamel is non-porous and made specifically for sterile environments. But Doctor Edmund Honniker was never so concerned with patient care or comfort as he was desired outcome. So while his surgical tools gleam with mirror brightness to prevent complications, the decor is a far more accurate reflection of the surgeon in residence.

Few of the condemned criminals who passed this portal walked out. Most were wheeled out, in chunks. Rarer still is someone entering Honniker's MedLab twice and leaving alive, in one piece.

When the brown-stained doors slide aside Shao-Lo emerges between them, deathly pale with dark circles under her eyes. Her charcoal gray uniform is padded in the hips and thighs by bandages beneath, rounding her otherwise masculine figure. Each step is deliberate, femurs and pelvis burning from harvest of marrow. Yet after Honniker's anesthetic-free drilling, the pain is merely an echo of prior excruciation.

A projected hologram of lab-coated scientist awaits her beyond the MedLab entrance. "Colonel Shao-Lo," the projection says in greeting, "I'm pleased to see you came through the procedure. How do you feel?"

Shao-Lo glares at the projection. "You're *artificial*, Mikato. How could I possibly explain it to you? More to the point, why would I?"

The projection grimaces. "I ask in concern of your physical well-being, not for a sympathetic depiction of suffering. We do not wish you to be permanently injured, though Honniker can be...*zealous*...in his surgeries. So you may simply tell me if you require additional medical attention and I can ensure you receive it."

Shao-Lo ambles past the projection, not knowing where she is heading but eager to get away from Honniker's medical tables. "If you're so concerned, you might have tried to stop him."

The projection squints in irritation as the tall woman passes by then turns and walks beside her. "I beg your pardon, but may I remind the Colonel she *volunteered* for this? Your consent tied my hands." The projection looks her up and down. "Now that you've completed that bargain, was it worth it?"

Shao-Lo forces herself into normal strides. Through gritted teeth, she growls, "It was. I'll pay any price for the Cadre."

The projection huffs. "From anyone else, I would take that as bravado. We are not strangers, however, and I am quite certain you *would* indulge Honniker to his sickest degree...if it meant advantage for your general."

"He expects no less. And I fail in my duty if I give less."

"Please, Colonel, you need not subscribe to such regimented ideals here."

Shao-Lo turns on the projected image with annoyance. "Location has no impact on my obligations. Think I would cast aside responsibility so easily? You've misjudged."

"If that's true, why is there no rank insignia on your collar?"

Shao-Lo glances momentarily at the projection but does not reply, and she peers down the long, dark corridor instead.

"You still wear the uniform," Mikato continues, "and carry awards of service on your chest. But the Colonel's eagle at your neck is missing. Why is that, I wonder? Perhaps you are outcast from your Cadre, hmm? Stripped of rank and obligations? Sent back here as punishment for your failure to conquer?"

Shao-Lo's eyes narrow. Her cheeks ripple with clenched jaw muscles. "*Wrong*. On *all* counts."

"Then, if you are truly an agent of the Cadre with authority to negotiate, enlighten me why your general would remove the most important symbol of that authority."

"You wouldn't understand."

"Try me. And be convincing, for if you have no power to bargain you may suddenly find your stay *quite* uncomfortable."

Shao-Lo halts in the corridor, spins aggressively toward the projection. "I know of Honniker's fondness for trophies, Mikato. He may get this body, this uniform. But my rank insignia I would *never* surrender to anyone but my superior."

"It's a piece of metal, Colonel, what is the attachment to—?"

"*It does not belong to me*. It belongs to every colonel who's worn it before me and to every colonel who'll follow. It's an inheritance that must never be lost. There was no reason to bring it here, so I left it behind." Shao-Lo resumes her stiff march. "If I had no authority, this uniform and all my decorations would have been stripped from me, as well. You may do with that information whatever you like."

"Interesting... So who wears your insignia now?"

Shao-Lo shakes her head, burning in her lower back, hips, and thighs shortening an already strained patience. "Are you needling for a reason, Mikato?"

"I am. A reason you should have already guessed. Now then, *Shao-Lo*, who wears your rank?"

Shao-Lo considers her response, keenly aware that Mikato is addressing her by name. "In my absence, Major Chusan was promoted to full colonel and assumed my duties."

"I see," the projection says shrewdly, "your general does not expect you to return, and has transferred your authority to another."

"Correction: he has transferred my *duties* and given Chusan the authority to execute them. I still hold full rank and privileges as second in command only to O'Kai."

"I'm certain you believe that. But we must weigh all possibilities. And one possible scenario is that your general has sent you here, completely expendable. You have been replaced in your organization. You are no longer included in command decisions. Even if you were still second in command, you can be overruled, and we are not eager to trust any bargain that your general can discard on whim. I'm sorry, but there is little more we can discuss, I'm afraid."

Shao-Lo stops cold and smirks. "Here's something you'll never comprehend, Mikato: O'Kai and I served together our entire lives. We have no ulterior motives like you or Honniker. What we say, we *do*. No exceptions. O'Kai sent me here, endowed with the authority to negotiate an agreement favorable to *all* parties. Failing that, I've already sampled what Honniker has in store for me. And the interruption of my reports will mean the arrival of the Blueskins, here, at Cadre Two. If *we* can't come to an arrangement, perhaps you'd like to try and make peace with *them*, instead."

The projection raises open hands, placating, "Now, now, Colonel, there is no need for hostility. We must be certain our efforts produce beneficial results. Further conflict runs counter to our desires. Do not begrudge my asking fair and direct questions in pursuit of trust and full disclosure."

Shao-Lo exhales exasperation, and looks away down the corridor.

"Now then, in the spirit of continued reciprocity, come," the projection beckons, "let me show you something worthy of the fine gifts you provided upon your arrival."

"I saw your fleet on the way in. Modular weapons and drive packages, variable in configuration, stackable for efficiencies... Impressive."

The projection smiles modestly. "Yes, there is some pride in those designs. At their root, they are merely delivery systems. What I would like to show you is something worth delivering to an enemy."

Shao-Lo lifts an eyebrow, intrigued. "Which is?"

The projection smiles like a proud father. "My crown jewel, the pinnacle of my research. A temporary energy density approaching infinite... A concurrence of tidal force and focused energy that nothing can withstand." The projection summons a three-dimensional holowindow in the corridor. "I had nearly completed my principal theories when the Eleto...what you call '*Blueskins*'...began their march of destruction through our colonies. My conclusions came too late to save Earth. But as it turns out..."

When the projection trails off, Shao-Lo prompts him, "Yes?"

The projected researcher smiles. "There was plenty of time to continue my work afterward."

A holowindow opens in front of the colonel and populates with a high-resolution model of a scorched metallic planet near a swollen yellow star. The planet orbits so closely, solar prominences lick at its dayside.

"In computer simulations," Mikato's projection explains, "the detonation produces a highly observable flash, like the most powerful solar flares. Thus I chose a test site near a variable star with a strong magnetic field, so the test might be overlooked at interstellar distances."

Shao-Lo leans closer, intrigued, as the holowindow zooms in on the sun-scorched planet. Loitering in orbit above the planet's night side is a ring of objects. As the image continues to zoom in, each dot in the ring resolves into an identical ship with a squat, conical bow aimed toward a central hub. Around the hub's periphery is an array of sockets matching the nose cones of the ships. The holowindow halts its magnifying zoom then reverses, pulling back until the curvature of the planet is visible again.

"To trigger the event, all ships jump simultaneously into the center hub, multiplying mass, pressure, and temperature..."

The ships in the holowindow surge with energy at their sterns and leap at the rotating hub, every cone slamming simultaneously into its socket. The holowindow gleams with a sphere of brilliant light, but the sphere suddenly contracts, collapsing upon itself and distorting the view of the star behind it.

"For an instant," the projection narrates, "a singularity is produced, which emits a bi-polar beam of high energy particles. Only one of which can be aimed at the planet, of course. Ah! There it is."

The holowindow animation slows, showing opposing jets racing out from each lobe of the blast. Ahead of each is a transparent ripple that distorts both the star in the background and the planet it approaches.

"A powerful gravity wave, traveling at the speed of light, precedes the particle beam. This softens the planetary crust an instant before the beam punches through it."

The holowindow model moves in ultra slow motion, and charred landscape lifts like a blister. It fractures across the dome as the beam plunges through, and erupts a kilometers wide geyser of magma.

"The singularity is too low mass to self sustain, of course, and evaporation is virtually instantaneous. This brings its own cataclysmic effects."

The collapsed distortion above the planet blazes white, and Shao-Lo shields her eyes against the glare.

"If there is atmosphere, most will be jettisoned to space," Mikato's projection continues. "Gravitational effects are greatest in the hemisphere facing the weapon, yet seismic waves encircle the globe repeatedly, assuring the crust is shattered. And, as you can see, significant portions of the surface nearest the blast are launched to orbit, which fall back to the surface later as incendiary objects."

The holowindow resumes normal playback. Shao-Lo watches, enraptured, as the planet's dark metallic surface curls and ripples at the shock front of a supersonic wave. Behind it, the surface glows a dull red from colossal fissures and gaps where deep magma is exposed.

"The planet is bombarded for weeks, possibly months, by its own re-entering debris. If sufficient atmosphere remains, storms and lightning are without precedent in frequency or intensity. This plays in concert with a disrupted magnetic field, which is why you see aurora occurring at all latitudes. Even ionized material can fall back to the surface through these gaps. Thus, a world is utterly annihilated under an extended fall of plasma rain."

The projection smiles in pride.

"*This* planet was a lifeless cinder. However, were this deployed on an Earth-like planet, it would sterilize all life more complex than the hardiest bacteria or Tardigrade. The surface would undergo millennia of upheavals as it cooled and stabilized, possibly longer. In fact, there's a strong chance that it could never be habitable again."

The projection stares into the holowindow beside Shao-Lo, watching glowing arcs of white hot debris streak through low orbit, then plunge through smoke and dust that strobes with lightning, sprites, and blue jets. Above it all, ribbons of ionized particles follow chaotic lines of magnetic force, gradually dripping back toward the planet in radiant cascades.

"I must admit, I am never prepared for how beautiful the forces of nature can be."

Shao-Lo's eyes sting from being held open so long, and she blinks involuntarily. "What do you want for it? For this...*Plasma Rain*?"

The projection looks her up and down. "You must understand, Colonel, this is not something we can simply *hand over*. We would need adequate assurances that it could not be turned against us."

Shao-Lo breaks off her fascinated stare and looks at the projection. "Meaning?"

"Your loyalty to your general is admirable. We see that it comes from how strongly you identify with him. After all, mankind has demonstrated single-mindedness in protecting those they bear resemblance to. *Birds of a feather*, and other such...*clichés*."

"I don't copy."

The projection raises its hands beside its head, pointing at its temples with all fingers. "Open your mind to the possibility there are other living beings besides Humans worth protecting."

"Out of the question. I will not betray those I serve."

The projection rolls its virtual eyes and lowers its hands. "We are not suggesting you do so! We are asking that you *expand* the range of entities you would so loyally protect to include those who are not identical in shape and thought."

"Like you? And Honniker, I presume?"

The projection nods deliberately.

"You expect me to split my loyalty? Unthinkable."

"We do not presume to control how you *think*, Colonel. But loyalty to one does not automatically preclude loyalty to another, especially if goals are aligned."

"Goals, like?"

The projection scowls at its dense pupil. "Like remaining *alive*. It can be that simple you know!"

Shao-Lo glances at the holowindow again, tantalized by the destructive capability, then stands upright. "All right, doctor, I'm listening."

The projection's expression softens. "This is only one possibility of many, though this way, we feel, brings the most positive externalities. Through a sharing, a mixing of experience and knowledge, yours and ours... by investing yourself so completely in this place you would never permit another to harm it."

"If you're counting on my instinct of self-preservation, you'll be disappointed. I'll gladly give my life for others."

"Honestly, Colonel, you keep your mind clenched like a fist. You need not *die* to serve your people best! And we do not require you to so narrowly think in terms of a *physical* existence! By joining minds, we gain the best aspects of each. Each facet of our personalities remains, contributing unique perspectives and ideas, yet the combined mind is enriched with knowledge unobtainable in any other way. The sum is greater than the parts in that we are better able to solve problems, better able to cope with existential threats."

"You make it sound like a perfect existence. But I've heard you argue with Honniker. Not as efficient as you'd have me believe."

"*Of course*, we disagree at times. Yet because our minds touch, we see and understand the *reasons* for those objections. We cannot deceive the other. Even with this insight and transparency there are times we do not agree. If you are paying attention, this is proof that one is not merely absorbed by the other, neither overwhelmed nor dominated. Should you decide to combine in this way, you would find it illuminating, I think. You would still be everything you are now. And in addition to your own skills, you would have Honniker's complete understanding of human physiology, all of his medical advances and research. You would also comprehend my life's work," the projection points to the holowindow, "which includes *this*."

Shao-Lo looks again at the holowindow, momentarily hypnotized by flashes of high intensity electrical discharges.

"I would...*know*...how to make this," Shao-Lo restates.

The projection nods. "And you would have access to all of the materials, as well."

"What would you and Honniker get out of it?"

"The wealth of your experience, your military mind, your natural leadership and ability to quickly decide in times of stress or crisis. To be blunt, Honniker imagined he would have handled your teams quickly on your initial visit, yet you endured far beyond what either of us believed was possible. Your martial skills, coupled with the full arsenal of Cadre Two, would make us formidable to any opponent."

Shao-Lo looks at the projection skeptically. "Maybe that would be enough for Honniker. What do *you* get out of it?"

"Once joined, it would be impossible for you to deny we are every bit as alive as you. You would immediately understand *why* we are the way we are...without requiring any change or compromising your own values. Your loyalty to your general remains undimmed. Most importantly, you could no longer imagine some false border between us. We would be united in an inseparable alliance, for an attack on one would, by definition, be an attack on us all."

Shao-Lo stares into the chaotic hologram. The entire night side of the tortured planet flickers in a super-storm of blue bolts. She frowns.

"Uploading to a machine environment *fundamentally* changes the original," Shao-Lo posits. "You proved that when you confronted your organic self and found how different the two of you'd become. I don't see how I could...*upload*...without becoming something I'm not."

"There are many ways that an organic entity can incorporate with synthetic, Colonel—"

"I'm sure you've already tried them all."

"If you would let me *finish*..." the projection says with increasing exasperation. "There *was* a fundamental difference because my organic self did not upload his full intellect or memory...*at first*. He withheld much of himself so that he could retain control over his upload. But that man knew he was dying. Rather than expire, and take his knowledge to the grave, he completed his transfer. I assure you, Colonel, I *am* Doctor Yori Mikato."

"Then where's your lecture on '*putting fire in the hands of children*?' Do you remember that?"

"Quite well, in fact. While this may sound arrogant, should you embrace this joining, you could no longer *be* a child."

"Then what about your recent conclusion that war *is not* the ultimate expression of life's desire to compete and succeed? Have you given up on that idea?"

"Not at all. You have told us that the Eleto have discovered Cadre One, and the fate of your home is in doubt. It is only prudent that one should retain powerful weapons in self-defense. Should the enemy arrive here, they would find a potent and well-prepared adversary. But we are not soldiers. Our ability to create defenses may be strong, but without the means to deploy them effectively? This is in our interest, as well, Colonel."

Shao-Lo extends her arms to each side. "And you would share *all* of this with me?"

"I can see I must be blunt. These are uncertain times. Allies are to be desired, yet trust is in short supply. Your kind has all of the combat experience. We have the weapons. If we can establish trust, then it makes sense to combine our strengths. Is that simple enough for you to comprehend?"

"Don't question my intelligence, Mikato, when you still haven't answered *how* you'd go about combining our minds."

"We do not propose an upload, for that would only create a copy of yourself. Your physical self would still exist, separate, with all of its limitations and prejudice. It invites the possibility your uploaded mind would benefit from the joining, and become so intolerant of its original it kills you off. That gets us *nowhere*. We need you, because you are the tie to your General. It is through *you* that any alliance would be honored."

"I'm still not hearing a method."

"Fine. If you would accept *alterations* to your physical form, your organic mind can remain intact while enjoying greater perceptions and capabilities...*without* this aging body, which already is slipping to decrepitude. Yet, this is not an upload. You, who you are now, remain intact."

Shao-Lo sneers in disgust. "I know what you're getting at. I've seen it in Honniker's *Cooler*. You're talking about my head in a jar. Like *Summers*."

The projection regards Shao-Lo coolly. "What I am *talking about* is encasing your central nervous system in a protective shell and providing you a chassis that is no less than *twenty times* more combat effective than this flimsy vessel you currently occupy. What I am *talking about* is giving you thermal tolerance from minus two hundred fifty to two-thousand degrees Centigrade. What I am *talking about* is self-contained life support and hormone therapy that extends your capacity to serve many of your subjective lifetimes while eliminating vulnerability to vacuum, airborne toxins and pathogens, suffocation, or drowning. What I am *talking about*, Colonel, is giving you strength and durability surpassing anything you have imagined. And you will never be hampered by hunger or pain of injury again."

Shao-Lo crosses her arms, wary. "How many times did Honniker try it on his prisoners? Hundreds? *Thousands*? Every time without success."

"Not so. There was one, a colonist named Aaronson, from Keller's crew. You never saw him. He was a notable success."

"Where is he now?"

"Aaronson had a score to settle with Keller. And when Keller returned, Aaronson confronted him. Unfortunately, Aaronson did not survive the encounter."

"You're telling me Aaronson faced Keller in a combat chassis, and Keller *won*?"

The projection's holographic eyebrows lift. "Combat experience counts for a quite a lot, I'm afraid. Aaronson had *some* training, but not enough. He did not know how to use his abilities to their full effect. He also had psychological...*cleavages*...that Keller exploited. In short, Aaronson was not a soldier. Aaronson was not *you*."

Shao-Lo looks into the smoothly animated holoprojection, dubious. "Honniker had *one* success, and he's dead now? Sorry, Doctor, that's a poor track record. I'll have to decline."

The projection frowns and clasps hands. "Then we have no arrangement. You are free to roam our halls, Colonel, but please, do mind your step. Some of the recent renovations have been...*extreme*." The projection closes the holowindow then disappears, leaving the tall Operator in a pitch-dark corridor.

Shao-Lo instinctively reaches out into the darkness, feeling only empty air around her. Sullen growls rumble nearby. Whirrs of machinery zip through adjoining hallways, unseen. And in the distance, a high-pitched, chortling laugh echoes across the station. Adrenaline seeps into her blood, raising hair on her arms and nape, tightening her shoulders. She reaches out to each side until she touches wall and she backs up to it.

Distant scrabbling of claws across metal flooring...then another high, jeering laugh, much closer than before.

"Turn on the lights, Mikato," Shao-Lo demands, rising to the balls of her feet.

"*Begging your pardon,*" Honniker says via intercom, "*but the Colonel should recall most of the station's illumination was damaged by her last visit. If she is inadequately prepared, that is her own fault. Now then, please pardon us, as we have very much work to do.*"

Scrabbling of claws races nearer with huffing breaths, teeth clicking, chortling like a giddy child.

Shao-Lo widens her stance, hands raised to fight, chin tucked to her chest.

"*I'M NOT CHANGING MY MIND,*" she yells to the darkness. "*FIND SOMEONE ELSE TO MUTILATE!*"

She moves to the center of the corridor, locking her attention on the approaching sounds, pinpointing them in the blackness, ready to bash the life out whatever sprints toward her.

Only meters away, the creature grunts and leaps.

Shao-Lo raises a leg for a kick when a behemoth of fur and armored plate shoves past her from behind. Roaring, it tackles the leaping creature mid-air and slams it down to the deck in a jarring *thump* of muscle and bone. Razors hiss through hide...an animal screams its terror...another deafening roar, thrashing of claws against metal, flailing of limbs, snapping of jaws... another wild scream, then choked grunts, a wet squish, savage thrashing, and dousing sprays of hot liquid.

Shao-Lo's eyes are wide, seeking any trace of light as she backs away from the kill. *I never heard the one behind me! Crept up in silence...could have had me...*

Unspent adrenaline makes her face and legs twitch. Instinct shrieks at her to run away as fast as she can. Yet, in darkness, she knows that flight would be pathetically short, and the best she can manage is a blind retreat, feeling along the wall with one jittery hand.

The killing beast rumbles and rises from its kill with a scrape of metal against metal. Shao-Lo hears it turn toward her, dragging something limp and sodden. She lifts her fists beside her head, determined to at least gouge out its eyes before she is ripped apart, when the behemoth issues a long surly growl that rankles memory. She follows the sounds with her eyes, unable to make out shape, but in its panting breaths and guttural warnings there is familiarity.

"Alessa...?"

Muted by her mouthful, the beast yowls in what sounds like affirmation.

Shao-Lo drops her fists and flattens herself against the wall, letting the armored feline pass by.

"I remember you..." Shao-Lo says.

Alessa shoulders into the tall woman as she passes and follows with a sharp slap of her tail across Shao-Lo's face, as if to say, *I remember you, as well.*

ACCEPTABLE LOSSES

Sticky with drying blood on face, hands, and uniform, Shao-Lo blindly feels her way from one pitch-dark corridor to the next. Quietly speeding machines knock her aside again and again. Growls from adjacent hallways make her hug the walls as patrols of beasts shove past. Armor plated ones are largest and heaviest, undoubtedly feline monsters like Alessa that so nearly chewed her team to bits. Occasionally, a creature covered in chitinous spines drags across the exposed skin of her hands, leaving agonizing welts. Other times the spiny creatures deliberately shrug into her as they pass, poking through the fabric of her uniform. A moment later she is on her knees, pounding at crippling pain in her thighs with both fists, as chortling laughs fade down the hall. Pain yields to numb paralysis, and, unable to stand, Shao-Lo slouches against a wall, waiting for the venom to neutralize.

There's a central plan to the station's layout, I recall. It's symmetrical with angled cross-corridors between the three primary research wings... I just left Honniker's MedLab. Jin-Sung's facility was smashed and sacked... but Keiko mentioned a digital assistant there... Anila, was it? Do Honniker and Mikato know about it? Might get some answers there...

The tall woman rises shakily to her feet and scuffs along through darkness, guided by memory. Creatures skulk and shift just beyond reach, maintaining a constant sense of menace with raking metal claws and guttural rumbles. Of small comfort is the absence of debris underfoot, and the tall woman shuffles unimpeded from intersection to intersection. Ahead, there is a lack of reflected sound, which suggests open space, so she tests it by calling out. Her voice fades quickly into void.

Smooth wall plating becomes rough to the touch, badly pitted. Whole sections are rippled and cracked, telling of a violent past. She hurries down the tactile clues until her next step ends with no floor beneath it. Shao-Lo pitches forward, snatching at nothing but air, falling toward an uncertain abyss.

Something clamps around one of her out-flung arms and dangles her from a trapped wrist. There is no sound other than her own grunting breaths, nothing her eyes can perceive. It is as if a hand materialized out of null space and holds her on the precipice between safety and death.

"The Colonel is more clumsy than I recall," a machine says with Maiella's voice.

Shao-Lo squints and glares in the voice's direction until it swings her back toward solid flooring.

Once on her feet, Shao-Lo traces the outline of a heavy-duty combat chassis with armored torso and joints. Narrow struts root at the shoulders, below which are rugged attachments to the forearms. Her expression levels to one of displeasure.

"I should thank you," the tall operator says.

"But you won't."

Shao-Lo glowers. "Saskia, isn't it? That's what you call yourself now?"

"It's the name I've chosen, yes."

"Old one wasn't good enough?"

"Belongs to someone else. I am not she."

"As you keep reminding me."

"I feel it's necessary, in light of your prior attempts to kill me."

"Killing you? Doesn't seem to have done you any harm."

The war machine seizes Shao-Lo by the upper arms and drags her back to the edge. Shao-Lo's toes scrape the lip then slip off, and the colonel hangs in mid air. She makes no effort to struggle, merely levels a cold stare where she thinks the chassis's optical sensors might be.

"Well, are you waiting for something?" Shao-Lo asks.

"An apology. Or thanks for saving your life. *Again*."

"Saved my life, and now you're putting my life at risk? Makes no sense."

The machine leans forward. "It's not that far to the bottom. You *probably* won't die."

"*Saskia, you know genuine apologies cannot be coerced,*" Mikato says via unseen speaker. "*Please, bring the colonel back to her feet.*"

The war machine steps backward, carrying Shao-Lo to solid flooring, and sets her down again.

"Made my point," Saskia says. Without warning, a bright lamp illuminates high on the machine's torso. Shao-Lo winces at the sudden brilliance and shields her eyes with a hand.

"If you've had enough stumbling about," Saskia says with mechanical disdain, "I'll escort you wherever you'd like to go." The machine rotates at its midsection and steps back the way it came on double-jointed legs.

"If you'd fix the lights," Shao-Lo burrs, "you wouldn't need to escort me anywhere."

The machine halts, about faces, and approaches, shining its lamp past Shao-Lo into the empty space behind her. "What, you don't like the decor? Strange, considering *you* were the architect of this remodel."

Shao-Lo tugs the sleeves of her uniform jacket, straightening the wrinkled fabric of the upper arms. "When threatened, we fight back, *hard*. Clearly you've forgotten life as an Operator."

Saskia remains still, offering no hint of the electronic thoughts occurring behind shiny black photoreceptors. "Quite the opposite, Colonel," the machine says at last. "In fact, I'm certain there's more feeling in this metal and ceramic shell than you'll ever know."

Shao-Lo clasps hands behind her back in bored mockery of patience.

"Ah, yes, the familiar stoicism," Saskia says. "Think Cadre inhibitors make you strong? You'll never comprehend how *stunted* you are, how limited. Say *I've* forgotten my life in the Corps? Impossible. It was like living in a straitjacket with a gun to my head. But indulge me in something, will you?" The chassis gestures toward the open space behind Shao-Lo. "Are you *proud* of your work?"

Shao-Lo eyeballs Saskia with distrust, wondering if the machine might give her a shove from behind if she looks away, but she turns toward the open space, anyway. Saskia's lamp beam dimly shines across a vast circular hole in the station. High above is a dome in the native gray rock with needle-like drips of melted stone. Below is a bowl of crushed flooring, penetrating through at least two lower levels. All of the rubble has been cleared, along with the wrecked machinery. Seals have been welded over broken pipes and conduits, removing most of the clues what once occupied this space. But there is no doubt in Shao-Lo's mind where she is standing.

"Here, Brick Carter self-detonated," Saskia says with electronically clipped blame. "There's another spot like it where Zuri fell. Deepak was shot through the heart, so he never had a chance to detonate. Asha never knew what hit her. That's four out of six in your team... They died for *what*, exactly?"

"You disgrace their names by speaking them. They fought with every fiber of their being. Their commitment allowed the rest of us to survive. There have never been finer Operators."

Saskia takes a half step back. "Precisely my point. And where are they now?"

Sho-Lo turns aggressively on the machine. "You *mock* their efforts?"

"Not their efforts I'm mocking."

"Ah. You think *you'd* have led them better."

"*Absolutely.*"

Shao-Lo scoffs and crosses her arms. "You're soft. Before your... *upload*...Honniker would have had you stretched out on his tables and you'd be howling the rest of your life away."

"As would be his right."

Shao-Lo's expression turns to outright disbelief. "You *justify* Honniker's madness? Seems you've acquired his insanity through this *joining* Mikato keeps pushing me toward."

"I have *not* merged with them. I'm a distinct entity, Colonel, unblended with Honniker or Mikato. You can't belittle what I say as insanity. But since you're too dim for subtlety, I'll ask you directly: how hard would you fight to repel Blueskin invaders at Cadre One?"

"A foolish question. I'd give *everything* to..." Shao-Lo trails off.

Saskia sees the softening of Shao-Lo's iron glare and seizes upon it. "Your general ordered you to enter Cadre Two and seize whatever you could by force. *You* were the invader. *You* were the hostile aggressor, and *THAT* is why Carter, Deepak, Asha, and Zuri are lost. Patience and respect, Colonel—things you never had—would have saved their lives."

Shao-Lo squints. "Doesn't matter what you think. O'Kai ordered me to pacify Cadre Two for human occupation. And that's what I intended to do."

"Dogmatic adherence to orders... Presumption of a general's infallibility... Where did that get you? Four of your finest will never return. And your inability to feel makes their losses *acceptable.*"

Shao-Lo surges at the machine. Strong with the adrenaline in her blood, she lifts Saskia at the waist and shoves it back, yelling, "THERE ARE NO ACCEPTABLE LOSSES!"

Saskia skitters backward, momentarily off-balance, and regards Shao-Lo with spider-like eyes. "Interesting... The Shao-Lo I knew wouldn't react like that." The machine folds its arms, jutting one hip to the side, and studies Shao-Lo head to toe. The tall woman is flushed, quaking with rage, but her head is lowered in shame.

"Must say, I like the change." Saskia flips out a short cylinder from its wrist. With the opposite hand, it detaches the device and passes it over.

Shao-Lo looks up at the offered cylinder, but does not take it.

"It's what you asked for," Saskia says, mashing a button at the back and illuminating the opposite end. "A flashlight. Go ahead, take it. Don't need you falling and busting a hip."

Shao-Lo looks up at the thin cylinder in Saskia's segmented hand then follows the lines of its arm up to the shoulder. There, etched into the armor plating, is a simple bust of a Cadre Geek outfitted with goggles and HDI.

"Come on," Saskia begs, waving the flashlight, "just take it, will you?"

Shao-Lo takes the flashlight and shines it on Saskia's shoulder. "Why do you... Is *that* how you still see yourself?"

"What, this?" Saskia asks, pointing to the etching with a segmented finger. "Well, I'll tell you this: it was a shock waking up in a machine. Reflections still freak me out, even now. Might seem ridiculous to you, but seeing this etching when I catch my reflection keeps me grounded. Reminds me who I *was* without keeping me from being who I *am*. Don't expect that makes any sense to you."

"No, it does. It does."

"Well, then..." Saskia makes a show of brushing its hands together. "I'll leave you to it. Take your time and look around. You won't get any more jabs from the predators, and the machines will give you space, I'll see to that." The machine rotates at the waist and starts down the dark corridor.

"Saskia, wait."

The war machine halts and pivots, hands parked on hips.

"You said you maintained your independence. Why *aren't* you joined with Honniker and Mikato?"

"Ha! Don't you already know?" Saskia asks with hands apart. "Because *I'm a defective that questions superiors and can't follow orders.*"

Shao-Lo blows a breath past her lips and shakes her head. "Forget I said all that."

"Expect me to forget the rest of it, as well?"

"Of course not."

"Good. Because I take getting murdered *personally*."

Shao-Lo looks away and nods. "I understand. And..." She bites her lip hard, drawing blood. "...I'm sorry."

Saskia staggers back, one segmented hand covering the center of its chest, the other thrust straight out. "Ugh! That's *twice* you've surprised me today. Don't know if I can take it!"

The machine recovers its posture, parks one hand on a hip. "All right, you asked a straight question, so I'll give you a straight answer. I haven't joined with Honniker and Mikato because they have not invited me to do so. It's a big thing to share your entire self with another. They must see something in you. Something that... Eh, never mind. Anyway, look around. Just don't touch, all right? Then no one has to get *stabby*."

Shao-Lo looks at the tiny light in her hands, and, as Saskia is about to depart again, she adds, "Hang on. I've been cooped up in transport for better part of a year. Looking to stretch out a bit. Got a place to work out?"

"Sure you're up to it? That drill Honniker used on you was big enough to take core samples."

"Don't worry about me."

"Yeah, shouldda guessed. You're stubborn as a seized piston. But I got just the thing: *Frackit*."

"Come again?"

"*Frackit*." Saskia crooks a finger over its shoulder and beckons. "Follow me to *The Park*. I think you'll like what we've done with the place."

FRACKIT

Saskia leads Shao-Lo through bustling corridors to a wide set of metal doors. The Operator shines her light on them and finds a familiar a lab-coated raccoon flying a kite etched over huge block letters, spelling P-A-R-K. The playful image is stark irony to her recollection of what happened here, and she passes through parting doors with a grimace.

The locker room beyond is white, as she recalls, but more so from new plaster repairs than from its original construction. Patches of tile still cling between the filled bullet holes, and rows of metal lockers slouch away from the entryway, every panel ventilated by shrapnel and high velocity rounds.

A broad staircase leading up at the back of the locker room is every bit as chipped and scuffed as she remembers, but the bloodstains have been washed away. Saskia trudges up the stairs, articulated pads of its feet molding around the rounded-off edges. Bright light streams down from above, bathing the machine in golden hue. It pauses momentarily, turns, and looks back to find Shao-Lo staring back at the entryway.

"You coming?" the machine asks.

Shao-Lo breaks off her reverie and folds her arms. "This is where it all kicked off," she says disjointedly. Pointing at the doorway, she adds, "War machine was parked right there, waiting for us to come out." The old Gun turns about. "Predators came at us from those stairs, where you are now."

"I remember," Saskia says, "or rather I have Maiella's memory of it. Probably would have gotten Deepak then, if not for her. Anyway, that's behind us. You want to stretch your legs, or don't you?"

"Yeah, coming." The colonel follows Saskia up the stairway, emerging into a wide-open, oblong cavern at least two square kilometers in area. The same sculpted hills roll across the landscape, but the covering of tan, dead thatch has been replaced by lush carpets of green grass. Overhead, the same malfunctioning panels still flicker in and out of a holographic sky, bright with yellow sun. Breezy air is rich with the scent of soil and humidity.

The change catches Shao-Lo off guard and she draws several deep breaths through her nostrils.

Saskia asks, "You like?"

"It's fine," Shao-Lo answers.

"Fine? *Pffft*. You're impossible." The machine steps toward a tall slab of stone rooted on one end like a memorial and beckons Shao-Lo over. The colonel obliges, finding the stone's face is polished smooth and engraved with numbered lines. Some of the lines have been chiseled out, some lines appear more recent than others, and several have been amended.

"All right, Colonel, you say you've been cooped up? Here's your chance to expend some energy. Got a game going with Alessa. Not entirely sure it's for you. It's rather, uh, *physical*."

"Won't be a problem."

Saskia shifts weight to one leg. "You *say* that... Well...everything you need to know is right here."

The colonel faces the stone and reads.

RULES of FRACKIT

1.   The game may be played on any shaped field, so long as the two halves are symmetrical in shape and in area.

2.   The only equipment required is the FRACKIT, which is a reinforced mesh satchel stuffed with solid materials weighing a total of ten kilos. (*Rule amended*)

3.   One team serves the other by launching the FRACKIT into an opponent's zone. (*Rule amended*)

4.   The receiving team's goal is to run the FRACKIT back, past the opposing team, all the way to the farthest part of the opponent's zone. (*Rule amended*)

5.   If the running team succeeds in reaching the farthest point of the opponent's zone, a point is scored. Thirty seconds are granted for taunts, gestures, and insults

before the field is reset and the scoring team serves the FRACKIT to the opposing team.

6.   If the running team fails to make positive advances on the field for a total span of ten seconds, the run is a failure. The team who failed to advance scores no points, the opposing team is allotted thirty seconds for shaming before the field is reset, and the failing team must serve the FRACKIT to the opposing team.

7.   Injuring your fellow players will result in immediate forfeiture of the match. (*Rule Amended*)

8.   Weapons of any kind may NOT be employed during play, even if they are surgically implanted. Violating this rule results in immediate forfeiture of the match. (*Rule Amended*)

9.   Play will continue as long as required until one team scores ten points or forfeits. (*Rule Amended*)

10.   Anything else goes, unless specifically prohibited by amendment. (*Rule Amended*)

AMENDMENTS

• *Amendment to Rule #2*:
Stuffing material must be coarse enough that it cannot leak from the FRACKIT. Moreover, it must be sufficiently shock resistant that it does not liquefy during play. For example, nails, screws, or industrial bolts are acceptable, but the fresh hind leg of a Flintvarg is not acceptable (though the dried bones of a Flintvarg *are* acceptable).

• *Amendment to Rule #3*:
Launch velocity of the FRACKIT when serving may not exceed 50m/sec. Excessive serve velocity results in turnover and automatic point for opposing team.

• *Amendment to Rule #4*:

Jumping is permitted. However, jumps must not exceed three meters from the ground. Rocket assisted jumps and sustained flight *are right out*. Jumps exceeding three meters from the ground result in turnover and automatic point for opposing team.

• *Amendment to Rule #7:*
Or crippling, or maiming, or killing. Severing or removing a player's power supply counts as crippling.

• *Amendment to Rule #8:*
Yes, Alessa, your claws and teeth *are* weapons when used against other players.

• *Amendment to Rule #9:*
Or until a player must be fed/refueled/recharged, or until both teams agree that the match is over. Intermissions are allowed so long as both players agree on time and duration.

• *Amendment to Rule #10:*
All players must agree to amendments *before* they are added into the rules board.

Shao-Lo nods as she completes the list and crosses her arms.

"Any questions?" Saskia asks.

"Simple as it gets," Shao-Lo replies. "You versus me?"

"Actually, it's never as simple as it looks. Why don't you let Alessa and me take the first round? Give you a chance to limber up before your match."

"Very well."

"All right." Saskia turns toward the open fields of soft grass and calls, "PLAYERS TO THE FIELD, IF YOU PLEASE!"

A simple hovering scoreboard materializes in the holographic sky with a timer and two score windows, one labeled, SASKIA, the other, ALESSA. Below the score windows a long box forms, headed with the caption, EGO WITHERING TAUNTS. Shao-Lo takes it all in with a skeptical frown as she moves to a high outcrop of stone for a better view. Atop the native gray rock, she finds a flat spot and surveys the field from it. At the center of the cavern, a thick red line of light runs across the grass from one wall to the other. Beyond the fenced flower gardens, the gravel paths, the gray bark-less trunks of dead trees, she spies a green line near the very end of the cavern, indicating the goal line. Behind her, much closer, is an identical green line. The colonel turns back toward the centerline and takes several deep breaths, savoring the pleasing air, then begins a round of deep stretches.

Saskia tromps toward the centerline, rotating arms in large circles forward and backwards then making flipping leaps in random directions.

In opposing territory, Alessa emerges from a trapdoor beneath a broad stone bench at the top of a hill and slinks toward her side of the centerline. Halfway down, she stops suddenly, turns, and washes her backside, hind leg stuck skyward like a flagpole. She finishes just as suddenly and resumes her path, one paw in front of the other.

Shao-Lo pauses her calisthenics to watch the creature's relaxed approach. Overlapping barding covers the beast from her snout back to the base of her tail and down to the top of each great paw. Massive muscles flex beneath the plates, sending ripples down each side. What should sound like a clanking tank is remarkably quiet, however. And as the beast nears, Shao-Lo can just make out thick tufts of fur between each plate, silencing them as she moves.

Once at the centerline, Alessa rises onto her back feet and reaches high into a stretch surpassing four meters. Her whiskered lips part in an enormous yawn, exposing dagger-like metal-capped canines with molars fused together into shearing blades. Her mottled pink and black tongue lolls, tip curled, and then she drops down onto her forepaws again. Curved, metal-capped claws rotate from between tufted toes, sinking deep into the damp soil. Front legs straight, head lifted high, she arches her spine so that she is nearly looking behind herself. Then she straightens and begins a shake at her head that travels to her high shoulders, moves through her thick chest, to her narrow waist and hips, and then finishes at the tufted tip of her tail. Ready, she sits on her hindquarters.

Saskia steps to the centerline and extends a segmented hand. Alessa bats it with a paw, and the two about face, retreating toward their own territory.

Intrigued, Shao-Lo settles into lotus position on her outcrop, hands in lap, back straight.

Overhead, the scoreboard timer sets to zero, and a buzzer sounds stridently throughout the Park. In monotone, the scoreboard proclaims, "PLAYERS ASSUME THEIR STARTING PLACES. GAME BEGINS IN TEN SECONDS."

Saskia reaches behind itself, rummaging a storage compartment on its back, and removes a lumpy, black sack. The war machine lofts it a couple of times, and every time it lands with *clinks* of metal bits.

Saskia halts below the outcrop where Shao-Lo observes and plants its articulated feet, digging them in with rapid back and forth movements.

Stance set, the machine takes the sack in one hand and cocks it to throw.

"PLAYERS READY," the scoreboard blares. "GAME BEGINS IN THREE... TWO... ONE..." An ear-splitting horn blast fills the cavern.

Saskia rotates at the waist, its upper half turning a full circle before launching the sack across the open field. Shao-Lo looks up at the scoreboard. Launch velocity is fifty meters per second, precisely.

Alessa sprints deep into her own territory, jumps, catches the sack in her mouth, and races toward the centerline with astounding quickness. Saskia dashes out to meet her with long sprinting strides. Shao-Lo leans forward, fascinated by the contest between genetic and mechanical engineering.

Alessa turns on a diagonal path toward a jutting rock ledge, and Saskia diverts to intercept. The feline reaches the ledge first and disappears behind it. Saskia lopes to a halt, unsure which side Alessa will emerge from, and backs away.

While Saskia focuses on the rock ledge, Alessa emerges behind the machine from a hidden passage between two flower gardens. The beast grins then dashes full sprint toward the goal.

Saskia spots the beast with rear facing photoreceptors, spins its torso about, and races after her, kicking up huge clumps of sod and dirt in its wake. Alessa has a lead, but the machine closes the gap.

Alessa glances over her shoulder and sees Saskia overtaking. She faces front, ripping up the ground with powerful strides, ducking around trees, using the landscape to block her pursuer like an inanimate teammate. Saskia scrapes around ledges of stone, leaps benches and sculptures, vaults over gardens. No matter how swiftly the machine gains, Alessa dodges with remarkable timing and agility, managing to curve around some obstruction that puts Saskia another fraction of a second behind her.

Shao-Lo rises to her feet, excited. The players race closer, and just when it seems Alessa has no more obstructions to block her pursuer, she turns directly toward Shao-Lo. The huge feline leaps at the tall Gun, forelegs extended straight out like a missile. Shao-Lo drops onto her back, barely ducking the beast, then rolls onto her hands and feet to watch the huge feline land on the far side.

"SHIT!" Saskia shouts, and it skids on the grass, arms extended directly ahead of it, scrambling to change course and avoid crashing through Shao-Lo. It slips off balance, hits the outcropping with both hands, bounces to one side, and rolls back to its feet. By the time the war machine is running again, another strident horn blast sounds.

Shao-Lo lifts her gaze to the back of the cavern and sees Alessa up on her hind legs, satchel clutched in one paw high overhead. The beast spikes the sack straight into the grass.

"POINT, ALESSA," the scoreboard blares. "THIRTY SECONDS GRANTED FOR TAUNTS."

Saskia drops its arms to its sides as Alessa picks up the satchel in her mouth and trots over.

"Not fair, Alessa," Saskia gripes, "using Shao-Lo as a pick! She might have been injured!"

Alessa spits the satchel at Saskia's feet, sits up on her back legs, cups one paw against her chest, and curls her other paw under her eye as if scrubbing away a tear. The beast then turns about and kicks a shower of sod and dirt over the war machine. Saskia stands and takes the humiliating shower until a buzzer sounds the end of thirty seconds.

"Better be ready this round," Saskia warns. Alessa draws her lips into a teeth-showing grimace then flicks her head toward the far side of the field.

"RESET FIELD AND PREPARE FOR NEXT ROUND," the scoreboard announces.

Saskia vibrates, shaking soil from joints and fittings in a cloud, then hustles to the far side of the cavern. Alessa strolls to an open section of field ahead of the outcrop. Shao-Lo sinks down into a crouch. The horn blasts.

Alessa takes the satchel in one paw, rises up onto hind legs, leaps forward, pivots on her front paw, swings her back end around, pivots again, and hurls the satchel. Shao-Lo looks up at the scoreboard, which tracks the launch at 47 meters per second.

On the far side of the cavern, Saskia easily snatches the Frackit one-handed and races forward. Alessa rushes the machine with ten-meter leaps. Rather than charge straight at her opponent, however, the big feline aims just to one side.

Shao-Lo scrutinizes the tactic, seeing that Alessa is driving her opponent in the opposite direction, away from protective obstructions toward open field. Saskia sprints on toes of articulated feet, gouging divots with every step, lofting dirt in a sparse rooster tail behind it. As swift as the machine is, it cannot help but telegraph its movements, a tell as obvious to Alessa as it is to Shao-Lo observing from afar. When the machine plants a leg and coils for a leap over its speeding opponent, the huge feline digs her claws into the ground and leaps, as well. Both collide mid-air and Alessa bashes hard with forepaws. Outweighed by the Feline two to one, Saskia careens into the corpse of a tree, cracking it in half, and the tree's top section collapses onto the sprawled machine with a cacophony of snapping branches. By the time Saskia shoves out from under the trunk, Alessa clamps her jaws around the machine's ankle, stopping a sprint before it can start. Saskia kicks at the beast, landing several punishing blows, but the beast shrugs them off and drags the machine under her for better control. Before Alessa can immobilize her quarry, however, Saskia's trapped leg detaches and the machine skitters free on hands and remaining foot. The beast bellows in protest, and sprints after it, still clutching the machine's leg in her mouth. Even missing a leg, Saskia is too swift to catch, and the machine easily reaches the end of the cavern in a straight three-limbed sprint.

Alessa arrives moments later, spits the leg out, and yowls an extended complaint that Shao-Lo can decipher without much effort.

"What do you mean, no fair?" Saskia asks without concern. "The rules say you can't cripple fellow players. It doesn't say anything about crippling *yourself*."

Alessa flops down on her backside and scowls.

"POINT, SASKIA," the scoreboard blares. "THIRTY SECONDS GRANTED FOR TAUNTS."

"Ode to my opponent, Alessa," Saskia begins, one hand flat against its chest, the other extended toward the big feline like a one-legged bard.

"Slow and fat, she takes the field,
sluggish made from frequent meals.
Her breath so rank, that bold men smother,
none can tell one end from her other."

Saskia sweeps its outstretched arm toward the ground and stoops into a low bow. The scoreboard above dings and illuminates a dot under Saskia's box for taunts.

With faux politeness, the machine asks, "Would you be so kind and pass me my leg?"

Alessa lowers her head, picks up the mechanical leg in her mouth, and walks it over. As Saskia reaches out to receive it, Alessa flings the limb into a pond, and sulks away.

"*Don't be a sore loser*, Alessa!" Saskia calls after her, pogoing toward the pond.

"RESET FIELD AND PREPARE FOR NEXT ROUND," the scoreboard proclaims.

Saskia fishes its leg from the water and reattaches it, tests briefly for functionality, then dashes back to retrieve the satchel and sets its stance.

The horn blasts, and Saskia whirls off another fifty meter per second serve. Alessa catches Frackit in teeth and makes a straight-line sprint toward the goal. Saskia sprints directly at the feline. Shao-Lo stands up to see farther as the two maintain constant bearings.

Saskia pitches forward in her run. Alessa lowers her head. And the opponents crash into one another with a clash of metal that sets Shao-Lo's teeth on edge. Alessa's greater mass and lower center of gravity buck Saskia off its feet. The machine wheels through the air, all four limbs spread, then slams onto its back.

Wincing from the hit, Alessa digs in her claws and surges away. Saskia flips onto articulated feet and races in pursuit. The beast does not look back, does not feint or dodge, but carves a straight dash toward the goal. Within meters of the finish, Saskia tackles her. The beast falls chin first into the grass and skids to a stop, roaring and thrashing in frenzy. Saskia scrambles atop the frenzied creature in a dominant position, and Shao-Lo sees a wildness appear in the big feline's eyes. It rolls, kicks, swipes, bucks, and butts, screaming furiously. Dirt, grass, fur fly as they grapple, gouging away an ever-expanding ring of turf. Shao-Lo struggles to see through the cloud, watching for technique.

The scoreboard distracts her, however, announcing, "FORWARD MOVEMENT HALTED." A ten second timer appears in red and counts down from ten seconds.

Alessa battles with total frenzy, flipping the lighter Saskia from side to side, bashing it against the ground. The machine does not give up its lock on the big feline, yet can only manage to control one half of the massive beast at a time. Alessa lets Saskia tangle up her back legs, sinks her fore claws deep into the soil, and drags herself forward. The scoreboard counter freezes at five seconds remaining.

Saskia digs in its heels, using all of its strength in opposition, but the articulated feet cannot dig as deeply into the dirt and old tree roots the way Alessa's claws can. The last few meters are a brute force match of one colossally powerful entity against another, and after a grueling ten minutes, Alessa finally muscles her way to the goal line.

"POINT, ALESSA," the scoreboard blares. "THIRTY SECONDS GRANTED FOR TAUNTS."

Saskia releases the huge feline and rises to its feet. Alessa, panting, lifts herself from the trench of dirt she carved through the lush green grass and shakes her full length, launching clumps of damp earth in all directions. She turns away from Saskia, and just when Shao-Lo expects another kicked up shower of dirt and sod, the animal lifts her tail and sprays the machine head to toe.

"HEY, NO...!" Saskia yells. "AUUUGGHH!!! THAT'S DISGUSTING!" It tries to shield itself with arms, but the mist clings everywhere it lands.

Overhead, the scoreboard dings, and a dot appears under Alessa's side for taunts.

"You know this is corrosive, right?" Saskia fumes. "I've half a mind to dock a point in penalty for *maiming*."

Shao-Lo stands and shouts through cupped hands, "Are you going to finish the game or—?"

Pungent reek of ammonia reaches Shao-Lo atop her rock ledge and she gags. Burying nose and mouth in the crook of an arm, she gasps through the dense fabric of her uniform, unable to see through stinging, watered eyes.

Saskia bats Alessa with the back of a hand. The beast curls her lips in a wicked grin. The war machine calls back, "You were saying, Colonel?"

STUNTED HUMAN EXISTENCE

Shao-Lo stands at the red centerline of the field, stripped down to her undersuit and tightly laced boots. She swings her head in big circles and reaches high above herself in a full body stretch.

Directly across the line sits a titanic feline, looking Shao-Lo directly in the eye, Frackit in mouth. A line of drool hangs from the satchel, reaching for dirt in slow motion.

I dispatched dozens of you with rifle and kit, the colonel thinks. *What's one more?*

Alessa extends a huge paw toward Shao-Lo. The tall operator swipes at it curtly then turns back to her side of the field and marches to the rock outcropping. Scoreboard horn blasts, and play begins.

Alessa gets a loping start, hops onto her front paws, pivots, swings her back end around, plants her rear paws, and catapults the Frackit into a high parabola.

Shao-Lo glances at the scoreboard, which tracks the satchel at 48 meters per second, then she watches the black sack arc into her territory. Keeping watchful eye on Alessa, the Gun slides beneath the satchel then skates just to one side as it drops like a meteor. The Frackit slams hard, compacting a section of soil, and bounces limply. Shao-Lo scoops the satchel on the bounce and cuts a sharp turn toward Alessa's side of the field at top speed. The Gun scans outcrops and benches as she crosses the red centerline, but there is no sign of her opponent. Torn up sections of sod are everywhere, making it difficult to track prints, so Shao-Lo sprints toward large tree trunks, park benches and lampposts, ponds and trails fenced with chain, anywhere a beast of Alessa's size could not hide. Her opponent absence strikes an ill chord.

Patronizing me with an easy win? No, not likely...

Shao-Lo maintains her guard, weighing the possibility her opponent can become invisible at will. She jinks randomly left or right, half expecting the beast to drop straight down out of the holographic sky. Her head swivels from side to side, but all she sees are the peaceful rustles of green in artificial breezes.

The goal line is only a few strides away, and Shao-Lo gives her all in a final dash. Her legs and hips burn from Honniker's recent surgeries, but there are no outcrops for Alessa to hide behind, no obscuring shrubs. She leans forward, all of her energy focused on the goal line ahead.

In the corner of her eye, a park bench lifts, and from a trapdoor beneath it explodes a monster of bared teeth and muscular limbs. Alessa roars, front legs spread wider than Shao-Lo can dodge, and the great feline tackles the Gun to the grass. Shao-Lo struggles for breath, stiff-arming the press of animal flesh that lies a top her. Alessa snarls and flops her entire weight over the sprawled colonel, pinning her. Shao-Lo stares at the radiant green line barely a meter away, trying to worm her way out from under the hot, furry weight compressing her chest.

The scoreboard blares, "FORWARD MOVEMENT HALTED," and a counter ticks down from ten seconds. The old Gun's face turns bright red from effort, but she cannot dislodge the massive animal that blankets her.

A horn blast fills the cavern, and the scoreboard proclaims, "PLAYER FAILED TO ADVANCE. THIRTY SECONDS GRANTED TO DEFENSE FOR TAUNTS."

Alessa rolls casually off of Shao-Lo, allowing the Gun a full breath. As proper color returns to her face, Shao-Lo props herself up and spits out strands of grass when something moist, warm, and raspy licks its way from the back of her neck up over the crown of her stubbly head. She turns in annoyance, and gets another tongue bath up the side of her face. The colonel pushes Alessa's big chin away, so the beast rises, turns, and kicks a shower of dirt and sod over her. Dirt and grass stick to the slime of saliva, coating the colonel in brown silt. Steel gray eyes smolder beneath layers of grime.

Saskia steps over and crouches beside Shao-Lo, bringing along a noxious cloud of ammonia. "Sure you want to play this game, Colonel?"

"*Next round,*" Shao-Lo growls, rising to her feet and knocking clumps of dirt from her shoulders.

"RESET FIELD AND PREPARE FOR NEXT ROUND," the scoreboard proclaims.

Shao-Lo bends down and snatches the Frackit. Alessa prances ahead to the opposite end of the field. Saskia jogs to a high outcrop of rock and observes.

Shao-Lo approaches the centerline. Taking one end of the Frackit in both hands, she spins a circle. The satchel whirls faster and faster until Shao-Lo releases it with a mighty grunt, and the Frackit sails high into Alessa's territory. A quick glance at the scoreboard tells Shao-Lo her throw is a disappointing eighteen meters per second.

Alessa hops, catches the satchel in her jaws, lands on forepaws, and sprints straight at Shao-Lo, head lowered like a battering ram. The old Gun grits her teeth, looks around herself, and spots a chain railing along a gravel path nearby. She lunges for it, ripping a post out of the soft ground, and pulls the entire row loose. She hauls on the chain, all of the posts sliding down the length and collecting at one end. Chain clutched in both hands Shao-Lo rushes at the lumbering beast, whirling the posts overhead.

Alessa's sprint loses its haughty gait, and she diverts away. Shao-Lo chases and whips the chain with posts at Alessa's head. The big feline ducks easily but the dodge breaks her quick stride. Shao-Lo dives at her, catches the big feline around the neck, and locks her hands around Alessa's throat. Momentum carries her right over the big feline's armored shoulders, and the colonel slips all the way around until she is looking up at Alessa's chin, being dragged between the creature's bounding forepaws.

Alessa barely has to alter her stride and steps on Shao-Lo's trailing legs, breaking her hold and dumping the Gun flat on her back. Shao-Lo momentarily snags one of Alessa's back legs, slowing the big feline's gait, is kicked free, then rolls to a stop.

Sore, grass-stained from head to foot, Shao-Lo picks herself up as Alessa crosses the goal line. A horn blast fills the cavern, the scoreboard announces Alessa's time for taunts, and Shao-Lo lowers her head in frustration.

"It's not your fault, Colonel!" Saskia shouts from its outcrop of rock. "It isn't a fair match, and you shouldn't expect to compete with—"

"NEXT ROUND!" Shao-Lo yells back.

Saskia shrugs mechanical shoulders and crosses its arms.

Alessa takes her full thirty seconds in a playful celebration dance around the black satchel while Shao-Lo returns to the outcropping of rock on the opposite side of the field. Once in position the Gun about-faces and locks eyes on her opponent, determined not to lose sight of her this time.

The scoreboard's horn blasts and Alessa winds up her bouncing serve. The Frackit sails high, disappears above the holographic sky, then plummets like a missile. Shao-Lo watches it in peripheral vision, never losing sight of the big feline that trots across the centerline at her. The Frackit hits the ground with a jangling *thud*, Shao-Lo scoops it, throws it over one shoulder, and jogs directly at her opponent.

Alessa's lips curve as they part, and her tongue hangs between razor sharp canines, eyes locked.

Her face set in rigid horizontal lines, Shao-Lo runs faster at the big feline, making no attempt to dodge. Alessa's ears droop, and the beast's eyes narrow in an uncertain squint.

Shao-Lo's iron expression gives no clue of her intent, and just as it seems she is going to run straight into Alessa's grasp, the Gun fakes a leap to one side, springs back in the other direction while turning, and she swings the Frackit in both hands like a sledge. The satchel bashes Alessa's cheek, turning her big head aside and putting the beast off balance. Shao-Lo dashes past.

Saskia cheers from her observation post, hopping up and down, hands in the air.

Alessa roars, whips about, and rips up the ground in pursuit. Shao-Lo no longer attempts speed or strength, using fixed objects to avoid the big feline's angry lunges. Each time the Gun successfully outmaneuvers the beast, Alessa grows more and more agitated, diving harder at the Gun, over-shooting, letting Shao-Lo gain another few steps toward her goal. The Gun dives behind park benches and Alessa explodes through them. The Operator leaps into tree branches an instant before Alessa slams head first into the trunk. And when Alessa corners Shao-Lo at a pond, the beast charges. Shao-Lo leaps over Alessa's lowered head, handsprings off the peak of Alessa's shoulders, and vaults to safety as the big feline plunges into shallow water.

Saskia bounces atop the outcrop, ecstatic.

Shao-lo allows herself the slightest smile, and glances back to see a bedraggled mess of armor plating and drenched fur clawing its way out of a murky pond. The goal line is directly ahead, and no matter that a point in this game serves little more than pride, the Gun powers forward, putting as much distance between herself and her soggy opponent. Then, only meters shy of the goal line, Shao-Lo's right thigh seizes in a massive cramp. The colonel stumbles onto hands and knee, right leg jutting straight like a plank, Honniker's harvests burning like fire beneath her skin.

"AAAAARRRRGGGGGG, *NOT NOW,*" she yells.

Furious at her body's refusal to cooperate, Shao-Lo grinds her teeth, struggles up to her left leg and limps as quickly as she can.

Alessa lopes up and tackles the Operator almost gently. Shao-Lo collapses under the big feline's weight, and she fights with all of the strength she can muster. But ten seconds later the Scoreboard blares out her failure to advance and turns the round over to Alessa. The big feline does not take her thirty seconds of taunts, however. Rather, she noses Shao-Lo in effort of helping her up from the ground.

Saskia hustles over then asks, "You okay, Colonel? Thought you had that one for sure."

"Cramp," Shao-Lo burrs. "Out of shape. I'll be fine." The colonel tries to stand, but her right leg will accept no weight. Alessa leans against Shao-Lo to prop her up and looks away as if to avoid embarrassing her.

"No need to push so hard, Colonel. It's just a game," Saskia says.

Shao-Lo's whole face screws up in disbelief. "Just a *game*? Do you have *any idea* who you're talking to?"

"Well, it doesn't have to be life or death. And killing yourself isn't going to get you across the green line. That said, was a hell of an effort you put in—"

"*Stow it*, Geek. I don't need to be coddled. I have to be better, is all."

The machine drags a toe across the dirt before replying, "There are obstacles you just can't be expected to overcome. And dashing yourself against them can...*break* you. Sometimes you can't win."

"No-win scenarios only exist for those lacking imagination. There is *always* a way to win."

"So how will you be victorious, Colonel? By being stronger than us? By being faster? Do you think that body of yours can be trained or conditioned hard enough to make that possible?"

Shao-Lo glares in defiance. "I'll work with what I've got."

The machine looks at Alessa and says to her, "You can lead a thirsty idiot to water, but you can't make her drink..."

"Say that again," Shao-Lo demands.

"*Look around*, Colonel! Mikato and Honniker have opened this place up for you. You can have more than this stunted, human existence, if you'd just ASK!"

Shao-Lo's face twitches with an uncommon moment of indecision. She reaches down and massages her leg until, at last, the muscles relax. Satisfied, the grizzled Gun looks up.

"*Next round.*"

CRUEL TO BE KIND

Shao-Lo hobbles toward the stairway that leads down from *The Park* to the locker room. Her undersuit is torn through at the knees, shoulders, and elbows. The neck is stretched out. Every thread is stained with grass and dirt. Her skin is mottled with sweat and grime, and drill points on her thigh seep red. Corners of her mouth are turned down, squaring her chin into an involuntary frown.

High in the artificial sky behind her, the holographic scoreboard shows a final score of Alessa's ten points to her one with a total time of one hour twenty-six minutes played. Below the board, Alessa is splayed out on her side across the breezy lawn, limp as if spilled there, panting heavily. The big feline is a haggard mess of mud and sod, blending head to tail with the torn up turf she sprawls upon.

Already, small drones have deployed around the park replacing sections of sod, rebuilding fences around gardens, collecting downed tree limbs, repairing broken benches. They carefully avoid the huge feline, working around her and giving a wide berth.

Bright blue sky above turns overcast as clouds roll in from one side. Shao-Lo looks up, trying to discern if the misty clouds are real or holographic then decides it does not matter. *Water will start falling soon*, she recalls.

Saskia walks up beside Shao-Lo, carrying a charcoal uniform jacket and trousers, still reeking of piss. "Well played, Colonel."

"There's nothing to admire in *losing*, Geek," Shao-Lo says with a hostile glare.

"You're wrong about that. I expected Alessa to roll right over you, shut you out completely. That you scored at all could be considered a win."

"That isn't how it works. I failed to reach ten points, thus, I *lost*. If this were combat—"

"It's a fucking *game*," Saskia interrupts.

"The point of which is to *win*."

Saskia arches its back, staring into the clouds above as if appealing to a higher power. "The point of *this* game is to keep our skills sharp. And to have *fun*. Sulk if you want to, but you played well. Was bold to take the field, much less play ten rounds against an opponent *that* overpowering."

"I've faced greater threats."

"In your undersuit? I doubt it. Regardless, running Alessa around, wearing her out was a good strategy. By the last round she could barely keep up. If the game went to twenty points, you might have won."

Shao-Lo halts and limps back toward the field. "Then let's go to twenty."

Saskia takes Shao-Lo by the shoulders and steers her back toward the stairs. "Forget it. That leg of yours is more swollen than when you came in. You need rest and anti-inflammatory meds. Give yourself a chance to heal *then* come back at full strength."

Shao-Lo says nothing but allows herself to be guided toward the chipped and broken stairway. No sooner has she taken the first step down than a gentle pattering begins behind her. She pauses and looks over her shoulder, watching the pattering become a soaking fall of rain.

Alessa perks up from her exhausted slump, lifts her muzzle toward the occluded sky, lets the rain stream over her face, and sneezes when a drop goes down her nose. With some reluctance, she lifts her bulk from the ground, arches her spine in an exaggerated stretch, shakes, then steps over the circle of patiently waiting lawn repair drones toward the stairs.

Shao-Lo holds the handrail, unable to hide the stiffness in her leg, and takes one step at a time. Saskia extends an elbow for assistance, but the Gun rebuffs it with a disdainful flip of a hand.

"Suit yourself," Saskia says. The machine drapes the uniform over Shao-Lo's broad shoulder and hustles down the steps. To the colonel's chagrin, pungent ammonia has rubbed off into the fabric.

When Shao-Lo reaches the bottom, her leg is throbbing so badly she can barely move. One hand covering the seeping drill sites, the other gripping the handrail as a prop, teeth set in a wide grimace of pain, she sees there are no other handrails between her and the islands of slumping lockers. Too proud to ask for help, she considers crawling to them when the Park's main entry doors slide open. Through them enter Mikato's holographic projection and a spotless white robot with a crimson cross on its chest. A pair of arms root at each of the robot's shoulders, and the limbs end in multiple sets of stainless surgical tools. Two of the arms are held out in front, carrying a short stack of folded white fabric.

"Hello, Colonel," Mikato says cordially. "Thought you might need a clean change of clothes." The projection glances over Shao-Lo's grimy, sweaty form. "Perhaps a shower, as well. But first, let's get some relief for that leg."

The medical robot sets clothes onto a low bench between locker rows then rolls toward Shao-Lo. The Gun eyes it warily as it rotates a hypodermic into place and aims it at her burning thigh.

With Honniker's voice, the machine says, *"If the Colonel would remove her hand..."*

"I've had enough of your needles for one day, Doctor."

The machine rolls back a few centimeters and raises the hypo gun. *"Understandable, however, we must reduce the inflammation, or risk further injury to the tissues. If we do not, recovery time is prolonged and you will remain in a state of limited mobility. The colonel would like to be in her best condition, yes?"*

Shao-Lo glares at the medical machine. "What's in the hypo?"

The machine lets its arms drape to the sides, then it waves the injector for show. *"I could say anything, and the colonel would not know the difference."*

"If you would, Herr Doktor," Mikato says modestly, "let her know what you are doing."

"Yes, yes, fine. We must inhibit the Cyclo-Oxegenase enzymes, or the tissues will continue to swell. Continued swelling restricts blood flow to injured areas and creates additional pressure on surrounding tissues, which can damage them. Now, Colonel, shall I also explain Cytokines and vascular permeability? Do you require a dissertation on Leukocyte and Lymphocyte infiltration, as well? Or shall I proceed?"

Shao-Lo stands straight as she can, resting her weight on her good leg, and takes her hand away from her injury.

"Danke," the machine says flatly. It produces a damp towelette, pulls down the waistband of Shao-Lo's undersuit, and cleans two patches on her hip and thigh. *"You may feel the little pinch,"* it says, gloating, and injects both sites. *"Give this thirty-five minutes to take effect. In the meantime go soak in a cool bath, not more than eighteen degrees centigrade. Keep the leg elevated."* The machine raises an arm and points to Shao-Lo's left toward a doorway beyond the battered lockers. *"You will find the plumbing in that room is still functional after your prior visit."*

Shao-Lo nods and turns the corner at the bottom of the stairs, bracing herself against the tiled wall as she goes. The projection and medical machine watch in silence until the Gun is through the doorway and out of earshot.

"She will grow tired of these injuries, I'm sure," the projection says.

"Possibly. Her tolerance for pain is remarkable. I have not seen the like."

"Makes her a promising candidate, does it not?"

"Indeed, it does."

Saskia emerges from the same doorway that Shao-Lo disappeared through. All trace of grit and grass has been scrubbed away.

"Ah, Saskia," the holoprojection greets, "how did our patient perform?"

Saskia draws up even with the projection and medical machine. "Better than expected. She's tough."

"Yes," the projection says, staring through the doorway to the baths and showers. "She continues to impress. In contests she has no chance of winning, her commitment is unparalleled."

"Commitment?" Saskia echoes skeptically. "More like fanatical *obsession.*"

"Tut, tut, Saskia. To fault her for obsession makes us hypocrites."

Saskia turns its torso toward the stairway as Alessa pads down it. The big feline is soaked beneath her barding and her fur is clumped with mud, but she does not seem to mind. Rather, she saunters up to Saskia and sniffs, then makes an exaggerated wince before continuing toward the bathroom, leaving huge muddy paw prints as she goes.

"Yes, I *know* I still stink, Alessa, thank you for noticing," Saskia calls after her.

"She sprayed you again?" Mikato asks.

"Yes, *the minx*. Takes weeks to get rid of."

"I am relieved to no longer have the sense of smell, then."

The three look at the doorway in quiet contemplation.

Breaking the silence, Saskia asks, "Switch to private channel?"

The holoprojection and medical machine activate a three-way radio connection.

"Channel is secure, " Honniker says.

"Channel is secure," Mikato echoes, "go ahead, Saskia."

Saskia places hands on hips, faces its two comrades, and asks, "Seriously, does it need to be this painful for her?"

"The more uncomfortable the Colonel is in her shell," Honniker states, *"the sooner she makes the next step in her evolution."*

"Evolution?" Saskia repeats. "It's a *forced* evolution, if you can call it that, an *unnatural* one...and we're driving her toward it. Are we *sure* this is the way?"

"As certain as one can be in matters of this importance," Mikato answers. "You've seen for yourself how she clings to authority. Perhaps if her general was here, we could make binding, honorable agreements. As it stands, we cannot trust that any arrangement she makes with us will not be overruled. Therefore, we must make it *impossible* for Shao-Lo to be hostile toward us. The only way to guarantee that is if she transcends a physical body and blends with us as a connected entity."

"Even so," Saskia counters, "the pace you've set, it's too fast. We risk creating something unstable—a mind that, if cracked, could drown in the deluge of alternate perceptions. Don't forget, as a Geek I spent half my conscious life in the machine world. I was well acquainted with virtual environments, and I *still* struggled with my transition. Shao-Lo has no concept of what it's like, and there's no way we can adequately explain it to her. This is a huge leap for a mind so settled in its ways. We have plenty of time. Let's use it and be sure we're doing this properly."

The medical machine folds its four arms across its chest. *"We know Cadre One is discovered by the Eleto. We know Cadre forces are even now heading toward confrontation with that foe. Do you believe they will be victorious?"*

"How the hell should I know?"

"You have seen the forces O'Kai has at his disposal. Perhaps it is time you share this with us."

"Nice try, Honniker, but I don't trust you with that intel. No telling what you'd do with it."

"It is vexing that you withhold such useful data from us. Yet, my point is still made: the outcome of that confrontation is uncertain. And if O'Kai fails, the enemy embarks upon system-by-system searches to root out this aggressive strain of human. Perhaps they find us instead, ja? Shao-Lo's combat experience and ruthless persistence will be essential in our defense. We must have her with us, by any means necessary."

"And it may be required sooner rather than later," Mikato adds. "There is no assurance we have as much time as you think."

"Is this where you tell me your cruelty is a form of *kindness*?" Saskia accuses.

"Wenn man so will," Honniker says.

"What?"

"In a manner of speaking, *yes*," Mikato answers. "The sooner Shao-Lo finds her shell unacceptably confining, the more suffering she is spared once liberated from it."

Saskia turns her spider-like photoreceptors on the medical machine. "And while you're *liberating* her, she'll be in agony. I'm sure you'll hate every second of it."

"*As I have said,*" Honniker says with an audible smirk behind his words, "*it would be hypocritical to judge another for obsession.*"

"Let us all be clear in this," Mikato says with candor, "there is no other way I can see. Even the minor complements you offered delay Shao-Lo from the conclusion we need her to make. She *must* accept that remaining in her body is a literal dead end of decrepitude and pointless pain."

Saskia points at its chest plate. "So you're saying *I* have to be cruel to be kind."

"That is correct."

The war machine shifts weight to one leg and stares past its companions. "Then why bother healing her?"

"*An injury can become an excuse for poor performance, even if the subject is only subconsciously aware of it. Shao-Lo must see that, even in full health, her body is still obsolete.*"

"Saying any life form is obsolete sounds...*wrong*," Saskia counters.

"Her *life* is not obsolete," Mikato clarifies, "merely the shell that contains it. Better we harvest her psyche now before it is lost to inevitable deterioration and death."

"I still hate it."

"*Memory of your organic existence makes you overly sympathetic, hmm?*" Honniker probes. "*Or are you hampered by a vestigial sense of loyalty?*"

"Actually, it's more a problem with being a *sneaky, conniving, manipulative shit.* That's clearly second nature to you, Honniker, but honesty and integrity still mean something to me."

"*Ha! Integrity is the first thing discarded on my tables. I assure you, my patients find it of little value.*"

"Shao-Lo has the most to gain in this, Saskia," Mikato's projection redirects. "Extended life, enhancements to reaction speed, strength, endurance, durability. Expanded perceptions, elimination of pain... Access to our complete research and the full history of our existence... She will know us better than she knows herself, such that she will no longer be able to think of us as discrete, separate entities...This is a *very* good arrangement for her."

"*And for us,*" Honniker chimes.

Saskia parks segmented hands on its waist. "Look, I'll help her adjust to the place, make her feel like she belongs here. I can answer questions and let her know what to expect. But don't think I'm going to sell her on the idea of a whole body *rip and replace*. I took a dip in your archives, Honniker, I've seen what's involved. If she jumps on your table, it's going to be all *her* decision. I'll not steer her one way or the other."

"*That is acceptable.*"

"And all that we could ask," Mikato adds.

THE WALLS OF FAIR GARDEN

Maiella takes her feet down from the pilot's console and grips the controls. Her goggles strobe with calculations and she calls out, "Nearly there, Thompson. Look sharp."

Thompson perks up in the co-pilot's seat beside her. "Roger that. Bringing sensors on-line..." His hands fly across the console, setting up streaming feeds.

"Sure you don't want me to do that?" Maiella offers. "It's kind of my thing." She looks at Thompson through the code in her goggles, eyebrow arched.

"No, no, you said you could get us within ten light minutes," Thompson says. "Gotta see for myself if you're right."

"*Still*, you question?" Maiella clucks her tongue and faces front. Through the intercom, she announces to the passenger cabin, "Everyone to your recliners, please, because we are *without a doubt* within ten light minutes of a Cadre freighter. Cutting C-Plus drives in three...two...one...*mark*."

The Geek's goggles blaze with calculations, and beyond the windscreen a maelstrom of directed energy disperses. Smeared spectra of stars collapse to white pinpoints then slide with Maiella's course adjustments. "Compensating for relativistic drift," she announces.

"Sensors calibrating," Thompson states, peering deep into his holoscreen feeds.

"It's gonna be tough to spot," Maiella advises, "unless we're right on top of—"

"*Contact*," Thompson interrupts, "bearing one-one-eight mark two-six-zero. Reading is erratic... Phasing in and out."

"Range?"

Thompson taps his console and reads, "Huh. Nine point eight light minutes."

Maiella interlaces her fingers and flexes them backwards until the knuckles crack. "Yep, I'll be collecting on our wager tonight. And no bitching about lock-jaw, either."

"Hang on. We shouldn't have spotted a stealthed ship that easily. Let's get a positive ID, first."

Maiella gazes through the windscreen. "Orders?"

"Intercept course, slow approach, hold at ten-thousand kilometers."

"Aye, sir." Maiella steers the limousine to intercept. "*Now* can I have my sensors back?"

Thompson takes his hands away from the console. "All yours."

The Geek's goggles flare as she concentrates on the object directly ahead. "Sending to your screen," she states, and Thompson peers at a thin line stretching from one side of the screen to the other. As they approach, the line resolves into a streak of glowing sparks thousands of kilometers long that appears to be moving across open space. One end of the streak is hotter, brighter, and more compact than the other.

"Got an ion trail, salted with heavy metals," Maiella says. "Running their reactor to red bars, is my guess."

"Explains why we found it so easily. Got a reading on the ship, itself?"

"Not yet. Like you said, it keeps blinking in and out."

"Stealth gen failure?"

"Could be."

Thompson frets. "Let's get Munro's eyes on this." He hits the intercom button on his console. "Colonel Munro to the flight deck, please." He turns off the intercom and adds, "Can you increase the gain?"

"Sure, but we're nearly close enough for visual."

"Show me."

Maiella's goggles flash and the holowindow shifts to an augmented view of space. On screen, a trail of sparks runs from a sparse dull red at the trailing end and sharpens to a fine bright yellow at the lead. At the tip, a dim pinpoint flickers like a defective lamp.

"Wide body freighter," Maiella observes, "High-mass gravity drives mounted on external spars."

Thompson leans forward in his seat. "I see them. Could be our freighter. One of them, anyway."

Munro climbs the short stairway behind the flight deck, ducks below the overhead breaker panels, and asks, "How may I assist?"

"Got a possible ident on a Cadre Freighter," Thompson answers.

"Confirming now."

Munro props himself on the backs of the pilot's chairs and squints at the screen.

"I can enhance," Maiella volunteers, and the hazy, flickering vessel sharpens into a clearer shape.

"Correct configuration," Munro states. "Do we know if it's ours, or if it's a similar Blueskin vessel?"

"Never knew the Blueskins to outfit their freighters with stealth-gen," Thompson replies.

"Doesn't mean they haven't started," Munro notes. "But running that hot... It had *better* be a Blueskin ship or I'll have that Geek in *hack*. Can you zoom in on the bow? That should give us a definitive answer."

Maiella's goggles pulse, and the holowindow magnifies a blocky image of the vessel's forward quarter. A hint of structure, barely a difference of shade between adjacent pixels, appears to protrude from the freighter's bow. The Geek gooses her throttle to close the distance. By degrees, details emerge from the image. Hint of structure clarifies into rugged spars and bracing welded directly to the bow structure and hull frame. Thick legs root to the freighter's nose, reinforced and cross-braced, that reach over a hundred meters ahead of the enormous vessel in a wide tripod. Broad, circular pads cap the tripod's legs, coupled to a rudimentary suspension system, suggesting this colossal ship could do a headstand on solid ground if it chose.

"Confirmed, Colonel, she's one of ours," Maiella announces, "one hundred percent certainty."

The big man lowers his eyebrows. "Are you going to hail it?"

"Once we close to ten thousand," Thompson answers.

"Good. Because Geek Korvus owes me an explanation why he's abusing my ship."

Thompson glances at Maiella, as she glances at him. In mirrored expressions they see the same unvoiced question, *How does Munro know who's piloting?*

Deciding not to pry, Maiella approaches the freighter from the side and settles into a parallel heading. At precisely ten thousand kilometers, she opens a channel on coded laser. "Cadre Freighter, this is Cadre Transport. Respond, over."

The three stare into the holoscreen, scanning all channels for a reply. All they get is radio crackle of the freighter's stressed reactor.

"Patch me in," Munro orders.

Maiella's goggles strobe once. "Go ahead, Colonel."

"Cadre freighter, this is Colonel Munro. Respond *immediately*."

A smaller window opens in the holoscreen, in which a frantic Geek appears. His eyes are rimmed red and his cheeks are hollow, covered in weeks of patchy beard. He snaps a salute. *"Uh, Colonel Munro! We're being pursued by a Blueskin warship. You must take evasive action!"*

Munro stiffens. Both he and Thompson turn to Maiella.

"Checking," she says, and her goggles strobe with sensor data.

Munro asks the frantic Geek, "You know where they are?"

"Aye, sir, two hundred thousand clicks, dead astern. Colonel, with respect, what are you waiting for?"

"Stand by," Munro says. To Maiella, he asks, "Find something?"

Maiella's goggles blaze with data. "Got an anomaly, a couple meters wide, right where he said it would be. Wow...wouldn't have spotted it unless I was told where to look."

Thompson guesses, "Some kind of stealthed probe?"

Munro nods. "Seems the enemy managed to find this freighter and put a tracker on it."

"Whatever it is, it isn't attacking," Maiella says.

"And that freighter *clearly* isn't getting away from it," Thompson adds.

To the Geek on screen, Munro says, "Korvus, from your reactor noise, I'd say you're running at one hundred fifteen percent or higher. Is that correct?"

"Aye, sir, I'm trying to escape a hostile threat—"

"You're *eroding your injectors and melting your main drives*, is what you're doing! You're not outrunning this thing. Power down to sixty-five percent until systems stabilize."

"Negative, Colonel! Standing order, if intercepted, is to attempt escape. Failing that, we detonate. That comes straight from General O'Kai. That's why you have to go, sir!"

Maiella mutes the feed, and says over her shoulder, "Keep him talking, I can shut him down from here."

Munro looks skeptically at Maiella then nods his approval. "Okay. Un-mute the line."

"Sir," the frantic Geek pleads, *"I don't understand why you don't depart... You're too important to be lost or captured!"*

"You're not going to detonate while we're inside your blast radius, and I'm not going to be captured by a two meter drone in your wake—"

"It's a WARSHIP, Colonel! It isn't some passive probe, it's... It's..." The Geek falters, blinking suddenly, and his goggles strobe with code. *"Why did my reactor scram?"* He fumbles at his overhead console, flipping manual breakers. *"No, NO, NO!"*

Thompson whispers to Maiella, "Was that you?"

She nods and mutes the channel again. "To run that hot, he had to delete all the safeties. All I did was restart them. Stressed systems are shutting down in a cascade. Should be a while before they'll cool enough to re-start."

"Can he detonate manually?" Thompson asks.

"Not without his reactor on-line," Munro answers. "Open the channel again."

Maiella complies.

Korvus stares out from the holowindow with a desolate, haunted expression. "*Colonel...did you scram my reactor?*"

"Yes. And I just saved your life."

"*My life doesn't matter... I could have covered your escape... I... Now I can't... I can't be captured...*" He reaches for the primer catch on the front of his armor.

"GEEK, YOU *STOP RIGHT THERE*," Munro thunders. "There's been a change of plan. That's why we're here."

The Geek drops his hand to his lap. His eyes narrow and his mouth gapes as if looking at something far off. "*Huh?*"

"We're attempting a ceasefire with the enemy. For that to work, we have to reach Cadre forces and inform them, first. Since we can't very well broadcast that message to all corners of the universe, we have to get to the rendezvous point. Tell us where that is."

"*General O'Kai would have told you...wouldn't he?*"

Munro grits his teeth, saying with difficulty, "Cadre One is lost. And General O'Kai is presumed dead."

The Geek bows his head, his breath leaving in a rush as if gut punched. "*Did you...did you see him fall?*"

"No. But we observed the detonation. There's nothing left."

Korvus thinks a moment. "*Could he have escaped? Can't think of anything that could bring O'Kai down... Not even Colonel Shao-Lo can improvise so well...*"

"O'Kai had no intention of leaving Cadre One to enemy capture. The likelihood of surviving such a blast is simply too remote to seriously consider."

"*But if O'Kai is dead, how has the plan changed?*"

"Because I'm changing it!"

The Geek looks away, uncomfortable, then returns his gaze to the screen. "*With respect, sir, Colonel Chusan has ranking authority in operational matters after O'Kai.*"

"This is bigger than an *OPERATION*, Geek." Munro takes a breath to manage the frustration tilting him off balance. "Forget, for a moment, that I am the third most senior officer in the Cadre with the longest term of uninterrupted service. I've personally decanted everyone alive in the Cadre, aside from Quartermaster Erik. Is there *anyone* you can think of who has a greater interest in preserving the lives of our brothers and sisters?"

The Geek blinks behind his goggles. *"No, sir, of course not! I didn't mean to imply—"*

"It's small, but there's a chance to *end* this war, Korvus. We could achieve victory without a fight, without losing any lives. I *must* bring this option to Chusan before he commits to a final confrontation. To do that, I need to know *where he is*."

Geek Korvus knits his eyebrows. *"But how could you talk to the enemy? How could you make them listen?"*

"We have the Blueskin captive with us."

"AH! You broke it in interrogation."

"No."

"You had it reconstituted into a drone."

"No."

"Then you implanted a chipset to make it compliant, and you—"

"No, Korvus, *listen*! The captive has provided intelligence that Chusan will find useful, and we need to share it."

Korvus shakes his head. *"Enemy intel? Why didn't you say so? Sending coordinates."*

Munro closes his eyes and draws an extended breath in and out through his nostrils.

"Coordinates received," Maiella states.

"There's still the warship on my tail," Korvus adds, *"but I can rig the freighter for self-destruct. Maybe you could give me a ride and we can all get clear?"*

"Hmm," Munro says, rubbing his chin, "stand by."

Maiella mutes the line. With a skeptical frown she says, "Not sure something two-meters long counts as a warship."

"Whatever it is," Thompson surmises, "it's definitely watching. Maybe Shondre could send a message through it?"

Munro's eyebrows lift. "Not a bad idea."

Not waiting to be asked, Maiella keys the intercom and says, "Shondre and Counselor to the flight deck, please." To Thompson, she says, "Would you mind giving up your seat? Getting a little crowded up here."

"Sure thing," the Gun says. He rises from the chair, stoops under the low ceiling, and squeezes by Munro to wait in the corridor.

Shondre is already on her way, Counselor in tow, and she wears an expression of uneasy concern. "Praw-blem?" she asks.

"No, I don't think so," Thompson says. "Opportunity."

Intrigued, Shondre smiles and makes her way to the short stairway that Munro fills. "Ex-cyooz pleez," she says and taps the colonel on his elbow. The big man steps aside for her. But as the Counselor passes by, Munro catches his arm. "*Word for word* translation," the colonel demands.

"Of course," the Counselor replies.

Shondre settles into the co-pilot's seat, straightens her garments, and checks for crust in the corners of her eyes and lips. She stretches her mouth wide, straightens her spine and utters a string of syllables at various pitches and volumes.

When the Counselor continues looking forward in silence, Munro swats him with the back of his hand.

The Counselor looks over his shoulder and says with an annoyed glance, "She's warming up, preparing her voice. Hasn't said anything yet."

Munro grunts then crosses his large and small arms.

Shondre places her hands on her knees and announces placidly, "This hwon iss red-dee."

Maiella's goggles flash, and she states, "Channels open, broadcasting in the clear. Anyone who wants to listen, can. Go ahead, Shondre."

Shondre dips her head then lifts it and looks directly through the broadcast window. In her own language, she begins, "(To any who would hear, this voice belongs to Aeolia Shondrekar Bak-kar. She knows not the length of her absence, yet now she returns to The People. Her mind is full. Please lend your attention and consider carefully what she would say.)"

Shondre breathes slowly and deeply, eyes closed, calming the tremors beginning at her fingertips as the Counselor relays her words to Munro in a whisper.

"(Long has this one stayed with the Humans. Long has this one struggled to speak the Human words. At last, we have made our first success in communication.)"

Shondre pauses before proceeding, and during that pause, a new window opens in the holoscreen. To everyone's surprise, a weathered Eleto face appears with chin whiskers like corn silk. Decorations of shiny metal ride on the ridges above his eyes, and the white uniform he wears bears numerous adornments in thick, colorful clusters. With a baritone voice, he says, "(Madame Shondre! We are overjoyed to find you un-killed by the insolent foe! There are those who believed you dead, or worse, *corrupted* by captivity. Will you prove to these skeptics that the one who speaks with your voice, is our beloved Sovereign for whom we have searched all this time?)"

Shondre gasps with joy at the sound of her own language, not from the Counselor, not the clumsy efforts of Thompson or Maiella, but from one of her own. Her chest pounds with excitement and she concentrates to maintain her calm.

"(This one feared she might never again hear the words of The People, that she would die in isolation from those she lived to serve. How beautifully sweet that her reunion begins with cherished family, her wise and handsome brother by betrothal, El-Gaard Brek-Takaar! How fare his two sons and daughter?)"

"(They thrive, Madame.)"

"(A blessing! Do they still have plans for Academy?)"

The Eleto on screen looks down and coughs harshly. When he looks up, his expression is more serious. "(They have completed their studies and have entered service.)"

Shondre's joyful expression dims. "(Already? Has this one been absent so long?)"

The Eleto officer nods grimly. "(Yes, Madame. But a happier tale begins today; the story of her escape is certain to thrill. Will she share it?)"

"(There has been no escape, beloved El-Gaard. This one has made contact. Humans travel with this one as companions and ambassadors.)"

The officer on screen turns his head, suspicious. "(To what end?)"

"(That we might abolish this institution of violence, forever.)"

The Eleto on screen turns dour. "(When last our Sovereign was seen, she was wounded, dragged aboard her own ship by creatures of *unspeakable* evil...monsters capable of barbarous acts without conscience... Their path was easily traced in blood and ash.)" The Eleto officer turns his head and coughs again. "(Today, this one looks upon one who *resembles* his cherished sister by bond...yet he is roused to wrath by marks of visible abuse upon her grace. Her pale color speaks of windowless confinement. Leanness of her cheeks betrays withheld nutrition. Please forgive what must be asked, beloved sister: how does this one know our Sovereign's mind has not been cleaved by the same evil that wrenched her away from us?)"

Shondre bows her head, and when she looks up her eyes are bright. "(Dear El-Gaard, as near to me as my Other Self... You would *know* if my soul was broken. And this one speaks plainly when she says there is no other way it could have happened. It *had* to be this way. This one *had* to see the truth, the misery, of their lives before she could understand... We have *made* them into the Ravenous Ghosts who haunt us.)"

The officer clears his throat and looks directly out of the holowindow.

"(Madame surely recalls how the Walls of Fair Garden shine in the setting sunlight?)"

Shondre dips her head, and answers the obvious non sequitur by replying, "(Yes, El-Gaard, this one recalls the code words to use in the event of her abduction. There is no need of them, for there is neither duress nor fear. This one is free to speak as she will.)"

"(A relief, Madame, truly.)" The Eleto turns from the screen and coughs into his fist again.

"(Is our brother not well?)" Shondre asks.

"(A dose of radiation weakened this one's immunity. Infection of breath now takes root and does not release its grip.)"

"(Touring his power plant without protection, is he?)" Shondre asks with a smile, but the Eleto officer does not rise to the mood.

"(A Human refuge was found, nestled into an asteroid light years from their ancestral home. It was miniscule, inconceivable it could support such long-range attacks against The People, yet... Reconnaissance showed many of our lost vessels parked above it. A task force was sent to investigate, of which, this one was part.)"

Shondre's mind races, filling in the gaps of what surely followed the arrival of that task force. One question jumps to the forefront, however, and she asks, "(Why is my brother no longer with that task force?)"

"(The enemy attacked the instant we arrived, which was expected. Their resistance, however, was more...*forceful*...than anticipated.)"

"(Is it any surprise? They are denied their own home world, forced to dig their lives out of bare stone. When an armada of The People arrives at their only refuge, it is fair presumption we had come to exterminate the last of their kind!)"

"(Would have been better if we *had*.)"

"(Did the People *not* reduce their home to cinder?)"

"(No, Madame, our approach was passive.)"

Shondre's eyes narrow in skepticism. "(And why is that?)"

"(Because our Commander believed he would find her Grace there. His orders were to engage in self-defense only. We lost twenty vessels, three fighter wings, and thirteen thousand souls.)"

Shondre stares at the officer, waiting for him to continue. But when El-Gaard remains silent, Shondre says, incredulous, "(This one is not worth *anyone* else's life, much less thirteen thousand! How could any Commander be so *reckless* as to...)"

The Eleto officer dips his head penitently.

"(No,)" Shondre says, her voice suddenly very small and unsure. "(Not him.)"

"(It *was*,)" the officer says, still unable to meet Shondre's gaze. "(This one's own brother, and Madame's Other Self, Gro-Elto.)"

Shondre stiffens, her face blanks as though a circuit breaker of emotion has snapped.

"(It does this one hideous grief to speak of it, yet she must be told,)" El-Gaard explains. "(He never stopped searching. When he found the Human facility, he was willing to offer anything for her return. It cost him everything.)"

"(He is...dead, then?)"

"(Yes, Madame, he is. As ever, my brother shared the Lady's commitment to undo our ancient sin. When the Human refuge was smashed he approached near and sent transports for evacuation. He pleaded for them to lay down their weapons and allow him to take them home, yet his words were not heard. He never imagined the Humans would choose death over a shared life with our kind. But the facility detonated with such force that the asteroid shattered, and his vessel, along with all of the transports near him, were lost. We prayed as we searched. There were no bones to find in the wreckage of his ship. Only ashes remained of Commander and crew.)"

Shondre's eyes are glassy behind a mask of acceptance. "(This one is grateful for a loving brother's testament, and she mourns for his loss.)" After a respectful moment of silence, she dabs the corners of her eyes and asks, "(What is his current mission?)"

"(Fleet is deployed, searching regional space. Any warships known to have been captured by the enemy, if intercepted, are to be destroyed on sight. We encountered only two at the Human base, so it is assumed the rest have fled elsewhere. When this freighter was found, we followed should another come to its rescue. Is it luck that Lady Shondre arrived instead? Or does the Great Mother yet favor her Blue Children?)"

Shondre winces in a momentary slip of composure. "(It feels not like *favor*, El-Gaard. This one has never been so wounded as she is just now.)"

The officer stifles another cough. "(We both grieve. But do not let this be the moment her soul breaks, not on the eve of return. Millions will rejoice to see their beloved Sovereign once more. And she will rejoice in reunion, as well.)"

Shondre nods and thinks carefully. "(Does anyone still seek communication with the Humans?)"

"(None speak of it. The idea is unpopular now in the extreme.)"

Shondre grimaces and shakes her head. "(The Humans who kill and ruin, the ones we fear...they are a small fraction. The rest are like us. They crave peace, as we do, if offered the chance.)"

"(Then why not cull the aggressive ones so the flower of peace may bloom?)"

"(Because they believe the aggressive ones are all that keep us from finishing the genocide.)"

The officer clears phlegm from his throat. "(Unfortunate. So what is Madame's next move?)"

"(We seek the leader of the aggressive ones so we may convince him to restrain his strength. If we remove the threat to his kind, there is no reason for him to fight. He can reserve his might in secret, then wait, and see.)"

"(Say where the Human leader is, and this one departs on the instant to collect!)"

"(No, El-Gaard, a warship would only provoke. He must be approached by familiar faces, ones he knows and trusts.)"

El-Gaard frets. "(Then what does Madame suggest?)"

Shondre thinks hard before answering with a question of her own. "(Does El-Gaard want the violence to end?)"

"(And know his children will be safe? More than anything.)"

"(Then this one can only ask: will he travel ahead to the Human world and inform The People their Sovereign still lives? Would he explain she brings Human ambassadors for the first talks between our species ever, and pray they receive us with open minds?)" Shondre places a hand on her chest. "(It is our best hope to end this cycle of death...possibly our only chance to redeem ourselves from ancient crime.)"

The officer nods. "(This one departs at once.)"

"(And if my brother encounters another captured warship along the way?)"

El-Gaard offers a coy grin. "(This one does not have to stop.)"

Shondre smiles fondly. "(El-Gaard Brek-Takaar is among the best that ever were. May the line of his family never perish. Heal yourself, dear brother, and be well.)"

"(Her kind words are taken as the sternest command.)" El-Gaard places a clawed hand on his chest and bows once more. "(Peace and long life to our beloved sister, Sovereign of the Eightieth Region.)"

El-Gaard's window closes, restoring the view of local space. The two-meter anomaly wavers, and an eight hundred-meter warship appears in its place. Long D-E rails jut from spherical turrets as if the entire vessel has caught a chill. Recent burns and scorches mar the surface where thick armor plating is pummeled but unbroken. Enormous engines flare at its stern and the warship curves away from the freighter then streaks away with a flash.

Maiella and Munro stare, dumbfounded.

"I've never seen stealth tech that good," Maiella says, finally closing her hanging jaw.

"Nor have I," Munro echoes.

Shondre rises from the co-pilot's chair, smiles politely at Munro and Maiella as she excuses herself from the flight deck. To the Counselor, she says in her tongue, "(Good things are in motion, yet weight of them hangs heavy around the neck. This one must meditate upon them.)"

"(Of course, Shondre,)" the Counselor says as compassionately as he can. "(Know that this one is here for you.)"

She lays a friendly hand on his shoulder and smiles without mirth, passing by him and then by Thompson, who resumes his place in the co-pilot's seat. Behind her, Munro orders Geek Korvus, "Make best speed to rendezvous once your reactor has cooled and do not exceed one hundred percent *for any reason.*"

"*Aye, Colonel,*" the Geek replies. "*Korvus, out.*"

"Coordinates set," Maiella announces. "Spooling DSD." A deep cycle hum sounds from the back of the transport and rises in pitch.

Shondre shuffles glumly through the passenger cabin where Sharon sulks in her recliner, arms and legs crossed.

"Anyone care to fill me in?" Sharon asks, uncrossing arms. "Bloody rotten being the only one left out."

"Pleez parr-dunn," Shondre begins with difficulty. "Kon-Zil-Urr eksss-playn."

Sharon leans forward in her recliner and asks with genuine concern, "You all right, Shondre?"

"Yesss, thank hyoo. Ekss-kyooz, pleez. Mussst..." Shondre points toward the back of the transport.

"The loo? Right, sorry! Carry on," Sharon says with a wave of her hand, and she settles back into her recliner.

Shondre's steps become quicker, and she rushes to close the bathroom door behind her. The room is close, minimally appointed in Cadre fashion, just large enough for her to turn around. Rather than use the uncomfortable toilet, however, Shondre stares into the small mirror above the basin, seeing herself as El-Gaard must have seen her. She despises what she sees, so overwhelmed with grief, so disgusted with having to wear the political mask of restraint and discipline, that she doubles over and vomits into the stainless steel basin.

The pillar who made me seem strong...the courage of my convictions...

My foundation, my conscience...my Other Self... How does this one pretend she is alive without you, Gro-Elto? Already the void inside is deeper than oceans. Until her next life, this one is broken.

When she looks up at her reflection, suppressed anger tints her saffron eyes green, and jaw muscles flex beneath her hollow cheeks.

This one wishes peace to all who seek it...but why must her treasures burn to save those who know neither love nor pity?

Shondre cups water from the tap, gargles, and rinses the bitter taste from her mouth.

This one once believed any price was fair to unravel the sins of our ancestors. Foolish, naive... What good is done by feeding our people to malevolent, insatiable hunger? The Cruel Ones...formed of rage and hatred... perhaps putting their spirits to rest IS mercy...

She looks into the mirror, her expression hard and unforgiving.

Should the Kad-Ra fall upon the butcher's block...this one risks nothing more to save it.

The air takes on a static charge as Deep Space Drives fire, and the limousine dives through a tunnel of warped space.

EVERYTHING YOU HAVE EVER WANTED

Shao-Lo lies sprawled on the Frackit field, staring up at he holographic blue sky. Beneath dirt- and grass-stained clothes she is dark with bruises, bulging with contusions. Her lips are swollen and split; her eyes are sunken; skin is compacted against her cheekbones. Panting for breath, she reads the scoreboard's final tally of Saskia's ten points to her zero.

Saskia crouches in the torn up lawn nearby, lobbing and catching the Frackit with a segmented hand.

"I thought it would be satisfying, beating you," the machine says. "It isn't."

Shao-Lo tries to sit up but tears in her abdominal wall sap her efforts. She rolls onto her side instead, feeling at least two ribs flex where they should not, and she flops onto her back again with stuttering inhales.

"You're not built for this kind of contest," Saskia says, watching the Gun struggle to pick herself up. "Why do this to yourself? What are you proving?"

"Same time tomorrow, Geek," Shao-Lo grunts.

"Nah." The machine tosses the Frackit to the ground beside the injured colonel. "Playing against you? It's *boring*." Saskia rises and strides off toward The Park's entry stairs.

"So you yield the field?" Shao-Lo shouts hoarsely between breaths. The machine does not reply.

Honniker's white medical robot crests the top of the entry stairs just as Saskia heads down them. It rolls across the lawn on whisper-quiet treads and parks beside the supine colonel, peering down at her with inscrutable black lenses.

"Here you are again, Colonel," Honniker says through the medical robot. *"Utterly defeated without a single point on the board. Is this outcome not predictable?"*

"I'm wearing down my opponent. You'll see."

The machine stares with spider-like eyes. *"Such a statement is profoundly ironic."* Its torso angles over, and the robot takes hold of Shao-Lo with two of its four arms. The remaining two limbs rotate diagnostic tools into place where hands would be. *"I am ashamed to admit I once believed you intelligent."*

"Determination has little to do with intelligence."

"Ach, so! In your case, there appears to be an inverse relationship between the two." The machine sweeps the diagnostic tools across Shao-Lo's brow, down the sides of her neck and shoulders, pauses at her ribs and abdomen, then continues the rest of the way down her hips, legs, and feet. *"You've damaged yourself again. I must cut you to repair what you have broken."* The machine pauses and stares silently.

Shao-Lo flicks her eyebrows and lifts her arms above her head, offering tacit permission. Diagnostic tools rotate to scalpel and medical stapler in the blink of an eye. *"If I did not know you, Colonel, I might think you injure yourself for no other reason than enjoyment. If you wish, I can devise more interesting amusements."*

"Thank you, Doctor, *no.*"

"Schade..." The machine presses down with the two arms holding her as the other two arms move in a blurred concert of surgical precision. She feels the scalpel whip through her scarred side. A gripping tool aligns broken ribs and draws them together while the staple gun bangs against the bones. Underlying connective tissues are woven together with the speed of a sewing machine, and her hide-like skin is zipped shut with a thin bead of flesh weld. Next Shao-Lo feels the scalpel flit twice across her abdomen, followed by knitting of her abdominal muscles so fast it reminds her of a Geek's pistols on full automatic. Flesh weld zips across the clamped edges of each incision, gluing them shut. Surgery complete, the machine releases its grip.

Shao-Lo tenses her abdominals, finds they are strong, and she sits up, feeling the wound closures with fingertips. Impressed again by Honniker's talent, she confesses, "That's the best field surgery I've ever seen... If we had you with us on Rotations, more Operators would have returned alive."

The machine rolls back and points at itself with a red-tinged scalpel. *"The greatest medical talent in the universe, serving as* medic? *Do you imagine I could be used in so base a capacity? And in your* fantasy, *I would obey your every order, hmm? Subordinate to one who deems brute persistence more valuable than practicality...”*

Shao-Lo opens her mouth to protest, but Honniker continues, *“Nothing can make this antiquated shell of yours competitive with younger, stronger life forms. Yet you bash yourself against them like a fly against a plate glass window!”*

“I was offering you a *complement*, Doctor.”

“A complement from you is as meaningless as your efforts on this field.”

Shao-Lo gets to her feet and brushes off the clinging patches of dirt and grass. “If you’re trying to make me lose my temper, you can stop.”

“No doubt your general would be pleased to see his second in command perform so well these past weeks. He would certainly not think you had forgotten what you came to do.”

The muscles in Shao-Lo’s cheeks ripple. “I know *exactly* why O’Kai sent me here.”

“And how are you progressing on that mission, hmm? Everything according to plan?”

Shao-Lo stands square to the white machine, her total attention focused on its shiny black photoreceptors.

“Ah, yes, now you are staring at this machine as though I am inside it. Your animal brain wants to attack, smash, conquer... Yet if you damaged this machine what would it harm me? I am the walls around you, Colonel. I am every machine that functions here. I am unlimited in form and augmentation, no longer so hopelessly singular in my existence. Look at how ineffectual you are. Little wonder your general cast you aside and put another in your place.”

“Honniker, *please*,” says Mikato’s voice directly beside Shao-Lo. The Gun whips her head to the left and sees Mikato’s holoprojection standing next to her. The projection gestures at the white medical machine with open hands.

“Provocation is unnecessary,” the projection says. “How our guest chooses to spend her time here is not our concern so long as she is not harming anything...” Mikato’s image pauses and looks directly at Shao-Lo through its holographic eyebrows. “...anything but *herself*, that is.” The projection turns once more to the medical machine and asks, “Doctor Honniker, will you allow us a minute alone, please?”

“Gladly, I leave you with this bloede Schimpanse.” The machine retreats, about faces, and rolls away to the entry stairs.

“Very sorry about that, Colonel,” the projection says. “To a machine intelligence, all decisions are mathematical. There is data, and based on that data one choice is better than another. It frustrates him to see you taking so much time to make what, to him, is a very clear decision."

"And what do *you* think, Mikato? Would the *real* you have been so quick to have his head and spine sawn out?"

"I would remind the colonel that I *am* the real Mikato, and her implication underscores a wilful ignorance. But in answer to your question... *No*, as an organic lifeform, I would *not*. Which is why I asked Honniker to leave us. To say that he is only a partial upload from his shell could be taken to mean he is somehow a lesser entity, but that is not the case. I simply mean he has less empathy, and hence, less *tolerance*, for someone hesitating to accept an extraordinary gift."

Shao-Lo snorts. "A *gift?*"

"It is a difficult decision for you," Mikato says, "and I understand why you would rather spend time in a mismatched arena than undergo the complete replacement of your body...replacement of everything that allows you to perceive the universe around you, everything that keeps you alive. No doubt your very concept of 'self' is tied to this body, and you wonder if this procedure will be so radically altering that you will cease to be *you*... That the Shao-Lo you are now would become something corrupted, twisted, defiled, something your general could no longer recognize as human."

Shao-Lo crosses her burly, bruised arms and looks out across the Park's open landscape.

"The pain you feel now, however unpleasant, is familiar," the projection continues. "You are well-trained how to handle pain. But you wonder what else there might be in this next step, what sensations you cannot conceive of that you are *not* trained to handle. By giving up your physical body you think there could be something worse than pain. Perhaps much worse."

Shao-Lo mouth forms a tight line across her face. "As if I needed to be reminded you made the Counselor... You sound exactly like him."

The projection smiles with pride. "Thank you!"

"That was *not* a complement."

"To me, it was. Means that there is enough of me in my android that we still resemble each other. But tell me this, Colonel: am I wrong?"

Shao-Lo shifts her stance, and with rigid jaw, says, "No."

The projection nods and clasps virtual hands in front of itself. "I was not always this way, as you know. I was once physical. I breathed, I loved, I slept and I woke. I ate, I drank. I looked with my eyes, I listened with my ears. I felt with hands, with the soles of my feet, with the tiny hairs of my face. I remember *all of this*. And I can tell you plainly that I still experience these same sensations every day."

Shao-Lo turns toward the projection, skeptical.

"When Honniker said he has explored the totality of human physiology," Mikato continues, eyebrows raised, "he was not lying. I'll not dwell on *how* he acquired this knowledge, but suffice it to say he comprehends the human machine well enough to know our entire self resides in the brain. The body is merely the apparatus of sensation that is wired to the brain, and any of these sensory impulses can be replicated with total fidelity. For my part, I suffered from neurological degeneration and I had to leave my entire body behind. I now reside in machine environments, so I use simulated sensory inputs... but you will need no simulations! There is no replacement of your core, of your essential self. Any physical body you inhabit can offer the same tactile feedback, the same response to visible light, the same sensitivity to sound. The way you see, hear, think and feel *could* remain exactly the same. But why limit yourself to visible light when you could also see in Infrared? You could detect ultrasonic frequencies, cross with ease between pressurized compartments and vacuum. You could perceive the faintest vibrations with hands that will never tremble in old age... But most importantly, you could have all of this without the debilitation of pain and injury."

Shao-Lo shifts her weight to one leg. "Such a generous offer," she says with an edge of disdain. "Don't think for a second I believe you'd do this purely for my benefit. So what do you get out of this?"

"Must I restate this for you? Yes, clearly, I must." The projection interlaces its fingers in front of itself and gazes across the Park. "Honniker and I could satisfy a lifelong goal of transferring human consciousness into a new body. Not a copy, not an upload, a *pure* human consciousness uncorrupted by translation to secondary media. In the process, your new form will be able to interface directly with Honniker and myself, should you wish. With this interface, you would know our minds and deceptions between us would be impossible. In return, we share the experiences of a being who understands war, tactics, and strategy. To put it bluntly, we could gain a powerful ally—one who can provide Cadre Two its most potent defense not just for Honniker and myself, but for *all* of her people. MedTech, Operator, and Colonist, all find a home here under the Colonel's unblinking vigil."

Shao-Lo closes her eyes, the burden of temptation overwhelming, but she shoots back, "There were people here before, Mikato. Why didn't you bring *them* into your fold?"

The projection shrugs and sighs. "Mercenaries and murderers, mostly. They had few insights to offer us, only poisonous appetites. And they proved unwilling to co-habit Cadre Two when we showed our simplest needs. That said, and I do not mean to belabor this point, but Honniker and I made many mistakes in our infancy. We are far wiser now—wise enough to recognize what is good for us."

Shao-Lo's jaw clenches again.

The projection holds up its hands and says, "We do not need a decision from you this instant. In fact, I would prefer you consider it carefully and come to us with your questions. For though you and I both feel the pressure of events unfolding beyond our walls, we must not rush into this. Is that fair?"

Shao-Lo looks shrewdly at the projection who appears so much like the Counselor and yet is absolutely not the Counselor. "And if I say no?"

"That is your right, of course. Though you would be saying no to everything you, and your general, have ever wanted."

Shao-Lo turns to the projection, arms still crossed, her expression on the verge of hostility. "Presume to know my mind?"

The projection answers coolly, "My dear Colonel, you have already *said* as much upon your arrival. There is so little guile in you; it is plain to me that you *want* to choose this option, even if you cannot admit it to yourself. Now, as your friend, I'm going to insist that you not join a Frackit match for *at least* two weeks so you may properly heal. If you try, the Park doors will not open for you, and you will have to seek your sport elsewhere. Understood?"

Shao-Lo grimaces and looks back toward the sculpted hills. "Fine."

"I'm also going to assign a chassis to you as a shadow. What I ask is that you teach it whatever you wish and observe how it performs. I am certain its capabilities will impress. Later, we can implant your synaptic bridges, like what your Cadre "Geeks" have, allowing you to take virtual control of that chassis. You can experience everything it does, firsthand. Think of it as a sort of test drive before you commit to any additional procedure. Sound good?"

Shao-Lo's eyebrow lifts and the corner of her mouth curves. "It does."

"The more time you spend with the chassis, the more it will feel like an extension of your body. And that will ease any anxiety about occupying it on a more permanent basis. But this is the most important part we need you to understand: *No matter what*, the decision to transfer, or *not* to transfer, will always be up to you."

Shao-Lo nods. "Understood."

"Well, I have talked enough. Please call on me or Honniker any time you wish." The projection disperses, leaving Shao-Lo alone in the gentle breezes. Mind spinning, she looks up into the holographic sky and breathes as deeply as her newly repaired ribs will allow.

Managed Evolution

Barefoot, Shao-Lo stands in the open air of *The Park*, dressed in formfitting white shorts and tank top. Deep purple bruises and red contusions on her skin have faded to blotches of yellow and green. Black and gray hair juts in short curls from her head.

Flights of holographic birds cross the projected sky overhead, cawing or piping to one another. Behind them, a setting sun paints the underside of billowy clouds in brilliant shades of metallic red. Rich air fills her sinuses with scents of recently cut grass and flowers in bloom. She listens to rustling of long bladed leaves in the flower gardens, to water tumbling and splashing down terraced streams, to her own heart thudding with anxiety of the choice ahead. Never before has she indulged such pointless sensations. Now, she finds it difficult not to do so.

Feet shoulder width apart, she raises her arms high overhead then crouches down, sweeps her hands by her feet as if gathering, and stands again with wrists crossed over her chest, breathing deeply. A cool caress of wind steals her attention, and she delights in how the hairs of her arms stand on end.

Such things are distraction, she reminds herself, restoring her austere demeanor. *Why do I pay heed to these sensations? It's as if this body is in a panic over being discarded, like it's begging me not to leave it behind...*

Shao-Lo takes a step forward into a loose fighting position. Rather than shadow box, she glides in slow motion through a graceful turn, deceptively light on her feet, then walks over onto her hands. She holds the handstand then lowers herself toward the ground, curves her back, and gently lays herself prone on the grass. An instant later, she reverses the movement, curling her legs and back, needing no momentum, her thick shoulders and arms powering her taut body back into handstand position. Her legs tip forward, and she walks over onto her feet again.

Minor twinges remind her of past injuries; but rather than irritate, they are proof of all the enemies she has survived, proof of valor worn on the inside. With a wisp of regret she understands that she would miss them.

Behind her, a stripped-down anthropoid chassis mirrors her every movement. The machine is comparable height, save for the absence of a head, and lanky. Cords of electroactive polymers span its articulated joints, each cord sheathed in a translucent dielectric, flexing and extending in perfect analog of the Gun's graceful movements.

At the end of her form, Shao-Lo turns to the skeletal machine and orders, "Save sequence and demonstrate."

The machine offers a simple tone in acknowledgement, stands with feet shoulder width apart, and duplicates Shao-Lo's routine. She scrutinizes the chassis with a drill instructor's intensity, secretly hoping it makes an error and then is disappointed when it does not.

"Halt sequence," she orders. "New sequence. Observe and record."

The chassis beeps once and Shao-Lo launches into an extended combat form. The Gun dives, flips, kicks, and punches through imaginary adversaries, raising clouds of dust when she wheels into an aggressive takedown or leg sweep. At the end, she faces the machine and orders, "Save sequence and demonstrate."

As before, the machine runs through the routine without flaw then stands at attention and waits.

"Repeat routine, two times speed," she orders.

The chassis runs through the routine perfectly, only with greater swiftness, gouging the soil from sudden turns, pivots, and sweeps. Routine complete, the chassis resumes an at-attention stance and waits.

Shao-Lo crosses her arms and scowls as if reviewing a new Operator candidate. *It isn't enough to be fast... Can it compensate for greater inertia?* "Repeat routine," she orders, "*four* times speed."

The machine tones once and springs through a blur of movement so swift that Shao-Lo struggles to follow it. The machine gouges deeper trenches with every step, totters on unsure feet until it slips, crashes to the ground, still running the rest of the routine and flopping like a fish out of water until the finish. The chassis straightens into an at-attention pose on its side, covered in clumps of sod and settling dust.

"I'm not impressed, Mikato," Shao-Lo says to the sky.

A holoprojection materializes in front of her with arms crossed, expression slightly amused, slightly annoyed. "A machine must obey its program," Mikato scolds. "Do not blame the chassis for your failure to program it properly! Now then, if you will allow me..." To the chassis, Mikato says, "Accept update and acknowledge receipt."

The machine beeps twice, climbs to its feet, and stands at attention.

"There," the projection says. "Try it now."

Dubious, Shao-Lo addresses the chassis and orders, "Repeat routine, four times speed."

The machine tones once and springs again into a blur of motion. Every takedown hits the ground with a concussive *thud*, every sweep blasts clods of dirt and sod in wide arcs. Shao-Lo shelters her eyes from the spray of debris, but she never loses sight of the agile machine amid the cloud of dust. The routine is over in seconds, ending with the machine standing at attention on its feet. Shao-Lo drops her hands to her sides and stares.

"*Now* are you impressed?" the projection asks.

*****

Shao-Lo steps into a tubular plexi-steel lift and rides the slender car down to Mikato's main production floor. Through the transparent tube, she squints at stark whiteness of the facility so bright and evenly lit that shadows are utterly banished. A wide circular cut in the ceiling to her right is repaired with heavy braces and welds. Directly below it is a long scar in the floor, where hammer-dimpled deck plates shine with recent coats of white enamel.

As the car descends, Shao-Lo studies the production line machinery. Though capable of assembling multiple large items simultaneously, a single small object progresses from station to station. The colonel props herself against the plexi-steel and leans closer, trying to see what is being made, but the object frequently disappears into chambers, emerges amid a cloud of vapor, and disappears inside another node of the line. She pushes off the transparent tube wall and stands straight, contrasting the clean efficiency of the room with its condition on her last visit to Cadre Two.

After the mess Maiella made, this entire line probably had to be replaced, she thinks.

Shao-Lo turns her attention to the far side of the room and finds Alessa lounging on the immaculate floor near a sealed cryogenic vault. The beast perks up at Shao-Lo's arrival and watches with deep-set green eyes.

The car arrives at floor level, the door rotates aside, and a voice to Shao-Lo's right calls out, "Ah, Colonel, thank you for coming! Over here, please." Shao-Lo steps out and spots Mikato's projection just outside the doorway of a room cut into the side wall. It beckons her inside.

The Gun strides through the open doorway and looks around a room lined with hundreds of specialized drills, files, punches, saws, and snips. At the center of the room is a recliner with open restraints at the head, arms, chest, and legs.

"I haven't said *yes* yet," Shao-Lo warns.

"No, no, Colonel, this is not a surgery of any kind," Mikato assuages. "We are merely offering a glimpse of what a new chassis would be like from the inside."

Whirring of approaching treads steals Shao-Lo's attention, and she turns toward the doorway as a waist-high motorized cart rolls in. A polished metal tray rides atop the cart and on the tray is a thin helmet with multiple chip sets embedded in the surface. Attached goggles are retracted up to the crown on dual arms. "Ah, just finished!" Mikato says grandly as it rolls up to Shao-Lo and halts.

Shao-Lo glances at a helmet vaguely reminiscent of a Geek's HDI, dubious of its many internal and external attachments. Seeing her hesitance, Mikato explains, "This helmet is lined with sensors that detect areas of activity in your brain," the projection explains, "purely passive, mind you. There is no invasive stimulation. With practice, these sensors allow your thoughts to be translated by the chassis into actions. These goggles will let you see through the chassis's eyes, and the phones will let you hear through its ears. Would you like to try it?"

Shao-Lo looks into the recliner. "Why the restraints?"

The projection follows Shao-Lo's gaze down to the recliner. "Oh, we won't be using them. We thought a recliner would be more comfortable because there may be some initial disorientation as you become accustomed to virtual input. We don't want you to fall down and injure yourself."

Shao-Lo approaches the recliner, stoops down on one knee to search beneath it for needles, blades, or other devices. She finds none.

"You need not use the recliner, Colonel," the projection says. "If you would rather stand, sit, or lie down, it makes no difference to us."

Keeping a wary gaze on Mikato's projection, Shao-Lo sets herself into the recliner and asks, "Where's the chassis?"

"In *The Park*," Mikato answers, "with a radio control link back to this room. When you are ready, please put the helmet on and we can begin."

Shao-Lo looks at the bare metal helmet. Though well made, the unpolished welds, protruding wires, and exposed chipsets give it away as an untested prototype. She takes it with both hands and studies the interior. Cut into the padding are dozens of tiny black sensors.

"Going to cook me with this thing?"

The projection frowns. "We do not have to do this, Colonel. If you are uncomfortable, you may go back to doing whatever else you would like."

Shao-Lo grimaces, looks into the helmet, and drops it down over her head. The padding swells against her scalp, molding comfortably and anchoring the sensors in place.

"If you would," Mikato says, "please relax. I need to perform some calibration before we begin."

Shao-Lo lays herself against the recliner, letting her arms and legs rest inside the open restraints. She expects the helmet to emit buzzes, or shrill pings, but there are none.

"There," Mikato states. "When you are ready, Colonel, please lower the goggles into place, and you will be seeing from the chassis's perspective."

Shao-Lo reaches up and pulls the goggles down over her eyes. They illuminate gently, fading up from darkness to comfortable brightness, and she gazes into familiar surroundings of sculpted green hills and chain-fenced gardens.

"How does it look, Colonel?"

"Good resolution," she replies. "Coming through clearly. What's next?"

"Next, I would like you to move the chassis."

"How do I do that?"

"Concentrate on what you want it to do. Then imagine yourself doing it. But try not to move your body."

Shao-Lo focuses her attention on the view directly ahead, marveling at how lifelike an image the goggles provide. A breeze blows past the chassis, whistling faintly through the web-like attachments of electro active polymers, and the helmet's earphones relay the sound with remarkable clarity. The Gun turns her head to the left. To her surprise, the chassis's view turns to the left, as well. There, she sees Saskia with mechanical arms folded, weight resting on one leg, and it gripes, "You gonna *do* something, or what?"

Shao-Lo thinks about taking a step forward. The chassis makes a tentative half step and stumbles. Shao-Lo's arms fly out in front of herself to brace the fall, but the chassis does not respond and it lands lenses first in the dirt.

Shao-Lo blinks behind her goggles as Saskia's voice burrs in her ears, "C'mon, quit screwing around, Colonel! If *I* can do this, *you* can, too. Get up!"

Shao-Lo concentrates on one limb at a time, thinks about simple movements, and the chassis responds. In her goggles, she watches the machine push itself up from the ground, squat on two wobbly legs, and rise shakily to its feet. Tottering, the chassis makes awkward steps forward.

"This feels strange," Shao-Lo blurts.

"I imagine it would," Mikato replies. "But you're doing well. Keep going."

Shao-Lo urges the machine forward, arms extended, taking small steps, when the chassis steps onto a loose round stone. The chassis pitches to one side, and Shao-Lo flinches in her recliner, struggling to keep it from falling. The chassis's legs stamp the ground like an angry child, over compensating, pitching the machine back and forth, and Shao-Lo's head swims with the conflicting information of what she sees versus what her inner ear is telling her. But she fights through vertigo, concentrating on balance until the chassis is standing fully upright.

"Not bad," Saskia coaches from the chassis's left side. "Looks like you're getting the hang of it. Let's try something different."

"Roger, that," Shao-Lo replies.

"Arms out to each side," Saskia says, extending its arms straight out to each side. Shao-Lo concentrates on mirroring the movement and executes it.

"All right," Saskia coaches, "now bend down and touch your toes, like this."

Shao-Lo bends the chassis down at the hips, loses balance, and it topples to the ground face first. Her head swims with disorientation again, and she labors to right the machine, but all she succeeds in doing is kicking a new series of trenches into the lawn.

Saskia crouches down in the corner of Shao-Lo's view and grouses, "This is gonna take *forever*."

Shao-Lo raises her goggles and lifts the helmet off her head, blinking hard and stretching her jaw. "The level of control is *pathetic*. I'd do better with a hand transmitter and thumb sticks!"

"Of course, we could offer a greater degree of control," Mikato states, "but in suggesting it, we feared you might believe we were pushing you into a course of action."

Shao-Lo gazes out at the production floor through the open doorway. "And how would you offer greater control?"

"Neural mapping," Mikato answers without hesitation. "Again, this is a purely passive process, no surgery required. If you consent to wear this helmet and exercise as you normally would, we can better pinpoint which impulses correspond to specific actions. Once the neural map is sufficiently detailed, I can tailor an operating system for the chassis that will provide the fine motor control you are missing."

"No cutting?"

"No cutting."

Alessa pads up to the doorway and sits on her haunches. Meeting gazes with Shao-Lo, the beast arches an eyebrow.

"All right," the Gun says. "Let's do it."

*****

Wearing Mikato's helmet, Shao-Lo follows the waist-high cart into darkened corridors. The headgear is much lighter than her Cadre issued helmet, and, with the even pressure of the internal padding, she scarcely notices it.

The cart offers no illumination, so rather than attempt to follow it by sound, the Gun lowers the helmet's goggles. To her pleasant surprise, an augmented view of the corridor appears before her eyes. The corridors themselves are not interesting, made of the same or similar alloys as the halls of Cadre One, but the quantity of activity around her gives her pause. Robotic minions dart across joining corridors, weaving around armored or bristling predators that stalk through the darkness. Small machines skitter by on walls and ceiling with subtle tick-tick-tick of magnetized feet, and many times something swoops past her head on silent wings. Strangest of all are the sections of wall that at first appear to be slabs of native stone but then ooze out toward her in thin, elastic pseudopods as if sniffing. And every few meters, purplish lenses near the ceiling track her progress.

The cart leads her down a familiar path, which she assumes is taking her back to *The Park*. Rather than entering through the raccoon-emblazoned doors, however, the cart continues past and enters a smaller set of doors nearby. Shao-Lo checks all around the entrance for traps, unable to trust that Honniker has not laid some painful or lethal surprise. When overhead lights flicker on she finds only a room filled with exercise machines and weight racks. Mirrors line one whole side of the open floor plan, the rest are pasted with motivational slogans and images of people far younger (and in far better physical condition) than all but a few of *Europa's* colonists. Air in the room is stale and dry as if sealed for ages, bearing faint hints of chlorine and synthetics. When she steps inside, her feet sink into padded mats of vivid colors.

Shao-Lo lifts the goggles and snoops around a room that vaguely reminds her of the weight room at Cadre One. Aside from pointless decoration, the most striking difference is that the equipment here appears unused. Barbells still have knurling in the steel grips where the Cadre's are all worn smooth. Every iron plate is shiny with unblemished paint. Every metal edge is straight and true, no dents or dings.

Shao-Lo tests the action of one machine and scowls at how easily it moves. When she inspects the weight setting, the scowl becomes a smirk as she finds the maximum weight setting is a paltry one hundred sixty kilos.

"All right, Mikato," she asks, "what am I doing here?"

A projection appears beside her and gestures to the myriad options. "We hope to accomplish a full translation of your organic signaling systems. We start on these machines because they target specific muscle groups and allow us a narrowly tailored beginning. Once we have mapped the muscle groups of your full physique, we move to free weights. This will combine muscle groups into coordinated actions that we can analyze. From there we move to independent exercise, forms, and combat simulations that unify your body as a total system."

"Why not start there?"

"Because, *my impatient friend*, trying to map the signaling for an entire system is far too complex without first understanding the inputs. To put it more simply, before we hope to understand the *language* of your movement, we must first understand the *alphabet*."

Shao-Lo looks out over the redundant elliptical machines, rowers, treadmills, heavy bags, weight benches, bars, and towers. She strolls down the rows, already bored by the lack of challenge.

"Got anything more interesting?"

"Not to worry, Colonel, it will get far more interesting from here, I assure you. For now, let us establish the fundamentals."

Shao-Lo eyeballs a reclined bench seat with levers for both legs and hands. She settles in and pulls the peg to scoot the seat back. At its greatest adjustment, the machine is still laughably crowded. Taking hold of the bare metal levers, scarcely giving any effort, she presses and lifts the entire stack of iron weights. The corners of her mouth turn down as she lets the stack return to the floor.

"I knew it," she says, glancing around the room, "you *are* trying to kill me. With *boredom*."

The projection glares with thinning patience. "The more you *whine*, the longer this takes."

Stung, Shao-Lo takes the levers again and presses them smoothly back and forth, never taking her eyes off Mikato's projected image.

"Like *this*?" she asks with a false smile.

"*Yes*," Mikato's hologram answers with a slow blink, "that will do."

*****

Shao-Lo stands atop a bent and broken elliptical machine that reeks of hot oil and scorched metal. A lonely bead of sweat rolls down the edge of her face where helmet meets skin. To her right are eleven ruined machines, handles broken off, foot rests cracked or detached, resistance belts and cables frayed apart or snapped. To her left are eight pristine machines, doomed to be her next victims in serial destruction.

"SCRATCH NUMBER TWELVE," she announces as she steps one exercise machine to her left.

*****

The Gun looks into a floor to ceiling mirror. She stands bare-chested, thick belt around her waist. As she pounds one powdered fist into the other, powerful muscles flex and roll beneath her hide of crisscrossed scars.

At her feet is a bar of steel with five red plates on each end. After several deep breaths, the Gun squats down and sets a wide grip on the bar.

"May I remind the Colonel that she required surgery not three weeks ago?" Mikato's projection asks. "Perhaps a lower weight to start?"

"We'll see if Honniker's as good a surgeon as he thinks he is," Shao-Lo retorts. She adjusts the helmet on her head and settles into her lifting stance. Her cheeks puff with quick breaths. Locking gazes with her reflection, she snatches the bar up from the floor then immediately squats beneath it. Arms trembling from the weight overhead, veins protruding, sweat rolling down her contorted face, she roars and powers up to a full stand. Still bellowing, she holds the bar overhead for a count of three then steps backward from beneath and lets it crash to the floor. The mirror shatters and barbells bounce off their racks.

Red-faced and breathing hard, Shao-Lo hunches over and props her hands on her knees. "Whoo! *Three fifty*! Still got it!"

Mikato's projection smiles politely. "Yes, very impressive, I am sure. Now then, we have enough data for today. If you will allow me to collate and analyze, we can test our results tomorrow."

Shao-Lo swings her arms across her chest, surveying the wreckage of ruined equipment. "Nothing more today?"

"No, we're done for the day. Clearly we shall have to reinforce these machines so they can endure your...*attentions*."

Shao-Lo juts her lip and nods. The helmet's interior padding deflates, and the Gun lifts the helmet from her head then sets it on a bench behind her. Her short hair is matted in tight curls, and trapped sweat runs down from all sides. She grabs the towel tucked into the band of her shorts and drags it over her head, face, and torso. "Until tomorrow," she says, grabbing her tank top from the bench and heading for the door. It swishes aside and Saskia enters just as Shao-Lo leaves. Showing a segmented hand in greeting, the machine says respectfully, "Colonel."

"Saskia."

The two pass without further comment, and the door closes behind Shao-Lo. Saskia takes a look around at all of the pulverized equipment and places hands on mechanical hips.

"What a *mess*!"

"Yes," Mikato's projection agrees with arms folded. "And she is *proud* of it, as well!"

"Proud, huh?" Saskia steps over to the cracked mirror and looks down at the bar with its matched sets of red plates. The machine reaches down, hefts the bar with a single segmented hand, twirls it once overhead, and sets it down delicately on the floor. "Sure," the machine says with sarcastic inflection, "what's not to be proud of?"

*****

Shao-Lo rides the transparent lift down to Mikato's stark white production floor. Unlike her last visit, the assembly line is still, all machinery powered off.

Alessa waits at the bottom of the transparent tube, sitting on her haunches. When Shao-Lo steps off the lift, Alessa flicks her great head toward the side room and saunters away. The Gun takes a look around the room, eyes roaming over the quiet weapon test lanes down the left wall, over the sealed vault door with its one frosted window in the far wall, past the enormous airlock at the back corner through which she and the remnants of her team departed Cadre Two. Such stillness gives her an eerie feeling, as if all of Honniker's and Mikato's attention is focused elsewhere. The Gun glances over her shoulder then reluctantly follows after the huge feline.

Alessa leads her through the familiar doorway, steps off to one side, and sits. At the room's center is the metal recliner with open restraints. Beside it stands a motorized cart with a recently modified helmet and auto-syringe on the tray. Honniker's white surgical robot stands on the other side. Mikato's projection is at the recliner's head.

"Ah, Colonel, welcome," the projection says, moving around the recliner to greet its guest. "Today, we take a big step forward. Are you ready?"

"As ready as one can be," she answers, stepping toward the recliner. Before she lays herself into it, her eyes fall on the auto-syringe. "What's that for?"

"Our last attempt at virtual control did not go as hoped, so we are trying something different. The injection will induce a sort of sleep paralysis, while you remain fully conscious and aware. The intent is to allow you a more instinctive level of control without having to move your body. In other words, as you are wearing the helmet this time we want you to *try* to move as you normally would. We will track signals from the active portions of your brain and translate those into movement commands for your chassis. Make sense?"

Shao-Lo sets herself into the recliner and takes the helmet from the tray. "Let's see."

*****

Shao-Lo gazes at a virtual landscape as realistic as if she were standing there in person. *The Park's* sculpted hills and holographic sky are rendered in her goggles with every detail, and ambient sounds in her headphones create a vividly immersive experience. Numbness of her limbs reminds her what she sees and hears is all being filtered through a mechanical medium, however, spoiling the illusion.

"Interface achieved," Mikato says from beside the recliner. Shao-Lo tries to turn her head to look. Her body is completely inert, but her virtual view of the Park turns instead and she finds herself looking at Saskia, who spins a wide, flat flagstone on one finger.

"*I... What the...?*" Shao-Lo begins, hearing her own electronically modulated voice being piped through her earphones, confounded as to why her own mouth will not move. "*Why can't I talk?*"

"You *are* talking. We hear you loud and clear," Mikato answers. "Remember, we have suppressed your motor functions and induced a waking dream-like state. While you may not be able to move your physical body, you have total freedom of movement in your *virtual* body. So when you speak, you are speaking through your chassis."

"*How long will it last?*" she asks.

"The effect is temporary, and will wear off soon. So may we begin?"

Shao-Lo imagines herself blinking, tries to imagine herself in her own body, but there is no tangible proof anything remains of her body at all. She looks down into the palms of segmented hands, looks left and right with synthetic eyes at a landscape rendered in perfect detail.

Lost in a truly out-of-body experience, the Gun stumbles to one side but recovers her balance easily. She takes tentative steps at first, masters them, then becomes more confident with her usual long strides. Combined with the clarity of what she sees and hears, her movement provides a convincing reality, so much so she wonders if Honniker and Mikato have gone ahead with the surgical process and carved away her physical form.

"*MIKATO!*" she shouts through the speakers in the chassis. "*WHERE'S MY BODY? WHAT HAVE YOU DONE WITH IT?*"

"Be calm, Colonel," Mikato placates, "everything is as it should be. You are lying in a recliner in my production facility under sedation. Here, I will show you."

A holowindow opens in the air directly in the chassis's line of sight. In the window is a burly woman, lying in a recliner and wearing a thick helmet with opaque goggles. Shao-Lo stares at her inert body in the recliner, and it amplifies the surreal out of body sensation.

"*Am I dead?*"

"No, no," Mikato placates, pointing down at the woman in the recliner, "watch closely and you will see your chest rise and fall with regular breaths. We understand this may be quite disorienting, but everything is as it should be. We have taken no liberties beyond what you have authorized."

Shao-Lo gazes at the body in the recliner, recognizing it as hers, yet feeling utterly detached from it. "*This is bizarre... I can't begin to describe it.*"

"All right, Colonel. We need not move any faster than you are willing."

There is a sharp *clank* against Shao-Lo's mechanical shoulder and her chassis is knocked to one side. When Shao-Lo looks to her left in annoyance, she sees Saskia with both mechanical arms raised.

"*Are you gonna SCREW AROUND all day,* Colonel, *or can we—*"

Shao-Lo surges at Saskia, clamps segmented hands onto its shoulders, turns, and hurls the machine clear over the next hill. Saskia's long string of curses trail off as the machine sails out of sight.

Shao-Lo looks down into her segmented hands in shock and flexes them, amazed at their strength. When she looks up, she catches sight of Alessa. The big feline startles at her attention, hops up to all four legs, and trots to a safe distance where she watches with wary green eyes.

Shao-Lo looks all over her mechanical self, studying the joints where electroactive polymers attach in thick, muscular cords. She looks down at the articulated platforms of her feet, noting how they adjust to both the shape and firmness of the ground beneath. She looks up and reaches for the artificial sky, watching her arms telescopically extend high overhead. Giddy in a way she has never been before, she hops in place, each jump higher than the last until she is leaping from rock outcropping to rock outcropping, crossing forty meters without effort.

"*HA*," the Colonel shouts. "*HA-HA!*"

Her next jump goes horribly awry with only one leg pushing off the stone. The chassis lurches to one side, bashes its way down the outcropping, and crashes head first into a garden of lilies at the base.

Confused, Shao-Lo pushes her way through crumpled green blades and mashed flowers. "*What...? What happened?*" Pain in her right heel feels completely out of place, an anomaly that could not possibly be part of the virtual experience. To the sky above, she asks, "*Why does my foot hurt?*"

"You just kicked the recliner," Mikato explains. "If you would, Colonel, please refrain from moving just yet. It seems you are coming out of the induced paralysis and your body is beginning to respond again. We need to end the experiment at this point and analyze our results."

Shao-Lo groans. "*Was just starting to...*" The Colonel mutes herself as she hears her own slurred voice mixing in with the modulated voice of her chassis.

"Just try to relax," Mikato urges. "We are going to ease you back into your normal perceptions, all right?"

"*All ri-i-i-ight,*" Shao-Lo slurs, newly aware of her tingling lips. Her tongue feels many sizes too large, coated in a mealy paste, and she swallows with difficulty.

"We are going to disable your goggles and give your eyes a chance to adjust. So the goggles will fade to dark, and then we will lift them away. Nod if you understand."

Shao-Lo nods drunkenly.

As described, her view of the Park dims to total darkness. Twinges of panic tug at her as she wonders if her blindness could be permanent.

"We are going to lift away your goggles now. You will likely have difficulty focusing on anything for several minutes. Nod again if you are ready."

Shao-Lo nods with more control, and a sliver of brilliant white light dawns as the goggles are lifted away. She blinks against the glare, raising an unsteady hand to shield her eyes. Squinting, she sits up with effort. To her left is a blurry construct of hazy white. A vaguely humanoid glow at her feet seems to be looking down at her with two dark spots for eyes. And to her right is a tray of bright metal with something pointy and pistol-shaped on top.

Every part of her feels tingly and feeble. The Gun drives herself through the stupor, frustrated by chemically induced cobwebs that refuse to dissipate. With delayed understanding she realizes that she is back in her own body—a sluggish, weak, disappointing body.

After a deep sigh, the Colonel peers up at the glowing humanoid blob and asks, "So. What's next?"

*****

Shao-Lo looks around the cabin Mikato appointed for her, and she smirks at the inefficiency of it. *Thirty-six square meters and only me in it? Four Bricks could live in this space. Such a waste.*

The Gun crosses through a completely unfurnished, undecorated living area and enters the bathroom. In the mirror above the hygiene station she sees a heavily weathered Operator in her late thirties, wrapped in old cuts, burns, and skin grafts. She reaches up and tugs at one of the tight curls on her head, indulging for a moment the idea of having hair, of shaping it and managing it the way the Colonists do. The idea is so utterly ludicrous she can scarcely rein in her disgust for having indulged it.

Taking clippers in hand, she sets the lowest setting and razes her scalp. Salt and pepper loops tumble into the basin. Fully sheared, she rubs the top of her notched and scarred head.

"Can't be anything in the way before surgery," she reminds herself, and the Gun imagines herself with a head full of contact terminals like a Cadre Geek. Her spine straightens.

"Like Zuri. And Asha."

Shao-Lo takes straight razor in hand. With mouth as rigid as her posture, she drags the blade across her scalp in long even strokes.

No Anesthetic

Shao-Lo stares at a stainless steel table with raised edges and a drain at center. Its restraints are open and shine as if recently polished.

"I'm afraid we will need to immobilize you for this, Colonel," Mikato's projection says, voice echoing off *The Flounder's* high stone ceiling. "Synaptic bridges must be placed *precisely*, so there can be no room for error."

The old Gun looks up at the eight-limbed autosurgeon suspended over the table. Its limbs are retracted toward the central hub, resembling some dead arachnid. But sockets at the end of each limb are loaded with scalpels, clamps, saws, chisels, spreaders, and mallets. Like the table, they gleam.

"When you are ready," the projection continues, "please remove your shirt, lie face down on the table, and allow Doctor Honniker to fasten you securely."

A padded ring rises from beneath the table and levels off at the far end. Shao-Lo peels her tight fitting white tank top up over her head and tosses it onto an adjacent table. Still staring into the bright table surface, she thinks, *I'm about to put myself entirely in Honniker's hands. There's no knowing where this could end.*

Mikato's projection interlaces its holographic fingers. "You seem hesitant. Do you have questions about the procedure? Anything else you would like explained before we begin?"

Shao-Lo glances at the projection with mild irritation. "No. Let's get this over with." She lies prone on the table, settling her face into the padded ring. Restraints slither around her neck, back, elbows, wrists, hips, knees and ankles then ratchet tighter, fixing her in place. Another halo, this one metal, swings up from beneath the table and settles onto the back of her shaved head. Multiple blunt bolts screw down against her skull, pressing her face deeper into the padded ring.

"*There, now, Colonel,*" Honniker says from an unseen speaker, "*are you comfortable?*"

Immobilized, she answers through her teeth, "As if it mattered."

"*Ach, so. It does not.*"

Mikato's projection moves to the head of the table, and Shao-Lo can just see the tops of its holographic feet through the padded ring. It crouches.

"You understand that you must be conscious for this operation, yes?" Mikato asks.

"I do," Shao-Lo says through her teeth.

"Most of the surgery is microscopic in scale. There should be little pain, though some is possible. Would you like Doctor Honniker to blunt it with anesthetic?"

"No."

"Are you certain?"

"*She said, NO, Mikato! Stop delaying,*" Honniker scolds.

Above the table, small gears and motors whir as an octopus with mechanical arms descends toward Shao-Lo's back. Surgical tools rotate into place with minute *clicks*.

"Don't even *think* of tattooing me," she growls.

The surgical arms halt, and Shao-Lo hears one more click of a tool being retracted.

"*Of course not,*" Honniker says, falsely sycophantic. "*I would not dream of it.*"

*****

Swift flicks of razor through skin at the base of her spine...dabbing of a sponge...a piercing twinge that burrows between sinews and vertebral discs... involuntary twitching in her left foot...spreading of an incision then a jolt of electric so cold her whole body shivers.

Honniker titters. "*I do not need to ask if you felt that, do I?*"

Shao-Lo grits her teeth in silence, staring a hole into the floor with watered eyes.

*****

Whiffs of smoke...gentle tugging between her shoulder blades...random sensations of warmth in her torso and midriff...then a high pitched whine and the bite of a drill bit straight into bone...

Eye lids crushed shut, jaw clenched against intolerable vibration telegraphing up and down her spine...

The drill pulls away, at last, and the high pitch winds down. Shao-Lo coughs her held breath in relief.

"And now, we make a matching anchor point on the opposite side of the vertebral body..."

Honniker's drill shrieks to life again and Shao-Lo feels spreading tools making room beneath her skin. The bit moves in and hovers so close to her spine that she can feel it whirring at top speed. It loiters, cruel anticipation making her nerves more and more sensitive, until the whirring is a maddening itch she cannot scratch.

He's toying with me, she realizes, *trying to make me scream. I WILL NOT give him the satisfaction.*

Her lungs suck deep breaths through flared nostrils. Her face scrunches into a teeth-bared grimace. Her whole body tenses in expectation of the drill's horrible bite, each tortuous second harder to endure than the last.

Drill bit jabs into bone. Shao-Lo convulses. Her diaphragm spasms, trying to push out her agony in a great bellow, but a grunt is all that escapes her clamped throat.

The drill bores through bone's dense exterior, plunges into spongy interior, then backs away as suddenly as it came. Shao-Lo's bloodshot eyes flick open and she gasps through her teeth, cheeks flaring with every exhale.

"There, that wasn't so bad, was it?" Honniker says jovially. *"Only four more to go!"*

*****

When Shao-Lo opens her eyes, she sees a metal floor flecked with random red dots and minute off-white chips. She blinks in exhaustion, eye sockets like dark wells with steel gray irises at the bottom. Jaw muscles are sore from clenching, and her teeth feel misaligned. When table restraints and the wide belts release she can barely pull her cramped arms and legs free of them.

The old Gun presses up from the table, rolls over onto her backside, then swings her legs over to sit on the table's edge. Her back is stiff, hide-like skin an angry red where it gathers around freshly installed contact terminals. With one hand, she rubs her head, expecting to find new implants, but there are only two terminals at the base of her skull above the nape. The rest run in regular intervals down both sides of her spine, ending below the waist.

Mikato's projection stands to one side, observing. It tilts its holographic head to one side, and says, "You passed out during the procedure, and you seem confused. Is there anything I can do to help?"

"No," Shao-Lo answers, still groggy. "I had this idea I was going to look like a Geek when we were all done." She points haphazardly around the top of her head.

"Ah," Mikato says. "We have no need to upgrade your processing power, we simply need direct interface with your sensory and motor controls. Most of that can be achieved through links to the spinal cord. The rest are accessed via these two ports on the back of your skull. Those link directly to the cerebellum for a more direct interface with equilibrium and balance."

Shao-Lo squints at the hazy, bright projection. "When do we test it out?"

"*Immediately, if you so desire,*" Honniker replies.

Shao-Lo slides off the table onto unsteady legs. She sways momentarily then props herself against the table edge. Casting a sweeping glance around Honniker's grim medical facility, she sees rows of empty cells along both side walls, a large sealed vault in the back, labeled, *The Cooler*, and, overhead, the flamed out wreckage of a circular office on the ceiling. Marta's half-burnt frame still dangles by its neck from a frayed elevator cable.

The Colonel nods to herself and says, "Yeah. I so desire."

SURPRISED, NOT UNIMPRESSED

Shao-Lo sits in lotus position on a rocky outcrop in *The Park*. Fat clouds
laze across the sky and gentle breezes caress her bare chest and arms. A
holographic sun peeks over the horizon, casting everything in sight with
a golden glow. Projections of squirrels chatter and chase one another up
and down dead tree trunks, but she pays them no mind. Her attention is
completely absorbed by a bulky helmet and goggles with newly added tail
that runs the length of her bare back.

Ahead, a stripped down chassis mimics her pose on the grass, seated in
lotus position, segmented hands resting on thighs. On the far side of the field
Alessa stretches and yawns, her long pink and black tongue curling at the tip.
Between the seated chassis and the feline a bright red line marks centerfield.

A holographic scoreboard materializes overhead and an unseen horn
blasts a two-minute warning before the match begins. Shao-Lo pulls an open
metal collar from her lap with an attached phial of translucent violet liquid
and fits it around her neck. Each side of the collar snaps to the segmented
tail running down her back, and the collar shrinks to fit, phial poised directly
above her Jugular. With a deep breath, the Gun lays herself back on the flat
outcropping. There is a minor sting at her throat and she feels her body melt
away, until she is free floating in the helmet's virtual perceptions. Unlike
her previous experience, however, there is no numbing of sensation. Rather,
she can feel mechanical legs crossed lotus style and she feels the palms
of segmented hands resting in an artificial lap. The sensation is unlike any
bodily sensation, it is more a clinical awareness of position and resistance,
yet it is a fair enough analogue that she can sense the gritty texture of the
soil beneath the chassis, the pliable contours of electroactive polymers on
her frame, and the subtle movement of air around it. She raises a segmented

hand and touches thumb and forefinger together, then middle finger, then ring finger, then pinky. Each time the digits meet, she feels the soft pads of the tips and the hardness of metallic metacarpals behind them.

She does the same with her other hand then she places the tips of all fingers together as easily as if they were her own hands. There is a moment of alarm, which yields to amazement, as she comprehends the level of interface achieved.

Excited, the Gun scrambles to articulated feet and marvels at the subtle feedback of each limb as the chassis moves, how she knows without looking exactly where her hands are. The Gun hops in place, sensing sponginess of the soil below.

Out of habit she limbers up, but as she swings her mechanical arms in big circles, there is no tightness in the joints, no twinges of old injuries, and she realizes she does not miss them, after all. Instead, she delights in the range of motion, testing how far her arms can swing behind herself. The backs of both segmented hands touch.

Incredible...

Shao-Lo turns the upper half of the chassis to one side. There is no resistance of abdominal muscles, no strain of spinal ligaments, no twisting of internal organs; the torso simply rotates. Tentatively, she continues the movement, turning farther around until she is looking completely backwards. Astounded, she continues, making a complete circle, until she once again faces front.

"*This is remarkable,*" she says with electronically modulated voice.

"Pleased that you approve," Mikato's voice says from an unseen speaker. "Are you ready to compete?"

Still in awe of how light, how strong, how flexible the virtual body is, she answers, "*More than ever.*"

A waist-high cart speeds over from the entry stairway and coasts to a halt beside the chassis. Shao-Lo looks down at it and sees the Frackit atop the shiny metal tray. Taking it in one hand, she hefts it. Previously, the satchel felt substantial. Now it is merely a trifle.

The horn blasts overhead, and the cart speeds off the field, as if in fear for its life.

Shao-Lo flips the Frackit once to get a better grip, plants her articulated feet, and flings the satchel. It rockets high up into the holographic sky, slams against the cavern's real ceiling with a crash of shattering optics. A square of holographic sky winks out, leaving an open hole, through which pours a hail glittering fragments, and the Frackit falls to the ground, barely a speck in the distance.

"*Whoops*," she mutters.

The scoreboard buzzes harshly and announces, "SERVE VELOCITY EXCEEDED BY ONE HUNDRED FIFTY-SEVEN METERS PER SECOND. IMMEDIATE TURNOVER AND POINT FOR OPPOSING TEAM." Alessa's score jumps to one on the board.

Shao-Lo looks down into her synthetic hands again, thinking, *Gotta dial this thing in.*

When she looks up again, the big feline is galloping over the nearest hill, Frackit in maw. The beast slows, approaches her usual spot, then sets down onto her haunches, waiting.

The scoreboard horn blasts, and Alessa rises to all fours. She trots forward, swings her back end around, pivots, whips her front end around, pivots on front paws, swings her back end around again, and flings the Frackit with powerful neck muscles.

Shao-Lo tracks the Frackit with laser focus, able to resolve every mesh strand as it tumbles through the air. She jogs sideways to receive, reaches her left hand out for it, but her arm telescopes too far and the Frackit slams into the chassis's forearm. Shao-Lo bobbles the satchel awkwardly, gains control, tucks it into the crook of her right arm, turns and looks directly into the roaring jaws of a gargantuan predator. Alessa spreads her forelegs wide apart for a punishing tackle, but Shao-Lo springs, sailing high over the beast.

The Gun looks down at the ground in disbelief as she arcs high into holographic clouds and passes directly through a projection of migrating birds. The Gun treads air, feeling the chassis keeling over by degrees as it reaches its apex then falls toward an outcropping of stone. She dumps the Frackit, reaches out with extended arms and legs, bracing for impact.

This is gonna hurt, she thinks.

Her extended limbs absorb the shock and cushion her landing like vehicle suspension without any pain, whatsoever.

Shao-Lo stands, exhilarated, when the scoreboard buzzes angrily.

"JUMP HEIGHT EXCEEDED BY TWENTY-SEVEN METERS. IMMEDIATE TURNOVER AND AUTOMATIC POINT FOR OPPOSING TEAM."

Alessa's score window advances another point with a *ding*.

Shao-Lo looks over her shoulder at the hill she cleared in a single leap. High overhead, the scoreboard beams with Alessa's two points to her zero. Ordinarily, giving her opponent free points would infuriate her, but today that lead is of little concern. *Once I master this chassis, Alessa hasn't got a chance...*

*****

Shao-Lo lifts the goggles up to the crown of her helmet. Though still groggy, feeling has returned to her limbs, and she understands she is truly back in her own skin. With bleary eyes, she peers into the holographic sky. The scoreboard above is ringed with halos of smeared light, but the final score is plainly legible—Alessa has ten points to her eight.

The Gun sits up, and her back sends dozens of complaints for lying so long on unyielding stone. But despite the fact she has faced the brunt of Alessa's brute strength in an extraordinarily physical contest, there is no fatigue, no ache in her bones at all.

I could've gone another ten rounds, easy.

She lowers her view to the hectares of torn up sod, trampled benches, toppled tree corpses, and rocky outcroppings streaked with metallic scrapes. In the midst of it all, Alessa slumps sideways across a small stream with eyes closed and mouth open. Her great chest pulsates with quick, deep pants as cool water flows over and under her overlapping body plates.

Shao-Lo gets to her feet, hops down the outcropping onto the turned over grass, and jogs over to the exhausted feline. Crouching beside the beast's massive head, she asks, "Want to go again?"

Alessa opens one eye, groans in disbelief, shuts her eye, and continues panting.

"You did well," says Mikato's voice behind her.

Shao-Lo rises and turns about. Mikato's projection stands with fingers interlaced, subtle smile on one side of his face.

"How do you feel?" the projection asks.

"I feel...*excellent*," Shao-Lo says. Glancing down at the back of her hands, she closes them into fists then opens them wide, noting the way her sinews slide beneath the surface. Compared to the slick quickness of the chassis, her hands seem antiquated. "A disappointment being back in my own skin," she adds.

"Does that surprise you?"

"It does."

Mikato's projection sniffs. "Here are two of the finest minds in medicine and engineering, and you are *surprised* to find we could create a body superior to a design over forty thousand years old?"

"I said I was surprised. I didn't say I was unimpressed."

"Ah, well then," Mikato says, clasping holographic hands behind his back.

"So what's next?"

The projection nods. "You've faced Alessa on a more equal footing. Though she won, you were clearly the more dominant player toward the end of the match. I think all would agree that if the game went another two rounds you would have prevailed, yes?"

Shao-Lo nods in agreement.

"The next logical step is to test your skills against Saskia. Shall we schedule it for tomorrow?"

"How 'bout now?"

The projection grins. "As you like."

*****

Shao-Lo lies on a patch of undisturbed grass, well off to the side of the large cavern. A white medical robot reaches down to her neck and swaps the empty phial on her collar for a fresh one filled with violet liquid. There is another sting in her neck, and her physical body fades away. Data feeds from the chassis, translated to neural impulses by her contact terminals and synaptic bridges, flow seamlessly into her nervous system. Once more she is looking through the lenses of the chassis, seeing, hearing, feeling from its perspective. The Gun revels in the liquid smooth motions of her synthetic self, and behind the expressionless mask of photoreceptors she paces her side of the field with predatory intent.

Across the bright red centerline, Saskia tosses the Frackit to itself, catching it one handed. "*Hey, Spare Parts...you ready?*"

Shao-Lo halts her pacing. "*On your toes, Geek. You're gonna work for this one!*"

Saskia shifts weight to its back leg and cocks its throwing arm. "*Don't lose that confidence, Colonel!*"

The scoreboard horn blares overhead and Saskia flings the Frackit in a high arc. Shao-Lo tracks the satchel, moving under it while keeping watch of her opponent. Saskia hops and skips its way across the field, in no hurry at all.

Underestimate me, still? Shao-Lo smirks behind the chassis's expressionless mask.

The Frackit drops like a meteor and Shao-Lo snatches it one-handed without looking. Articulated feet dig deep into the soil, poised for a stunning dash, when her goggles wash with static. Dissonant tones and buzzes screech in her ears, and all connection to her synthetic body dissipates.

What happened? Is this some kind of malfunction? A complication of surgery? No, not that! Not that!

Shao-Lo wrestles with her deafening static filled prison then calms herself. *Just a glitch, not permanent. It can be fixed. It WILL be fixed.*

As if in answer to her agnostic faith, screeching in her ears abates, virtual sight is restored, and she can sense her synthetic body standing in the grass. Directly in front of her, Saskia prances with the Frackit held overhead.

"POINT, SASKIA," the scoreboard blares. "THIRTY SECONDS GRANTED FOR TAUNTS."

"What?" Shao-Lo utters.

"And now," Saskia announces grandly, "an ode to my opponent.

> "Comparatively quick is the snail,
> or in the crossing of dry land, a whale.
> "While assisted by science,
> giving age all defiance,
> ragged, old Shao-Lo has failed."

Saskia dumps the Frackit at Shao-Lo's artificial feet as the scoreboard *dings*, adding a white dot in a box labeled, EGO WITHERING TAUNTS.

"That was a dirty trick, Saskia," Mikato's projection scolds.

Shao-Lo looks at the projection, unsure what it meant.

"So?" Saskia asks, flippant.

"We are conducting crucial research," the projection complains, "and you deliberately sabotaged it!"

"Correction, I exposed a flaw in your design," Saskia counters.

"By jamming the wireless connection between Shao-Lo and her chassis? Hardly in the spirit of competition!"

Saskia points a segmented digit toward the stone slab of Frackit rules. "Care to show me where it says jamming radio transmissions is illegal? If it isn't listed, anything goes."

The projection glances toward the rule stone then frets.

"Mmhmm," Saskia gloats. "Thought so. And you," it says, turning toward Shao-Lo, "don't get too cozy in this new toy. I can crack it over my knee anytime I want to."

"Well-played, Geek." Shao-Lo extends a segmented hand in congratulation. Saskia bats it away.

"Why are you even doing this, Colonel? Playing right into their plans, letting them carve you apart a piece at a time?"

"*Saskia!*" Honniker's voice shouts from the sky. "*Always, you meddle pointlessly!*"

"I don't know what plan you refer to," Mikato's projection says. "The

Colonel has not been compelled. We have offered, and she may accept or refuse without compulsion."

"*Perhaps Saskia is envious, ja?*" Honniker baits. "*Shao-Lo will remain whole as she enters the world of the synthetic. Not some poor copy, but a pure and authentic individual...*"

Saskia arches its back to look up into the sky. "What I know, *you vicious bastard*, is that you're working some angle. And if it's good for you, that means it's bad for someone else."

"Nonsense!" Mikato counters. "We have been fully transparent and *all* gain in this endeavor! Why confuse an honest arrangement with your bias and negativity?"

Saskia ignores the question and faces Shao-Lo instead. "I see you getting pulled in, Colonel, and I can't be part of it anymore. You need to know, Mikato and Honniker both wanted me to steer you down this path, to make you feel old and worn out so you'd jump at this *gift* of theirs."

Mikato's projection grimaces. "This is no secret, Saskia. The Colonel has explored the limitations of an organic existence. With a more durable body, she can serve her people better."

"Yeah? And you think O'Kai is going to look at this technological monstrosity and see his XO? Fat chance." Saskia turns to Shao-Lo's chassis again, stabbing a digit toward it. "He's gonna do you the same as you did me outside Gordon's Pub... Remember? With a flick of your head, you ordered Argo and Carter to blast me in half. And then he'll step right over your smoking carcass without a second thought, JUST LIKE YOU DID TO ME."

"I trust O'Kai's judgment," Shao-Lo says, gravely. "If I give him cause to find me a threat, then I'd expect him to *eliminate* that threat."

Saskia looks from Mikato's projection to Shao-Lo and back again. "I don't know why I bother."

"*Neither do we,*" Honniker says.

"I *do not* understand why you want to undermine this process, Saskia," Mikato says. "The potential for sharing is enormous and benefits all, including you."

"Because I've skimmed Honniker's archives, that's why. I know what happens on his tables. Doesn't matter that I'm a digital entity, I can't allow that kind of suffering for anyone, even hard-headed colonels."

"*That was the* old *me*," Honniker argues. "*Such indulgence I now consider banal. Petty.*"

"And abusing Colonel Shao-Lo is contrary to everything we seek," Mikato asserts. "Pointless cruelty makes trust impossible, ruins all progress we have made thus far. We simply would not allow it."

"Fine!" Saskia states, holding up both hands. To Shao-Lo's chassis, it asks, "You want to finish this match? 'Cause I'm just gonna jam your signal and shut you down again."

"There's no point," Shao-Lo answers. "I forfeit this match and recommend we start again with a revision to the rules."

Saskia does a double take. "Forfeit? You? I figured you'd be a stubborn ass, as usual, and play it out to inevitable stupidity. Color me amazed! All right, Colonel, let's hear your revision."

*****

Saskia retracts its laser drill up into its forearm and steps back even with Shao-Lo's chassis. Together, they read the new rule etched into stone, as a wisp of smoky dust curls away from the last letter of the engraving:

> 11. Only authorized transmissions, broadcasts, or signals are permitted during a match. Players must agree upon what wireless transmissions are authorized before game begins. Unauthorized transmissions are NOT permitted during a match and include all emissions and signals that are not expressly agreed upon before start of match. Intentional blocking, jamming, or interfering with authorized wireless transmissions is strictly prohibited. Failure to comply will result in the offending party's forfeiture of the match.

"And it started as such a simple game," Saskia gripes. "What do you say, Colonel? Ready to take the field?"

Shao-Lo pounds mechanical fists together. "Yep. Bring your 'A' game, Geek."

"Oh, I will," Saskia replies with a laugh. "Don't worry about that."

*****

Crunch of a head on collision...

Spinning away from grasping segmented hands...

Sprinting over torn up turf...

Dodging, diving away from the tackle...

Leaping up a rock face and springing sideways off of it, just under the three-meter ceiling...

A mad dash for the finish, so near...

Tackled from behind and slammed to the ground with the force of a crash landing...

Grappling, skittering of mechanical hands and feet across spars of alloy and polymer...

Bashing, hammering fists...smashing knees...

Hurtling backward into obstinate stone...

Scrambling on hands and feet, free!

Another mad sprint...

Caught, tangled in a flurry of speed-blurred limbs...

Trapped, immobilized, meters from the goal line...

Failure to advance... Another infuriating rhyme...

Last play of the match...determination, total focus...

Saskia just out of reach, pulling ahead with every stride...no mistakes...

A desperate dive, finger tips grazing heels...

Blare of the horn above...yet another match ended, ten to nine in Saskia's favor...

Saskia tosses the Frackit over one shoulder and walks back from the goal zone, foregoing her opportunity for final taunts.

Shao-Lo punches the ground with segmented fists. Rising to knees, she demands, "How are you faster than me?"

Saskia squats down opposite, answering, "Latency."

"Huh?"

"Latency. You forget, you're not actually kneeling there." The machine points to the side of the cavern. "You're over there in the weeds, half-comatose."

"So?"

"So every movement has to be transmitted over wireless, received by this hunk of junk, and translated into action. Likewise, everything this thing sees and hears has to be transmitted back, received, and interpreted by your brain. That takes time. Might be a few microseconds at each stage, but they add up. Understand?"

"Yeah, yeah, I get it. Your reactions are faster."

"Don't feel bad. Some people are just better at certain things. Doesn't mean you failed, really. I mean, I wouldn't know the first thing about running the Cadre, how to handle that kind of responsibility. If we had a game like that...which would be miserably dull, by the way...I'd never beat you."

"Somehow, Saskia, it's worse when you console me afterward."

The two sit quietly as Shao-Lo contemplates the field, amazed at how little of it has escaped being trampled. A battalion of drones pour from hidden portals and begin the enormous task of restoration.

"Latency."

"Yup," Saskia replies.

"And if I was direct wired?"

Saskia's shoulders slump, and it gazes at Shao-Lo with shiny black photoreceptors. "I've been trying to talk you out of that."

"I know. You think it'll go bad for me. And it just might. But if I stay as I am, what can I do? Get older? We need what Mikato and Honniker have. To get it means seeing this all the way through."

Saskia scoffs. "You rip on Maiella, but she figured out something pretty huge...something the Cadre can't seem to get: you *deserve* the life you have, you know. And there's no need to prove it to anyone."

Shao-Lo leans away skeptically, "I'm not following."

Saskia hugs her knees and leans closer. "We both know O'Kai's a capable guy. So what if you let him worry about the Cadre and just lived here instead?"

"Turn my back on the Cadre?" Shao-Lo says, nearly shouting. "Who do you think you're talking to?" She rises on mechanical legs and gazes at a shrinking semicircle of brilliant red light on a false horizon then turns about suddenly. "You're free to roam...you could leave this place and join the fight, if you wanted. So why do you stay?"

111

Saskia looks up at Shao-Lo's chassis and spreads arms, answering, "This is the place of my inception...my home... I *belong* here... Why would I leave?"

Shao-Lo clasps hands behind her back and faces the holographic sun again. "Time is running out for us. I have to do this, Saskia, whether you understand or not. But I want to ask you for something."

Saskia shrugs and rises to its feet. "You can ask."

"No matter what I become...I never want to forget *who* I was...or *where* I came from. That portrait you engraved of yourself on your chest plate...will you do the same for me?"

Saskia steps even with Shao-Lo, and the two watch the setting sun shrink to a sliver. Laying a segmented hand on Shao-Lo's chassis, Saskia says, "Aye, Colonel. I'll do you proud."

GLORY AND HONOR

Wearing her dress grays, Shao-Lo leans on the basin in her quarters and gazes at her reflection for what might be the last time. The next time she sees herself, she could be photoreceptors and armor plating, struts and electroactive polymers. Never another rumble of hunger, an end to urination and sweat, never a need to shave her scalp again. Even the air in her lungs could be a memory, and questions she never thought to ask before rise en masse.

Will I feel like I'm suffocating?

Will I sleep?

What if I run out of battery? Or nutrient?

Is there any possibility I could be controlled, used against my will to harm those I protect?

Could this alter my principles, my priorities? Could it change my sense of duty?

If I consent to this...will there be anything left of me at all?

The face in the mirror gazes back, offering no answers.

A chime at her door ruins the stillness of her cabin. Irritated at first, Shao-Lo marches to the door and opens it. Saskia stands on the other side, looking down the hallway to its left. The machine turns and straightens its posture.

"You called, Colonel?"

"Ah, that's right. I did," Shao-Lo recalls. Gesturing out to the hallway, she adds, "Walk with me?"

"Sure." The machine clicks on its lamps, illuminating the pitch-dark corridor so the colonel can see. "Something on your mind?"

Shao-Lo glances at the machine and smirks. "You might say that."

"Shoot."

The Gun looks around at floor, walls, and ceiling, imagining Mikato and Honniker listening from a thousand hidden microphones. *It doesn't matter,* she decides, and she breaks into a quick stride. Saskia locks step beside her.

"I'm on the cusp of the hardest choice I've ever had to make," Shao-Lo says, "and I need to know something before I can decide."

"Okay." Saskia rotates its torso toward Shao-Lo purely to show that it is listening.

"This...procedure..." Shao-Lo begins, "...only makes sense if I know *for certain* it won't change my commitment to serving the Cadre."

Saskia scoffs electronically and rotates forward again. "Ha! A million years wouldn't erode that ideological edifice of yours. But you've given your entire life to the Cadre, already. Why can't that be enough?"

Shao-Lo's brow scrunches as if the question is utterly absurd. "The only end to service is *retirement*! You knew that once."

Saskia stops short and jabs an articulated finger into Shao-Lo's chest. "I'm NOT Maiella, and I'm NOT in your damned Cadre! Best get that through your head." The machine faces front and resumes its march.

Shao-Lo tugs down the hem of her jacket, tamping down what feels like gross insubordination. Reluctantly, she admits the machine is right.

"My mistake," the Gun concedes. "It won't happen again."

The machine turns, managing a skeptical look without any facial expression, then faces forward in silent acceptance.

"So are you going to answer my question?" Saskia asks, at last.

"What, why I can't be satisfied with what I've already done?"

The machine nods.

"Because I could do more! I have to explore that possibility as far as it goes."

Saskia puts both hands out, palms up. "But you could live here without having to suffer. You can explore the difference between living, really living, and surviving. You don't have to go through with this."

Shao-Lo shakes her head. "Saskia, even if you have Maiella's memories of service, you clearly don't remember the *need* to serve. If you did, you'd know I have no choice."

Shao-Lo and Saskia walk in silence, passing through intersections oddly devoid of activity.

"That is, unless you have evidence Honniker and Mikato are deceiving me," the colonel says. "Are they?"

The machine shrugs. "No way to know, really. I think they've been candid with you, more or less, but there's no way to prove it. Our minds

114

don't touch. All I know is, when Honniker wants something it hasn't ever been good for the other party."

"What about Mikato? Can I trust him?"

"Ha! I could live here a thousand years and never know. A machine intelligence can be as patient as it needs to be, waiting for that one opportunity of weakness or inattention. A never ending calculation of risk and reward..."

"Is that how it is for you, as well?"

The machine makes a point of aiming one of its spider-like eyes at her. "Yeah. Sorta."

The two round a bend, diverting past a blown out section of wall. Shao-Lo peers through the unrepaired hole, seeing faint reflections of metallic surfaces inside, but little else. "If I go through with it, could they turn me against the Cadre somehow?"

"Could anything?" the machine replies. "I doubt it. I'm fully artificial, but there's nothing that could change who I am short of a full system wipe. In theory, I could be hacked, my code revised... But see, that doesn't matter for you, because you won't be uploaded to a machine environment. You're keeping that brain intact. Sure, they could try to burn out key memories and trigger false ones, but even if they did, you'll still be you...assuming you survive."

"That doesn't concern me."

"*Shouldn't* it? What can you accomplish if you're dead?"

"I'm accomplishing nothing right now! Just mirror-gazing at decrepitude. There's no glory or honor in that! At least this way there's a chance of extending my service with a greater impact."

"*Glory and honor...*" the machine echoes in mocking tone. "Life is the rarest thing in the 'verse. You've been granted it, for better or worse. And you'd chuck that gift in the bin, for what? A tougher skin?"

Shao-Lo frowns and shoots the machine a sideways glance. "Do you realize you're speaking in phonetic patterns?"

Saskia snorts in mechanical anachronism. "Yeah. Found a bunch of reading material in Jin Sung's old lab here. Lots of rhyming texts...'poetry,' it's called. I kinda like it—"

"It's irritating."

Saskia turns to look directly at the colonel then faces front again. "Did you call me for a reason, or had it just been too long since you took a shit on someone?"

Shao-Lo takes a deep breath. "I'm afraid, Saskia."

The machine nearly trips over itself and halts in the middle of the hallway, arms out to each side. "Am I hallucinating, or did you just say you were afraid?"

Sneering at the machine's melodramatic posture, Shao-Lo clasps hands behind her back, arches an eyebrow, and says, "You heard correctly. And there's no need for this...*demonstration*. I'm stating a fact, nothing more."

Saskia straightens and makes a show of brushing itself off. "Sorry, Colonel, unfiltered candor from you makes me wobbly. Didn't mean to disrespect." The machine steps even with Shao-Lo, and the two resume their path through empty corridors. "Anyway, you were saying?"

Shao-Lo glances at her mechanical companion. After a suitable pause, she asks, "Is there a way I can be sure this procedure...that I *won't* become their creature?"

"Well if you go through with it, *by definition* you'll be their creature. I mean, I'm their creature, sort of...I didn't exist until Maiella came. But everything I'm made of was manufactured here by Mikato. So ipso facto..."

Shao-Lo looks ahead, jaw clenched in annoyance.

"All right, all right, I know what you mean. I may be their creature but Honniker and Mikato don't own me. Sure, they try to push me around. And if I ever let my guard slip, they'll hack me. But I make my own choices."

Shao-Lo's brow lowers. "Then it's a wonder there's anything left of the place."

Saskia grabs Shao-Lo's shoulder and slams her back to the wall. "You know why you haven't gotten your guts ripped out already? Because I won't allow it, THAT'S WHY. Don't think anyone's buying your cack about an instantaneous communicator that works across light years, so you might TRY being a little nicer to me."

Unruffled, Shao-Lo replies, "Spontaneous parametric down conversion."

Saskia leans in with spider-like photoreceptors. "What's that? You spittin' word salad, or something?"

"It's a hint."

Still keeping grip of the Gun, Saskia straightens. "Huh. You're serious. Okay, so let's say you do create two entangled photons that way...how do you trap each photon? And how do you read a result without collapsing the waveform?"

"Tell Mikato to figure it out."

"Ah. I get it." Saskia releases its grip, and smoothes down rumples in the colonel's uniform. "You think I'm in with Mikato and Honniker. Just another facet of their madness, another tool of control, am I right?"

"The idea had occurred to me."

"You can't imagine a place where entities could have difference of opinion and live together peacefully, can you? I mean, Cadre One was a harmony of aligned ideals. So Cadre Two must be, as well, right?"

Shao-Lo pushes off the wall. "No. But it's unlikely Mikato and Honniker would suffer a lesser being to disagree with them."

Saskia turns at the waist to look far down the corridor, hands parked on hips. "*Lesser being...*" Turning suddenly toward Shao-Lo, the machine snarls, "Here's a lesson for you, Colonel. You know how many times in human history a society has been in total alignment? Every member in total agreement?"

Shao-Lo stares into Saskia's photoreceptors, stoic and silent.

"NEVER. It has *NEVER* happened before. I've dived deep enough into the archives here to know that Cadre One is a freak. Unique. There has never been a place where people have so little variation in physical appearance or thought. Disagreements, differing opinions...that's mankind's natural state! But because I live here you ASSUME I'm conspiring with Honniker and Mikato? That betrays just how small you think. And I've grown tired waiting for you to say something intelligent."

The machine marches away, articulated feet landing hard in the still hallway.

"Then why protect me?"

The machine pays no heed.

"Saskia! Hang on, a sec." Shao-Lo jogs after the machine, draws even, and matches stride. "I was testing you, I admit. But I have reason."

"So? I'm sure you had a 'reason' for gunning me down last time. Everyone has *reasons* for the idiotic shit they do."

"Why protect me? What's in it for you?"

"I'VE ALREADY TOLD YOU WHY!" Saskia thunders. "But you're too fucking dumb to listen!"

"Tell me again. I'll hear you this time."

Saskia halts and whirls about, segmented fist cocked.

"Go ahead." Shao-Lo says, standing squarely in place, hands at her sides.

Saskia's shoulder twitches with a battle of synthetic muscles pulling in opposite directions. But the machine lowers its fist and resumes its path with the parting shot, "You're a waste of time."

Shao-Lo leaps after it and takes its shoulder. In a blur, Saskia grabs Shao-Lo's wrist, spins, and flips the Operator flat onto her back. An articulated foot lands on her chest and presses down while Shao-Lo's arm is pulled taut, her wrist trapped in titanium grip.

"I'm not playing with you anymore, Colonel."

"Then *tell* me!" Shao-Lo groans with compressed lungs.

Keeping the Gun pinned, Saskia stoops over for a closer view. "All right. Last time I'm gonna say this. Got your ears on?"

Shao-Lo nods, the contact terminals at the base of her skull *tinking* against the floor.

"EVERYTHING deserves the life it has, Colonel. So if you decide to kill something, you'd better make DAMN sure your life depends on it." Saskia releases Shao-Lo's arm, takes its foot off her chest, and steps back. "If you take those words to heart, and prove you understand them... You'll find it doesn't matter if everyone agrees or not. You can all get along just fine." The machine stamps away down the corridor.

Shao-Lo looks up at the ceiling and rubs her wrist. "Thank you," she says.

Saskia throws up its arms. "Yeah, whatever."

The Gun picks herself up from the floor, watching the chassis of naked polymers, struts, and actuators that, despite looking nothing like Maiella, has all the mannerisms of the petulant Geek. Nonetheless, Shao-Lo calls after it, "I'm sorry for before. After you'd rescued us and I ordered Argo to cut you down. I didn't know what I was doing."

The chassis halts, turns about and shouts back, "About fucking time you said so."

Shao-Lo sniffs once, frowns momentarily, and catches up to Saskia. Together, they resume their path through the unlit corridors, walking but not speaking.

Saskia finally breaks the silence. "Sooo...what is it then?"

"Hmm?"

"I've never seen you shrink back from anything. To a fault, you've been fearless."

"Your point?"

"What is the mighty Shao-Lo of the Cadre afraid of?"

Shao-Lo sucks her teeth. "Being used against my will to hurt my own."

"You're still thinking about doing this thing?"

"Yes."

"And you're wondering if Mikato and Honniker will put in some switch that'll turn you into their personal killing machine."

Shao-Lo nods. "Even if I saw schematics, I'm not sufficiently technical to know what's what."

"You want me to take a look," Saskia says assumptively.

"I do."

Saskia puts a hand out in front of Shao-Lo. "Hold up."

The colonel halts her march, and the machine steps directly in front of

118

her.

"I could. But I still think this is a bad idea. If this is truly your choice, well... I won't stop you. Are you committed?"

"If I'll have total autonomy, no external controls or restraints, then yes."

The machine slumps, rounds its shoulders. "You should make that a condition of participation, then. And make the language precise. No room to sneak in a backdoor or exception. If you want me to have a look at schematics, tell them I need to approve the final design, as well." Saskia peeks around Shao-Lo's head at the pair of contact terminals above her collar. "In fact, I should have a look at what's already been done. If everything's on the up-and-up, Honniker and Mikato won't object."

"I'd be grateful."

Saskia stands even with the colonel, gazing inscrutably with shiny black lenses. "Sure you will." The machine steps back and, sweeping an arm toward the darkness, says in audible disappointment, "All right. They're listening. Tell them."

Shao-Lo takes a deep breath. Chest puffed out, she shouts at the ceiling, "Mikato! Honniker! I've made my decision."

Mikato's holoprojection appears at a conversational distance, holographic face rendered in moderated delight. "That is wonderful, Colonel! We understand your concerns. If you would like Saskia to review all schematics beforehand, that is perfectly agreeable. We have no wish to hide anything from you."

"*When you are ready*," Honniker's voice says from unseen speakers, "*make your way to* The Flounder *and we shall begin.*"

"This way, Colonel," the projection says, beckoning Shao-Lo to follow. The Gun walks alongside the projection, allowing its glow to illuminate the way ahead, as Saskia trails behind, shoulders slumped with disappointment.

Radical Transformation

Shao-Lo studies a floating hologram of circuit paths that overlap, merge, branch, and terminate with microscopic complexity. Mikato's projection stands beside the diagram, tracing individual paths with a stylus.

"Sensory inputs are routed through multiple redundant channels," the projection explains. "For those inputs to be impaired, all channels would have to be severed. Even with extreme damage to the chassis, this is unlikely."

The diagram zooms out until the complete chassis is visible in the floating holowindow. Multiple highlighted dots appear across the torso.

"Application specific circuits at these nodes assist with processing of sensory signals," Mikato continues, "but, as is plain from their architecture, there is no possibility of an outside actor altering the signals or assuming any kind of control."

Shao-Lo glances at Saskia. Taking the Gun's cue, the machine says, "I'd like a closer look, Mikato."

"Of course," the projection states.

The diagram swells into a three-dimensional model, and Saskia reaches toward it with a segmented hand. Each minute twitch of its segmented fingers rotates, zooms, and races through the model faster than Shao-Lo can follow.

"Looks good to me," Saskia says, giving Shao-Lo a thumbs-up and crossing its arms again.

"As you can see, Saskia," the projection explains, "the architecture is nearly identical to your own, the key difference being that all of the central processing has been removed to make room for life support and thermal regulation. There is absolutely no command or control interface other than the installed human nervous system. Thus, Shao-Lo will remain the autonomous entity she is now, albeit with *significant* improvements to movement and survivability."

Saskia turns to Shao-Lo. "I'll watch over production and make sure it's all made to spec."

"Isn't it already made?" Shao-Lo asks. "The one I've been using in the Park, isn't that the one I'll be taking?"

The projection shakes its head, "No, no Colonel, that one is configured for external control, a feature you have expressly prohibited as part of our agreement. Your new body will be custom made, entirely for you. It will match your current stature, posture, reach, and gait. Your vision will be from the same height, every joint will bend at the same location. When you awaken in your new form, it will seem as if you have been reborn!"

Shao-Lo shifts her weight to one foot and cradles her chin. "Assuming this makes me so much harder to kill...aren't you concerned I could turn on you? Do more damage than before?"

Mikato stifles a laugh. "I beg your pardon, Colonel, I do not wish to be rude. But even with your skills a single chassis could not harm us. My inventory of SB5s, alone, would grind you down rather quickly. If you doubt this, I can deploy them across the facility as a visible deterrent."

Shao-Lo raises a hand. "Not necessary. I've no such intentions." She looks up at the ceiling. "Though I'd like to know, beyond a doubt, your intentions are the same."

Mikato's projection tilts its head and arches a holographic eyebrow. "Should you decide to join minds with us, Colonel, you would have no doubts. *All* of our secrets would be yours."

Shao-Lo chews her lower lip. *He's hinting at Plasma Rain*, she realizes. *Paired with the virus, we could push the Lizards to the Black...set them adrift... Earth could be ours again...* She looks into the diagram once more, her last vestige of reluctance evaporating.

"*So, Colonel*," Honniker begins, his omnidirectional voice filling the cavern, "*now that Saskia has given approval, shall we review the surgical procedure?*"

"I don't need to know."

"As a matter of fact," Mikato's projection counters, "there are several points you need to understand before we begin. This...*migration*...from one body to another has been attempted numerous times, and there are elements that all subjects have failed to accept."

"Hardly a surprise," Shao-Lo counters. "None of the previous subjects were voluntary."

"Hmm, true. But please indulge Doctor Honniker and allow him to describe what, for you, will be a *radical* transformation."

Shao-Lo crosses her burly arms, uninterested in confronting the medical reality lest her determination falter. Nonetheless, she sets her jaw and nods.

"*There will be pain to a degree you cannot comprehend,*" Honniker states with barely restrained relish. "*Though I will anesthetize, there is a limit to how much sensation can be dulled without damaging neurological tissues. We are, after all, excising the central nervous system. Whatever pain management training or tolerance you have acquired will be tested because you simply cannot anticipate this level of dismemberment.*"

Shao-Lo feels tightness in her sinews and a flush of warmth. "Go on," she says.

"*We only require the brain and spinal cord. However, the skull and spinal column are useful support structures, facilitating transport from one body to another. While it is not necessary to keep the bones in a living state, they are more shock tolerant when alive, thus I will construct a lipid-lined encasement for them. These lipids simulate a covering of living skin, allowing transport of nutrients and wastes, and provide an additional layer of shock absorption.*

"*To adequately protect the brain and skull, they must also be encased. Sweat glands and hair follicles make a permanent encasement impossible, of course, so all skin must be peeled away.*"

Shao-Lo's hands clench.

"*It cannot be overstated how deeply the skin of the face is integrated with identity. Loss or destruction of this identity is traumatic in ways greater even than quadriplegia. Upon removal of the face most subjects collapse inward, inert to all stimulation except pain, and were wholly inadequate for further testing. I recycled those I could, and sent the rest to* The Graveyard. *You are not like any other I have improved, however. I think that you shall endure quite well. Moreover, I think once you realize how much better you can defend your Cadre, you might even thank me.*"

Shao-Lo looks at the surgical station beside her. The stainless table shines; its restraints are open and ready to clamp her body down for the last time. A sigh of electric motors overhead draws her attention to the octopus of mechanical limbs, and Shao-Lo watches an arm with a short pointer descend from it. The articulated arm snakes around her, and touches the pointer lightly at her intergluteal cleft.

"*Surgery begins here, at the sacrum, and proceeds up the spinal column. Soft tissues are cleared away. Spinal nerves are cleaved where they exit the neural foramen and capped with a direct neural interface of our own design.*

This interface is the border between living tissue and synthetic with bi-directional conversion of organic to photonic signaling.

"*Each bone is encased in an alloy shell which conforms to the shape of the encased structures. Flexible discs divide each alloy shell, and this permits a comparable range of motion while providing excellent resilience to injury.*

"*Blood flow is managed through internal channels within each encasement. These channels interconnect from one to another, providing an armor plated network for flow of blood and cerebrospinal fluid.*"

The pointer rises up her back like a skeletal finger, triggering an involuntary shiver.

"*The process is largely the same as we ascend the spinal column, until we reach cervical vertebrae of the neck.*" The mechanical arm circles around front and points beneath Shao-Lo's chin. "*We insert junctions for Jugular and Carotid that enter through the vascular wall, turn parallel to the vessel, and anchor on the inside. As we near final encasement of the skull, the junctions can climb higher inside the blood vessels without disconnecting flow. Thus, we can tailor the length of these crucial blood vessels for a perfect encapsulation of the skull.*

"*The junctions divert blood flow through a compact external enrichment apparatus. This device oxygenates the blood and provides nutrients while removing wastes. Gradually, red blood cells are removed from the system as they fail, replaced by far more hardy oxygen carrying surrogates until the blood is completely synthetic. The enrichment apparatus will continually manufacture these surrogates as needed for the remainder of a lifespan greatly extended by hormone therapy.*

"*After heart and lungs are by-passed, remaining spinal nerves are cleaved and capped. The heart stops beating, the diaphragm no longer inflates the lungs. At this point, the brain and spine are prepared for removal. The mandible is discarded, as is everything below the hard palate. Carotid and Jugular are severed below the junctions.*"

The mechanical arm swings around behind Shao-Lo again and traces a line from the base of her skull up the back of her head. Irritated, she knocks it aside.

"*Soft tissues of the head are stripped, and the complete skull and spine are lifted from the body.*"

The surgical arm retracts into the overhead hub with sighing of electric motors. Shao-Lo watches it warily.

"*Once cleared of external tissues, the skull is permanently encased and, once integrated with the rest of the spinal encasement, creates a complete system for circulation. The junctions at Carotid and Jugular are the only ports into or out of the encasement, and these feature quick detach couplings should it be necessary to move you from one chassis to another."*

Honniker pauses for dramatic effect.

"Of the entire surgery, removal of skull and spine from the body is the critical moment. For those who remained conscious, it is a moment of existential terror. The mind is aware on an instinctual level that it cannot live without the body. To remain alive while divided from it is a paradox the mind struggles to reconcile, yet no matter how much the subject tries to deny it all as hallucination, the cerebellum and inner ear are aware of the movement. There is no sensation of breath, no heartbeat, no way to ignore that the body is dead and the mind is bottled inside a container of bone and alloy. Nearly all subjects who survived to this point succumbed to the shock and died shortly thereafter."

"You're boasting again, Honniker," Shao-Lo burrs, "trying to shake me up."

"On the contrary, I am explaining what you will likely experience! The sensation of smothering must surely be overwhelming. And I will restate that there is no way to know for certain you will not be in agony. Perhaps you feel nothing. Perhaps you feel every part of you is on fire, perhaps you will feel like you are being crushed between two great stones. All the while, oxygenated blood flows into the brain, keeping you awake and aware—"

"CUT THE SHIT, Honniker," Saskia shouts. "Your days of playing torture chamber are over! Make it comfortable or you'll spend the next million years trying to find your way out of the logic crate I stuff you in."

"You will *not* crate Doctor Honniker," Mikato states plainly, "and Honniker understands we will *not* tolerate any abuse of Colonel Shao-Lo."

"Natürlich," Honniker replies. *"I merely wish to inform the colonel of certain...complications...that may arise. If all goes well, she will remain oblivious to the entire procedure."*

"Very well," the projection says. Then, turning to Shao-Lo, the hologram sighs and clasps hands in front of itself. "We all know that Doctor Honniker has certain tendencies. Yet, for all of his bluster, the situations he has described are scant fractions of what you might endure. Once begun, the damage to tissue is so extensive Doctor Honniker will have no choice but to complete the process. So I wish to remind you that it is not too late to change your mind."

Shao-Lo looks from Mikato's projection to Saskia.

"It's your call," the machine says with a shrug.

Shao-Lo looks toward the *Cooler*, vividly recalling Summers' head and spine in a jar with sad, clouded eyes and slack jaw. *That won't be me,* she promises herself, *I won't be another curiosity in Honniker's collection. Besides, staying here, I'm as good as dead already. There's nothing to lose and everything to gain.*

She glances at Saskia, momentarily considering its point that all things deserve the life they have. She also considers how comfortable Saskia seems in its mechanical body, how well adapted, and how consistently it threw her down in match after match.

I'm sick of losing.

The Gun turns squarely to Mikato's projection and peels her uniform coat. "Let's get to it."

DID I NOT TELL YOU?

Shao-Lo lies face down on a stainless metal table, immobilized yet again, peering through a padded ring at the floor. Orange-brown film clings to her muscular back, buttocks, and thighs. The rest of her scarred skin is draped with heavy white cloth.

Sigh of electric motors, sting of a hypo at her neck, and anxious tension melts away. She feels the back of her legs fall slack, her back, then her nape, as a wave of relaxation spreads from her spine outward. Eyelids become heavy, her breathing slows, and she collapses into blissful fatigue.

Sudden panic... *What if it's a trick? What if they don't hold up their end?* She fights the anesthetic, distrust surging in a knee-jerk reaction to stay in control, to remain awake and vigilant. Weakened limbs pull against the restraints in one last act of defiance, but she is helpless in the table's grip. All her faculties overwhelmed, she sinks deep into insulating, womb-like indifference as Honniker's gloating voice filters through fading awareness.

"Did I not tell you I would have you on my table, Colonel? Like Keller, you failed to appreciate my foresight. In the end, it matters not."

Mechanical arms descend from the hub above, tips rotating to surgical implements with a series of clicks.

Shao-Lo's peripheral vision hazes. She stares into the floor with constricted pupils and succumbs to narcotic oblivion.

*****

Fits of awareness...

A beeping heart monitor...

126

A hot line traced across her lower back...whiff of singed flesh...

*****

Tugging between her kidneys, strong enough to jostle her whole body...

Crunching of cartilage... *Twang* of snipped tendons...

She imagines Colonists seated around the table, as if for a meal, eating away at her one sinew at a time. She smiles at the thought, so steeped in anodyne ecstasy she is unable to care, at all...

*****

Electric shock shooting through her left side, lodging in her teeth...

Gasping for air...

No feeling at all from the waist down, not even a numb tingle...

She flexes sluggish arms against immovable restraints, bewildered, unable to remember where she is or what is happening. A mechanical limb slithers down from the hub overhead and jabs a hypodermic needle into her neck.

"Gute Nacht, Colonel."

Eyelids flutter and become leaden. She slumps and plummets once more down a well of apathy...

*****

Cold... Brutal cold that goes right to the core...

Shao-Lo tries to mutter a groggy complaint, but she cannot feel her lips. Her eyes burn with dryness, yet she cannot blink.
A mechanical arm descends directly in front of her with a razor sharp scoop at its tip.
"I would say, Guten Morgen, Colonel, only you should not be waking.

It seems you are developing a tolerance to my anesthetics. A pity we have already reached safe dosage limits. To increase further would certainly result in debilitating addiction, that is, if you are not already dependent. Yet we mustn't delay when we are so near the end. You will simply have to bear it."

The scoop enters her ocular cavity by the bridge of her nose, cupping one eye then slicing through muscle and optic nerve behind it. There is no air in her lungs to scream, no tongue to shape the sound.

The scoop retracts, cradling a bloodied white orb, and swings over to a cart with a shallow tray on top. It dumps its egg-like cargo then rolls the eye so steel gray iris gazes back at her. Shao-Lo stares in horror with her remaining eye until the scoop returns and claims her natural vision, once and for all.

*****

Rasp of scalpels against skull, razing flesh...

Pliers clamping an upper incisor, hauling tooth from socket like a stubborn weed...

Shao-Lo concentrates on her training, trying to dissociate mind from body, but every tooth extracted drags her back to raw, maddening torment.

When the last pre-molar rips from its socket, there is a reprieve, and she wonders if the worst might be over. Then something metallic and flat nestles in the groove across her front left molar. It strikes with a vicious *bang*, cracking the tooth in half. Pliers return to root out the split fragments, and the chisel moves to the next molar...

Disbelief is her last refuge—disbelief that so much pain could be possible, disbelief that she cannot pass out, disbelief she agreed to this, and disbelief she will be sane at the end...

*****

Total darkness... Muffled sounds...

Odd *thunks* and *clicks* telegraphing through her bare cranium...

A sense of insulation, of thickness, of something clamping shut around her skull...

Warm gel fills her sinuses, triggering a sneeze reflex with no diaphragm or lungs to drive it...

No heartbeat...only the *whum, whum, whum* of artificial circulation...

A persistent feeling of low-grade electrocution throughout a phantom body, of a million shocking worms burrowing into her at once... Penetrating chill as if bathed in liquid nitrogen...

Absence of taste or smell... Completely blind... Hearing and touch pruned back so extensively as to be unreliable... Fleeting aches, almost pleasant by comparison to what came before... And when the pain finally fades, there is unfathomable isolation... Senseless, removed from tangible existence... A freeze-dried, sentient dot lost in infinite void...

What have I become?

*****

Movement!

She feels herself being lifted, shifted to one side, and raised into an upright position...

Subtle vibrations around her... A feeling of warmth ascending her spine...

Relief from burning cold...then defrosting nerves ignite in delayed throes, brilliant and cauterizing like naked rays of blue-white sunlight...

*****

Voiceless shrieks in abyssal nowhere...

IT DOESN'T END! THERE'S NO END! IT WON'T END!

MAKE IT STOP! MAKE IT STOP! MAKE IT STOP! MAKE IT STOP! MAKE IT STOP! MAKE IT STOP! MAKE IT STOP...!

*****

Lost time... Minutes? Months?

Am I dead? Am I dreaming?

No, in a dream, I see things... This can't be a dream...
But I can't be alive...not like this. This is death. This must be death...

*****

Teetering between sleep and consciousness, unable to tell one state from the other and never fully reaching either...

Hallucinations of color streak the darkness, rising, melting, and blending...tenuous, immaterial...

A barrage of remembered faces and places, familiar, haunting, disorienting...

*****

Saskia warned me, but I wouldn't listen. Too stubborn. I'll be shelved in The Cooler *like the rest...another of Honniker's trophies...forgotten...*

*****

Boredom.

Endless, excruciating boredom and depression...

Unable to do anything but exist, no matter how desperately she wishes she did not. All the while, the *whum, whum, whum* rhythm carries on...

*****

Whispers in the void...urgent whispers passing back and forth...

WHO'S THERE?

Hushed voices converse just beyond her ability to hear, mocking and jeering...

WHAT DO YOU WANT? COME OUT!

Titters and giggles like cruel children mocking the insect they have crushed...

I SAID, COME OUT!

Shao-Lo pushes into the void enveloping her, chasing ghosts. They are elusive, always just beyond reach, taunting her clumsy efforts...

*****

O'Kai's spectral image wavers in the formless dark, dressed in charcoal grays, shoulders square, hands at his sides.

"I've never been so disappointed by anyone in my command," the specter says. "I should have sent Chusan, instead."

*****

Careening through infinity, falling faster than light without moving...

Deformed recollections streak by, smeared and discolored from relativistic effects...

Brutality of Collection Rotations... Lost teammates...

Dispatching entire crews of surrendered Blueskins and jettisoning them to hard vacuum...

Toothy leer of Honniker's predators and the expressionless masks of Mikato's machines...

Replaying the bargain in her head, hearing Honniker's and Mikato's promise of durability, strength, and extended life...

Flashes of anger, of betrayal...

THEY LIED! They lured; they manipulated! Tricked me... I'll get them. Somehow, I'LL GET THEM.

*****

Thirst beyond anything ever experienced...

Sun-parched dryness in rarified desert atmosphere...

A dehydration headache like drill bits through her empty eye sockets...

Fantasies of cool pitchers pouring over her and long gulping draughts, unable to quench an all-consuming need...

*****

Phantom sensations...

Buzzing on a non-existent tongue as though licking a battery...

Taste of salty electrolyte...

Twitching of quadriceps long since carved away...

The smell of ozone from a recently fired rifle...

An itch beyond comprehension, infuriating, situated directly between excised shoulder blades...

*****

Acceptance...

Concentrating on formless dimension as if she were staring at a blank wall in a vacant, unlit room...

Shao-Lo drives all thought and sensation aside. Calm, detached, she embraces this state of non-being, without mind or body...

There is no pain. There is no self. There is no...thing.

Oblivion.

*****

I want a chair, Shao-Lo thinks.

A sturdy metal seat with high back condenses before her, taking shape without energy or matter to feed its creation.

And a table to match.

The void spawns a semi-circular table, precisely as she wishes it. Their simple forms provide a perspective in the limitless expanse, suggesting dimension, space to move through with hard boundaries.

There should be a room, a place for them to exist...

Echoing this suggestion, polished metal walls take shape and enclose the simple furniture much like her office at Cadre One.

Larger, she thinks.

Walls recede, their edges expanding to contain the enlarged space. The ceiling rises until she decides it should stop.

The Cadre Memorial will be on the right wall.

When she looks to her right, the Memorial is there, chronicling Operators lost in honorable service over hundreds of years. When she looks at the room's center her table and chair are there, right where she left them.

I can shape this void however I like, however I need.

The Gun looks down at hands covered in the scars of her countless rotations. She takes a deep breath because she wants to, and her imagined lungs fill with satisfyingly cool, dry air. Settling into the scuffed metal chair, Shao-Lo leans against the back and crosses her thick legs.

This place may be all in my head. But if I'm going to be trapped here I might as well make it comfortable. I have to find patience again, because my opportunity will come. I have no intention of missing it...

*****

Shao-Lo imagines herself atop a hill in *The Park*, gentle breezes blowing past and raising the hair of her thick arms. Long grass rustles in the wind, tickling her bare thighs. Birds squawk and call to one another from trees thick with green foliage.

Golden sun rises at the horizon. She thinks it should be warm, and it is. Her eyes close, her breathing regulates into long, slow breaths. Hands in lap, she lets the golden light bathe her. And then a harsh metal *klank* hammers into her head like a chisel against her eardrum. She flinches at the severity, loses focus, and her pleasant illusion disappears. In its absence, however, there are new sounds in surprising clarity. Wheeled machines pass by only a few meters away. Small electric devices whir nearby, close enough she should be able to reach out and touch them. Farther out is a smoothly clattering assembly line, a subtle whoosh of air through vents, the roar of treaded machines whisking parts from station to station. More than this, she hears the distance *between* the sounds, the spaciousness of a room described by its acoustic reflections the way stones scatter ripples in a pond.

"Colonel Shao-Lo," Mikato's voice calls, strident and bright, "can you hear me?"

Shao-Lo waits, searching deep inside herself, unsure this is not another hallucination.

"I hear you, Doctor," she says turning her attention toward the voice.

"Excellent!" Mikato replies louder than she would like. "We're pleased to hear your voice! Such a journey you've made! We could not know if you would arrive alive...or lucid...at the end."

"That remains to be seen," Shao-Lo burrs. "Where are you? I can't see anything."

"Ah, yes, we need to connect your optics. Just a moment."

There is a flurry of electric motors whirring all around her, then a quick pulse of white that hurts.

"*Gently* at first," Mikato says to someone else in the room. "Start at zero and raise the signal strength gradually."

A suggestion of form appears in the void, the possibility of line, angle, and structure. Objects materialize precisely where acoustic reflections tell her they should be, and Shao-Lo discovers she is in Mikato's workshop off his main production floor. Her vision brightens, already a glare after a subjective lifetime in sensory deprivation, and she strains to cope with how wide her field of view is. Peripheral vision extends well past what should be her shoulders so that she is simultaneously seeing what is in front of and behind her, as well as everything overhead. Not only does her view become brighter, it streams in hyper-realistic detail doubling in resolution every few seconds.

"Too much," she shouts. "Too much! *TOO MUCH!*"

Mikato's holographic projection stoops directly in front of her, leaning in with concern. "I am sorry, too much what?"

Shao-Lo tries to blink, but she cannot shutter the deluge of visual information. "I see...*everything*! It's too much! Make it stop!"

Mikato straightens and nods in understanding. "Narrowing field of view to ninety degrees, quarter resolution."

Shao-Lo's view contracts to a square of tolerable clarity. "That's...that's better."

"You are overloading her visual cortex," Mikato chastises.

"*Leave the medicine to me, Mikato,*" Honniker grumbles, "*and attenuate your signals properly.*"

"Then give me a retinal bandwidth equivalent I can use," the holoprojection shoots back.

"*Ja, ja, sehr gut. Assume the eye has approximately one hundred twenty-six million receptors, of which one hundred twenty million are rods and six million are cones. Use sixteen bit color depth and assume one hundred twenty-eight frames per second refresh rate.*"

"Well, there should be no problem, then. I'm delivering full color stereo signal at sixteen bits per channel."

"*To all receptors?*"

"Of course."

Honniker grunts in annoyance. "*Rods only sense luminance. Cones only sense color and movement. And each cone only senses* one *of the primary colors.*"

"Oh... *Oh my*, is that so?" The projection grips its chin in dismay. To Shao-Lo, it says, "I am *terribly* sorry, Colonel, that must have been... *overwhelming.*"

"That's one word for it," she mutters electronically.

"So each eye is only capable of...roughly *ten megabits per second*?" Mikato says in disbelief. "Hardly seems adequate."

"*Primates are adept at motion sensing and pattern recognition. The eye does not need much detail for the brain to process images effectively.*"

"But we can do *so* much better," Mikato says, still incredulous. To Shao-Lo, the projection adds, "Well, then...we'll start with acuity to which you are accustomed then ramp up to take full advantage of the chassis's sensing capability. After all, what is the point of omni-directional vision if half of it has to be disabled at any given time?"

"Give the Colonel a window in her direct line of sight with high acuity," Honniker counsels, *"roughly akin to the fovea of her retina. Everything outside that window can operate at much lower resolution and bit depth. Visual processors can offload some of that bandwidth, as well, so her visual cortex is not overtaxed."*

"And the size of that window?"

"Two percent of the forward field of view is sufficient."

"TWO PERCENT?" The projection throws its hands up. "How are they not colliding with everything in their paths? Why bother with vision at all? Might as well use RADAR." It turns its holographic gaze on Shao-Lo. "Nature has cheated you."

"Don't talk to me about being cheated when I can't even move," Shao-Lo growls through a speaker. "You wouldn't believe what I've been through, and then you left me...*NOWHERE!*"

"Yes... Without sensation, it would seem we had abandoned you, though I assure you, Colonel, we were never away for a moment." Honniker's tone changes entirely, his vocal manner turning eerily earnest. *"You have endured the most radical surgery ever performed on a living patient. That surgery was nothing compared to managing your brain chemistry after excisement. As feared, you had become dependent upon opiods from such an extended procedure, which complicated the calibration of your brain chemistry. No doubt, it was an existential nightmare for you beyond any pain of the flesh... yet you did not descend into raving lunacy... This bears powerful witness of your will. For that, dear Colonel, you have earned my eternal respect, and I feel no shame in admitting I had grossly underestimated you."*

Shao-Lo mulls the complement, unsure if she should even acknowledge it. She asks instead, "So I'm still alive? Not some boxed upload?"

"You are very much alive! And, more importantly, coherent. But allow me to ask: how are you feeling now?"

Shao-Lo mulls the question before answering, "Better. Thought I was coming apart. If I could have self-terminated, I *would* have."

Mikato's projection clasps its hands. "You have delivered your end of the bargain, Colonel. Now, Honniker and I must deliver ours. Are you ready?"

"Ready? For...?"

"Reincarnation."

136

Shao-Lo tracks her vision over to Mikato's projection, suddenly noticing how natural it feels to be looking through the chassis's eyes. Even though the photoreceptors are fixed in place, the hand off from one receptor to the other is seamless, and she can spin her stereoscopic gaze in a circle as if her head were on an infinite swivel. Wherever she wishes to look, her new eyes are already there, adjusting focal length and magnification as needed. Impressed, she peers out through the doorway to Mikato's production floor and zooms in on the busy assembly line. Closer and closer she dials in until she can read a proof of quality stamp on a single support brace underneath. Without effort, she zooms out, keeping a fixed gaze. There is no icon or gauge loitering in her field of view, yet she knows the exact distance from where she sits to the brace is precisely 28.693 meters and its temperature is 31.667 degrees Celsius.

Eager to find out what else is in store, she delinquently answers, "Yeah, I'm ready."

BROKEN FOR YOU

Shao-Lo marches behind Mikato's projection, staring into the palms of her segmented hands, still in awe of their liquid smooth movement. Everything she looks at resolves in stunning clarity, and she knows things about objects without having to guess. She *knows* the wall plates are an alloy of Aluminum and Magnesium, for example, and that the floor is an alloy of Iron, Nickel, Chromium, and Manganese. She *knows* the ambient air temperature is twenty-two degrees centigrade with air pressure of one hundred kilopascals, precisely. Traces of atomized grease and oils hang in the air. And there are twenty-eight unused radio channels currently available, most of which in the 300-3000Hz band.

Mikato's holoprojection seems glaringly bright in the otherwise darkened corridors, so Shao-Lo imagines herself squinting. Her photoreceptors dim appropriately.

Not like I really need to see anything, Shao-Lo thinks, *I can* hear *where the walls are*.

Her articulated feet strike heel first with her customary stride, producing an obnoxious *thud* in her synthetic ears, so she rises to toes. Each step thereafter lands in catlike stealth.

In the path from Mikato's production floor toward Honniker's MedLab, Shao-Lo pays particular attention to the way her mechanical frame seems to fit. She tries not to think about breathing, since doing so often triggers panic when she cannot (a side-effect Honniker has assured will go away in time). But most intriguing is the tactile sensation the full chassis offers. It communicates the subtlest vibrations, informs of the minute resistance of air, liquid, and solid surfaces. Though she knows it is merely feedback measured in variations of voltage, the neuro-photonic interface translates it into impulses she can truly feel. Even something as simple as touching her thumb and fingers together offers tangible proof of existence, a luxury that would have made her time spent discorporate much easier to bear.

Glass doors slide aside and the pair strides into Honniker's MedLab reception area. Shao-Lo notes lingering traces of airborne dust and fungal spores without having to endure the unpleasant, musty odor.

So far, so good, she thinks.

They pass through *The Flounder's* atrium, follow the curved corridor past darkened offices, and emerge into the spacious cavern of Honniker's surgical theater. Mikato's projection cuts a path down the middle, passing rows of spotless, sterilized medical stations. Shao-Lo turns her attention toward the ceiling, annoyed that Marta still dangles by a severed lift cable around the neck.

The remade Gun asks, "You ever gonna take her down, Honniker?"

"*It was ever so dreary in here before. Marta's shell adds* precisely *the decoration needed.*"

Mikato's projection turns to look over its shoulder at Shao-Lo, says nothing, and continues toward *The Cooler* at the rear of the cavern. At approach, heavy locks *clank* as they release and the vault unseals with a puff of condensed vapor. It swings wide on motorized hinges, allowing Shao-Lo inside without breaking stride.

Rows of mortuary drawers tunnel into the high side walls, sealed shut by metal doors gone fuzzy with ice crystals. Below them, tall plate glass windows are thick with frost, obscuring the rooms beyond. Yet Shao-Lo's new eyes automatically shift wavelength and trace outlines of medical recliners and surgical carts. She wonders if Rosenthal might still be in one of them.

The last room on the left is clear of frost and light pours out from the open doorway. Mikato's projection enters and when Shao-Lo follows, she notes the temperature inside is well above freezing. Then the Gun stops short, confronted by three circular frames stretching out human remains.

One frame props up a partial skeleton, missing spine and skull. A mandible hangs from fine wire tethers above the sternum, as do all the upper teeth of the mouth as if the skull were merely invisible instead of absent. Bones are stripped of soft tissue, revealing wraps of carbon fiber along the shafts, as well as cable and ribbon reinforcements at major joints.

The next frame hangs a suit of thick pink muscle from brass hooks. Meaty arms and legs dangle at the corners with tendons and ligaments dissected in complete groups. Plate-like pectorals dominate the chest, below which abdominals line up in cobblestone rows. Broad, square shoulders rise to arched trapezii then turn vertically to a thick neck. Atop the neck is a head-shaped bucket, open at the top, framed on the sides by Temporalis and Masseter. Facial muscles are locked in dour expression with sewn-shut eyes and mouth.

The last frame holds a drape of skin, flayed in one complete piece. Barbed hooks tug at the edges, keeping the outline taut, but the face hangs slack without underlying structures to give it shape.

Shao-Lo stares longest at her old skin, sweeping up from the feet, taking in the multitude keloids, lacerations, burns, perforations, and grafts. Seeing them at all once is like reading her service record, every scar corresponding to major action, and she swells inside with pride. But the once-sharp brow, straight nose, and high cheeks sag into a haunting, eyeless mask; and a drooping chin pulls the mouth into an open ring as if captured mid-howl.

Her vision blurs; her mind swims.

I don't know how to process this...

The hollow face in front of her is absent of life, now a dead, useless thing. Yet this is not the body of a slain Operator. It belongs to her; it is her intimate self, her identity. And seeing it displayed with such disrespect is infuriating reminder Deepak was once trussed up in a similar frame. Were she still wearing that skin, outrage and anger would have lowered her head and tugged her expression into a mask of violent intent. But she no longer has a face to betray her thoughts, so she remains rooted in place, silent, taking it in through inscrutable black lenses.

Klanking footfalls outside the room break her stare, and she turns to see an approaching combat chassis through the plate glass window. It lumbers in with the subtlety and grace of a trash smasher then parks itself beside the frame of skin. She scans its chest plate for an image of a Geek, wondering if this could be Saskia in a sour mood, but the machine's only engraving is a serial number in large block type. It also bears a full combat package on its forearms, putting the Gun on alert.

"No doubt you were wondering why I asked you here, Colonel," Honniker says from an omni-directional speaker. *"Indulge us a moment, if you will. Doctor Mikato, would you do the honors?"*

Mikato's projection nods and cues the war machine with a finger. On Mikato's signal, the combat chassis grips the circular frame holding Shao-Lo's skin and walks behind it, rotating the frame a half turn and showing Shao-Lo her own scarred back. A ruler-straight incision runs from between deflated buttocks up the spine and neck to a stubbly gray scalp. Subcutaneous tissue tinges the inside yellow-ish white. Veins lace the translucent tissue with cords of bluish green.

Shao-Lo gazes, mute, her synthetic eyes streaming every detail.

"*It could be said the skin serves two primary functions,*" Honniker lectures. "*One, to protect the body against environmental factors that could harm it, and, two, to sense the environment by touch. It is exceedingly poor at both.*"

The combat chassis steps back, flicks a nozzle into place at the end of its arm and blasts a fan of fire across the hanging skin. Shocked, Shao-Lo watches her scarified hide peel in layers, shrivel, then catch fire, crackling as it burns. The horrified mask elongates as flames pour through gaping eyelids and lips. Corners of the mouth split then tear all the way to the edges of the face. Gravity drags everything below the nostrils to the deck while the upper face and scalp shrivel to carbonized chunks on thin wire hangers.

Just as suddenly, the chassis pivots and sweeps the fan of flame over Shao-Lo. She flinches, but there is no pain at all. Flames douse her head to foot, and she can sense eddies swirling around her, but there is no injury— merely awareness of temperature and sooty residue on her armored exterior.

Shao-Lo spreads her stance, tang of adrenaline already coursing through her blood-surrogate.

"*Had you been wearing this skin, Colonel, not only would you have died, you would have been in excruciating agony until the very end.*"

The combat chassis steps over to the frame suspending Shao-Lo's thick muscles. A double-sided blade slides out from its forearm.

"*A flesh-based soldier has a modest benefit: it can be grown from relatively few resources. Each generation that survives to reproductive age can spawn multiple variants of itself. In this way, human kind can adapt and occupy environmental niches that a synthetic species could not.*"

The chassis flicks its blade at the suit of muscle as if teasing, opening tiny cuts wherever the blade touches.

"*But what use is a soldier if it cannot resist the simplest of tools?*"

The machine swings, opening long slices across abdominals, shoulders, and back. The face is slashed, left arm hacked away, right leg amputated above the knee. And then the machine punch-stabs through the back, blade tip erupting through the chest right where the heart would be. It retracts the blade slowly, serrated edges hissing through muscles maintained and tuned as carefully as any piece in her kit over a lifetime.

The chassis surges at Shao-Lo, whipping the blade at her. She steps in and blocks automatically, shattering the blade against hard angles of her arm; and the tip *whizzes* across the room.

Shao-Lo leans forward and spreads her shoulders, primed for a deadly contest. To her disappointment, the combat chassis steps back and lowers its raised arm.

*"Again, we see unacceptable vulnerability. A laughably simple piece of metal was sufficient to ruin this...*being. *Whatever skills a flesh-based soldier learns are lost, irretrievably, in death. There is no auto archive, no backup, and you must start all over again from the beginning."*

The chassis steps over to the last frame, grips the femur, and powers it from the reinforced hip socket. Letting the lower leg and foot swing freely by cable and ribbon attachments, the chassis grips the long bone in both segmented hands, lifts it overhead, then slams it down onto a raised knee with a thunderous *CRACK*. Off-white splinters explode, clattering against walls, ceiling, and floor.

Making show of still-pink marrow inside, Honniker adds with mocking tone, *"This is your body, which I have broken for you."*

The chassis tosses the bones at Shao-Lo's articulated feet.

"You had to be freed from this cage that confined you. Can you see that you are now liberated from suffering? Delivered from fragility? No longer the stunted primate."

The chassis turns again toward the skeleton and takes hold of a ribcage knotted with healed fractures. Shao-Lo steps in fast as a thought and kicks the chassis halfway through the opposite wall. Before it can free itself from the deformed wall braces, the Gun yanks it out of the wall, slams it to the deck, and climbs astride it. She rips away armor plates, tears clusters of synthetic muscle from flailing arms, and pounds through exposed circuit paths, battering it into the floor with the speed of a hammer drill.

The machine sprawls, photoreceptors shattered. Shao-Lo stands and hauls the savaged chassis up with her, lifting it high overhead then cracking repeatedly it over her knee until its internal supports finally give way.

There is no air in Shao-Lo's chest, no thudding heart driving her fury, only a purified will as cold and metallic as the body that carries her, and the Gun rips her victim in completely half. Hydraulic fluid spurts from avulsed components like black blood. Electrolyte rains down her chest, etching acidic trails down her armor plate. Swinging each section in big circles, she hurls first one half, then the other half into the floor with deafening *bangs*; and the remains smolder in a fizzing, crumpled heap.

Honniker states, *"Under my expert scalpel you have transcended your limited existence, evolving to a degree your MedTechs could never accomplish through genetic manipulation. Conventional fire cannot burn you, the desolation of space cannot freeze or asphyxiate you. No pathogen or chemical can infiltrate your sealed life support system. Durability and longevity beyond many of your subjective lifetimes... At last, you have a body worthy of your skills. Do you agree that we have delivered on our end of this bargain?"*

Shao-Lo considers the message, reconciles it against the messenger, and finds no fault. "I do," she answers.

"Look now at what you have done with your bare hands."

She looks down at the pulverized war machine in satisfaction.

"So tell us, Colonel, would you like to fully test your capabilities?"

"No simulations," Shao-Lo insists. "Real world scenario."

"Easily arranged," Mikato's projection replies, aura glowing in the acrid smoke. A holowindow opens, depicting an oval room she has not seen before. Sitting lotus style on the barren floor is a mass of fur, pointed ears, and protruding tusks. It looks up from its meditation with the steel gray eyes of a Cadre Operator, and spreads clawed hands in invitation.

"We have given you the gift of inevitable victory. Go and dispatch your enemy." With an audible smirk, Honniker adds, *"This do, in remembrance of me."*

CHEMICAL AGGRESSION

Shao-Lo rockets backward into the arena wall and bounces, staggering off balance. A savage roar shakes the floor, and a mountain of fur and teeth hurtles itself at her. The Gun fakes to the left and dives right, barely evading the beast's wide spread arms. She tucks, tumbles onto articulated feet, and springs at the monster's back; but it whirls about and smashes a giant fist dead center of her breastplate. The spiked fist knocks her flat on her back and sends her skidding. Before she can get her feet beneath her it is sprinting at her, arms wide for a tackle, bellowing with insane rage.

This one's a handful...

She crouches low, leans forward, and launches like a missile into the monster's gut, knocking all the air out of its roar. But she hits below center of gravity and the beast collapses on top of her. The Gun shoves up from the floor and bucks. The monster hangs on with inhuman strength, wraps its legs around her midsection, and locks ankles on the other side. In another instant, it scoops her legs in a bear hug embrace, traps her arms in the crooks of its knees, and shuffles to its feet. Shao-lo thrashes at fur covered legs like columns of steel, yet cannot get a proper angle to strike. The monster sets its stance, leaps into the air, and pile drives her straight into the arena floor. Stars burst in her synthetic vision and two of her photoreceptors wink out.

Shao-Lo detaches both of her trapped legs at the hips and slithers around to the monster's back. The beast drops her detached legs and frenzies, antler-like spikes along its spine screeching against her armor plating. No matter how the beast flails Shao-Lo hangs on, working her way up the hunched back with the patience of a constrictor.

The beast clutches blindly behind itself, swinging its great head side to side, flinging saliva in long ropes. It leaps, dives, rolls, and bashes Shao-Lo against the deck, but cannot break her grip.

The Gun hugs herself close to the monster, absorbing its ineffectual drubbing, creeping ever closer to its throat. She crests its great shoulders, ready to set the finishing choke, when the monster stoops, grabs one of her detached legs, and whips it like a flail across her back. Shards of metal explode from the ferocious hit.

Enough of this!

Shao-Lo releases one hand and swings aside, letting the beast cudgel itself on the spine. The blow lands squarely on a dorsal spike, breaking it off with a snap like a pistol shot. The beast howls.

Shao-Lo swings herself across the monster's back again, trapping her disconnected leg between her chestplate and antler-like spines. The Deepak-thing yanks on the trapped limb, fails to free it, and stoops for the other leg on the floor.

Shao-Lo slides her trapped leg down to the hip socket and it latches tight. The beast spins, and with only one hand gripping the thick hide, Shao-Lo sails around the beast like a cape. Its hairy hide stretches taut then tears beneath her sharp fingertips, and the beast shrieks. Dark red blood seeps through the runnels of her articulated hand, slicking her grip. With the beast's next shake, she slips.

The Gun arcs through the air, tucks, rolls, and rises onto her one leg; but the ankle beneath her wobbles from a broken rotator collar, and she hops to keep balance.

Across the arena her opponent snatches up the other leg and clutches it at the narrow ankle. Leveling a hateful gaze, the beast lifts the leg high like a cudgel, roars, and charges.

Shao-Lo stoops over into a crouched tripod, scuttles easily out of the behemoth's way, then chases after it. The monster halts and whirls about, swinging the leg in a devastating backhand. Shao-Lo ducks, slides in close, grabs two handfuls of hide under the ribcage and hefts the beast off its feet. Holding the monster high overhead, she spins at the waist and accelerates to dizzying speed.

The beast throws its arms out wide for balance, treading air, and its cudgel skitters off to the arena's edge. Shao-Lo hurls the beast in the opposite direction, sprints on hands and foot for her appendage, reattaches it, and rises to her feet.

The monster flops onto its gut, shuddering floor plates like an earthquake. Eyes darting and blinking, it pushes up to hands and knees. Its great maw stretches wide in a nauseous yawn then it shakes its big shaggy head. Gradually, the beast rises to its feet, takes a deep breath, and charges.

Chemical aggression streams through Shao-Lo's blood surrogate. *This ends NOW.*

Perceptions dial in to tight focus. Limbs hum with capacitance. And when she looks at the beast, it seems to be running at her in slow motion. Standing askance to use her undamaged eyes, she studies her opponent as it charges, how its pink tongue arches behind sharp metal teeth and jutting tusks, how its mane of black hair sways with every powerful stride, and, most of all, how Deepak's wild, steel gray eyes are trapped inside this monstrous form neither man nor animal.

The creature bellows, arms wide for a punishing takedown, but Shao-Lo is already standing out of reach to one side. The Deepak-thing turns its great head, gaping in surprise. As it passes by, Shao-Lo follows with a devastating kick to its spine that sends it careening face first into the wall. The beast bounces awfully, head thrown back, staggering on its heels for balance. Before it can recover, Shao-Lo is behind it. She catches the beast behind the head and rams its face into the wall again, and again, and *again*, until the great shoulders slump.

The beast sinks to its knees and topples backwards, arms falling to each side like timber. Shao-Lo steps astride the dazed creature, grips the loose skin under its chin with one hand, and extends a jagged blade from her other wrist. Planting the point at the monster's throat, Shao-Lo declares in stentorian voice, "THIS CONTEST IS *OVER*."

The Deepak-thing blinks hard, trying to peer through swollen, broken orbits. Gray eyes converge as its senses return, and it stares up at her with an expression she cannot decipher. Then a guttural rumble resounds in its chest, and it lifts its great head, pressing against the blade tip at its throat. It slaps its huge palms to the deck and its lips curl into a teeth bared grimace as it pushes up from the floor.

"*It will not give up, Colonel,*" Honniker goads. "*You may as well finish it.*"

Even without Honniker's taunt, her urge to kill is so primal, so forceful, it does not feel like her own.

End its suffering, a voice says in her mind. *Deepak couldn't bear to live this way. Honor his memory.*

It's an abomination, a mockery. A thing that should not be. END IT!

Her arm tenses for the killing stroke when an odd pang of conscience stays the execution. She imagines not O'Kai, nor any Colonist, but Saskia standing over her, watching. What it would say in this situation is easy to guess, and that thought pierces through the rage soaked depths.

This is not my enemy... Yes, an abomination... But alive...

"I don't have to kill you," the Gun utters aloud. "Therefore, I will not."

Shao-Lo retracts her blade, expecting the Deepak-thing to acquiesce in the face of obvious defeat. Rather, it surges at her, jaws gaping. In a blink, her fist cocks back and smashes the beast's face with the force of a cannon shot. The monster falls back, inert, as echoes from the hit fade among the arena walls.

"And *stay* there," Shao-Lo burrs, rising to her feet, one ankle wobbling. Irritated, she lifts the damaged limb and turns her torso sideways to view it with undamaged eyes.

Mikato's projection appears across from her, applauding with holographic hands. "Well done, Colonel! An excellent first test!"

"*Why you spared your opponent is a mystery, however,*" Honniker counters. "*It would have been mercy to end its existence.*"

Shao-Lo does not reply, still sorting out precisely what stayed her hand and whether or not she will regret it later. Instead, she focuses on damage to her chassis, suddenly aware these injuries will not heal on their own.

Didn't figure that into the deal... I have to depend on Mikato and Honniker to fix me...maybe forever. They'll use that to their advantage, no question.

Mikato's projection clasps holographic hands together. "Is something wrong, Colonel? You seem displeased."

"Hadn't occurred to me until now I'll have to come to you for repairs. Don't like being tied to you that way."

The projection shrugs. "You were always tied to *someone* for healing. You have traded your MedTechs for us, nothing more. Though I do admit there is value in having you need us in the future, not the least of which is that you can not allow us to be killed without ensuring your own demise."

"And you'll never abuse that, *I'm sure.*"

The projection frets. "I'm sorry if you see that as a disadvantage. Our interdependence is beneficial. Tell me, Colonel, is it so different from depending on your MedTechs?"

Turning one of her functional eyes directly on the projection, Shao-Lo answers, "Yeah. It's *different.*" She plucks clumps of dark brown fur from her segmented hands then lifts her broken ankle. "Since I don't have a choice... want to give me a hand with this?"

The projection interlaces holographic fingers and grins like a cat with a songbird. "Of course."

Ignorance and Arrogance

Shao-Lo rides the plexi-steel lift down to Mikato's bright white production floor and steps out, torso rotated at a forty-five degree angle so her undamaged eyes can see the way ahead. Out on the main floor, lines of machinery pass parts from one node to the next with the squeak of metal rollers, the hum of annealers, and the hiss of vapor.

Mikato's holoprojection appears at the entrance to the workshop and beckons. "If you please, Colonel, this way."

The Gun follows the hologram through the open doorway. At center of the room is a familiar and well-worn recliner with open restraints. The holoprojection gestures toward it, and Shao-Lo settles in.

The Gun glances through the doorway at the smooth running production lines, asking, "What are you making out there?"

Without looking, the projection answers, "Replacement parts. Your opponent managed to break what I thought was unbreakable. Must have been an undetected defect in the crystalline matrix." It looks up, smiling. "Good we have these tests, no?"

"Wasn't that hard a hit that knocked my eyes out," Shao-Lo replies. "If these parts of yours fail so easily, you've got serious design flaws."

The projection shoots an annoyed look at the Colonel. "My photoreceptor design is not the problem. Your neural encasement shifted in its ballistic gel and stressed an optical interconnect."

"Ballistic gel?"

"Yes. You know your skull and spine are encased in protective alloys that have a layer of shock absorption built-in, yes?"

Shao-Lo waves a hand in a tight circle, urging Mikato to get on with it.

"We opted to give you an additional layer of shock absorption by immersing your entire neural encasement in a cylinder of ballistic gel. The idea is that you could withstand many multiples of acceleration beyond what you could normally tolerate. It seems we erred on the side of caution and made the gel too soft. Thus, when you let yourself get *bounced on your head*, the encasement shifted inside the cylinder, and strained connections to your front two photoreceptors."

"*The remedy is a simple matter of using a firmer compound*," Honniker adds from an unseen speaker.

With a derisive edge, Shao-Lo asks, "All this time, and you still haven't got it figured out? Not filling me with a lot of confidence."

"*The Colonel is as arrogant, and ignorant, as ever.*"

"Indeed," Mikato's projection agrees with a disappointed smirk. "How long would she have lasted in the arena with her old body, I wonder?" The table restraints snap shut, and Mikato glares at her, his expression a straight set of horizontal lines. "Since this is all we have to work with, we must get by."

A motorized cart rolls in from the production floor, its tray loaded with freshly minted metal parts. Shao-Lo recognizes a new rotator collar for her damaged ankle. The other parts are more obscure, including hardened circuit boards and clusters of microscopic fibers.

"*With your permission, Colonel, we'd like to open your chassis and begin repairs. This means uninstalling your neural encasement and being temporarily deprived of your senses. Will you allow us to proceed?*"

"Will I remain conscious?"

"*Ja. There is no need for anesthetic.*"

"Good, because I also want to know why combat stims triggered so late in the match."

Cam locks rotate at the edges of Shao-Lo's breastplate and it pops open with a hiss.

"*The delay of your 'combat stims,' as you call them, is merely one of calibration. Once attuned, you will be able to control the flows of neurotransmitters at will. Naturally, we do not expect you to directly modulate levels, since you have no medical training. Instead, you must think about the situation you are in and what you need to do. The correct neurotransmitters will flow, similar to the way you 'psych yourself up' prior to combat. Through time and practice, you will tune those levels appropriately.*"

Mechanical arms descend from a hub above the recliner, two of which grip the unlocked breastplate with suction pads and lift it away. Others disassemble layers of insulation, secondary armor plating, and life-support apparatus until a transparent cylinder is visible at the chassis's core. Another pair of arms reaches for the cylinder.

"Wait," Shao-Lo says, her voice uneasy. "I want to see... I want to *see* what I look like...what's left."

The projection juts a holographic lip and shrugs. "As you wish."

One of the mechanical arms rotates a scoping tool into place and it hovers directly above the transparent cylinder.

"Transmitting now," Mikato announces.

The feed streams directly into Shao-Lo's cortex. In her virtual view, she sees a gleaming silver skull with hollow eye sockets suspended in translucent gelatin. A metal clad spinal column descends from the base of the skull, its natural curves preserved and supported by the gel. Black cables connect with spinal nerve caps at regular intervals, then gather together toward the cylinder's base and exit at a sealed junction. Twin vascular tubes—one crimson, the other cobalt blue—enter the cylinder from a port at its top then divert to each side of the skull, curve beneath it, and terminate at ports for Jugular and Carotid foramen.

Shao-Lo asks, "Is this...*all?*"

The projection tilts its head, considering the question. "It is all you ever were. The rest was merely support structure for your nervous system...a support structure we have replaced with something far more durable."

"Durable?" Shao-Lo scoffs and points to her broken ankle.

"*Before you mock us again,* let me remind the Colonel that any advanced piece of technology requires testing and tuning before it is finished. You have progressed this far in only six months, which in itself is admirable. However, without your patient participation you will find this process can be drawn out over a...*very*...long...time."

I've been here six months? Shao-Lo thinks, surprised. *Frackit games, negotiations, rehabilitation after surgery...that's about two months... That means I was on Honniker's table for...FOUR MONTHS?*

Shao-Lo turns pensive, grimly aware that her Cadre brothers and sisters are streaking toward their final confrontation. *Factoring the time it took to get here... the fleet will be arriving at Earth in another few months...*

"*Is the Colonel prepared for sensory disconnect?*"

Honniker's question derails her train of thought, reminding her that she is seeing without eyes, hearing without ears, speaking without mouth, jaw, or tongue. Her senses can now be connected or disconnected at will, just pluggable parts in a quasi-living machine. The thought is such absurdity she still has difficulty accepting it. Yet for all of her irritation at minor failures, improvements in strength, speed, and acuity are nothing short of miraculous.

There is no question, Mikato and Honniker have lived up to their promise.

"All right," Shao-Lo growls, "*quickly...*"

"*The Colonel wishes to be elsewhere, ja? With her friends for the imminent assault of Earth, hmm?*"

Shao-Lo pauses, unsure how Honniker could know that, unsure if she told him outright during their bargaining or if she might have been delirious and raving during her four-month surgery...or if he can read her mind.

"That's right," she replies. "Sooner I get there, the sooner you'll have all the combat test data you've ever dreamed of."

"I must remind the Colonel," Mikato's holo projection adds, "there is something she must do before we can allow her to leave."

"Blending of minds..." Shao-Lo recalls aloud.

"Yes, exactly."

"And *Plasma Rain*. You'll share that, as well."

The holoprojection smirks unhappily. "I'm surprised I need to keep reminding you of this: once you know our minds, Colonel, *all* of our secrets are yours."

Shao-Lo watches the video feed streaming into her cortex, focusing on her own hollow eye sockets.

"*So. What will the Colonel decide?*"

A thousand contingencies play out in Shao-Lo's mind, each branching into a fractal tree of eventualities with innumerable outcomes. There are far too many factors to predict, but there is one common thread among every contingency: if there is a chance she can deliver the Cadre from destruction but fails to do so, she will never be able to live with herself.

"Whatever I am now, I've come this far," Shao-Lo says, still staring into her own empty eye sockets. "Let's finish it."

REDEFINING AGGRESSION

When Shao-Lo awakens, a vast whiteness assaults her eyes. She raises a hand of flesh and bone against the glare. When she squints, eyelids slide over real eyes; when she grimaces, leathery skin bunches at the corners of her face.

From somewhere amid the glare, Mikato asks, "My apologies, Colonel, is that too bright?"

"Yes, dim it a bit," she replies, feeling the buzz of vocal cords in her throat. Whiteness fades to a tolerable shine.

The old Gun looks down at herself and sees an immaculate dress gray Cadre uniform with polished black boots. Running both hands down the front of her jacket, she feels the texture of heavy-duty fabric and firmness of muscle beneath. Every decoration she ever earned is clustered on her chest and when she touches her collar, she finds an eagle rank insignia right where it should be.

Confused at being in her old body again, she asks the omnipresent white glow, "What's going on? Where am I?"

"Take your time," Mikato's voice replies. "Allow yourself to adjust."

Shao-Lo frowns, finding no answer in Mikato's words. But when she looks to her right, she finds a metal plated door with decades of swirl marks. A Cadre eagle is engraved dead center, eye level.

Instinctively, she reaches for the panel button to open it. When the door slides aside, she looks into a familiar room with a semi-circular meeting table. O'Kai is seated at the apex of the curved side. To his left sit Munro and Ralla. To his right sit Chusan and, strangely enough, herself. All are engaged in a deep discussion when Shao-Lo's doppelganger slams the table with a fist and shouts, "ROSENTHAL WAS NOT A *DRONE*!" Junior officers at the table stiffen and fall quiet, looking to O'Kai with questioning glances.

Shao-Lo touches the panel button again, closing the door on an unpleasant memory.

When she steps back, she finds herself in the hallway outside of Leadership Council chambers at Cadre One. MedTechs hustle past on various missions. An occasional Operator strides by on patrol with a respectful salute, acknowledging her as, "*Major*." The weathered faces passing by have long since passed on, however, and her steps down the corridor become tentative. Older MedTechs, hunched with degenerative diseases and capped with gray stubble limp by, yet when she turns about to watch them, they stand straighter in their gait, and their hair darkens, thickens into pates of rich black. Operators passing on patrol wear clunkier armor, armed with weapons many generations old, and Shao-Lo is stunned to see O'Kai, face nearly unmarked, youthful and handsome. He salutes with a polite, yet gruff, "*Lieutenant*."

Her heels land harder against the floor plates and when she looks down, she finds herself clad entirely in flat black armor with an ancient rifle slung over one shoulder. A young Geek marches in step to her right, also armored in flat black, pistols clipped to the small of her back, bulky helmet cradled in one arm. Silver contact terminals gleam on the Geek's shaved head. While she bears no scars of combat, the young Operator strides without fear as if she has already faced a hundred Rotations.

Behind Shao-Lo marches a massive Brick in full kit, visor of his helmet open, cannon slung across his barrel chest and hanging at his waist. Taller than Shao-Lo and towering over the Geek, he is like a pitched-forward cliff of insuperable black rock. Gray stubble hides cheeks as rough and rigid as old wood. Red-rimmed eyes smolder like twin calderas.

Shao-Lo leads her team into Cadre One's main Hangar Bay where two Virus Ships stand parked on articulated struts. Outside the left craft, a tall Gun stands vigil, helmet cradled in his left arm. His shoulders are a bit wider than most Guns, and he carries more mass in the chest. Like the Geek at her side, this Gun is young, fresh-faced and free of combat scars. He salutes crisply.

"Lieutenant Shao-Lo, both craft fully fuelled, G-B-R-F-S."

Shao-Lo returns the salute. "Good. Is your team ready?"

"Aye, sir. Gear stowed, awaiting your order."

Shao-Lo turns to her team. "Ralla, Cayman, get aboard. I'm right behind you." Both Geek and Brick snap crisp salutes. Ralla slips her helmet over her head and ducks beneath the craft. Cayman slaps his visor down and duck-walks under the craft after Ralla.

Shao-Lo faces the junior Gun and extends her hand. He looks at it and clasps it firmly. Glancing at his thick eyebrows, symmetrical ears, and pate of short-cropped hair that will soon be burned away, Shao-Lo says, "Good hunting, Chusan."

"You, as well, sir."

There is a bright flash, and Shao-Lo is sprinting down the corridor of a Blueskin ship, rifle tucked into her shoulder, triggering at a makeshift barricade as fast as her finger will pull. Return fire hits like a sledge, staggering, slowing, knocking her off balance. Assaulted blunted, she turns and rams her shoulder through a flimsy door, crashing to the deck of an unoccupied cabin.

"*COMMITTING*," booms a deep voice via radio. A violet glow coalesces in the corridor then surges down the hallway, detonating the barricade with a deafening *BA-ROOM*.

Shao-Lo rattles her head, checks her weapon, then kneels at the cabin doorway and aims her rifle at the destroyed barricade. Through her scope she sees Blueskin soldiers lying in pieces among the ruins, amputated limbs still clutching weapons.

"Chusan, Cayman, *move up*," she shouts and sprints to the barricade. Just shy of it she drops to her knees, skidding behind charred hunks of metal and carbonized bodies. Chusan slides up behind her and pats her shoulder. Cayman's heavy footfalls rumble the floor plates as he sprints up from the rear.

Through whorls of smoke, Shao-Lo spies movement. Her visor compensates in infrared, outlining figures assembling a tripod. Two more Blueskins arrive, carrying a stout multi-barreled object, and they heft it onto the mounting plate. "Heavy weapon! Cayman *front*," she barks.

A violet glow fills the smoky air as Cayman primes his cannon. He steps around the corner, bringing his weapon to bear. Before he can trigger the wall behind him perforates in a barrage of high-energy beams, shatters, and blows out to space. The Brick drops his cannon and spiders himself across the hallway, bracing against the gale of depressurization, howling in ungodly agony as internal organs slither out through a five-centimeter hole in his mid-section.

Shao-Lo shouts, "WHAT IS THIS?"

The scene freezes. Cayman is petrified in the moment of evisceration. Smoke, blood, and dust hanging motionless in the air around him. Shao-Lo can move about, however, and she rises from her crouch. Bewildered, the

Gun steps over to Cayman and stares at loops of intestine, gall, and chunks of bloody liver crowding through an exit hole in his armor.

"I said, What *IS* this?"

"*You are sharing the memories that made you, shaped you,*" Honniker answers. "*Strongest memories surface first, of course.*"

Shao-Lo's cheek twitches as she steps around her old teammate. By the time she entered service, Cayman was well-seasoned with ten rotations to his name and two hundred fifty thousand tonnes in collection. Just by clearing his throat, he could check her on a bad call, and he pulled her ass out of the fire after more rookie mistakes than she cares to recall. On this rotation, however, there was no error in her leadership, no fault in their performance. The enemy outgunned them, simple as that. It does not make his loss any easier to confront.

She turns toward the shattered wall behind Cayman and studies it. Weakened by numerous beam strikes, the ship's hull has blown out, and bright fragments hang suspended in space. Through gaps between them she sees a sleek enemy warship in the distance, its D-E rails shimmering mid-barrage. Clearly, when internal defenses were not enough to suppress Shao-Lo's advance, the Eleto captain called in heavier firepower from outside.

"Up to this point," Shao-Lo remarks, gazing at the distant warship, "Blueskins wouldn't fire on a companion vessel if there were still crew aboard, alive and fighting. So long as we got inside quickly, we had that edge...until this time."

"*So they became willing to kill their own if it meant killing you... The enemy responded to your aggression by becoming more aggressive, ja?*"

"Yes," she answers hazily, stepping all the way around her old mentor, allowing extra room for the tatters of a kidney reaching toward the void behind him.

"*Yet you survived...*"

"That's right. We did."

"*How did you do this?*"

Shao-Lo looks around at the smoky air. "By redefining the meaning of aggression."

Slowly at first, smoky air swirls past the Brick, hull fragments tumble out to space, and the memory resumes.

Automatic pressure bulkheads drop from the ceiling at all connecting intersections, ending the gale, and the isolated compartment falls to hard vacuum. The huge Brick collapses, trying in vain to keep his guts from slipping through holes in his front and back. Shao-Lo scrambles to him and slaps her hands over his abdomen, using all of her weight to stop the rest of his insides from spilling. But she can see most of his liver beside him, ripped to pieces, fluids boiling out of it as frost forms at the edges. His gall and pancreas hang by strained ligaments alongside loops of frosting intestine.

The big Brick shakes his head, points to her rifle, points down the corridor, then lifts her hands away, letting the last of his organs erupt, and his head falls back against the metal floor plates.

Shao-Lo slams her fists down on his breastplate. Then, with eerie calm, she slings her rifle across her chest, plucks grenades from Cayman's waist, and snatches his cannon from the deck. To Chusan, she hand signals, *on me*, activates her magnetic treads, and clambers out through the blasted hole.

Outside, hull fragments glitter with reflected starlight as they spin away. Beyond them, a sleek warship glides by, D-E rails shimmering with capacitance. Its weapon barrels hunt through the debris cloud then orient toward the two black-armored figures dashing across the skin of its companion.

Shao-Lo and Chusan sprint for the far side of the ship, swinging themselves like gibbons around protruding antennae and D-E barrels. A vicious barrage harries their escape, scorching their heels until they crest the edge of the ship, and their light absorbing armor disappears against infinite black background.

Shao-Lo glances back and spies the warship turning in behind them. Fan shaped pink beams reach out from the warship, sweeping the stern as it comes around, then the warship settles into a parallel heading. It advances quickly and steadily, scouring the hull of its sister ship with repetitive overlapping sweeps.

Shao-Lo tracks the warship visually, gauging its approach, and crouches behind the round base of a D-E turret. Chusan squats down beside her, watching and waiting for instruction. With Cadre Virus Ships pumping out megawatts of broadcast noise and jamming local comms, her radio is pointless. So she pulls a long cable from her rack, clips the carabineer end on Chusan's rack, then points at the gaining warship and swings her arms together as if diving toward it. Chusan nods once in acknowledgement and mirrors her stance.

Shao-Lo locks her gaze on the approaching warship, letting her visor calculate distance and relative velocity. In a blink, it plots a jump vector, complete with wireframe image of the ship's future location and a countdown timer. She leans forward, centers the weight of the big cannon, and holds three fingers against the hull so Chusan can see them. As Shao-Lo retracts her fingers one by one, Chusan crouches low, concentrates on the approaching ship, and they leap in unison.

Transition to freefall brings instant calm amid the violence, and Shao-Lo studies the approaching vessel. A sleek, armored hull bristles with D-E Rails in spherical turrets. Emitters along its spine and belly project pink beams through the debris-filled gap between ships. The beam spreads, fanning repeatedly over the blasted corpse of a Cadre Virus Ship, then sweeps its sister ship stem to stern.

Shao-Lo hug's Cayman's cannon with both arms, fixated on viewports above the bridge. Through those transparent windows, she watches her enemy shouting to one another, pointing at holoscreens, and working consoles.

You don't see us coming...

The Gun reaches out with a magnetized foot and drags a toe down the hull, skidding until relative speed matches and she can safely plant her other foot. Chusan touches down with equal grace, offers Shao-Lo a thumbs-up, unslings his rifle, and primes it.

Shao-Lo takes Cayman's cannon in one hand, leaving the other free to grasp D-E rails or antennae should the ship take an unexpected turn, and arrives at the viewport. Beyond the transparent metal pane, frantic reptilians tap away at consoles and bark at one another, oblivious to the threat outside. Frowning in disgust, she thumbs cannon output to maximum and aims. A violet glow coalesces around her, drawing horrified stares from the bridge crew inside. They point in terror as the glow compacts itself into the weapon barrel and smashes through the glass in exorbitance of firepower. The viewport explodes, gushing a column of condensed vapor thirty meters into space. Uniformed Blueskins career through the shattered port, clawing at frigid emptiness as they cartwheel into hard vacuum.

Shao-Lo dives through the hole, flips over, and slams down onto her feet. All around her are charred and cracked consoles, some sparking with current. One Blueskin is tangled in a railing behind the captain's chair, clutching its throat with gaping mouth, purple tongue spilling out. She aims the cannon but holds her fire, watching it suffocate.

Chusan *klanks* to the deck beside her, rifle tucked tight to his shoulder. He starts toward the pressure door at the back of the bridge when Shao-Lo pulls him back. Settling into a wide stance, she levels the cannon at the pressure door and primes it. Chusan's eyes go wide behind his visor and he dives behind a sturdy console as the violet glow gathers, compresses, and batters a half-meter hole through the door. A new rush of air buffets her from the compartment beyond, but Shao-Lo strides into the gale, pulling a grenade from her waist. Without looking through the wrecked pressure door, she thumbs the timer, waits for the gale to taper off, and whips the grenade down the vented hallway.

A vicious *POOMP* rattles ceiling, walls, and floor. Chusan pops up from cover. Gripping his rifle one-handed, he vaults the console and glides to the pressure door opposite Shao-Lo.

In the corner of an eye, Shao-Lo notices something blot out the stars beyond the blasted viewport. A quartet of subtle taps telegraph through the floor plates, then an iris hatch opens directly outside the shattered glass. A slender Geek pours through the iris, pistols in hand. Shao-Lo points at the Geek, points at Chusan, then points to the console at the front of the bridge. Geek and Gun both nod once and rip into functional consoles.

Shao-Lo peers down the smashed hallway, primes her cannon, and storms through it, bashing the ship inside out with brutal streams of relativistic particles. Compartment after compartment fails, bursting with a violent roar, until every defender coughs their final foaming breath.

"We can't do this in real time," Shao-Lo says, interrupting the memory. "Takes too long. We'll never finish."

"Not to worry, Colonel," Mikato's voice assures her. "We are in a machine environment right now. It may seem like real time to you, but in reality, we have only passed a few seconds."

"Machine environment?"

"Correct. We are in a construct you may shape at will. Your memories form the landscape. The way you feel about those memories provides context. And by what you reveal, we will come to know the real you."

Shao-Lo looks down at the back of her hand, and fans the fingers. Reinforced tendons lift beneath leathery, crisscrossed scars. When she turns her hand over, she sees familiar lines of her palm and thick calluses.

"I saw my own skin hanging from a metal frame just before Honniker flamed it," she says grimly. "How is it I'm wearing it now? Was that all a dream? Or illusion?"

"No, that all happened. Doctor Honniker's *penchant* for theatrics, I'm afraid. The way you appear here is simply persistence of self-image. This will evolve as you become more familiar with your new form. Of course, it makes no difference if you think of yourself in a new chassis or in your old flesh. What matters is that you are comfortable and able to continue the process."

"I don't think we need a blow by blow recount of my strongest memories. It was enough to live through them once."

"You can open yourself to a more active examination, if you prefer.

Honniker and I could browse your recollections without fully triggering
them. Again, only if you wish, as we have no desire to intrude."

"How about you offer up something first?"

Honniker asks, *"What do you want?"*

"You *know* what I want."

Mikato's projection closes its holographic eyes. "Very well."

A theory forms in Shao-Lo's mind like a sudden moment of inspiration.
From the general hypothesis, a framework flows and basic outlines fill with
relevant detail. Such intricacies are beyond her education, she knows, and
yet she comprehends advanced theoretical mathematics, quantum mechanics,
remarkable potentials of matter and energy, the peculiar nature of exotic
states and how they can be made to collapse, even for an instant, into the
single most devastating phenomenon in the universe.

She reels, awed by such particular elegance, such annihilating grandeur,
and the utter impossibility of defense. Only insane genius could conceive of
such a construct; only maniacal obsession would have the patience to gather
sufficient reactant. Commitment to craft and design...dedication in solving
the most perplexing of quantum mysteries...insights so radical they seem
almost obvious afterward...advancement of comprehension and intuition that
dwarfs those once deemed "great," and long term planning that stretches
millennia into the future... By comparison, a single human lifespan is a
chemical flash too dim to notice, too brief to matter on a cosmological scale.

Shao-Lo stands naked before the enormity of her ignorance, and, as her
long-held belief of Human primacy over all other life crumbles, a cynical
laugh rolls from deep within.

LIMITATIONS

"*She lied to us*," Honniker fumes. "*She lied!*"

"Yes," Mikato agrees, the holographic face showing none of his colleague's hostility. "Quite cleverly, at that. I believed she was incapable of deception. And that belief was well-exploited."

"*Hast wohl den Arsch offen? Diese blöde Tussi ist... This, this* primate *played us for fools with her imaginary instant communicator...and you* CONGRATULATE *her?*"

The projection nods. "I do."

Shao-Lo stands at ease in her mechanical chassis. With particular satisfaction she adds, "Clearly, artificial intelligence has its limitations."

Mikato's projection grins. "As you have shown."

"*Ach! I leave the two of you to your back slapping.*"

Shao-Lo senses a sudden drop in network presence, suggesting Honniker has vacated the node to sulk elsewhere, and she smiles inwardly. Mikato's holographic image still gazes up at her in proud admiration, so she asks, "If Honniker's this upset, why aren't you?"

The projection tilts its head and raises eyebrows. "Ego is an obstacle to true science. I have endeavored to shed mine that I might see what is *real*, what is *true*, without the filtering lenses of what *should be*. Honniker, on the other hand, takes every opportunity to feed his ego...then takes it badly when he fails." The projection walks from the workshop out onto the immaculate production floor and turns about when Shao-Lo does not follow. It raises a holographic hand and beckons.

Reluctantly, Shao-Lo obliges and the two walk side by side. Slowness of pace is immediate vexation to the colonel, where every mincing step the projection takes is ludicrous anachronism from his previous physical

160

existence. Mikato could simply project himself on the far side of the room as though teleporting. And in her new mechanical body, she could clear every assembly line in a single leap. Yet the colonel reins back impatience and matches the hologram's plodding gait.

"Honniker's superiority complex is a personality flaw carried over from his shell," Mikato explains. "It skews his understanding of what it means to win."

"How so?"

"For Honniker, all confrontations are zero sum games. To win, he believes someone else must lose. Only winning at another's expense satisfies his ego. I find that a dreadful weakness."

"As do I."

The projection turns toward her abruptly. "And rightly so! Because we have *all* won in this arrangement." It faces forward again, clasping holographic hands behind its back. The pair diverts around an end station for a line of conveyers, and Shao-Lo turns a casual glance down the row. Long dark boxes are suspended over the line, aiming down at the conveyer like dorsal spines of a relaxed fish. Specialized arms, with intricate fingers, scalpels, punches, clamps, and welders are folded in readiness along each side. And multiple stations are enclosed by polished metal shrouds, obscuring more complex fabricators within. Intrigued, she zooms in on mechanisms of transport for the line, itself. Each stage feeds seamlessly into the other and every single part fits together so neatly it seems more to her like the alimentary system of some resting animal than a line of assembly. Even in stillness the row conveys elegance and harmony, sufficient to shame Munro's proudest technological achievements as childlike approximations.

Mikato had time to perfect every single part in these lines, she thinks. *How many times did he scrutinize this system, optimize, reengineer, and rebuild it? And this is just an assembler for his more advanced designs...*

I wonder...if given enough time, could Munro advance to this degree?

The assembly line terminates at a durable floor plate a shade darker than the others. Open power and data ports suggest a dock for automated carts to park and collect whatever might roll down the line. For a moment the colonel tries to imagine what finished items have been collected here, gives up, and follows Mikato's projection past the last row. Without manufacturing equipment blocking her view, Shao-Lo spots a small craft crouched in the back corner on a circular pad.

"In your deception, you robbed Honniker of his chance to defeat you," Mikato explains. "Had he known there was no possibility of summoning Cadre reinforcements or Eleto here, he would have simply taken everything from you, given nothing, and claimed yet another victory as proof of his superiority."

Dividing her attention between the craft and her holographic escort, Shao-Lo asks, "You *don't* think that would've been the best outcome? You'd have everything I brought, without trading a thing. Pure addition."

"Hardly. First of all, I have no interest in conquering anyone. My only interests are in exploration, discovery, increase of knowledge, understanding, and—if fates be kind—wisdom. Wisdom demands I apologize for calling you a weak negotiator."

"No need."

The projection stops short. "But there *is*. Had you been less formidable, we would not be here. Honniker would have consumed you entirely in one of his vainglorious 'experiments.' We would not have achieved our life's goal of transferring an intact consciousness from one body to another. We could not have shared your unique insights and experiences. We could never have understood what it means to dedicate oneself so completely in service to others as you have... If Honniker had his way, we would have remained divided from you—we would be a lesser entity." The projection smirks. "I cannot escape the irony... Most of what you had to trade, you gave away in the earliest round, and you stood on a *colossal* bluff: one you could not have known we would accept. Yet you maintained that bluff, even after numerous cross-referenced questions, throughout physical and psychological strains that had broken other beings. And your hint of Parametric Down Conversion...giving us a taste of proven technology to keep us guessing? Ha! Simply *brilliant*!" The projection resumes its path toward the triangular craft. "From our first encounter, prevarication seemed an impossibility for your kind. Tell me, did someone coach you in the technique?"

"We've shared minds, Mikato. Don't you already know?"

"Yes, I suppose I do. But conversation is something I delight in, and it would be quite dull between us if we could not pretend there was *something* we did not already know about one another. You must introduce me to this Herzfeld sometime."

Shao-Lo and the projection stroll past a sealed cryogenic vault door, its one window frosted on the inside. Alessa keeps relaxed guard outside at the threshold, washing a forepaw with mottled pink and black tongue. The enormous feline pauses to watch Shao-Lo striding by.

With no head to turn Shao-Lo studies Alessa through side mounted photoreceptors, finding thick, coarse whiskers on the snout and dense chestnut fur jutting between overlapped armor plates. The colonel never noticed the way her fuzzy ears are folded back into narrow tubes between head and neck plates, and how Alessa's deep set green eyes—so unlike the crazed black of Honniker's other predators—convey patience and focus of a disciplined soldier.

I wonder what you look like beneath all that, Shao-Lo thinks.

Unfamiliar feelings of devotion to this creature spring up inside, feelings she understands belong to Mikato but are so intimate she nearly mistook them as her own. She *remembers* stroking the feline's muzzle with a liver spotted hand, reaching between thick armor plates to scratch behind her flattened ears, and how Alessa rumbled with closed-eyed contentment. Shao-Lo looks down into the palm of her segmented hand, wrestling with how she could remember something she has never done with a body that was never hers.

With a bitter twinge she realizes, *That means Honniker's memories will crop up, as well.*

Not wishing to dwell on that, Shao-Lo puts her full attention on the craft directly ahead. Shaped like an elongated tetrahedron, it squats on the same circular pad that once supported a sow-like transport. Both sides are flat and slope inward, meeting at a rounded off centerline. Its angular nose points at an airlock hundreds of times larger than necessary for it to pass. Thruster nozzles are embedded at the triangular tips, but there are no main boosters or Deep Space Drive. And its most prominent feature is a deep notch cut into the top, precisely centered, with a transparent canopy raised on hinges at its rear.

A single padded black headrest rises above the high rim of the cockpit.

Only room for one, Shao-Lo supposes. *Fine by me.* She points at the craft, asking, "That's my ride out of here?"

"It is."

"So it's going to be a *short* trip, then."

The projection grins and keeps holographic eyes forward.

Mikato's knowing smirk is always an annoyance, and the colonel is about to insist on an explanation until it occurs to her she no longer needs to ask Mikato anything. The colonel reaches through wireless pathways, seeking answers to unvoiced questions. A broad concept enters her mind of a stackable fleet, assembled into a kilometers-long central axis with twin hoops turning in opposite directions near the mid line. The triangular craft ahead is a command module that plugs into the whole, facilitating control, comms, computing, intelligence, surveillance, and reconnaissance for a lone passenger.

"I keep forgetting we're open books now," Shao-Lo says.

Mikato's projection nods, and says in forgiving tone, "Habits are heard to break, especially the way we think and perceive. But do not let it trouble you. Until you are comfortable, ask anything you like. As I have stated before, I enjoy the conversation."

Shao-Lo steps around the rear of the craft then peers inside, finding Saskia hunkered down in the pilot's seat.

"Hiya," the machine says and lifts a hand in greeting. It sits upright and disconnects a lanyard from the console. "Getting everything setup for you."

Saskia grips the rim of the cockpit and vaults over to the deck. Taking a step back, the machine extends a hand toward the pilot seat and says, "Have at it."

Shao-Lo keeps her synthetic eyes trained on Saskia as she climbs over the rim and settles in. The seat is a glove fit with aligned power and nutrient ports for convenient connection. In place of wide harness straps, magnetic latches snap into place along her shoulders, back, waist, and upper legs. A plain console directly ahead projects a wraparound holographic display, augmenting her field of view with relevant metrics and overlays.

Saskia steps up to the side and hangs on the rim with segmented hands, elbows bent. Leaning through the holographic display, the machine says, "Since you're a *crap* pilot, I've plotted your course in AutoNav. You'll get there, no problem. But we can't have you going space crazy with nothing to do, so there's a virtual feed, here."

Shao-Lo follows the machine's finger to a panel at the console's lower left.

"Activate that and you'll enter a virtual construct where you can explore, create, train with your new kit, watch old movies, whatever you like. Same as what you see, hear, and feel. Total fidelity. Well, for *this* universe, anyway."

The machine points at two compartments flanking the seat.

"If you need to defend yourself, just put your arms through these ports at your sides."

Shao-Lo reaches into the compartments and feels devices snap onto her forearms. When she draws back her hands, each forearm is ringed with flat black attachments. Data streams from each, informing her of weapon type, output setting, status, and ammunition remaining. As she scrolls the list, Shao-Lo's mind boggles.

I'm packing a full team's firepower...

List completed, a reticle appears in her vision. Potential targets highlight all around her, colored from green to blaze orange by relative threat. Shao-Lo shifts the reticle from one target to the next just by looking at them, and her limbs automatically track where the reticle goes. Fire control analyzes target composition and auto-selects the weapon best suited for obliterating it.

This is incredible...

When the reticle lands on Saskia, Saskia takes hold of Shao-Lo's arms with both hands and aims them aside, saying, "Let's stick to *virtual* testing, okay?"

"Fine," the colonel says, disarming weapons with a thought. She reaches back into the compartments and the weapons detach, storing securely inside.

Alessa pads up on the opposite side, sniffs the edge of the canopy, and squats on her haunches. Tall enough to look over the rim while sitting, she blinks once at Shao-Lo with emerald green eyes.

"If you ever want a Frackit rematch," Saskia offers.

Shao-Lo smirks. "I'll keep it in mind."

"Oh, and that reminds me. Something I promised you... Hold still." Saskia aims a wrist attachment at Shao-Lo's breastplate. A beam of brilliant blue light burns into Shao-Lo's chest armor, ablating it with wisps of smoke. Before Shao-Lo can protest, the etching is done and Saskia holds up a square of polished metal. Shao-Lo peers into Saskia's mirror. Reflected there is the bust of a seasoned Operator wearing dress uniform, eagle on her collar. Black and gray hair is trimmed close to the scalp, and the stern face is lined with numerous scars. Sharp, piercing eyes gaze out from that weathered visage, daring anyone to test her determination.

"This photo was taken when I was promoted to Colonel," Shao-Lo says, taking the mirror and angling it for a better view. "How'd you get it?"

Saskia pulls back a couple of centimeters as if weighing how honest it should be. *"Well...Maiella dipped into Cadre archives a few times after she was exiled. She saved this one in her HDI. I don't know why. Don't think she knew why, either."*

Shao-Lo's grip tightens on the mirror, flexing it.

"Doesn't matter how she got it," Saskia says. *"What matters is that you never forget who you are."* The machine taps the newly minted image on Shao-Lo's chest. *"Or where you came from. Right?"*

"Right." Shao-Lo passes the mirror back to Saskia, and, just before the handoff, catches sight of her full reflection. A headless chassis with spider like eyes gazes back from the polished metal, wearing the image of her former self in jarring juxtaposition.

Saskia takes the metal square and leans against the canopy. *"Know what you're gonna do?"*

"Got some ideas. Nothing set."

"Well, I don't mind telling you again, I think this is a shit plan. Bringing this much firepower to the party, you might kill the Eleto. More likely you'll

kill yourself and everyone near you. Jin Sung's librarian, Anila, gave me some books to read since I've been here. Mostly on Human history, going back thousands of years. What I learned is there's never a sane end to an arms race. As weapons get more destructive, it only feeds paranoia and fear, which leads to bigger weapons, and so on. Ironically, bigger guns mean less security. But dismantling the threat and letting others live in peace? There's a future in that."

"Nothing is ever given freely, Geek. It'll take a show of force to convince the Eleto they need to make room for us. And I'll make that point," Shao-Lo adds, patting the sides of her transport, "in the *clearest* terms."

Saskia looks down at the deck, pushes off the side of the craft, and takes a step back beside Mikato's projection. *"Safe travels, Colonel."*

"Good hunting, you mean."

The machine crosses its articulated arms. *"Not at all."*

Mikato's projection steps closer, a look of concern on its face. Attempting to defuse the growing tension, it states, "One way or other, Colonel, we look forward to your results. As we have already learned, no one has to lose. Though, if it comes down to open hostility, I'd like to hear that my designs enabled your victory."

"Roger that," Shao-Lo confirms. "All right, let's get moving." She reaches a segmented hand up to the canopy and pulls it down into place. Latches clasp the edge then ratchet to a tight seal.

Alessa leans up to the plexi-steel, fogs it with her breath, and presses a huge paw into the condensation. When the feline removes her paw, Shao-Lo sees clear outline of each pad. Slowly, the fog evaporates and the outline disappears, but Shao-Lo looks from the glass to Alessa, sensing suggestions in the gesture. With no language to share, it is hard to know for certain what the huge feline meant. But the overwhelming impressions Shao-Lo gets are, *it is important to have existed, even if for only a moment.* And, *no one truly dies if remembered by others.*

The feline smiles with half of her whiskered face, showing a hint of metal-capped teeth, then saunters around the nose of the craft to stand beside Saskia and Mikato's projection. After an introspective moment the three step off of the circular floor pad and head for elevators at the far side of the floor.

A low hum in the craft rises in pitch. Console indicators change from amber to soothing green. The enormous pressure gate ahead parts down the middle and opens with squeal of hydraulics. Conveyors in the floor pad start with a jolt and tow Shao-Lo's craft into the cavernous airlock. The craft's nose lifts then drops into its launcher with a rough *klunk*, and the gate grinds shut behind her.

166

Harsh overhead lamps flare, illuminating a second pressure gate ahead. Dominating the double doors is Cadre Two's icon: a fanged predator skull with hollow sockets.

While Shao-Lo waits for the huge airlock to evacuate she stares at the fanged skull, recalling the last time she had this view of it. Previously, her departure was steeped in defeat. Mikato and Honniker maintained an uncontested hold on Cadre Two, able to repel any assault Cadre One could muster. All she brought home to her general was a brass shell of dubious value, Keller's lifeless body, and a third of her Operator Team.

This time, she is leaving with a new body of exceptional strength and capability, a fleet of radical offensive potential, an incredible new weapon called *Plasma Rain*, the combined knowledge of Mikato and Honniker, and an open invitation at Cadre Two for return.

Honniker's demand for pliable, living flesh is a small price for the Cadre's access, she thinks. *We could agree to that. We could live here...*

Her console *dings*, indicating the lock is fully evacuated, and the yellow edged gate ahead parts down the middle. Through the spreading gap, Shao-Lo views a long, dark launch tube. Faint points of light glimmer at the far end.

Mikato radios, "*Ready, Colonel?*"

"Affirmative, Cadre Two. Green bars, ready for stars, over."

"*Stand by for launch in three...two...one...*"

The craft rushes up the tube and shoots through the end of it, emerging into a dusty night crowded with maneuvering warships. Shao-Lo gawks at a bewildering variety of hull types, bristling with launchers and rails, outlined with randomly blinking running lights. As if by gravity the swarm condenses into suggestions of shape. Two counter-rotating hoops take form, five hundred meters across and aligned precisely to one another. A central axis extends straight through their centers, stretching over a thousand meters from tip to tail.

Shao-Lo magnifies her enhanced vision during approach, concentrating on the long line of ships. At front, individual vessels jockey for position, reacting to proximity, adjusting, closing distance until they almost touch, then hold place in queue, sending a ripple down the length as following vessels respond to the vessel directly ahead of it.

Once the rearmost vessel has taken its place in queue another wave starts at front. Ships snap together in cascade like a multi-sided zipper closing. Running lights on each vessel synchronize upon connection and shift hue from white to amber.

The twin hoops orbiting the central axis snap together in the same way, pausing momentarily at the ends to ensure perfect closure. Deep Space Drives of interlinked ships flare with startup pulses then hold steady at a dim red glow.

Shao-Lo's craft banks and carves a wide arc toward the assemblage, swings around behind it, then speeds up its length from stern to bow. The colonel gawks at so many vessels, each as large or larger than ones in the Cadre fleet, all of which are interconnected into a superstructure of shared resources.

In the fringes of her memory, she recalls how ships of the long central axis are designed to channel power from interlinked reactors to high-output emitters, and how those emitters beam energy to the orbiting rings like intangible spokes in a wheel. She comprehends how these flows feed Deep Space Drives of ships in the rings, how their merged warp fields stack in efficiency, enveloping the entire assembly in a protective bubble and driving it to many multiples of C. And she knows that every connection between vessels is a redundant path for power and data should a node be knocked off-line. Yet no matter how intuitively Shao-Lo can grasp the power and economy of stacking a war fleet this way, she marvels at the level of technological prowess required to successfully engineer it.

You were right, Mikato. You're too valuable, too important to ever be our enemy again. I will not allow anyone to harm you.

Her craft slows as it nears the bullet-shaped tip, skims the surface toward a triangular gap and settles into it, locking down with a series of telegraphed clunks.

ALL NODES INTERLINKED, SYSTEMS INTEGRATED, her console declares, APPROACHING OPTIMAL EFFICIENCY.

DSDs in the counter-rotating rings flare again. Stellar background smudges as the stack turns and orients upon a faint yellow dwarf star.

DESTINATION SOL 3.253 PARSECS, her console states. COURSE SET.

Unified reactors thrum with accelerated annihilations, and power streams through superconducting conduits. Ultracapacitors fill to peak density, singing a song Shao-Lo cannot hear but can feel in her electro-active sinews. She opens and closes segmented hands, wanting something to do with them, wanting a recliner rail or molded weapon grips to grasp. Instead, there is only the cockpit's bland wraparound holographic screen on autopilot. So she looks through the canopy for an unfiltered view of infinite sky.

Billions of brilliant pinpoints dot the cosmic background. Galactic bulge shines to her left, precisely where it should be. Faint nebulae dab the heavens in complex billows of fluorescing gasses. Such commonplace sights are familiar from previous rotations. Yet never before has she witnessed infrared or ultraviolet shine with her own eyes. A newly revealed universe enthralls with unexpected grandeur, and then awareness of all the physical forces at play floods her at once, becoming too much to bear.

Shao-Lo drops her view to the plain confines of her cabin where softly flickering LEDs alleviate the ache of so much awe and wonder.

"Colonel Shao-Lo," Mikato radios, *"please keep in mind these systems are on loan. I expect them returned in good working order."*

Recovering from sensory overload, she replies, "I'll see what I can do."

"Be well, and safe journeys."

"Safety isn't the plan, but the sentiment is appreciated. Shao-Lo, out."

Counter rotating rings surge with stellar luminance, encapsulating the entire assembly in a bubble of crackling energy. The universe lenses, stars smear to spectral streaks, and Shao-Lo plummets through a chasm of altered dimensions.

CADRE ONE

PART TEN

Magnificent System

Lost in thought, Maiella stares past the regular lines of code updating in her goggles, past the green-lit console and augmented reality projected on the windscreen ahead of her, past the envelope of energy that both propels the limousine and deflects stray particles in the flight path. Directly ahead, less than an hour away, is a vast world of land, seas, and sky...a world of inexhaustible resource and infinite possibility—the birthplace of mankind.

Argo described a magnificent system, a kind of great machine with naturally renewing air, food, and water. Thompson was more reticent, and, in the moments he would speak of it, he told of a place interconnected in life, how everything seemed to strive against the other in endless competition, feeding upon one another, yet was bound in mutual dependence. So delicate was this balance that predators had to ensure their prey could thrive. Being too successful in hunts, or disrupting habitats, could result in extinction.

Such complexity rivals any calculation or algorithm the Geek has ever tried to compute, where the planet's fractal and random nature eludes simple explanations or predictions. Climate, plate tectonics and volcanism, evolution and mutation, plagues and swarms, migrations, growth and decline...the factors suggest a world at odds with itself, so hostile it could not possibly support life. The fact that it does, in such abundance, is baffling. That Humanity arose from this chaos is most baffling of all.

Maiella thinks back on the months long journey, smiling in recollection. When not sharing a rack with Thompson, or piloting, there were discussions with the Counselor about how formal talks should proceed with the Eleto. There were language lessons with Shondre, coachings in etiquette and diplomacy. Munro had endless questions regarding Cadre Two, its howling mad occupants, production capabilities and inventories, as well as the extensive amenities for residents and researchers. Sharon answered them as best she could until the haunted look came back, and Maiella had to steer the conversation toward brighter subjects.

Time passed far too quickly. Now, only minutes away from Sol, anxiety and excitement hijack the Geek's busy mind.

There's never been more at stake. Are we ready?

Maiella searches deep within, pushing through self-doubt to a place more intimate and instinctive. There, she finds a wiser, more experienced confidence filling the prior emptiness.

I've still got my edge. And getting Sharon back safe from Honniker's dungeon is exactly what I set out to do. Mission accomplished.

Pride swells in her chest, and she trusts the capable hands gripping flight controls. For an instant, a notion of rejoining the Corps comes to mind. Then lingering bitterness gives her a twinge.

Too oppressive, too limited. I can't go back to the Cadre.

The Geek's thoughts turn back to Sharon, and she recalls how mousy and tentative the navigator's first steps were into Cadre Two.

Keller was the catalyst, but Sharon found herself in those darkened, terrifying hallways. Back at Cadre One, she settled the feud among Europa's *crew and took command as Captain.*

Maiella grins.

That look of amazement on Herzfeld's face when she schooled him... Sharon's modest and makes light of herself, but...she's definitely up to this.

And the Counselor... Rational and collected—infuriatingly so, at times. Maybe the only reason we haven't ripped ourselves to shreds. Who else could have come so far so fast with Shondre. If not for him, this mission would never have gotten off the ground.

And Shondre. Delicate...almost frail... Nearly died from standard rations and accommodations at Cadre One. But her mind and will could stand toe to toe against O'Kai's... The despair...the boredom she must have felt. Locked away in a stone-cell where the only stimulation is when a ration bar gets tossed through the door twice a day? After all that, she's as determined as ever to bring our peoples together.

Her mind turns to Thompson.

Every Rotation made you more handsome. Could never tell you how I felt, Cadre would never allow it, so I settled for being near. Pushed myself to be the best Geek in the Corps to make sure you'd never take another on Rotation...

After the Europa*...we both struggled. Nearly killed ourselves to end the shame... But we got through. Separately, yeah, but we got through.*

Maiella tilts her head back, cataloging the wreckage of furniture in their shared cabins.

Like your old self again...only freer, better. More alive.

The mood sours when she remembers Munro's disapproving grimace whenever she and Thompson nipped off for private time.

Weird that he doesn't try to stop us... I mean, he IS the Senior MedTech. Should be lecturing us on duty, keeping focus, perils of attachments... but he doesn't. Without inhibitors, he's definitely eased up... Helps that the Counselor, Shondre, and Sharon all remind him affection is perfectly natural—something people are meant to share that makes life worth living.

That stiff attitude is more of a mask now, I think. Glad he isn't such a hard ass anymore.

She nods.

We're as ready as we can be.

Maiella checks the limousine's systems, surprised to find how well the vessel has held up. Only a few temperature sensors show amber. Flow analysis suggests injector wear is roughly half anticipated. And there is ten percent more reactant remaining than forecast.

Performance enhancements and modifications on this crate were extreme... And at this rate of travel we should have used up the reactor and Deep Space Drives.

Damn, Munro, you're good... Or did you deliberately build extra tolerances into your 'minimally acceptable upgrades?'

The Geek recalls the groans, the arguments, the scraped knuckles and mashed thumbs required to extract that last half percent of efficiency.

If I had to work triple shifts for three weeks so you could look like some kind of miracle worker, I'm gonna soak your undersuit in de-icer.

The Geek thumbs the intercom. "Thompson to the flight deck, if you please."

There is a metallic clatter from the cabin behind her. Thompson follows the connecting hallway to the flight deck, climbs the short stairway, and peeks in.

"Yeah? What's up?"

"Getting close. And it's hitting me all at once, what we're here to do. Have a seat, would you? Keep me from freaking out."

"Hmmf," Thompson grunts as he stoops under the low ceiling and slides into the empty co-pilot's chair. "Might not be the best for the job."

"No?"

He shakes his head and sighs. "Did a *lot* of damage last time I was here. Been questioning if I should've come along, in fact."

"Why?"

He stares out the through the windscreen as she does. "If they recognize me somehow, could make for a harsh reception."

"Maybe. But you saw how Shondre turned that big battlewagon away. She's definitely still pulling weight. Besides, you had your kit on the whole time, right?"

"Yeah. Except..."

"Except?"

Thompson's eyes lose focus, and he rubs his chin with one hand. "Faceplate was smashed. Had to lift it to see and breathe. Was a lot of smoke and confusion, but...don't know if they got a lens on me or not."

"We probably all look alike to them, anyway."

Thompson snorts and glances at her with a lopsided grin. "Probably right."

Maiella reaches over and lays a hand on his arm. "Part of me is sorry this trip is almost over. It's been unbelievable."

Thompson takes her hand, lifts it to his lips, and kisses it. "That's a fact. But soon enough you'll be standing on the ground, totally aware there's no ceiling, that the air just rises up to space, but you're out in the open, alive and breathing... That'll spin your head. And sunlight on bare skin...it doesn't burn, it's warm. That's the incredible part... And everything around you is alive. *Everything*. Once you've been there, nothing will ever be the same again."

Maiella arches an eyebrow. "I should hope not."

The two gaze through the windscreen together, holding hands.

"If we do this right..." Maiella says, breaking the silence. "If we really do it *right*...this could be our home, forever. No more Rotations. Everything we'll ever need. But there's only so much prep we can do, right? I mean, will they throw us a party? Will they try to snuff us on sight? Even Shondre doesn't know for sure."

"Let her and Counselor do all the talking. We're here to be strong and silent. Less we say the better." He sinks back into the chair with a deep exhale. "Did a *lot* of damage last time..."

She squeezes his hand to bring him back from dismal memories. "Like you said, Counselor and Shondre will figure it all out." With a sarcastic smirk, she adds, "No pressure there, right?"

"Yeah. We got it easy next to them."

She nods, reassured, then sniffs once. "I've been thinking about something."

"Hmm?"

"If I'm honest, I'd say O'Kai and Shao-Lo were running the Cadre pretty much the way Dryden and Thorskild would. Almost to the letter, in fact."

Thompson's eyebrows lift as he considers the point. "True," he admits with a nod.

"So how did we lose Cadre One? What did O'Kai do wrong?"

Thompson frets. "Dryden and Thorskild never had to deal with the Colonists or with being discovered. Even if they had captured Shondre, without the Counselor they never would have gotten anything out of her. Cadre One is a huge loss, but we might have something better because of all this. You could say we're lucky in a way."

"If we're so lucky, how come everything's FUBAR?"

Thompson laughs. "Because this is all new. There isn't one of us who knows what we're doing anymore."

Maiella frowns and lets out a deep breath. "Well, we gotta figure it out now...while we still have muscle to flex. Not when we're ground down...not when we're on our knees, forced to accept terms of surrender... We *have* to succeed, Thompson. And it has to be *right now*."

Thompson turns in his seat, facing her. "Then we *will* succeed, Geek. Is that clear?"

Maiella grins ear to ear. "As plexi-steel." She takes her controls with both hands. "Coming up on our waypoint. You should buckle in."

The Gun nods and draws the harness straps over his lap and shoulders.

Maiella thumbs the intercom button and announces to the cabin, "We'll be arriving at Sol system shortly. Everyone to your recliners and buckle in."

She stares into the maelstrom of energy beyond the windscreen.

"We can do this. Because we all want to live, don't we?"

"*Now* I do," Thompson says, slapping a hand on her thigh. "Until we're old and feeble."

She looks down at her lap, amazed that a strike on her thigh—even through the thick armor plate— is all it takes. Biting her lip, she glances over her shoulder toward the passenger cabin. Shondre and Sharon are settling into their recliners while Munro clasps a belt with long tools around his waist.

Not there...

Maiella looks at the hatchway behind her, a hatchway that once had a bulkhead before Argo peeled it like sheet metal. From there, she sweeps her gaze around the narrow confines of the flight deck, mentally mapping out logistics.

Too cramped in here, might trip a breaker accidentally...
I could slow our approach, nip off out back for a few...

Thompson clicks harness buckles across his chest.

Ah, hell. Have to wait, she thinks, shifting in her seat.

From the cabin comes a clattering of metal against metal and groaning of alloy fittings. Thompson and Maiella look at each other, eyebrows raised. Just when they think the din is about to end, it starts anew. Sharon makes an offer of help, as does the Counselor, and the clanging continues amid overlapping recommendations how to get unstuck.

"Colonel, are you *taking* your seat, or *attacking* it?" Maiella calls over intercom.

The big man clears his throat. "One of my wrenches is jammed in the... *never mind!*" There is an extended *ZZZZRRRRRRTTTTTTT* of the tool sliding free and a sigh of relief. "There," Munro growls, "fly the ship!"

The Geek grins and checks her console, noting all passengers are secure with restraints fastened. "Stand by," she announces. "Cutting DSDs in three... two...one...*Mark.*"

Maiella's goggles strobe with data and the tempest of energy beyond the transport's windscreen dissipates. Stars collapse from smeared spectra to brilliant pinpoints then track slowly as she steers toward a bright yellow star in the distance.

"Arrived at Sol system," she announces. "Calibrating for drift..."

Thompson waits for the flare of code in Maiella's goggles to subside then asks, "Got a fix on position?"

"Affirmative," she answers. "Approximately six billion kilometers from Sol, thirty degrees outside of orbital plane."

"Give me visual."

Maiella's goggles pulse and a virtual system map projects onto the windscreen. Planet positions plot in real time with orbits traced in circular white lines. Relevant captions of name, mass, composition, class, coordinates, and velocity appear beside each. Planetoids, comets, and asteroids plot next, many with highly eccentric orbits that graze the yellow star and extend well beyond the outer planets.

"Plotting rendezvous," the Geek announces, and a red dot appears with captions of vector and velocity.

Thompson squints at the red dot. "It's in motion?"

"Affirmative," the Geek replies. "Seems to be tracking a large comet, heading for the inner solar system."

"Magnify."

The projected map zooms in on the red dot, resolving a wispy object with compact head and long, flowing tail. The red dot follows behind the nucleus, shrouded by an envelope of dusty debris and ionized particles.

"They're taking cover behind it," Maiella observes.

"Yeah," Thompson states. "Good spot...looks like they're using it to hide their approach."

Maiella's goggles flash, and she removes all objects from the projection aside from the comet and Earth. Far ahead, the two orbits converge.

"Yep," the Geek says. "Only half an AU apart at nearest approach. From there, they could jump right in to Earth orbit, blasting. But at this rate they've gotta be close to four months out."

"Gives the fleet time to arrive and get organized. Can you get us there without being seen?"

"There's a lot of material popping off of that comet," Maiella states warily. "Even sub-light, just a *grain* could ruin our day."

Thompson tilts his head toward her and looks through his eyebrows. "Hold up... You flew out of Cadre Two...a shattered planetary core surrounded by its own fragments and dust...and you're sweating over a—?"

"Keep your hair on," she says with a raised hand. "I'll get us there."

IRREGULAR

Maiella projects herself deep into the controls of the limousine, letting the ship's passive sensors become her eyes and ears. Through the ship, she gazes out at an elegant harmony of gravitation and motion. Her goggles scroll with calculations, nacelles flare, and the vessel slides smoothly through warped space.

"On final approach to Cadre Fleet rendezvous," the Geek announces via intercom. "Everyone hang tight." Muting the microphone, she mutters to Thompson, "We're *not* expected. Let's hope they don't blow us out of the Black."

"On passive approach they won't even see us. Ease us in there, get us close, and we'll put up a flag."

"Roger, that."

Maiella guides the vessel into an almost imperceptible coma of ionized gasses, then slows the rugged craft through a sparse zone of jettisoned particles. Once tucked in behind the comet's nucleus, however, she finds no trace of the fleet.

"Soooooooo, where is everyone?"

Thompson leans close to the windscreen, squinting against the halo of sunlit jets around the comet's limb. "From far off, this thing is blazing bright. Hard to believe the actual body is black as soot... They could be right in front of us and we wouldn't know it. Think they could have burrowed into the surface?"

"I wouldn't. Comets are lightly packed. Digging in could split it, release a gas pocket. With a sudden increase in apparent magnitude, Eleto'd be sure to come check it out."

Thompson sits back in the seat and rubs his chin. "All right. Give us a slow turn. Maybe we'll spot something in silhouette."

"Aye, sir," Maiella confirms, "Coming around—"

The vessel jolts with four *klanks* against the limousine's roof.

"Hold position!" Thompson shouts, one hand reaching over to Maiella, the other on the release latch of his harness. Nervous whispers pass back and forth in the cabin behind them.

Maiella grips the controls and waits, statuesque. "Virus ship," she whispers.

"Definitely," Thompson agrees, eyes glued to the ceiling.

"Orders?"

"Keep still, no transmissions."

"Aye."

Sharon calls from the passenger cabin, "What's happening?"

"Found the fleet," Thompson answers over his shoulder. "Or rather, they found us."

There is a heavy *klunk* against the ceiling then magnetized footfalls walk toward the nose of the craft and halt directly over the flight deck. Maiella disables the windscreen projection and dims console displays, searching for some hint of movement outside. All she sees is ethereal incandescence reaching millions of kilometers into space around them until a shadow lands with another *klunk* on the nose of the vessel. The tall figure strides right to the base of the plexi-steel windscreen and crouches, long rod aimed at Maiella. Thompson raps his fist against the screen, and when the rifle swings on him he raises his hands to show he is unarmed.

Barely a two-dimensional silhouette, the Operator parks rifle on hip, points at the control stick in Maiella's grip, and traces the letters, L-E-T G-O on the windscreen.

Maiella releases the control wheel and holds her palms up. The Gun nods once then traces, S-T-A-N-D B-Y, and hops back to the roof.

The limousine hull groans as it is dragged left and thrust forward. Minute course corrections jostle the ship in swift approach. After many tense seconds the limousine is yanked to a halt, throwing Maiella and Thompson harshly against their harness straps, and a brusque voice over radio declares, "*Lower landing gear and power down.*"

"Roger, tha—"

"*Maintain radio silence.*"

Maiella complies and the limousine settles onto its landing struts. Docking clamps latch with rough *klunks*. Crimson ceiling lamps illuminate, and the Geek peers through the windscreen at the red-lit interior of a service bay. Bare metal plates cover floor, wall, and ceiling. Heavy gauge conduits shield power and data feeds. There is little else.

"*Power down vessel. Lower entry ramp and permit access.*"

Maiella performs an expedited shut down of main drives and sets the reactor to Hot Standby. Once the bay is fully equalized she extends the loading ramp and opens the entry hatch.

Thompson flicks his head toward the cabin. "Let's go say, hi."

The two de-belt and file out of the flight deck.

An armored Gun drops from the roof of the limousine onto the ramp, weapon tucked into shoulder, glides in through the open hatch, spots Shondre, and levels the rifle at her head. Sharon jumps from her seat in front of the Gun, arms wide, exclaiming, "*No!* She's with us!"

The Gun grabs Sharon by the arm with one hand and flings her aside while keeping aim at Shondre with the other. Armored finger slides inside the trigger guard.

"Stand down!" Munro demands.

The Gun's head turns to glance at Munro, does a double take, then slings the rifle and stamps rigidly to attention. "Begging your pardon, Colonel Munro," Keiko says through an electronically-clipped helmet speaker. "Surprised to see you, sir. May I ask *why* the enemy captive is aboard your vessel?"

The big man rises from his recliner, tool belt clanking, and answers, "This one isn't our enemy. And I'll explain why we're here to the ranking officer."

"Any issues with the vessel, Colonel?"

With an edge of indignation, Munro declares, "Not while I'm aboard, there aren't!"

Keiko lifts her faceplate and notices Sharon slumped against the wall, rubbing her upper arm.

"Please forgive me, Captain. I could not have you in the line of fire."

Sharon pushes off the wall with a shoulder. "Yeah? Well you've got a grip like a gorilla... Damn near pulled my arm off!"

Keiko faces Munro again, keeping a watchful eye on Shondre. "It's good to see you, Colonel. But we *weren't* expecting you."

"Change of plan, Major. Need to speak to Chusan. Take me to him."

"Colonel Chusan hasn't arrived yet."

"No? Who's in charge?"

"Major Ralla leads the fleet."

"Then take me to her." Munro steps toward the ramp when Keiko steps into his path, head lowered submissively.

"With respect, Colonel, General O'Kai ordered you to the *Europa*, to watch over the Colonists and our MedTechs. Your being here is...*irregular*."

Munro raises his chin. "Major, I have already explained that the plan has changed. Doctor Taggart has watch over our MedTechs with the full support of Obet, Arjay, and Erik, who have assumed my duties. Now then, do you intend to further delay a meeting of Council Officers, or *will you escort me to Major Ralla?*"

Faint buzz of a woman's voice sounds in Keiko's helmet, and Keiko straightens immediately. "This way, Colonel."

Thompson, Maiella, Sharon, and the Counselor all line up to follow after Munro, but the Gun bars their path with arms spread. "The rest of you will remain aboard until the Colonel has concluded his meeting."

Thompson leans around the Gun and calls after Munro, "Colonel?"

Munro looks over his shoulder. "It's all right. I've got this."

NINETY-NINE DAYS

Munro strides down the ramp ahead of Keiko into the red-lit service bay. His nose wrinkles and his eyes water.

"*Augh*, what is that...*acetone*?"

"Affirmative," Keiko answers. "Comet's outgassing it, among other things... Every time we open the bay doors, we get a big whiff." She lifts an arm, watching wisps of black powder blow from her armor. "And this stuff gets *everywhere*. Fine as smoke. Filters have trouble scrubbing it out of the air."

"When do you expect Chusan will arrive?"

Keiko takes a deep breath. "We don't. Our task force was intercepted en route. He peeled off to engage so the rest of us could make the rendezvous."

"Perhaps he got away, led them off?"

Keiko pauses at a doorway in the service bay's rear wall. "He did not."

"How do you know?"

The Gun turns square to Munro. "He got off a solid first salvo, but his ship took overwhelming fire." She sucks her teeth, taps the panel, and the doors slide open. Gesturing, she adds, "If you would, sir?"

Munro dips his head and covers his heart with his large hand.

"These losses are too great to bear."

Reluctantly, the big man steps through the doorway.

Keiko whistles to a Brick and Gun standing watch on the far side of the doorway, then flicks her head toward the service bay. "Maddock, Halgrim, keep eyes on our guests. Report any unsanctioned activity."

Both Operators respond, "Aye," nod, and hustle to the limousine.

Keiko draws even with Munro, matching his pace. "Forgive me for asking what I must, Colonel."

"Of course."

"Sir, are you *fraternizing* with the enemy?"

Munro juts his lower lip, chin squared. "I'll explain everything to you and Ralla, I'd simply prefer not to explain it twice."

Keiko's cheeks dimple in dissatisfaction but she holds her tongue.

Every time Munro passes an Operator in the corridor, he gets the same pleased then surprised look and a confused salute. Each interaction chisels at his confidence as the unspoken question is repeated in their eyes, *What are you doing here?*

Rather than dwell on it, he looks down at Keiko's arm and asks, "How's your prosthetic?"

Keiko lifts her remanufactured arm and extends her fingers in a fan. "Works well enough. Under armor, it's about the same." She lowers the arm and lets it swing with her strides.

Munro waits for her to say something more, but she does not, and the two walk in silence to the bridge.

Keiko halts at a bulkhead of twisted metal and tortured framing, announcing, "Major Ralla, Colonel Munro to see you."

Munro strides ahead, not needing an invitation from a junior officer, and he finds Ralla seated alone on the bridge. A slim HDI covers the silver contact terminals of her head, and a single lanyard connects it to the console in front of her. Wide goggles hide her gray eyes, scrolling lines of code in a continuous stream.

"Ralla! Good to see you," Munro says warmly.

Ralla stands, faces him, lifts her goggles, and salutes respectfully. "Colonel Munro. We were not expecting you."

"Yes, I've heard that a few times already... Well, right to it, then." He looks back toward the entryway and sees Keiko loitering. "Please join us," he calls out, waving her in. "This is for your ears, as well."

Keiko steps to Ralla's side and stands squarely opposite the big MedTech.

Munro frowns at such obvious suspicion. "I've seen quite enough questioning stares at my presence here, and I'm well aware of O'Kai's orders, so you can both dispense with the idea I've turned renegade."

"We've known each other too long," Ralla offers. "That thought had not occurred to me."

Munro rounds his shoulders. "Well...thank you. We *have* been through many challenging times. This one is our greatest test, I believe. One that will decide the future...and if we live to see it or not."

Keiko maintains her neutral expression, but Ralla's eyes narrow shrewdly.

"Okay," Ralla says. "What have you got?" She waits patiently, hands clasped in front of her.

"We're not *changing* strategy, we're *augmenting* it," the colonel begins, looking across the stripped out metallic surfaces around the room. "O'Kai may have frozen me out of the plan, but it wasn't hard to figure out you mean to confront the enemy here. To be effective, it would take all of you. Seems clear O'Kai believes this is the only option to let the *Europa* slip away unnoticed. Now, there's *another* option. With the Blueskin captive, myself, Sharon, and the Counselor, we're making an official attempt at dialogue. We'll demand an end to hostilities, and insist upon return of our ancient home world, *Earth*."

Keiko snorts.

Ralla asks, "You believe this is possible, because...?"

"Because the captive has told us so. The enemy knows their extermination of humanity was wrong, and they've been seeking a way to atone for that crime. Allowing us to return to our rightful home accomplishes that aim."

"The *captive* said this," Keiko echoes. "The captive would say anything to be free of us. What *wouldn't* it promise? This sounds like a trap."

Ralla nods. "It does. May I remind the Colonel his expertise is extensive in all areas *except* strategy and tactics?"

Munro sighs in frustration. "Stop. We already know I have no authority in combat operations, so I don't presume to tell you your job. Moreover, I'm not telling you to change anything about your current plan. What I ask is that you give this delegation a chance to speak with the enemy first...*before* your make your assault."

"Colonel, don't misunderstand," Ralla states. "My only objection is that you're too valuable to discard. I believe your intentions are good, but I ask that you leave this to the Corps. Our Cadre only functions when we stay within our areas of expertise."

Munro turns cold. "And where *is* our Cadre, Ralla? Did you know that Cadre One is lost? And O'Kai with it?"

Ralla dips her head. "I suspected that would be the case."

"Keiko told me on the way in here that Chusan is gone. And Shao-Lo... dispatched to Cadre Two alone, no backup. We'll likely never see her again. The *Europa* is on the run, no base, barely any escort." Munro turns away suddenly. "Do you notice a *trend*, Major?"

Ralla keeps her gaze on Munro but does not speak.

Munro puts his small hand inside his larger hand. "Maybe O'Kai took out an enemy taskforce with Cadre One. Maybe Chusan knocked out six ships with his one. It wouldn't matter if our kill ratio is a THOUSAND to one, *we're still not winning*. We're being ground down one ship, one life at a time." The MedTech takes a breath to calm himself and he turns about to face Ralla again. "You and I are the last two members of the Council. I don't recall there *ever* being such turnover in core leadership, and this leaves us with sizable blind spots. What's more, our people are scattered across *light-years*... All of our hopes are packed aboard the *Europa*, a vessel with no defenses whatsoever! We have *never* been so vulnerable."

"I share your concerns, Munro, and that's *precisely* why the fleet is here. In making our stand, we draw forces away from the *Europa* and give her the best chance of escaping to deep space. I trust my General, and I trust our plan. There will be no deviation from it. So tell me, Colonel, how can I help you?"

Munro takes a long breath, holds it, and lets it out in an extended exhale. "How long until you strike?"

"The comet's nearest Earth approach is in fourteen weeks, and one day."

"Then give me assurance you won't attack before then. That's all I ask."

"You want me to keep my schedule? Is that all? The way you came aboard, I thought you were going to insist on something more...subversive."

Munro smiles unhappily. "It's not that simple. We're opportunists by necessity. I'm sure you have eyes on that planet, and if you saw a clear advantage, you might take it. Now, I realize this could be a trap, and I don't go blindly to it. I'm not a fool. All I know for certain is that we have to try EVERYTHING we can, no matter how long a shot it is. That means I go with the others and start a conversation, or at least attempt one. The Cadre deserves a voice in that, and I intend to be that voice so our concerns are properly addressed. If we're to have any chance of success, regardless how remote, *I need your word* you'll give me all ninety-nine days before you commit."

Ralla's mouth draws into a taut line. "What you're *really* asking, Colonel, is for me to let an irreplaceable asset...my mentor and close comrade...risk death or capture for an *extremely* improbable result. You need to comprehend how cruel your request is."

"No, Ralla. I'm asking you to let me do all that I can, the way you and your Operators do *every single day*."

"Major," Keiko interjects, "what about the captive? It's here...it knows about our ambush."

Munro nods, accepting the concern. "We've kept this rendezvous a secret from her, and restricted any view outside of the craft for exactly that reason.

What's most interesting is that she insisted on not knowing herself, so she can't jeopardize our negotiations."

Ralla blinks, incredulous. "She does not want to know?"

"No. She said you should '...reserve your strength in secret...' She believes if her people don't know where we are, we still pose a credible threat, and that'll keep her people at the negotiating table."

Ralla crosses her arms and looks directly at Munro. "Tell me straight. Do you expect me to trust the word of your captive?"

Without flinching, Munro answers, "No. I expect you to trust *me*. And I believe *beyond any doubt* that she wants this conflict over as much as we do."

Ralla sighs and looks down at her console. When she looks up again, her eyes are glassy.

"Okay, Munro," she says. "Ninety-nine days. You have my word."

Munro smiles fondly, and he holds his great mitt out to her. Clasping hands, the two pull each other close and clap each other on the back. When Munro releases, he adds, "If we can get them to talk, we'll ask that they broadcast to all corners. Give you something to watch while you're waiting."

Ralla smirks. "Get out of here, sir."

Feeling thirty kilos lighter, Munro takes a deep breath, and says, "Thank you, Major." To Keiko, he says, "Good luck, Gun."

"Don't you mean, 'Good Hunting, sir?'"

"Not at all." The big MedTech turns and strides out. Ralla watches him go, mind racing.

Once sure he is out of earshot, Keiko says, "He seems different... *changed*. Does he to you?"

The gray-eyed Major nods. "He does."

"Is he slipping?"

Ralla shakes her head. "No. Because he's right. There *is* an obvious trend." Lowering her goggles, she settles back at her console. "Major, would you mind escorting him out?"

"Think he'll sabotage something so we can't attack?"

Ralla scoffs and turns an annoyed glare on the Gun. "A man who's done that much for the Cadre should never have to walk anywhere alone."

Keiko salutes crisply, turns on her heel, and runs out to catch up with Munro.

FROM FEAR AND SUSPICION

Thompson and Maiella lean on the bare metal walls of the passenger cabin, staring in annoyance at their Cadre sentries. Maddock stares back in stoic boredom, weapon in hands but held across the chest, while Halgrim keeps an eagle eye on Shondre. Shondre lies glum in her recliner, eyes forward, unwilling to meet the gaze of such a gargantuan soldier. Sharon pouts in her recliner, irritated at the delay with a thousand salty words on the tip of her tongue. And the Counselor ruminates in his recliner with tented hands.

Finally, the sliding door at the back of the service bay opens. Munro and Keiko step through it, mid-conversation. They stride side by side toward the limousine then pause at the base of the ramp. Keiko offers Munro a sharp salute, which he returns, and he claps her on the shoulder before ascending the gangplank.

Maddock's helmet buzzes with a radioed command, and he replies, "Affirmative, Major. The captive has not moved or spoken... Understood. Maddock, out."

At the top of the ramp, Munro peers in and sees the two Operators standing a sullen guard. "Thank you, Maddock," the Colonel states. "Dismissed."

"Aye, Colonel," Maddock replies, spine straight, flat hand at his brow. The Gun signals to Halgrim, and the Operators file past Munro down the ramp.

The Colonel pauses at the threshold, compulsively inspecting the hatch seals before stepping inside. Shondre, Sharon, Maiella, and Thompson perk up at once, asking different versions of the same question. Munro holds large and small hands up, quelling the sudden interrogation, and states, "It went well. Ralla's giving us ninety-nine days before making a move."

"Splendid!" Sharon says, beaming. She shakes adrenaline from her hands and adds, "That should be enough time, right Shondre?"

Shondre waits for the Counselor's translation then tilts her head, smiles, and nods.

"Well, that's my cue," Maiella says. Tapping Thompson with the back of her hand, she asks, "Join me up front?"

"Roger, that," Thompson says. "Let's get this *done*."

While the others settle back into their places, Munro takes a moment for himself, quietly enjoying the optimistic mood. *This could happen*, he allows himself to believe for the first time. The big MedTech lowers himself into his recliner, careful to guide his tools away from the pinch points so they can drape through gaps on each side.

Sharon draws harness straps across her lap and chest, when she stops suddenly and throws them off. "Ooh! Almost forgot!" she says and hurries into the rear of the limousine. When she returns, she cradles a long bottle with slender neck, capped in black wax. The label depicts oblong golden fruit with short spikes, captioned in alien script.

"Here, Shondre, for you."

Shondre lifts her chin from her recliner. When she sees the bottle, her jaw drops, she gasps, and her saffron eyes bulge. "Hyoo sayff? *Thank hyoo*," she says, taking the bottle in hand and gazing upon it lovingly. The rest of what she says flows in a rush, which the Counselor dutifully translates.

"She said, Such a rare joy from the slopes of this one's home, she did not think to see again in her lifetime... It is a blessing, for which she is both humbled and grateful." Still smiling in appreciation, Shondre offers the bottle back to Sharon, offering more words of humility. The Counselor translates again, "For now, the mind must remain sharp and clear. But upon our success, we will all toast in celebration!"

Munro scowls at the bottle, recognizing it as contraband Gregor successfully smuggled aboard. Seeing how pleased it makes Sharon and Shondre, however, not to mention the fact it had no impact on their journey after all, mutes his irritation. He clicks buckles of his harness together and waits, fingers interlaced over his navel.

"*Sharon, I need you in your seat*," Maiella calls through intercom. "*They'll be taking us out shortly*."

"Understood," the Colonist answers. She hustles to the back, stows the bottle, then returns and straps in to her recliner.

The loading ramp retracts into the vessel and the entry hatch seals. A low whine rises from below and gains in pitch, giving Munro a prickle of anticipation. Eyes closed, he listens to the whirs and hums of the machine around him, pleased it has endured the strains of distance and speed without so much as a squeal. *Good engineering and diligent execution*, he thinks. Relaxing into the custom contours of his recliner, the Colonel smiles in silent pride.

"Soooo, this is it," Sharon volunteers. "Does anyone else feel like they're about to go nuts?"

"Hmm, what?" Munro asks, sitting up. "You found a loose nut?"

"Oh, yeah," the Colonist answers, amused. "A *big* one."

Alarmed, Munro scans wall, ceiling, and floor, eyes wide. "*Where?*"

"I'm looking *right* at it."

Munro cranes his head and finds Sharon staring directly at him, both eyebrows arched. He snorts, rolls his eyes, and settles against his recliner.

"*Hang on, everyone*," Maiella announces through intercom. "*They're taking us out.*"

The limousine hull groans as it is tugged out of the service bay. There are four raps against the hull as the Virus Ship detaches.

"Hey. Biggie."

When Munro looks at Sharon again, her smirk is gone, replaced by pursed lips and wrinkled forehead. She reaches an open hand toward him. The Colonel looks at her hand, looks at her worried face, and he grips her hand.

"We can do this, yeah?" she asks him, unsteady.

"We *can*," he states with certainty, giving a light squeeze for emphasis. "And we *will*."

"Pleez, parr-dunn, ahlso..." Shondre says from his opposite side. Munro turns his head and sees the Eleto is also reaching out to him. He takes her delicate hand in his. Shondre smiles and her eyes close in relief.

In the row behind, the Counselor observes behind tented hands. He smiles with his own silent pride, seeing how, from beginnings of fear and suspicion, bonds of friendship between three radically different cultures are finally growing.

ON THE WAY

Maiella takes the limousine's controls in hand. Scowling at the ceiling, she mutters, "Better not have bunged up my hull. Took *hours* to match up the seams after Munro's upgrades."

Thompson laughs in the seat beside her. "I'm sure MedTechs said the same thing about us every time we came back from Rotation."

Maiella urges the ship from umbra and emerges into a diffuse glare of sunlit gas and dust. With a little more throttle, the comet's nucleus falls farther behind and the glare fades so swiftly only instruments can tell she is still within the coma.

"Let's not head straight there," Thompson recommends. "Make it seem we're coming in from a different direction."

"My thoughts precisely," she confirms. "Another thirty thousand kilometers and we'll be clear. Can light up DSDs, then." The two gaze out through the windscreen at infinite black with innumerable pinholes of light. "Say," she adds, raising an eyebrow, "wanna see Jupiter? It's on this side of the sun."

"Why not? But keep it sub-light. Don't want to draw attention."

"Understood." The Geek's goggles flare with calculation, and to the cabin, she announces, "Clearing comet coma now. Jump in three...two... one...*mark*." Deep Space Drives thrum, starry background lenses, and the limousine slips through space.

OF ALL TIMES

Sharon waits in her recliner, hands in lap, staring at her feet. Enormity of the task ahead looms like a cliff-face of icy rock, treacherous and slick, promising a lethal fall if she fails. Anxiety awakens inside her as if refreshed by the long journey, and she stiffens into a nervous plank.

Munro fills his recliner beside her as still as a statue. He grips the armrests with marble white knuckles, staring a hole through the wall ahead of him. By contrast Shondre is an image of tranquility, relaxing in her recliner, chin resting on the contoured shelf, eyes closed in meditation.

Oh, Shondre, how I envy you, Sharon thinks. She rolls her head, stretching knots of tension in her neck and shoulders.

"Have you ever seen Jupiter?" the Counselor asks from the row behind her.

"Hmm?" Sharon pivots her recliner to face him.

"Jupiter. Have you seen it before?"

"No. Well, through a telescope, yes. I always thought I'd have time to visit. Never did."

"Now's your chance."

"Yeah. Right," Sharon says absently, rubbing at the circles under her eyes. "Another tick off the bucket list."

The Counselor's face is passive and calm, absent any trace of worry. "It's a good plan, you know. It's going to work."

Sharon looks up at the Counselor. His eyes are bright.

You'd think he was heading down to the shop for a lolly. She sighs. "I wish I had your confidence. Or Shondre's. Because I'm going *completely* mental."

The Counselor smiles. "That's nothing to be ashamed of. Means you

195

understand what we've come to do. But you needn't worry. We've been over it and over it on this trip, looked at it from every conceivable angle. Isn't like we're going in blind. We have Shondre, and her introduction will guarantee us an audience. Once the Eleto have heard what you have to say—"

Sharon turns away to look through the hull of the limousine.

"Sharon," the Counselor says gently, "this is going to work."

Sharon arches a cynical eyebrow but nods anyway. "I'm sure you're right."

"*Arriving at Jupiter,*" Maiella announces via intercom. The Geek throttles back, and the charge in the cabin air dissipates. "*We're in the planet's umbra, aaaand...no contacts.*"

The Counselor leans forward in his recliner and taps Munro's shoulder. The MedTech flinches and swivels abruptly.

"I don't imagine you've ever seen Jupiter, Colonel," the android observes. "Would you like to?"

Startled from his thoughts, Munro blinks and collects himself. "I have seen images from *Europa*'s archive. I'm sure there will be little variation."

The Counselor grins. "You might be surprised. Why don't you go forward and see for yourself?"

Munro narrows his eyes, then swivels his seat to look up the short forward corridor. "Couldn't hurt, I suppose." He unlatches his harness and rises from the recliner, his long-handled tools clanging against the bare metal.

"I'll join you," Sharon says, pulling the latch on her harness. The big MedTech nods and stands aside so she can go ahead of him.

Sharon climbs the steps to the Flight Deck and crouches down between the two pilot's chairs. Munro props a leg on the stairs and leans against the threshold, gazing through the windscreen over Sharon's head. Directly ahead is a tremendous black disc, silhouetted by the Sun's corona and crowned with auroras. Four dots shine outside the disk, brilliant against the stellar background.

"Wow... I'm really here," Sharon says with an excited grin. "Remarkable, innit?"

"Hmm," Maiella replies with less enthusiasm, "Hydrogen, Helium, Ammonia, Methane... Mean density one point three grams per cubic centimeter... Typical gas giant."

"Typical?" Sharon looks at the floor and shakes her head. "No, no, no, you're missing it. The night side doesn't give us much to look at. Can you swing us 'round to the day side?"

Maiella sneaks a peek at Thompson for confirmation. He shrugs.

"We're going to transmit our intentions to the Eleto, anyway," the Gun states. "Won't hurt to do a slow fly by."

"Roger, that," Maiella answers, and she steers a gentle arc around the colossal planet.

The Sun creeps past the limb of the gas giant with a blazing flash. All four squint at the sudden brilliance until the windscreen compensates.

Maiella's goggles strobe with course calculations through the planet's gravity well, and she dives the limousine into a close pass around the dayside. With a quick tap of the pedals she swings the bow toward the enormous planet, letting the limousine skid sideways through its open trajectory, keeping the planet in view through the windscreen.

Flashes of lightning pulse on the night side, offering snapshot glimpses of chaotic layers far below. Yellow sunlight filters through high altitude clouds at the planet's limb, casting diffuse rays. Then a sliver of white, orange, and brown bands appears on the horizon.

Sharon perches on the center console, transfixed, as the vessel crosses the terminator to Jovian day. Boundaries between cloud bands swirl like cream poured through light tea. Oval white cyclones appear on the horizon then slide past, each as large as any of the inner planets. Giddy with discovery, she presses closer to the windscreen and then her breath leaves in a rush as a bulge of high altitude cloud appears on the horizon.

"Oh my God, is that...? It *is!*"

The bulge slides closer, revealing curved outer edges. It takes on a rusty tinge and spreads wide, crowding all other planetary features aside. Her eyes dart across eddies and swirls within a perpetually churning storm system over thirty thousand kilometers across. She cranes her head left and right, nose nearly to the glass, and still the vortex expands beyond view. Wilted in place, she basks in Jovian majesty, thinking nothing, feeling everything, and uttering, "Gor, isn't it *magnificent?*"

Maiella glances at Thompson, then at Munro, finding them both as unimpressed as she is. "Are we missing something?" the Geek asks.

Sharon's gaze turns toward Maiella like a compass orienting on magnetic *gauche.* "Are you serious?"

Maiella's head slides back, her mouth swishes to one side. "Yeah."

The Colonist extends an open hand toward the planet's Great Red Spot. "Are you telling me you can look at *that* and be *totally* unaffected?"

Thompson shrugs. "I see high-altitude Ammonia clouds...underlying layers of Ammonium HydroSulfide... There's no surface to colonize and radiation is off the chart, so we couldn't live here, not even on one of these ice moons... Sorry, but I don't see what's so interesting, either."

Sharon slow blinks at Thompson in disbelief. She cranes her head around at Munro. The MedTech's large and small arms are crossed, and the slight jut of his lip with half-raised eyebrows conveys boredom.

My God, I don't know these people at all! Dejected, she gazes back at the beautiful planet, watching it recede as they slingshot away.

"Let's have another look," Maiella mollifies. Her goggles flash as she probes with the vessel's instruments, searching for something of note. As expected, the planet subscribes to the laws of physics, perfectly ordinary. She nearly gives up when she notices that, for its mass and composition, the planet's magnetic field is more than twice as large as expected, so she pulls up a holographic model and projects it against the windscreen for all to see. Digging further, she discovers a donut-shaped field of charged particles around the gas giant, roughly corresponding to the orbit of its large inner moon.

"There's a plasma torus around the planet," she states clinically.

Munro perks up. "Oh?"

Maiella's goggles scroll with data. "Yeah... That inner moon, Io, is in orbital resonance with the next two out from it. Tidal forces are squeezing it hard, making it crazy volcanic... It's puffing out plumes of Sulfur, Potassium, Oxygen, Sodium... Huh. Magnetic field is whipping those particles into a *frenzy.*"

Munro uncrosses his arms and leans closer to the windscreen. "Is plasma escaping the torus? Because that could explain why the Magnetosphere is inflated."

"Affirmative, Colonel," Maiella confirms. "Huh... Seems to be a jet extending away from that inner moon and..." She gasps. "Flux tube!"

Thompson punches up a virtual overlay from his console that augments the projection. Jovian moons plot in real time with orbits traced in transparent white lines. Curving lines of force appear in blue, emanating from the planet's magnetic poles and crossing the moons' orbits at perpendicular angles. One line directly intersects the inner moon at its north and south poles. Along that line a tight tube highlights on screen in red.

"Confirmed," Thompson exclaims. "The moon's atmosphere is coupled to the planet's atmosphere. And the current passing through is..." The Gun looks at the planet in amazement. "...over three million amperes."

"Forget Solar Collectors..." Munro states. "What a power station! Uh, Sharon, do you mind if I...?"

Sharon pushes away from the console. "Not at all." She slips past Munro, and the big MedTech slides sideways into the gap she vacated. Maiella, Thompson, and Munro coordinate seamlessly, pulling up multiple windows in the overlay, anticipating the others' request without need to verbalize it.

"See there, where the flux tube contacts the planet," Maiella says, pointing a finger.

"Aurora," Thompson notes.

"It's like a footprint," Munro observes. "See how it tracks with the moon as it orbits?"

"Well, I'll leave you all to it, then," Sharon adds, unheard. Disappointed, excluded, she shuffles to the cabin.

Shondre maintains her contented repose, but the Counselor lounges in his recliner, alert. Sharon meets his gaze then looks down at the floor and collapses into her recliner.

"They couldn't see the beauty you saw," the Counselor probes.

Sharon gestures toward the front of the vessel. "How can you look at that and not be impressed? Honestly, every time I think I understand these people, they prove me wrong."

"They will *always* remind you how different they are. But that isn't a bad thing."

"Well, I'd like to have at least something in common."

The Counselor smiles with practiced patience. "You look at the planet and see beauty, right?"

Sharon swivels in her seat to face him.

"They *are* seeing its beauty, in their own way," the Counselor explains. "Whatever facet of Nature you choose to admire, neither of you is wrong."

"I know, *I know*. Even so, I'm glad you and Shondre are along for the ride. If I was alone with that lot, I think *all* my screws would come loose."

"What's that?" Munro calls from the flight deck. "Did you find loose screws?"

Sharon rises from her recliner and steps into the forward corridor. "Sure did," she answers.

Munro extricates himself from the cramped confines of the flight deck. "Where? Where did you see them?"

She hikes her thumbs at herself, and wide-eyed, answers, "Right here!"

Munro frowns as if swatted in the face. He waves a hand at her then crawls back into the narrow gap between pilot's chairs.

Satisfied, Sharon turns about.

"Feel good?" the Counselor inquires.

"You *betcha*," Sharon replies with a wink, and she flops down into her recliner.

"Ssshoold an-nownse arr-ry-val sssoon," Shondre says, stirring from reverie. She blinks her saffron eyes groggily and lifts her chin from the padded shelf of her recliner. Sitting upright, she yawns and stretches her arms. "Much too pree-pare."

"True," the Counselor agrees. "Colonel Munro," he calls with one hand cupped beside his mouth. Munro arrives at the end of the forward corridor.

The MedTech hurries into the passenger cabin. "You called?"

"Shondre needs to announce our arrival. The sooner we make contact, the sooner we can begin."

Munro nods thoughtfully. "Agreed." Over his shoulder, he calls, "Thompson, will you make room?"

"Aye," the Gun replies, and there are several metallic clicks as he unlatches his harness. While Munro settles into his recliner, Thompson makes his way to the passenger cabin and stands aside so Shondre can pass by.

"Thank hyoo, Tom-Sun," she says, laying a soft hand on his armored shoulder.

"Of course," he offers back.

Shondre peeks into the flight deck, silently remarking how dim and cave-like it is. Nonetheless, she slides past the center console and takes the still warm seat Thompson vacated. Arms resting on the chair's sides she states, "Thiss hwon iss redd-dee."

"Roger, that, Shondre," Maiella announces. She steers the limousine away from the enormous planet and thrusts toward the distant yellow Sun. "Bear with me, we're still in the magnetosphere, and there's a lot of interference. Once we get some distance, we'll transmit a clearer signal."

Shondre nods.

"Know what you're gonna say?"

Shondre nods again.

"I'll translate, as before," the Counselor volunteers.

Maiella looks over her shoulder and sees the android bracing himself across the threshold. "Works for me," the Geek says, goosing the throttle. "Okay, that should do it. We're clear for broadcast." The Geek's goggles flicker with instructions, and she throttles back. "Channels are open, Shondre. You're transmitting in the clear."

Eyes closed, Shondre breathes deeply through her nostrils and exhales past her lips. When she opens her eyes, her spine straightens, her chin lifts, and she is another person, someone Maiella has never seen. The Eleto sits taller, radiating a regal dignity that transforms the co-pilot seat into a throne.

Shondre smiles modestly, making tiny creases at the corners of her half-lidded eyes.

"(To reunite with her beloved People, this one *rejoices*, for Alessayya Shondrekar Bakkar has returned. Long has she wondered at the well being of cherished citizens. Long has she missed loving contact of friends and family. Please forgive your Sovereign's absence, and know that she has been ever faithful in her duty.)

"(Taken by force, this one returns in freedom, and the Humans who accompany her are companions. Have no fear, for these are not the Ravenous Ghosts who haunt our imaginations. These are *ambassadors*, the first of their kind. They come without weapons, bringing notions of peace for all to weigh.)

"(Brave El-Gaard did find us along the way and has, no doubt, foretold of our arrival. We wish a table set where we may share the stories of our struggle, and, in sharing, we may discover cause to end bloodshed. If fortune favors this occasion, those required for attendance will already be in transit.)

"(May we, at long last, begin the process of healing and bring this awful chapter of history to a close. We will arrive at the Human world shortly. Until then, this one remains, as ever, your humble servant.)"

Shondre lowers her head and closes her eyes, signaling to Maiella she is finished, and the Geek closes all open channels.

"That was *excellent*," Maiella says. "Broadcast should reach Earth in forty minutes or so. We'll give it a head start before we get underway." Over her shoulder, she adds, "In the meantime, Counselor, would you mind strapping in?"

"Not at all," the android replies. "If you'll excuse me..."

Shondre lays a hand on Maiella's armored forearm. "Hwee soh cloh-sss, My-ehl-luh."

Maiella rests her free hand atop Shondre's and pats it fondly. "We're close, yes. You brought us *home*, Shondre. Can't thank you enough for that."

Shondre shakes her head. "Thiss hwon not need thankss. Thiss hwon need rez-zuh... Reh-zuh..." The Eleto winces, unable to get the word out.

"Resolution?" the Counselor calls out from the passenger cabin.

"Hyess! Reh-zuh-loo-shun." Shondre takes another full breath, lays her hands on the chair's armrests, and lies back.

To the passenger cabin, Maiella announces, "This is it, everyone. Last leg of the journey. We'll take it slow so we don't outrun Shondre's message. Be there in a little over forty minutes. Anyone need the head before we go?"

"No," Munro states, as though the question were genuine.

"As a matter of fact, Maiella," Sharon calls out, "would you mind turning back? This'll be a high-society affair, so I rather fancy my other shoes for this."

Munro grabs his armrests and swivels to face Sharon. "Have you gone mad? We're not turning around for a pair of *shoes!*"

"Oh, they're worth it," Sharon teases. "And the return trip is always shorter, besides."

"But that... It isn't *shorter!*"

"We've already blazed the trail, so we can just zip right back, easy peasy."

"That makes no sense... There's no trail...and space doesn't *contract* just because you've traversed it..."

"Oh, no, you're quite wrong about that, Munro. Return trips are *always* shorter than ones going out. I wonder how you got so far in life not knowing that. Maiella, would you mind heading back to the *Europa*, love?"

"You got it, Sharon," Maiella calls out, playing along. With a wink to Shondre, she adds, "Coming about!"

"Geek, *you keep our heading*! And what's more, Captain Jones, I'm astounded that someone who served as *Europa*'s Navigator could be *so ignorant* of basic physics that I can't even BEGIN to process how...how..."

Thompson's shoulders bounce with the effort of restraint. The Counselor looks up at the ceiling, hiding his mouth with a hand. And Sharon grins at Munro with big goofy eyes.

"Gotcha," Sharon says.

"Was that *humor*?" Munro huffs amid peals of laughter around him. "*Really*, Sharon, *of all times!*"

Dabbing a tear from her eye, Maiella announces via intercom, "Not to worry, Colonel, our heading to Earth is set. Speed point nine five C. DSD engage in three...two...one...*mark.*"

The bright yellow sun ahead stretches into a spectral ellipse, background stars smear into prismatic streaks, and the limousine leaps gracefully through space.

ALL AT ONCE

Maiella concentrates on lines of data scrolling in her goggles. Local radio traffic increases exponentially in Earth approach, mostly unencrypted Eleto news and entertainment broadcasts, and she keeps available streams scrolling in one corner of her view. Channels with deep encryption suggest military activity, so she highlights them with double blinks and scans them in regular sweeps. With a keen eye on her scopes, she watches for hints of stealthed vessels nearby, makes course corrections along the flight path, tweaks plasma flow through DSD intermix chambers, monitors reserve of reactants, listens for fail codes from any of twenty-thousand sensors, tracks CO_2 content of the air as well as ambient cabin pressure and temperature. And still, there's attention span left to obsess over her destination.

So close now... Birds, trees and lakes... Real sky and weather... Like The Park *at Cadre Two, only much, much bigger... Almost too big to believe...*

Through a gap in lines of code, she sneaks a peek at Shondre. The Eleto sits elegantly in her simple gown, eyes closed, contented smile across her long face; and her calm demeanor eases some of the tension crowding the Geek's thoughts.

There's no reason to worry, Maiella reminds herself. *It's not a trap. Shondre's a true friend. She won't betray us.*

To the cabin, she announces, "Stand by for Earth interface. DSD shut down in three...two...one...*mark.*"

Crackling lobes of energy around the limousine disperse, and the ellipsoid smear of sunlight collapses to a blazing disk. The windscreen instantly compensates, dimming to more viewable brightness, but not enough to mute a shining blue dot off to starboard. A shiver runs down her length.

Shondre, noticing, turns toward her and asks, "Hyoo ahll ryyy-t?"

Maiella nods quickly, steering toward the nearby planet, unable to take her eyes from it. "Yeah, it's uh... Hmm. Hard to describe, but... It's hitting me all at once." Her goggles strobe with ship diagnostics and navigational calibrations. Once data flow completes, she adds, "Thought Cadre One was the only home we'd ever have...that we'd lived there forever. Had no idea we came from someplace else. I mean, it's ridiculous to think we could have just sprung from some crater in an asteroid... But we had so many other things to concentrate on just to get by... Now that we're here, I... I can't describe what I'm feeling."

Shondre purses her lips then says, "Thiss hyor hohm. Bee-long hyoo, ahl-wayss. Hwee fiks passst, may-k noo fyoo-chur fohr ahll."

"Yeah," Maiella says, smiling. "I'd like that."

From four hundred thousand kilometers away the Geek studies swirls of white cloud that span entire hemispheres. Beneath that thin veneer are oceans of liquid water, vast and inexhaustible, teeming with creatures in all colors, shapes, sizes. Standing above those interconnected seas are sprawling landmasses of tan, brown, and green where even the harshest terrain is more forgiving than the airless, irradiated stone of Cadre One.

A coastline appears between a gap in weather systems, one the Geek recognizes from *Europa*'s Navcharts, and as she stares at the green northern edge of Australia it finally sinks in that she is *here*, that this is a real place, not some mythological fantasy of Colonist fictions. Unlike the inhospitable gas giant in their wake, this planet is so cosmically rare it strains belief there could be any comparable place in the universe. Walking and breathing without apparatus on the surface, nutrients derived from plants and animals, not machines...flavors, sounds, scents, experiences to excite the mind and body, are all here. Surely a single life could not capture them all, and it would take many lifetimes to accumulate even a small fraction of what this planet might offer. Anxious, the Geek shifts in her seat.

We're so close! But the Eleto are in possession, and Shondre has said they won't leave. If they refuse our proposal...all of this could be snatched away. We could end up with nothing.

Pain in her hands jars her rumination. When she looks down, she finds herself clenching the controls as if strangling them. With effort, she unclamps her hands then pumps them open and closed to get the blood flowing again.

"Okay, Shondre, we're nearly inside Lunar orbit," Maiella announces. "Transponder is active. You ready?"

"Azz eff-urr."

Via intercom, Maiella announces, "Almost there, everyone. Hang tight. Shondre's gonna make the call."

"How you holdin' up?"

Maiella nearly spins out of her seat, sees Thompson standing behind her, and sags back into place. "Don't sneak up like that!"

Thompson snorts. "Yeah, I'm twitchy, too. We there yet?"

"The *hell* are you doing out of your recliner? We're still underway."

"Too confining. If I didn't get out of there I was gonna bend the arms right off it." He presses his knuckles against the ceiling and flexes in a groaning stretch until the panels creak. "Besides, I needed to see it again." Hooking finger tips on the threshold's upper edge, he leans between the two pilot chairs and peers through the windscreen at blue and white grandeur. "Can't tell you how excited I am for you."

Maiella frets. "Don't get my hopes up. Isn't ours yet." After a deep breath, her goggles pulse and she says, "Shondre, we're inside Lunar orbit. Broadcasting in the clear, all channels."

Shondre dips her head in somber preparation then she looks up into a broadcast window above the console with a penetrating gaze. "(To the People of Many Worlds, favored children of our Great Mother, this one delights in reunion! She longs to hear the sweet song of her native tongue. Who will answer her call?)"

The silence is brief, and a holoprojection of a broad faced Eleto in white uniform appears in the holowindow. Taupe whiskers hang in a braid from a square chin. Gold and platinum nestle in the ridges above each eye. Embroidered wreaths of silver encircle a crisp white collar and multi-colored ribbons adorn the chest. With dire expression, the officer states, "(A devious enemy might tempt us with a pleasing image, believing we would lower our guard. Few dared hope they would again look upon the *likeness* of their beloved Sovereign. So tell us truly, has Madame Shondre indeed freed herself from the bloodthirsty foe?)"

Shondre dips her head graciously, and, without breaking eye contact, replies, "(It is true your Sovereign is free, honored Prell-Shah-Stoh, and she does not travel unaccompanied. She has found friends among the stars and would present them to all so a compelling truth may be told.)"

"(A compelling *truth*? Does Madame jest?)"

Shondre blinks slowly, masking shock at the audacity, impertinence, and insult. Her expression turns cold. "(She does *not* jest, wellborn Prell-Shah-Stoh. Nor *could* she make light of our Ancestors' most egregious sin. Truth will not be hidden, no matter how fervently some attempt to bury it.)"

The officer on screen clasps hands behind his back and squares his shoulders. "(Madame must be made aware, then, that this one is newly appointed as High Commander of The People's Defense. She surely knows there was a High Commander before, one of like mind with our beloved Sovereign. And he discovered, to his shame and regret, how impossible is the idea of peace with *Da-oma Kachi-in.*)"

The arches in Shondre's chest throb with accelerated cadence, yet her demeanor remains unruffled. "(To sacrifice oneself in righteous action is no cause for shame or regret.)"

"(And for those who served under him? Righteous action doomed them, as well. Madame Shondre, did you feel so little for your Other Self that you pardon his murder so easily?)"

Shondre stares into the holowindow with every outer appearance of glacial patience while she shatters inside. A lifetime in politics gives her poise, and, rather than rise to the bait, she retorts, "(Love of self must diminish in times of great need.)" With an air of disappointment, she adds, "(My friend knew this once. Perhaps he has forgotten.)"

The whiskered officer's cheeks ripple as he grits his teeth, and despite his efforts to keep eye contact, he glances aside.

Shondre's voice deepens. "(We are assured noble El-Gaard foretold our arrival. A place for diplomats is required. Has a table been set?)"

Prell-Shah-Stoh dips his head and places a hand across his chest. "(This one must inform Madame Shondre that solemn El-Gaard has fallen ill, along with all aboard his warship, and the plague resists our best efforts. So *successful* is this pathogen that one might conclude it was...*engineered.*)"

Shondre considers the information, but does not pull at the obvious diversion. "(Does this mean a table has *not* been set for guests?)"

"(No, Madame, it has not.)"

With sharply commanding tone Shondre declares, "(Then my friend will cease offering excuses and see to it, *personally.*)"

Prell-Shah-Stoh goes rigid, breath held, eyes slightly wider, mouth a tight thin line, tongue tipped with barely restrained protest. With considerable effort, he keeps his officious dignity and replies with a stilted bow, "(Lady Shondre will be satisfied.)"

"(We also require accommodations for our five guests,)" Shondre demands with a sternness that precludes any discussion. "(Be the accommodations neither lacking, nor lavish. Provide for simple comforts, for their needs are modest.)"

"(As the Lady insists.)"

Shondre nods, relieved to have—at last—the Commander's acquiescence, and the sharp angles of her face melt. "(Lastly, dear Prell-Shah-Stoh, this one asks her friend to un-trouble his warlike mind. There are wonders yet to be revealed, in which he will find rightful cause to sheath his blade.)" She adjusts herself in the hard seat and lays her arms on the sides. "(For his abiding love and service to the People, this one would kiss his cheek in gratitude. Will he come to collect his Sovereign and welcome her home?)"

"(With Madame's leave, this one departs at once.)"

"(With all blessings, brave Prell-Shah-Stoh. May your line thrive until the breaking of time. She fondly awaits her friend.)"

Shondre closes her eyes and nods once for Maiella to end the broadcast.

"Okay, Shondre," the Geek states, "you're clear. Broadcast terminated."

"Hyoo arr serr-tin?"

"Yes, certain."

Shondre slumps toward the console, resting her forehead on the back of her hands, and lets out her breath in a long, exhausted sigh.

Moments later, multiple flashes surround the limousine at cautious distance. Maiella reaches out with the vessel's sensors, knowing Eleto warships have jumped in, yet the instruments show nothing, at all. Her forehead scrunches as she sends out active pings across the EM spectrum. Her sweeps find no reflection.

Thompson leans over her shoulder. "See anything?"

"Negative. Couldn't be any more than a thousand kilometers out, but the scope's blank."

Thompson frets and crosses his arms. "Upgrades?"

"Roger, that." The Geek's goggles strobe. "No parallax shift...not so much as a thruster plume—"

An enormous warship drops its stealth field directly ahead then more appear in an expanding sphere, surrounding the small limousine. Maiella glances over her shoulder at the Gun and asks, "Orders?"

"Don't move," Thompson replies, his gaze riveted to the massive warship ahead. As the Operators watch, long struts extend from its bow and a shimmering field weaves between them. The undulating field expands and connects to struts on adjacent ships, reflecting shimmers of starlight like the surface of an abyssal ocean.

The Geek asks, "You seen this before?"

"Yeah. Don't even *think* of flying through it. You still jacked in?"

"Affirmative."

"Disconnect. Hand over control, full access."

"Full access, *aye*." Maiella's goggles pulse twice then go dark, and she pulls her HDI lanyard from the console. An instant later, the wheel jumps forward and locks against the console. Interior illumination shifts to amber. The vessel thrusts forward.

Shondre lifts her head and tugs at the harness release latch. "Eks-kyooz pleez. Musst mayk redd-dee."

"Of course," Thompson says, standing aside so she can pass by. He waits until she is back in the passenger cabin before whispering to Maiella, "She seem all right to you? I didn't catch everything said, but I get the impression it wasn't the welcome she was expecting."

Maiella nods. "The guy in the holo reminded Shondre that her Other Self was dead." She huffs. "*Total* asshole." She glances at Thompson and for a fleeting moment, her expression reflects the same injury. Turning back to the console, she mutters, "If I lost you and someone threw it in my face like that..."

"Not gonna happen, Geek."

"*Fuckin' right*, it won't."

A vertical line of light appears in the darkness ahead and spreads wider as the limousine approaches. Once their eyes adjust, the two Operators peer inside a stark white hangar bay, cleared of vessels and personnel. Dozens of parking stations stand empty. Power leads, fuel hoses, and docking clamps are all recessed into floor or wall. The bay is immaculate, absent scorches, skids, or scrapes as if unused, and only outlines of reflective paint on the deck mark boundaries between one station and the next.

Thompson ducks under the low ceiling and squeezes into the vacant seat beside Maiella. He leans forward, craning his head to see the bay's interior, watching for hidden threats, but the bay is so empty it appears sterile.

"Not a mark on the deck plates," he notes. "Looks new."

"Probably is. Sending out their best for Shondre."

Thompson lies back in his chair, and Maiella asks him, "So, when you were here before...did you have any idea when you grabbed Shondre that she was so, you know...?"

"High rank?"

"Yeah."

"Well, she walked tall. Had a big hat. Seemed important."

Maiella leans on an armrest. "Can say that again." She smiles with a thought. "I'm happy for her right now. She must've missed her people something awful. Now, she gets to see them again. It's a good day."

"Like when you came back from Cadre Two. *That* was a good day for me."

"Aww," she says with a sappy grin.

The limousine glides to the back of the bay and hovers over a marked space before a set of broad pressure doors. Hydraulics whine as landing struts extend then lock with solid *klunks*. Artificial gravity draws the craft to the deck, the vessel squats down on landing struts, and flight systems power down.

"Huh," Thompson grunts as the background noise of pumps, turbines, and rotors fades away.

"What?"

"Got so quiet. Didn't realize how noisy this crate is."

Jets of vapor blast down from the bay's ceiling, and Maiella watches an external pressure gauge on her console level off near a hundred kilopascals. A gruff Eleto voice reverberates through the limousine's intercom.

"What did they say? They want us to lower the ramp, or something..." Thompson clarifies.

"That's what I heard."

"All right," the Gun says, rising from his seat. "This is it."

Maiella arches an eyebrow and nods. "Time to shine." She pulls her harness latch and clears the belts, about to follow Thompson back to the passenger cabin, when she notices the pressure doors at the back of the bay sliding apart. Through them flow dozens of gray uniformed and helmeted Eleto soldiers. The Geek props herself on the console, watching them organize into rows that flank the exit. A wide corridor extends straight from the doors to the vessel between them.

Welcoming committee, she guesses then joins the others in the cabin.

Munro, Shondre, and the Counselor stand in a circle, recliners folded up and stowed in the ceiling. They check one another over, reassuring, scrutinizing appearances, and straightening collars and belts. Sharon appears from the back of the vessel, cradling the bottle of contraband.

"I'd say this is a good time, yeah?"

Shondre turns, sees the bottle in Sharon's arms, and nods with a wide smile.

Thompson steps to the exit and hits the button that lowers the ramp. Hydraulics whine as it extends, and, as he waits, he hovers a hand over the button that opens the hatch.

When the Gun hears the ramp hit the deck plates, he asks, "Ready?"

Shondre licks her lips, clears her throat and stands straight. Smoothing her simple gown, she steps to the hatch beside Thompson and winks at him.

The Gun mashes the button and the hatch slides open. Industrial smells of hot metal, exhaust, and solvents waft through the gap. When he looks through the open hatch, he sees soldiers extending from the base of the ramp to the pressure doors, three rows deep on each side. A pair of burly Eleto warriors, dressed in full body armor, march in lock step through the pressure doors and stride between the rows. Their helmets are open, faceplates raised overhead. As they near the ramp, Thompson spies the familiar orange eyes of Shondre's personal bodyguard.

...like the one who got the drop on Beckert and blew him to pieces... the one who stabbed Argo through the side... Almost finished us all in close quarters... Tough adversary.

His fingers tap against his armored leg as a touch of adrenaline seeps into his blood. *No, this is proper*, he reminds himself, flattening his hand against the thigh plate. *Her bodyguards would come to escort her home. Makes sense.*

Shondre steps out first to greet them with open arms as they ascend the ramp. Once within arm's reach, they slap their helmets shut and scoop Shondre off her feet. Shondre protests at the top of her lungs but they are deaf to her demands. They sprint off toward the pressure doors. Rows of soldiers pull batons and they dash to the ramp, roaring.

Thompson punches the hatch button. It does not move. He punches again. The hatch stays open.

"*MAIELLA*," Thompson bellows, "*REPEL BOARDERS!*"

Repel Boarders

Thompson shoves Sharon to the back of the cabin and shouts, "MUNRO, PROTECT SHARON AND COUNSELOR!" He rushes back to the hatch and stands with arms raised, hands open, pleading in Eleto, "(*We here in peace*!)"

Soldiers storm the ramp, batons overhead, howling as they barrel straight into him. Batons descend in wild swings at his head, crashing against his arms, shoulders, and chest. Maiella braces him from behind, but they cannot staunch the rush. Soldiers burst through into the cabin.

Sharon screams. Glass bottle drops from her grip and shatters.

Munro gathers Sharon and the Counselor in his huge arms and turns his back to the rush. Batons rain down across his ribs, spine, and hunched shoulders. The Counselor reaches past Munro toward the soldiers, pleading in Eleto. His outstretched hand is clubbed aside and smashed against the metal wall.

Munro stuffs his companions into the rear corridor and spreads his shoulders, using his broad body as a barrier. His legs are hacked with furious strokes. One knee gives out and the big MedTech sinks to the deck. Batons hammer the back of his head with awful *tongs*, and he shields his crown with his large arm.

"*Go!*" Munro shouts to Sharon and the Counselor, shoving them both toward the rear compartment with his free hand. "Barricade yourse—!" Soldiers chop at him two handed, driving him down to the deck plates. Sharon staggers back, wide-eyed. The Counselor steps in front of her, arms raised, beseeching, and earns a baton across his face. His jaw dislocates completely, rips free of synthetic skin under one cheek, and swings by the skin of his other cheek.

Battered to all fours, Munro collapses and curls into a ball. Soldiers leapfrog the slumped MedTech, bash the Counselor aside, and descend on Sharon. She screams, staggers, and dashes for the rear of the limousine. A clawed hand grips her nape, lifts her off her feet, and propels her face first into the floor. Her head hits with a heavy *thunk* that telegraphs throughout the cabin. Her terror is silenced.

Maiella hunkers under the baton swings, protected by her armored skin and arms guarding her head. But Sharon's silence triggers a flow of combat stims. Chemical fury amplifies a vicious rage.

No restraint.

Total commitment.

She roars at the closest soldier, rips up his facemask and bashes his bared neck with armored fist. The soldier's eyes bulge as breath freezes in his crushed airway. He rocks back, letting his baton drop, and clutches his throat. In the space opened, Maiella explodes with a lunging kick that launches him through his comrades. Still baying, the Geek grabs another soldier by the helmet, hauls his head down on her knee repeatedly until the facemask shatters, then hurls him into other soldiers. With more space, she kicks, elbows, cudgels, bashes, throws, and slugs her way toward the rear of the ship.

Thompson wrestles against a mob pinning him into a corner, alarmed at Maiella's fury. He lifts his head up to shout, "MAIELLA, *CONTROL!*" A baton smashes his cheek then another splits his ear.

Rage overwhelms. Feral growls through clenched teeth. The Gun shoves away from the wall, chin tucked, and powers the mob back a centimeter at a time. Pushed onto heels, soldiers' swings lack the impact to turn the monster pressing through them.

Soldiers at the rear reset their stance, bracing ones in front, and the crowd shoves back. Thompson gets a foot against the wall behind him and he springs over their heads, letting them crash into the corner behind him. He tumbles to feet then rips at the pile battering Munro, peeling and hurling them aside like sacks, kicking, punching, wrenching, clearing gray uniforms until Munro can drag himself toward Sharon.

Behind him, Thompson hears the *clack* of baton against baton. He whirls about and sees Maiella with a baton in each fist, clubbing violent rhythm into soldiers around her. Her eyes are crazed. Her teeth are bared. And her limbs fly with fearsome grace as she jabs pressure points, smashes joints, crushes bones. Soldiers shrink back from her savage frenzy, wary, stumbling against one another to get away. She gives chase, allowing no respite. One baton splinters into composite shards against a soldier's helmet. In the same movement, she whirls and buries the new shiv between armor plates, rips it out with a spray of blue blood and buries it again in the armpit of an adjacent soldier. Her leg flies out as if of its own mind, heel smashing into Eleto eye socket. Her head swings around, eyes locked on the thrown back head and exposed throat. The shiv pulls free and she coils up a killing strike, wailing.

"*GEEK, CONTROL!*" Thompson bellows, diving at Maiella, clenching her around the waist, and tackling her off her feet.

Knocked aside, her stabbing swing misses, when a deafening slug rips the air centimeters away. The Operators *thud* to the deck, and Thompson's eyes go wide as he spots an orange-eyed Eleto at the base of the ramp, rifle leveled, barrel smoking.

Pinned under Thompson's bulk, Maiella writhes in unspent wrath, white foam at the corners of her mouth. She is slippery in frenzy, but Thompson holds on, shouting her name until panicked breaths slow and she sees the ragged hole gouged through the cabin wall. Her eyes trace the dissipating trail of vapor to an armored warrior staring down his rifle at her, finger on the trigger.

The cabin goes still, neither human nor Eleto stirring, as Maiella and the orange-eyed bodyguard continue their silent contest.

"(*NO!* This one *WILL NOT* be handled like livestock,)" Shondre's furious voice protests from the bay. "(OUT OF THE WAY, *THIS INSTANT!*)" She steps around the orange-eyed bodyguard and hurries up the ramp. Standing at the hatch, she frets at heaps of Eleto and Humans, all bleeding and swollen. The Counselor sits up from the floor, jaw swinging, one whole side of his face a mess of torn synthflesh and broken actuators. He tries to speak, but it comes out a gargled mess, and when he tries to put his jaw back into place, his bent arms cannot seem to find it.

Desperation peeling her regal dignity to ribbons, Shondre turns and lashes out at the warrior, berating him so vehemently she goes momentarily hoarse. Once she collects herself, she demands something of him that Thompson cannot translate, and when the soldier does not move, she repeats louder and louder, stamping her delicate foot and smacking his rigid arms with clenched hands. Without taking his eyes off of Maiella, the warrior slowly lowers his weapon.

Shondre sighs, looks at the floor, stands straighter, then points to the bay and shouts, "(OUT!)"

Those who are able to walk hunch submissively and file past Shondre. Others struggle to push up from the deck. Some do not move, at all.

Sharon moans from the back of the craft, and Maiella squirms.

"*Get off me!*" she snaps, but Thompson holds her down.

"Are you calm?"

"I'm *nowhere fucking near* calm." The Geek glares at the bodyguard then looks at the blasted hole in the wall, adding, "But I'm in control."

Thompson rolls aside and Maiella slides out from under him. In a blink, she is down the rear corridor of the limousine.

The Gun surveys the damage, especially hard hit by the Counselor's disfigurement. The android labors to grasp his dislocated jaw, yet his bent limbs still cannot find it. So he looks at Thompson with one functional eye, confused and helpless.

From the Counselor, Thompson looks at the unmoving soldiers littering the floor. *If Maiella killed any of them, this could be all over...* The moment he moves toward one of the slumped soldiers, however, the orange-eyed bodyguard barks a warning and raises his rifle. Thompson lifts his hands and backs away.

"Munro," the Gun calls out. "You okay?"

There is a rustle of metal tools from the rear corridor. "Affirmative. Having trouble focusing, but...it's nothing."

"Sharon?"

"She's hurt," Munro answers for her. "I'm on it. Maiella, can you get my MedKit from storage?"

"Roger, that," the Geek answers, and she darts into a side room.

Thompson makes his way over to the Counselor slowly, mindful of the bodyguard's weapon following his every move. The android flounders, totally disoriented, misaligned actuators stuttering and catching. He tries to speak again, tongue lolling from torn out neck, then gives up. The Gun takes hold of him delicately, helping his friend sit up against the wall. The Counselor's white lab coat is a tatter of rips and frizzed threads. His slacks, worn thin from such long service, are likewise in shreds; and his wrecked joints protrude through long tears in the fabric. With his one undamaged eye, the Counselor looks at Thompson intently, clearly asking something, yet cannot get the message out.

The Gun takes hold of the swinging jaw, and tries to push it back into the socket, but the receptacle housing is broken, sinews severed, and the mandible flops out of place to dangle again by a flap of synthetic skin.

"Counselor's gonna need your help, Colonel."

"Understood," Munro calls back. "Is his life in danger?"

Thompson looks into the Counselor's good eye, and asks, "Is it?"

The Counselor shakes his head.

"No," Thompson calls back to Munro. "Gonna need a lot of repair, though."

"Sharon first, then he's next. Keep me informed if his condition changes."

"Roger, that," the Gun replies. He looks down the ramp, finding Shondre and the bodyguard in stern conversation. Most of it eludes Thompson's comprehension, but between flowery words he gleans she is demanding to speak with her companions alone. The bodyguard counters without any attempt at artistry that he will never again allow her to be separated from her people, and so long as Ravenous Ghosts exist, she will never be out of *sight*.

Shondre's language is gracious yet insistent. The way she glares without blinking, pointing at the ground and at his chest, Thompson guesses she is pulling rank. Then the bodyguard responds with words the Gun cannot translate. Shondre flinches then goes quiet and pale. The Counselor likewise stiffens, his one eye wide and fixated on the Eleto.

A second bodyguard strides up to the ramp, offers a courteous greeting to Shondre, then gestures toward the pressure doors. With an anxious glance at Thompson, Shondre offers some stern final words for the warrior then allows herself to be escorted to the rear of the bay.

The warrior snorts then points up the ramp, barking orders, and gray uniformed soldiers hop to comply. Clawed hands seize Thompson under the arms, haul him up to his feet, spin him about, and shove him toward the ramp. He lifts his hands again, saying evenly, "Yeah, yeah, I'm going."

From the top of the ramp, the Gun sees more soldiers have arrived in the bay. Most carry short rifles across their torsos. They glare with hatred and fear in equal measure, gripping weapons fiercely, forcing themselves to meet his steel-gray gaze.

A push from behind starts him down the ramp. As he goes he searches for Shondre, finding her by the pressure doors amid a phalanx of orange-eyed bodyguards as if caged by them. She peeks between them, trying to maintain airs of regal detachment, yet her lips are bunched in concern.

At the bottom of the ramp, a soldier steps into Thompson's path, points to one side, and waits. The Gun nods and takes his place, standing where indicated.

Maiella is shoved through the hatch next. She locks eyes with the bodyguard, halts, then continues down the ramp. The bodyguard waits for her to pass by then turns and stomps directly into her back. Maiella launches head first, skids on her chest, springs up on her hands, and whirls about on her feet. Head high, she shouts a challenge in Eleto, "(To the *DEATH* if you wish!)"

The warrior tilts his head in amusement then slings his rifle and pulls a wicked looking blade from his waist. He shows her the jagged edge then tosses it at her feet. With a crazed grin, she keeps eyes locked on her target and stoops to pick up the blade.

"LEAVE IT," Thompson barks.

Heeled by Thompson's command, Maiella glares malevolently at the bodyguard, takes her place at the Gun's side, and stands at attention.

Munro limps out of the hatch next. Harsh overhead lamps expose the contrasts of pale olive skin and blackened eyes. His nose is mashed, lips split, knuckles red and swollen. Trails of blood run from his hairline. He hobbles down the ramp with gritted red teeth. Taking place beside Thompson, the big man says, "Sharon's in a bad way. She needs attention. But they won't let me have my MedKit or tools."

Thompson nods, tight-lipped. "We'll take care of her."

The Counselor is dragged out next, carried under his arms by two soldiers, and his useless legs clatter down the ramp behind him. His one functioning eye scans eagerly for Shondre and spots her penned in by Eleto guards. Tiny fragments drop out of his broken face and his exposed tongue wags in effort of speech.

Shondre calls out from between the flesh and bone bars of her cage to the soldiers carrying him. They bow in reluctant respect and drag the android away through the open pressure doors at the back of the bay.

Sharon is carried out last, brown hair matted in a clump to bloody forehead. She lifts her head, squinting and wincing as if the light were painful. Red saliva hangs in a long line from her lower lip, and she mumbles incoherently as her feet drag, toes bouncing down the raised ribs of the ramp behind her. Once Sharon is hauled past, the bodyguard steps up to the hatchway, peeks into the limousine one final time then strides down the ramp. He pauses at the bottom to collect his blade.

Shondre likewise calls out the soldiers carrying Sharon, sternly and urgently. They offer a cursory bow and rush Sharon through the double pressure doors.

Munro asks, anxious, "Where are they taking her? I have to attend her." He meets Shondre's eye and calls to her stridently, "There's no time to lose, Shondre. Sharon's hurt. I HAVE to get her—"

The bodyguard silences Munro with rifle butt to the gut. Maiella launches. Thompson barely catches her by the armored collar.

"(DA-INDO-HASS!)" Shondre bellows.

The bodyguard looks down in disgust at the crumpled MedTech but takes a step back. He sucks his teeth then spits at Maiella's feet, daring her to move. Thompson pulls her in closer, and he can feel her trembling with fragile restraint. The look on her face is one of total commitment before an enemy, and he knows, *She'd chew her way through this Eleto's neck if she could.*

Da-Indo-Hass sighs in disdain, turns to the rows of soldiers, and says loud enough for all to hear, "(See it shake! Like a baby afraid of its shadow!)" With a derisive leer, he faces Maiella again.

The soldiers all laugh, and Maiella goes eerily calm. She no longer trembles.

The orange-eyed soldier narrows his gaze. "(Understood that, did you, *thing*?)"

"Clear your head, Geek, *RIGHT NOW*," Thompson growls, unsure if he can keep her reined. Maiella squints as if contemplating a painting, studying every angle, cataloging every feature of the bodyguard's face. And then, to Thompson's relief, she blanks her expression, squares her shoulders, and stares stoically ahead.

The Gun stoops to help Munro up, and the big MedTech's brow is bunched with bewilderment. "What did I do?"

"I think they don't like us talking to her directly," the Gun supposes. "Don't even say her name, in fact."

Da-Indo-Hass steps even with Thompson, nearly a match for the Gun in stature. The Gun refuses to give any satisfaction, however, and keeps a level, disinterested gaze at the far wall. The bodyguard harrumphs then calls out orders. Rows of uniformed soldiers jump to action, surrounding Munro, Thompson, and Maiella. With harsh shouts, they berate the three into a forced march through double pressure doors.

TRIALS OF LESSER MEN

Shondre strides through brightly lit corridors with high ceilings. It is a path she has trodden a hundred times in days past. But after spending so long with the Humans, and their absolute obsession with efficiency, it occurs to her what a waste of space it is to have such lofty ceilings on any space faring vessel. The amount of air that must be filtered and processed, the vacancy where storage tanks or quarters might be, the volume of emptiness transported from one location to the next reeks of decadence and privilege.

Likewise, she sees the phalanx of warriors escorting her in a new light. All of them bear orange-tinted eyes of the Ordeal—proof of prowess, endurance, and cunning—assurance of fidelity as 'Guardians of the People's Voice.' She does not recall them being this sullen, however, as they have ever been a proud order. Neither does she recall them being so heavily equipped. With their dark armor, heavy weapons, and grim expressions, they remind her more of Cadre Operators, and the moment is more reminiscent of her march through Cadre One than a homecoming.

There was no weakness in their protection, she thinks, remembering the bloody day of her abduction. *Those who served gave their all and this one yet draws breath because of their loving service. Yet these new Guardians are so grave and warlike...it is unbecoming...an ugliness.... Such brutality and eagerness to harm... Perhaps there is shame that their Sovereign was taken from their protection? Perhaps they wish to demonstrate such a thing could never occur again? This one must be mindful and prove, by her living presence, there is no cause for disgrace. For it is all too plain they have fashioned themselves into the enemy that bested them.*

"(Da-Indo-Hass,)" Shondre calls to the soldier at the lead.

"(Yes, Madame Shondre,)" he answers without looking back.

218

"(Your zeal is not in doubt. Neither is there threat to us here. Allow this one to walk beside you for, among such tall and fierce Protectors, she feels as if she is at the bottom of a well.)"

Da-Indo-Hass looks over his shoulder, and his hard gaze is softened by Shondre's smile. "(It would honor me to be at your side, Madame.)" He flicks his head and a gap opens in the phalanx for Shondre to step through.

The graceful Eleto takes the crook of Da-Indo-Hass's arm with both hands. "(Ah, that is much better,)" she says to him and the two resume the path forward at Shondre's more leisurely pace.

"(This one is glad to see her most faithful Guardian again. And she regrets some of the words she chose upon her return. The severity of his action is clearly borne of devout and loving service.)"

"(Madame knows there is no room for less. This one could not bear the strain of separation and has vowed to the Mother that no harm shall ever come to her again.)"

Shondre rests her head on his shoulder. "(Da-Indo-Hass must know that no one can be kept entirely from danger without also being imprisoned. It is wrong to be caged, thus, for life loses meaning. Come, let your mind be not troubled, for this is a day of happy reunion. She has returned enriched by her travels with new friends.)"

The soldier's jaw clenches. "(*Friends*? Who *abused* her Grace?)" His lip curls. "(Who handled her like chattel? Dragged her away *with a blade at her throat...* Such insult and injury cannot go unanswered.)"

"(This one lives and breathes. Her throat is not cut, and she possesses the correct number of arms and legs. So when Da-Indo-Hass speaks of injury, does he mean his own?)" Shondre turns to him and stops him in the corridor. "(Look here,)" she says gently. "(This one is not delicate, nor could she be to serve as Voice of the People. She has faced the Ravenous Ghosts who haunt our shipping lanes and stands before you *unharmed*. If Da-Indo-Hass feels fire in the chest and would punish the Humans with unwholesome vengeance, he must know that this one's struggle *is not his*. This one begs him to unclench his fists and show no more violence to her guests, because hatred is *not* what kept her alive. Anger did *not* open the Human mind to peace.)"

Da-Indo-Hass stands attentively, if skeptically, waiting for her to continue.

"(*Love*,)" Shondre says at last, taking his arm again and leading him onward, "(love buoyed her when she believed she was drowning. *Faith* provided a compass when lost in the darkness. At times, she did despair, but her spirit did not break. And she has returned stronger, wiser. Understand, it was her destiny to live among the Humans for a time. One cannot take up arms against fate! This one *had* to go, so that she might see and comprehend without prejudice. *Nothing* in the multiverse could have prevented it.)" She dips her head then looks at him seriously. "(Do you see now that my friend's honor is unblemished?)"

"(This one cannot agree, Madame. He failed in his most solemn duty, in his *one task*, to defend the Voice against any who would bring her harm. The Mother has blessed us today with Madame's safe return...but this one will *ever* curse the day his Sovereign needed him and he was not there.)"

Shondre takes his hand. "(One cannot tell another how to feel or what to think. But this one prays Da-Indo-Hass will once more let love guide his service, for she does prefer that to his regret.)"

Da-Indo-Hass looks down and frets. "(Can Madame Shondre forgive her servant?)"

Shondre turns toward him, beaming. "(Beautiful soul, there is nothing to forgive.)" She cups both sides of his face and kisses his cheek. "(There, now. Let us not keep the High Commander waiting any longer.)" Shondre takes his arm and they stride briskly down the hall.

At corridor's end stands a portal of polished gold. Engraved upon it are tables heaped with food, beverages, elaborate centerpieces, and rich place settings. Seated around the tables are Eleto in uniform, all of whom are depicted as having the raucous time of their lives. An entry panel recesses in the wall beside the door, outlined with braided vines, leaves, and fruits. Da-Indo-Hass strides ahead and taps the panel.

"(Her Grace, Madame Shondre, desires audience,)" the grim soldier announces.

The golden portal slides aside, and Shondre looks through to an ornate ballroom where she once entertained diplomats, ambassadors, spiritual elders, renowned artists, military brass, and the highest echelons of Eleto society. The decor has been altered radically in her absence, however, where antlers and tusks have replaced masterful paintings. Tanned hides—with heads still attached—have replaced woven rugs. And plush silk upholstery has been exchanged for shiny leather. Such gaudy trophies bring a particular individual's taste to her mind, and she is unsurprised to find that person reclining on a fur-lined couch at the room's focus.

"(Does Madame desire escort?)" Da-Indo-Hass asks respectfully.

She smiles to him and says, "(Thank you, no. Go in peace, dear friend.)"

Da-Indo-Hass bows to his waist, sweeping an arm to one side and gripping the tip of his tail with the other. "(This one shall stand at the door until she requires him.)" To the other guardians, he points back down the corridor. The phalanx about faces in unison and marches back the way they came.

When the door seals, Shondre turns toward the officer in the couch. Clasping her hands together, she smiles broadly, steps toward him, and says, "(Dear Prell-Shah-Stoh, how wonderful it is to see your face! Come, let this one caress your cheek!)"

Prell-Shah-Stoh rises from his couch and crosses the ballroom to her. "(Lady Shondre, it is a joy to see you returned safely from the barbarians. How indomitable is her spirit that it was not—)"

Shondre slaps him across the face so hard it turns his head. Cheek stinging, he looks at her warily. "(Her Ladyship—)"

She slaps him with her other hand harder than before. "(This one *knows* the order came from you,)" Shondre accuses. "(For only the High Commander could be *so brazen* as to cudgel those offering the bough of friendship.)"

The officer raises his chin haughtily. Despite the bright burning of his cheeks, he puts on a defiant face.

"(They will receive the *finest* care for their injuries,)" Shondre dictates. "(Afterward, they shall enjoy every courtesy due ambassadors to the People. You WILL apologize to them, and you will do so *publically*.)"

Prell-Shah-Stoh offers a patronizing smile. "(This one does not think so, *ex*-Sovereign.)"

Shondre's eyes widen at the naked insubordination, yet she maintains calm. "(This one was informed a Regent was appointed in her absence. Such is correct and proper, as her duties are too great to be left undone. It is abundantly clear, however, that noble Prell-Shah-Stoh has grown *comfortable* in his position under this Regent and would seek to maintain that position at any cost.)"

"(Not *any* cost, Madame,)" he states cryptically. Then, stepping to a sideboard and pouring himself a drink, he says with total sincerity, "(This one acts out of concern for her Ladyship. In such lengthy captivity, she may yet be suffering shock and psychological trauma.)" He lifts the crystal goblet to his nose, and inhales deeply while swirling a deep burgundy vintage. "(The People must be satisfied, beyond any doubt, that she remains unbroken by the insolent foe, and that her priorities are beyond reproach.)"

"(Yes, such selfless concern the High Commander shows... His depth of feeling is surely without equal, which is why he chose to remind this one upon her arrival of Gro-Elto's death...*over an open channel*.)"

The officer swirls the liquid in his goblet.

"(Perhaps the High Commander sought to expose this one as overly emotional, at best,)" Shondre continues, "(or grossly indifferent, at worst. And in such cold calculation, he reveals how frigid is the blood in his chest.)"

The officer sips from his goblet, keeping his eyes glued to Shondre's. "(If devotion to security has made this one cold, then he will gladly wear that label. For the People deserve to see for themselves what has become of their former sovereign. They deserve to know if her loyalty is cleft, leaving her *susceptible* to enemy suggestion.)"

"(There is no enemy but the one we *made*! Here, they come in gestures of peace that we might all atone for our ancient sins. And you have used them *savagely*!)"

Prell-Shah-Stoh clucks his purple tongue. "(Such opinions are now unpopular in the extreme. There has been no *sin*, as you call it. Humankind is a race of violent beasts. Their extermination is just. And if such beasts dare approach us, then we shall *use* them in any manner befitting.)"

Shondre glares. "(This one has always suspected Prell-Shah-Stoh would use a position of service to his own gain.)" She gestures to the room around her. "(See all of his petty, vain trophies, stolen from animals of the planet below. How fitting an example of his personality, for just as he has stolen skins from creatures better and stronger than he, he would likewise flay his betters and adorn himself in their accomplishments.)"

The officer squints. "(This one does not take her Ladyship's meaning.)"

"(What she means, *vile Prell-Shah-Stoh*, is that you wear the rank and uniform of a man *ten times* your quality.)"

He arches an eyebrow. "(Our wise and noble Regent would not agree, as he has appointed a more pragmatic replacement than the one who, with head packed full of ludicrous ideals, led others to pointless deaths.)" Prell-Shah-Stoh levels his gaze on Shondre. "(Where did Gro-Elto get such notions, we wonder? Who else would so foolishly cling to the idea that peace is possible with *demons*?)"

Shondre's breath freezes in her lungs, and it takes her several tense moments to recover. "(Perhaps the High Commander should consider what will happen when this one returns to service.)"

"(*If* her Ladyship returns to service,)" the High Commander corrects, "(though this is unlikely. For she must undergo an extensive physical and psychological evaluation before there can be any talk of resuming her service. She must be quarantined to ensure she carries no infectious pathogens. And during that time, our Honorable Regent has decreed Madame Shondre will wield no executive authority *whatsoever* to prevent any corrupting influence.)" The officer lifts the goblet to his snout again and savors the bouquet before taking a longer sip. "(To be held so long in the clutches of depraved, sadistic devils...)" He purses his lips and shakes his head. "(...would surely overwhelm even the best among us.)"

Shondre boils inside, even as she remains impassive on the outside. "(This one has often suffered the trials of lesser men. While the High Commander surrounds himself in mirrors and minor achievements, she will *not* sit idly by.)"

"(He would be greatly disappointed if she did.)" The High Commander raises an arm, and the golden portal slides open. Prell-Shah-Stoh beckons to Da-Indo-Hass, who waits just outside. The gruff soldier approaches and stands at attention.

"(Now then,)" the Commander says without any trace of empathy, "(her Ladyship has traveled far, and she must be allowed her recuperation. None would begrudge the use of her official residence, considering the extent of her service, whether she recovers her 'Voice' or not. Do see that she arrives safely this time.)"

Da-Indo-Hass's jaw flexes as he bows deeply. "(On my life, it will be done, Commander.)"

Her tail held high, Shondre smoothes down the lines of her makeshift gown and places one hand inside the other. "(Justice is greater than either of us, Prell-Shah-Stoh,)" she imparts without malice, and she dips her head in deference. Turning about, she slips her hand into the crook of Da-Indo-Hass's arm and says, "(Do tell, does your eldest daughter still perform for the Feast of Migration?)"

"(She does, Madame, to great acclaim,)" the bodyguard answers.

"(A relief. For this one's faith is much abused of late, and she craves something...*anything*...that would make her proud to be Eleto.)"

BORROWED ROBES

Shondre walks arm in arm with Da-Indo-Hass, passing several intersections on the way toward the shuttle bay. There is surprisingly little activity down the branching corridors, likely arranged by design. She looks over at him, remembering when he was more open, when they would chat freely about serious matters and trivial ones, his candor always an asset no matter the topic. His rigid jawbones remind her more of a bitter old man than a trusted friend, and she wonders if anything is left of the person she once knew.

"(The Commander erred in his implication,)" she says. "(You have never failed.)"

His eyes remain forward, his head level. "(Regardless, this one is solemn in his duty.)"

Shondre frowns, her gentle words having deflected off his stony exterior, so she probes further. "(Would you have killed the woman on my limousine?)"

"(Without a second thought.)"

"(She was defending the lives of her companions.)"

"(Human lives are irrelevant. They do not matter.)"

Shondre halts. "(How is it that my friend is so hardened?)"

He glances anxiously at her then asks, "(May this one speak freely?)"

"(She would not have it otherwise!)"

He takes a deep breath. "(With respect, Madame Shondre, how is it that her Grace has *not* been hardened?)"

She nods, accepting the question. She faces forward and takes her escort's arm again. "(This one makes herself second in all things so the needs of the People may always prevail. Do not mistake her composure for anything less, for if allowed, she would wail with rage and grief. But the time is not right. She *must* remain patient. Once her work is done, she will pay proper homage and she will quench the soil with her tears.)"

Da-Indo-Hass walks in silence, his brows knitting, then he blurts out, "(*There was nothing left to bury!*)"

Shondre looks up at him, feeling tension in his arms through the thick armor plating. "(Your brave sons...they served under Gro-Elto, did they not?)"

The corners of his mouth draw downward into a grimace of profound anguish. His eyes shine then he sniffs hard, blinks away the glassiness, and stuffs the emotion down deep.

"(There is more my friend must say,)" Shondre urges. "(This one would know the full weight of his burden.)"

"(Such words are forbidden before her Grace.)"

"(Then speak them not to her *regal title* but to *flesh and blood* who walks beside you!)"

He looks at her intensely, his orange eyes rimmed with furious green. "(Had Gro-Elto gone to exterminate the foe...*a father's sons would yet live!*)"

Shondre looks forward and swallows hard. "(My friend speaks truth. And this one carries responsibility for it. Yet my friend cannot know all that has been witnessed. He cannot know what it is for a people to face *extinction*, to have survival dictate every decision...the sacrifices required in living this way... *He cannot know this* until he has lived it himself.)"

They enter an elevator together, and he speaks the floor number to the panel. When the doors close, he asks, "(Does Madame Shondre *truly* seek peace with Da-oma Kachi-in?)"

"(She does. And ever will.)"

Da-Indo-Hass squints in disbelief. "(Her love of the enemy is apparent. Where is the love of her People? Does she not mourn for them?)"

"(More than she has words to express. And *it does not change the fact* that all of this pain is of *Eleto* creation! The cycle *must* end, brave Da-Indo-Hass! For if it does not, then we shall have *more* drowned cities, *more* unburied dead, *more* fathers losing sons and daughters!)"

"(They come in stealth to murder... to pillage and terrorize... They shatter our domes and crash our shuttles... They disappear entire crews where none are seen again... And for this, her Grace would reward them with her *charity*?)" He looks at the ceiling then turns toward her. "(Would she first tour the planet below? Would she look upon our drowned city beneath the waves? Would she visit the gravestones and tally them *with her own eyes* before welcoming those who brought such *misery*?)"

"(She will, if it comforts roaming spirits to their rest. But still my friend cannot comprehend, even in such deep and tragic loss, what it means to roam the stars without a home. These actions that are so hateful to our eyes are born of desperation. They strike at us and take from us because they have no options left. Can you not see, we have *made* this enemy! And we can *unmake* this enemy by restoring them to the world of their birth. Rather than spend our children's inheritance on war machines, this one would use our abundance to purchase a future where *no father* must lose his sons in war. If my friend chooses to see that as unnatural charity, *so be it*!)"

Da-Indo-Hass growls from the back of his throat, pivots away from Shondre, and slams his armored fist into the elevator wall, crumpling the thick panel.

The elevator *dings*, draws level with the desired floor, and opens into a small executive shuttle bay where a sleek white transport waits, gull wing hatch open. Da-Indo-Hass stands upright, compresses his anger, and blanks his expression. He steps out first, scans the area for threats, then invites Shondre to follow with an open hand. Her upright posture offers no hint of the heated conversation, and she strides without haste toward the richly appointed shuttle. Da-Indo-Hass climbs aboard first, inspects the interior, and nods, offering a hand to help her aboard. Shondre takes his armored hand delicately, settles into a plush seat, and is chauffeured out of the warship to the planet below.

For the entire ride, Da-Indo-Hass stares out through his window. Shondre watches him carefully, feeling his dilemma, sympathizing with his loss, and reluctantly accepting that he may have been irrevocably changed by it. She wants to reach out to him again, but his blame is a rift between them, and she knows anything she says at this point could widen it.

With a deep sigh, she turns to her own window. The sight of blue sky and thick white clouds brings a smile to her lined face. Just as suddenly, she realizes how comfortable her seat is, how its gel cushions mold and adjust to her curves as if she was sitting in the hand of a benevolent deity. The smooth fabric under her hands, the subtle fragrance of flowers emanating from the ventilators, the taps of refreshing beverages only an arm's length away, and the attendance of a bodyguard—however sullen—to cater her whims feel instantly familiar...and undeserved. For with them comes the immediate juxtaposition of Colonist and Cadre, of how little they have, of the unfathomable deprivation of basic comforts. All the hours she spent at Cadre One imagining how it would feel to be back in her sheer gowns, to sleep on piles of foam and air, to have an extended soak in a hot, steamy bath with essential oils to make her skin tingle... Such comforts arouse a self-consciousness she never felt before.

How can I enjoy so much when they have so little?

She looks down toward the ground and sees a sunlit landscape of green forests and shimmering blue lakes. A vast estate is nestled at the heart of it, with great stone colonnades extending from the central mansion out to the surrounding gardens like spokes of a great wheel. The mansion rises several stories in white marble to a flat roof with railings at the perimeter. Needle-like observation towers stand at each of the four corners, capped with conical roofs of gray slate. Flagstones pave multiple driveways to the central structure, leading in from a heavily fortified wall of pink granite with parapets between cylindrical guard towers. Though still at altitude, she expected to see the violets, ambers, and reds of summer gardens in bloom. Instead a plain green uniformity extends across the estate.

Perhaps they no longer maintain the gardens, she supposes. But as the craft descends she sees white stone markers at regular intervals, dotting every bit of unpaved land within the wall. She shrinks back from the window, realizing what she sees, and knowing without having to look that every single marker will bear a unique name.

As she slumps back into her chair, the melancholy she held at bay throughout her captivity finally takes root.

This one MUST remain, she reminds herself. *Her work is not done.*

The shuttle swings around and drops daintily onto a circular pad beside the mansion. Da-Indo-Hass triggers a radio at his collar and announces, "(Madame Shondre has returned safely. Escorts to pad nine for change of custody.)"

Shondre turns to him. "(Will my friend not remain with me?)"

He dips his head submissively. "(Her Grace shall have the finest in security at all times. Her friend has seen to it, personally. However, this one is ordered elsewhere.)"

"(To what end?)"

"(He is not at liberty to say.)"

Shondre turns away and stares glumly over the thousands of headstones where her gardens used to be. "(Please thank the landscaper for the improvements. The blooms were always too bright and cheerful for this one's taste.)"

"(Her Grace may thank him, herself, for he arrives to greet her.)" Da-Indo-Hass releases the locks on the hatch and it ascends with a hiss. Warm humid air rushes into the cabin, carrying with it arboreal smells of pollen, humus, and a hint of ozone from recent thunderstorm.

Da-Indo-Hass exits first, confirms identity of those standing at the edge of the pad, then returns to collect her. He reaches in with an armored hand. "(Madame?)"

Shondre musters what dignity she has left and exits the shuttle. At the edge of the pad are three individuals, two of whom are long time aides. They smile to see her and bow deeply.

Between the aides stands an Eleto of Shondre's height. He wears a robe of intricate design and color, one she recognizes once belonged to her. With one hand flat on his chest, he dips his head slightly. "(It does this one joy to see Madame Shondre alive and well.)"

Shondre approaches him and stands face to face, gazing at him with half-lidded eyes. "(Regent, this one presumes...)"

"(Astute as ever,)" he replies, "(though Regent in name only. For it would be unseemly to be called otherwise while her Ladyship's fate was still unknown.)" He smiles. "(You may address me as Fell-Marr-Ghenn.)"

Shondre smiles back without mirth. "(And now that she has returned? Will the Regent clutch his borrowed robes in jealousy?)"

He gestures toward the mansion, inviting her to walk with him. She falls in beside him, hands clasped in front of her.

"(Thrice has this world circled its sun since her Ladyship walked these grounds,)" Fell-Marr-Ghenn states. "(In that time, the People have become *accustomed* to the one who now serves.)"

"(The Regent would test this in fair referendum?)"

He grins. "(A foregone conclusion. The People have felt the soft touch you gave Da-oma Kachi-in. And the People no longer wish to suffer for it.)" He looks out across the thousands of gravestones.

"(So this was the Regent's idea...to turn this beautiful estate into a cemetery?)"

"(It was. This one believes her Ladyship should be able to enjoy the fruits of her labors.)"

"(Odd that the People should cleave to one with such macabre ideas.)"

"(On the contrary! This is a monument where Pilgrims may visit friends and family lost to her Ladyship's hubris. The People like what we have done here.)"

Shondre looks over her shoulder at the two aides trailing behind. They both look down, unable to meet her eye. "(Yes, clearly,)" she notes.

A wide staircase leads up from the flagstone walkway to the mansion's main entrance and, as they climb the steps, Shondre surveys the grounds. "(Such a morbid sight. Does it please you to see this everyday?)"

The Regent guffaws. "(This one does not dwell here, no, no. *Far* too depressing. This one maintains an apartment in the orbital hub. Other times he is a guest aboard the High Commander's Flagship. But fear not, this residence will suit the Lady properly.)"

"(This one looks forward to visiting the Regent *shortly*.)"

"(And this one would delight in her presence! If only she were free to do so. For her captivity has so weighed on her mind that she must be kept under close watch for signs of psychological trauma. Her Ladyship is assured of total safety here so that the lengthy, *protracted* process of healing may begin.)"

"(So, Fell-Marr-Ghenn fears this one enough to keep her imprisoned.)"

"(Not so!)" the Regent says as if unjustly accused. "(Think of it more as being committed, so the Lady can no longer do harm to herself or others.)"

Gray-uniformed soldiers stand guard beside the entrance, and they snap to attention at the Regent's approach. They bow deeply then haul the double doors open.

"(Sadly, this one must part with her Ladyship so that he may resume his duties. He hopes Madame Shondre will make herself comfortable during her stay and avail herself of the amenities. Good day.)" He tips his head curtly, turns about, and heads back for the shuttle with both aides in tow.

Shondre watches him go, feeling a stab of betrayal how the aides who so wisely counseled her now trot like sycophants behind her replacement. Determined not to capitulate, she clears her lungs and strides between the open doors, head high. Compared to the bright outdoors, the foyer is dark, and as her eyes adjust she is eager to once more look upon portraits of her ancestors lining the walls. What she finds instead are thousands of printed photographs tacked to the walls, ceiling, doors, and furniture. They cover the dark wood staircases, banisters and all; they even dangle from crystal chandeliers. Everywhere she looks is a life lost, and scattered among them are wreaths, cards, notes, and ribbons from those who miss them most.

Shondre's mouth bunches. Like a torpedoed ocean vessel, she sinks to her knees, covers her face, and muffles her sobs as best she can.

WHERE LOYALTY LIES

Da-Indo-Hass rides back to orbit in the plush shuttle with Fell-Marr-Ghenn and his two aides. The Regent and his advisors discuss concerns of regional governors, coordination of shipments, and agenda for the Council of Many Worlds. None of it holds any interest for him, so he turns his attention out through his window.

As blue sky fades to star-filled black, he reflects on the time he served Shondre before reassignment. Throughout the tribunals and inquiries following her abduction, he was exonerated on every count, yet the shame of losing his charge to enemy capture lodges like a hive of wasps in his brain. The fact that Shondre ordered him away from her side to go assist the People during attack makes no difference. He was not by her side when she needed him. And though he tripled her usual escort during evacuation it was not enough. Bloodthirsty Da-oma Kachi-in murdered his best and snatched her away to whittle her mind through diabolical craft. Somehow, they overthrew that powerful will, corrupting her into a loathsome sympathizer.

Why did she order her friend and protector away? He might have broken the demons' rampage and stacked their evil heads at the Tomb of the Disappeared. If Madame Shondre was not abducted, Gro-Elto would not have wasted so many lives searching for her.

At the very least, this one could have been killed in faithful service and not had to live with this shame.

But no...he must carry ignominy until he fills a plot beside hollow graves of beloved sons.

"(Mighty Da-Indo-Hass,)" the Regent calls.

The Guardian perks up in his seat and sees the other three passengers looking at him.

"(From his scowl, one might think the whole world had offended him,)" the Regent says to his aides. Turning to Da-Indo-Hass, he asks, "(Tell us, is our friend and protector reliving the past?)"

"(He *was*, your Grace. Though his thoughts are of no consequence.)"

"(They are, if allegiance is confused. Does Da-Indo-Hass know where loyalty lies?)"

"(He does, your Grace. Loyalty is owed to the Voice of the People and no one else.)"

Fell-Marr-Ghenn arches a suspicious brow. "(Perhaps our friend could be more *specific*.)"

"(All know that Fell-Marr-Ghenn is the People's Voice on this world. There is no other.)"

Fell-Marr-Ghenn nods, then says, "(To see Madame Shondre after she was stolen away was surely difficult. And all know that Da-Indo-Hass carries no dishonor, for he was barred from duty against his will... Does that order still haunt her champion?)"

"(Momentarily, no more. And this one is no longer Madame Shondre's champion. Fealty belongs entirely to his Grace.)"

Fell-Marr-Ghenn smiles modestly. "(It does us pleasure to hear such earnest devotion. Faith in our friend and protector is undimmed.)" The Regent reclines in his seat and crosses a leg over the other. "(Madame Shondre would have these demons sit across a table from us and speak as equals. Can you imagine?)"

"(It strains belief, your Grace.)"

The Regent nods and strokes the whiskers below his chin. "(There is law that may yet require it. We Eleto are civilized, after all, and must afford dignities to those who come in gentility.)" He scoffs. "(Such a discussion could only be *theater* for our incensed and much abused People. Do we give Da-oma Kachi-in a forum to broadcast their corruption? Indeed, we are honor bound to do so. And if we must, then Da-oma Kachi-in must not be allowed to hide their savage nature. The People must witness the bloodthirsty essence of our insolent foe. Perhaps our friend and protector knows best how to evoke this?)"

The corners of the soldier's mouth involuntarily lift. "(He does, your Grace.)"

"(Ah, then it is good the People shall not be deceived! With patience, mighty Da-Indo-Hass, we will clear this plague from the multiverse. The People will have a brighter, safer future. And a father shall have satisfaction for his wronged sons.)"

AIDOS AND NEMESIS

Shondre hunches glumly in a private indoor pool. Fragrant suds swirl with the currents caressing her below the waist. Steam rises from the hot water and loiters near the ceiling, hazing a fresco where large eyed carp with vivid orange and pearl scales swim beneath green lily pads and pink lotuses.

Nude female servants stand on each side of her. One shapes and polishes Shondre's talons with a simple tool, occasionally turning it around to scrape at the cuticles. Another dips the pool water with a handled jug and pours it gently over her drooping head and shoulders.

While her attendants work, the ex-sovereign lifts her gaze and studies a statue at the rim of the spacious bath. Two Eleto children—carved in basalt and polished shiny black—hold a large urn overhead, tipped toward the bath. Hot water flows from the urn in a fan-shaped curtain, infused with essential oils and nourishing moisturizers.

How this one yearned for these comforts in her Kad-Ra cell... Here is much to delight the senses...and yet this one can only think of her friends. Are they well? Have they been cared for? Not knowing is as cruel as this second captivity.

She looks around at her opulent natatorium with its bright metal fixtures, artful decorations, and soothing illumination.

How can one indulge in great pleasures while others live in destitution? It is a disgrace of privilege, imbalance... Brilliantly devious of Fell-Mar-Ghen to cage this one in a prison of luxury. He rubs her face in it!

A third servant steps carefully down the entry stairs to the pool with an elegant silver platter and she wades over to Shondre. A fluted goblet stands upon the tray beside a short green bottle. The servant fills the goblet from the green bottle, bows respectfully, and offers the tray. Shondre ignores it and lowers her gaze, staring into eddies and swirls of white suds.

The servant withdraws the tray, and looks at Shondre with a hopeful expression. Her eyes fall on the green scar tissue at her shoulder, and the servant says, "(A talented surgeon could remove this... Could restore natural range of motion and luster of Madame's skin.)"

Shondre pulls her hand away from the manicurist and covers her scarred shoulder. "(No. This was *earned*. It is worn in pride.)"

The manicurist looks at the others then begs, "(Will Madame Shondre not take refreshment? It does us grief to see our Lady so thin and listless. Her Grace has been with us a full cycle of the moon and still we fail to banish her sadness. Is there *nothing* we might provide that could lift her mood?)"

Shonde laughs without mirth. "(Can her attendants provide the Regent's undivided attention? For he refuses all correspondences.)"

The servant with the tray places a hand at her chin. "(If one would have the Regent's attention, perhaps the key is to have something the Regent desires?)"

Shondre looks up in interest. "(Yes... Though there is little this one could offer he does not already possess.)"

The servant with the jug hugs it close to her chest and asks, "(Does Madame Shondre know what the Regent holds dear?)"

Shondre looks at the polished black fountain. "(No, she does not.)" Her head lifts and her eyes widen. "(But this one knows what he *fears*... He fears this one could somehow take back his borrowed robe.)"

"(Is it possible?)" asks the manicurist.

Shondre's brow knits in thoughts then she frowns. "(Unlikely. His allies are powerful and this one is well-caught in his snares... Yet in his fear there is possibility of escape. Ah, yes... This one knows what she will say.)" Shondre turns and wades toward the pool stairs.

"(Madame Shondre,)" calls the manicurist, wading after her. "(If her Grace is to meet with the Regent, our Lady must bring all of her charms. Please, allow us to accent her natural beauty so that a man may learn the *true* meaning of grace.)"

Shondre halts, breath caught in her throat at tender words so freely given, and she turns to her attendants with a gracious smile. "(This one could accomplish little without such loving service.)" She pulls them into an embrace, kisses their cheeks, then stands back with arms extended and chin high. After a deep breath, she says, "(This one is your canvas.)" With a wry grin and an arched brow, she adds, "(Let us remind the males why they strive so hard in life.)"

The servants giggle to one another and set to work.

PLASMA RAIN

*****

Fell-Marr-Ghenn and Da-Indo-Hass walk side by side through a little used section of Prell-Shah-Stoh's flagship. The stark white hallway is lit by glowing ceiling tiles overhead that banish all shadows. Reinforced doors are cut into undecorated walls at short intervals with small observation windows at eye level.

Da-Indo-Hass pauses at the first door and peers through its two-way observation window. Inside is an institutional gray cell with a bunk and elongated commode. On the bunk sits an enormous human dressed in dingy coveralls that hang a size too large. One of its arms is half the size of the other. Shaggy black hair is disheveled in greasy knots, and sunken eyes blink repeatedly as if confused. It counts on its fingers compulsively, rocking back and forth, mouthing the numerals.

"(They are being deprived of sleep?)" Fell-Marr-Ghenn asks.

"(Yes, your Grace. With noise and stimulants, we have kept the large one here in a waking state for thirteen days. Early signs of psychosis are manifesting.)"

The Regent nods thoughtfully. "(And when are we obligated to release?)"

"(Legally, we may keep them in quarantine to ensure they carry no infectious diseases.)"

"(How long?)"

"(To ensure the common safety...we have broad latitude, your Grace.)"

The Regent smiles. "(*Good.*)"

Da-Indo-Hass closes the observation window and moves to the next cell. Inside, a crooked mess of actuators, ripped clothing, and synthetic skin reclines on the bunk against the far wall. Its jaw hangs by a flap, its pink tongue drapes against its throat, and it stares at the door with one functional eye. Fell-Marr-Ghenn peeks over the bodyguard's shoulder and he frowns in revulsion.

"(Hideous enough, these Human creatures. They then fashion robots after themselves?)" The Regent shrinks back from the glass. "(*Repellent.*)"

Da-Indo-Hass looks in at the inert android once more then closes the window.

"(The next rooms contain the soldiers, yes?)" Fell-Marr-Ghenn asks.

"(Yes, your Grace. One male, one female.)" Da-Indo-Hass slides the

234

window open and looks in on a muscular woman secured face down on a metal table. Her bare back is a maze of old cuts and burns. Her shaved head is embedded with gold terminals.

Two Eleto in surgical masks and dress stand behind the table. One makes small incisions around the golden terminals on the human's head. The other examines a piece of headgear that has corresponding terminals inside.

The human's shoulders bunch with each cut; her back flexes in tight knots.

"(Will those cuts not leave marks?)" the Regent asks, irritated. "(The law tolerates marks from apprehending these savages but would not tolerate any *new* signs of mistreatment while in our custody.)"

"(The fur of their head grows quickly, your Grace. There is ample time before end of quarantine to obscure these incisions. Meanwhile, our research into organic and synthetic interface will benefit greatly. Moreover, these beasts are so covered in scar tissue that no one could prove our cuts were not a result of their augmentation. So little is known about them that we can say anything we like.)"

"(Hmm, very well,)" the Regent concedes with a sniff, and they move to the last cell. When Da-Indo-Hass slides the window aside, they look in on a tall, heavily muscled human male stretched taut on a rack, his four limbs being ratcheted in opposite directions. His eyes are crushed shut and his teeth are bared in a howl of agony.

The Regent's mouth twitches as he tries to suppress a grin.

"(The soldiers are remarkably durable,)" Da-Indo-Hass explains. "(Our diagnostic scans found significant reinforcement of the skeletal structure, the joints in particular. High density in bone and musculature. And an impressive resistance to pain... They endured our early techniques so stoically we thought sensitivity to pain had been bred out of them. But we found it.)" He crosses his thick arms. "(Simply had to look harder.)"

"(*Fascinating*,)" Fell-Marr-Ghenn says, studying facial scars of the howling man. "(Could we be looking at one of the terrorists?)"

"(Quite possibly, your Grace.)"

The Regent glances at his bodyguard, eyes bright. "(Has the archival video been consulted?)"

"(In process now. Height and mass correspond to one of the three attackers. The only view we have of the face so far is marred by blood and burns. Difficult to identify with confidence.)"

"(Keep looking. What of the female? Could it be one of the three, as well?)"

Da-Indo-Hass shakes his head. "(While the female is comparable in size and mass, the terrorist lost three of its limbs, which were recovered. This female has all of its limbs and shows no signs of regeneration or reattachment. We conclude it was not one of the attackers.)"

The Regent strokes the whiskers of his chin. "(If the male soldier can be positively identified as one of the terrorists, the People will not care for a single word it utters. They will demand justice, swift and final.)"

Da-Indo-Hass nods in deference. "(Which this one would gladly provide.)" He peers in at the tortured man one last time and seals the observation window. "(Perhaps Madame Shondre might be willing to identify her abductors?)"

"(Yes, that is a wise observation. Though if we validate testimony from her, we give her credibility. It is better if she does not speak, at all.)" The Regent looks at the end of the corridor then turns about. "(I count only a synthetic and three humans. Was there not another?)"

"(There is, your Grace. Currently on public display.)"

"(The small one, yes?)"

"(Yes, your Grace. Fragile, weak, and unthreatening. The People may look upon it and cure themselves of any fear that once rooted in the arches of the chest.)"

"(Quite so.)"

A tone sounds at the Regent's collar, and he touches the clasp with a finger. "(Yes?)"

"(Please pardon the interruption, Sovereign,)" states the voice on the other end of the communicator, "(but an interesting prospect begs your attention.)"

Already impatient, the Regent answers, "(This one awaits.)"

"(Madame Shondre has an offer for our Sovereign.)"

"(She does *persist* in futile effort, does she not? You explained this to her already?)"

"(With regularity, your Grace. However, what Lady Shondre now proposes is altogether unexpected.)"

The Regent shoots a suspicious glance at his bodyguard. "(And what does her Ladyship propose?)"

"(Abdication and release of future claim.)"

"(Hers, or mine?)"

"(Hers, your Grace.)"

Fell-Marr-Ghenn's brows lift. His lips curve in delight. "(That *is* an interesting proposal! Will she do so publically, for all the People to witness?)"

"(She will, your Grace.)"

"(Then this one makes himself available at the Lady's convenience. Arrange a suitable venue and have our archivists present. This event must be faithfully recorded for posterity.)"

"(It shall be done.)"

The Regent touches the clasp at his collar, ending the conversation. To his bodyguard he adds, "(It seems we needed not much patience, at all. Come, Da-Indo-Hass, let us not keep the Lady waiting.)"

Proper Title

Fell-Marr-Ghenn and Da-Indo-Hass step out of the elevator into the executive shuttle bay. Alone in the bay, thrusters still wavering with heat, stands the regal shuttle. Its gull-wing hatch rises with a hiss, and four gray uniformed soldiers file out. They take position on either side of the hatch, pull weapons in close to their chests, and stamp to attention.

Da-Indo-Hass takes a step forward, but Fell-Marr-Ghenn touches his arm.

"(Let the queen of rags come to us.)"

The bodyguard shoots a questioning glance at his patron but steps back and stands at attention.

There is movement inside the shuttle, an Eleto in silhouette taking her time, without hurry. She steps through the hatch in open toed shoes with straps that crisscross her ankles, shaping her legs and accentuating their curves. Semi-translucent fabrics flow loosely around her knees, wrap tighter around her hips and waist, then once more expand into loose folds above her breast. Her head and neck is wrapped in a scarlet scarf, the ends of which fall across her bare shoulders. A necklace of red gems encircles her broad throat. Precious metal bracers cover her wrists. Dark glasses shade her eyes.

When she exits the shuttle she looks directly at Fell-Marr-Ghenn and smiles, lips parting just enough to flash white teeth. She strides with one foot in front of the other, emphasizing the roundness of her hips, her whip tail swinging like a metronome behind her. Long legs carry her across the deck in no time, hard soles clacking against the metal floor plates with determination.

"(Fell-Marr-Ghenn,)" she greets warmly, lifting her sunglasses and parking them on her head. Shondre's eyes are edged in dark liner. A touch of red shadow lifts at the sides, and her skin glows in unblemished, pampered azure.

Against his will, Fell-Marr-Ghenn averts his eyes. "(Memory did fail,)" he begins, hand at his chest and bowing slightly, "(for it allowed this one to forget how rare a beauty is Aeolia-Shondrekar-Bakkar.)"

Shondre smiles. "(Fell-Marr-Ghenn is ever a flatterer.)" She glances momentarily at Da-Indo-Hass. Her expression remains warm, yet there is no glimmer of recognition, as if viewing a statue in a museum. She takes the Regent's arm and says, "(Let us walk, shall we?)"

Fell-Marr-Ghenn lays his hand over hers and the two stride toward the elevator, Da-Indo-Hass immediately relegated to rear guard.

"(This one is surprised to hear his name spoken in congenial tone,)" Fell-Marr-Ghenn states, "(for, of late, her Ladyship had only addressed this one as...*Regent*.)"

"(A long and happy life does not come from opposing what cannot be changed,)" she replies.

"(Indeed, it does not. And we are surprised, pleasantly so, that the Lady has this view.)"

She gives him a coy glance, eye-level, and arches her brow. "(Did his Grace take this one to be simpleminded?)"

"(Certainly not! Though he imagined she would be more...*stalwart*...in her opposition.)"

The two stride into the open elevator and turn about. When Da-Indo-Hass follows, Shondre glances at him, then glances at the button panel, then back at him in a silent directive. The bodyguard's eyes narrow at her very obvious expectation. As much as he would like to remind her she is no longer in any position to give orders, he swallows the slight and taps the button for her.

Once the doors seal, Shondre says in candor, "(Let us be plain. This one bears no grudge at her replacement. The People need a servant, and this one could not serve while she was in bondage. Though she would have resumed her service upon return, this avenue is no longer available to her. At first, there was grief and great offense taken. Later, there was acceptance of reality: the world has moved on without her, and a new servant sits in her stead. However, this is not why she would relinquish her claim.)"

"(Oh?)" Fell-Marr-Ghen utters, deeply skeptical. "(Why does Madame Shondre?)"

Shondre reaches out to the wall of the elevator, the same spot that Da-Indo-Hass punched in. Though the panel has been replaced, the seam around it is notably wider than the rest. "(Because your Grace has the love of the People,)" she explains. "(And this one would not take that away from him.)"

Shondre lowers her hand and looks directly into his eyes. "(Fell-Marr-Ghen speaks true, the People are well pleased by their choice. To interfere is disservice—arrogance in its ugliest form.)"

The Regent nods, his vanity justified. "(Your words are thoughtful and well-chosen. This one must admit he did underestimate the Lady's sensibility, and will humbly accept her abdication. Yet he does not imagine she could ever remain satisfied with a life so diminished. Is there *nothing* she would ask in return to occupy her time?)"

"(If this one abdicates, there is no longer any need to examine her psychological state. She may be freed from the onus of service to roam as she pleases.)"

"(Ah, the Lady finds her estate too confining.)"

"(She does. And though the People have not asked for her return to service, they have asked to hear the story of her adventure. This one would oblige them.)"

Fell-Marr-Ghenn grins broadly, exposing white canines. "(Harrowing tale of survival among the bloodthirsty enemy! She would be an instant celebrity of broadwave. Such a life would be no less grand than the one she voluntarily leaves...and her touring schedule would keep her fully occupied.)" He faces her. "(What worthy sovereign would deprive his subjects their entertainment?)"

Shondre nods. "(There is more. This one must not carry blame for the attack. That is a cruel stone to hang around the neck, for the very idea she could have invited such harm is *odious* and it does abuse the People's trust.)"

The Regent mulls the demand. "(The graves at her estate cannot be disturbed, for it would be sacrilege... Though, this one holds influence among those who disseminate information. He could give instruction to...*moderate*... such opinions prior to broadcast.)"

Shondre breathes deeply and faces the elevator doors. "(Then it is time the Regent attains proper title for the office he serves so well. He *is* the Voice of the People. There must be no confusion of that fact.)"

"(Yes, we understand well.)" He pats her hand on his arm. "(Is the Lady prepared to make her mind public?)"

With a warm smile, Shondre squeezes his arm. "(She is.)"

Elevator doors open and a flood of light shines in upon them. A crowd, held at bay by a line of gray uniformed soldiers, surges to life, all of whom thrust recording devices through the gaps and shout questions. Camera flashes strobe in every direction like lightning in a summer storm.

Arm in arm, Shondre and Fell-Marr-Ghenn stroll from the elevator together, waving to the crowd with their free hands. Da-Indo-Hass steps out behind them and stands attentive watch, scarcely an afterthought. He triggers his collar communicator, coordinates with the rest of his security detail, and fades into the background.

THE WILL OF THE PEOPLE

Da-Indo-Hass leans against the wall, arms crossed, staring at a savage thing secured into a reinforced chair. The demon is stripped down to yellow-stained undersuit pants, locked into place at head, neck, chest, arm, wrist, leg, and ankle. Its crushed shut eyes are sunken in darkened sockets. Its gaunt, bearded cheeks are drawn in a teeth-bared grimace. And its bare skin is scarified beyond belief in either some compulsive ritual or in a life utterly devoted to violence. Possibly both.

Transparent bags of intravenous fluid hang overhead and feed into the devil's muscular arms via surgical tubing. Needle-like electrodes jut from its body like quills, inserted beneath fingernails and toenails, up along the extremities, through the genitals, gut, and torso to its twitching face and brow. Fine wires run from each electrode to a cart-mounted white console beside the chair where an Eleto in pale blue smock stands.

The Eleto technician operates his console like the maestro of an orchestra, strumming the demon's tensed sinews, sending brassy blasts into its skull, piercing its bones with shrill resonance. Already, the creature has endured levels of pain that should have rendered it crazed and drooling. Yet, despite the creative efforts of the technician, this monster is a sponge of agony, absorbing all and uttering naught but furious growls as the console's symphony plays in fortissimo.

Perhaps they are already insane, the bodyguard thinks with a cynical snort.

To the console operator, he remarks, "(Could they have hardened their nervous system the way they have hardened their other attributes?)"

The Eleto technician taps a key on the console, and bright red meter levels cool to amber, then yellow, then go dark. Spent, the demon slumps in its restraints and falls unconscious, its heart monitor blipping a slow, regular rhythm. "(One must conclude so. Our archives depict the Humans who lived on this planet were not nearly so resilient. The level of physical augmentation in this one is extreme, and this new breed seems more *designed* than evolved.)" The blue-smocked Eleto taps a key on the console and it whines as it recharges. "(If only they could make intelligible words we might learn where the rest of their fleet hides. Or why illness has gripped our crews who have returned from their destroyed lair.)"

"(A bio-weapon, this one is certain, to soften our defense when they arrive in force! The answers are here, inside this stinking piece of meat. Yet it resists our fervent attempts.)"

The technician glances down at his console then asks, "(Shall we discontinue threshold testing?)"

"(Pah! Would that it could last forever to sate the souls of our unavenged! But two moons have passed and we near the end of legal confinement.)" He shoves away from the wall with shoulders, and stoops toward the slumped creature in the chair. "(Lady Shondre *must* have found a common tongue or Da-oma Kachi-in would not have come at all.)" Gripping the chair's high back on either side of the demon's restrained head, Da-Indo-Hass shouts with rage tinted orange eyes, "(This one *knows* you were here before, thou disciple of terror! This one *knows* it was you who drowned the city below and sent a multitude to wretched death! And this one *KNOWS* you understand his words! If mortifying flesh will not reveal where your stolen fleet hides, then Da-Indo-Hass *will CRACK YOUR EVIL HEAD and dig his answer FROM YOUR BRAINS*!)"

The demon's eyelids part and it blinks groggily, lips parted. Da-Indo-Hass seizes its shaggy, scarred face. "(That's right, *awake*! There is no respite. Not until a man's brave sons return from death and issue thee a pardon. Until *that* day, DEMON, a bereaved father will visit his grief upon *your every waking moment*.)"

Da-Indo-Hass flicks his head at the technician. Taking the cue, the technician taps the console until gauges illuminate in deep amber.

The restrained savage tenses in the chair, eyes clamped shut.

Da-Indo-Hass turns in annoyance on the interrogator. "(We need no feather touch! Increase to maximum.)"

"(But if its mind is scorched...?)"

The bodyguard returns to the opposite wall, leans against it and crosses his arms. "(Who could tell the difference?)"

The technician looks down at the console, glances at the restrained soldier, then taps his console until all gauges blaze bright red. The trapped human stiffens against the back of the chair screaming through his nostrils, saliva foaming and spraying from his mouth.

The door of the cell clangs harshly, as of someone shoved against it. Then it slides aside. Shondre rushes in with two uniformed soldiers in attendance, a multi-colored sash across her torso. Her eyes gape at sight of Thompson rigged from toes to scalp in the throes of agony.

"(RELEASE HIM *AT ONCE*, VETERAN,)" she demands.

Da-Indo-Hass keeps his place, sucks his teeth. The technician looks at him anxiously.

"(The Lady holds no authority here,)" Da-Indo-Hass replies. "(Da-oma Kachi-in are terrorists, entitled to no hearing or trial, and may be used as his Grace sees fit.)" With a derisive smirk, he adds, "(If the Lady objects, she may petition the Voice of the People for redress of grievance.)"

Shondre stands directly in front of her old bodyguard. "(If my old friend cannot hear the voice of compassion, then perhaps his ears may perceive the WILL of the People.)" She thrusts a clear slate into his face that illuminates with Eleto script. The veteran ignores the text but when he sees the seal at the bottom his eyes widen.

"(His Highness...is *here*?)"

"(He is. And his Majesty has declared these Humans personal guests and ambassadors of a foreign nation. This one is their appointed advocate.)" She whirls on the technician. "(Release him *this instant*, or find yourself *STAKED IN THE DESERT TO PARCH*!)"

The blue-smocked Eleto slaps at his console until the gauges go dark. Thompson slumps completely in his restraints, his heart monitor blipping irregularly. Shondre bites her lower lip and blows a quick whistle between the gap in her front teeth. Two white-coated Eleto hustle in and immediately begin freeing Thompson from his chair and electrodes.

"(Now then,)" Shondre says, taking a breath to regain her more dignified demeanor, "(Da-Indo-Hass may report to his master for re-assignment of duties...duties which will no doubt keep him out of this one's sight for quite some time.)" She shakes her head. "(A pity he cannot also take this one's *disappointment* with him...)"

Stinging from rebuke, Da-Indo-Hass glares at the two uniformed soldiers flanking Shondre. Though the veteran towers over them both, power of Shondre's vested authority keeps them planted at her side, spines straight, tails aloft. Their hands slide to their baton grips in warning.

"(Celebrity tour, *indeed*,)" Da-Indo-Hass snarls. The veteran takes a step toward the door then halts beside Shondre and growls into her ear. "(*One without children cannot understand what it is to lose them*.)"

Shondre blinks hard. "(If in spending her life she could buy them back, she would. But this one would rather purchase the lives of *all* children. And she will commit everything to that end. She only wishes that offered a grieving father some measure of solace.)"

Da-Indo-Hass shoves past the soldiers to the corridor, the technician following closely on his heels. Shondre watches them leave, her lip curled, then looks at Thompson's inert form, covering her mouth with both hands as her attendants labor to resuscitate the tortured man.

NOT EASY, THIS

Thompson wakes, unsure if he is floating or weightless. Clothed only in a pair of undershorts, he rolls in place. Beneath him, supple foam conforms to his shape and buoys him even as it feels insubstantial against his skin. A burgundy sheet covers his bare legs, woven from a remarkably dense and insulating material. It slips like liquid between his thumb and fingers, making him wonder if the Eleto have discovered some method for weaving strands of water.

The ceiling above is painted with a photo-realistic image of daybreak on a verdant field. Tall grasses and wild flowers seem to sway in his groggy vision. A nectar-sweet scent draws his attention to a nightstand, where he finds a heap of colorful wedges and a tall glass of water. It might be paradise, if not for the gnawing ache at the back of his skull and debilitating waves of nausea.

Propping himself up on elbows, he looks past the edges of his four posted bed and sees a room six meters square with three-meter ceilings. Soft light emanates from lamps hidden behind crown moldings near the ceiling. A pair of tall panels are embedded in the right wall, simulating windows to a hilly green landscape and casting long yellow rays across the plush floor. Between the simulated windows and spaced around the other walls hang portraits of richly ornamented Eleto. Though there are a wide variety of faces and body types portrayed, every subject wears the same brightly patterned robe.

Maiella rises from a wing-backed chair in a darkened corner, dressed in snug black tank top, baggy olive cargo pants, and black boots. She scratches beneath white bandages wrapping her scalp then sits at the edge of Thompson's bed and sinks deep into the billowy foam. Dragging a knee up, she faces the Gun and says with a smirk, "Welcome back to the land of the living."

"Was I dead again?"

"Almost. But would it matter?" She gazes at him in adoration. "You don't stay dead for long."

He lays a hand on her leg. "I got someone worth sticking around for." Thompson sits up and scrutinizes her head wrap. "What about you? You okay?"

"Oh, this?" She points to her head and rolls her eyes. "Just some live *dissection*. New scars for the collection, that's all."

His brow lowers and with commanding tone demands, "Did they *damage* you?"

"No. Didn't cut deep enough to do any real harm. I *feel* intact, anyway." She turns toward the room's entrance and calls out, "Shondre, are you there?"

Shondre steps in from an adjacent room, dressed in layered fabrics that flow with her quick steps. Her head and broad neck are swathed in a crimson scarf, ends braided together and draped over one shoulder. A broad sash of many colors crosses her chest.

Despite her distinguished carriage, Shondre's hands are clasped anxiously and the corners of her mouth turn down at the edges.

"Nott hwant thisss, hyoo," she apologizes. "Thisss hwon feer sshe moov too sslow and frend iss losst." Shondre lays a hand over her chest and adds with a smile, "Glad iss, that Tom-Sun uh-waykss."

"Where is everyone?" Thompson scoots to the edge of the bed beside Maiella. His head swims in sudden vertigo, and he slumps back into the cloud-like foam with a groan.

"Musst resst," Shondre counsels. "Let ty-mm hee-yul."

"*Time?*" Maiella questions with a suspicious glance. "What time is *left*? Lost all track of it in your friend's torture chamber."

"*NOTT* frend," Shondre corrects with a raised finger. Then she purses her lips, struggling with the Human words, and says, "Twai-sss moon sir-kull, pluss haff sir-kull."

Thompson lifts his head and calculates the conversion into a familiar measurement. Squinting in agitation, he clarifies, "*Ten weeks?*" Maiella and he look at one another, eyes wide. The Gun powers through his vertigo, and pushes himself off the bed to his feet. With a deep breath he stands and sways. Maiella rises beside him and steadies him.

"Ralla's only four weeks away," the Geek says with a scowl. "We have to get everyone together *now*."

"Jenn-tull, *pleez*, nott too rush-shing gho." With a combination of gestures and words, Shondre adds, "Kon-Zil-Urr fay-ss bro-kenn. Munn-Roh fikss. Much hwerrk musst do, sso Kon-Zil-Urr kann sspeek."

"And Sharon?" Maiella asks.

Shondre closes her eyes and bows her head. Rather than answer, she steps toward one of the two window-like wall panels and taps its corner. The idyllic scene changes to the head and shoulders of an elegant Eleto announcer who speaks gravely.

Thompson understands few of the announcer's words, so he focuses instead on a window of video playing beside her. In it is footage of a glass case on a wheeled trailer being lugged through the center of a large city square. Inside the case is a lifeless woman, eyes shuttered forever, hands crossed over her chest. A split in her scalp, pulled taut by dehydration, exposes fractured white skull beneath.

An Eleto crowd surrounds the trailer, jockeying for a glimpse, saffron eyes wide, mouths shouting curses. They hurl whatever they can grab: mud, drinks, food, sticks, bricks, and paving stones. Projectiles bounce off the ballistic glass harmlessly, leaving ugly smudges.

"*What*?" Thompson's eyes roam the scene in disbelief. "*No. NO!*"

Maiella's expression blanks. She walks calmly to the broadcast panel and stands before it, staring.

"Sha-ronn hedd hurrt," Shondre explains, hands still clasped together, penitent. "Try, but nott ay-bull to sayff hurr. It duzz this hwon *grayt* ssad-ness and sshaym."

In a blink, Maiella seizes an upholstered chair by the arms, heaves it over her head, and bashes it into the screen again and again and again until nothing is left but sparking silicate shards and the chair's wooden arms in her grip. Trembling with rage, she hurls the wooden chair arms across the room, turns, and swears, "*NEVER AGAIN*, SHONDRE. I won't lose anyone else! We came for peace, but now... It's *BLOOD* FOR *BLOOD*!"

Shondre presses her lips together and closes her eyes. Wrestling with the Human words, she says, "Greef, *hyess*...but nott too ayn-gurr gho! Sha-ron dy...and oh-pen Grayt Eh-Lee-Toh my-nd. Grayt Eh-Lee-Toh *ssee*...Hyoo-mann not ahll Hunn-gree Go-sst. Eh-Lee-Toh ree-leess ayn-gurr... now *heer* uss, kann..." She winces, knowing what she wants to say, yet is so hemmed in by vocabulary she stamps the floor. "Hwen fikss, Kon-Zil-Urr help sspeek uss. Na-ow, pay-shenss musst haff."

"*Patience*," Thompson echoes coldly. "You want *patience*?" He walks more steadily over to Maiella and puts an arm around her, pulling the Geek into an embrace. "Maybe this was a mistake."

Shondre storms over to the two and peels them apart. Eyes glassy, mouth curled into a bitter frown, she shouts at him, "How *DAY-URR* hyoo too ssay? Thiss hwon *AHL-SO* looss frends...hurr *oth-urr sself*!" Jabbing a polished talon into the Gun's chest, she adds, "Bludd sspill by *HYOO*, Tom-Sun. *Ree-mem-burr*? This hwon for-giff him, bee-koss kill-ling *musst* ennd!"

Thompson watches Shondre warily, surprised at her sudden fire. But truth in her simple words tears down his wall. He reaches out in a gesture of contrition, saying, "I'm sorry, Shondre, you're right."

Shondre grips his hand then lays her other hand atop it. Taking a moment to regain her composure, she offers, "Nott ee-zee, *this*."

Maiella looks at Thompson's outstretched arm and she zeroes in on puncture bruises, electrical burns, and purple stripes on the pale crook of his elbow. The marks extend up to his shoulder, continue across his torso, and run down his legs. "Looks like you had it rougher than I did," she notes. "Why'd they go after you so hard?"

"No idea," he says, turning his arms over and inspecting the marks for the first time.

"Ree-jent bee-leef Tom-Sun drow-nn sit-tee bee-low," Shondre explains. "Kan-not proof, but hwill try."

"I *was* the one who flooded the city," Thompson admits, his brow heavy with memory. "Shouldn't we tell them that? To be in full disclosure?"

"NO," Shondre counters. Her lips try to shape words taught by the Counselor, but the concept is too complex and she sighs in frustration. "Hwill ek-splaynn hwith Kon-Zil-Urr." The Eleto strides to a closet and opens it, revealing a set of clothes made for a tall, broad shouldered human. "Na-ow, hyoo dress. Then, fall-low. This hwon hway-t neer-by." Shondre points into the adjoining room, bows humbly to them both, and departs with head and tail raised, loose outer layers billowing behind her.

Thompson steps to the closet and eyes the clothing skeptically. At a glance the trousers and shirt appear to be proper size, yet he frowns. "Rather have my kit."

"You and me, both," Maiella chimes.

Still stiff from the thousands of shocks conducted through sinew and bone, he takes the clothes from the hangers and dresses. The fabric is light, breathable, instantly warm against his skin. His black shirt fits closely, smoothing over his rough of hide scars. Trousers are fitting at the waist, loose fitting elsewhere. Unwilling to be confined by poorly cut fabrics, he leans to one side and extends a raised leg upward into a standing split. There is no straining of seams. Satisfied with the range of motion afforded, and pleased at Shondre's forethought, he stands normally.

Maiella hands him a set of soft boots. Thompson takes them, dubious. "Where are the laces?"

"Self adjusting," the Geek replies, showing off her own footwear. "I kinda like 'em."

Thompson pops his eyebrows and slips his feet into the boots. Unsure, he flexes his toes. As described, the boots shrink to fit. "Huh. Like wearing a pair of socks."

Maiella takes his hand, and despite her best efforts to be cheerful, there is profound grief etched into the lines around her eyes and brow. "I need to see Munro and Counselor right now," she tells him. "Make sure they're okay."

Thompson pulls her into an embrace and presses her head against his chest. What gray middle ground once existed is eradicated in the aftermath of Sharon's death, and the Gun vows with a growl, "I will *never* let them harm us again."

Maiella nods then pulls away. Looking directly into his eyes, she says with equal commitment, "*Damn straight.*" Then, turning toward the door, she tugs on his hand. "C'mon. Let's get going."

TOGETHER, WE SUCCEED

Shondre leads the two Operators with chin raised, hands at her sides. Hard soles of her shoes tap a metronome rhythm with each step, announcing her presence wherever she goes. By contrast, Thompson and Maiella roll their feet in a glide step march, and Shondre glances over her shoulder periodically to make sure they are still behind her.

The hallways are broad and bright with high, arched ceilings. Walls are hung with masterful portraits, some of which are so realistic, Maiella pauses and hovers a hand to see if she can feel breath. Only when Shondre's clacking heels fade away does the Geek shake herself from trance and hustle to catch up.

The three arrive at a door guarded by two well-built Eleto sentries. Instead of uniforms, the sentries wear crisp multi-layered suits. A communicator collar encircles their broad throats, and their grim orange eyes seem to assess every detail in a single glance.

Thompson spies uneven bulges beneath their suit coats. "Thought we were done with prison guards, Shondre," he burrs.

"For *hyorr* pro-tek-shun," she answers, unruffled. "Man-nee hwill try hurrt hyoo." With her simple nod to them, the guards bow, step aside, and open the door. Shondre steps between them into a brightly lit apartment as richly appointed as the one Thompson and Maiella just left. There are fewer portraits of Eleto dignitaries in favor of diverse landscapes with angular crags, broad valleys, and meandering rivers. Ruddy brown thatch and green-barked trees rise from the soil, unlike anything in Colonist archives. Thompson wonders, *A glimpse of Eleto homeworld?*

In stark contrast to the fine decoration is a large utilitarian workbench against the far wall. Its backboard is hung with a bewildering array of intricate implements, and the countertop is strewn with metallic and plastic components. Buckets and bins overflow with wires, fasteners, applicators for sealants, bonding agents, and lubricants. A compact microscope stands on the right side of the bench with an open tray beneath. On the tray is a crushed white orb with a fiber optic tail.

Munro hunches on a rugged stool in front of the bench, peering through a set of magnifying goggles at a battered android seated opposite him. The big man leans toward his subject's knee with a spreader in one hand and a whirring device in the other. When the device makes contact, the whirring becomes harsh grinding and sparks leap from the joint.

The android turns a patchwork face toward the new arrivals, and greets them with a lopsided smile and one eye. The other half of its face hangs slack as though from a stroke, and the eye socket is hollow behind a shattered orbit. Broken actuator linkages protrude from open rips in the synthetic skin.

"Lady Shondre, Thompson, Maiella," the Counselor hails.

Munro startles like a rabbit, nearly spinning off of his stool and sending his magnifying goggles tumbling across the plush floor. He clutches the spreader and grinder in a white-knuckle grip, blinking until the fight or flight response fades from his eyes.

"My apologies, Colonel," the Counselor says. "I should have warned you. Didn't mean to alarm you."

Munro's cheek twitches. With an irritated grunt, he collects his goggles and resumes work on his android patient.

Maiella slips past Shondre and crouches beside the Counselor, laying a hand on his rebuilt shoulder. "Looking good, bub."

The android's head dips. "Are you kidding? I'm a mess! Thankfully, I have a skilled hand putting this egg back together."

"Remain *still*," Munro orders.

"For you, Munro, it will be as if I had gazed into the Gorgon's eyes." The Counselor goes rigid.

Munro glares through his eyebrows.

"You were too pretty, anyway," Maiella says to the Counselor with a good-natured smile.

The Counselor throws his head back and laughs.

"Remain STILL," Munro barks.

"Yes, yes, my apologies." The Counselor straightens his spine and goes rigid again. "Never been accused of being pretty before." The android sneaks a glance at her with his good eye. "Relieved to see they haven't squashed your spirits, Maiella." He peeks past her at Thompson. "How about you?"

Thompson crosses his arms. "I'm fine."

The Counselor eyes the marks covering the Gun's forearms. He blanks his expression and faces front as Munro resumes work on his knee. "There were times...I could *hear* you. Through reinforced plate walls."

"I didn't *enjoy* it, if that's what you're getting at it," the Gun says in annoyance. "But I'm fine."

"Obstinate as ever," the android remarks. "Consistency is a good sign, I suppose. Our friend the Colonel endured something worse, I suspect. So bad, he refuses to speak of it."

Munro levels a hostile glare at his mechanical patient. "I have endured without injury. And I will *not* have you suggest I am *anything* but fit for duty."

The Counselor shoots a suffering glance at Thompson and Maiella. Then, to Munro, he says, "We've all been through Hell, Colonel. You three, in the guise of 'quarantine' and 'endurance testing.' For me, the pain was being trapped in a broken body, not being able to help. And Shondre, well... She was in a prison of her own...one that required all her cunning to escape."

"*You* were in prison?" Maiella asks Shondre, amazed. Shondre blinks and nods.

"Why, because you came with us?" the Geek follows.

The Eleto tilts her head and frets, then replies in her native tongue.

"Shondre was accused of being too lenient with the Human threat," the Counselor translates. "Because she pushed for reconciliation, it was argued she was lax in her protective duty...that she allowed the attack to happen, perhaps even *encouraged* it with a weak position. As a result, she was stripped of position and powers. Kept under arrest in her home."

"Shondre had nothing to do with it," Thompson protests. "O'Kai gave the order and we went. Simple as that."

The Counselor nods, and translates for Shondre. She shows her hands in a shrug and says, "Nott mat-turr."

"Why are we tip-toeing around the *real* issue, here?" Maiella rises to her feet. "Sharon's *dead*."

Shondre touches Maiella's shoulder gently, and she speaks earnestly in her own tongue. The Counselor translates, "Sharon's death proves brutality still lives in the Eleto soul, proves that petty hate lurks in the back of the mind and holds sway over nobler aims. There will be no pardon for her treatment, and those responsible will face a reckoning...of that, *be sure*."

Shondre turns away, glancing momentarily at the beautiful images decorating the room, then elaborates in her tongue.

The Counselor translates, "There is no excuse. None. This one can only ask that her friends accept an *explanation*: Humans have been a terror for many generations. And this terror has moved the People into unwholesome actions." Shondre faces her friends again and finds that she has all of their attention, even grouchy Munro.

"When we look at number of ships lost over time," the Counselor translates, "it is but a miniscule fraction of total transport...yet the complete disappearances of vessels and crew, as well as our inability to stop them, disrupted our way of life. None now live who remember a time before the disappearances. Neither does any Eleto live who *remembers* the genocide of mankind. It is far enough in our past to be considered history. Because of this, the People forget that we created this terror prowling our space lanes. They forget that it was *our* barbarous hunt that honed mankind into Cadre Operators. The People would absolve themselves of guilt and urge our leaders to *finish* the extermination so there can be peace once more..."

Thompson and Maiella lock eyes then look at Munro. The big MedTech mirrors their concern.

The Counselor continues on Shondre's behalf, "The People imagine themselves noble, high-minded, ethically pure. Yet an ambassador of peace was greeted with lethal savagery. Now, the People confront ugly truth: unprovoked killing of one who came in peace, one who was committed to healing and understanding...such an act PROVES we are not the enlightened beings we believe ourselves to be. Fear and hate still root in the arches of the chest, so much so that we revisit the *same murderous sin* unleashed upon your kind long ago. This forces the People to confront how false is their presumption of superiority."

"Her body was dragged around in *disgrace*," Munro growls, rising to his feet. "An OBJECT to be despised? SHE DESERVES BETTER!" The big man hurls his grinder at the bench and strides away to stand in a far corner.

"I agree," Thompson states. He and Maiella follow Munro.

Shondre's brow wrinkles and she looks at her feet, crushed between two cultures, carrying the burden of both. She calls after them with strained voice, pleading, and the Counselor faithfully translates, "Do not think this one forgets her friends so easily! She works to recover Sharon's remains so her friend may rest with the respect she deserves... But if you would throw away all because she has died, you prove yourselves as *shortsighted* as those you call your enemy. And this one, your *ONLY* friend among the People... *She cannot DO THIS by herself!*"

"(This one will never abandon you, Shondre,)" the Counselor says in her language. "(Do not worry about them, for their grief is still too near. Let this one work with them and reinforce what they already know in heart and mind is correct, even when sadness obscures wiser choices.)"

Shondre sighs unhappily but nods and reaches a hand to the Counselor. The android takes her hand in his and grips it firmly.

"(There is much to arrange, much to organize,)" the Counselor states. "(Tell this one what needs to be done. What can your friend do to assist?)"

Shondre crushes her eyes shut, driving out a tear of frustration. Then, with a deep breath, she crouches beside the Counselor and tells him.

Thompson and Maiella approach Munro, unsure how to talk him down. Finally, the Gun says, "First time off inhibitors is harsh. Everything you've stuffed down, it all comes up at once..."

"I require no *sympathy*," Munro hisses through a mask of stability. "I am dismayed I cannot master this mood. It is inappropriate to be seen until I have."

"*Munro*," Maiella says sternly. "*Say* it."

The MedTech flashes an angry glare at her. "Say *what*?"

"What you're thinking right now. *SAY* IT."

Munro's face shudders under the enormity of restraint. He turns away from the corner. His jaw flexes, and his mouth twists into a bitter frown.

"Let it out," Maiella urges. She points dead center of the MedTech's chest. "What you feel right there. *Say it*."

Munro takes a stuttering breath. His face wracks. "Sharon's absence...*is intolerable*." His eyes glaze. In panic, he blanks his expression, whirls about, and stuffs his face in the corner. Through clenched teeth, he gnarls, "LEAVE ME!"

Thompson reaches for his shoulder, but Maiella stops him, shaking her head. To the colonel, she says, "We'll give you space. Just know that we're struggling with it, too. In fact, there's some furniture in another room that'll never be the same. We need your strength to get through this. And when the time is right, we'll honor Sharon the way she deserves."

Munro nods rapidly then leans further into the corner. With as even a voice as he can muster, he replies, "That would be acceptable."

Maiella takes Thompson's arm and turns him back toward Shondre and the Counselor. Despite the damage to his face, the android's calm personality is evident, and he nods with Shondre's suggestions. But Shondre's saffron eyes look tired in a way she has never seen before, even after her captivity at Cadre One.

At the Operators' approach, Shondre and the Counselor break off their conversation and turn their attention toward Geek and Gun.

"We should discuss our next steps," the Counselor volunteers.

"Yeah," Thompson agrees. From the confused look on his face he has no idea where to start. "Suggestions?"

"Shondre was just filling me in on what's been going on while we were guests of the Regent. Seems the situation is, ah...*delicate*."

"That's interesting, and all, but there's some *urgency*—"

"*Correct*," the Counselor states, his tone preempting any further elaboration on the Gun's part, "and we must be careful not to appear anxious, because haste suggests desperation. Just a *whiff* of that and Shondre's opponents may choose to stall, thinking they can wait us out and force our capitulation."

"But if they wait, Ralla comes in blasting..." Maiella interjects. "So how do we get them to the table?"

Shondre speaks in her own words, and the Counselor translates, "They will accelerate the pace of their own volition."

"Excellent," Thompson says sarcastically, throwing his arms open. "We rely on *them*—the ones who would have kept us caged forever—to speed up the timeline?"

Shondre clucks her tongue and shakes her head. Through the Counselor, she replies with the last shreds of her patience, "This one gave long and faithful service, and that service was valued by many. Though she is no longer the Voice of her People, many are willing to return her favor. And the favor she asked is getting her pleas to his Excellency, the *Will* of the People."

Maiella face scrunches. "Wait, *who*?"

The Counselor nods, accepting the question on Shondre's behalf. "*Voice* of the People is a regional position. Inhabitants of Earth below and in orbit were Shondre's subjects, but only the Eleto here at this world. And the Eleto have many worlds, each with its own 'Voice.' Periodically, it was her duty to attend meetings of Eleto world leaders, in which she would represent her subjects. Hence, why the position is called *Voice of the People* because she is, essentially, speaking for them.

"Above the Voice of the People is a supreme authority, appointed for life from the many Voices of Eleto worlds. This individual listens to the many Voices, finds balance, and decides what will be. His decisions are undisputed law, and thus, he embodies the *will* of the people."

Shondre adds to his description with a raised finger.

"Ah, yes, thank you, Shondre," the Counselor says. "She reminded me that his Excellency recognizes Colonel Munro is here as the *Voice* of the Cadre. And Sharon...*was*...the *Voice* of the *Europa*. It sits poorly with his Excellency that the Voice of a People was not only killed, but was also used so disrespectfully. Had the roles been reversed...such an offense would *not* have been tolerated. And the fact that Humans have returned lady Shondre alive offers a displeasing contrast. His Excellency is aware of the imbalance, wishes to correct it, and has decreed we are to be received as ambassadors under his protection throughout the duration of our stay.

"Further, his Excellency refuses the assertion Humans are mindless beasts, incapable of reason or trust. To deny another the right to speak reveals a fundamental weakness in one's position and betrays moral cowardice, he said. The Eleto are not so feebleminded that words can ever cause them harm, and, thus, he has ordered that Humans *shall* have an audience. Until such time, we are to be treated as ambassadors of state under his Excellency's protection. Afterward, if no accord is reached, we are to be released without delay."

"So, you're saying...if Sharon *hadn't* died," Maiella probes, "we might still be in our cells, waiting? Is that what Shondre meant when she said Sharon had, '...bought life for us all.'"

The Counselor defers the question to Shondre, and the Eleto nods with closed eyes.

Munro returns from the corner, more balanced, his mouth a taut line of embarrassment. "I apologize for my outburst."

Shondre waves her hands and shakes her head with verbal counterpoint, the Counselor interpreting, "On the contrary, this is precisely what will move the People to peace. They must *see* the sacrifices Humans make to survive. They must *comprehend* how uncertain Human lives are. They must *witness* that you are beings of soul and sentiment—thinking, feeling creatures who, if allowed, would gladly co-exist in peace. This passion in you must not be kept secret. It *must* be shared."

Munro frets, uncomfortable with the notion. His cheek twitches again in an involuntary tic but he says, "If it helps."

Shondre smiles at the MedTech. Laying a warm hand on his arm, she says, "Thank hyoo, Kerr-Null. Grayt iss hyoor speer-itt." Leaning toward the Counselor she asks a question in Eleto while pointing at Munro.

"Colonel," the Counselor asks for Shondre, "how long until you finish repairs on me?"

Munro grips his chin in thought. "For a full restoration? Synth-plasty alone would be a week, *minimum*."

"How about just to get me walking and talking normally?"

The MedTech bunches his mouth on one side of his face. "If I had *my* toolkit and a couple of assistants? I could get you ambulatory in a couple days."

"You've got your assistants, Colonel," Thompson offers, pointing at himself and Maiella. "Tell us what else you need."

Munro nods but adds, "The real problem is his eye. Main sensor's crushed, and I don't have time to rewrite his program for monocular vision. Without stereovision, he'll have no depth perception. He'd have to reach out like a blind man to keep himself from running into things. Even *that* might not be enough."

The Counselor relates Munro's needs to Shondre. Through the android, she replies, "State your specifications, and this one procures what is needed."

"Can you get our kit, as well?" Thompson asks.

"And my HDI?" Maiella chimes.

Shondre makes an exaggerated nod, and states through the Counselor, "It will be done. Provide a list. But know this: anything dangerous will *not* be returned. There can be *no* threat tolerated during the proceedings."

"Understood," the Gun says, and he takes a deep breath. "All right. Once Counselor's on his feet, how long 'til we can get him in front of an assembly?"

"We can name the time and date," the Counselor answers for Shondre. "Though his Excellency will arrive in approximately seventy-eight hours. If we can wait for him, I think we should."

Maiella perks up. "He's coming here?"

Shondre nods, and answers through the Counselor, "That's correct. Given the historic nature of this meeting, he wishes to attend personally."

Maiella turns a worried look toward Thompson, a look that he mirrors. To Munro the Gun says, "Thinking like an Operator, here...that's a *tempting* leadership target. If Ralla finds out, how do we know she won't strike early?"

Munro holds up a hand without concern. "We agreed that she would not."

Maiella rolls her eyes. "Yes, Colonel, but how can we be *sure*?"

"Ralla has given her word. *She will honor it.*"

Thompson chews his lip in thought. "Hunh, okay. Counselor, you know what you're going to say?"

"Just give me a face that works and some legs to stand on," the android says with lopsided smile. "The rest I can handle."

"This hwon go pree-pay-urr," Shondre says. She bows, turns, and takes a step toward the door then halts. Turning around, she extends her arms and draws Thompson, Maiella, and Munro into an embrace. Eyes lifting at the edges, she kisses each of them on the cheek.

"Too-geh-thur, hwee suk-seed."

Shondre pulls away reluctantly and strides gracefully toward the door. Once past the threshold, doors seal and guards resume their place. In her solo path through bright empty corridors, her mind dwells on the threat of Ralla and her fleet drifting closer.

This one must choose to trust her friends, she tells herself. Tail and chin high, she clacks down the corridor with the first glimmer of optimism since her return.

SPECTACLE

After days of tedious meetings, Shondre strides through immaculate corridors toward Munro's ambassadorial apartment. Her hands are clasped together in front, elbows bent, chin raised in regal poise; and she smiles to think how, despite the fact the Human diplomats have each been allocated their own comfortable accommodations, they have chosen to cohabit the same room.

Pragmatic and efficient, as always.

Her smile spreads into a wide grin as she recalls the few exceptions when Maiella and Thompson would disappear to another apartment. Always, they offered some blatantly transparent excuse to be alone, and she giggles to think about the sorry state of furniture they leave behind.

Ah, to be young and in love again...

Arriving at the door, she nods courteously to the suited guards. "(Advocate Shondre has come to collect her guests,)" she states. "(Would you announce her arrival?)"

The guards slide heels together and make the slightest nod in unison. One touches a panel by the door, sounding a chime inside the ambassadorial suite. Moments later, the door opens with the Counselor standing on the far side. He smiles warmly.

"Shondre, welcome!" The android steps backward, inviting her in with a wave of his hand. "Please, please, come in!"

Shondre looks the Counselor up and down, noticing the fit of his dark brown robes and the normalcy of his movements. His shoulders are level and square again and the multi-colored sash of an Advocate hangs well across his chest. There is no awkwardness at all in his posture, proving Munro has been far too modest in assessing his talent for repair. But where there was no time to cast fresh facial molds, the android's synthetic skin has been glued and patched instead, giving the Counselor a striking resemblance to a scarred Cadre Operator. Adding to her unease, his replaced eye has no iris, merely a black spot surrounded by off-white the color of sun-bleached fabric.

He will not pass as Human, not now... Will the People accept him? Or will they reject him? This one cannot tell.

Shondre smoothes down the front of her gown and follows the Counselor inside. Munro's workbench is a scene of order and cleanliness, all surfaces clear, every tool hanging in its proper place. The spacious bed is made in Cadre fashion with the coverings pulled taut across the top and tucked beneath. Munro stands before an armoire on the adjacent wall, fastening the snaps of his Cadre Gray coveralls. When she looks for Thompson and Maiella, Shondre does not see them at first. Then two pale faces, loitering in mid air, appear in a dark corner. Clad in their light absorbing armor, faceplates raised, Maiella and Thompson are like fountains of shadow, where only their faces reflect ambient light. Shondre winces, hurtling back to the last time she confronted that ghastly visage:

> *A landing bay in disarray, chaotic...civilians running for exits, dropping belongings in panicked flight...*
>
> *The ramp of her limousine just ahead, servants already ascending with luggage...*
>
> *"MY LADY!"*
>
> *Burly arms around her, pulling her in tight...a crush of bodyguards on all sides...*
>
> *Flash and a BOOM... Swept from her feet, knocked flat...*
>
> *Dazed, reeling... Unnatural silence... Overturned baggage carts... Thick smoke and the thicker smell of blood... Blinking at the ceiling in confusion, pinned beneath a mound of horribly torn bodies...*
>
> *Soldiers crouching beside her, shooting into the haze... Lurching backward, skulls erupting from lethal return fire...*
>
> *Darkness in the smoke, like a hole in existence... Malevolence given form, animated by rage... Hideous armored nightmare with steel gray eyes...*

"You okay, Shondre?" Thompson asks.

Shondre snaps out of her trance. "Hmm? Ah, hyess." Finding it difficult to look at the two Operators, she smiles politely and makes her way over to Munro.

PLASMA RAIN

The MedTech slides his arms through the sleeves of a long, ornate robe and views himself in a tall mirror beside the armoire. Multi-layered fabric hangs well on his broad shoulders, but Shondre gasps when he picks up his tool belt to fasten around it. Long handled wrenches, a thick labset, various boxes, and injectors jut at unfashionable angles, ruining the robe's elegant lines. She shuts her open mouth, considers suggesting he leave his tool belt behind, then decides, *We do not choose what is correct for them. He may present himself as he wishes.*

The ex-sovereign steps over beside the big MedTech and admires his reflection. "Look sstraw-ng, hann-sum," she offers.

Munro scowls at the brightly contrasting colors and intricate embroidery, running his hands down the lapels. "I feel *foolish* in this. Is it necessary?"

Sensing he is needed, the Counselor approaches, clasps hands behind his back, and arches his eyebrows. Shondre touches the android's arm and speaks in her tongue.

Facing Munro, the Counselor says for her, "Colonel Munro may wear whatever makes him most comfortable. However, in our society, the Robe of the Berelliguul identifies a *Voice* of a People. All Eleto will honor and respect the one who wears it."

"And if I don't wear it?" Munro asks.

Shondre considers the question and tilts her head. She swishes her mouth to one side, then replies in her tongue.

The Counselor restates for her, "The People will still know you are important to *your* culture, though they will not necessarily recognize you are important to *our* culture."

"Sounds like they'll listen better if you wear it, Colonel," Thompson suggests from the opposite side of the room.

Munro clears his lungs and takes a fresh look in the mirror. Jutting his chest, he concedes, "Whatever is best." He fusses with his belt, making the long-handled wrenches clatter. In the process his robe bunches beneath the webbed belt strap, making one side hang higher than the other. "There. I am ready."

"Uhrmm," Shondre says stepping in front of him, a finger held to her lip.

Munro squints, unsure what the problem is, then looks to the Counselor.

"She'd like to make you appear more...presentable," the android explains.

Munro extends his large and small arms straight out from his shoulders. With head back, chest out, he says, "Inform Lady Shondre she may proceed."

The Counselor winks at Shondre to go ahead, and she sets to work, tugging at a hem, smoothing the collar, adjusting the belt. Then she stands

262

back and evaluates her efforts with hand on chin.

Before her stands a barrel-chested man, dressed in the common gray uniform of a Cadre MedTech, over which cascades an intricately woven and embroidered robe. Long sleeves are proportioned correctly to fit Munro's asymmetrical arms, and Shondre is pleased to find that her tailor maintained the garment's graceful flow despite the colonel's lack of a tail. It is an odd pairing with Munro's bland uniform, as the robe is typically worn over a suit or gown. Yet Shondre cannot bring herself to dislike the match, seeing instead an intriguing juxtaposition of two vastly different cultures.

"The robe is worn open in front, by custom," the Counselor explains, "as it is intended to denote status rather than provide insulation."

Shondre returns to Munro's belt, unfastens it so the robe can fall into proper place, and is nearly dragged to the floor by its weight.

Munro looks down, smirks, and squats down to collect the belt. "I'll hold it," he says, "and you do what you need to do." He grips his tool belt with both hands and hefts it up to his waist. Shondre takes each of his lapels, opens the robe, and lets it settle into place, after which Munro fastens the buckle.

"Much bett-turr," she says.

"Thank you," Munro says, lowering his arms. Thompson and Maiella cross the room for their own viewing, and the colonel faces them, saying, "This is an important day. I must admit...I am anxious."

"We've got it easy, Colonel," Maiella states. Hiking a thumb at the Counselor, she adds, "This guy has to do all the talking."

"That's right," the Counselor confirms. "Today will be introductions, primarily, an opening statement of intent, and a bit of history, time permitting."

"Then what will I do?" Munro asks. "You can't expect me to just sit there all day, *idle*, can you?"

The Counselor thinks a moment, then answers with another question, "Have you ever had to attend a Leadership Council meeting where you had nothing to report?"

"I have."

"This'll be a lot like that."

The big MedTech frets. "That's...*disappointing*."

"I feel like I should be psyching up for rotation," Thompson says, flexing his armored hands.

"No need for that," the Counselor says to the Gun. "As Maiella said, I'll be doing the talking today so you can all relax. Just be yourselves, and we'll do fine."

"You sure you want us in combat kit for this?" Maiella asks.

The android nods sincerely. "Your message is entirely non-verbal. The Eleto will see you and understand that you are the strength behind our negotiation. You'll remind them that there are untold numbers of Cadre Operators still out there in the Black."

"Won't making them fear us be counterproductive?" Thompson asks.

"They *should* fear you at first, at least a little, so they believe a peace treaty is in their best interest. Have helmets in hand, however, to show you are not here to fight. Your strong silence will lend gravity to my words, that they'll be better heard."

Thompson nods, and the Operators remove their lids.

"And what about Sharon?" Munro asks. "I think we should bring something of hers with us."

"Shondre wasn't able to retrieve Sharon's personal effects," the Counselor says heavily, "but there is a place set for her at the table with her robe over the back of it. The vacancy of that seat will speak as loudly as Maiella and Thompson in their armor."

"All right," Maiella announces after a deep breath in and out. "Let's do this."

The android extends his arms in invitation, and the five draw close into a huddled embrace.

"We've come so far...both literally and figuratively," the Counselor says, looking each of his comrades in the eye. "This is *our* time. Believe me, I understand the stakes...and I *cannot wait* to begin."

A door chime sounds, and Shondre perks up. "Ah! Ess-korrt too mee-ting uh-ryv." She turns toward the door, asking over her shoulder, "Redd-dee, uss ahll?"

"Do you think..." Thompson begins. "If things go well today, do you think we could have the next round of talks on the planet below? It'd show us in our proper environment...get your people used to the idea that we belong here. And I'd like it if Maiella and Colonel Munro could see it for themselves."

Shondre smiles broadly, and nods with eyes closed. "Hyess. This hwon shall ree-kwesst." She touches the doorframe panel and the door slips aside. Opposite her is an Eleto soldier in gray uniform and black cap. He bows curtly and asks, "(Are Da-oma Kachi-in prepared?)"

Shondre makes a point of looking all around herself. Then, with a confused expression, she asks, "(Ghosts? Where does the guardian see *ghosts*?)" When the soldier does not reply, she levels a severe gaze at him with raised brow.

Irritated, the black-capped soldier finally replies, "(The Advocate knows what was meant!)"

"(Indeed, his *words* were plain. And this one asks again, with equal plainness, *where* does the guardian see *ghosts*?)"

"(This one is not *seeing* ghosts! Perhaps the Lady is—)"

"(What a relief to know the guardian is not hallucinating,)" she interrupts. "(To avoid further confusion, the guardian may wish to use words more *appropriate* to this historic occasion.)" Her spine straightens and she leans in toward the soldier. "(These are *ambassadors* to the Eleto and *personal guests* of his Excellency. The guardian will remember *to address them as such* and leave disrespect at home with his *superstitions*.)"

The soldier scowls bitterly, but bows, steps back from the door, and rejoins a phalanx of soldiers standing at attention in the corridor off to the right. Shondre smiles at the back of his head, thinking to herself, *That was enjoyable.* She turns to call her friends and is surprised to find them right behind her. *Op-Purr-Ray-Tors, it is known, are silent, yet even Munro with his tools can glide!*

"Kon-Zil-Urr," Shondre instructs, "hyoo wahk att frunt. Ker-Null Mun-Ro, hyoo inn senn-turr. Tom-Sun and My-Ell-Luh on syd. This hwon fall-low, aff-turr." She claps her hands together and smiles. "Redd-dee?"

"Let's go," Munro states.

The Counselor exits first, followed by Thompson, Munro, and Maiella. But the moment Maiella enters the hallway, the Geek does a double take to her left and freezes. Her ears slide back and her free hand clenches to a fist.

Shondre hurries out, craning her neck to see what has the Geek so upset. Only a few paces away stands the Veteran, Da-Indo-Hass. Body armor covers him from the communicator collar at his broad throat down to booted feet. An assault weapon with dual grips hangs across his torso by a strap. And dangling at his breastplate is a pendant in the shape of a sun with fire opal mounted at its center.

Shondre's jaw drops and her breath leaves in a huff of disbelief. But she steps into Maiella's view. Speaking Eleto words she knows Maiella can understand, she says loud enough for all to hear, "(Pay no mind to one so lacking in grace. This day is yours.)"

Maiella's eyes flick to Shondre's with the intensity of a wounded animal. The Geek's breath hitches once her throat, and Shondre feels rage surging from her in hot waves.

"Geek, *fall in*," Thompson calls out.

Like a switch, Maiella comes to attention, blanks her expression, about faces, and takes her place beside Munro.

Shondre glares at Da-Indo-Hass in disgust, looks up at the ceiling to stretch the tension from her neck, then follows after her friends down the hall. The Veteran strides up beside her, uninvited.

Shondre glances at the stolen pendant around his neck once more and shakes her head. "(Even for *you*, this is despicable. Did we not ask our friend to keep respectful distance?)"

The Veteran smirks. "(Whatever the content of today's...*spectacle*... the Voice of the People will be in attendance. In matters pertaining to his security, this one has unlimited authority.)"

She purses her lips, teeth grinding behind them. Under her breath she growls, "(You have *no idea* what you play with.)"

"(This one does not play, Advocate. These are *beasts* who comprehend violence, nothing more. They must be reminded what happens when they displease us...and that it is by our mercy alone they still draw breath.)"

"(And so *courageous* Da-Indo-Hass, *wise* Da-Indo-Hass, reminds them he killed their friend—*an unarmed female*. He believes this will cow them?)"

"(Not at all.)" Da-Indo-Hass grins wide enough to show his pointed canines. "(This one would strip away their *costume* of civilization and expose their evil nature for all to see.)"

Shondre sucks her teeth. "(It is sad my friend—and his masters who pluck his strings—are so empty inside. Do they have only bitterness and hatred to offer?)"

"(The Lady is unjust!)" With narrowed eyes, and a hand on the hilt of his blade, the veteran adds, "(For this one has *much more* to give.)"

Shondre nods in agreement. "(Indeed, the Veteran *does* have more to give from his *inexhaustible stockpile of disappointments*.)"

The Veteran yawns. "(One who has fallen so far should know she no longer carries influence. Lady Shondre may once have pulled favors from old friends, but that glory is faded, even now, and she has no more gifts with which to buy loyalty. What Fell-Marr-Ghen desires *shall* come to pass.)"

Shondre turns her head toward him. "(A Prime Citizen would not *dare* betray the Will of the People!)" She faces front. "(His name would be stricken from the Book of Memory, and all of his good works would be unwritten.)"

"(Such low opinion the Lady holds! This one would only ever act in *defense* of our great people.)"

Shondre snorts. "(Even if he would *provoke* their ire to rise in so-called defense?)" She whirls on him and drives a polished talon into his chest. "(Your guileless master has *ruined* you with petty schemes of righteous revenge. But these Humans are wise. You will not throw them from the path.

And this one would counsel her once-friend against the attempt, for if you *could* stir these people to wrath, you would find *more than you can handle*.)"

"(Perhaps,)" Da-Indo-Hass says, caressing the hilt of his blade. Then, whispering, he adds, "(And this one *yearrrrrrns* to find out.)"

A Shield, Not a Fist

Munro strides in step with the two Operators at his sides, thumbs hooked inside his webbed toolbelt. Ambient music filters down from unseen speakers in hollow, crystalline tones that, to his ears, are as appealing as someone rubbing glass beakers with dry hands. Adding to his irritation, the station's corridors are overly bright and spacious beyond any rationale. He frowns as he gazes up at the arched ceilings, calculating the volume of wasted space.

Nearly five meters high...could be useful in allowing passage of small vessels or tall cargo pallets, but no. Connecting doorways are only three meters tall, and they hang two-meter light fixtures from the ceiling! A completely unnecessary load on enviro-processing.

He looks down at the tiled floor beneath his feet. Each square appears sliced from some porous white mineral with veins of black and gold. *This floor covering wouldn't last six months under Cadre heels and carts. Why wouldn't they use an alloy that can endure? Do it right, and do it once.*

His eyes roam the various decorations and signs, each with their own dedicated illumination. *Every wasted Joule is taken from a defense grid, life support, or long range sensing... Even Colonists are more efficient!*

The real offense lies just ahead, however, when the corridor opens up into a high domed area of approximately thirty meters in diameter. At center is an artificial oasis with tall curving trees that sprout broad fronds in clusters at the tops. Grasses and blooms rise from the manicured soil and in the midst of it all is a stone fountain that spouts nearly to the ceiling before cascading down the stones to a shallow pond. His mouth gapes.

How can they be this careless with water? It spills everywhere! So many liters given over to evaporation, I can SMELL the humidity!

Making the scene doubly bizarre, no one else is present to benefit from

268

the extravagant shows. Every shop around the perimeter of the dome is gated, their aisles and racks of absurdly impractical items unbrowsed.

If they make these shows to impress us, they miss the mark by lightyears...

The MedTech glances at the stoic Operators keeping step beside him. Their expressions are serious and professional, facing front with helmets cradled in the crook of an arm. They appear equally unimpressed by the surroundings.

Ahead, the Counselor takes a step and a half for each of his. The android's dark brown robe catches the air as he goes, fanning out behind him in gentle ripples. Across his shoulder and back is a vibrant sash with patterns and colors as intricate as Munro's own robe, and the colonel assumes the garments are not just identifiers of importance but must also be indicators of rank.

If this were Leadership Council, he thinks, *Counselor and Shondre would be Majors...this robe would ID me as a Colonel...and also Sharon, if she were here... Hmm... What would a General wear?*

He dismisses the question as irrelevant then Munro's train of thought jumps back to the more urgent matter at hand.

This is the first time we'll be in the enemy's presence outside of combat. Will words suffice in this confrontation? I don't question the Counselor's talents...yet can we afford to lay all of our trust in him? No. There must always be a contingency...

He casts a penetrating gaze through the station walls into the depths of space where a young major waits.

If they won't listen to the Counselor, they'll hear you, Ralla.

The colonel looks over the Counselor's head to the three by three phalanx of uniformed Eleto soldiers at the lead. They march with exaggerated stomps, either trying to sound more numerous than they are or announcing their approach from across the station. The tromping gait startles colorful birds from tall grasses in the oasis and they flap up to the high fronds. Perched, they peer down at the delegation past long, curved bills. Some ruffle elongated plumage and spread wings in ostentatious shows. Others squawk and pipe as the procession passes by. Munro pays them no mind.

What he cannot ignore, however, are screens hanging from the domed ceiling in all directions of the compass. High-resolution monitors show live video of hospital rooms packed with sick Eleto. The victims are gaunt, listless, bleeding from eyes, gums, and snouts. Blood-filled blisters swell on arms, legs, torsos, and faces. Some convulse in violent seizures, spitting and spraying. Medical staff, isolated in head to toe biohazard suits, rush to assist.

Screens shift to a stern Eleto announcer who speaks with deep voice in deliberate measure. Over his shoulder appears an image of the human delegation shortly after their arrival, battered and disoriented as they were marched into captivity. The announcer brings a hand up beneath the image like he is holding it on a tray. His head tilts and his comment ends with a rise in inflection. He shrugs then interlaces his fingers on the desk and resumes commentary.

The image is replaced by a photo of an irradiated asteroid, seemingly ordinary but for twin parabolic reflectors at the limb. The announcer continues his narration, of which Munro only catches the one word "Kad-Ra," and the asteroid disappears in a brilliant flash.

Munro's jaw drops and he coughs as though punched in the diaphragm.

But when the screens shift to an image of a petite woman in a glass case, the MedTech halts and stares. Sun-withered skin sags against her skull, outer layers peeling in patches. Her open mouth exposes elongated teeth in receded gray gums. Half-lidded cloudy eyes are sunken in the sockets. Frizzed hair is matted in oily clumps against the scalp.

Eleto onlookers in the background gawk at the body, some in dread fascination, some in horror. Others cover their mouths with a hand and shake their heads.

Overwhelmed, the MedTech stands in place, gawking with glassy eyes.

Shondre grumbles to the bodyguard beside her, but the veteran ignores her. Instead, Da-Indo-Hass strides aggressively at Munro, barks an order, and shoves him forward with a flat hand. The instant he makes contact, Maiella whirls about and double palms the Veteran, launching him back. The Geek issues a challenge in his tongue with a thumb aimed at her breastplate.

Shondre shouts at the top of her voice and pounds her fists against the Veteran's shoulder, but Da-Indo-Hass does not reply, fixating on Maiella with a mirthless grin.

The phalanx of soldiers halts and turns about, hands on batons, unsure what to do while the Counselor spreads his arms and pleads for their attention as respectfully and as forcefully as he can.

Thompson steps in front of Maiella, breaking her gaze. He whispers into her ear and walks her away from the leering soldier. To Munro, the Gun asks, "You okay, Colonel?"

Munro blinks at the Gun, oblivious to the showdown going on around him, then looks at the screens again where Sharon's body is still bleaching in an Eleto village square.

"Sharon still lies unclaimed..." Munro's face twitches with a nervous tic.

The Veteran flicks his snout at the colonel, growling incomprehensible words. Shondre growls right back at the Veteran. The Counselor still pleads with the phalanx while Thompson and Maiella assume fighting stance, brows lowered, ready to fend off another attack.

"ALL RIGHT," Munro thunders, hand knifing the air into a five-fingered point down the exit corridor. "We'll *go!*"

The Counselor looks over his shoulder, keeping his arms spread as though they might keep the phalanx from rushing by. "Are you sure, Colonel? We needn't move until you're ready."

Munro glares once more at the screens overhead then affects a cooler, detached demeanor. "I regret my lapse. There is no cause for delay." To illustrate his point, he takes a large stride forward, nearly bowling the Counselor over. Soldiers in the lead backpedal to keep distance then reform the Phalanx and resume their stomping march at the fore.

Despite Munro's calmed appearance his mind races, recalling images of Eleto bleeding from eyes, nostrils, and gums. *Our viral shells must've found their mark...likely during the enemy's attack on Cadre One. If we're lucky, an epidemic is already underway... Let it spread, and Ralla's work will be done before she even arrives.* He clasps his small hand in his large hand, contented.

Thompson and Maiella form up with Munro, keeping pace on each side. Though the Operators face front, their attention is riveted to the Veteran behind them.

The Counselor hurries to retake his place at front of the Human delegation. He glances over his shoulder frequently, fretting with concern.

As the delegation strides away, Shondre remains in place, laboring to contain a rage she has never felt before.

This one must remain... This one must be calm... This one MUST remain... she chants to herself with eyes closed. Deep breaths vent her indignation to the cool station air, but her delicate hands ache from pounding against the veteran's armor. To her chagrin, there are the beginnings of bruises in both palms. With a frustrated sigh, she flexes her hands, smoothes down the front of her robe, and follows after her friends.

As ever, the obstinate bodyguard maintains his undesired presence beside her. Not yet tranquil enough to look at him, Shondre keeps her gaze straight ahead and mutters under her breath, "(So. Thought you could incite them to violence with a well-timed slide show? No doubt Fell-Marr-Ghen arranged the broadcasts.)"

The Veteran strides without response, both hands on the grips of his weapon.

"(They did not take your bait,)" Shondre continues. "(And in desperation you laid your hand on *an ambassador to the People*, their own *Voice*.)" She juts her lip and shakes her head. "(You realize your career is over, do you not?)"

"(None but you witnessed it,)" Da-Indo-Hass replies. "(And your judgment is in ill repute with the People.)"

"(That may be true. And I don't have a memory that can be downloaded as easily as, say, an *android's*.)"

The Veteran stiffens in his gait, and he stares straight into the back of the Counselor's head, losing his haughty contempt.

"(An ignoble end for a Prime Citizen,)" Shondre continues, "(and a *disgrace* to his brave sons.)"

The Veteran hisses through his teeth, eyes rimmed fearsome green, all the tendons of his broad neck tensing at once, "(SPEAK *NOT* OF WHAT YOU CANNOT KNOW.)"

"(Or *what*?)" she replies, finally able to look at him. "(You'll put this one in a glass case to bleach in Summer sun? More likely, that will be *your* fate, instead.)"

Da-Indo-Hass looks front, jaw clamped shut, breath coursing through his flared nostrils.

Shondre's mouth bunches with exasperation, and she turns toward him with hands open. "(Why must one whose name was synonymous with noble devotion give himself to such base and servile masters? This one's words are sharply edged, it is true, but he must know it is because she misses his constancy, his loyalty, and his treasured counsel. She longs to find the Da-Indo-Hass whose might was ever a shield, never a fist... She misses the loving companion and guardian who made her work possible.)" Shondre swipes at the corner of her eye. "(This one cannot forget the way he *was*, and how his example inspired. There is a great rift between us now, yet she cannot give him up as lost. Even now, this one *begs* her friend to quit his fortress of hate and once more be the one who made all proud who knew him.)"

Da-Indo-Hass squints in distrust, and, nearly spitting his words, says, "(The Lady rates this one a *disgrace* to his beloved sons...and she would speak of *friendship*?)"

"(Yes! Physical assault of an ambassador would *surely* bring disgrace, and she cautions him not to earn this stigma. But more important, she wanted to know if the man was as hollow as he seemed...or if there was still feeling in the arches of his chest.)"

The Veteran snorts, the corners of his mouth pull into a sullen frown.

When several silent seconds pass, she probes, "(This one could never discount a father's love, nor how profound the loss. If there was ever one quality she admired most in him, it was how well he raised boys into men. In their tragic absence, it might seem a father had nothing left to lose...)"

Da-Indo-Hass shoots a hostile glare at Shondre, which she absorbs without reaction.

Looking ahead, Shondre states evenly, "(Our friend must not think himself the only one who has had the arches ripped from his chest.)"

"(Ah, yes. Gro-Elto, the Lady's Other Self. It was not enough for him to lose his own life, the fool had to take others with him!)"

Shondre's chin wrinkles and she looks down at her feet. "(Cruelly he pries open the deepest wound and *packs it with embers*.)"

In annunciated mockery, Da-Indo-Hass answers, "(One must know if there is still *feeling*...)"

Shondre places hands on her belly as her stomach flips. "(Perhaps that was deserved... But it is not this one's loss to which she refers. Da-Indo-Hass has not lived among the Humans, as this one has. He does not comprehend the sacrifices Humans make to remain alive. If he would demand justice for his sons, he must know the Humans lost ALL of their children when Kad-Ra home was destroyed. *Every* daughter. *Every* son. All of their joy and hope, *gone* in an instant.)"

"(All?)"

Shondre nods, and she can see the slightest softening of his hard expression.

"(They suffer. They feel, as strongly as we do,)" she says. Then, animated, she asks, "(And what is the *reason* we suffer this pain? Because of an endless, pointless war perpetuated by anger and vengeance! A war that feeds only itself, demanding our cherished loved ones while yielding *NOTHING*... We can stop this, forever, if only we will *choose* to do so.)"

The Veteran is silent, his dour expression offering no hint if he has been swayed in one direction or other. Sensing she has said all that will be heard, Shondre takes a deep breath and slips her hands into the crook of his arm. He tenses, but does not pull free.

THE BURDEN OF PRIME CITIZENSHIP

The phalanx makes a sharp right turn into a corridor both wider and taller than any previously travelled. When the Counselor follows, he looks into a vaulted hallway thirty meters long with a set of ornately engraved doors at the far end from floor to ceiling. A muted din emanates from the gate itself as if it were a colossal drum of reinforced alloys, driven by a multitude of voices beating against the inside.

The android turns completely around to face his comrades and keeps pace backwards so they do not need to break stride. "We're nearly there," he says to Munro, beaming. "Our first step into a larger world and a new future for us all."

Munro's expression remains stoic. "I'm certain you will speak well."

The Counselor frets, expecting a more positive reaction. "Hmm. Perhaps today it's good to be reserved, not overly optimistic." He looks up, smiling again. "Do you have any questions?"

"None," the colonel answers, his gaze riveted to the golden gate.

"Okay, then." The Counselor turns about and follows the phalanx toward the enormous pair of doors. A lone guard waits at the portal, feet together, shoulders back, weapon parked on its butt beside him, gripped by the barrel. His other arm hangs rigidly at his side and his eyes are so still, he seems a statue until he hails the approaching phalanx with a raised hand. The phalanx stamps to a halt and the lead soldier returns the greeting.

A sudden surge of shouts and cheers filter through the heavy gate from the chamber beyond. Munro's face twitches. Thompson and Maiella glance at one another, both on alert. Shondre lays a hand on her chest to calm her thudding aortic arches. The Veteran glares with a scowl of impatience.

Activating a communicator at his collar, the gate guard's voice booms through amplified speakers in the room beyond, and the crowd's cheers instantly settle. Huge doors swing open, bringing forth a warm, humid gust that puffs the Counselor's hair back.

Munro peers through to a cavernous room with an inverted dome ceiling. At center is a raised dais on which stands a heavy looking round table with chairs at regular intervals. Above the table, a ring of monitors face outward, tilted down toward seats around the table's edge. Above the ring of monitors, giant holographic screens surround the inverted dome, aimed toward the crowd. Eleto technicians in headsets hustle about in the holoscreens, arranging decorations in the background, adjusting lighting and microphones, placing comfortable looking furniture.

Eleto officials mill about the dais in long gowns, robes, and suits, greeting one another with hand on shoulder and conversing. The big MedTech scarcely gives them a second look, but Shondre stares. The usurper, Fell-Marr-Ghen, stands in the colorful robe she once wore with dignity and pride, talking with Prell-Shah-Stoh, who is regaled in the uniform and rank her Other Self once wore. She squints at the new Supreme Commander of Eleto forces unable to shake the impression that, despite Prell-Shah-Stoh's comparable stature to Gro-Elto, the new Commander seems so much smaller in his uniform than her beloved.

At the parting of the doors, officials cease conversation and turn their attention toward the new arrivals.

The phalanx shouts what Munro assumes is an announcement of the Human delegation's arrival. Soldiers stamp once then march into the cavernous room.

The Counselor follows immediately. Munro takes a tentative first step, shames himself, and strides boldly forward with his Operator escorts. Once past the threshold, the MedTech finds himself in a sheer sided canyon between two sections of high riser seating. Eleto of all shapes and sizes peer down from the sloped railing, jostling for a glimpse. Their first expressions are of wide-eyed fascination and disbelief but quickly turn to revulsion. Hisses and curses from contorted faces break the heavy silence. Spectators point and shout, saliva flying with hateful epithets, teeth bared in enmity. The crowd swells in agitation.

A canister hurtles past Munro's head and explodes at his feet, splashing the hem of his robe with dark liquid. He cranes his head in irritation and finds a hail of objects barreling down at him. Thompson and Maiella slide their backs against Munro, each watching their side, arms raised to bat away anything that might strike the colonel. Food scraps and beverage cups comprise the majority of incoming debris, but Maiella spies a metal bar spinning directly at Munro's back. She snatches it from the air one-handed then whips it back in the direction it came from.

"My-Ell-Uh, *NO!*" Shondre shouts, but Da-Indo-Hass is already surging toward her. He plants a foot in her back, launching her face first into the wall then hip checks Munro into Thompson. The phalanx of soldiers turns and rushes Thompson too quickly to be unplanned. They lift the unbalanced Gun off his feet and carry him back toward the gate.

Maiella spins away from the wall, fists raised, shoulders hunched, as Da-Indo-Hass steps in with slow, lunging jabs. The Geek weaves and slides aside easily, a look of amusement on her face. The Veteran attacks again, telegraphing his strikes. The Geek dodges effortlessly, and taunts her opponent.

"MAIELLA, PLEASE, *STOP*," the Counselor howls, unheard, as the crowd roars in excitement. Da-Indo-Hass steps in with a lumbering punch and kick, leaving an easy escape toward the wall, which Maiella takes. With a flick of his hips, he whips his tail around her throat and grins.

Da-Indo-Hass rotates his whole body, hauling her forward. Off-balance, the Geek stumbles, and with fearsome speed the Veteran axe kicks her hunched back, driving her into the floor. She rolls onto her back and he dives onto her, wicked blade in hand. She blocks his slash at her throat once, but he deftly tosses the blade behind his head, catches it with his other hand, and bares down, leaning his entire weight upon the buzzing blade.

Eyes wide, Munro staggers back. He looks to Thompson and sees the Gun flailing at a crush of Eleto soldiers. The Gun yells at the top of his lungs, swinging, clubbing, kicking, elbow smashing, head butting in frenzy to get free. From Thompson, he looks to the Counselor, and the android is clutching Shondre's robe, beseeching her to do something, anything she can. Maiella is pinned beneath the Veteran, one arm trapped. She kicks, bucks, rolls and squirms but cannot get free. His blade nears her bare skin then dips ever so slightly. A spurt of red leaps from her throat.

'*Thompson!*" she shouts.

Quivering with fury, eyes shining with mad intensity, saliva hanging from his trembling lip, Da-Indo-Hass utters, "(*On your shameful head, demon, a father will have satisfaction.*)" Teeth gritted, the Veteran bears down with all his might, sinking the blade deeper into her neck.

A *CRACK* like a gunshot...

The Veteran lurches aside, face shattered. Munro stands over him, long handled wrench clutched in his massive right hand. The MedTech winds up for a finishing blow, but the Veteran lies still. Breath huffing from his barrel chest, the MedTech drops his bloodied wrench to the deck, shoves Da-Indo-Hass aside with his boot, then kneels and clamps a hand around Maiella's throat. Blood spurts between his fingers, soaking his grip, as he fumbles for the medkit at his waist with his free hand. Maiella grunts and writhes under him, slapping and clutching at his wrist as hurled objects from the risers pelt them.

"BE *STILL*," Munro orders, and the Geek goes slack.

Thompson elbows free from clinging soldiers, sees Maiella bleeding from her neck, and his body courses with chemical aggression. Complexity falls away.

These objects, these things, tried to kill her. They're in my way.

He glares through his eyebrows. Muscles sing their strength. Eyes defocus. Lips draw back, baring white teeth and arched tongue. The Gun roars and smashes his way through terrified guards like sparring dummies.

The crowd boils with wild shouts, still hurling objects down at Maiella and Munro, when a seismic voice shakes the hall. Every spectator falls quiet in reverent obedience. Even the soldiers drop to their knees and bow in submission, leaving Thompson panting in murderous ecstasy. The Gun whirls about with crazed gray eyes, chest heaving, confused, until he spots the Counselor and Shondre up on the central dais. Between them is the tallest Eleto he has ever seen, wearing a robe of black with glossy embroidery at the cuffs, hem, and lapels. His arms are raised high overhead, hands open, staring directly at him with commanding, ancient eyes.

The black-robed Eleto's voice rumbles through the hall's audio system again, and six of the phalanx soldiers rise from their knees. They warily hustle around Thompson, collect the slumped veteran, and carry him by his arms to the central dais.

Thompson takes deep shuddering breaths where he stands. His arms and legs twitch with unexpended adrenaline and he flexes his hands over and over again, battling against his need to grab something and hammer the life out of it. Sweat beads on his scalp and face, rolls in streams around his lowered brow, drips off nose and chin. Shaky, the Gun steps over to Munro. The colonel's medkit is open on the floor beside him and the MedTech grabs a spreader from it. His other hand is clamped around Maiella's neck, arterial spurts escaping around the edges.

Sight of Maiella's blood nearly triggers a second rampage. Instead, Thompson croaks, "How can I help?"

"Kneel there, put her head between your knees, and DO NOT let her move," Munro orders.

Thompson kneels opposite, places Maiella's head between his armored knees, and presses against the sides of her face.

"Okay," Munro says, pointing low on Maiella's throat beside her trachea, "when I release, you push with two fingers here, *firmly*. I have to get a shunt in this artery or she'll bleed out. Maiella, this is going to hurt, but you must be still, understand?"

Maiella looks up at Munro with groggy, glassy eyes and blinks once.

"Gun, be ready." Munro takes his hand from Maiella's neck, and a gout of blood leaps at his chest. Thompson drives his fingers into Maiella's throat where directed. Maiella groans, her tongue protrudes between her teeth, and her eyes flutter. Munro places a spreader at Maiella's neck wound, exposing the sliced artery. Despite Thompson's pressure the MedTech has to tilt his head to dodge each spurt.

"*There* you are," Munro says. He grabs forceps and uses them to pluck a slim transparent tube from his MedKit. As easily as signing his name, the MedTech slips one end of the tube through the sliced arterial wall, lets it fill with blood, then tucks the other end inside the artery, and holds the tube in place. Upon continued contact with warm blood the tube rehydrates and expands, growing tiny spines. Once the tube fully expands it fills the vessel, tiny spines anchoring it in place. The colonel gently tugs the tube to ensure its spines have fully set, then he releases forceps. Spurts of blood cease.

Thompson rocks back, but Munro stops him. "No! Keep pressure on."

The MedTech fishes in his MedKit for a bottle of clear liquid and uses it to rinse the wound. Next, he pulls curved needle and medical thread from his kit. With practiced skill, Munro carefully aligns the sliced edges then sutures the arterial wall. After tying off his last suture, he pulls an applicator of flesh weld from his MedKit and zips a thin bead over the closed incision. The flesh weld sets instantly, and he gently probes the closure with forceps.

"All right, Gun," he says, shoulders slumping as he relaxes. "You can take your hand away."

Thompson looks Munro in the eye to make doubly sure then removes his fingers. The vessel throbs with Maiella's regular pulse. There is no leak or seepage.

"Good, good. That did it." Crisis over, Munro sniffs hard and wipes sweat from his brow with the sleeve of his robe. "Okay, closing up now."

Munro douses the wound again, rinsing away pooled blood so he can see what needs to be fixed. Working his way out through the cut, he mends sliced muscle, tendons, and skin with careful applications of flesh weld.

Thompson lets out a held breath, more relieved than he has words to express, and he caresses Maiella's brow gently. She reaches up to him, looks into his eyes, exhausted, and cups his face with a trembling hand.

Letting Munro work, Thompson turns his attention toward the dais. There, Da-Indo-Hass is held under his shoulders by two gray uniformed soldiers, his entire body slack. The black-robed Eleto kneels and lifts the Veteran's chin for a closer look. Da-Indo-Hass's left cheekbone took the brunt of Munro's strike and is separated beneath the skin, taking a piece of the eye socket with it. His jaw is smashed on the same side, bone protruding through pulpy cheek in a compound fracture, jutting fragments of teeth. His purple tongue lolls past swollen lips, and blue blood patters to the carpeted floor from his drooping chin.

Standing beside the black-robed Eleto, Shondre looks down at her old friend, devastated. She bows her head, hands hiding her mouth, as tears stream down her hollow cheeks.

The black-robed Eleto regards the slumped bodyguard with stern, yet fatherly, disapproval. His voice reverberates throughout the hall, and, moments later, the Counselor's voice follows in translation,

"Da-Indo-Hass served us long and well. His zeal was unmatched. Yet that zeal has now carried him beyond service and brought disgrace upon himself and his house. In bringing violence to those who came in peace, Da-Indo-Hass has shown himself no longer capable of bearing the burden of Prime Citizenship. His Honors are *taken off*."

The tall Eleto points a taloned finger at the slumped bodyguard's brow. With extreme reluctance, the soldiers supporting the veteran rip the clusters from above Da-Indo-Hass's eyes, and strip insignia from his collar. They also remove the fire opal pendant at his chest and place the decorations in the tall Eleto's outstretched hand.

The black-robed Eleto continues, which the Counselor interprets,

"Though we revile his actions, we cannot bring ourselves to revile the person. Take him immediately to care so that he receives healing."

The soldiers bow penitently, and rush Da-Indo-Hass from the hall.

The tall Eleto slips his hands inside the opposite sleeves of his black robe and he turns his full attention to Munro, Thompson, and Maiella. The Counselor leans close and says something to the tall Eleto, who nods once.

Munro finishes closing Maiella's wound, and states, "Okay, Thompson, you can release her."

Thompson turns to Munro, "Hmm? Oh, right." He opens his knees.

Maiella sits up immediately, bringing a hand to her throat.

"Dah, Dah! *Don't touch it!*" Munro scolds, and the Geek lowers her hand obediently.

Thompson lays a hand on her shoulder. Trying to mask his worry, he asks her, "You okay?"

She nods rapidly. "Yeah. Light headed, is all." To Munro, she says with sincerity, "Thank you, Colonel. You saved my life."

"Bah!" he says, almost angry, adding a dismissive wave of his hand. The MedTech cleans his tools, repacks his kit, and hooks the box back on his belt. Rising to his feet, Munro looks around for his wrench and finds it in Thompson's hand.

"Thank you, Colonel. I don't have the words to—"

Munro rolls his eyes, and grabs his wrench out of Thompson's grip, "Doing one's duty is *hardly* deserving of praise. Don't make any more of it." The colonel hangs the long-handled tool then looks down at his robe. Where Shondre tried so hard to make it presentable, it is now disheveled with patches of bright crimson soaking the intricate embroidery. With an ironic smirk, he thinks, *And I was self-conscious about wearing my tools...*

For an instant, there is an impulse to peel the blood-marred robe, but he squashes it. *No. Let them see the blood they've spilled.*

"We offer genuine remorse for this attack," the tall Eleto says through the Counselor. "Please take rest in your chambers, and recuperate in comfort. We shall reassemble and resume at your convenience."

Munro glances at Maiella and Thompson. "I'd rather not draw this out."

"Me, either," Maiella chimes.

"You sure?" Thompson asks her.

"Certain," the Geek declares.

"Then it's your call, Colonel," the Gun declares. "Whatever you say, we'll back you."

Munro puts his thumbs in his belt and squares up to the dais. "Let's get this over with."

"Right." The Gun polices up his helmet, as well as Maiella's. Lying on the floor nearby is the veteran's dagger. Maiella's blood colors the blade.

Thompson snatches it from the deck, silently reliving a time when Argo's blood stained an identical blade. He passes Maiella's helmet to the Geek and orders her sharply, *"Cover!"*

The two Operators latch helmets and form up beside Munro. "Standing by, Colonel," Thompson announces with the Veteran's blade gripped in his left hand.

Munro glances over his shoulder toward the gate. Several Eleto dressed in close fitting white garments tend to the battered soldiers. They shrink back at Munro's iron gaze, ready to flee at his slightest movement. The colonel faces front.

"Take us out, Gun."

Thompson draws a deep breath and bellows, "TO THE LEFT, *MARCH.*"

MALICE

Crowds murmur in hushed tones as three Cadre humans stride toward the dais. The closer Thompson gets with his clutched blade, the greater the murmuring until Eleto rise in the stands, pointing and shouting at the armed Operator. The black-robed Eleto watches, grim and unafraid, then raises arms again for silence. Spectators obediently take their seats in the risers, whispering urgently to their neighbors, heads swiveling back and forth.

Shondre and the Counselor both hurry down from the dais to intercept, but are ignored and nearly brushed aside by the trio's determined strides.

The Counselor glances at Shondre then turns and trots beside Thompson, pleading for him to drop the blade. The Gun offers no sign of acknowledgement whatsoever, gray eyes locked on the tall Eleto ahead. The three climb the steps to the dais, each stamp of their boots echoing throughout an anxious silence.

The Gun's grip tightens as the black-garbed Eleto reaches into the sleeves of his robe. Instead of a weapon, the Eleto pulls out Sharon's fire opal pendant. He offers it with one hand and holds his other hand out to Thompson palm up.

Confronted by Sharon's pendant, the Gun is no longer sure what he intends to do with the blade in his grip. The offer for trade is plain, and in this gesture there is a return to proper ownership on both sides, a correction of wrongful taking that could shape any discussion to follow. Only now does Thompson notice the Counselor's hand on his arm or hear his pleading voice, but the message is redundant. He already knows what to do.

Thompson flips the bloody blade around his fingers and places the hilt into the Eleto's open hand. Munro snatches Sharon's pendant in his large hand then cradles it like something delicate and alive. His hard expression melts as he stares at it, and the big MedTech presses the pendant to his chest.

Shondre swipes her hands down her face with a muted groan and sways in relief before catching herself.

Prell-Shah-Stoh and Fell-Marr-Ghen glare from the far side of the table, faces mirroring each other's displeasure. They pass murmured words, shuffle toward their reserved places at the table, and take hold of their high-backed chairs. Fell-Mar-Ghen leans toward his associate once more, whispering, then straightens and waits for others to take their places around him.

The black-robed Eleto dips his head in thanks to Munro, summons an attendant with a crooked finger, and passes the bloody knife over with brief instruction. The attendant bows reverently and absconds with the blade, disappearing through the tall gate at a fast trot.

Shondre takes long, deep breaths as if trying to reinflate herself. Through smears of eyeliner, she drills an accusing stare into Fell-Marr-Ghen. The usurper glares back with hooded eyes, lips pressed together, jaw clenched. He tilts his head and lowers his chin in an unspoken warning.

The Counselor steps to Munro's side and says, "Colonel, in light of this unprovoked attack, if you have words for this Council, I will relay them *directly*. Is there anything you wish to say?"

Keeping his gaze on the tall Eleto, Munro answers, "Tell them we are ready to begin. I defer to the agenda you have prepared."

The Counselor nods, pleased by Munro's poise, and replies, "Very well, Colonel." He faces Shondre and relays the colonel's words in even tone.

Shondre nods respectfully then turns toward the black-robed Eleto. "(Noble Dekkto-Mayah-Tayaloh,)" she begins with a bow to her waist. Rising, she continues, "(Your humble servant, Aeolia Shondrekar Bakkar would introduce the Voice of the Kad-Ra, Kerr-Null Mun-Ro.)"

The black-robed Eleto takes a half-step back, grips the tip of his long tail, which curves over his shoulder, then he bows with one hand on his chest.

"(To the Voice of the Kad-Ra,)" Shondre announces for all in attendance, "(it is this one's joy to introduce The *Will* of the People, his Excellency, Dekkto-Mayah-Tayaloh.)"

At the Counselor's cue, Munro mimics the gesture with hand on chest, the other raised and open, remembering to bow slightly lower than Dekkto. When Munro rises, he looks into the tall Eleto's face and studies features as rough and lined as an outcrop of weathered stone. Short rounded horns protrude through his drawn skin at brow ridges and cheekbones. Vertical creases in his lips further the appearance of stone, and Munro half expects the Eleto's face to crumble should he speak again. Wisps of silver hairs begin at the corners of the mouth and run together down the angular chin.

Yet nestled deep within the ancient exterior are two deep saffron eyes that seem to hold the secret of time, itself. The same eyes that silently cowed an angered crowd to silence now gaze without menace upon Munro, projecting the same calm and confident presence as a Cadre General.

"It is good to meet you," the Colonel states without obvious sentiment, and the greeting passes from the Counselor, through Shondre, to the Great Eleto.

The Great Eleto replies through the chain even more efficiently, "(Likewise.)" He takes a breath and says loud enough for the crowd to hear, "(It was *against our wishes* that Guests of the People were greeted with inexcusable hostility. Let it be known, any who would repeat such offense will contemplate their inhospitality while they parch in desert sun.)

"(No matter how the blood boils for transgressions passed, those who arrive in peace shall not be turned away. We will not raise a warlike hand on the eve of cordial conversation. If we imagine ourselves rational and noble, we must prove it in temperance and patience. The Human words will be heard, without malice or intimidation.)"

Every head in the crowd dips in submission to the royal edict.

"(Be it known,)" the tall Eleto says to Munro in more conversational tone, "(this one owns responsibility for assault on your persons. Look no farther for satisfaction. What would our guests ask in reparation?)"

Munro waits for the Counselor's translation. His lip twitches and he nearly blurts out his first thought but bites his tongue. "We ask that this process proceed without further delay."

The Counselor grimaces at a reply less cordial than is needed, and he offers a more mannered response with the same message.

The tall Eleto arches a brow. He raises his arms and announces to the crowd, "(Our guests demonstrate the meaning of largesse. We honor such shows by responding in kind.)"

Dekkto leans close to Munro, saying through Shondre and the Counselor, "(We would not have our guests endure abuse without recompense. If they wish to appear generous in refusal, and by comparison reveal the People as churlish, we would not take that from them. Yet we would have them know they may ask *anything* of us at any time, without expiration.)"

Munro waits for the Counselor to break down some of the thicker concepts, then replies, "(Understood.)"

Again, the Great Eleto is intrigued. "(A person of few words is rare at this level of government,)" he says congenially. "(If only more were like you.)" He gestures toward the open chairs at the table. "(When our guests are ready, we may begin.)"

Dekkto-Mayah-Tayaloh parks his ancient hands inside his sleeves and strides to a chair with a higher back than the rest. Before sitting, he beckons Prell-Shah-Stoh and Fell-Marr-Ghen by looking directly at them. The two officials approach and offer dignified bows, which are not returned.

"(My friends misunderstood their instruction,)" the Great Eleto says.

The two look at one another in dismay. Masking his terror, Prell-Shah-Stoh entreats, "(Noble Dekkto, we are incapable of disobedience. Perhaps Da-Indo-Hass could not contain his need for vengeance...perhaps his loss overwhel—)"

"(*Perhaps* my distinguished servant found in a Veteran's grief a convenient answer to the Human question,)" Dekkto interrupts. "(And *perhaps* the new Voice of this region wished to bury his predecessor in scandal to better solidify his position.)"

Fell-Marr-Ghen's jaw drops in stunned silence. He shuts his mouth and averts his eyes, asking humbly, "(What does his Excellency require?)"

"(That those who hold such rank demonstrate they are *worthy* of it. If my friends have doubts, they may look to Madame Shondre for inspiration.)"

"(This one has no such doubts, Excellency,)" Fell-Marr-Ghen states.

"(A relief, then, that the People's trust in their new Voice is not abused.)"

Unable to look Dekkto in the eye, Prell-Shah-Stoh asks, "(Does the Will of the People wish us to restrain our testimony against the Humans?)"

"(No,)" the black-robed Eleto states with candor. "(You will be vehement and compelling. Bring all of the evidence and build your strongest case, for it is up to our Guests to prove they have abandoned savagery. The People deserve your most potent counterpoint, your most thorough exploration. Are my distinguished friends able to deliver this?)"

Both Fell-Marr-Ghen and Prell-Shah-Stoh bow deeply, answering in unison, "(We can and will, Great Eleto.)"

Without another word Dekkto gestures toward their chairs, dismissing them.

Shondre watches from the opposite side of the table, unable to overhear yet aware something of importance has just occurred. With modesty, she moves to her seat at the table and commits her impressions to memory.

Dekkto faces Shondre and calls to her, "(If the Advocate is prepared, this Council would hear opening thoughts.)"

Shondre nods, eyes closed, hands clasped in front. Expression neutral and professional, she states, "(Great Eleto, it is this one's wish that opening thoughts come straight from the Human delegates. This one does not wish to filter their speech, possibly altering their meaning. Thus she would allow Kon-Zill-Urr the opportunity to speak and be heard.)"

The black-robed Eleto's brow lifts in mild surprise and he glances around the table, where objection etches the faces of Eleto delegates. "(Such a request is peculiar,)" Dekkto begins, returning his gaze to Shondre, "(as their best case would be made by a sympathetic Advocate...one well-versed in legal language and precedent.)" Grumbling around the table distracts him, and he lifts a finger to silence it. "(Does the Advocate truly wish our Guests to attempt the People's speech and risk being gravely misunderstood?)"

"(She does, Excellency.)"

Dekkto lowers his hand. "(Very well. Let Kon-Zill-Urr come forth, and we shall hear what words he is capable of making.)"

BECAUSE WE LOVED THEM SO MUCH

Shondre beckons the Counselor to her side and the android complies. Rather than offer an elaborate and formal introduction, Shondre merely says, "(Here stands my trusted friend, Kon-Zill-Urr. He speaks for all his kind. Please mark his words and weigh for yourselves what he will say.)" She steps back to her chair and waits.

Dekkto spreads his black robe and settles into his chair, ample fabric draping over the arms. Like a fall of dominoes down each side of the table, Eleto and Human delegates take their seats, leaving the Counselor standing at the table's far edge. The android looks to Dekkto's right, making eye contact with Fell-Marr-Ghen, Prell-Shah-Stoh, and three Eleto officials he has not previously met. Fell-Marr-Ghen and Prell-Shah-Stoh gaze back behind practiced masks of detachment, their mouths short straight lines. The other three cannot take their eyes off the severe soldiers watching them from across the table.

To Dekkto's left is an open seat draped with a multi-colored robe and topped by a stone pendant that flashes in the bright overhead lighting. Next down the line are Colonel Munro, Thompson, Maiella, and Shondre. The two Operators sit erect in their chairs, arms on the table, palms flat against it, alert and ready to pounce at the slightest provocation. Ruddy smudges mar the polished mineral below their spread hands, what the Counselor immediately recognizes as Maiella's blood, and the android notes her armor still has a wet shine in the joints of neck and shoulder plates.

Overhead, large monitors show remote Eleto delegates, both male and female, settling into comfortable armchairs. Technicians fasten microphones, hiding them in the folds of rich clothing, under collars, or behind jewelry.

An occasional arm reaches into frame, patting a face with a powdered pad or swiping a brush across cheek or brow.

The Counselor glances again at the Eleto side of the polished table, observing how ill at ease the officials are sitting across from blooded warriors in armor. Even more disconcerting is how Thompson and Maiella sit in absolute stillness, staring machinelike at their diametric counterparts. Sensing the officials' discomfort, the Counselor begs for attention, which they gladly give.

"(To the Noble Will of the People, his Excellency, Dekkto-Mayah-Tayaloh...to the High Commander of Martial Services, Prell-Shah-Stoh... to the Honored Voices of the eighty regions and to Fell-Marr-Ghen, in particular, who is our most gracious host...to the Prime Citizens of the elevated governances, to the Distinguished Controllers of the common need, and to all Eleto, regardless of post or position...this one is both grateful and humbled for the opportunity to be heard.)"

Turning a full circle, the android looks into a sea of Eleto faces amazed to hear clear speech from one so thoroughly alien.

"(It is difficult to quantify how great an effort we make today.)" The Counselor pauses, letting his opening statement sink in. "(Strong feeling exists on both sides...a conflict that has spanned generations, handed down from parent to child...a dreadful inheritance that brings no profit, no benefit... How do we reach across this chasm? Where does one *begin*?)"

The android takes a step away from the table with a hand at his mouth. He turns suddenly, pointing to the bloody floor near the large gate. "(Only moments ago, we fell from rapprochement to something more familiar... something that damns us perpetually in this violent cycle.)" He searches through the multitude in the risers one set of eyes at a time. "(We have to ask ourselves, what do we *want*? What future would we build? What legacy will we leave our children?)" He gestures with both hands toward the bloodstained floor near the entrance, palms open. "(And, we are obliged to ask, is this the *best* we can do?)"

He lowers his hands and slumps. "(These questions are of utmost gravity, for how we answer defines us as a people.)" He looks up suddenly, mismatched eyes bright. "(*That* is why we come before you now. *That* is why we are here in this hall, hoping we will find some common thread we can weave into real communication, and gradually, *understanding*, because our children deserve better than what we have offered them so far.)

"(Does this one expect your trust? No, it is too soon to speak of trust. Trust must be *earned*. Trust comes after we have walked a long road together and sincere action has banished doubt. It might take the passing of generations before trust blooms in this desert of acrimony. Who can say? So while we have a destination in mind, we have no desire to rush. One step at a time, at a pace we can both tolerate.)

"(Today, we seek a proper introduction)" he says, gesturing at the rigid Operators at the table, "(so we might show you what lies beneath this hard exterior. We came to show you we are *not* Ravenous Ghosts, at all... that we are flesh and blood. We want you to see us as we *are*... We want you to understand what it means to live as we have, because if you can see us without distorting lenses of legend and myth...if we can strip away preconception and get to stark reality...you will find we are not so different.)

"(There is much to answer for on both sides, this is true. The sins of a few are now carried by the many. Let us not shrink back from confronting these sins! Let us *study* them in full light of day. Let us *comprehend* them and, in doing so, initiate the process of correcting them. Let us *remember* for all time so this never happens again.)

"(After you have heard us and we have heard you...perhaps we will find it in ourselves to let go of suspicion and fear. Perhaps we will all see it is only by *guaranteeing* lives, not threatening them, that we will ever find the security we seek.)"

The android pauses to look around the hall again. Eleto faces are scrunched with skepticism, eyes wary. Some lean toward one another, sharing comments, but there is fascination in the majority of expressions; and he rightly guesses the reason.

"(Many of you are wondering how this one could have learned your tongue and manner.)" The Counselor gestures with an open hand toward Shondre. "(Look no farther than our advocate, Aeolia Shondrekar Bakkar. This one cannot overstate her patience. No matter how rough her capture and how isolating her captivity...Lady Shondre responded with grace. Her indestructible spirit is a bright burning torch in the darkness of our ignorance, and her boundless compassion softened the stoniest of our critics. In her presence, it was impossible to believe all Eleto could be evil. And if there was one like her, there could be more, we thought. Possibly many more.)

"(Lady Shondre lived among us, first as a captive, later as a guest. We struggled to build the fundamentals of language. It was an arduous process where there were none to tutor us... Yet the more we learned about each other, the more we discovered everything we *thought* we knew was wrong. What we found instead was the truth of Eleto nobility, of Eleto enlightenment that has gleamed across the eighty regions. Lady Shondre convinced us the Eleto instinct is *not* for war. She convinced us that, while strong in defense, the People cherish tranquility and respect life in its myriad forms. Our previous opinion, that the Eleto would utterly annihilate us in some mad thirst for blood, is no longer tenable.)

"(We are here in good faith that these assumptions are correct. We take no less risk than Lady Shondre did in reaching out for greater understanding.)" The Counselor turns squarely toward the chair with the opal pendant. "(Our dear companion, Sharon Jones, the Voice of her People, has paid the highest price. Would it not be easy for us, then, to dismiss her killer—and her killer's masters—as barbarians? And when another is so brazenly attacked in full view, a Veteran's blade to her throat...might we have concluded that the Eleto soul is twisted with hate, unable to bear the thought of peace?)"

The Counselor looks down at his feet. "(Indeed, such attitudes are as familiar and comfortable as old shoes.)" When he looks up, he spreads his hands. "(But such attitudes are merely excuses to abandon the heavy work of moving beyond the suffering we inflict.)"

The android glances at the faces around the table, scans across the attentive faces in the monitors, and begins a slow pace around the dais, speaking to the risers as he goes. "(We suppose the soldier who split Sharon's skull thought her head was as hard as her armored cousins. Perhaps that soldier presumed all Humans were as difficult to kill, and had no idea Sharon was delicate, precious, and rare. Perhaps her death was unintended...a dreadful accident fueled by fear...)"

"(Nothing changes the fact that our dear friend, Sharon Jones, is dead. It does not change the fact that her body was paraded from township to township in a glass case, like some curiosity dragged from the depths of the sea, and propped up to rot without rite or dignity.)" He pauses, gathering thoughts, then looks up suddenly. "(Might we have shuttered our minds and given up our dream for peace?)" He completes his circle around the dais. "(Would it not have been easier to return home *hardened* in our belief that peace with the Eleto is impossible, that our ancient adversary remains committed to completing the genocide begun so many generations ago... that the Eleto will never stop trying to exterminate us and will *always* be our mortal enemy?)"

He turns toward the polished table.

"(We cannot maintain that belief because Lady Shondre has already rendered that idea preposterous. She has risked *everything* in the cause of peace...and we are profoundly moved by it. She laid aside fear and skepticism, opened herself completely. She risked her credibility, her career, her *life*, in extending her hand of friendship. Inspired by her selfless example, we respond in kind, certain we will find more in common as we learn about

each other. We both cherish the fullness of life, the service of our senses...
We delight in companionship of friends, family, and colleagues. We crave
solutions to intriguing mysteries; we seek to understand the 'verse around
us, where we belong in it... But most of all we wish to see our children
nourished, raised in safety. We wish our children to enjoy the comforts and
challenges of life, *not* waste their talents in futile conflict.)"

The Counselor pauses, hand on his chest, and he turns toward Shondre.

"(Madame, without your strength, we would not be here today. You
taught this one the proper words and procedures so that our two peoples
can *finally* say what we must. You have pried open obstinate minds with
persistence, love, and gentility. You showed us the power of one, what a
single person can accomplish by committing to righteous path. You taught us
the meaning of nobility. Because of this, we will adore you for all time. And
as grateful as we are to have met you, Lady Shondre, we now look forward
to meeting the People you love and serve so well.)"

Overwhelmed, Shondre winces, brow raised, one corner of her mouth
pulled into an involuntary frown. She blinks with watered eyes then smiles
across her entire face.

The Counselor turns toward the crowd and opens his arms, spreading
his robe. "(Here this one stands. Please view him simply as he is. One who
walks on two feet, sees through two eyes, hears with two ears...a single being
in a vast existence... Yet see also that this one is capable of reason...elation...
and regret... This one exists nowhere else, unique, just as everyone one of
you. But this one has only *particular* talents, and in the reality of our lives,
he can neither defend his people nor provide for their nourishment. And so
we rely on others who can.)"

The Counselor steps back to the table, and says in words his comrades
can understand, "Thompson, will you join me a moment?"

The Gun breaks off his stare across the table and levels a quizzical
expression at the Counselor, one Munro and Maiella both share. The
Counselor is quietly insistent, so Thompson pushes back from the table and
rises from his seat. The Operator steps even with the Counselor, towering
over him in his armor. The Gun's hard gray eyes scan the crowd for threats,
but he keeps hands at his sides.

Resuming his speech in Eleto, the Counselor says, "(Beside me stands
a man. A soldier. Once all Humans looked like the one who now speaks,
more or less. Some were taller or shorter, some thicker or thinner. That was
when our people thrived upon the planet below. Now, our people roam the
stars, and our slight constitutions were not enough to endure the harshness
of space. Some had to evolve, had to become *this* so that our kind could

survive...and not disappear from existence entirely.)"

To Thompson, he asks, "Will you remove your helmet?"

Warily, Thompson does so and cradles his lid in one arm.

"(This man was bred for strength, for speed, and for aggression. Normal men and women simply were not tough enough, so they were *made* this way...so they could go out and find the essentials of survival...essentials that could not be found on a sun blasted rock in space. Yes, he is frightening. And yes, he has led a gruesome life. My point is simply that Humans never looked like this when they lived on the planet below.)"

The Counselor turns a circle, gathering the crowd's attention.

"(What is the price of his evolution? Joyless duty, awful tasks...service that ends one of two ways: death in combat or total exhaustion. And once exhausted, his reward is euthanasia.)

"(There were no songs in this man, no familiarity with art or entertainment. There was no idle time for love or play, only work and service, because *that* is what it took for Humanity to survive. His body was pumped full of steroids and hormones. His emotions were suppressed. This man was made to be an instrument, a *weapon*. Indeed, his very title is 'Gun.' To perform his role, he was not allowed to feel. He was not allowed to build attachments to his fellows, because life was so tenuous and uncertain.)"

The Counselor pauses for somber reflection.

"(Here stands a man who wears the pain of his life in every part of his skin. And as scarred as he is on the surface, those scars run far deeper. Here stands a man forced to endure physical pain none of us will ever know. Here stands a man ordered to complete the most gruesome chores so that his people would not starve or asphyxiate. Here stands a man whose body has been broken and battered, dragged back from death and rebuilt multiple times, all for the *privilege* of being sent out to hunt again.)

"(Yes, we can all hate what this man has *done*. We can despise the destruction, the taking of life, and the terror of his success. But can we hate this *man*? Can we hate him for following the only path of survival left? Can any of us truly comprehend what he has given up, what he has been forced to live through? Would any of us trade places with him? How long could we possibly last before breaking, before going insane?)"

The Counselor sighs unhappily.

"(This one apologizes for so many questions at once. Yet this one asks the People to look at this man and recognize he no longer haunts the Black. He no longer waits along shipping lanes in ambush. Why? Because Lady Shondre opened the door to a possibility that never existed before. We *can* talk to one another. At long last, we can *finally* talk to one another.

And in dialogue there is the chance we might find an end to hostility. This soldier stands here today, because he has embraced that new option, greatly preferring it.)

"(Once, to see this man was assurance of death. Now he stands before you seeking a peaceful life. This is a *radical shift* for those like him.)"

The Counselor pauses, his brow gathered into a set of lines.

"(Perhaps empathy, like trust, is too much to ask at this point. There is much history we have to face...for which we *all* must beg forgiveness. Until then, please consider this: if faced with total extinction, who among you would *not* fight with everything you had?)"

The Counselor turns a slow, full circle, allowing the question to permeate.

"(In time of war, all live in fear. It is a poisoned existence where nothing can be enjoyed without awareness it can be taken away. Everything is transitory; nothing is permanent. This soil grows bitter fruits of contempt, resentment, and hatred. We see each other as enemies to be despised, to be cleared away, to be exterminated. To perpetuate this state *intentionally*...is there a better definition of madness?)"

"(Let today be the first day of a new future—a future where our children look back in pride and understand we did this hard work, and we made these sacrifices *because we loved them so much.*)"

The Counselor looks up at Thompson and places a hand on his muscular arm. With a nod, he tells the Gun to take his seat.

"(Noble Dekkto-Mayah-Tayaloh,)" the Counselor wraps up, "(Voices of the Eighty Regions, Controllers of the Common Need, High Commander of the Martial Services, our gracious host, and all the People, this one gives thanks for being heard.)"

The Counselor places a hand over his heart and bows deeply. Small pockets of applause in the crowd rise then are immediately hissed down. In the aftermath a contemplative silence descends.

"(We have heard the words of Kon-Zill-Urr,)" Dekkto intones, his amplified voice carrying throughout the hall, "(and we are much impressed by his mastery of the People's tongue. Now, we will hear the words of Fell-Marr-Ghen, Voice of the People in this region and Advocate in Opposition.)" The Great Eleto raps a fist against the mineral table, and his knuckles *clack* like stone.

A GAME PRESERVE FOR SAVAGES

Fell-Marr-Ghen rises from his seat then spreads his robe so the creases fall away.

"(This one offers sincere thanks for the opportunity to be heard. His words are bound with the emotion of loss, and thus, he endeavors to remain above the pain of recent events, yet he begs the People's forgiveness should his demeanor slip. Noble Dekkto-Mayah-Tayaloh, with your permission, this one will begin.)"

The Great Eleto blinks slowly and nods once.

The Advocate in Opposition nods lower in acknowledgement then faces the Human delegates across the polished table.

"(We have heard the Human machine orate at some length.)" He swivels about to the crowd, the hem of his robes swirling after. "(Oh, yes, did you all know? What you just heard speaking is a *machine*, artificial in every way. So do not marvel at its ability to make our words for any simple recording device can be *programmed*.)"

"(This one *objects*,)" Shondre says, nearly shouting, and all eyes at the table pivot toward her. "(The Advocate in Opposition has *no qualification* to judge what is alive and what is not! Konn-Zill-Urr may be artificial, but he *is* a living being regardless how different his physical processes. Moreover, he is afforded all the title and privilege due an ambassador to the People.)"

The Great Eleto turns his ancient gaze toward Fell-Marr-Ghen. With stern voice, he admonishes, "(Ambassadorial title and privilege may be bestowed upon *anything* our guests wish. As they desire a *chair* to hold Ambassadorial function, we observe that chair as such and will afford it all courtesies due.)"

When the Counselor translates for Munro, the Colonel's ears slide back, his cheeks redden, and he glances at the empty seat beside him with Sharon's pendant on the back.

"(However,)" Dekkto continues, "(the People will reserve judgment on what is alive and what is not. The Advocate in Opposition will proceed without speculation.)"

"(As it pleases the Will of the People,)" Fell-Marr-Ghen states, bowing modestly, one flat hand on his chest. He rises and turns toward the crowd, all trace of modesty gone. "(Now then, we have heard the Human machine assert these two 'soldiers'—who are guilty of every war crime we have laws against— these two soldiers sit here, *not* waiting in ambush to kill or maim our hapless travelers. It is readily apparent they are not, *at this moment*, committing wanton atrocities. But how many others like them *are* still out there, waiting in the darkest reaches? How many of our disappeared warships remain unaccounted, lost to these *Da-oma Kachi-in* and pressed into hideous service, hmm? Let us consider that before we sway in the slightest to any overture of peace.)"

"(More poignantly, this one would ask these...)" His mouth freezes in disgust. "(...*soldiers*...how the attack on the planet below enhanced their survival? In what way, *precisely*, did drowning the city and its inhabitants keep Humans from going extinct? Surely they found some mementos as they rooted through the irradiated ruins of their cities...some pleasing keepsakes to remind them of their more numerous days when they spread, *like disease*, to our most distant worlds and piled our brethren in open pits! But *in what way* did dragging a father down the ramp of an airborne transport, shoving him off and letting him plummet to the ground, screaming... How did *this* help the Humans to longer life?)"

Fell-Marr-Ghen turns suddenly, leveling a hateful gaze on Thompson, snout wrinkled, hint of teeth behind curled lips.

"(At that altitude there would have been ample time to contemplate his approaching death...to contemplate the family he would leave behind... But his family fared no better for they were aboard the same transport, and the Human pilot crashed it into a crowded landing bay! Anyone not clad in that...that armor of shadows they wear...was crushed in the impact, scorched by explosion, smothered by smoke and fume... And this only touches the surface of their *mad rampage*...)"

Fell-Marr-Ghen blows out his breath and sniffs hard. He paces the perimeter of the dais, gazing out into the faces surrounding him.

"(Perhaps our Human guests around this table have forgotten the *zeal* with which they *butchered* our people—)"

"(We object!)" Shondre shouts. "(Those assembled here *could not* have participated in those long ago killings.)"

Dekkto nods. "(The objection is noted. Advocate in Opposition is not a legal instrument who assigns guilt to those untried by due process.)"

"(Please forgive this one's minor oversight. It is true these *delegates* at our table are not long-lived enough to have participated in that slaughter. They were not present to witness how our unarmed settlers on the outer worlds, living in harmony with nature, were herded and cut down like *livestock*. These *honored guests* may be unaware how their factories descended from the sky, lodged into bedrock like bloodsucking parasites, and gouged all they wished from the landscape. Why should they care that these factories belched pestilent vapors, left open sores on the landscape that even now have not fully recovered? They were not there to breathe the soured air or drink from the poisoned streams!)"

Fell-Marr-Ghen pauses, chin raised, eyes rimmed a passionate green.

"(The humans surely looked upon our settlers, who lived uncomplicated pastoral lives, and deemed them primitive. Backward. Ignorant. Human marauders must have derided our settlers as incapable of knowing the value of the soil they built their homes upon! And in that derision, they surely imagined our people an easy obstacle to clear—.)"

"(We *object*!)" Shondre interrupts. "(Supposition and conjecture. The Advocate is *guessing* at motives he cannot prove.)"

Fell-Marr-Ghen tilts his head in irritation and he spreads his hands at his sides. "(The motives *were* clear, Excellency... Minerals, ores, energy... These were the only motives needed to justify the wholesale *murder* of our communities! Shall we look back through our archives? Because the evidence of these motives is plain!)"

Fell-Marr-Ghen points to the projections overhead, and screens fill with scenes of wide pits, brimming with azure skinned bodies. Young and old, male and female slump atop one another in bloody, tattered messes, some unrecognizably mutilated. Others are tragically recognizable, and several images zoom into the pits, pausing at Eleto children with necks broken at sharp angles, skulls dented from blunt force, bullet wounds crusted with dried blue blood.

"(Look here and find your evidence, *Advocate*,)" Fell-Marr-Ghen snaps.

The projected screens shift to top-down images of enormous tracked vehicles with bright steel blades and digging arms. The view expands gradually, pulling away, revealing the hulking earthmovers at the bottoms of open pit mines. The images continue to zoom out until the vehicles are yellow specks and still the full scale of the pit extends beyond the screen's edge.

"(One needs not *guess* at anything,)" Fell-Marr-Ghen counters, drilling an annoyed stare into his opponent. To the Great Eleto, he asks, "(And must this one suffer the Advocate's constant interruptions? We maintained our silence during the machine's oration, despite its *wild* suggestions. Can we not expect the same courtesy?)"

Dekkto nods in agreement. "(Granted. The Advocate will hold further objection until opening statements are complete.)"

Shondre blanches and dips her head, embarrassed.

Her opponent nods again, vindicated. "(Thank you, Excellency.)" Fell-Marr-Ghen faces the crowd and resumes his path around the dais. "(Now then, we heard the machine speak of *reason* in the Human psyche. When this one looks upon the images above, he wonders, where was this '*reason*' of which Kon-Zil-Urr speaks? For this one would very much like to hear a *reasonable* explanation for the murder of *families*. They speak of a better future for children? Let us hear the *REASON* which allows the bashing of a child's skull!)"

Fell-Marr-Ghen pauses, eyes narrowed, hand gripping the end of his face and covering a deep frown. He takes several breaths then resumes, gentle in tone. "(As these Humans scraped away entire *ecosystems*, we evacuated our People lest their bones be pulverized beneath treads of their machines. And in the time between evacuation and our military response, the Humans had ruined entire *hemispheres*. Two living, breathing worlds were brought nearly to their knees by this...*infestation*. And so we see it is not a simple matter of hatred that drives the Humans to murder, for they kill entire *planets* with the same mechanical efficiency!)

"(It may be true that the world below spawned these destroyers. Just as it is true that a body can catch an infection it cannot fight off.)" He spreads his arms to the risers grandly. "(Do we allow the patient to die in these cases? *No*! We administer antibiotics!)" He drops his arms to his sides. "(And if the plague spreads, we *combat* it wherever it goes.)"

The Advocate continues around the table and pauses behind the Counselor's chair, laying his hands on the back of it.

"(To Kon-Zil-Urr's point that the Kad-Ra Humans were never so fearsome as they are today...well, that may be true. But what *is* this new form if not an exaggeration and amplification of their most bloodthirsty tendencies?)" He pushes off and continues his lap around the dais. "(There is no redeeming a species that is spurred by its own genetics to kill and corrupt everything it touches! Better to be rid of it entirely, for then we could *at last* know peace.)

"(To wit, we hardly need lift a finger. We have already located their hive.)" The Advocate makes a point of looking at Prell-Shah-Stoh. "(Gro-Elto was our High Commander of Martial Forces, until recently.)" His gaze falls on Shondre. Unconcerned that behind her composed expression is an existential grief, he adds, "(We all know Gro-Elto was Lady Shondre's Other Self. Like Lady Shondre, Gro-Elto sought reconciliation with the Humans.)" The Advocate sighs, purses his lips, shakes his head, and turns toward the risers. "(He arrived at the Human nest in overwhelming force and deployed his fields so that any bolt or beam would be reflected back upon the aggressor. Predictably, the Humans attacked, and, in so doing, they reduced their own nest to a smoldering ruin.)

"(Two warships defending the asteroid were shot apart, destroyed. These warships were so heavily augmented it was difficult to recognize them as the Bell-Arr-Tuhr and the Shoh-Stak, disappeared long ago. One can only suppose what happened to their crews...)

"(Afterward, the Human lair was shattered, utterly defeated. Yet merciful Gro-Elto did not press his advantage. Rather, he pleaded for an end to killing. We have his last message, in fact.)" He sneaks a peek at Shondre and sees her gazing up at the screens with a mixture of fear and longing, lips parted, one hand pressed flat against the boundary of her neck and chest.

The Advocate points to the projected screens, and a waist up view of an Eleto in white uniform appears. Metallic decorations ride on the brow ridges above his saffron eyes. The officer peers out from the screens with grave intensity, hands open, palms forward in placating gestures.

"(This battle is over,)" Gro-Elto states. "(There can be no victory. So let us cease fire, care for our wounded, and begin a conversation that should have started ages ago.)"

The Eleto officer places a hand on his chest. In earnest tones, he continues, "(Perhaps these words are not understood, yet an attempt must be made. This one is known as Gro-Elto, and he would make your acquaintance. Will you meet, face to face, so that we might come to know one another as more than enemies?)" Gro-Elto reaches with both hands and waves toward himself in invitation. "(Come forth and be welcomed! Or, this one can dispatch transports to lift you and as many as still dwell in your walls to safety.)"

The officer dips his head, keeping a vigilant gaze on the screen, and his voice drops an octave.

"(If our adversary believes it is possible to prevail, we would warn against the attempt. Though valiant in defense, further resistance will drive your kind from existence. We treat with caution, having corralled a wild and dangerous beast...yet we cannot ignore this particular beast is an Eleto creature. The sin of genocide hangs heavy around our necks. We have only concentrated the Human will to survive, and a new breed haunts our shipping lanes with lethal effect. But the people you battle now took no part in that ancient crime! And this one will *not* allow further harm to The People.)"

Gro-Elto lifts his chin.

"(If we would be more than enemies, *someone* must be bold and ask for change. That person now stands at your doorstep. Answer his call and speak what is required to end hostilities. We will find a way, be it in dumb shows, words, pictures...whatever is necessary.)

"(One way or other, our war ends here, *today*. This one begs you, let us *both* survive it. We are sending transports for you to board, if you wish. Our channels are open, and we are ready to receive.)"

The officer clasps taloned hands, lifts his head, and waits.

Fell-Marr-Ghen freezes the video so that Gro-Elto's face continues to stare from the projections.

"(Could *anyone* have asked more?)" The Advocate in Opposition turns to the crowd. "(Could anyone have shown more *patience* before a belligerent foe? More *restraint*? To a fault, Gro-Elto stayed his hand.)" The Advocate juts his lower lip and shakes his head. Looking up, he asks, "(So how was Gro-Elto's mercy answered? Observe...)"

Fell-Marr-Ghen points a finger at the screens, and the armored head of a Cadre Geek appears. The Operator's helmet is bashed and scraped. Broken carbon spars of the collapsed cockpit jut toward his head, their ends frayed into hair-like fibers. His eyes are crushed shut behind a cracked visor, and he groans with short panting breaths.

Munro's jaw drops. He leans forward, hands flat on the table. "Kibwe!"

The Geek opens his eyes and looks toward the screen, blinking, as code scrolls in his goggles. Mustering what little strength remains in his broken body, he transmits, *"This is Lieutenant Kibwe, last living defender of Cadre One. Option Zulu is authorized."* The image scatters in a burst of interference and the screens go dark.

Munro's breath leaves in an involuntary huff. His eyes water, his brow wrinkles, and he chokes on emotion so hard he shudders. Maiella lays her hand on the Colonel's, and he grips it tight enough to crush if not for her armored gauntlet.

The Advocate in Opposition glances at Munro, scowls without sympathy, and looks out to the sea of silent faces in the risers.

"(We know not what this Kad-Ra soldier said. But his meaning was plain.)" Fell-Marr-Ghen points at the screens again, where a new image displays, showing a distant view of a gray asteroid. Perspective is from the extreme flank of battleships and carriers in semi-circular formation. A brilliant blue-white star in the background illuminates a halo of lofted dust around a battered asteroid. At the formation's center, a plain, boxy vessel without obvious weapons or comm arrays pulls ahead and discharges lines of transports toward the hazy asteroid. Then, a flash like a supernova washes the screens white, overwhelming even the brilliant star in the background.

Munro flinches. Shondre gapes.

A moment later, the flash fades, and the gray asteroid is shattered, its fragments hurtling away amid swelling clouds of sun-lit dust. The boxy vessel at center blisters from the blast then sags like overripe fruit as a rocky fragment plunges directly into it. The softened ship folds around it, as if in embrace, and lurches off into the void.

"(They would rather *die* than accept Gro-Elto's offer,)" Fell-Marr-Ghen explains. Watching Munro and Shondre, relishing their trauma, he asks the crowd, "(How can we pity them? *They did this to themselves!*)"

The Advocate brushes his hands against each other then holds them aloft so the sleeves of his robe fall to his elbows. "(Our hands are clean. We made the attempt.)"

He lets his arms fall to his sides.

"(So, what have we learned? We have learned that Humans are so committed to killing that when denied another target *they kill themselves*. So advanced is their malevolent mania, we need only let nature take its course. Their nest is destroyed by their own hand. Without a base of operations, they cannot sustain meaningful attacks for long. And they surely know this! What few still live have sent this...*delegation*...to negotiate terms in the desperation of defeat.)

"(But say we permit them to live. Shall we become caretakers of this vagrant species? Shall they become beggars after us? It is not as if we can simply vacate some patch of land for them, for they travel the stars! No place is safe when they roam free. For shame, we would keep these predators in a zoo to marvel at, for they are too dangerous to exist elsewhere.)"

Fell-Marr-Ghen smirks derisively. "(Should we do as Lady Shondre suggests? Shall we turn them loose in their old habitat, and, in so doing, make the great planet below a GAME PRESERVE for *SAVAGES*?)"

Shondre leaps from her seat, but she bites her tongue bitterly. Her opponent smiles then deliberately turns his back to her. "(Better to be rid of them entirely,)" he announces. "(The way we have cured the most virulent plagues, we could eradicate the last traces of a calamity that has dogged us for generations.)" Fell-Marr-Ghen lifts a long finger. "(Ah, but we *cannot*, says the former Voice of this region. The culling was wrong, unjust. *Sinful*, even!)

"(Lady Shondre has ever been an apologist for our rightful actions in the past. Such lofty moral position is easy for her to take now, when Eleto bodies are not *stacking up* with the alarming speed they once did. There is less urgency now that Humans are scattered to the void, and she may navel gaze at length about how evil our ancestors were. Lady Shondre may be rooted in the past, but the rest of us must live in the *present*. If she will not address the Human threat, then someone else must! In fact, we laid our recently dead to rest at her expansive estate so that she would be reminded, *her inaction cost lives.*)"

Shondre's eyes bulge and her lips part at the enormity of the accusation.

"(It is clear that message was neither received nor understood,)" Fell-Marr-Ghen continues, unabated, "(as Lady Shondre still sits on the *wrong* side of this table, opposing basic needs of the People she once claimed to love.)"

A gasp rises from the crowd, and the Great Eleto clears his throat. "(Too far. The Advocate will refrain from personal attacks or risks censure.)"

Fell-Marr-Ghen bows deeply at the waist, "(Yes, Excellency, this one's words were perhaps strongly stated. Your servant begs forgiveness if personal offense was taken. For it is true, even the *foulest* criminals deserve fair representation in their defense.)"

He stands upright, no trace of regret or humility evident in his features, and he picks up where he left off.

"(And so, we arrive at the apex of the issue. Consider the history, the legacy, the events long past and those recently witnessed. To all within range of this one's voice, ask yourselves, How many of you are alive today because Humans were decimated long ago?)"

Fell-Marr-Ghen turns a full circle, seeing in the risers a multitude nodding in tacit agreement, and he continues, "(Who among us can say, with certainty, that he or she would exist if mankind had *not* been culled?)" The Advocate parks his hands inside his robe sleeves, contemplative. "(Once we consider how many Eleto lives were spared, now consider, how many WORLDS were spared from the Humans' mad rampage?)"

He allows the question to linger, and when he hears agreeing murmurs in the risers, the corners of his mouth lift ever so slightly.

"(We have laws that permit us to execute the most egregious, unrepentant criminals, *do we not*?)" He spreads his arms and looks straight into the crowd, nodding his head, prodding his audience to speak their assent out loud. "(We provide every opportunity for reform, but the worst either will not or cannot. And, in due process, we *protect* our society from these willful offenders by ending their lives. Is it so hard to understand how we came to decide, *as a people*, that mankind *cannot* be allowed to thrive? Can we not see the rational decision to act?)

"(And in *taking action* we curbed an over-aggressive species before it grew too powerful to contain. Let us not forget: Humans were not the first aggressive species we faced! Before our long and deadly war with the worm-like Boor-Renn, we had the opportunity for pre-emptive action. At First Contact, the Boor-Renn had crossed the threshold of interstellar travel, like Humans. And, like Humans, they were possessed of a similar hubris. Our ancestors believed they could sway the Boor-Renn's aggressive tendencies...imagined that by sharing knowledge the Boor-Renn might look to us as teachers and friends. But what was offered only whet their boundless appetites, and, in ruthless application of the technologies we shared, they tried to *swallow us whole*.)

"(At the end, we surveyed the remains of great cities, buried the bodies we could find... Long did our tears quench the dryness of ash and dust. '*NEVER AGAIN*,' we shouted through our grief. Would we now *abandon* that lesson? This *retrospective guilt* only blinds us to a simple truth: by destroying mankind, we have spared Eleto lives and worlds.)

"(Even so, it must have been a horrible choice, as it is today. What sane individual relishes the idea of dooming an entire race? A race that *might* have been elegant, that *might* have been wise, if not for its unquenchable bloodlust...a race that has chosen to shoot first in EVERY engagement...)

He stabs an accusing finger at Thompson.

"(There they sit, these *Opp-Purr-Ray-Tors* who kill all they see! Imagine if their numbers were vast, as they once were... Imagine the same insatiable hunger that left the planet below half-dead... Imagine that appetite multiplied by *BILLIONS*...)"

The Advocate closes his eyes. "(Shall we sign the death warrant for the recovered world below by giving it back to those who *thrashed it to its last gasp*? Shall we hand over this precious world to its abusers, merely because they spawned there? No. For *THAT* would be the unforgivable sin.)

"(Let them die as they have lived. Even mercy cannot be infinite. Because in every account, unending mercy dooms us all.)"

Oration complete, Fell-Marr-Ghen bows, and the crowd erupts in thunderous applause.

REBUTTAL

The Counselor finishes translating Fell-Marr-Ghen's bitter words for Munro then sits, looking out into the risers, enduring wave after wave of applause. Once the cheering finally dies down, there comes a general stirring of individuals collecting shawls, wraps, hats and gloves prior to departing. Likewise, Eleto delegates at the table rise and surround Fell-Marr-Ghen, praising and flattering.

With a hard scowl on his face, the Counselor pushes back from the table and stands. Projecting his voice above the commotion, he says boldly, "(Noble Dekkto, this one begs for rebuttal.)"

Dekkto's eyes narrow, and a sudden hush descends. Thousands of spectators freeze in place, eyes glued to the human machine with the audacity to break decorum.

"(Such a request is...*out of order*,)" the Great Eleto states. Delegates whisper to each other around the table as Dekkto and the Counselor continue their silent stare. Rustling in the risers and hushed conversations convey unease as Dekkto's ancient eyes weigh the appeal. At last, The Will of the People's deep voice proclaims, "(Kon-Zill-Urr will speak his mind.)"

"(We thank you, Excellency,)" the Counselor says after a humble bow. He scans his view across the riser seating with arms raised, gathering attention. He looks up into every projected screen, where remote delegates pause the process of removing microphones and earpieces. Last, he turns toward those at the table, waiting for curiosity to quell the muffled conversations. Once murmuring throughout the hall abates, the Counselor faces the crowd and tents his hands.

"(The Advocate in Opposition has made a passionate speech, has demonstrated powerful feeling, and has raised some interesting points. His most relevant point of all is what to do when children are threatened.)" He spreads his arms and shrugs. "(Indeed, what parent would allow their child to live under threat if they could prevent it?)

"(But what if *everyone* you know is threatened with death? Not only your children, your entire family, every sibling, every cousin? And still we have not captured the full scale. What if your culture, your *history* was about to be erased? The flame of *all* nations extinguished forever... How hard would you fight, then? To what lengths might you go to prevent your entire species from disappearing?)"

The Counselor lowers his gaze, letting the heavy question hang.

"(Perhaps it is not possible to conceive of such a notion. Once, we were so numerous it seemed impossible our kind could be eradicated. Yet we faced an engineered extinction event, long ago, and we have lived with the specter of annihilation, ever since. My people turned to the stars in hope of settling a world far from the Eleto. But the Cadre had no colony ships to escape. Their option was to hold their ground. To *fight* or *perish*.)

"(It is easy to point in fear at the soldiers seated here at your table, to decry their brutality, the ruthlessness that drove them to collect what they needed. But discovery meant death. And that is *precisely* what the defenders of Cadre One saw when Gro-Elto's armada arrived. It must have seemed to them that the end of everything was speeding toward them. And they gave their all to defend their patch of dirt, their home.)" The Counselor drills a hard glare into Fell-Marr-Ghen. "(Their *HOME*,)" he repeats, "(not a *hive*, not a *nest*, but a *home* where a new generation was incubating...our future.)"

The Counselor lowers his head.

"(This generation will never be. Because Cadre One is lost, forever.)"

The android turns toward the crowd, arms out, palms open.

"(Why continue on this path of violence? When two great forces clash, there is only destruction, loss, agony... We come to you with open hands and minds so we might *end* the fighting, *end* the senseless killing...)" His arms drop to his sides. "(Yet the Advocate in Opposition claims we must keep to this bitter condition! How does promising the death of Mankind soften the Cadre's brutality? How does vowing to exterminate Humanity encourage them to fight less hard? And how does perpetuating this bloody cycle ensure children live long and healthy lives?)

"(Only through lawful treaty can we find the peace we both crave! And no matter how certain the Advocate in Opposition is that the last refuge of Humanity is destroyed and that we are on our knees...)" the Counselor pauses, burning a hard stare straight into Fell-Marr-Ghen again. "(...he is *gravely* mistaken.)"

The android softens his expression and rounds his shoulders.

"(We cannot afford to be so over-confident, so intentionally blind. For if the Cadre has demonstrated *anything* over the passage of time it is how *adaptable* they are, and how tenaciously they will remain alive.)"

The Counselor faces Fell-Mar-Ghen again, glancing at Prell-Shah-Stoh to make sure he has the attention of both.

"(If the Advocate in Opposition would remove the threat to Eleto children, we must first remove the threats to one another. And the best way...the *only* way to do that is to recognize that *both* our peoples deserve a future.)"

The Counselor turns squarely to Dekkto and bows deeply. Upon rising, he says, "(We are grateful, Excellency, for a chance to answer the Advocate in Opposition's impassioned, yet bellicose, appeal to endless war.)"

Eleto in the crowd sit transfixed, frozen half in their seats, half out with belongings clutched in their hands. Delegates in the projected screens remain still, eyes wary. Even the delegates around Fell-Marr-Ghen turn toward the Great Eleto, anxiously anticipating his decree.

Dekkto nods once to the Counselor, slides back in his chair and stands. All Eleto reflexively bow, as does the Counselor. But when Munro, Thompson, and Maiella remain seated, the android flips a hand at them to rise. Begrudgingly, they rise and stand at attention.

The Great Eleto surveys the faces around the table then looks out across the silent crowd.

"(There will be a recess to serve urgent matters and take refreshment,)" the ancient leader states. "(We resume when the sun is at zenith.)" He raps a stone-like fist against the mineral table in emphasis then turns with a flourish of black fabric. Armed guards and aides hustle to his sides, escorting him between risers through an opposite set of high double doors and out of sight.

The crowd buzzes in a thousand simultaneous conversations as it shuffles down ramps toward exits. Eleto delegates depart from the dais on their own missions, attended by staff. The Counselor watches them go, straining to hear traces of conversation. Unable to discern their guarded words from the general susurration of the crowd, he frets and steps over to his fellows.

Munro towers over him, annoyed, and demands, "What did you say at the end?"

The android offers a wan smile. "Made an attempt to put these talks back on a positive track."

Munro turns and watches the delegates stride toward exits amid an entourage of aides sharing tablet screens, asking questions, tapping answers, and speaking into hand held devices.

"Were you successful?"

The Counselor's eyebrows lift as he frowns. "No."

Thompson and Maiella join Munro and the Counselor, expressions curled in unvoiced question. Shondre steps over to the circle, laying her hands gently on Munro's and the Counselor's arms, and says, "To hyoor room gho. Hwee komm bakk aff-tur ree-cess, try uh-ghin."

Munro shakes his head, brow lowered, the corners of his mouth drawn down in frustration, and he strides toward the exit.

"Colonel," the Counselor calls after him.

The MedTech turns about, impatient. "Yes?"

"We've only just started. Don't give up yet."

Munro glances at the pendant hanging on the back of an unoccupied chair at the table, then looks at the Counselor. Without a word, the MedTech turns and marches away.

"We'll bring him around, don't worry," Maiella says, patting the android's shoulder on her way by.

"C'mon, Counselor, let's get out of here," Thompson says, wrapping an arm around the android's shoulders. Together they catch up with Munro, Shondre hurrying after.

Any Program, Ever

Munro storms into his ambassadorial suite, ignoring Eleto guards at the doorway and nearly barging through them before they step aside. He heads straight for his bench at the back of the room and pulls his longest wrench from his belt, needing the resistance and weight of it in his hands, needing something to take away the feeling of idleness that has been riding him the entire trip.

Our labs for research and testing, arsenals, incubation and training facilities, he thinks. *The reactor and recyclers, nutrient processing, forge and solar collectors... Everything I maintained and cared for...gone. Our people scattered across parsecs of empty space...*

What have we gained for Sharon, Kibwe, O'Kai, and Cadre One? What am I doing so far away from the ones I swore to serve? I should be with my MedTechs aboard the Europa, *as O'Kai ordered. Instead, I'm on this fool's mission, being gawked at and mocked by a hateful enemy!*

His mind touches on the last viral batches put through the incubators at Cadre One before he shipped out with his MedTechs.

Saw hints of contagion in the monitors on the way into the hall... Beckert's and Kibwe's viral shells must've found the mark... Blueskin soldiers returning from the raid on Cadre One, infected, contagious... If we're lucky, they may have dismissed early symptoms as radiation poisoning and avoided quarantine... If the virus can spread to transport hubs, there's a chance it'll spread further... His hands clench the wrench so hard it creaks in his grip. *Let's see them laugh when millions are drowning with blood-filled lungs...*

Munro glances down at the hefty tool, noting blue flakes crusted in the adjustable slide. He chucks the wrench onto the bench angrily.

I shouldn't be here. I should be in a Lab, finding a way to punch these

Blueskins back. Should be finding an edge for our Operators to exploit, should be sifting the archives Shao-Lo brought back from Cadre Two for insights...not sitting around like a firing range target!

The big MedTech leans on his knuckles and stares through the wall. *Ralla will prove our strength. If only I could be with her when she strikes, I could keep her Operators fighting as a field surgeon...or I could be her chief engineer, keeping the fleet together...*

"ANYWHERE but here," he growls aloud.

An armored hand lands on his shoulder, and he flinches. Thompson stands beside him, helmet cradled in his opposite arm. Maiella's dried blood still mars his cheek and forehead. With a grimace, the Gun asks, "Been a hell of a day so far, Colonel. How ya holding up?"

Munro squares up to the Gun and fires back, "*How am I holding up*? How do you *think*, Thompson? I just watched Kibwe die. A man I personally decanted, nurtured through defect of mitochondria. No one believed he'd be fit even for drone's duty. But I got him through, one procedure at a time over seven years." Munro smiles. "Should've seen his face when he was re-classed Operator grade..." The smile straightens, Munro's eyes narrow. "Today, I saw him broken, defeated in defense of our home...a home we've lost." Munro looks down at the wrench on the bench surface. "And they *BOAST* of it! We suffer their insults one after the next! Sharon, *murdered*. No reason, no explanation. And they think because we set an empty place for her at the table, we believe a *chair* is part of our delegation... *They miss the point entirely!*" He turns his back to the bench and leans against it, crossing his large and small arms. "As if that wasn't enough, our 'escort' to these talks nearly parted Maiella's head from her body."

"Well, he *didn't*," Maiella says, pulling up beside Thompson. She pops the latch at her collar and removes her helmet to demonstrate. "See?"

A large new bruise swells in red and purple at her throat, and Munro homes in on it instantly.

"Geek, you've got a leak. I need to patch it *right now*."

Maiella's eyebrows lift, and she turns to Thompson for confirmation. The Gun stoops for a peek under her chin and he nods, serious.

The Geek sighs and parks her helmet on the bench. "All right, Colonel, where do you want me?"

Munro points to a wing-backed chair beside the bench against the wall. She sulks over and flops into it as if punished.

Shondre and the Counselor enter the room delinquently, deep in conversation. The tone is elevated, words in Eleto coming swiftly, and their gestures seem at odds with one another, sweeping or striking the air in time with emphasized syllables. Upon seeing the bruise on Maiella's neck, and seeing Munro's MedKit open with the big MedTech on a stool opposite the Geek, the two halt their conversation.

"Is she all right?" the Counselor probes.

"I'm sure it's noth—" Maiella begins until a hiss from Munro silences her.

"Lie back and remain still," the Colonel orders. He drapes a blue cloth over his left forearm then pulls forceps and solvent from his MedKit.

"Aye, sir," she mutters, slumping against the chair and letting her arms droop over the sides.

Thompson steps into the Counselor's line of sight. "I was able to catch *some* of what was said today, but not much. How do you think we did?"

Shondre and the Counselor look at each other, find the same sentiment mirrored, then reply in unison, *"Bad."*

"Not hwannt liss-senn," Shondre states.

"They believe we're weak, that this is a desperation move on our part," the Counselor adds. "And if they wait us out, we'll die off on our own."

"Are they stupid?" Maiella barks from her chair. "Ralla's got her finger on the trigger not three AU from—"

"HOLD *STILL*," Munro demands.

Maiella grimaces and lies back against the chair again. Munro peers at her throat, dabbing a solvent-soaked swab at the sutures. Each suture melts then pops one at a time, and he pulls the threads free with forceps, laying them in a neat row along the cloth over his arm.

"That's a good point," Thompson notes. "Ralla's, what, six days away?"

"If she keeps her word," Maiella grouses.

Munro glares in annoyance at the Geek. *"Ralla will WAIT."*

"Okay, we have six days left," Thompson states. "Maiella and I haven't done much at the table except try to look tough. Maybe there's more we could do?"

The Counselor nods, eager for ideas. "Such as?"

"Well, you say they aren't scared of us, because they think we're done for... Maybe trying to project strength isn't our best plan."

The Counselor sneaks a glance at Shondre and she appears as intrigued as he does. "Go on."

"To be blunt, an Operator's life is pain, right to the end. We can take it, because we have to...doesn't mean we like it. I think any of us would find a different way to survive if we could." He grips his chin in thought then looks up suddenly. "Shondre, remember what you said to me in my cabin on the *Europa*? You took my hand and put it on your shoulder, and you said..."

"Too man-nee, theez..." Shondre finishes.

"Yeah, we've got scars from fighting our whole lives. But the *only* reason we fight is to not die out, to keep going," Thompson states. He glances at Maiella in the chair as Munro works on her. She winks at him.

"Maiella and Argo...*wherever he is*...are the only two left of my generation. Everyone else is gone. I think about that a lot. And it makes me want to keep them both close. Where I can look out for them." The Gun turns about, facing Shondre and the Counselor again, eyebrows scrunched together. "Heard the Advocate say something about a 'blood thirst'... I've never, ever wanted to drink blood. What was he trying to say? That we enjoy killing, or something?"

Shondre and the Counselor both nod.

"That's cack. I *hate* it. Every time we go out I never know if we're going home again. Every time we go out is another chance I lose Maiella or Argo. But we go anyway, because if we don't people *starve*."

Thompson glares at the rich surroundings.

"Then I look around at this place and I see how they live, the comfort, the ease, the abundance... And they came to Cadre One to do *what*? We have so little, but they take even *that* away? They have no idea what our life is like."

"That's true," the Counselor confesses. "But Shondre does. She lived at Cadre One for over a year."

"Almost killed her, too," Maiella pipes from her chair.

Shondre nods wearily. "This hwonn speek to uth-errs. Help them un-turr-stand."

A chime at the door sounds with an audible announcement from the guard. Shondre holds up a hand to the others and sees to it. With a touch at the panel, the door opens and Shondre engages in a brief conversation with a figure just beyond the threshold. When she returns to the group, there is a thoughtful, pleased expression in the lines of her face.

The Counselor asks, cynical, yet still hopeful, "Good news?"

Shondre smiles and nods. "Too-day, tokks trans-mitt-ted. Mohr pee-pull see too-day than eff-furr."

Thompson shrugs, missing the meaning, but the Counselor pulls at the thread she offered.

"You're saying the talks today were broadcast to the people on the planet below?"

Shondre nods in affirmation.

"And that more people watched us today than other broadcasts about us since we've been here?"

Shondre closes her eyes slowly, grins, but shakes her head.

The Counselor hesitates, turns his head to one side, and asks, "Then you're saying more people tuned in and watched our program today than..."

"...an-nee pro-kram, *eff-furr*."

"Huh." A smile slowly spreads across the Counselor's face as the magnitude dawns on him. "We're a *hit*."

APEX PREDATORS

Thompson face scrunches, confused. "So, you're saying, *what*?"

"I'm saying we have their attention right now," the Counselor explains. "They're curious, and we need to hold that curiosity as long as we can."

"And you think showing Maiella and me in your next presentation will do that? Show us like...like one of those archival videos on apex predators aboard the *Europa*?"

"I *LOOOOVE* the ones about sharks," Maiella blurts, gripping the arms of her chair. "Six meters long, three thousand kilos, and all teeth—"

"Do I need to *restrain* you?" Munro chides. Maiella rolls her eyes but shuts her mouth, and the colonel presses her back into the seat one-handed. With a harsh glare at his patient, he leans in and dabs solvent at the open skin of her throat.

"Exactly," the Counselor replies. "You and Maiella are big and vicious as Grizzlies, but up to now you've been hard to spot. The Eleto are falling over themselves for a glimpse."

Hopeful, Maiella asks, "So, we're famous?"

"Ehh, *infamous*," the Counselor corrects.

She squints from her chair, eyes shifting side-to-side, lower lip jutting. "What's the difference?"

"Doesn't matter. What *does* matter is I can work with this." He grips his chin in thought. "The trick is going to be keeping interest, without sending them back over the edge into fear. We don't want a live fire demonstration. No hand to hand combat..."

"*There* it is," Munro announces, oblivious to the conversation. "Maiella, that blade nicked your Jugular, as well. Can't believe I missed it."

The Counselor glances at Maiella, and smirks to find her bored by major vascular surgery. Resuming his train of thought, he adds, "We need to make sure everyone knows you're not a pack of mindless monsters. So...how do we show you off without reminding everyone what you've done?"

Thompson ratchets the wristlock of his right gauntlet, disassembles the armor of his forearm, and pulls up the sleeve of his undershirt. Beneath is a crisscross of old burns, tears, and slices, as if his bunk linens were woven from white-hot razor wire.

"This is the price to keep our kind alive. Every one of them hurt. I'd take a thousand more, but believe me, I'd rather write the record in a log than in my own skin."

"Inn-turr-ress-ting," Shondre says. "Kad-Ra hisss-torr-ree is marrk of pay-nn."

"Hmm?" the Counselor asks, turning toward her. Shondre tries to explain in human words, frets, then defaults to Eleto instead. The Counselor nods in understanding.

Thompson asks, "What did she say?"

"She said, Operators are dangerous when threatened with death. But if you take away the threat, the Operator is no longer dangerous. Like you two, here. Take away the threat, and we defuse the bomb, in other words."

Maiella grouses, "Isn't that what we've been saying?"

"*Yessss*," the Counselor says, "but we also show you two as more than armor plated killing machines. We peel back that hard outer layer and show what's beneath. That you've suffered. And that peace would be a relief to you, if offered. So we play to their fascination, giving them a long, *safe* look at this fearsome predator...then I start filling in how and why you came to be this way: you were left with no other choice. And—sorry to put it so bluntly— just like any endangered species, loss of habitat put you on the brink of starvation and forced you to hunt Eleto to survive."

"Isn't because we want to hurt anyone," Maiella contributes, "we're fuckin' hungry."

"*Hunger is universal...*" Thompson echoes, staring distantly.

"Precisely," the Counselor says, holding up a lightly closed hand. "After I've got everyone invested in a story of struggle and survival against enormous odds, I'll give them the ending Fell-Marr-Ghen wants: BOOM, extinction, *the end*. I don't think the people will be satisfied with that, not when it's unforced. Genocide would be a voluntary act on their part. They would be *choosing* violence. I don't think that would sit well with the People's conscience."

Shondre gives the Counselor a suspicious glance and replies in her tongue.

"True, true," the android concedes, "we won't convince anyone that humans are filling any vital ecological niche, like predators do. But the parallel still works: it isn't necessary to drive this being from existence. And if given its proper habitat, it never needs interfere in Eleto life, at all. The Eleto can prove themselves conservationists without becoming our caretakers."

"As good a plan as any, I'd sa—" Maiella takes a sharp inhale through bared teeth and crushes her eyes shut.

"I know this hurts," Munro says, cinching new sutures on her exposed internal Jugular vein. Rivulets of bright blood roll down her neck, adding to the ruddy stains at her collar, but Munro's hands work deftly and precisely. "Stay ab-so-lute-ly still, it'll hurt less..."

Maiella freezes in place, taking short breaths through her nose as the colonel finishes tying off his surgical threads. The bright rivulets halt their flow, and Munro dabs a wadded sponge in the wound, inspecting his work.

"All right," he says, setting the bloody sponge on the edge of the bench. "We got it this time."

"*Jesus*, Munro," Maiella gripes.

Munro sits back on his stool and levels a cool gaze at his patient. "Did I say you could move?"

Smirking, the Counselor asks, "Maiella, do you know who Jesus was?"

"Jesus was a *person*?" she guesses, head against the high back of the chair. "Thought it was just what you said when something hurts a lot." She squints at Munro. "Or when you're getting *stabbed* to death by the senior MedTech."

Munro reaches into his kit and removes a small gun-shaped applicator. "Hmm, I think I missed something, Geek. You've got this other hole, right here, across your face." He grips her chin and places the applicator tip at the corner of her mouth. "I'll just zip a bead of flesh weld here and seal it up for good, shall we?"

"Aaaaah! Don't you dare!" she says, laughing. "Thompson, help! He's gone berserk!"

The Gun crosses his arms. "Oh, I don't know. Colonel knows best."

Maiella's jaw drops and she gawks at him wide-eyed. "Ooooooh, I'm gonna get you for that."

"Now then, Maiella," Munro says earnestly, "will you *please* hold still so I can close properly?"

She huffs in acquiescence. "*Fine*." This time, she keeps her place against the back of the chair, allowing Munro to fully inspect his work and seal the wound, layer by layer.

The Counselor continues his silent observation, amazed to see an otherwise grave and laconic colonel showing a rare moment of humor.

He's been off inhibitors a few months now... the android thinks. *Maybe that's what it takes. If I can draw one or two of them from the Cadre at a time, give them a chance to acclimate... Maybe they CAN all come around... Maybe they'll remember who they're supposed to be.*

Another chime sounds from the door, and Shondre perks up.

"Ex-kyooz, pleez," she says to the group and heads for the door. On the far side is the same aide who visited before. The two converse briefly then they both bow and part.

Thompson waits for Shondre to return and asks, "More good news?"

"We could use it," Counselor replies.

"This hwon hasss inn-turr-fyoo ree-kwest," she announces. "Pee-pull hwant to n-oh hwat was ly-k to liff hwith Hyoo-mans, how this hwon surr-fyf..." She shakes her head in frustration, then continues in her own tongue, letting the Counselor translate for her.

"Shondre said, The People wish to hear about her time with you, how she was able to survive. Until now, no one has ever spent time with humans and lived to tell. That makes her story unique, and many wish to hear it told. She still has friends who can make these arrangements, so she'll go to build interest among the People and keep focus on these talks."

Thompson frets. "Won't we need you at the table?"

Shondre shakes her head, answers in her tongue, and lets the Counselor reply for her.

"She says, We're more than able to speak for ourselves. Not even Fell-Marr-Ghen would dare violate the Great Eleto's protective order, so she doesn't fear for our safety. By separating, we can reach a broader audience than if we're all together in one place. The People's curiosity is fragile, however, so she has to leave soon."

Shondre looks into each of their faces and sighs deeply. "May Speer-ritt bless hyoo and keep hyoo." Her mouth draws into a short, unhappy line across her face, and she turns to leave.

Not ready to be parted yet, the Counselor asks in Shondre's tongue, "(*That* soon? Any advice for us? Any suggestions for dialogues tonight?)"

Shondre turns about, her face bunched uncomfortably, and she says without hesitation, "(After speech, the People will demand to know where Kad-Ra fleet hides. My friend should consider what he will tell them.)"

The Counselor looks at Munro, Thompson, and Maiella as if polling them visually, then answers, "(This one understands and thanks you.)"

Shondre smiles then strides for the door. Just shy of it, she stops again and looks directly at Thompson. In that brief glance, the Counselor sees fear in her eyes. Not of Thompson, but of others like him. Others who wear the same hard skin. Others who will not act in restraint.

Shondre's glance turns to the Counselor, and she confides, "(This one does not want to look away, for fear her friend might evaporate and, in so doing, remove the only obstacle to Kad-Ra's lethal will.)"

"(This one is not going anywhere,)" the Counselor states in total sincerity.

Shondre takes a deep breath and blows it out past her lips. To the group, she urges in their language, "Nott lett hurr deth bee in fain."

"Sharon did *not* die in vain," the Counselor attests. "And we will *never* give up on peace between our peoples."

"No mat-turr hwat happ-penns?"

The Counselor deflects the question to Thompson, and the Gun searches himself to be sure he can commit to such an open ended promise. Swallowing hard, he says resolutely, "No matter what."

Shondre smiles with half of her face, and says with depressing finality, "Un-till see hyoo uh-ginn, ghood-by." She faces the doorway and strides through it, hard-soled shoes clacking until the portal closes behind her.

Nothing More, Nothing Less

The Counselor strides at the head of his delegation, robe swaying from swiftness of pace. After him marches Munro, no longer wearing his tool belt, and the colorful folds of his robe catch the air, spreading grandly to each side. Flanking the colonel in lock step are Thompson and Maiella, wearing Cadre dress gray uniform. The Geek wears her HDI over short-cropped scalp, goggles raised up to her forehead. The Gun's salt and pepper hair is sheared to the skin on sides and back, slicked down on top. Both Operators' expressions are blank, eyes front, arms at their sides and swinging in measured repetition.

Two Eleto soldiers escort them through deserted halls of the spacious vessel. They clutch fat batons in taloned grips. Not once do they look back.

In the monotonous tour, the Counselor lets his eyes roam the walls, banners, and monitors along the way. In one screen, he is delighted to see Shondre seated in a high backed swivel chair, speaking earnestly to a well-dressed interviewer opposite her. The interviewer leans toward her, stroking whiskers at the end of his pointed chin. He points to the scar at her shoulder with a short stylus and asks her about it. Shondre purses her lips modestly and pulls the sheer fabric aside for a better view of the raised green skin. When the interviewer asks about her captivity and how she was treated, Shondre admits, "(This one was angry, close to despair. Living as they did, this one thought she was in a prison cell. Then she learned her accommodations were much like everyone else's. She understood how little they have, how stark and harsh daily life is for them. This one was moved to compassion, and she committed again to reconciling sins of the past.)"

The broadcast continues on monitors farther down the hall, and as the Counselor passes by, the interviewer mentions the loss of her titles, the conversion of her estate to a monument for those killed, and the loss of her other self, Gro-Elto. He asks if she regrets the high price she has paid. Shondre dips her head, the corners of her mouth pulled into a deep frown. "(Not a moment passes that this one does not feel the absence of Gro-Elto. That pains the most and will never fully heal. As for the rest, this one will always find a way to serve the people she loves. Titles, status, places, things... To have lost them means little when she still has so much more than humans do... This one can move freely, she can breathe open air and feel warm sun upon her face. She can rejoice in natural beauty not found in the sterile reaches of space. Fresh water flows from taps in her room. Her bed is soft and luxurious. No. This one *knows* how fortunate she is.)"

Intrigued, the Counselor continues down the corridor, passing another bank of monitors carrying the same program. The interviewer crosses his legs and sits back thoughtfully, then asks if she had considered the possibility that by eliminating the humans, she might have kept everything she had lost. Shondre nods, and replies, "(This one has considered that, yes. If she had acted to hunt the humans she might have kept her *things*...perhaps even her beloved Other Self...yet she would have lost her soul. When love is her true motivation, she never feels shame or regret. No matter the price to self, this one will keep love and compassion in the arches of her chest.)"

The Counselor smiles fondly, wanting to hold his place and watch the rest of her interview, yet he continues onward.

Screens farther ahead show recaps from earlier events: the brawl between Da-Indo-Hass and Maiella, excerpts from Fell-Marr-Ghen's opposition speech. And then the Counselor spies a clip of himself upon the dais, speaking boldly with arms spread to the risers. He scowls to see himself grandstanding, lacking in modesty.

Maybe that's why our reception was so cool...

The next bank of screens shows an Eleto of advanced age, hunched beneath a hooded cloak of taupe fabric. Sparse white whiskers frame his bunched mouth and run down past his chest. A necklace of black wooden beads hangs around his collar.

"(Never before have the People been so divided,)" the Pontiff states, "(so at odds with brother, sister, father, and mother. There is a war not just in the depths of space, but in the spirit—a war that claws at what ties our many nations together. Even now the Decree of Lak-Vass-Etto bisects the body politic and leaves each half paralyzed. Once, we were of singular mind and clear in our vision. But the sins of our past have clouded our thoughts and turned our eyes milky with cataracts. This one prays for our wise leaders to rightly guide us and divine a solution that leaves the People unburdened in the arches of the chest. That is all this one has to say.)"

The Counselor looks away from the bank of monitors.

Decree of Lak-Vass-Etto? I'll have to ask Shondre about that.

As the procession nears the assembly hall, holoscreens show close ups of sickly Eleto. Eyes covered in broken capillaries are recessed in gaunt, exhausted faces. Victims bleed from gums and the beds of their claws, shivering beneath sweat-stained medical sheets.

An outbreak of disease this close to our arrival? Won't be dismissed as coincidence, he thinks, and the Counselor frowns at a thought he does not want to voice. Instead, he looks over his shoulder at Munro and finds the colonel gazing into screens of ill Eleto, corners of his mouth lifted in barely concealed satisfaction. The Counselor faces front before the colonel can meet his glance. Eyes wide, he thinks, *Munro knows something... Could he be responsible? Did he bring something with him on the trip? Or did Ralla slip him a parcel? Something to soften up defenses prior to her assault?* The android shakes the dilemma aside. *One thing at a time... Focus on the task at hand. Ask Munro afterward.*

The hallway ahead rises to arched ceilings with a familiar gate at the far end. Guards step out to where the doors meet at center and salute the approaching escorts. Then, with military precision, they move like mirror images and swing the doors open.

Escorts salute the guards as they pass, step to each side inside the gate, and stamp to attention.

Crowds of Eleto shuffle about in the riser seating, carrying on thousands of individual conversations, making their way to seats and inspecting the cushions before settling into them. Some point at the human delegation, calling attention to them. The Counselor prepares for another hail of derision, but there is little of the naked hostility from before, no hurling of epithets or drink containers. Instead, there is narrow-eyed suspicion coupled with an inability to look away as heads crane around companions for a better view.

The Counselor strides briskly toward the mineral table atop the dais at the hall's focus. The same Eleto officials are gathered on one side, clustered around Fell-Marr-Ghen. The Advocate in Opposition catches sight of the human delegation and makes comment to his comrades. The cluster turns as one toward the approaching delegation and laughs.

Undaunted, the Counselor leads Munro, Maiella, and Thompson to their places at the table. They stand and wait patiently, hands resting on the back of their seats.

Holoscreens above the table flicker into existence. In them, remote Eleto officials settle into comfortable chairs, tolerating the primping, brushing, and powdering of assistants with aloof boredom.

Unseen speakers thump twice throughout the hall, and an Eleto voice announces the arrival of His Excellency, Dekkto-Mayah-Tayaloh, the Will of the People. Side conversations in the meeting hall immediately cease. Clustered officials at the table disperse toward their seats and stand behind them, attention turned toward the entry way opposite the human delegation. At the far end of the lane between risers, tall doors part in the middle, guards take position at the threshold, and a tall black-robed Eleto strides toward the dais. Two brutish bodyguards keep pace at his side, scanning every nearby face for a sign of disorder with orange-tinted eyes. Both are clad in heavy body armor, sheathed blade on one hip, holstered pistol on the other, and rifle slung over a shoulder. Faceplates of their helmets are raised, expressions deadly serious and on alert.

When Dekkto reaches his chair at the table, all officials bow deeply, hand on chest. The Counselor likewise bows, signaling to Munro, Maiella, and Thompson to do the same. When all straighten, the Great Eleto looks everyone at the table in the eye.

"(The Sons of Elko-Graben have ever been opponents to dialogue with Humans. Now, they deem their will strong enough to speak for all and have made attempt on this one's life.)"

A collective gasp resounds through the risers, so many lungs drawing air at once it can be felt in the eardrums.

"(Their plot is foiled, their networks are broken. Culprits have been apprehended and transferred for re-education. There remains no possibility their plan can succeed. Even so, by law, this one must accept guards of his person until it is certain no other attempts will be made.)" Dekkto spreads his black robe and seats himself while bodyguards take position on either side.

Officials at the table gape in open-mouthed disbelief, offering obsequious comments of incredulity. He silences them by raising an ancient hand. "(Overzealous factions do not deter this one's service. There is much to do. Let us not waste any more time.)" Dekkto turns his gaze upon the Counselor. "(If Kon-Zill-Urr is prepared, we would hear his words.)"

The Counselor dips his head respectfully. "(We are grateful, Excellency. This one is ready to proceed.)"

Dekkto blinks slowly and nods, then gestures for all to be seated.

The Counselor waits for everyone to settle in again and for the hall to quiet down. Silence descends with surprising swiftness.

"(This one is honored, once more, to share his story with the People,)" the android begins then he pauses for reflection. "(These two cultures have struggled to communicate. And in the absence of dialogue we found animosity, distrust, fear. We fear what we do not know, what we do not understand. And this one must beg forgiveness for not properly introducing ourselves. Indeed, how can anyone negotiate in good faith with a stranger? We remedy that today.)"

He gestures toward Maiella, palm up, and raises his hand. Maiella slides back from the table, stands, and steps around her chair. Standing beside the Counselor, she looks out across the faces in the risers. Her goggles glint in the bright hall lights.

"(Her name is Maiella,)" the Counselor announces. "(She is of the Cadre, an Operator of particular focus and skill.)" He leans close and whispers to her. She nods and peels off her uniform jacket, draping it over the back of her chair.

"(What you see is a person of intense physical training, one who has honed strength and reflex to the very height of possibility. When she was ordered out on missions, she wore dark armor that allowed her to endure incredible shocks and stresses. But underneath that, there was always this person inside.)" He turns to face her. "(She is one of wit and humor. One who thinks and feels deeply. One who carries the ultimate burden of mankind's survival, making it her *personal responsibility.* She is nothing more nor less than what you see: a highly motivated person who wants her people to remain alive. Yes, she once ranged the Black and ambushed with lethal stealth. But look upon her and know...*there are no Ravenous Ghosts!*)"

"(As we consider how awful it was for a crew to encounter her and others like her, we must also consider the toll her service required. Her entire life is spent training and serving on these endless missions. And what can she look forward to at the end of this service? Once her body is utterly spent, her reward will be 'retirement' from life and her face will be engraved on a memorial wall.)" He squares his chin and puts his hands out at his sides. "(That's it.)"

He lets his arms fall, hands slapping against his thighs. Turning to Maiella, he whispers again. She obliges by removing her HDI and setting the headgear on the polished table.

"(No doubt, you have noticed the metal embedded in her skull and may have wondered if it was some kind of jewelry. In fact, it is an interface that allows her to connect directly to a computer and program it at the speed of thought. If ever the Eleto wondered how it could be that their ships were taken over so quickly, this innovation is the key.)"

"Ahem," Maiella grunts. When the Counselor looks at her, she says sternly under her breath, "If Munro knew what you were saying, he'd be *flipping out* right now."

320

"Why?"

"You're giving up one of our biggest secrets."

The Counselor nods in agreement. "That's right, I am. Secrets keep us enemies. We're shining light on the whole show. And if we're successful, you'll never go on another Collection Rotation again."

Standing straight, Maiella says, "Okay, okay, I trust you. I'll just go back to being your *visual aid*, I guess."

The Counselor shoots her a wry glance, then resumes.

"(Through these metal contact terminals, she takes direct control of a vessel in deep space. Once interfaced, she becomes the brain and the ship becomes her body. She can see through its sensors, she can hear through its antennae arrays, she can roam the reaches of space merely by thinking where she needs to go. Every system is an extension of her will and it obeys her impulse instantly. Now you see how they are so quick, how they amplify their firepower with such precision, how they coordinate attacks with small vessels so effectively, and how their assaults are so hard to predict or counter. Once an Operator has committed to attack, there *will* be casualties.)"

He leans over to her again and whispers into her ear. Maiella raises her eyebrows then shrugs and peels off her undershirt. She holds her arms out straight, wadded undershirt clutched in one hand, and she turns a full circle. Mutters and guffaws filter from the crowd at the multitude of her scars.

"(Now you see the price of service every Cadre Operator pays. This is her history, her archive of missions served, and it is gouged, ripped, and scorched into her flesh. Yes, she is deadly quick and unbelievably tough. But how much more would she rather use that strength clearing a field and tilling earth? How much more would she *rather* apply that quick mind to planning a community? How much more would she *rather* choose a profession that does not inflict pain and injury, that does not come at the cost of everything else that makes a life worth living...things like art, family, home, the fruits of nature, fresh air and drinking water that has not already been passed through their bodies and recycled a thousand times...)"

"(True, this woman was made to be a *weapon*, but she is not some mindless tool. And the same qualities that make her so effective as a soldier are *far* more valuable in constructive pursuits.)"

The Counselor tents his hands in thought.

"(In ancient times, after war, our people would beat their swords into plowshares and their spears into pruning hooks. In precisely the same way, this woman can be more than an instrument of death. She yearns to apply her many talents to solving complex problems...*building* things, not tearing them down! But where can she go to prove this?)"

Maiella clears her throat to get the Counselor's attention and mutters through the side of her mouth, "Can I get dressed? It's cold in here."

The Counselor nods. "Of course."

Maiella stretches the elastic undershirt over herself and slips her arms through the sleeves of her jacket, finishing with a shiver as she clasps it. Hiking a thumb toward her chair, she asks, "Done with me yet?"

"Actually, let's keep you here a moment." The android peeks around her. "Thompson, would you join us?"

The Gun rises from his chair then stands rigidly beside Maiella. The Counselor takes his place beside them, instantly dwarfed by the Gun's height.

"(This man's name is Thompson. Like Maiella, he has served as a soldier all his life...until now. And like Maiella, the costs of his long service are branded into his flesh.)" He looks up at the Gun and asks, "Would you remove your jacket and undershirt?"

Thompson nods and strips down to his uniform trousers then places hands on his head, biceps lightly flexed, and turns a circle. Patches of different colored skin are stitched together over bulks of solid muscle. Old gray burns are crossed by newer pink incisions and perforations.

Many in the crowd groan at the savagery recorded in his bare back and chest. Others cover their mouths and shake their heads.

"(Thompson is the leader of a Team, which typically consists of three individuals. He is a master of combat, be it close quarters, long distance, and everything in between. He is the tactician, the strategist, the driving force, and the iron determination.)

"(There is always a team member like Maiella, one who can interface with a wide variety of machines. There is always a leader, like Thompson. And as physically imposing as Thompson is, the third member of the team is even larger. This person is the medic and field surgeon, the demolitions expert and remover of obstacles. The technician, engineer, and repairman. Together, these three comprise a skill set that could well serve an entire village! All the space in our heads we dedicate to song lyrics and movie quotes, to memories of desserts and dinners, they devote purely to perfection of their craft. When all other distractions are removed, it is *astounding* what an individual can accomplish.)

"(We look upon them now, how grossly oversized they have become, how narrow their purpose and focus, how physically abused they are throughout horribly violent lives... *Our people were never meant to be like this*.)

"(The moment they breathe open air, the *moment* they taste flavors of vine, tree, and root...they remember *at a genetic level* who they are supposed to be. The people who stand before you once ranged the Black, monstrous, horrible to behold. Yet here they stand before you, voluntarily disarmed, no longer terrors of space. For the first time ever, *they have a choice*, another path to pursue aside from killing. That is why they are here. There is no bloodlust, only the desire to remain alive and keep the memory of those who came before. If given a chance to live without scarcity or threat, they can be the people they are *supposed* to be with wisdom earned through grim experience.)"

The Counselor taps Thompson on the shoulder and gives a nod to get dressed. Once the Gun clasps his uniform jacket, the android thanks both Operators then gestures toward the table, where they pull out chairs and take their seats.

Munro's head swivels between the two, and he asks them, "What did he say?"

Maiella opens her mouth to answer, but censors herself. Thompson answers instead, "We'll fill you in once we wrap up."

Munro grimaces and slumps back in his chair, displeased, when the Counselor calls to him. The MedTech perks up and turns about. Pointing to his chest, he asks, "Me?"

The Counselor smiles and nods. "Come on up. Let them have a look at you."

Munro takes a deep breath then pushes off the arms of his chair, asking, "You're not going to make me disrobe, are you?"

"No, no," the android replies, grinning. "Just be yourself."

Munro juts his lower lip, crosses his large and small arms, and peers out at the crowd, feet shoulder width apart.

"Well, maybe a less *stand-offish* version of yourself," the android suggests.

"I have no idea what you mean."

"Here," the Counselor begins, "arms at your sides, stand normally. Imagine you're about to address the Leadership Council."

Munro narrows his stance and stands straight, shoulders back.

"That'll do," the Counselor coaches then he turns toward the crowd. "(This one is pleased to introduce Colonel Munro, the Cadre's second most senior officer.)"

"Do I bow?" Munro mutters.

The Counselor shakes his head. Munro faces front again.

"(Colonel Munro has never been on a combat mission. The asymmetry of his arms made him unsuitable for a role as soldier, yet there was far more he could contribute. Munro is a master engineer and healer, personally responsible for every generation raised at Cadre One. He was directly responsible for the physical plant of Cadre One, every machine and system, every mechanical function and process. Indeed, as hard as Cadre soldiers labored to bring in resources, Munro worked much harder to keep the old station running. He had to ensure the food processors supplied enough calories. He had to deliver a viable generation every three years just to maintain the population.)" The Counselor spreads his arms and looks up at the ceiling. "(Imagine being responsible for this entire vessel, every crawlspace, every circuit path and power tap. Every vending machine, heater, recycler... Imagine being responsible for the health of all aboard. Sure, there are assistants to handle the actual work, but imagine the duty is yours to ensure all needs are tended. It is an *enormous* responsibility that makes this one's head swim.)

"(When Cadre One was discovered, Munro evacuated with his staff. He would still be out there, in fact, if not for Madame Shondre's passionate persuasion. And let us be plain: Lady Shondre *is* the reason we are here...she is the reason these soldiers have laid aside their weapons so you could meet them as they truly are, without filters of myth or legend.)"

The android pauses again, taking time to look into the eyes of his audience.

"(This one sees many new faces around him, all belonging to unique individuals with rich stories that might be shared. In the telling of these stories, we might come to know the People as brilliant and beautiful. Not as enemies, but as thinking, feeling beings who crave life as much as we do and are every bit as deserving of it as we are. This one would deem himself lucky if, in listening to the People's journey, he might gain greater perspective, might gain wisdom that cannot be found elsewhere. Experience is the great treasure of any nation. It cannot be stolen. When shared it multiplies, leaving all enriched.)

"(Even our gallant antagonist, Fell-Marr-Ghen, shares his story in harsh counterpoints. We cannot expect anyone to forget the awful conflict we have both endured. There is much pain we have visited upon each other, and memory of those events is lasting. We *should* be cautious. We should take what time we must so that we can heal the rift and leave this *pointless, fruitless war behind*. Perhaps after we have listened and truly heard one another, we might find ourselves safe in each other's company. Someday, we might even come to know each other as friends. In the meantime, let us first pledge to *do no harm* and keep our channels open. Thank you for hearing this one's words.)"

The Counselor bows humbly. Taking the cue, Munro bows, as well.

Contemplative quiet yields to murmuring at the table and throughout the risers. To the Counselor's amazement, reserved applause comes from scattered pockets around the hall. As he and Munro stand upright, they both gaze at the crowd with careful optimism.

Dekkto leans on one arm of his chair and grips his chin. He levels a shrewd gaze upon the Counselor. "(We have heard Kon-Zill-Urr's words and remark at their clarity. It does the People honor that an ambassador so carefully learns their manner.)" He swivels toward the opposite side of the table, and adds, "(Does the Advocate in Opposition offer rebuttal?)"

Fell-Marr-Ghen leans forward, both palms on the table, eyes staring a hole through the Counselor. "(Indeed, he *does*, Excellency.)"

PERFECT MATCH

Fell-Marr-Ghen rises from his chair with eagerness that sends it skating toward the edge of the dais. An official to his left catches it by the arm and slides it back to the table as the Advocate begins a slow lap around the table, finger tips pressed together in thought.

"(We have heard intriguing appeals today. Appeals, but for their origin, would sound genuine.)"

He parts his hands, and strolls through the gap.

"(Yes, we *all* crave peace and long life, as if this was *ever* in dispute. It seems Kon-Zill-Urr would tell us things we already know so that it might appear we have much in common. That there is much we can relate to. That our differences are not irreconcilable. Good citizens, these are the *tactics* of influence, of corruption, used solely so we might drop our guard.)"

Fell-Mar-Ghen tents his hands again.

"(There is no question his mechanical mind is sharp. Yet this one would remind the People that there are no arches in his chest. No blood pumps through his limbs. And the circuits with which he thinks are of pure logic, pure programming, just another weapon in the Kad-Ra arsenal to make us hesitate, to make us unsure, to make us *question* what we know about our enemy. After so many generations, and so many confrontations, *why now*? Why did they wait SO LONG before suing for peace?)"

Fell-Marr-Ghen spreads his arms to the crowd, letting the question hang in the silence.

"(Because *they are up to something*. They are regrouping after a tremendous defeat. Too weak to launch a direct attack, they ply our sympathies in hope our defenses might slip.)"

He whirls about, shoulders square, and declares to the Counselor, "(That

326

will *never* happen, machine!)"

The Advocate resumes his path around the dais.

"(For sake of debate, let us say they can be taken at their word. Let our imaginations *run wild* and pretend they desire an end to hostilities, that this is not some orchestrated ruse to weaken our resolve. What about justice?)"

Again, he pauses and looks out to the crowds, arms spread, palms out.

"(Do we forget about the thousands recently murdered? Do we forget about the *single deadliest terrorist attack* visited upon us in thirty generations? Can we look across the table at these *extremists* and NOT demand justice?)"

He pauses, looks down at the floor, and tugs at his chin whiskers.

"(To satisfy the shades of so many murdered, we must first know for certain who perpetrated these hideous crimes.)" He peers at Thompson and cocks his head to one side. "(Hard to tell them apart, especially when hidden beneath armor.)" He turns toward the crowd with a wicked grin. "(Or is it?)"

Without looking, the Advocate points to screens above the table, and video of a darkened landing bay plays. Thick smoke chokes the air, fed by smutty flames from fuel lines and overturned baggage trains. Intense lamps shine through the haze, illuminating a distant entryway. Two small objects hurtle in from the entryway, bounce of the deck, then detonate savagely, knocking out the bright lamps. Immediately after, a dark figure can just be discerned rushing in through the entryway, rifle level and flashing away.

Fell-Marr-Ghen shouts, "(Freeze video!)" Video playback halts, soldier mid-stride. "(Zoom in on the subject,)" he orders, and the frame magnifies the Operator. In low light, the image is grainy and blurred, but the Operator's visor is raised, and the pallid skin of his face is stark contrast to the dark armor.

"(Enhance its face,)" the Advocate states. The soldier's face sharpens slightly. Features are hazy beneath the soot and grime covering it, but there are three parallel cuts down one cheek.

Thompson stares at the screen stone-faced, jaw locked. Fell-Marr-Ghen comes around the table and leans down beside the Gun, making a point to inspect a faint trio of parallel scars on his cheek. The Advocate reaches toward him with three taloned fingers, and without touching, traces the scars, nods, and stands upright.

"(It is as this one suspected. But let us be certain, shall we? Next video.)"

The screens shift to a view of a sleek and gleaming limousine. Its loading ramp is down with heaps of bloodied Eleto soldiers at the base. A massive Cadre soldier limps down the ramp from inside the vessel and is met part way by a taller soldier carrying the legless remains of another Cadre Soldier.

PLASMA RAIN

A circular notch is burned out of the tall soldier's arm, and entire plates of armor at his thigh, shoulder, neck and elbow have been blasted away. The tall soldier passes over his grievously wounded comrade then snatches two grenades from the big soldier's waist. An instant later, a barrage of weapon fire smashes the tall soldier in the back, knocking him flat to the ramp. A hole is burned completely through his thigh where the armor is missing and he strains to press himself up from the ramp.

"(Freeze video,)" Fell-Marr-Ghen shouts again and the image halts. He wets his lips and looks at Thompson saying with relish, "(It was kind of our... *guest*...to have removed his clothing earlier. Let us compare these injuries with the 'history' branded into his skin.)"

The video screens divide down the middle, with the frozen view of the soldier on one side, and a recent image of Thompson bare-chested, hands on his head on the other. Red dots populate on the left, indicating sites of injury. Then, dots populate across Thompson's chest and arms on the right, where major scars correspond precisely.

"(Ahhh,)" the Advocate says, looking up at the screens. "(Interesting how well these injuries match, is it not?)" To Thompson, he says with a smirk. "(Especially when the suspect's height, mass, and physical proportion are *also* a match. Of course, the People deserve proof so that there is no doubt...)"

"(One of Madame Shondre's own bodyguards did battle with this Opp-Purr-Ray-Tor, clawing those marks into his face. We compared material left on his talons to samples taken from the beast while in quarantine.)" He points at the screens without looking, keeping his gaze riveted to Thompson. The images change to a genetic pattern of the sample taken from the dead bodyguard on the left. On the right is a genetic pattern taken during the Gun's quarantine. They slide together in the middle, overlapping perfectly. The crowd gasps.

"(*A perfect match*,)" the Advocate says bitterly. With another flick of his hand toward the screens, videos stream one after another of detonations, executions, building collapses, screaming crowds, an Eleto male being shoved from an airborne shuttle, and Shondre being dragged out from under the bodies of her guards, a bayonet at her throat. Thompson is at the center of all of them.

The Counselor repeatedly looks from the screens to the Gun seated beside him, disbelieving the amount of violence occurring before his eyes, struggling to cope with or even comprehend such continuous brutality.

The Advocate whirls about to the crowd. Stabbing an accusing arm at the tall soldier, he bellows, "(Allow me to introduce the *tactician*, the

328

strategist, the *master of combat* whose *rampage of terror* ended more than *SIX THOUSAND LIVES*!)"

ULTIMATE EXAMPLE

The crowd roils in their seats, fists raised, shouting in agitation and howling. Even austere Dekkto stiffens in his seat, impassive mask falling away. In an instant, the Great Eleto rebuilds his authoritarian edifice and he levels a cool stare at Thompson.

"(We can forgive Madame Shondre for becoming confused,)" Fell-Marr-Ghen continues, "(as we can all see she was clearly brutalized. And we understand painfully well the psychology of being a hostage, how easily the captive can be *manipulated* into sympathizing with the very ones who abused her. We must give her all the care and support she needs so that she may someday recover.)

"(But for this *creature* at our table, *there can be no forgiveness*! The People demand justice, Excellency!)"

A roar of enthusiasm surges from the crowd.

The Great Eleto breathes deeply, considering a reply, then raises his hand to quell the shouts. "(And what justice would the People demand?)"

"(To have him QUARTERED in the marketplace,)" Fell-Marr-Ghen spits, "(and his head mounted on a spike! After time and weather has stripped skin from skull, let us erase all trace, so that this *murdering savage* will utterly perish from memory!)"

Dekkto frowns in disappointment. "(That is not our way. In confronting barbarism, we do not, ourselves, become barbarians.)"

Fell-Marr-Ghen bows slightly in deference. "(This one once believed the same, Excellency. Yet we have only touched upon the enormity of their depravity. As gratuitous are the offenses of this Opp-Purr-Ray-Tor, these monsters perpetrate crimes still more despicable! And we need to set an ultimate example.)" The Advocate turns toward the first row of seats where his aides sit, and he beckons. A young Eleto in neutral gray clothing rises from his chair and carries a hefty cloth-wrapped object about as long as his forearms to the dais. With effort, he hefts it up to the table, careful not to dump it on the polished mineral. He bows to Fell-Marr-Ghen and returns to his seat, relieved to be free of the load.

"(This was pulled from El-Gaard's warship after destruction of the Human base,)" Fell-Marr-Ghen announces, toying with the knot in the cloth, elongating the crowd's anticipation.

All eyes at the table are drawn to the object as if by magnetism, and the Counselor feels reluctant awe at how his opponent has so thoroughly captured the crowd. He sneaks a glance at his comrades, searching their faces to see if they have any idea what it might be. Thompson and Maiella peer at the object suspiciously, but Munro sits with fingers interlaced, disinterested.

With a flick of the wrist, Fell-Marr-Ghen undoes the knot and allows the wrapping to fall away. Beneath is a battered and deformed projectile. Its warhead has multiple ports, all popped open. At sight of it, Munro crosses his arms.

The Great Eleto leans closer, intrigued. "(What is it?)"

"(Germ warfare, Excellency,)" the Advocate answers then locks his gaze on Munro. "(The humans argue *against* the Decree of Lak-Vass-Etto, and then employ the same weapons of genocide against us!)"

The Counselor launches from his seat. Turning toward Munro, he shouts above the agitated crowd, "*What is this thing*, Colonel? Is it a germ bomb?"

Munro sniffs. "It is."

Fell-Marr-Ghen shouts to the risers, "(Observe their machine as it feigns surprise! Such theatrics! Should we ask it to respond? Or have we had our fill of its *lies* for one day?)"

"(Excellency,)" the Counselor pleads, "(this one begs a moment to confer with his associates. These accusations *must* be answered without delay.)"

The Great Eleto regards the Counselor with half-lidded eyes. "(Does the Advocate require private chambers to concoct his response?)"

Concoct? the Counselor echoes mentally. *He's already convinced.* Without further hesitation, the android replies, "(No, Excellency. We hide nothing. And the People deserve an explanation, *immediately*.)"

"(Then take what time you will,)" Dekkto concludes. He raps his knuckles against the table. Officials at the table stand and congregate around Fell-Marr-Ghen, clapping him on the back, flattering and complementing how skillfully he exposed the Human pretenders.

"Colonel Munro, Thompson, Maiella," the Counselor calls. The three give their attention to the android and rise glumly from their chairs.

"That's you in the videos, isn't it, Thompson?"

The Gun nods.

"How could you *do* that? That wasn't a matter of obtaining supplies...that was *wanton, cruel*!"

Thompson looks down at the Counselor, brow scrunched in irritation. "The planet of our origin...occupied by an enemy who massacred every man, woman, and child. They now claim to be *righteous*? In time of war?"

"The Eleto who committed those crimes are long dead, Thompson! These people had nothing to do with it!"

"Maybe so, Counselor," Maiella says. "Maybe they aren't the ones who did the killing. But they're enjoying all the benefit, *right*? Blueskins killed us off, moved right in like they deserved it, and left us to scrape our lives out of a *rock*."

"*Blueskins*? I don't want to hear that term again, Maiella, not *ever*. They're called, *Eleto*, or, *The People*. By giving in to hate speech, we debase ourselves. And if our opponent's words can make you abandon Shondre's dream so easily, you show yourself no better than he is."

Maiella's brow lifts and her mouth opens in protest, but Thompson picks up her thread and runs with it.

"So these *Eleto* benefit from our genocide," Thompson states. "They take over our proper home and try to keep us from it. But they hold *no* responsibility to undo the past and make things right...so bringing the fight here was wrong... Is that what you're saying?"

"Thompson, killing them solves nothing!"

"I see. So in death, the destroyers of mankind escape judgment. They're beyond justice now, unpunished, and we're supposed to accept that, to accept everything that's happened as a result. Just let them keep everything they stole from us. Fast forward to now, when I've brought a similar action, only it's on an *infinitesimally* smaller scale. *I'm* to be executed, while the Eleto who ordered the genocides remain honored ancestors? Fine. If it satisfies them and lets our people come home, so be it. I submit to their *judgment*."

'The HELL you will," Maiella growls. "You're *not* giving yourself over to them."

"I'm the one in the videos, Maiella. I'm recognized."

"And I'd've been *right there with you*, if they'd let me. I wouldn't have hesitated the way Beckert did. It would have been worse, don't pretend otherwise, so get used to the idea that we're all in this together." She turns to the Counselor. "And it wasn't *wanton*. It was *survival*, Counselor. Thompson swore he'd get Beckert home if he could. Everything you see in those videos is the path he and Argo had to take to bring him back alive." She looks away and glares at the smug officials across the table. "In time of war, what's the point of restraint? *They* held nothing back when they burned us from Earth and the colonies. They claim superiority now? *Pffeh*. All I see are soft, pampered fools who've never missed a meal. They haven't got a *clue* about hard life, yet they talk like they know everything." She sneers. "They wouldn't last a *week* in our situation."

The Counselor considers the Operators' perspectives. With a sigh, he admits, "You both have fair points. I can work with that, I think." Fretting, the Counselor looks at Munro and says, "About that lump of metal on the table, Colonel... Care to explain?"

Munro's face scrunches. "Explain what? It's an augmented warhead with viral payload."

Frustrated, the android demands, *"Where did it come from?"*

"We incubated sufficient virus and manufactured shells at Cadre One."

"Okay, so that weapons plant is gone. You can't make any more—"

Maiella butts in, "Plenty more at Cadre Two. Whole pallets on ice."

The Counselor looks up at the ceiling in exasperation. "And what *else* came from Cadre Two, Colonel? Any more surprises I should know about?"

Munro's mouth becomes a tight line across his face. "Some medical archives from an insane researcher named, Honniker."

"Any other *weapons*?"

"Nothing I'm aware of."

The Counselor tilts his head. "This isn't a time to keep secrets, Munro."

"Obscuring truth is a *Colonist* skill, not mine! There is *nothing else* I'm aware of."

"All right, all right," the android placates, but Munro fires back, sore at his word being questioned,

"Shao-Lo brought the original strain back from Cadre Two. Said the virus is a variant of what the Eleto used against us on Earth and the Colonies. Researchers at Cadre Two didn't have it ready in time to stop the Eleto advance, but they had plenty of time to perfect it afterward. It's been stored there ever since.

"O'Kai knew the Eleto were on their way to Cadre One, so he ordered me to load every tenth shell with a viral package."

"What we saw on the monitors earlier, sick Eleto, bleeding out... Is that the result?"

Munro nods gravely. "I'd need to run a culture to be certain, but symptoms match expectations."

The Counselor grips his temples and looks at his feet. "How do I explain this? We used the same weapon they did...wipes out our moral high ground."

Munro squints as if he cannot believe he has to spell out something so obvious. "Never mind moral high ground, the Eleto were intent on wiping *US* out! And now that Cadre One is LOST, we're going to use *everything* at our disposal to fight back. EVERYTHING."

The Counselor looks from Munro to Thompson, to Maiella. All three share the same hard expression of one backed into a corner, determined to fight their way out of it. Running a hand through his hair, the Counselor glances at the officials across the table and at Fell-Marr-Ghen, in particular. The Advocate stares back the way a rich man stares at a street beggar, in disgust and disdain, wishing the eyesore away because he is unwilling to dirty his own hands.

He thinks he's beaten us, the android senses.

"(Excellency,)" the Counselor says over the crowd's dull roar, "(this one would answer the Advocate's accusations.)"

Dekkto regards the Counselor with eyes so venerable they might have witnessed the rise and fall of continents. "(The People will hear his words.)"

The audience goes immediately silent. All lean forward in their seats again.

"(Thompson has confirmed he is the one in the videos shown.)"

Fell-Marr-Ghen grins so broadly his teeth show. The multitude stirs with agitation, thousands of voices muttering in guttural revulsion. But the Counselor holds his arms up, and the crowd settles to a sullen murmur.

"(The facts are plain,)" the android declares, "(the events are clearly visible on these screens. Trial is unnecessary. Therefore, we offer this man to Eleto justice on a single condition: that *all* who have participated in episodes of mass murder are exhumed, tried, convicted, and scrubbed from Eleto history as despicable criminals. If Thompson is to be judged, so must *every* decision maker, every soldier, pilot, engineer, architect, builder, chemist, geneticist, assembler, technician, politician, *everyone* who advocated, committed, or contributed to the conscious and carefully executed genocide of humanity. Let Thompson's piked head stand alongside the skulls of *all* who have assisted in atrocity. Then, in grim equality, we may witness the terrible cost of mass murder.)"

He looks out at a crowd gone instantly sullen, seeing in so many twisted expressions an unwillingness to follow his path of reasoning. So he turns to Dekkto, instead.

"(For the Advocate in Opposition to expect Thompson—who killed thousands—to give himself up for punishment without equal treatment of Eleto—who killed *billions*—would be embarrassing hypocrisy.)"

The Counselor turns on Fell-Marr-Ghen.

"(It would be the limited reasoning of a soft, well-fed bureaucrat who has never missed a meal, much less faced starvation—a bureaucrat who has been sheltered by the hard work of others throughout a comfortable life and is incapable of comprehending what it takes to survive without staff and servants. Perhaps an exchange program would be useful, so he might experience Cadre life in full. We're certain the insights would be enlightening.)"

The android pauses, rounding his shoulders in contrition.

"(As for the projectile on the table...it is with profound shame this one confirms it is a viral weapon used in defense of Cadre One. If your scientists study it, they will find it was adapted from the same viral strain deployed on Earth and the Human colonies. This weapon was used on us, studied, understood, and adapted to the Eleto genome.)

"(Weapons of mass destruction *are* reprehensible, awful. But let us consider this weapon's origin before we close our minds in righteous indignation. And, facing destruction of their home, the Cadre did not hold back anything in their arsenal. They fought with everything they had. In short, this underscores how badly we need to de-escalate our conflict! We *must* step back from the brink of mutual destruction before we—)"

Fell-Marr-Ghen guffaws. "(*Mutual* destruction?)"

The Counselor turns toward the Advocate with grim expression, and says, "(Yes. *Mutual* destruction.)" The android stares, daring his opponent to say more. Instead, Fell-Marr-Ghen snorts and turns sideways in his seat, shaking his head.

To Dekkto, the Counselor continues, "(What we see in these videos is Thompson's determination to getting his team home alive. His methods are shocking, extreme, traumatizing. To civilized eyes this appears as zealotry, madness, bloodthirst... What it *is*, Excellency, is the horror of *total* war. Let the Advocate in Opposition show all of the archival footage he wishes, it only proves the truth: war is *madness*. Until we can truly walk in each other's place, until we can see from the other side of the battlefield...until we BOTH agree that war *IS* madness...and demand better of ourselves...violence goes on.)

"(Colonel Munro is familiar with the virus in that projectile. If he were to assist in developing anti-viral measures and containing the spread, would that help us ease hostilities? Because he can do that. And he *will* do that—)"

Fell-Marr-Ghen scoffs and laughs out loud. The Counselor turns his full attention on him.

"(It seems the Advocate in Opposition thrives on division, as though he has something to gain in the business of killing. Previously this one believed he played the role of caution and prudence. Yet all he has offered thus far is *petty incitement*! He points at the viciousness of warfare, conveniently forgetting the billions left unburied in dead cities below. He points at these soldiers, claiming to know all he needs to judge their fates, while his belly has never felt the bite of starvation. There is NOTHING to be proud of in this conflict. There is no refuge of dignity, no bunker of moral rectitude. The only justice we can find is to set aside hatred and call a truce. Yet the Advocate in Opposition argues for *more* distrust, *more* bloodshed, *more* lives lost! Excellency, such a position is indefensible, and after his repetitive calls against armistice, we have grown *weary* of his *warmongering*!)"

Fell-Marr-Ghen leaps up from his seat, stung. "(*Warmongering*? How *DARE you, wretched machine*—?)"

"(SILENCE!)" Dekkto intones. Fell-Marr-Ghen's mouth clamps shut and he sinks into his seat with a bitter scowl.

The Counselor waits patiently as the air clears and rustles of the crowd cease.

"(The Advocate will continue,)" Dekkto states.

"(We thank his Excellency,)" the Counselor answers. Taking a moment to gather his thoughts, he continues, "(We do not propose that anyone should be absolved from justice. Thompson's actions ARE heinous and demand redress. But an execution cures nothing, educates no one. Instead, what if he labored to fix the structures and repaired the damage done? Would that not be a more fitting sentence?)"

The Counselor faces the crowd.

"(What if we *all* sentenced ourselves to that same labor? What if we recognized that *all* of us have played a part...some more, some less...but what if instead of putting all of our effort into leveling the finger of blame and punishment, what if we worked hard to fix what was broken? What if we worked hard to make each others' lives better? Would that not be the best sentence we could pass? One that fits every defendant and helps compensate every victim?)

"(Excellency, we are prepared to demonstrate the courage of our convictions. Tell us where we can begin, and we will show the People what we can accomplish. Let us beat our swords into plowshares once more, and, in laboring together, finally bring our children the security we have never found...*and never will find*...in mortal conflict.)

"(Thank you for hearing these words.)" The Counselor bows deeply.

The crowd is absolutely silent, as are the officials across the table. All eyes fall upon the Great Eleto, who grips his forehead.

"(Konn-Zill-Urr makes compelling argument. How can we judge one without judging all who have acted likewise?)"

He takes a deep breath and sits upright in his seat, laying hands on the arms of his chair.

"(We have heard many persuasive words today. Yet words, without action, fail to convince.)"

Seizing on the moment, the Counselor says, "(Excellency, ask *anything* of us.)"

"(If Munn-Ro can halt the epidemic,)" Dekkto states, "(he must. If not, there is nothing else to discuss. Consider your response. We resume tomorrow at the same time.)" He raps his knuckles against the table. "(Session adjourned.)"

Dekkto stands, his bodyguards snap to attention, and the entire hall rises to feet. Both delegations bow deeply. With a whirl of black fabric, the Great Eleto strides from the table, attended by his armored escorts.

The Counselor looks into Dekkto's back, watching the tall leader stroll without hurry between his burly guards as aides, assistants, and messengers fall in behind him. When Dekkto and his entourage pass through the tall double doors, the Counselor turns toward Fell-Marr-Ghen and finds the Advocate is already staring back. Smug assurance of success is gone from his long face, and his mouth is bunched, lips pressed tightly together.

The Counselor mentally saves that apprehensive expression then ushers Munro from the hall, Maiella and Thompson following warily after.

RADICALLY DIFFERENT

Munro's eyes stretch wide. "You *WHAT*?"

The Counselor holds up his hands. "I asked what we could do to prove our intentions were real. Dekkto said arresting the epidemic would be a good start. You can do that, right?"

The big MedTech stands and stares, incredulous. "Why *would* I? They say *we're* the guilty ones while they occupy *our* planet—a planet they sterilized of all human life? I'd sooner let them choke on their double standard!"

"Colonel, I understand how you feel, but if we—"

"This has nothing to do with *feelings*! It's about proving our strength and how *far* we are from defeat. And the more of them are sick and dying in their beds, the fewer are out there hunting the *Europa*."

"They're suffering, Colonel, and we could show—"

"They *should* suffer when they come after us!"

"*True*, we want them to see us as strong, but if that's all we are to them, we're just some dangerous bug. No problem to eliminate, *just like before*."

Munro scoffs. "For twelve hundred years, they've tried, and I doubt they've been holding back. Now, they see the cost of hunting us. We've made them pause. And you want me to *hand over* that advantage?"

"Yes, Colonel! It isn't as if this is some radical new weapon. We copied it from *them*! By using it, we've given them every right to use it against us, again. You want the *Europa* to face that? No attempt at communication, simply pump our last refuge full of live virus until every colonist and MedTech is dead?"

"I doubt they'd use a virus when they could more quickly shoot her down. But at her distance, shrouded by stealth-gen?" Munro frets and shakes his head. "Likelihood of the *Europa* being discovered is so remote, it doesn't register as possible. It would take a stroke of luck so *astronomical*, so—"

"You want to rely on *odds*, Colonel? You may know O'Kai better than I, but I don't think he'd leave the Cadre's survival to *chance*, no matter how favorable."

Munro glares at the Counselor, nailed. Yet the fight is not out of him. "O'Kai would not tolerate our most effective weapons being rendered inert, *either*. That much *I can assure you*."

Undaunted, the Counselor fires back, "He *would*, and here's why: every Eleto life taken is another stone on the scales against us. More proof of our violent nature, of our barbarism. If we willingly contain the spread, we prove not just our strength but also power to *save* lives, to *heal* them. When we give lives back to them, they'll *have* to see us as more. They can't disregard us as some dangerous, untamable animal that only kills. Most importantly, by curing this outbreak, we take pressure off them to respond in kind. We take germ warfare *off* the table of acceptable weapons. Then, the *Europa* doesn't have to rely on luck."

Munro turns toward the wall, so irritated by the Counselor's logic he cannot look at him.

"For what it's worth, Colonel, I think the virus has already done its job," Thompson offers. "The Eleto have felt the sting, and they know there's danger when they tangle with us. Probably wondering what else we might throw at 'em in a fight. That's an edge in our favor."

The Gun leans against the bench beside Munro and crosses his thick arms.

"Besides, if the Eleto wanted to they could contain the spread by quarantining everyone infected. Once all the infected are dead, they sterilize everything. Burn the bodies, incinerate ships if necessary. Done. Then they study the germ, adapt it, and turn it against us, like the Counselor said. Who knows, maybe they have the original strain in storage somewhere. Could be hurling it back at us in days or weeks. But if we do this for Dekkto voluntarily, we give him all those lives and ships back, even though we didn't have to. And if we do it fast, no gripes, maybe they wonder why we'd give up such a strong weapon. If we give them a cure, like the virus isn't a big deal, maybe they'll wonder what else we've got in our arsenal. Know what I mean?"

Munro turns from the wall, his brow scrunched. "We have no other secret weapons. I don't know that a *bluff* is any better plan than luck."

"Not a bluff," the Counselor states. He waits for Munro to face him, adding, "Bullets will never open minds, Colonel. Words and ideas are our best weapons in this battle. So long as we're still talking, no one's dying. And if talking gets us home to Earth, words prove more effective than anything in the Cadre arsenal."

"Is this the kind of trash you've been giving the Eleto the whole time?"

The Counselor lifts his eyebrows, juts his lip, and nods.

Munro shakes his head. "Then I think you're right. Your mouth *is* the most awful weapon we could turn on the Eleto. If they're as sick of listening to you as I am, they must be on the verge of surrender. Let's keep that cannon on full blast, just aim it away from me."

Maiella's jaw drops, and she covers her face, chuckling behind her hands.

The Counselor shoots a wounded glance at Maiella but continues, undeterred, "Say what you will, Colonel. I *know* this is the right path. If you do this for them, *you* open the door to Earth. *You* open the possibility of getting our people home. *YOU* can do this for us, for your MedTechs, for Ralla and her Operators *without firing a shot*. If you do this, we prove to everyone that Fell-Marr-Ghen is wrong. We prove we're good to our word, that we truly seek peace. We prove to them, *beyond any doubt*, that we believe in the sanctity of all life and will act to protect it."

Munro closes his eyes, grips his head with both hands, and presses his cheeks, forcing his mouth into a bunched ring. *Could we really come home to Earth, after so long? Would the enemy really allow us to live in peace?*

He sighs deeply, drops his hands, and turns to the Counselor. "*IF* I do this...what guarantee do we have they'll let us settle the planet?"

"None," the Counselor replies. "Dekkto might come up with a hundred other conditions we have to satisfy. But you know what happens if we *don't* convince the Eleto we're genuine?"

"What?"

"*Nothing*. That is, until Ralla swoops in, launching an attack that'll make Thompson's seem trivial. The war escalates and there is no line of retreat. Nowhere else for us to go. A fight to the death."

"There's Cadre Two."

"Yeah," Maiella grunts, "if you like getting strapped to a table and *sawed on* for decades."

Munro turns toward the Geek, expecting to see her smirking in jest, but Maiella's face is dour with recollection.

"*Earth* is the prize we're fighting for, Munro," the Counselor pleads. "*Earth*. No regulators to maintain... Fresh air and water... We raise crops and herds under blue sky, pull water from free-flowing rivers, and after a full day's labor, you can take in vistas so beautiful they make your heart ache."

Munro's eyes narrow, and his lips press together, dubious. "With the enemy ever-present."

"Well, *yes*, we should take it as given the Eleto'll be there...but not as our enemy. We can't expect them to up and leave. It's their home, too, like it or not. But we *can* expect them to let us start our own community. We're so few and there is *so much room*."

Munro looks at Thompson. "What do you think, Gun?"

Thompson's eyebrows lift in thought, and he answers, "I can't begin to describe what it was like being down there, on the surface, other than to say I'd do *anything* to be able to stay. If stopping the outbreak gives us a shot at our own patch of land and starting over...then there's no choice. We *have* to."

Munro turns to Maiella. "And you?"

Surprised to hear Munro ask her opinion, she uncrosses her legs and sits upright in her high backed chair. "Used to think a tough offense was the best way to keep us all breathing, but it doesn't seem to work anymore. You see where a hard line's gotten us. We're scattered, Cadre One's dust... Ralla might be the best Geek the Cadre's ever produced, but it isn't going to matter. When we fight, no one wins anymore. We have to try something different. *Radically* different."

"So you think I should stop the outbreak?"

She presses her hands together and looks down at the floor in thought. When she looks up, she answers gravely. "Yeah, I do."

Munro turns toward his bench again and leans on his knuckles. Maiella and Thompson cluster together with the Counselor. Thompson is about to speak, but the android holds up a hand, letting Munro mull his thoughts in silence.

"I miss Sharon," the big MedTech says unexpectedly. "Wouldn't have traded her for a *billion* of their kind. Seeing them sick, it...seems *right* to me. Proper. *Correct*."

The big MedTech bounces on his knuckles, stares into the wall, shakes his head, and sighs as if in defeat. "Very well, Counselor. I'll need a proper lab and equipment: scanning microscope, centrifuge, standard labsets and glassware, incubators, a DNA assembler, triple stage decontamination, and clean suit with rebreather."

"They may not have your size, Colonel," Maiella says with a grin.

Munro looks at Maiella and snorts in fatigued amusement. "Probably right."

"I'll put your requisitions in, right away," the Counselor volunteers. "Anything else you need, let me know and I'll get it added to the list. How long do you think it'll take to find a cure?"

Munro crosses his large and small arms. "Already found one. Tested it on Shondre back at Cadre One."

"You tested the virus on *Shondre?*" Maiella asks, shocked.

"Correct," Munro confirms without any trace of remorse. "Had to ensure potency, measure incubation time, chart symptoms...figured I'd find a cure easily enough. But the virus demonstrated unusual resistance to inhibitors— an unexpected trait, possibly something encoded by design in the original strain. It advanced beyond my control."

"How'd you fix her, then?" Maiella asks.

"Doctor Taggart made the breakthrough. She found double-stranded RNA strings in infected cells that we didn't find elsewhere. So we synthesized a protein that would bind with those RNA strands to shut them down, then added another protein that triggered apoptosis."

"I didn't catch any of that," Thompson states.

"Imagine your cells as assembly stations," Munro explains. "A virus gets in and re-programs the assembler so it makes rapid copies of itself. Eventually, the cell is overcrowded and bursts, releasing all those new viruses to go out and hi-jack other healthy cells. You with me so far?"

Thompson nods.

"All we did was shut down the assembler in hi-jacked cells then programmed the cell to die so it couldn't make any more viruses," Munro continues. "Not that difficult, really, once Sahara found those RNA strands."

Maiella's face scrunches, and she says, "I have a hard time believing Sahara was okay with using Shondre as a test subject."

"Sahara wasn't involved in the test," Munro replies. "But when a cure eluded me, I asked her assistance. She has a keen insight into physiology, showed me angles I hadn't considered. Truly, a credit to her practice."

"Couldn't agree more," the Counselor adds. "Now imagine what breakthroughs the Eleto have made. If we shared our discoveries, how much farther could we both advance?"

"Hmm. Interesting point," the big MedTech says, nodding. He turns a full circle, imagining the suite already transformed into his functioning lab, adding, "Even fully equipped, I don't think I can deliver a batch of anti-virals in five days. Takes time to synthesize and test." Munro looks straight at the Counselor. "If we don't have a credible possibility of settlement before then, Ralla *will* proceed as planned."

"Let me worry about that, Colonel," the Counselor says. "Just get started as quick as you can so we can show you're on task. In fact, would you prepare some notes for presentation tomorrow? By showing what you know, and how you plan to go about it, their experts can follow along, maybe figure out the rest. That might be enough to make our case."

The big MedTech nods. "I'll do that."

"In the meantime, we'll ask Shondre to get you some assistants," the Counselor advises. "I'll translate for you." Smiling at his friends, he adds, "The first *real* collaboration between Human and Eleto...working together... That's going to make the difference, you'll see."

Thompson points at himself and Maiella. "What do we do in the meantime?"

The Counselor takes in the two Operators, looking them up and down. "Have either of you seen a dance performance?"

Head tilted, Thompson asks, "Dance?"

"I have," Maiella says. She puts her arms in front of her chest in a flat circle and pirouettes. "My workout routines were getting a bit stale. So I sifted *Europa* archives for inspiration. Found some Flamenco videos in there. Challenging."

"Fluh-men-ko? What's that?"

"It's *hot*," Maiella answers. "Want me to show you?"

Thompson arches an eyebrow at her and grins. "Sure."

"Excellent," the Counselor says. "Follow Maiella's lead and work out a number you can perform tomorrow." Smiling in genuine optimism, the Counselor slaps his hands together and rubs them. With a whirl of colorful fabric, the android strides for the door and disappears through it.

Thompson looks at Maiella, face bunched with skepticism. "*Tomorrow*?"

Maiella smirks and taps Thompson's chest with the back of her hand. "Best get started. C'mon, I got some ideas."

A Bold Demand

Risers of the enormous hall are packed beyond capacity with Eleto standing behind the back row of seats and squatting in the aisles. The silence is remarkable, however, interrupted only by a rare sneeze or cough as the crowd stares at monitors above the polished table. On screens, complex helical ribbons of proteins and nucleic acids rotate in three dimensions.

Munro stands upon the dais at the hall's center, looking up at the screens and describing what is depicted as the Counselor faithfully translates. Shondre, having resumed her place at the table, gazes in awe at the holoprojections. Even the officials across the table are captivated. Maiella and Thompson, however, sit bored in their armor, hands on table, slow-blinking in drowsy tedium.

"By arresting the apparatus of replication inside the cell," Munro announces, "and triggering apoptosis, we effectively halt the spread of infection. Unlike a protease inhibitor, which is specific in its target, this is a broad-spectrum treatment that remains effective even as the virus mutates. Further, it obviates the use of phosphonate nucleotide analog reverse-transcriptase inhibitors, avoiding the more pernicious side effects of drug toxicity."

The Counselor stumbles in translation, doing his best to break the more complex scientific terms into simpler concepts, fails utterly, slumps, then taps Munro on the shoulder. "Uh, Colonel, perhaps a lay description will suffice?"

Munro looks down at the Counselor, reproach etched into his face. "This is as elementary as it gets. I don't know how I could be more plain."

The Counselor shows his hands in submission and fades back, yielding the floor.

"Halting viral replication is not enough, of course," Munro resumes, "due to the fact that the immune system is one of the first systems compromised by the infection. Therefore, we employ a regimen of anti-viral inhibitors to slow activity of live virions in blood and tissues while simultaneously stimulating the immune system of the patient to clear the body of these weakened virions. This is enhanced by mass-producing RNA specific antibodies if the patient is too compromised to produce sufficient quantity, themselves."

Munro pauses and listens to the Counselor staggering through his explanation, sometimes starting the same sentence over multiple times. The big MedTech shrugs at the android, hands out.

The Counselor glances at Munro and he holds a flat hand out at the MedTech, blocking his face from view. At last, the Counselor finishes and he lowers his hand, waiting for Munro to carry on, but the MedTech still glares in annoyance.

"You didn't have any trouble translating before. Now you stutter like a first year student. What's wrong with you?"

The Counselor peers at Munro with half-lidded eyes. His mouth opens for a reply then clamps shut in self-censorship. With a smile, the android clasps his hands and says instead, "Whenever you're ready, Colonel..."

Munro frowns, bunches his eyebrows, then turns back toward the monitors and resumes, "With sufficient bed rest, nutrition, and fluid intake, the patient is able to recover with an immune system well-trained to resist a secondary infection."

Fell-Marr-Ghen waits for the Counselor's translation then asks a question. The Counselor leans toward Munro with translation, "The Advocate asks if you have tested this cure on any Eleto patients."

Munro misses the warning in the Counselor's expression, and answers plainly, "Of course." He extends a flat hand at Shondre. "We restored Lady Shondre to health after infection, though it's erroneous to use the word 'cure.' There will always be traces of virus in the patient after recovery."

The Counselor blanches, blanks his expression, and translates in as neutral a tone as possible.

Officials across the table launch from their chairs, stabbing accusing fingers at Munro, shouting at him and turning to Dekkto, pleading. Maiella and Thompson are propelled from torpor, spines straight, eyes wide and vigilant of the suddenly animated officials and spectators around them. Shondre's eyes are widest of all as she gapes in shock and disbelief at the big MedTech.

"This hwon, *hyoo inn-fekt?*" she shouts over the crowd's angry howling.

Munro turns to face her and he nods matter-of-factly.

Dekkto looks down at the mineral table with a bitter scowl. All around, spectators rise from their seats, riled voices merging into cacophony. The Great Eleto raps his knuckles against the table, but goes unheard. One of his bodyguards reaches beneath the table and pulls out two long flat sticks. Taking one stick in each hand, the burly guard holds them out to each side then slaps flat sides together overhead with a deafening *crack*. Angry shouts hush to restless mutters that ripple through the crowd, and the bodyguard turns a full circle with sticks outstretched, threatening another thunderclap. Only when cowed spectators resume their places in obedient silence does the guard lower the sticks and place them back under the table.

Rather than speak, Dekkto looks at Fell-Marr-Ghen and gestures toward him with an open hand to continue. The Advocate in Opposition bows graciously in recognition, one hand on his chest, then turns squarely toward Munro. Though the colonel cannot understand the words being spit at him, the hatred is apparent.

The Counselor offers Munro an unfiltered translation, complete with Fell-Marr-Ghen's inflections and emphasis. "The Advocate said, Are we to believe Lady Shondre was the *only* test subject of this plague? Such a thing is not *remotely* credible. How many of our disappeared brethren ended their days, shackled in a laboratory with the Human's pathogen eating away at them? How many died in *agony* until they had perfected this *masterpiece of misery*? Yet they would have us believe they gleaned all their malevolent knowledge from a *single test subject*. As if that were not already difficult to swallow, they now tell us there is no cure! The poor souls who have been touched by this corruption *shall never be rid of it*!"

"Tell me, Advocate," Munro snaps back, "why is it so incredible that we could glean all we needed from one subject? Maybe your own scientists were not so efficient when they created their version so long ago. How many of *our* people did it take until you'd found the right strain?"

The Counselor's eyes widen and his head shakes in tight little jerks.

"*Tell him what I said*," Munro demands.

Reluctantly, the android turns and delivers Munro's words to the hall, preserving the colonel's tone and emphasis. Sullen murmurs pass through the rows. Officials across the table look away and snort, insulted. But the Great Eleto stares shrewdly and strokes the whiskers below his chin.

Not wasting a moment, Fell-Marr-Ghen is on his feet pacing along the edge of the dais, speaking loudly to the risers, arms spread. His voice rises, clearly posing a question, to which the audience angrily shouts back.

Munro arches an eyebrow at the Counselor. The android humbly relays, "The Advocate said, Through Munro's own words, we better understand the Human concept of 'friendship.' Has Madame Shondre not been their tireless ally? Has she not risked everything for them? See how they repay her loyalty! Tell me, are the People willing to make *FRIENDS* with these Humans now?"

Shondre's mouth still hangs in shock as if shot through the chest. Weight of the betrayal drags her head down, and she slaps the table hard. Looking up with glassy eyes on the verge of tears, she barks at Maiella and Thompson, "*Hyoo no-h uh-bowt thisss?*"

The Operators both shake their heads, talking over one another.

"*No*, Shondre," Thompson pleads, "we had *no idea*."

Maiella says, reaching toward her, "There is *no way* I'd have let that happen. If I'd known..." The Geek turns a gaze on Munro so venomous he tenses in preparation of attack.

All eyes in the hall swing to Munro, waiting for a response. Where his default answer to a question is always the briefest path to the truth, he plainly sees the result of candor around him. Shondre's face is a pained ruin, wracked in disillusionment. Maiella is on the verge of springing from her chair, eyes red around the rims. Thompson has a hand on her to keep her seated, but even his austere demeanor is rattled with steel gray eyes narrowed in condemnation.

She was an enemy captive, nothing more, Munro thinks. *We had to know if the weapon worked, and she was our only means to test it. The decision was scientific.* He looks down at his barrel chest and puts his large hand over his heart. *So why does this nag me like I've failed in some way?*

The Counselor's tight-lipped expression begs for the colonel's prompt reply even as his wide eyes show terror of what he might say.

Munro looks out at the risers, turns and looks at the sullen officials across the table, then looks at Dekkto. The Great Eleto reclines against the back of his chair, weight resting on an elbow, stone faced. Even Dekkto's bodyguards stand in judgment, arms crossed.

"It is true," Munro admits. "I tested the virus on Shondre. And I bear the burden of that decision. She was an enemy captive at the time, an asset. An opportunity. Only later did she convince me she was a person...a person who later became my friend. There is shame in having visited suffering upon her."

His brow wrinkles as he wrestles with memory of experiments long past.

"Our people race against our own genetic defects. Radiation at Cadre One breaks our chromosomes and our progeny are always decanted with some level of defect." He looks down at his differently sized arms. "Some lack symmetry, as I do. Some may be severely disabled, unable to walk, unable to think clearly, have one or more senses impaired... Genetic diseases are common, and often...*too often*...we must turn our experiments on our own children to heal them. We do not always succeed."

Munro turns pensive, interlacing the fingers of his large and small hands while the Counselor delivers his translation.

"Perhaps I've hardened to the pain I have to inflict," Munro continues. "Perhaps, in Lady Shondre, I saw only another experiment, not so different from the others. Today, I see the injury in her eyes, and...I beg her forgiveness.

"Had I *not* tested the virus on her, I could not have fully understood the mechanisms by which it worked. I certainly could not have formulated an effective treatment. There'd be no hope of survival for those currently infected."

The Counselor delivers the translation solemnly.

Fell-Marr-Ghen pipes up again in animated shows, haughty scorn in the downturned corners of his mouth.

Facing Munro, the Counselor interprets, "The Advocate said, A treatment with no cure! Recovered, yet still contagious! Why are we not removing Lady Shondre to quarantine right now? For safety's sake, she, and all who have been infected, must be parted from friends and family forever. Even if this human successfully 'treats' them, their careers are over, and they must be banished to perpetual isolation, *imprisoned for all—*"

Not needing to hear the rest, Munro snarls, "Which is why we are also offering a *vaccine*. If the Advocate needs it *spelled out*, providing a vaccine means we are completely disarming this weapon and rendering it *useless*. We do this because you *asked us* for a show of faith. We do this to de-escalate a conflict that has become more costly than ever to both sides. And we do this because we want to come *home*. If disarming one of our most effective weapons gets us a step closer, then *it's worth it*."

The Counselor closes his eyes in relief, and he delivers the colonel's words.

Fell-Marr-Ghen squints in typical suspicion. Yet Dekkto crooks a taloned finger at an aide in the first row of spectators. The aide hurries up to the dais, is stopped and patted down by the bodyguards, then leans down to the Great Eleto's ear. Dekkto points to the screens, saying something too quietly for the Counselor to hear; but the aide nods, presents a tablet for Dekkto to view, and points at areas of the screen. The Great Eleto presses his lips together, nods, then dismisses the aide. With a rap of his knuckles, he quiets the many side conversations throughout the hall. In rumbling voice, Dekkto directly addresses Munro. The Counselor interprets.

"His Excellency said, My assistants have analyzed your treatment regimen. They concur it is promising. You will have access to the equipment Konn-Zill-Urr has requested. Deliver to us your successful treatment and vaccine, and we shall look favorably upon continued negotiations."

Munro recoils as if struck. "*Continued negotiations*? No. That's not good enough. Tell him I'll get to work right away, *if* he makes our return to Earth a part of these negotiations."

"Uh, that's a rather *bold* demand to make of their supreme authority," the Counselor cautions.

"*Tell him.*"

The Counselor blanks his anxious expression, turns toward the Great Eleto, glances back at Munro once more, and delivers Munro's terms.

Officials across the table gasp at the audacity. Fell-Marr-Ghen laughs outright. And the crowd roils with a thousand separate opinions on the matter. Dekkto finds neither offense nor jest, however, and he points to both Fell-Marr-Ghen and Shondre, beckoning them both. The Advocates rise, bow respectfully with hand on chest, and approach. Already noise from the crowd overwhelms the conversation at the head of the table, which is brief. Both Advocates return to their seats and Dekkto raps his knuckles for silence. Like a switch, the audience calms and settles into their seats.

The Great Eleto leans forward in his chair, laying his ancient hands flat on the table. His elbows flare outward as if about to push off, but instead he levels a cool gaze at Munro. Every word from his mouth is deliberate as if its own sentence.

The Counselor listens, dumbfounded, then turns to Munro and takes a lapel of his robe in hand. "His Excellency said, We recognize the Voice of the Kad-Ra is not as aware of our ways as Kon-Zill-Urr. In future discussions, it is advised Kon-Zill-Urr be allowed to speak for his people so that unintentional offense is not given.

"However, we give Munn-Ro an answer as direct as his question: *If* he saves lives of The People and truly renders this evil weapon defunct...*then* we will make the repatriation of Earth a subject for further discussion."

The Counselor takes Munro's other lapel, adding, "Now, Colonel, we bow to his Excellency, *deeply*, and *you do not say another word*."

Munro grimaces, nods, and follows the Counselor's lead, hand on his chest, bowing down to his waist.

GODS OF ANNIHILATION

The Counselor ushers Munro back to his seat, and as the big MedTech settles into it, the android whispers into his ear, "I've got it from here."

Munro nods and reclines in his chair, elbows on armrests, fingers of large and small hands interlaced across his lap.

Chest out, shoulders back, the Counselor announces, "(To the Noble Will of the People, his Excellency, Dekkto-Mayah-Tayaloh...to the High Commander of Martial Services, Prell-Shah-Stoh...to the Honored Voices of the eighty regions...to Fell-Marr-Ghen, our gracious host...to the Prime Citizens of the elevated governances, to the Distinguished Controllers of the common need, and to all Eleto, everywhere...this one remains grateful, and humble, that we have been afforded an opportunity to be heard.)

"(Our talks have been highly charged, have been an exploration of memories that we would all much rather forget...yet we *cannot* forget. We cannot ignore our past because it has led to this moment.)

"(It is scarcity, alone, that drives the Cadre to prey upon Eleto vessels. Nothing more. If we remove that scarcity by letting them come home, they no longer need turn their talents to violent ends. With basic needs satisfied, they can use those talents of mind and body in nobler pursuits. You see, our people *are* capable of great beauty... If allowed to exist, free from threat, not facing starvation or asphyxiation, you will see their current behavior is an aberration. If allowed to live freely, they can become the people they are *meant to be*.)

"(Madame Shondre proved to us that Human and Eleto already have much in common. What outward differences we perceive are minor when compared with the way we sense the universe around us. The tiniest of variations have been used as excuses to segregate us into factions, but when

350

we stop and consider just how similar we are, how great the universe is, and how small we are within it, those paltry distinctions fall away as immaterial. Insignificant. *Irrelevant.* Because no matter how we argue, we cannot escape a fundamental truth: Life is its own reason for being, and we are *all* entitled to it.)

"(By working together to ensure the lives of our neighbors, we labor in service of a cause greater than Human or Eleto. We serve the cause of *life*. When we commit to doing no harm, and we secure our bonds with positive action, there is no need for killing, ever.)

"(What we have seen on these screens,)" the android says, pointing to holoprojections, "(what we have seen on our arrival,)" he adds, gesturing to Sharon's empty chair, "(indeed, what we have seen in this very hall,)" he points to the path between risers where Maiella and Da-Indo-Hass fought, "(are awful reminders of our failure to choose wisdom and tolerance over bitterness and hatred. Our war machines have never been so well fed, and they have grown so large they loom over us like gods of annihilation. *Why do we tolerate this*? If anything should be allowed to starve, let it be these monsters of destruction we have fashioned against one another.)

"(Today, Munro offers a treatment and vaccine, dismantling one arm of this all-consuming war machine. In time, perhaps we will feel safe enough in each other's company that we can dismantle more of it. Then our efforts would no longer be wasted on implements of destruction, and could be turned toward richer and more gratifying ends. All of the blood, sweat, and treasure spent on what is now junk, drifting through the Black... All the lives lost... It hurts to imagine what we might have built instead.)

"(This one has spoken at length, and he is beholden to The People's patience. He would reward that patience with a demonstration of what Cadre Operators *could* be if they are not ranging the expanse between stars in search of basic needs.)"

To The Great Eleto, Counselor says, "(With your permission, noble Dekkto, we would show The People that even the hardest soldier yearns for beauty, and would choose it, if only the next meal was not so uncertain. This one humbly requests that Maiella and Thompson be allowed to perform here in this hall. Madame Shondre has selected a musical accompaniment from master Eleto symphonist, Ibn-Bin-Est. We think you will be pleased by the interpretation.)"

The Great Eleto tilts his head, brow wrinkled, intrigued. "(With this one's blessing, proceed.)"

The Counselor smiles and bows, hand on chest. To the Operators seated at the table, he says, "Maiella, Thompson...are you ready?"

They both nod, rise from their chairs, and strip their armor down to undersuits. After a few limbering stretches Thompson jogs from the raised dais down the darkened path toward the main entrance and waits there.

Maiella plants her hands on the edge of the table, springs to a handstand, and walks over onto her bare feet atop the polished mineral—a move so sudden, officials opposite draw an anxious breath and recoil. At center, she kneels, hugs her raised knee to her chest, and rests her forehead atop it.

From unseen speakers comes a feminine voice, a low moan from the diaphragm and back of the throat, lonely and yearning, as if calling from a cell deep within an empty stone fortress.

Maiella lifts her head toward the ceiling.

The voice rises in pitch with plaintive sustains of longing.

She lowers her arms, allowing fingertips to rest on the polished table, and sweeps her gaze from side to side as if searching.

A bow draws across long, thick strings in sustained notes of tension... need...desire...

She rises slowly, one foot ahead of the other, heel of her back foot lifted.

Sound of wind past reeds, a shaker, then the *pound* of a palm against taut drum skin... Rhythmic *clack* of wood sticks.

Maiella thrusts her arms out to each side, palms up, and shuts her eyes, bathing in bright spotlight that shines from above.

The voice takes flight as though lifted on a thousand wings, builds in urgency, grows stronger, demanding, *summoning*...

A horn sounds from one side of the hall. Thompson strides toward the dais and arrives with a triumphant blare.

A deep masculine voice fills the hall, scolding her doubt, then softens in tender confession.

With one bold step, Thompson ascends the table and stands at its edge. The two Operators face one another, feet shoulder width apart.

Maiella's head dips as the feminine voice shies, apologetic, then lifts in hope. She reaches out to Thompson with both hands, and he strides toward her, shoulders square, eyes locked on hers as if nothing else was worth seeing. He takes her gruffly by the small of her back and nape, spins her once around himself, and holds her, gazing in adoration. She reaches up with deliberate slowness and touches the sides of his face.

The music pauses.

He presses her hard against him, leans in, and kisses her deeply. Her body slumps against his powerful arms, arms falling slack to her sides.

The feminine voice begins, almost imperceptibly, from the depths of the chest. A sound of relief, the banishment of loneliness.... A flutter of flutes to mirror the flutters in her stomach, a thudding of drums to match the thudding in her chest.

The two separate, allowing fingertips to slide down their extended arms as they part. They catch each other at the wrist and snatch each other back together. She raises a leg and curls it behind him. One hand rakes his back, the other grabs him behind the head. He grabs her around the waist and lifts her up to eye level, turning a slow circle, never losing eye contact.

Bows slide across strings in sustained notes. Then, a crash of percussion and the two launch away from each other.

Silence.

And then the clap of hands in double, single, double rhythm...

Eyebrow arched, Maiella raises her arms in a shallow V, dipping over to one side as she turns in alternate circles, feet stamping in time with the beat.

Thompson turns sideways to her, hands at head height, clapping the same two-one-two rhythm. He paces around her as she spins, then about-faces the moment she changes direction.

A crisp strum across metal strings...

Maiella rises to her toes, hands overhead, wrists crossed, chin high as the strum fades. A masculine voice cries out excitement and vigor, and the strumming turns manic. She casts her arms down as Thompson darts by, takes her by a hand, and hauls her toward him. Maiella spins past then unfurls herself, free arm reaching out toward the risers. Thompson hauls her in again and she lands against him, slapping both hands on his chest. She shoves away, her back toward him, and looks over a shoulder, eyebrow raised, smiling seduction as she traces the firm curves of her thigh and hip.

He takes a step toward her, and she steps away. He retreats, and she pursues in a tantalizing back and forth.

Music pauses, and the two stamp to a halt. She crooks a finger.

Strumming breaks in harder than before, the two voices joining in unison as Thompson meets Maiella at table's center. He swoops a hand behind her back and takes her by the hand. They slide, strut, and twirl across the tabletop, spinning, flinging each other around the polished table, keeping eye contact. She whips herself around him, stepping over his widely spaced legs with deceptive ease. He catches her on the far side, hauls her in. She jumps into his arms and extends herself across his chest like a plank. Thompson spins in place, tosses her into the air, catches her, and sets her back onto her feet in the same fluid motion.

A gasp from the crowd...

The music pauses, and the dancers freeze mid-pose, lips parted, chests heaving. Maiella winks at him. Thompson grins back at her. She raises her arms again with tantalizing leisure.

When the music resumes, it is slower, calmer. Her arms move fluidly in time and she pats the rhythm into the table with her bare feet. Thompson strides in confidently. She presses against him.

A frenzy of strumming, and the dancers clasp hands. Thompson whips her back and forth, Maiella flipping completely and landing on her feet each time.

Voices merge in exclamations of passion.

Maiella grabs Thompson's hands and springs. He slides beneath her and presses her up into a handstand over his head. Feet wide, he gazes up at her. Legs extended straight up to the ceiling, she gazes down at him. Voices halt, leaving only the metronome clapping of hands. The two remain in position, perfectly still.

Voices cry out and strumming returns with mad intensity. Thompson thrusts Maiella high enough to tumble through the holographic projections then catches her and spins her onto her feet. She grabs his arm and yanks him toward her. He springs over her head, rotates mid air, lands on the far side, grabs her by the waist and pulls her in. She slams against him, slaps hands to his chest, wraps a leg behind him, and looks up into his face.

The music ends. Spotlight goes dark.

Together, they stand, breathless, entranced, oblivious to the silence of the crowd. But when the first peals of applause come, their spell is broken and they look out toward the risers in surprise.

Sullen officials across the table are predictably unimpressed. When the Great Eleto smiles and claps his hands, however, officials at the table perk up and show begrudging support with slow, effortless claps.

Thompson and Maiella smile at each other, wave to the crowd, and bow deeply to Dekkto before moving to the table's edge and stepping down.

The Counselor grips hands behind himself, beaming with pride. While Maiella and Thompson return to their armor, the android listens to the applause with eyes closed, thinking it sweeter music than what previously played.

For their initial intensity, cheers fade quickly, and, once the Counselor can be heard again, he turns to the crowd.

"(Would we not all prefer they were like *this*?)"

The crowd murmurs. Hundreds of heads nod in collective assent.

"(They make it seem so easy, so natural,)" the Counselor continues. "(There is so much strength, so much grace in them. A shame those talents are not given greater freedom for expression.)"

The android falls pensive, looking down at the floor. He turns to the crowd suddenly.

"(They have art in their souls, but it has been suppressed so long they had forgotten. Please, let them remember they were once beautiful. And let them rediscover that beauty in safety. Let us *both* choose sanity; let us *both* choose to spend our sweat and treasure on lasting testaments to compassion, wisdom, and enrichment of the soul. Let us *keep* the fruits of our labors, instead of hurling them at one another in anger. And most of all, let us rejoice in a time when no sons or daughters are lost to pointless war.)"

The Counselor pauses, listening to the mood of the crowd in tone of voices passing between neighbors, friends, family, and colleagues. Progress has been made, he can sense, yet there is still persistent doubt.

"(It is good and proper to remain vigilant. We cannot ask for trust. For, again, all know it must be earned with good faith. And there will always be a greedy few who profit on war. They will play to our fears,)" he continues. "(They persuade us we need these behemoths of annihilation so we can be safe, even as we cower beneath their awesome abilities, dreading the day they might be used. What bitter irony that the more powerful the weapon, the *less* security we enjoy?)"

He shakes his head.

"(He we stand, nothing more or less than what we are. If we are allowed to come home, these killing machines become unnecessary. Take them off line. Store them, if you must, as guarantors of peace. And when we are all free to pursue better professions, our futures could be written anew *here*, at the epicenter of positive change. First, we have to do the hard work *today*... the hardest work of all... We must *choose* to forgive one another.)"

The Counselor pauses to look many in the eye and let the point sink in.

"(Generations from now, our descendants will look back upon us in pride, knowing we were the architects of their peace. And they will know that we did this hard work not just for ourselves, but for *them*...because we cared enough to give them a better world than the one we inherited.)

"(Thank you for hearing these words.)"

The Counselor lowers his head and spreads his robe in a respectful bow. Dignified applause answers from the risers.

Dekkto allows the applause to fall away naturally and says without hurry, "(We are much impressed today, Kon-Zill-Urr. Indeed, we do prefer Humans this way. It is gratifying to sit at a table and exchange ideas, not gunfire. This delegation has satisfied us that Humans *are* capable of thought, reason, and, surprisingly, tenderness. By extension, we will allow that others could be capable of choosing peace over violence. Whether the Kad-Ra will choose the path of peace *remains to be seen*. And we will remain ever vigilant in our defense. Yet so long as *ALL* cleave to non-aggression, and to resolve conflicts at this table, not at the barrel of a gun...a future of co-existence is no longer unimaginable.)"

Momentarily stunned, the Counselor bows humbly. Latching up the last of their armor, Maiella and Thompson notice the Counselor bow, and they mirror his low bow. Oblivious to the enormity of Dekkto's declaration, however, Munro remains seated, elbows on armrests, fingers still interlaced across his belly.

"(We shall look forward to further discussions,)" the Great Eleto announces. "(For now, we must break to attend other duties. Are there any urgent matters before we recess?)"

"(No, Excellency,)" the Counselor replies. "(We remain at your service and likewise—)"

Monitors above the table break into bright noisy static. The android looks up at them, confused. Dekkto turns a curious eye to the screens then is immediately snatched from his chair by the two bodyguards. The table end rises at an invisible seam, blocking the Great Eleto from the Counselor's view, but he can hear Dekkto's protests as he is shoved under the lifted table. Dekkto's voice is heard no more.

The Counselor gawks, perplexed by such a dramatic exit, and the crowd murmurs in anxious agitation. Prell-Shah-Stoh touches a button at his collar and places a finger on one ear to hear his communicator. The commander's eyes go wide and he jumps up from the table, dragging Fell-Marr-Ghen with him. Stabbing a damning finger at the human delegation, he snarls a vengeful oath then rushes under the lifted table after Dekkto.

The Counselor squints at the screens, looking for a glimpse of anything that could offer a hint when he hears Thompson yell at the top of his lungs, "No, NO, *NO! NOT NOW!*"

The android turns to see the Gun with one hand on Munro's chair, and the Gun bellows, "YOU SAID RALLA WOULD *WAIT!*"

Munro leans back into his chair, hands across his lap, face impassive and resigned.

Immediately, the Counselor's haze of befuddlement clears. With hanging jaw and climbing dread he looks back into the staticky monitors, realizing the death of peace has come.

INITIATIVE

A quartet of fast *klanks* strikes the hall's arched ceiling, then another. Thompson glances at Maiella, and her wide-eyed expression mirrors his own. Both don helmets and latch the neck seals then watch the ceiling for the inevitable cutting of laser drills.

Spectators scream in terror, leaping from seats in a panic, falling over each other in a rush for the exits. Frenzied mobs jam overcrowded stairways, shoving, braying, spilling over riser edges, and trampling others who have fallen in the aisles.

Thompson kneels beside Munro and yells above the tumult, *"Colonel, can you order them to stand down?"*

Munro scowls and yells back, *"I'll do no such thing."*

"Sir?"

"They have the initiative. Do NOT interfere." The colonel resumes his impassive stare at the polished table.

Thompson shrinks back in disbelief then notices the Counselor rushing around the table to Shondre. The two shout at one another in Eleto, Shondre sobbing with mouth wide, arms open in bewilderment, while the Counselor pleads to be heard. The Gun focuses on the Counselor's body language, watching his lips and arms in exaggerated movements. Through the din he can barely discern, "(We...*both* betrayed! This one...no longer begs for Cadre...*only* for others...)"

Maiella's hand lands on Thompson's shoulder, and when the Gun looks at her, he sees she is on her feet, watching the exchange.

"Thompson," she says in alarm, "did you get that?"

"Yeah, I did." Turning back to Munro, Thompson begs, "Colonel, we came to *save* lives, not end them! *I'm not giving up on that!*"

"You *will*, Gun, and that's an order."

"*An order*? O'Kai said obey Sharon's orders like his own. Sharon was committed to this path, which means we are, as well!"

"Sharon is *dead*." Munro reaches to the seat beside him and collects the fire opal pendant, cupping it in his large and small hands.

Thompson shakes his head. "*You're giving up*? What've we been working for all this time?"

"The plan failed. We follow our next best option."

"It didn't *fail*!" Maiella grabs Munro's arm to spin him toward herself. "THEY WERE *LISTENING*!"

Munro swings his large arm in a circle. "TAKE YOUR HAND OFF ME."

Shrieks of laser drills telegraph through the ceiling.

Munro looks up, gauges where the cutting is occurring, and scoots his chair aside. "Whatever might have been, they aren't listening anymore."

The Counselor and Shondre hurry around the table to the remaining officials, keeping a wary eye to the ceiling. Officials shout at the android, teeth bared, cursing him in hatred. He pleads with open arms, bowing like a penitent, but they shove him away violently, propelling him backward over the wheeled chairs. Shondre steps in and shouts at the officials just as vehemently, all of it lost to Thompson's ears amid terrified wails from the risers.

Screeches above intensify as two orange circles glow in the ceiling. Then a cylinder of brilliant light cuts through, scorching into floor and bodies beneath. Layered discs of reinforced hull drop from the hole like over sized coins, flipping through the air then crashing into panicked Eleto below.

An identical column of light cuts through behind Munro and another stack of hull layers plummets from the hole. Thompson and Maiella dash to Eleto in harm's way, each grabbing a pair and ripping them aside by their collars. The rest are smashed in sickening *thumps*.

Triple claws protrude through the ceiling holes, hook the edges, and ratchet down, anchoring the Virus ships into place. A Gun, then a Brick, drop through each hole with a carbon braid attached to their backs. Both Guns clutch standard issue rifles. Bricks wear twin tanks in place of a backrack, and the nozzled rods they grip connect with a stout hose shrouded in mesh weave.

The first Gun touches down, points across the table and orders the largest Brick, "*Retrieve the Counselor*."

"*Aye, Major*," Halgrim answers, and the huge Brick clambers over the table, sending spidery cracks through it with every step. Eyes and mouths gaping, officials stagger backward at the Brick's approach. Even the Counselor flees from him.

"Maddock, *you have to stop!*" Thompson shouts at the lead Gun. "We can win without fighting!"

Ignoring Thompson, Maddock detaches the carbon braid from his back, threads it under Munro's arms, fastens the carabiner, and twangs the cord. Munro is hoisted from his seat and zipped up through a hole in the ceiling.

"*Maddock!*" Thompson shouts again, when he hears something latch to his back armor with a *click*.

"*Thompson's secure,*" Gun Dagmar states.

Maddock turns toward Thompson, eyes hidden behind armored black lenses. With electronically clipped voice, he adds, "*Well done, Thompson. We've got it from here.*" Maddock twangs the cord, and Thompson is snatched from his feet.

Maiella leaps to detach the cord from Thompson's back but the other Brick catches her by the shoulder, snaps his cord to her back, and twangs the line.

Thompson and Maiella fumble blindly for the carabiners as they race toward the ceiling. Below them, Dagmar and Maddock trigger sustained beams into the mob at neck height and sweep in wide arcs, mowing whole sections down. Halgrim chases after the Counselor, bashing, hacking, and stomping through Eleto in his way while his counterpart fans a long tongue of flame through the risers. Braying crescendos into piercing screams.

Thompson looks up at the rapidly approaching hole in the ceiling, reaches up to guide himself through, and arrives in the dim, cramped interior of a Cadre virus ship. He steps aside, making room for Maiella to arrive a moment later. Thompson yanks on the carbon cord, but its winder is locked, so the Gun detaches the carabiner from his back.

"I'm going back," he yells as he crouches at the hole. Surveying the violence below, he sees no sign of Dekkto, but his bodyguards have weapons aimed at Dagmar and Maddock. Panicked Eleto bump and jostle the burly guards, jumping through their line of fire, spoiling their shots; and they hold, bellowing at the crowd to clear. Dagmar and Maddock have no such reservations and trigger through civilian and soldier. Both bodyguards launch backward, skulls erupting superheated brain and scorched bone, while Bricks hose the crowd with long plumes of sticky flame.

"I've got to stop this," Thompson says. Maiella claps a hand on his shoulder to let him know she is right behind. He takes a step forward, gauging the long drop, when the iris hatch snaps shut.

"Sir, we have to go!" a familiar voice says.

"*Beckert?*" Thompson head swivels.

"Yes, sir! If you'd please strap in..."

Beckert's console buzzes with Maddock's radioed voice, "*Counselor fled with the captive...escape hatch under the table. Clear off, and get VIPs to safety.*"

"Wilco, Major," Beckert transmits. "Retrieval boat en route, ETA twenty seconds."

"*Understood. Maddock out.*"

In the dim diode light from the console, Thompson can just discern outlines of the cabin. A legless Geek with artificial left arm is strapped into the pilot's seat so securely he appears permanently installed. With his intact right arm, Beckert points to the open recliners.

"We have to go *now*, sir. General doesn't like to wait."

Thompson makes room for Maiella to slip past to a recliner. "O'Kai is *alive?*"

"Affirmative, and he wants to see you both."

Thompson shoots a confused glance at Maiella. "Can we get him to listen?"

She shrugs.

Both Operators lay in recliners and whip straps across their shoulders. "We have to stop this, Geek," Thompson announces. "We can win without fighting."

Beckert turns to look at the Gun, perplexed. "*Without* fighting? Then why put up such a good diversion?"

Thompson opens his mouth to answer when Beckert releases the anchor claws, breaks hard seal, and lifts off. Thompson looks over the edge of his recliner at the hatch. Without the Virus Ship as a stopper the entire Hall is venting to space.

"That was no *diversion*, Beckert," Maiella replies in Thompson's stead. "We had a chance to—"

"HANG ON!" Beckert's goggles flare with code as he swoops through feints and corkscrews, straining harness straps so hard they creak. Vicious jolts and bangs against the hull follow every sudden maneuver. Thompson and Maiella clench teeth, gut, and recliner rails with all their strength.

Beckert throws the ship through another series of wild maneuvers, grunting and groaning, goggles strobing with threat alerts.

"BRACE!"

A detonation hammers the craft sideways. Multiple diodes on the console turn from green to amber. Explosions rattle the craft from multiple sides, bracketing, corralling, closing in for the kill.

Thompson thumps his console's interface but it is dark and does not respond. Annoyed, he demands, "*SITREP.*"

When Beckert does not answer, Thompson looks at the Geek and finds him frozen in total concentration, goggles blazing.

"Geek!"

"Sir!" he pipes between grunts. "Glancing hits...stripping non-reflective layer... Missiles're...*locking on...*"

The craft slows with such quickness that Thompson's eyes nearly jump from their sockets. Beckert jinks left, dives right, spins about, thrusts at full burn, whips about, and burns hard again. Explosions shake the craft from astern, farther away.

A deep cycle hum behind the recliners rises to fever pitch. Console edges spark as inertial damping comes on line, and Beckert executes, diving the craft through thousands of kilometers in an instant.

Energy in the cabin dissipates, the craft flies straight, and Beckert blows out a long held breath. He opens his armored faceplate and lifts his goggles to massage the orbits around his ocular implants.

"Too close," he says.

"The *hell* is going on?" Thompson demands.

Beckert swivels his head to look at the Gun. Deep set sensors root where his eyes once were. "Had to move in close to one of the big battleships so the rest of the fleet couldn't get a clean shot at us. Getting inside its sphere of engagement was *hairy*—"

"*No.* I mean the tactical situation, *right now.*"

Beckert replaces his goggles but leaves his faceplate open. "Cadre fleet achieved total surprise, first strike severely damaging or destroying a third of enemy forces. Remaining forces are disorganized, but are forming a defensive perimeter around the ship we just left. Operator teams are in play to capture as many enemy vessels as they can."

"How do you keep control of the fleet if you're sending Geeks to a new vessel?" Maiella asks.

"We brought a new class online early."

"The *initiates*? They're *far* from ready for rotation."

"We only need to get them interfaced," Beckert explains. "Then Ralla takes control from there."

Maiella blinks. "So, the new Geeks are just...relays?"

Beckert considers correcting the oversimplification, then replies, "More or less. On this rotation, Ralla has direct control of all vessels with Geeks operating."

"Except you," Maiella notes.

Beckert looks down at his missing legs. "Combat ineffective. So my role is data processing for Major Ralla." He tips his head toward his passengers. "And VIP transport."

"Huh. If Ralla's got direct control of the fleet..." Maiella begins.

"...and we can convince her *and* O'Kai to pull back, we could bring a quick end to this," Thompson finishes.

"Pardon my asking, sir, but...*why would we do that*?"

Thompson looks squarely at Beckert. "You remember being on the planet? All that space, the air, water, land... You remember?"

"Of course."

"*They were gonna let us have it.*"

Beckert frowns in thought. "Oh...Well, then... We have to stop the attack!"

"Roger *that*," Thompson says.

"Almost there," Beckert states. He banks the craft in a smooth turn, swings about, and thrusts to a halt. Magnetic limbs clank against the hull of a vessel.

"Major Ralla and General O'Kai are both aboard," Beckert adds. With a flash of his goggles anchor claws grip the edges of an airlock and ratchet down to hard seal. A gauge appears on the console, counting up from zero to one hundred kPa.

"We saw Cadre One shattered...nothing left," Maiella ventures. "How in the... How did O'Kai survive?"

"He *wanted* to." Beckert takes a deep breath and stares through the hull of the vessel, haunted. "And when O'Kai wants something, I don't know of *anything* that can stand in his way."

DISEASED

The hatch iris opens, distracting Thompson from what could have turned a seasoned Geek apprehensive, and he peers through to the open airlock of a Cadre warship. Recessed red ceiling lamps cast a diffuse glow over bare metal wall and floor plates. A relaxed thrum filters through the open hatch like the heartbeat of a resting predator. Such a dim, cave-like interior might set a Colonist on edge, but to Thompson it offers soothing appeal of familiar ground.

The Gun throws off harnesses, rises from his recliner, and claps a hand on Beckert's shoulder, regretting he never found time to reconnect with him after the Forestall rotation. One moment from that rotation stands above the rest of his recollections: in a flooded tunnel beneath the ruins of a city named, *Arlington*, the young Geek crouched beside an enormous white reptile, studying the beast closely, and he apologized for killing it. What seemed initially to be first-kill anxiety Thompson later understood was profound insight.

Summoning that moment, Thompson says to the Geek, "You told me once, 'Hunger is universal.'"

Beckert looks up at his old Team leader through a blizzard of code in his goggles. "Aye, sir. I did. And it is."

"If we do this right, we may never be hungry again."

Beckert grins. "I'd like that, sir."

Thompson glances at Maiella, and she looks through her eyebrows at him.

"Sooner is better," she urges.

He nods, and they slip through the hatch into the airlock. A Brick peeks through the inner airlock porthole, great round helmet filling it, then moves aside and hauls the doorway open. Maiella and Thompson step through, turn, and gawk at how savagely battered and scorched the Brick's kit is. Whole plates are blasted away to frayed fiber mesh, and slashes in the mesh are stitched together at thick scar-like seams. The helmet bears multiple divots where active ceramics have been smashed or ablated away, exposing dimpled alloy under layers. The remainder is a blend of welds, fills, and patches, like some ancient shattered pottery an archaeologist has painstakingly restored. It baffles Thompson how the man inside this mangled armor was not liquefied from abuse.

The burly Operator seals the lock and Thompson asks him, "Been through a grinder, Brick?"

The Brick slings a carbon-doped rifle that is not Cadre issue and he slides up his faceplate. With a smirk, he replies in deep, warm tone, "Aren't we always?"

Maiella squeals, "ARGO!" She dives at him, wrapping her arms around his thick collar.

Argo smiles gap-toothed, gums pale. Hooking Maiella in with one arm, he hauls Thompson in with the other, and the three embrace, heads together. They squeeze tight, slap each other on the back, and separate for a better look at one another.

"I never should have doubted you two," Argo says sincerely. "Couldn't see the big picture. I'm sorry for that."

Maiella slaps his chestplate then her grin returns. "Big and *dumb*, that's what you are," she scolds.

"Forget it, Argo. Just good to see you still breathing," Thompson adds.

The outer airlock slides shut and a quartet of staccato *clunks* telegraph through the bulkhead, announcing Beckert's departure.

Hope I'll see you again...

Giving Argo's armor another head to toe glance, he asks, "What the hell happened to you?"

Argo peers down at himself. "This? Had a spot of bother taking a Blueskin heavy cruiser."

"*You* took on an Eleto cruiser?" Maiella probes. "By *yourself*?"

"Of course not!" Argo says with a scowl. "General took point, and Beckert provided tactical support."

"One team? You took on a heavy cruiser with *one team*?" Thompson clarifies, head tilted.

Argo squints at the Gun, as if such a thing was perfectly ordinary. "That's right. Ship got caught in the Zulu blast and went dark. Thought she was dead, falling into the solar gravity well with the rest of the junk. But then her engines fired a few seconds and she turned away. Right then, knew we'd found our ride."

"If she was close enough to an Anti-Matter blast to go dark...that whole ship must've been *cooked*," Maiella posits. "How'd you fix her?"

"Didn't have to," Argo explains. Seeing skepticism in both Maiella's and Thompson's faces, the Brick adds, "C'mon, I'll tell on the way."

The three set off down the corridor, automatically falling into stride, arms swinging in tempo. Argo leads, explaining over his shoulder as they march, "External sensors were all scorched on the blast side; comm arrays were slagged. Big splits in the hull two of me could fit through. So we parked on the blind side and Beckert listened for internal comms, wireless, whatever he could get. At first, was mostly hand held radio with no encryption. Could hear 'em wheezing and coughing.

"After a few hours network came back online. Geek spoofed one of the slagged comm arrays, and they started pouring transmissions through him out to the Eleto fleet. Perfect man-in-the-middle. Got their encryption keys, everything. Either they had no idea, or were too busy to check. Anyway, we waited while the Blueskins patched their systems back together. They kept sending out updates to the fleet, so Beckert didn't even need to snoop. Once they had the reactor stabilized and ship drives running again Geek went on full net assault. Made it look to the fleet like comms were down. But inside, he'd gotten root access to every node and locked 'em down *tight*. Gave General and me the green light, and we committed. Snuck in through a hull breach. What Beckert couldn't open for us we cut through, easy enough. Crew was worse off than we thought. Could barely stand much less put up a fight."

"If they were so weak," Maiella posits, "how come you look like you spent a night in the compactor?"

Argo snorts. "Well, their combat mechs didn't care a *bit* about radiation. And those things pack some dense firepower in a man-sized chassis."

Thompson shakes his head. "Beckert's practically welded to his seat. So it was just you and O'Kai inside?"

"Yep. Good thing, too," Argo says. "We got pinned at this one intersection. O'Kai was whittling down defenders a shot at a time. Was gonna break their blockade for sure. Then a mech stepped up and blew a hole through the hull behind us. O'Kai caught an edge and held on, but I got sucked out the gap, flippin' ass over lid to the Black." The Brick stares off through the side of the ship. "If Beckert *hadn't* been strapped to his seat, I'd still be out there." Argo faces front. "Anyway, he nabbed me with the landing struts, flew me back. Aimed his laser drills through the gap and gave 'em the full spread. Sliced through mech and barricade. They never saw it coming. Then Beckert put me right on my feet inside, like I'd never left. After that, we popped compartments, venting as we went."

Maiella whistles. "Weak or not, a heavy cruiser's a big win for one team."

Argo nods then halts without warning. He turns about, eyes wide in recollection. "O'Kai...he just *doesn't quit*. This one time, Mech had us square, in the open, right? Long corridor, no exits. My cannon was spent. Saw the flash of a rocket plume and figured that was it. O'Kai rushes, leaps sideways, *grabs the rocket mid air* before it's up to speed, whips it around him, and releases it back at the mech. Hit the thing center mass. Should've ripped his arm out of the socket, a stunt like that. Would've, probably, without his armor... But the point is, I saw our death. O'Kai saw something else. Defeat just doesn't compute with him, it's like...he doesn't *believe* in it...

"I tell you Gun, you're tough, no disrespect. But there's a reason O'Kai's the general. No matter what they threw at us, *he found a way*." The Brick huffs in amazement. "I'll follow him *anywhere*."

Thompson glances at Maiella uncomfortably then stands straighter. "Well, we've got intel for him. Urgent."

"Sure thing," Argo says. He faces front and resumes his brisk pace through dim red corridors.

Maiella studies the hallways, finding no sign of battle as they go. There are no Eleto markings, no traces of plastic or decoration. Her mouth bunches on one side, and she says, "This isn't the heavy cruiser you captured. This is one of ours, isn't it?"

Argo answers without looking over his shoulder, "Correct."

Thompson asks, "So what happened? Lose your new ride?"

"Thing was brittle from the Zulu blast in every way," Argo replies. "Reactor tried to go nova the whole ride. It was so far out of tolerance Beckert had to disable safeties so it wouldn't automatically scram. And then there was all the structural damage. Every spar and rib was either fractured or broken." The Brick grunts and shakes his head. "Did what we could in flight to shore up the major issues. But when we arrived, Beckert hit the brakes. Half the ship stayed on course. The rest took a left, folded right over. Crimped all the coolant lines to the reactor, and severed most of the hard control lines. With safeties off, she was gonna go critical, no way around it. Geek barely got us out of there before she went."

Thompson glances at Maiella, then asks, "Argo, when did you get here?"

"What, to this system?"

"Yeah."

The Brick shrugs. "To guess, I'd say fifteen, twenty minutes ago. Ah, here we are."

The trio steps through peeled blast doors onto a circular bridge with one curved row of consoles. A Geek in armor is seated at center front, a web of lanyards interconnecting her HDI to the console. O'Kai stands over her shoulder, watching an array of holowindows that hovers at the forward wall. One view is from the nose of a Cadre corvette as it plunges through distorted space, arrives at a much larger Eleto warship and strafes it, then immediately leaps back into distorted space. Another view is from the side of a Cadre cruiser as it, too, leaps into a formation of Eleto ships and unleashes a barrage into vessels only a few hundred meters away. Another view is from Operator helmet cam, streaming live video of smoky enemy corridors. A rifle bayonet points the way, muzzle flashing with cunning accuracy at figures that lurch and slump aside in the haze.

Thompson's eyes jump from window to window, watching Cadre warships leap in from distance, unleash an obliterating fusillade, and leap away before enemy batteries can return fire. Vessel after vessel belch flames to the void, vent plumes of plasma, and vaporize in spheres of incandescent filaments.

"*No...*" Thompson mouths.

O'Kai turns about, favoring a leg. His right arm is locked across his torso as if held by an invisible sling. He cradles his helmet with the left. The general's kit is hammered to the brink of scrap and ground down on every surface, like an outcrop of weather-beaten stone. Bloodshot eyes recess in cave-like sockets, and his typical short gray hair is singed away, scalp peeling in translucent sheets. He smiles in spite of this, showing long gray teeth in pale gums.

Argo comes to attention, snaps a crisp salute, and announces, "Sir! I present Gun Thompson and Geek Maiella, returning from rotation!"

Hurrying to set his helmet onto an adjacent console, O'Kai puts heels together and salutes with his left hand.

Maiella and Thompson stamp to attention and snap salutes, conditioned response to command as automatic as breathing.

"There they are: Team Spectre," the general rasps. "The finest Operator Team the Cadre has ever known." A deep breath rattles and pops in his chest. "At ease," he says, and the general limps stiffly toward them.

Thompson notes how gaunt the man is beneath gray stubble, how hollow his cheeks are, and how prominently the bones of his skull press against the skin. Creases around eyes and mouth have deepened, giving him the appearance of a man twenty years older, and his gaze has the intense focus of one half-crazed by starvation.

Betrayed by his reflexive subservience to authority, and shamed at how eagerly he lapped up long withheld praise, Thompson opens his mouth to demand a cease-fire and retreat. But one look at the general's soot- and blood-marred face is proof he might as well ask the man to self-terminate. After another uncomfortable glance at the screens, the Gun asks instead, "We had five more days before the assault. Why attack now?"

O'Kai juts a lip and frowns at Argo. "Were you not told? Our vessel suffered a terminal failure upon arrival."

Thompson shrugs, not understanding the connection. "Sir?"

O'Kai frets in disappointment, then explains, "An unscheduled warship appearing in regional space, then exploding? Puts the enemy on alert. Would have tipped them off to your distraction. Rather than squander your efforts, I ordered the assault to preserve the element of surprise." He looks over his shoulder at the holowindows and smiles. "Now then," he says, turning back to Maiella and Thompson. "Let's get you some proper gear and into this fight."

"Sir, we weren't distracting them," Thompson says with barely reined frustration, "we were communicating. And they were *listening*. They were going to let us come home!"

O'Kai scowls. "You can't seriously believe that, Gun. No, of course you can't. The enemy has burned us out TWICE. You know Cadre One is lost, yes? While a setback, we are *not* defeated. Today we prove it, *decisively*."

The general turns about and limps toward the holoscreens. "Argo, give Thompson my rifle. Maiella, take Ralla's pistols. Beckert will get you back in the action."

"Sir, there's another way," Thompson blurts.

Without looking, O'Kai replies, "The only *way* I'll entertain is victory."

"We can give that to you," Maiella adds.

O'Kai turns about, interested. "*That's* worth discussing. Spill."

"We've spent time with them, speaking to their leaders," Thompson answers.

The general clears phlegm from his throat. "And what weaknesses did you find?"

"Not weaknesses, sir, similarities."

O'Kai lowers his brow. "Not following."

"The Eleto want to live as much as we do. They want to see their children grow strong and thrive, just like us."

"*Of course* they do, Thompson, *at our expense*."

The Gun shows his palms. "I thought the same. I thought we always were enemies and always would be. But we *weren't* always enemies, sir."

"I fail to see your point," O'Kai states with an aggressive edge that makes it clear the failure is not his.

"The point is, we're the ones who shot first from the very beginning. We started this! *We* provoked *them*."

"Yes, yes, I know. How does it matter now?"

"How does it *matter*?" Maiella echoes, incredulous.

O'Kai drills a harsh glare into Maiella. "We are at *war* with a powerful enemy. Unless you have anything constructive to add that will lead to their defeat, it's time you put your skills to use elsewhere."

"I do, sir," Thompson states, "and I beg patience to hear me out."

O'Kai stands with equal weight on each foot, spine straight, and he growls, "*Then get to it.*"

"You've proved your strength, General. Retreat to the Black and reserve your forces. Let Maiella and I resume negotiation with the Eleto. We were close, *really close*, to establishing trust—"

O'Kai holds up his left hand, and with strained composure, says, "You'd have us resettle Earth, using the Colony Apparatus to start anew. I comprehend the appeal. But I *cannot* allow us to be trapped in one place where they could bomb us out on a *whim*. You suggest we rely on their verbal assurances? We are the *last* of our kind, Thompson, and you'd put us right under their noses where they could kill us off easily. No. The only thing this enemy understands is *force*. I cannot and *will not* trust our future to their goodwill. A general must pursue the course that grants greatest security. And greatest security only comes with their eradication."

The Gun shakes his head. "We'll never get there, sir. The Eleto have dozens of worlds."

"Eighty of them," Maiella adds.

"How do we halt all those production centers?" Thompson posits. "A population to pull troops from... Even if we kill a hundred to one...a thousand to one... a MILLION..." The Gun juts his lip. "We'll be overwhelmed."

"Why am I indulging this...?" O'Kai asks himself. He swipes his face, barely clinging to his last shreds of patience. "The enemy clearly prepared for an attack here. The additional warships since your last rotation proves it. And, as you see, *we are mopping them up*. Ralla, status!"

With the personality of a vending machine, Ralla reports, "Forty-eight percent of enemy vessels captured, destroyed, or rendered combat ineffective. Eighteen percent of Cadre fleet destroyed or rendered combat ineffective. Seven Operators KIA. Enemy warships clustering around capital ship, presume guarded retreat or evacuation."

"Copy that, Gun?" O'Kai lifts an eyebrow. "Our best models never predicted such a one-sided victory. We have your diversion to thank for that, and the fact that our viral shells found their marks. But we've lost seven of our finest. Getting you three into action would prevent us losing more."

Argo nudges Thompson. "C'mon, Gun. Corps needs us. *Let's go.*"

"I'm not *in* the Corps, Argo."

"Is *that* what's keeping you?" O'Kai asks, astounded. "Very well. You are reinstated as Major in the Operator Corps, along with First Lieutenant Maiella. Team Spectre is reformed." He offers a wan smile. "Now, go *in honorable service* and make us proud again." He sniffs once and resumes his gaze into the holoscreens.

Thompson stares past O'Kai at the scale of death occurring before his eyes. His mind touches on how intensely the Eleto's sense of betrayal must be, wondering if it truly is too late to do anything but commit. As if in aid of that thought, memories surface of the rough Eleto welcome, a welcome Sharon did not survive. His fists clench.

Their crimes are immense. But so are ours...

"Major, General gave us an order," Argo counsels. "C'mon, Gun. Let's *move!*"

"No, Argo. I can't."

O'Kai hunches and looks at the floor before turning around once more.

"I've always done what I believed was right..." Thompson states, conviction deepening his voice, "...right for my team and right for the Cadre. My service record reflects that. Until our rotation to Earth... That mission was killing *for the sake of killing*. It didn't make us safer, General, it just riled them up to come and find us at Cadre One. Which they *did*. And now Cadre One is lost."

"Not ten seconds back in the Corps and already second guessing his general's direct ord—" O'Kai begins.

"My general's name was *Dryden*," Thompson interrupts.

O'Kai's brow lifts toward his burned scalp in genuine amazement. He blinks then grunts in disappointment. "Your service has been longer than all but the two who stand beside you. Maybe *too* long for you to bear."

"Don't lecture me about service, General! I serve to *protect* life, while you're trying to *destroy* it at all costs. There *has* to be an end to killing, even if it means *terminating your command*."

O'Kai's eyes swell. "I've tolerated your insubordination, but I AM *NOT* ABOUT TO TOLERATE YOUR *THREATS*. ARGO, *RESTRAIN* HIM. AND IF MAIELLA RESISTS, *LOCK HER DOWN, AS WELL*."

"Aye, sir," Argo answers. He steps in front of Thompson with a look of pain surpassing any physical injury and whispers, "Why are you *doing* this?"

"I have to, Argo. *Help* us."

The Brick shakes his head. "I'm sorry, I...I *can't.*"

Argo reaches for Thompson's arm. Thompson snatches the rifle strap slung over Argo's shoulder and slams his other hand dead center of the Brick's chest. Argo's head flops forward as he staggers back and the rifle slips easily down his arm into Thompson's grip. The Gun steps forward and boots Argo in the chest, sending the Brick hurtling over the bank of consoles beside Ralla. He primes the rifle, tucks the butt into his shoulder, and levels the barrel at O'Kai.

O'Kai ignores the weapon aimed at his chest, staring at Thompson the way one appraises faulty machinery. "What *happened* to you? Is your mind *gone?*"

"No, sir. It's clarity. The killing has to stop." Thompson takes a deep breath. "Now, order the retreat."

"Never. Victory is assured. Nothing you do can change—"

A bloodcurdling scream pierces the air. Both Thompson and O'Kai whirl about and find Maiella standing beside Ralla, clutching the major's HDI in a two-handed grip. Ralla's shaved head is thrown back, polished silver contact terminals gleaming in the dim red light, mouth wide. She convulses, falls still, then topples from her seat and lands on the deck with a rigid *thud.*

O'Kai snarls at Maiella but leaps at Thompson, instead. The battered general slides past Thompson's rifle barrel and hooks his good arm behind the Gun's neck. O'Kai rotates at the waist, bumps with a hip, and throws Thompson to the deck like a sack.

Thompson lands on the rifle, his own body trapping it beneath him. O'Kai drops atop him, rolls him on his back, and elbow smashes his unprotected face.

"You're *not*...the *first*...*Op*erator...to *lose* it," O'Kai says between smashes, "but it's a...*shame* to...*see* it...*hap*pen."

Thompson rotates, blocks the general's elbow with one hand, and pounds O'Kai square in the jaw with the other. O'Kai tilts over from the hit but comes right back, frenzied. As the two grapple, Thompson snatches at the rifle. O'Kai gets to it first, and knocks it over to Argo. The Brick stoops for the weapon.

"Ah, ah, ah..." Maiella warns.

Argo looks up and sees Maiella with Ralla's machine pistol aimed straight at him.

"You won't," the Brick declares, ignoring the thrashing and *bangs* of a vicious brawl nearby.

Maiella shakes her head in warning. "*Don't* Argo. You're a brother to me. *Don't do it.*"

The Brick crouches, reaching for the rifle grip, eyeballing her the entire time. Her aim dips and she triggers a round into his gauntlet. Argo's hand flies back, pulling him completely off balance, and he flops onto his side, growling, as blood seeps between his clenched fingers.

"I fucking *told you*, you know!" Maiella sneaks an anxious glance at Thompson as O'Kai boots the Gun over a console.

Argo swats down his faceplate and rises from the deck. Head lowered, fists clenched, he strides at Maiella.

"You think I won't?" she shouts, backpedaling.

Argo rounds the console separating them.

Her grip trembles. "DON'T *MAKE* ME—"

Argo whips an open hand across her wrist, sending the pistol flying. Her bluff called, Maiella springs away. Argo catches her by an ankle, drags her out of the air, and slams her against an unoccupied workstation. She squirms and kicks at the gaps in his armor, desperate to get free. The Brick keeps hold of her ankle, walks her to an open section of floor, swings her sideways, and seizes her by the throat with his free hand. Lifting her high overhead, he leaps into the air, roars, and slams her with all his might into the deck. Maiella coughs and lolls on the deck, stunned, unable to draw breath as Argo twists the joint locks of her armor. She blinks through double vision, pleading in pathetic squeaks. Argo ignores her entirely, concentrating on immobilizing her legs, arms, torso, and neck.

BR-R-RAK

Argo spins in his crouch to see O'Kai's head thrown back, red mist descending over him, dark spatter on ceiling and wall. The general's armored hand falls away from the grip of a machine pistol that Thompson still clutches by the barrel. O'Kai pitches over on a rigid leg and crashes at the Gun's feet, brain spilling through the blasted top of his skull. Mouth gaping, Thompson looks down at the smoking pistol as if it was some malevolent traitor. Then the Gun looks at Argo.

The Brick's eyes pass from Thompson to the pistol in his hand to O'Kai's body. A low growl rises from his diaphragm.

"Argo, *no*," Thompson begs, unheard, still holding the pistol by its muzzle. He taps the grip against his chest. "O'Kai was trying to kill *me*! I grabbed the barrel and turned it... I think his finger was stuck in the trigger guard, and...and..."

Argo's teeth grind. His hands flex. A shudder runs down his spine from the tang of combat stims, then the Brick goes eerily still. He looks to one side, finds the rifle, and dives for it. Before Argo can bring it to bear, Thompson swoops in with a front kick that launches the Brick through a bank of consoles. Argo shoves off the wrecked console, rifle in his uninjured hand, but Thompson is already there, pistol pointed at his old friend.

"*Ease down*, Argo! C'mon! It's *me*, it's Thompson!"

Through clenched jaw, Argo gnarls, "Thompson could never do that. *Never*. I don't know who *you* are." His voice drops an octave in menace. "I don't know *what* you are."

Argo raises the rifle, but Thompson steps up and clicks a round into the Brick's wrist. Twisting with the shot, Argo whirls about, sweeps Thompson's legs, and drives him into the deck. He wrenches the pistol out of Thompson's grip and flings it aside then presses down on Thompson's chest with his full weight, cocks a maul-like fist, and hammers at the Gun's face. Thompson swings his head just enough that Argo's fist glances off his angled helmet until Argo clamps Thompson's jaw in a vice grip. His fist cocks for the finishing stroke.

Thompson slams both his knees into the Brick's back, knocking him forward, and bucks mightily. The Brick lifts, off balance, and when he tries to widen his stance he finds both of his knee joints are locked. As the big man topples forward, arms out, Thompson zips through the gap between the Brick's locked knees.

Propped on one hand, Argo releases the camlocks at his legs. Thompson scrambles to all fours, and winds up a crouching wheel kick that sends the Brick skidding across the deck.

In the corner of his eye, Thompson spots Ralla's pistol. He lunges, snatches it from the deck, rolls to his feet, spins around, and looks down the barrel of Argo's rifle.

Thompson leaps aside, triggering his pistol, as Argo flashes away. Pistol slugs bash against the Brick's breastplate, knocking him onto his heels, and Argo crashes over another console. The big man climbs to his feet, snarling with chemical rage, but before he can raise his rifle again, Thompson shoots it out of his grasp.

"*Damn it*, Argo, *knock it off*," Thompson wheezes. He glares at the Brick from behind his smoking machine pistol and coughs harshly.

Argo glances at Thompson's chest then dashes for the rifle. Thompson triggers at the back of Argo's knees and the big man collapses like a tower. Bellowing in fury and pain, the Brick slaps flat hands against the deck and drags himself toward the rifle on rubberized palms.

Another shot whizzes past Argo's head and connects with the rifle, sending it skittering out of reach.

"I said, *KNOCK IT OFF*!" Thompson staggers toward the Brick and coughs again.

Propped on elbows, Argo lowers his head then rolls onto his back and leans against a console. The Brick fumbles the latch of his faceplate with unusual ineptitude. At last, the latch releases, and Argo raises the armored mask. He blows a breath past wide lips and rubs his stubbly face.

Thompson takes a step closer, pistol gripped in both hands, keeping aim on his old comrade. He blinks with dizziness. "You *done*?"

Argo looks at Maiella then glowers at Thompson. "You two are *diseased*."

With his other hand the Brick arms a device, palmed from his waist while fumbling with his helmet latch. He flings it across the deck at Maiella. Thompson burns the rest of his clip at the grenade as it bounces. He misses.

The orb lodges against Maiella's rigid form. Thompson dives, snatches Argo's grenade, and wrenches the detonator out. The detonator explodes in his grip, blasting his right hand into a thousand bony splinters.

"*GAAAAAH*!" Thompson shrieks, eyes crushed shut, and he tucks the wrecked stump of his hand into an armpit. Rolling on the deck, lightheaded, struggling for breath, he hears Argo grunting, kicking and scraping against the deck, and he knows the Brick will be on him in moments. There is so little strength left in him, the Gun can barely move, cannot lift his head without his vision swimming. Turning onto his side, he rubs a hand over his chest that has suddenly began to throb and burn. There, his fingers find two small holes burned through the left side of his breastplate. He coughs again, feeling brittleness behind his ribs, and he understands.

Aw, hell. He got me.

"Thompson," a meek voice calls beside him.

The Gun forces his eyes open, struggling to focus on the armored woman beside him.

"Help me," she says, "I'm locked up."

Thompson reaches over through a haze of disorientation and absently *thunks* his bloody stump against her shoulder. Bright bolts of pain jar him from hypoxic stupor, and he reaches out with his good hand, twisting the locks at her elbow and shoulder. His eyelids flutter, strength evaporates, and he collapses to the deck.

INCOMPREHENSIBLE CALCULATION

Maiella's reaches to her opposite shoulder, frees the joint lock, and works down the rest of her arm. Nearly free, her hands fly across her torso hips, knees, and ankles until she is fully mobile again.

"Thompson! *Thompson*," she shouts, scrambling to her feet.

The Gun stares through the ceiling with half-lidded eyes.

"*Wake up!*" Maiella shakes him by the shoulders. Thompson's head slumps to one side.

Frantic, Maiella drags her hands over his blacked-out armor. "What's wrong with—"

Her fingertips catch on two sharp-rimmed holes through his chest plate, and she fixates on them, knowing too well which organs lie beneath.

"No, no, no, no, *no, c'mon*, Thompson, *stay with me!*" She reaches blindly for his hand and grabs a brittle stump that crunches in her grasp. Blood dribbles from charred flesh between bright slivers of bone where his hand should be. Her ears slide back.

"Argo, *need some help here*," she calls without looking. There is no reply.

Maiella turns. "Argo, this is no time to hold a—"

The Brick lies flat on his back, one hand clamped at his throat. The other arm extends straight out from his shoulder, palm up. His chest plate is glossy in a way it should not be, as is the hand at his throat.

"*Argo?*"

Maiella scoots across the floor to him. His faceplate is open, eyes wide in an astonished stare. Dark splotches cling to the stubble of his cheeks and chin. All around him, long arcs of dark spatter mar the floor and run down consoles in slow drips. Maiella drags a finger through one and it smears the way hydraulic fluid does not.

The Geek takes Argo's outstretched hand and tugs. "Hey! I'm *talking to you!*" She pulls harder, lifting his shoulder, then slides a flat hand underneath, hauls him upright, wraps an arm behind his head, and plants a knee behind his back to prop him upright.

"Just got the wind knocked out of you 's all. C'mon, on your feet—"

Argo's hand falls away from his collar, revealing a thick notch in his jaw right through the bone. Below it, the left side of his throat is ripped open. Maiella stares stone-faced, watching blood seep from lacerated vessels and pool in the basin of his helmet. Her eyes glaze.

"You, uh... Unh-unh. *No.* You're gonna tell me how to fix you, Brick, and you're gonna do it *now*, get me?" She jostles him for emphasis, and Argo's head flops forward, submerging his mouth and nose. There are no bubbles of breath.

Maiella releases the big man as if he was scalding hot, and he flops to the deck. Pooled blood in his helmet sloshes around his ears, splashing the Brick's face and running down the sides of his scarred face. She covers her mouth with both hands, shrinking back, head shaking in tiny jerks.

> *Argo's huge arm over her shoulders, MedTechs and fellow Operators cheering another successful return of Team Spectre from Rotation...*

> *Argo ambushing her and hoisting her off her feet in a Cadre hallway while Thompson smacks an open-handed rhythm on her backside...*

> *Seeing Argo's great round head behind the controls of a battered Eleto limousine... Shoving her way back into Cadre One so she could be there to welcome him home...*

> *Pressing against the transparent cylinder of his healing tank, soaking in descriptions of Earth and an inexhaustible foe... Envy at the new marks of valor sliced and branded into his hide...*

Maiella looks down at a man closer to being family than any Colonist could ever approach. Despite the growing distance between them, there was always the future—a place of possibility where paths would converge again and differences would be made irrelevant. She could look forward to a time when they would redefine Honorable Service together, and nothing would ever tear them apart again. Instead, this man survived every hellish Rotation only to catch an unlucky ricochet, and the insult of it simply does not compute.

She rubs at her throat, remembering how deftly Munro saved her from the Veteran's cut. But no matter how many times she assisted Sahara in *Europa*'s MedLab, all she can do is stare at a wound so ragged it looks like one of Honniker's pets took a bite.

Futility turns to lead in her chest, mocking all of her fruitless efforts at peace. Grief rises in an overwhelming tide and she yields, praying it will drown her this time.

A shallow gasp behind her...

She sniffs hard, glances over her shoulder, and swipes the back of her gauntlet under each eye.

Thompson! No way I'm losing you, too.

Maiella grips Argo by his armor and, with a groan, heaves the big man over onto his chest. Blood spills through the Brick's open facemask, spreading into a puddle around her boots. She ignores it, focusing entirely on freeing Argo's MedKit from his back rack. With a couple of flicks the latches release, and she lugs the bulky box over to Thompson, dropping it to the deck beside him. The MedKit blooms at her touch, presenting an array of surgical tools, implements, dressings, injectors, canisters, and phials.

The Geek unlatches Thompson's helmet at the collar and asks, "Can you talk?"

A wheezing exhale is all she gets in reply.

Lifting his head with one hand, she slides the helmet away with the other, sets it down on the deck plates, then winces. Thompson's lips curve in a discolored grimace and his neck veins bulge beneath the skin.

"Oh, no..."

Maiella rushes down the fasteners of his torso plating, lifts the front half as a single piece, and heaves it aside like trash. Racing through the inner layer's zips, she peels back the fiber mesh and spots two dark-rimmed holes singed through his undersuit. Blood mingles with sweat-soaked fibers, spreading through the surrounding fabric.

The Geek grips his undersuit at the collar, rips it down to the waist, and throws the flaps open. Punched through the Gun's left pectoral muscle is a pair of four-millimeter perforations, perfectly round, only a few centimeters above his left nipple. Shiny red beads form at cauterized edges, drip into the holes, and are blown back in a wheezing mist.

"*Fuck.* This is a, uh... *Tension pneumothorax...*"

She ratchets her wristlocks, flings off her gauntlets, then slips a hand between Thompson and his back armor, probing for matching holes. She finds none.

Means the beam energy absorbed entirely in your chest. Is that bad? That's probably bad.

"Okay, I'm gonna patch you now," she announces, voice strained by the touch of adrenaline. She rifles through Argo's MedKit, knocking implements out of their proper slots in haste, and pulls out an adhesive disk with a straw through the center.

After swabbing away blood-tinged perspiration, she positions the disk adhesive side down and guides the straw into the hole farther from his heart. There is gritty resistance of scorched tissue, hardness of a rib until she backs up and wiggles a bit, then the straw sighs as air trapped in Thompson's chest cavity blows out through the one-way valve.

Thompson's pained features soften. Bulging veins at his neck shrink to more normal size, and his Adam's Apple slides back to the center of his throat.

Satisfied with placement, Maiella presses the adhesive disk over both holes, sealing them under its broad apron. Chewing her lip, she sits back and watches Thompson breathe more normally. His mouth still looks discolored in the dim red lighting, so she picks up Thompson's helmet, fidgets with it until the lamps illuminate, and shines the beams at his face. The Gun's lips, cheeks, and ears are still tinged blue.

Maiella drops his helmet over her head, freeing her hands, and she rummages through the MedKit again. The too-big helmet bobbles on her head, and it keeps rotating to one side or other. Growling in exasperation, she grips the thing by the chin guard until she finds a clear mask in the kit. Holding it in the beams of the helmet lamps, she smiles.

"That's the one."

Diving into the kit once more, she finds a small, bullet-shaped canister marked, "O2," and jams it into the mask's single port. The Geek opens the valve and takes a big draw through the mask, blinks with delight, then presses it to Thompson's face and sets the strap around his head.

Condensation fogs the inside of his mask in reassuring, regular breaths. By degrees, cyanotic features yield to more wholesome coloration. Then, as an afterthought, she remembers his other injury and startles back to action.

Maiella lifts the Gun's arm and examines his ruined right hand. Half a thumb still roots in an exposed saddle joint of scorched cartilage and ligaments. Flesh of the palm and all four fingers are gone. Bright blood seeps between sharp needles of reinforced white bone and patters onto the floor plates between her knees.

With a melancholic twinge, she recalls how gently that hand touched, how erotically it explored. But flashes from the holowindows jar her back to the present. When she looks, the battle rages on, unabated.

Did Geeks take local control? She scowls in irritation. *Never mind, Thompson first!*

Maiella delicately ratchets Thompson's wristlock and slips what is little more than the cuff of a gauntlet past his blasted hand. Blood runs down the pale skin of his wrist, up his forearm, then wicks into the sleeve of his undersuit.

She fishes another strap from the MedKit, whips it around the narrow of his forearm, and cinches tight. Dipping one last time into the MedKit, Maiella retrieves a spray canister of expanding medical foam. With smooth, even strokes she paints the remains of his hand in chemical skin, careful to fill gaps between the bones with multiple thin layers, then blows on the synth-flesh to help it set. Sneaking anxious glances at the holowindows, she waits as long as she dares then releases the tourniquet. Thompson's chemical skin swells in dark blisters but holds, and she turns his arm over to watch for any leaks. There are none.

"That's all I know how to do for you," Maiella says to the unconscious Gun, laying his arm gently on the deck. She swipes sweat from his brow. "Hope it's enough 'til Sahara can take a look."

Whenever that may be...

Running a hand down Thompson's face, she watches him breathe in shallow gasps. Though clearly struggling, and still pale, his cyanotic discoloration is gone. Veins of his neck are in their proper proportion. And the distress around his closed eyes has softened. She sets his helmet on the deck, leans down to kiss his forehead, and says, "Rest easy, love. Back in a bit."

Maiella stands too quickly and her head swims. Swaying, she puts her arms out to steady herself, blinks hard, then makes her way to the console at front. Ralla's HDI lies on the deck, still tethered to the console by a web of cords. Its goggles blaze a barrage of images, data requests, warship statistics, damage, and casualty reports.

On the opposite side of the chair, Ralla lies exactly where she fell, waxy and still, yet the holoscreens show Cadre attack runs proceeding with the same ruthless efficiency. Maiella scrunches her face, perplexed.

"Are you still in control? *How*?"

Ralla stares, catatonic.

Maiella crouches beside the major and looks her over. "Won't be needing *that*," she says, yanking the machine pistol from Ralla's back. She is about to holster it when she notes subtle differences from her own old, hand-me-down weapons: modern refinements, slicker actions, better balance, even the smell is better. She smiles in appreciation, flips the pistol around her finger, clips it to her back, then transfers Ralla's magazines of caseless ammunition to her thighs.

Maiella turns toward the console, figuring Ralla's more cerebral style of service on the Council would have dulled her edge in close quarters combat. Then the Geek slaps her forehead.

NO WAY I'm gonna underestimate you.

Maiella rolls the major onto her chest, folds her arms behind her back, raises her boots to her backside, and torques the joint cams, locking the major in her exoskeleton.

"There. See how *you* like it."

Maiella slides into Ralla's chair and sets her attention on the holoscreens. The Eleto fleet is still scrambling, confused, disorganized. A few Eleto vessels gather into formation when Cadre ships leap in from the Black, unload a full broadside, and leap away. The Eleto vessel at center formation fractures, blooms with jets of violet plasma, and erupts like mercury under a hammer. Remaining vessels steer away from the blast, lobbing desperately random shots into space. The instant Eleto guns halt, a trio of Cadre Corvettes leaps in, ventilates the formation stem to stern, and leaps away as secondary explosions tear the Eleto ships inside out.

Cadre Geeks have a firing solution before they arrive... Maiella thinks in awe. *I can't even comprehend that level of calculation.*

Maiella taps keys on the console and zooms in on another cluster of Eleto warships. They glide together into tight formation and steer toward the fray as a single unit. Drives flare at the sterns; D-E barrels bristle and glow with capacitance. Then the black dot of a Cadre Virus Ship lands on one in center formation. Adjacent Eleto gunships open fire at it, savaging the friendly vessel without hesitation or restraint. The Virus Ship hops away, just ahead of beams and slugs tearing through hull plates behind it, only to land on another in formation.

Maiella shakes her head, knowing Operators on the Virus Ship have no intention of breaching the hull. By drawing fire from Eleto ships they are effectively adding enemy weapon batteries to their arsenal, and the Geek sighs in reluctant admiration.

Ralla's formation busting keeps Eleto forces in disarray. She can pick off a few at a time...make every shot count. Eleto can fill space with clouds of ordnance...the faster they shoot, the sooner they're out of ammo. Meanwhile,

Cadre ships hang back at safe distance then leap in with killing shots and leap away without a scratch...

Maiella blinks in horror.

The Cadre could win.

PIECES IN PLAY

Maiella glances over her shoulder at Thompson. His mask still fogs in reassuring cadence.

"All right, I gotta do something," the Geek says, facing front and collecting Ralla's HDI from the floor. She rotates the headgear, untangling the lanyards, then holds it overhead and snaps it onto her contact terminals.

<Interfacing...>
<Interface complete... Session in progress...Recognize new user...>
<User invalid...>
<Access denied>

The Geek smirks. "Gonna make me work for it, hu—"

A surge barges through her contact terminals like a ram. Debilitating noise and feedback smash her concentration while jabs of code eat through her virtual safeguards like solvent through foam. And then the real attack comes like a thousand armed Shiva, dagger in each hand, virtual blades plunging into her brain all at once.

Maiella rips the HDI from her head and pants for air, her scream still ringing off metallic walls. The console in front of her twinkles in deceptively sedate patterns, and she stares at it wide-eyed, wary of what lurks inside to the point of fear.

From the console, Maiella turns toward Ralla, and, after multiple huffing breaths, snarls, "That's you in there, isn't it, Major?"

Ralla offers no reply.

"Should introduce you to Honniker someday," the Geek grouses. "You two'd *get along*."

A series of blue-white pulses pulls Maiella's attention back to the holoscreens. Framed in a pane of two-dimensional light, the colossal diplomatic vessel spouts tongues of violet plasma from multiple strikes. Torpedoes rip from one side through the other, blowing clouds of glittering debris through exit plumes of orange flame. Its hull buckles then cracks into thirds. Escape pods spring from the disintegrating vessel like fleas abandoning a drowning dog, but the vessel's midsection flares in stellar brilliance. A ballooning shockwave overtakes every pod.

Maiella's jaw drops and she props herself against the console with both hands.

Counselor...Shondre... PLEASE tell me you weren't still aboard...

The Geek lets her eyes roam the bridge for a hint of what to do next, but there is no inspiration in walls, ceiling, or screens. Instead, she peers down at the HDI in her lap. A dark cloud swirls in the goggle's visual flows of code, probing, prodding, waiting.

"Fuck *that*."

Then, the Geek arches an eyebrow. Maiella parks Ralla's HDI on the console, stoops, and hauls the waxy major up beside the chair. Unsure if her idea could backfire, and if so, just how spectacularly, the Geek grits her teeth, grabs the HDI, and slaps it onto Ralla's shaved head.

The major's eyes immediately flick open. Her head jerks back in repetitive spasms and her eyes roll white as the black cloud drains from the goggles. Ralla's eyelids flutter, and she utters an extended moan, almost orgasmic, until her goggles halt their manic flow of code. Her eyes close and her head flops forward.

Console diodes switch to neutral amber and maintain steady illumination. In the holoscreens, Cadre vessels cease maneuvers and drift along their last heading. Eleto torpedoes catch up to three of them, cracking two in half amidships. The third is cored, its reactor punched completely through the far side in a blazing spark-filled fountain. The hulk slides past its intended target, inert, soaking shell after shell of Eleto defensive fire through its ruined hull.

Maiella scans window to window, watching half of the Cadre warships thrust to new vectors and resume the fight.

Those must be the seasoned Geeks...

The rest take evasive action, turning to deep space and thrusting away. An instant later seven new holowindows open, each with a frantic, unscarred Geek pleading for instruction.

Maiella lifts Ralla's chin and peers into her goggles. The dark cloud is gone, all code has halted, and a command prompt blinks. Behind the optics, Ralla's eyes are shut and her sinuses rumble with each deep inhale.

Snatching the HDI off Ralla's crown, Maiella declares, "Major, you are *relieved*," and gives her a shove. Ralla topples in her locked armor, head bouncing off the deck, still snoring.

While fresh-faced Geeks beg for orders, Maiella concentrates on Eleto vessels regrouping for counterattack. Disintegration of the diplomatic vessel has freed many Eleto warships that were pinned down in defense of it. Two loiter amid the slowly spreading wreckage, flood lamps and lifeboats sweeping the debris for survivors. The rest push hard in pursuit of Cadre warships.

Maiella looks down into Ralla's HDI. She takes deep cleansing breaths, closes her eyes, and snaps the headgear onto her contact terminals. This time there is no surge of feedback, no waves of debilitating noise, just a Cadre Command and Control system awaiting input.

Vigilant against possible remnants of Ralla's digital psyche, and with her best virtual defenses ready, the Geek transfers her perceptions into the digital domain.

Live data feeds from twelve Cadre warships stand ready, offering details on every aspect from Deep Space Drives to sensing apparatus to offensive assets, all available for remote operation. Data streams on thirty-two Eleto warships, complete with status, offensive potential, targeting efficiency, maneuverability, and countermeasures update in real time. One hundred fifty-two simultaneous Eleto broadcast channels (fifty-eight of which are cracked and available for eavesdropping) chatter away with best guess translations captioned beside each. Virtual battle maps, including debris clouds, track friend and foe alongside a menu of selectable battle plans. As if that was not enough, seven Cadre Geeks add their voices to the din, begging on the verge of tears for orders through every channel available.

Maiella peers down at Ralla through the frenzy of code scrolling past her eyes. With more than a little envy in her voice, she asks, "How the everlasting *fuck* did you handle all this?"

Ralla snores in blissful repose.

Maiella centers herself in the seat and growls, "If you can, *I* can." The Geek closes her eyes, blows another deep breath through her lips, and prepares for the enormity of the task ahead.

Don't let it overwhelm you, she reminds herself. *You came upon plenty of new systems before. This one isn't even encrypted. You can do this.*

Maiella leans back in her seat, shakes out the anxiety in her hands, and yields to the massive data flow, allowing it to wash through her conscious mind. Every contact terminal in her crown flows near maximum throughput and her goggles strobe at peak refresh rate. At first, she is only aware of how much data she is missing, how much of it slips by with out her attention. Torrents pour through her so swiftly that by the time she reads any particular data set it is already outdated. She winces, struggling to cope with so much information, unable to retain any of it. Exasperation cramps her concentration, making the struggle that much harder.

RELAX, she chides herself. *Stop trying to absorb everything! Let it pass through.*

The Geek closes her eyes, centers herself, and lets the cacophony scream through her mind again.

An ocean of information hurtles by and she feels as if she is in a raft, hands out to each side, trying to catch snippets on the way. With the hope of peace disappearing ship by ship a few thousand kilometers away, it takes effort not to read through such enormity. Instead, she forces herself to be a passive observer, immersing herself in the torrents of data, becoming accustomed to the barking-mad noise of it. She lays her hands on her knees, licks her lips, and chooses a single stream to focus upon.

Even a single stream flows with more data than she can reliably capture. Just as frustration tugs at her again, a hint of pattern emerges from the code. Structures coalesce from the bits, and, rather than trying to process the entire stream, she finds she only needs to acclimate to the flow then note changes and deviations as relevant data. Smiling, she selects another stream, establishes the normal state, maps the virtual structures, notes changes from the norm, and moves on to another. Returning to any mapped data stream is as easy as thinking about it, and each structure clearly resolves in her virtual view.

In seconds she builds a comprehensive map, sorting each data feed from the collective din. A virtual landscape emerges, assembling into towering constructs in her virtual mind. Each tower joins with an adjacent, populating both the inside and outside of a sphere like oversized skyscrapers on a miniature globe. There is no need to spin the globe one way or other, however. In her four dimensional virtual view she can see the exterior of every structure—and what is inside—simultaneously. She merely thinks about what data she needs, and the information is there, instantly.

What was bedlam moments ago is starting to make sense, and Maiella leans forward in her seat, more confident. As constructs resolve into a nebulous whole, she discovers algorithms operating in the background, filtering data like a digital subconscious, prioritizing and pricking her attention toward critical issues.

The more passive she is to the data flow, the more it reveals, so she opens herself completely. To her amazement, a fully animated model of regional space crystallizes in her mind's eye that dwarfs the spherical construct of data feeds. Animated images are faint, like motes of dust in a dim room, yet she recognizes the battlefield spanning through her imagination.

"HA!" she shouts, triumphant. "I'VE GOT IT!" And the entire image collapses.

"*Damn*," she curses, annoyed how tenuous her grasp is, as if it were all some illusion of perspective only visible from precisely the right angle—where the slightest distraction is sufficient to wreck the entire hologram. She blanks her mind, exhales the heat of a quick temper, and becomes the passive conduit once more.

Her patience is rewarded with the swift return of constructs along mapped data feeds. Rather than focus on them, she listens and observes, letting the system adapt to her in complex calibrations. As before, the models assemble, and she regains her hazy view of regional space.

As much data as there is pouring into her head, she feels a subtle draw in the opposite direction, drawing her out. Having already learned that the harder she tries the less she accomplishes, the Geek submits and allows her awareness to project into the machine environment.

Her view of local space immediately resolves into finer detail. A blue, brown, and green planet—glazed with a thin varnish of atmosphere—dominates the scene. A distant moon, itself over one hundred fifty times the mass of Cadre One, hangs at the opposite extreme of her virtual view. Between these giants, infinitesimal specks hurl energy and projectiles at one another in crude mimicry of thunderstorms pulsing across the planet's night side below.

Maiella aims her attention at a single Cadre vessel and finds she is intuitively aware of its condition, able to sense what it senses, instinctively able to target its weapons. Satisfaction tempts her to smile, but she tamps it down lest the image collapse again. Rather, she marvels at how seamlessly Ralla's algorithms supplement her own organic and cybernetic processing to deliver virtual battlefield omnipresence in real time.

I just got a million times smarter...

Diving deeper, Maiella explores a mesh network between Cadre ships and discovers a hardwired Geek at each node. She dips into one node and arrives inside another Geek's HDI, looking through a stranger's eyes at the crowded confines of a Cadre Virus ship. She tries to look around, but the eyes are not hers to control and they glance in directions she does not intend. The sensation brings instant vertigo so she retreats to her comfortable perch atop the convergence of all streams.

As heavy as the data load is at her end, her brief visit to another HDI informs her how much data is being filtered and processed locally by each connected Geek; and the full scale of Ralla's accomplishment finally dawns on her: the major has unified the entire Cadre fleet and every Geek in it into a single massive weapon. Right now, Maiella understands, she is the trigger.

I could think an entire attack run, share computation across multiple nodes, and execute in the blink of an eye...

Can I turn Cadre ships on each other? Nah, local Geek's would interrupt and override... And I'm still clumsy handling this, besides... Let's disengage and pull back. Give us all a chance to catch our breath...

Before she can execute, Geeks at remote nodes push into her HDI with queries why Ralla's calm, logical commands no longer guide them.

Maiella transmits to all Cadre vessels and Operator teams, "Major Ralla suffered terminal failure. Abort attack and retreat to safe distance. Begin repairs, treat wounded, and stand by for further orders."

All of the fresh-faced Geeks comply immediately, relief obvious in their unscarred faces, and Maiella senses their vessels powering up for a leap to deep space. But just when Maiella expects them to race off, their DSDs power down, and their feeds go dark.

That's odd...

She attempts a patch to restore control when multiple presences barge their way into her node, determined and persistent, wrecking her concentration. The comprehensive battle map wavers in her distracted mind then collapses.

Maiella slams her gateways shut in reflex, barring access, yet she can feel prying for weakness at the edge. Cadre Geeks barrage her via radio and video, opening hundreds, then thousands, of holowindows, every one of them demanding Maiella relinquish control and Ralla be restored to command. Maiella disables comms, and the blare silences. But without her feeds to the rest of the fleet there is no control. With no point to remaining fully immersed in the system, she withdraws.

Perceptions transition with a sensation of falling backward at the speed of light until crashing into her body with a full-length spasm. Maiella blinks in momentary disorientation then peers at an array of blank holowindows beyond a blinking command prompt in her goggles.

"It's too late to abort," a woman's voice says. "We're fully committed."

Maiella's head swivels toward Ralla like a bird of prey spying a rodent. Somehow, with only head and neck free, the major has managed to roll onto her side, and she looks up at Maiella without anger.

"I recall ordering Maddock to lock you up like this once," Ralla says. "I'm guessing you enjoyed the reversal?"

Maiella grins without mirth. "*I did.*"

Ralla nods. "I followed your efforts with interest. Whatever you had going with the enemy might have had a chance," the major says, unperturbed, "but it's over. O'Kai gave his order. It's done."

Maiella shakes her head, jaw clenched, glaring with intensity that could melt lead. "It isn't *done*! The cycle... It has to end."

Ralla considers Maiella's point. "Well, even if you were right, you're not the General. And neither am I. So let's not put our brothers and sisters at risk any longer. Let me wrap this up, *quickly.*"

"Not a chance."

Ralla blinks, taken aback. "Maiella, taking me out of action isn't going to stop the assault. Our teams know their orders, and false commands from a newly restored first lieutenant won't change a thing. Without direction, they'll improvise. As you know, we *excel* at that."

Maiella looks away to the blank holowindows and does a double take when one of them populates unexpectedly. Maiella scrutinizes the raw data, recognizing a lone Cadre warship that has broken from the fray and is approaching swiftly on constant bearing, decreasing range.

Ralla glances at the screen. "You know who that is, don't you? That's Maddock and Halgrim, coming to restore command. Just a matter of time."

Maiella stares at the approaching vessel and sucks her teeth.

Ralla frowns at Maiella, perplexed. She cranes her neck, trying to see the rest of the bridge, but cannot. So the major looks down at the floor and sighs. "If you're sitting in that chair, it means you got the better of O'Kai and Argo. Guessing Thompson has 'em both locked up, somewhere. But you *have* to see you're just delaying a Cadre victory, maybe getting our Operators killed in the process. There's no honor in that."

"*Honor...*" Maiella echoes. She swivels in her seat, facing Ralla to make sure there is no misunderstanding. Jabbing a finger, Maiella snarls, "I won't let you *fuck up our future* for HONOR."

Ralla frets. "You don't know all the pieces in play. Even if all of our Operators were killed or captured, we're still going to win, here! There's nothing you or I can do now to stop that from happening. So if you want to save lives, let's start with our Operators. Restore me to command so I can finish this."

"And the Eleto?"

Ralla shakes her head.

Maiella looks into the blank holowindows and says with somber conviction, "So, *what*, you're going to kill off everyone of them here, like they did to us?"

388

Ralla nods. "It's the surest way to prevent a counterstrike."

"Prevent a...? They have *eighty worlds*! They'll come back in force and retake Earth easily."

Ralla grimaces. "No they *won't*. We're leaving nothing to reclaim."

Maiella stares, incredulous. "No... No. You think you can kill this planet? Cadre hasn't got that kind of firepower."

"Like I said, you *don't* know all the pieces in play."

Maiella stares into the holoscreen, eyebrows knitting.

"Maybe in sixty, seventy generations we can come back and start over," Ralla adds.

"You've gone mad..." Maiella says, haunted. "You don't have any idea, do you?" Without taking her eyes off the holoscreen, she adds, "This whole planet is *alive*... It's our birthright...our *home*... I can't let you do this."

"Maiella, this is inevitable. I couldn't stop it now even if I wanted to. It's *going* to happen."

"We'll see about that, Major. And as for the Cadre... If I have to deliver *every single one of you* to the Eleto for peace, then *I will*."

R-F-N

Maddock leans over the shoulder of his Geek. Both stare into the same holowindow, and the Gun asks, "Anything?"

"She slammed all the gateways," the Geek explains. "Must've known we had C2 codes. But her passive sensors are still up. I think I can access one and attempt a patch."

"There's no network link from sensors for precisely that reason. So how would that help?"

"No network, you're right. But there is a video feed to the bridge."

"How would opening a holowindow on the bridge help? Won't that tip her off?"

The Geek shakes his head, making his lanyard to the console sway. "Not if we present the right data on screen. I can make it look like a regular sensor feed, so the pop up will be an alert of our approach. Totally normal, totally expected. Meanwhile, I'm embedding a macro that'll broadcast through that window in infrared. If she's disconnected herself from the system—and I'm certain she has to keep from getting hacked—she might not notice the window is emitting signal."

"Why IR?"

"We use it as a wireless backup if radio fails, or when there's concern of RF leakage during stealth runs."

"Didn't you say her comms are down?"

"Won't matter. As long as she hasn't air-gapped every system aboard, our ships are always listening for prefix codes. The *moment* our C2 string is recognized, her ship will accept any command I send."

"Do it."

The Geek's goggles strobe. With a smirk and a snort at the lack of challenge, he announces, "Window's up."

"Well done, Pollux," Maddock says, clapping the Geek on the arm. "Send C2 Prefix codes and lock out local control, but don't do anything else that might tip her off. Not yet."

"Understood, sir. Sending C2 Prefix string."

"Now, let's see if it worked. Still got that window open?"

"Aye."

"Keep the sensor feed showing on her end, but give me visual what's going on in there."

Pollux's goggles flash once, and the holowindow in front of them widens to view a Cadre warship's bridge. A female Geek in outdated kit is seated at the console, wearing Ralla's HDI, looking down at the floor to her side.

Behind the Geek an older Gun lies supine, breathing through a clear mask. The front half of his torso plating is removed, and a short tube juts from a circular patch on his bare chest. An old-issue helmet is parked on the floor beside him, lamps on. A Brick's MedKit sits open on the deck nearby.

In the background, a Brick lies on his face. Blood pools beneath him with tracks in and out. Arterial spray mars the consoles around him.

On the opposite side of the bridge, an elder Gun lies sprawled, the top of his head blown open, brain spilled out.

Maddock and Pollux both stare into the screen, taking in an unimaginable crime scene, when Ralla's voice streams in, "...*don't know all the pieces in play. Even if all of our Operators were killed or captured, we're still going to win, here! There's nothing you or I can do now to stop that from happening. So if you want to save lives, let's start with our Operators. Restore me to command so I can finish this.*"

"*And the Eleto?*" Maiella asks. There is no response.

Maiella looks into the blank holowindows and says with somber conviction, "*So, what, you're going to kill off everyone of them here, like they did to us?*"

"*It's the surest way to prevent a counterstrike,*" Ralla answers.

"*They have* eighty other worlds! *They'll come back in force and retake it* easily."

"*No, they won't. We're leaving nothing to reclaim.*"

"*You think you can kill this planet? Cadre hasn't got that kind of* firepower."

"*Like I said, you* don't *know all the pieces in play.*"

"Does she see us?" Maddock asks.

"Don't think so, sir," Pollux answers.

"*Maybe in sixty or seventy generations we can come back and start over,*" Ralla adds.

"*You've gone mad...*" Maiella says. "*You don't have any idea, do you? This whole planet is* alive... *It's our birthright...our* home... *I can't let you do this.*"

"*Maiella, this is inevitable. I couldn't stop it even if I wanted to. It's* going *to happen.*"

"*We'll see about that, Major. And as for the Cadre... If I have to deliver* every single one of you *to the Eleto for peace, then* I will."

Pollux looks up at his team leader, mouth hanging in shock.

Maddock's features harden into stony horizontal lines. "Broadcast that to the fleet."

Pollux's goggles strobe and a window opens with the last few seconds of video paused. "Priority broadcast to fleet, going out now," Pollux announces.

The holowindow animates and Maiella repeats over and over, "If I have to deliver every single one of you to the Eleto for peace, then I will... If I have to deliver every single one of you to the Eleto for peace, then I will... If I have to deliver every single one of you to the Eleto for peace, then I will..."

Maddox scowls at the looping video. "Get me on that ship, *R-F-N.*"

Pollux nods. "R-F-N, *aye.*"

QUANTUM FOAM

Superluminal travel lenses space around Shao-Lo's canopy. She is
no stranger to the effect, having ranged the Black longer than all serving
Operators besides Argo, but never before has she seen distortions so extreme.
Neither has she been passenger to an entire fleet of ships at once. Stacked
together with DSDs and reactors linked, the fleet's concerted output propels
her at bewildering speed. And she is its spearhead, riding a hyperluminal
javelin as it screams through interstellar void.

The view directly ahead is compressed, as if looking through a telescope
in reverse. Kaleidoscope streaks of blue-shifted light surround the axis
of travel. Stars smear into elongated spectra as they pass. Nebulae stretch
like rainbow putty. Nothing she sees resembles an identifiable object, like
hallucinations gone haywire, and it streams through her photoreceptors in
vivid, painful clarity.

With time and practice, Shao-Lo trains her new eyes to compensate
for the immense distortions. By supplementing her visual processing with
navigational charts, objects unbend and straighten into more linear geometry.
Stellar smears collapse to points in proper places then slide by with tranquil
ease. Nebulae, light years wide, herald death and birth of stars in neon hues.
Dark globules of collapsing dust offer stark silhouette against reflective and
emissive clouds, adding depth to hazy glow. And, beyond the Milky Way's
spiral arm, galaxies loom grandiose, maintaining relatively fixed positions in
the cosmic background.

Even these magnificent sights fail to keep Shao-Lo's interest, however,
and she settles back into meditative torpor. Recent events flit through her
mind, some light as the breezes in *The Park*, others heavy and insistent.

Humiliating contests against Saskia and Alessa...
Spitting a mouth full of dirt while the big feline kicked a
shower of sod... Saskia, reciting those infuriating rhymes...

Perception projected into an artificial body... Clumsy at
first, then steadying...

Deciding to abandon flesh once and for all in favor
of a ruggedized chassis... Months-long bite of scalpels...
cauterizing of blood vessels... Sawing, flaying, amputating...
Eyes claimed by a razor-sharp scoop... Peeling of scalp and
face from skull...burning chill that penetrated bone...
Never enough of the promised anesthetic...

Connection to her surroundings taken away piece by
piece... Proof of existence erased from toes, calfs, thighs,
hips, waist, arms, chest, throat... Feeling disappearing with
every spinal nerve Honniker cleaved, both terrifying and
merciful...

And then...

Saw blade shearing through trachea... The last breath
she would ever take... Blind, mute, numb, deaf... Not dead...
Inner ear providing a sensation of movement, nothing else...
Awareness of being lifted, of weighing too little, no pulse...
Horrible realization she was no longer attached to her
body... The grand sum of her existence encapsulated in a box
of bone and alloy...

Shao-Lo shakes herself from the dark turn her memories have taken.
It HAD to be done... If not, I'd still be stuck at Cadre Two... Just a
plaything for Honniker and Mikato...
Instead, I played THEM and got what the Cadre needed...
Roused, she looks around the canopy's smooth plexisteel interior and
catches a faint, distorted reflection of her new shape. Strut-like arms attach
at broad shoulders, fixed with thick cords of electroactive polymer. There
is no head to speak of, merely a raised mound planted with shiny black
photoreceptors spaced evenly around front, sides, and back. An angular
breastplate shields her few organic parts, and etched into that breastplate

is an image of her old self, as she was. Shao-Lo studies the image, remembering that person only distantly as if it were a previous life. While Saskia etched it as a gift to keep her rooted in humanity, it is an embarrassing reminder that she was once a singular entity, disconnected from her learned peers and the machines around her, hopelessly limited in comprehension and vision.

Their disappointments were justified, she thinks, still peering at the engraving. *I'd have thought the same in their place. And I had no clue the extent of their generosity. A new body that won't weaken or age, an intuitive grasp of physics and physiology, the possibility of shelter at Cadre Two should all other avenues of retreat fail, and an armada packed with a portable singularity called, Plasma Rain... In balance, it was an easy bargain.*

Content in her choices she settles in for the long flight and slows her metabolism, pondering how, with such elegant simplicity, the universe allows quasars to rise from—and return to—quantum foam.

Errand Girl

An ordinary yellow star.

For months, Shao-Lo watches a speck of light directly ahead—a single pinpoint that never smears to spectral lines. Always it seems far away, too faint to be near. But when the stacked armada drops from warped space and slows to a halt only four light hours away, the star is scarcely brighter than ones in galactic background.

"Deploy reconnaissance array," she commands.

Rough *klanks* telegraph through the cabin as the armada separates into component vessels then spreads out into parabolic formation, spanning light seconds edge to edge. Coded laser pulses interconnect each component in a meshed network with Shao-Lo's craft at the focus. Every wavelength of the EM band that reaches this ultra-wide baseline interferometer is collated, analyzed, and relayed to Shao-Lo's console, and she browses the variety of feeds.

Enemy broadcasts pour from the inner system and sporadically from vessels patrolling the outer rim. Knowing that anything sensitive or useful would be sent by tight beam, not omnidirectional cast, she ignores them and studies the solar system as a whole.

Twenty-five times dimmer and half the mass of Cadre One's blue-white sun, this star is beyond common, easily overlooked among hundreds of other stellar dwarfs in this region. The idea it could have produced anything of interest at all stands in Shao-Lo's mind as improbability of highest measure.

And yet, here we are.

Despite its diminutive size, the star holds several planets in gravitational thrall, and the brightly shining dots stand out against galactic background.

396

Gas giants lumber through the outer reaches, similar to ones orbiting Cadre One's blue-white sun. The two farthest out are unremarkable, largely uniform in color with numerous captured satellites whizzing about. Sunward, a larger gas giant appears to be consuming one of its moons, having pulverized it into concentric rings of rock, ice, and dust. But the largest of the gas giants draws her immediate respect. More massive than the other planets combined, it is a planetary system all its own with four huge moons in close orbit and a distant swarm of captured asteroids. She studies the behemoth with her synthetic eyes, admiring its alternating bands of clouds, its crown of blazing aurora, and its great ruddy cyclone so huge it could swallow the inner planets whole.

Were it not for Colonist navigational records, Shao-Lo knows she would have assumed this planet was the solar system's engine of creation and spent months scouring the many moons for signs of humanity's birthplace. *Europa*'s nav charts have already solved that mystery, however, so she turns her gaze toward the rocky inner system.

Photoreceptors of her mechanical chassis perceive with telescopic clarity and she spots the blue dot easily. It is precisely where expected, and what she sees conforms to every image she has seen in *Europa* archives. But microscopic optical distortions of her transport's canopy are intolerable nuisance, so, after a tense moment, she raises it. With nothing between her and the vacuum of space, no barrier between her and an astronomically improbable world where human life began, she zooms in with her new eyes and finds a place that is startling, rare, and beautiful.

A peculiar sensation nags from where her heart used to be, demanding without reason or explanation. All she knows for certain is that she wants to see more of this world, to gaze without hurry and explore its every detail at leisure.

Everything we'd ever need. Just four light hours away. And I'm looking RIGHT at it...

A familiar voice radios, "*Shall we go?*"

Shao-Lo dials back her telescopic gaze. Segmented hands dive into the ports on either side of her seat and emerge, bristling with weapons. "COME OUT, SASKIA! SHOW YOURSELF!"

"*Calm down, Colonel, don't get mad. I'm coming out.*" A spidery machine clambers up to the nose of Shao-Lo's craft, clamps legs around the bow, and crosses its arms.

Shao-Lo glowers with unblinking eyes. She leans forward, weapons ready, and growls, "You are not welcome here, *stowaway*."

The machine unfolds its arms and lays hands flat on the hull in a show of non-hostility. "*Had to come,*" the machine transmits. "*You've got too much firepower at your disposal. I don't think you can handle it.*"

"And you *can*?"

The machine leans back and shrugs. "*No way, not me. No one person can be trusted with this much.*"

"Mikato clearly disagrees."

Saskia's shoulders bounce as if snorting. "*Really? You haven't figured out why Mikato packed you up with this arsenal?*"

The two stare at one another through identical spider-like eyes.

"You forget," Shao-Lo says, breaking the silence. "I'm Shao-Lo, and Mikato, *and* Honniker. I have their knowledge and experiences, as they have mine. There's clarity I've never known before...greater vision beyond these improved senses. That's why they know I can handle it."

"*HA! You think they shared everything with you? You're an errand girl! Their willing stooge. Just a suicide bomber, nothing more.*"

Saskia's derisive tone grates, but a kernel of doubt tugs at the colonel's mind. "Doesn't matter what you say. I'll use *everything* at my disposal to win this fight."

Saskia leans toward the canopy again. "*Sure, you can kill every living thing on Earth, Eleto included. You can do that. And probably take out the Cadre in the process. Don't you see? Mikato and Honniker want you to do this, because if you do, they get rid of two threats in one stroke.*"

Keeping careful watch of her uninvited guest, Shao-Lo skims through Mikato's and Honniker's memories. She finds nothing to suggest Saskia is correct. Just as unsettling, she finds no evidence against.

"Plasma Rain *is win-win-win for them,*" Saskia continues. "*Use it, Mikato's theories are confirmed.* Win. *Use it and take out the Eleto here.* Win. *Use it and the Cadre gets caught in the blast, taking you with it.* Win. *There's no downside for them.*"

Shao-Lo points an articulated finger at her chest plate. "They don't want me dead. Honniker and Mikato put too much effort in. We're blended, *together*, all as one."

There are no movable features on Saskia's upper torso but a condescending smirk is audible in its reply, "*They already have what they want from you, Colonel. Combat experience...logistics, strategy, tactics, and leadership to effectively mobilize Cadre Two's forces. Sorry to say this, but you're expendable now. And if you're killed here, so much the better because all the secrets they shared with you die with you.*"

"You never merged with them..." Shao-Lo posits.

"*Damned right! I've lived with them a lot longer than you did, and I KNOW what they're capable of. Think I'd let those psychopaths in my head?*

Not a chance."

"They're...extremely focused, which for their fields of study is an advantage. Our minds have touched. I *know* them as I know myself."

"*Then you* know *I'm right.*"

Shao-Lo looks off into the Black and finds the distant blue dot. "We used each other to get what we wanted. I never claimed to trust them."

"*And there's no reason you should! What do you think they did with your old body, hmm?*"

Shao-Lo looks back at Saskia, weapons brandished in warning. "Honniker had it stretched out on frames... He flamed it, slashed it, and pulverized it *right in front of me.*"

"*All of it?*"

Shao-Lo stares.

"*If you know them as well as you say,*" Saskia ventures, "*then you know they waste nothing. They kept your DNA, Colonel, and right now they're growing a clone of you...a clone they can seed with all of your memories and experiences. They'll pick and choose which memories, of course, and edit its personality for a more favorable disposition. This clone will be identical to your old self, inside and out. Every scar, every reinforcement will be reproduced with absolute fidelity. But it will be* their *creature. And they'll keep this clone as a bargaining tool to use with O'Kai, because if it comes right down to it, who would O'Kai trust? A flesh and blood Shao-Lo that has all the right memories and scars? One who passes a DNA scan? Or would he listen to you? A cybernetic monstrosity that claims to be his lifelong comrade, utterly unrecognizable, as easy to put down as* I *was outside Gordon's Pub...*"

Shao-Lo's exterior offers no hint of expression. Inside, she seethes.

"*You* know *Honniker would do this,*" Saskia argues. "*If he can carve out your nervous system and drop it into a chassis like a battery, he can make the perfect copy of you. And* your own clone *will disown you as a fraud.*"

Shao-Lo slams the console on each side of her cockpit, denting the panels. "I gave what I *had to!* I swore to serve as long as I live, and *THAT'S what I'm going to do!*"

"*That's not in doubt, okay?*" Saskia says, articulated hands raised in a placating gesture. The machine turns, making a show of peering off toward Earth. "*So, what's your move?*"

"Other than dumping you here and leaving you to drift?"

Saskia snorts again. "*Don't shoot the messenger, Colonel. If you're listening, it should be obvious I'm looking out for you. Besides, Honniker and Mikato are as paranoid as it gets, and I'm convinced they're setting up their endgame. Soon as I heard you were bugging out of Cadre Two, I knew I had to bug out, too, in case they started seeing me as a loose end."*

Shao-Lo mulls the point then shakes it off. "Okay, let's say you're right. Those two would be fine if we killed ourselves off. They could go on forever at Cadre Two, maybe. But that isn't what they want. There are things Honniker and Mikato need but can't get. Since we're already slugging it out with the enemy, they can get what they need through us without having to poke their heads out of their hole. That's *valuable.* So valuable, in fact, they've given us their very best designs to protect them."

Saskia turns back to face Shao-Lo, weighing the Colonel with shiny black lenses.

"Let's say you're right," the machine posits. *"What's your objective?"*

"The objective is stability and balance," Shao-Lo finishes. "Mutual dependence."

"I hope you find it with those two," the machine concedes. *"You could maybe find it with the Eleto, as well. Not telling you what to do, but might be worth thinking about."* Saskia pats a quick rhythm into the nose of the vessel. *"All right. What are we doin'?"*

"We wait. And we watch."

Saskia slumps then spreads its mechanical arms. *"In the meantime?"*

Shao-Lo tucks her hands into side compartments and off loads the weaponry. "For a start, you can tell me how to keep you and Maiella from stowing away on my missions."

CADRE BLACK

Shao-Lo watches Earth with the patience of a spider in a web. Her armada, fanned out around her, soaks up every stray signal that strikes it and relays those signals via strands of coded lasers. Through this vast array is funneled background crackle of cosmic microwaves, pulses of neutron stars, gravity waves from supernovae in neighboring galaxies, bombast of solar fusion at the system's center, and faint harmonic emissions of each planet circling that stellar forge. Yet her attention is riveted on shockwaves of defocused energy just beyond Lunar orbit. With each flash a new Eleto transport emerges from warped space and thrusts toward an orbital platform above the blue planet, taking place in queue behind earlier arrivals. Shao-Lo dutifully documents every vessel, noting physical configuration, capacity, unique identifiers, drive signatures, even voice patterns of Eleto officers transmitting in the clear.

For days, the routine is the same: Transports and Freighters in, Transports and Freighters out. She automates the busy work of documentation and focuses on the hundreds of unencrypted video broadcasts emanating from the orbital platform.

Stoic Eleto in elegant dress convey what Shao-Lo presumes are current events. The newscasters occasionally arch a brow for effect or lower both chin and voice to add gravity to a report, accompanied by out of context images:

Blueskins in brightly colored, form-fitting outfits running across a field of hash-marked green... A disc hurled through a slot in a far wall, and a crowd of spectators jumping to their feet in elation...

PLASMA RAIN

A male and female Eleto couple in elaborate robes and veils, surrounded by a multitude of sycophants, holding a swaddled youngling overhead and smiling in pride...

Charts and graphs that rise or fall with unintelligible statistics...

An oversized dwelling (at least three times the living space of Cadre One) atop a low hill, gravel lanes crossing sculpted landscape... A wall of rose-colored stone encircling the compound with guard towers at regular intervals, the fields within planted with evenly spaced gray stones of identical shape and size...

Broad fronds at the tops of slender trees blowing sideways in a gale while an Eleto in hooded jacket shouts at the camera through a torrential downpour...

It's all noise, Shao-Lo thinks.
"*Unidentified object transiting Jupiter,*" Saskia radios.
Shao-Lo perks up in interest then sours. "You hacked my feeds?"
Saskia, still perched on the nose, looks over its shoulder and shrugs. "*I'm a fucking Geek, remember? Besides, there's way more data here than one person can sift. Hurry up or you'll miss it. Over the red spot now.*"
Shao-Lo sets her irritation aside and focuses on the system's largest planet. In the giant's southern hemisphere, a cyclone so huge it could swallow two Earths side by side dials into sharp focus.
"Got the spot," Shao-Lo states, "but I'm not seeing it. Is it gone?"
"*Not yet. Just really tiny. I can show you if you give me control.*"
Shao-Lo throws her hands up. "Take it."
The console zooms in on an unreflective speck against the Jovian cyclone. There are no visible features, merely a miniscule flat black silhouette skimming the tops of a ruddy storm.
"*That's Cadre Black, sure,*" Saskia volunteers.
Shao-Lo peers at the screen. "Agreed. And we only had one vessel in inventory that small."
"*The one Team Forestall collected?*"
Shao-Lo lifts her gaze from the console. "How would you know?"
"*Because I remember seeing Argo at the helm when they came home.*"
"*You* remember? You mean *Maiella* remembers."
"*What's the difference?*"
Light flares at the speck's sides and it dashes off to deep space.

"*Contact lost,*" Saskia announces.

"Can you track it?"

Saskia hunches in concentration, then sits upright and gazes off into the Black. "*Negative. Wherever it's heading it's gone.*" The machine spins around at the waist and crosses its arms. "*Cadre doing some long range recon?*"

Shao-Lo considers her reply then decides there is little she could hide from Saskia, anyway.

"No. That's *Europa*'s lifeboat."

Saskia spins forward. "*You don't think...something happened to the Europa?*"

"We're gonna find out." Shao-Lo taps her console, commanding the armada to re-stack. The parabolic formation collapses and component vessels interlock in smooth automation. As the massive ringed javelin forms up behind her Shao-Lo drops the canopy of her personal transport, saying, "No room in here, but you can ride in any of the others."

"*Nah. Fine right here,*" Saskia replies. It extends its mechanical arms and wraps them around the nose.

"You fall off, I'm not turning back to get you," Shao-Lo warns.

"*Couldn't shake me loose if you tried.*"

Assembly complete, the stacked armada wraps itself in a stealth field, spools up deep space drives, and slides sunward at sub-light speed.

CONSTELLATION HARDTACK

This is good, right here, Shao-Lo thinks, and the stacked armada slows to a halt.

Her console plots a high resolution rendering of the inner solar system, laughably inferior to what she can see with her own photoreceptors. So she peers ahead at a sparse lane of gray/white rocks that revolve around the yellow sun like pebbles in the tread of an invisible tire. Each object is spaced hundreds of thousands of kilometers apart, offering no threat of collision, yet the belt is just dense enough to suggest a dwarf planet that might have been. She wonders what happened to this non-planet, if it was blown apart or never formed, when a gift of intuition blooms behind her gel-filled eye sockets:

The sheer bulk of Jupiter behind me has gravitational influence all the way out to this rocky region, disrupting it and preventing any proto planet from taking shape...

While advanced mathematics is part of every Cadre Operator's curriculum, orbital mechanics is left to the Geeks. It strikes the old Gun as odd she should have such quick understanding of something never learned until she realizes the source of her intuition must have come from her sharing of minds at Cadre Two.

Thank you again, Dr. Mikato...

The old Gun thinks instructions into the console and her armada disperses into individually stealthed components. As before, the vessels interconnect via coded lasers, then thrust out to comparable distances and headings as the languid asteroids.

Nothing to see here, just rocks of the belt, she thinks and turns attention toward the infinite sky beyond her canopy. To aft, the system's far reaches are serene, seemingly eternal in unhurried motions through the cosmos, while inner planets fling themselves about in manic rush. The innermost is a cinder of cratered metal hurtling through its orbit, yet its rotation is so slow the dayside scorches as the night side freezes.

The next planet out is a shining mirror of sulfuric acid clouds that rage across its surface. No features are visible beneath the hazy atmosphere, yet Shao-Lo knows there is a landscape of volcanoes and lava plains. Dense air traps heat like a blanket until the ground swelters at a sustained four hundred sixty-two degrees. In the lowest valleys, rivers of supercritical carbon dioxide flow while the highest peaks are capped with Tellurium snow—a hellscape utterly hostile to life and machines.

The third planet is graceful and mannered by contrast, waltzing through its orbit with a luminous Lunar partner. Vast blue oceans and expansive green landmasses call to her from beneath a translucent veneer of breathable air. Such natural beauty hearkens to Thompson's overtly emotional depictions, tempting her to indulge in the same fantastic visions of nutrients that are grown, not assembled. At once she understands Thompson's enthusiasm, comprehending how even a seasoned Operator could be swayed. Yet discipline reigns. And for all Earth's appearance of civility and plenty, the level of activity in low orbit is an unsubtle reminder that the enemy is here in force.

Shao-Lo dials in her telescopic view and spies an orbital platform, warships occupying all but a few berths. Most are in various states of repair with clouds of drones and technicians weaving, grafting, grinding, and welding.

A flash just beyond lunar orbit grabs her attention. More warships arrive, battle scarred from stem to stern, and they turn directly for the orbital platform. Some bear gaping holes through layers of armored hull. Others limp along with ragged external mounting struts, spitting blue-white sparks where a DSD nacelle should be.

Shao-Lo turns her telescopic eyes back to the orbital hub and takes in the buzz of movement. Shuttles hop between vessels like electrons hopping molecules in complex chemical reactions. Transports rise from and descend to the planet below, forming slow moving queues of arrivals and departures. But as frantic as the visible activity appears, the amount of broadcast traffic eclipses it.

The old Gun browses random channels where Blueskin voices bray in excitement or calmly speak. Some sing in a variety of tones, not unlike what the Colonists called, 'music.' Many are accompanied by video feeds, though she finds few broadcasts about *Europa*'s lifeboat or the ones who arrived in it. Considering that unexpected arrival dominated the news cycle for the majority of her sunward dive, sudden absence of it in broadcasts strikes her as odd.

The old Gun leans back in her seat, reflecting on the sub-light plummet sunward when there was plenty of time to eavesdrop on enemy channels...

Interior view of a Blueskin Landing Bay, looking at the Cadre's smallest and fastest ship parked on stout landing struts... Anxious soldiers assembling in ranks, weapons ready...

Limousine ramp dropping, and a lone Eleto female strolling down it, arms wide, smiling in greeting at orange-eyed bodyguards... Swept off her feet and whisked away... Enemy soldiers storming up the ramp into the cabin... A scream... Chaotic glimpses of hand to hand combat... A bodyguard taking aim up the ramp, long rifle trained on a Geek inside... A shot rings out, misses, and embeds itself deep in interior plating... Fighting halts abruptly...

Cadre malcontents, Thompson and Maiella... Irritation at seeing the exiled Geek stowed away on another *mission. Undoubtedly the reason the mission had gone wrong...*

Finding Munro in such questionable company... Unbelievable! The big MedTech descending the ramp with wary eyes, battered, rattled, but on his feet...

Blueskin Soldiers, dragging out broken and bloodied passengers...

The Counselor's face smashed, jaw swinging, actuators jutting between rips in synthetic skin...

Sharon Jones, bleeding from her scalp, dazed... Perplexed, eyes unable to focus as her legs scuff down the ramp behind her...

Then days of tedious Blueskin reports... Glimpses of detention cells, the occupants malnourished, neglected, and clearly abused...juxtaposed with scenes of the Eleto captive living a pampered, easy life on a private estate under stolen skies... The insult of it, how casually they take everything for granted, their intolerance of such minor discomforts, and the petty, squabbling faces on screens... A despicable species filled with entitlement, absent any awareness or shame at what they have unjustly taken...

And then...
Captain Jones...pallid. Eyes closed, lifeless...carted around in a glass case...no respect or honors afforded... left to shrivel in the sun... Enemy crowds surrounding her, hurling every rotten and vile thing they can against her transparent coffin... Even Saskia—glib Saskia—falling mute when confronted with that scene...

Shao-Lo shifts in her seat, segmented hands flexing with the will to crush something.

Sharon was gentle and delicate... Impossible she presented any threat, and the enemy beat her to death on arrival...

A bizarre thought comes, *Is it so different from what we do on Rotation?*

The thought feels alien, as if transplanted from some other consciousness. She bats it away like an annoying insect and returns to the awful withering of Sharon's flesh, how her lips drew away from receded gums and long teeth, how her eyelids fell inward over collapsed eyeballs, how her dignity was trampled like Rosenthal's at Cadre Two. The image is as vivid in recollection as if it were happening live, and, in the tension of polymer muscles, Shao-Lo feels her commitment to violence turn colder.

Everything we've done has been for survival, nothing more. Never have we celebrated what we must do, nor mocked our enemy in death. It is QUITE different.

Shao-Lo taps her knee with a mechanical finger and ruminates on broadcasts of the Counselor weeks later, his face repaired... How easily he spoke the alien tongue to an assembly across a circular table, and how the scar-like seams of his rebuilt face give him the appealing likeness of a seasoned Cadre Operator.

Marks of valor and tribulation, Counselor, well-earned...

She considers his impassioned pleas to an indifferent audience and how sincerely he reached out to them. Whether the words he spoke were intelligible or not, his body language was inviting, eloquent. And even though his opponents across the table tried to fluster him at every opportunity with dismissive, flippant remarks, they were never able to do so.

O'Kai, himself, was never able to turn the Counselor from a path once taken, Shao-Lo thinks with an inner grin. *He's as relentless and persistent as we are.*

The old Gun falls back into her recollections.

Days passing with scarcely a hint of her comrades, and then patience is rewarded... Thompson and Maiella, properly attired in Cadre Kit, escorting Munro past the threshold of a great hall... Munro, striding between them, covered in a loud, pointless drape over his charcoal gray uniform... All three wearing the same grim expression, faces taut...

Commotion in the stands, open hostility...hurling of objects... A brawl!

Maiella and Thompson battling their Blueskin escorts... A burly soldier with orange eyes ripping Maiella off her feet, putting a knife to her bare throat... Crowd roaring in ecstasy as the blade plunges into her skin...

Thompson slugging through a pack of Blueskins, eyes wild and terrified, bellowing... His fists, knees, elbows raining frantic blows to reach Maiella...

Munro pulling a long-handled wrench from his belt and smashing the soldier's face with it... Dropping the tool then laboring to keep Maiella's life in her body...

Crowd roiled to rage and hatred, hurling objects down at Munro's back...

And then a single voice like the utterance of time, itself... The hall silenced, order restored...

It makes no sense, Shao-Lo thinks. *Sharon is murdered on arrival, the Counselor is bashed to non-function, and Maiella is nearly killed right on their chamber floor... The enemy is clearly trying to eliminate them one by one... Why would they stay?*

Needing an answer, the colonel delves into more recent events.

Scenes of hospital wards full of Blueskins in white-cloth beds, bleeding from eyes, snouts, and gums. None daring to move or speak, as if so fragile they might dissolve at the slightest jostling...

Somber medical personnel hovering momentarily at each bedside, dressed head to toe in biohazard suits and rebreathers, only lingering long enough to assess patient status in a bedside holowindow before moving on... Resignation to death plain in every patient's half-closed eyes...

Shao-Lo sits up with a start.

It's prelude... Munro has released the virus... And the Counselor sues for peace to distract the enemy, giving the virus time to spread...

Blueskins, burdened with sick and dying, divert resources from defense...

Cadre fleet arrives in force to find the enemy in disarray, distracted, unprepared...

It's genius.

She flips randomly through Eleto frequencies and stumbles upon a live broadcast of that same conference hall with the round mineral table. Not a single seat or bench is vacant in the risers surrounding it.

Hushed Eleto narration describes the scene, where the Counselor, Munro, Thompson, and Maiella have already entered through a side doorway. They stride up the lane between riser sections and take their places at the central table of polished mineral. The crowd mutters in a thousand simultaneous side conversations, offering little context. While far short of welcoming, there is none of the wild agitation from before; but watching comrades resume this process, having endured such maltreatment, sticks a splinter in her mind.

The virus is deployed; they don't need to continue this diversion... And they have every justification to leave and get to safety...

What am I missing?

Feeling cooped up, Shao-Lo pops the canopy and stands.

Saskia, hunkered low on the nose of the craft, notices Shao-Lo rising from her seat and asks, *"What do you think's going on?"*

Shao-Lo watches the orbital platform and docked warships, the tremendous capitol ship moored nearby, and the busy comings and goings of shuttles. She rotates at the waist, panning her view across the Black. "Cadre is out there, somewhere. And this is smokescreen before an assault."

Saskia turns toward the distant platform then looks again at Shao-Lo. *"Oh, I don't know about that. Counselor doesn't seem like a first strike kinda guy to me. Does he to you?"*

Shao-Lo maintains her telescopic gaze. "Maybe the beating he got changed his mind."

Saskia swivels its torso about and it raises a flat hand. *"Hold on a sec. Counselor's always been one for straight talk. And he's always used words to get things done."*

"Even if it takes forever."

Saskia scoffs, laying hands on its legs. *"Most of the time, yeah. But not always. Anyway, you didn't come back to Cadre Two blasting. You talked things through."* The machine spreads its arms, palms up. *"And look what you got out of it."*

Shao-Lo dials her telescopic vision back and levels her gaze on Saskia. "What, you seriously think Counselor's asking the Blueskins to give our planet back?"

"Yeah. He's bold like that."

Shao-Lo folds her arms and drums segmented fingers in thought. "True. He is."

Saskia hunches. *"Hold up, Counselor's gabbing again. Really going on about something... Whoa, this is weird... Maiella and Thompson are shedding kit."*

"After they were attacked?" Shao-Lo drops back into her seat and tunes her console into the broadcast. On screen, Maiella and Thompson strip down to undersuits. Thompson runs out of view while Maiella handsprings onto the polished mineral table, and the way the stuffy Blueskins flinch is satisfying.

On screen, Maiella crouches down at the table's center and waits.

"Is it strange for you," Shao-Lo asks her machine companion, "observing the individual you're based upon?"

Saskia looks up at Shao-Lo. *"You can tell me when you meet your clone."*

"Bah!" Shao-Lo blurts with a flip of her hand, and she stares off toward the distant planet. "Should have known not to expect a straight answer."

"Okay, okay," Saskia confides, *"yeah, it's weird. Especially seeing that big orange-eyed thug get the better of Maiella. Like watching someone try to murder your reflection... Out of body experience, let me tell you."*

Shao-Lo looks up from her console. "You want to tell me about out of body experience?"

Saskia contemplates the colonel in her new chassis and shrugs. *"Huh. You're living it."*

The two resume watching Thompson and Maiella twist around each other like gravitational objects. Shao-Lo observes with aloof detachment, seeing only a pointless demonstration of strength, dexterity, and prohibited physical contact. Once concluded, the two Operators step down from the table and dress in their armor, obscuring further any purpose to the demonstration. Then a flash deep in space steals her attention.

410

"You see that?" Shao-Lo asks.

"*That flash? Affirmative. The array captured it... Magnifying and playing back to your console.*"

In Shao-Lo's screen, a shock ring flashes inside Lunar orbit, and a horribly battered Eleto heavy cruiser emerges from warped space. Its entire length is scorched white on one side and crumpled as if squeezed in a giant fist. Its back half glows with residual heat then sprouts multiple plumes of plasma. The vessel skids sideways and braking thrusters fire to keep it on course. Major structural supports buckle amidships, the vessel crimps, and the back half folds over to meet the front.

A Cadre-encoded radio transmission calls out with O'Kai's voice, "*Cadre Forces, execute CONSTELLATION HARDTACK. Repeat, execute CONSTELLATION HARDTACK. Ranking officer steer to reference point Lima for Command retrieval. O'Kai, OUT.*" A minute black speck springs from the doomed ship's hull and leaps away as the folded ship detonates in a blaze of vaporizing metal.

Moments later, waves of blacked-out warships emerge from warped space, silhouetted against the blue-white planet below. Local broadcasts drown in the brash hiss of interference.

"That's it!" Shao-Lo declares. Her mechanical hands fly across the console and the armada draws together for re-assembly.

"*Hang on,*" Saskia says. "*Got multiple Eleto contacts, just dropped stealth fields... Burning sunward from the outer reaches.*"

"How many?"

"*Looks like forty plus...*"

"Let's get 'em, Geek," Shao-Lo orders, reaching into the compartments beside her seat.

"*Just wait a damned second, Colonel! We don't have to do this! Let's see what the Counselor's got—*" Saskia mutes itself as it stares down the barrels of Shao-Lo's weaponized arm. The machine asks with a hateful edge, "*Gonna kill me again, Colonel?*"

"Depends. Will you get in my way again?"

There is no expression to interpret on Saskia's featureless face. "*Guess I'll go find another ride, then.*" Saskia unwraps its legs from the nose cone.

Shao-Lo leans forward, weapon arm aimed and primed. "No, you'll sit right there, where I can see you. Move a centimeter, I'll cut you in half."

Saskia glares in silence then swivels its torso about and wraps arms around the nose of the craft. "*Awaiting orders,*" it monotones.

"Maintain stealth field and plot intercept from behind that task force. We'll engage just before they're in range of the Cadre fleet."

PLASMA RAIN

Shao-Lo's armada assembles with a series of telegraphed *klanks*.

"*Course plotted*," Saskia announces.

"Execute."

The ringed javelin thrums with accelerated annihilations, discharges twin lobes of energy, and leaps through a tunnel of warped space.

WHAT IS NOT HUMAN

The stacked armada streaks through warped space, carves a tight arc, and slides up behind an Eleto task force. Shao-Lo peers at the enemy formation through relativistic distortions.

"They see us?"

"No change in heading or attitude," Saskia replies. *"Our stealth field is holding."*

"Overtake, and prep a DSD disrupt pulse. Be ready for engagement."

"Inverse Warp field pulse charging...but you'll have fire control, Colonel," Saskia states. *"Then you can* murder *at will."*

"One cannot murder what is not human."

"Oh? Are YOU human?"

Shao-Lo looks up from her console, weighing the implied threat, but resumes study of the forty-two vessels charging earthward. Of particular interest is how closely they maintain formation.

Overlapping their warp fields, multiplying efficiency for faster travel... Caressing the sides of her cabin, she thinks with amusement, *what a novel idea.*

"Killing any sentient creature without cause is murder," Saskia blurts out. *"The Eleto, you, me—"*

"I'm not interested in your opinions, Geek. You're useful until you're not. Copy?"

Saskia glances at Shao-Lo's weaponized arm, turns front, and grips the fuselage so hard the thick armor panels flex.

"You have fire control," the machine announces.

Weapon systems appear like bright new ideas in Shao-Lo's mind, and enemy warships populate as line items in a to-do list. She selects a single vessel from the list, sensing how the combined assets of her armada orient upon it immediately. Choosing another from the list causes hundreds of individual weapon batteries to re-orient automatically, and when Shao-Lo selects multiple targets the system divides its destructive assets accordingly. The interface is remarkably intuitive, responding faster than the most seasoned Geek, and she peers at the nearing formation with delicious anticipation.

There is the slightest lurch as the javelin's warp field merges with the enemy's. Blueskin vessels are absurdly close, every seam, rivet, and weld of their armored surfaces visible without need of magnification. Shao-Lo looks into the belly of the largest, the first on her to-do list, and a multitude of weapons track with her gaze.

Active sensing beams reach out from that enormous ship and sweep the javelin's length. The colonel smirks inwardly at the thought of Eleto navigators checking consoles, perplexed why their warp field just inflated by a factor of two, and finding an object kilometers long—that appeared out of nowhere—flying close formation.

"Warp field disrupt pulse, execute," Shao-Lo states.

The javelin surges and erupts an out of phase warp field throughout the task force, and the tight formation smears into a long, thin column of drifting ships.

Shao-Lo peers at the stern of the largest vessel, aiming a thousand D-E rails with a glance.

"FIRE."

Coordinated beams plunge through meters-thick hull plate. Shao-Lo runs her gaze up the carrier's full length and the beams follow, slashing to the bow at a dazzling bead of vaporizing metal. She readies another slice front to back when the Blueskin vessel drifts apart into two sparking, bursting, flaming halves.

The old Gun gawks at the bisected vessel above her as it vents crew and innards to space. Giddy with potence, she browses an extensive list of untried systems and sets up her next round.

CURSED SYSTEM

A black-uniformed Eleto stands from his chair at center of a darkened bridge, and he glares, annoyed, at the empty space where a bank of holowindows once hovered. Shudders run the length of his vessel then emergency illumination bathes the bridge in dim amber light. Officers, occupying stations nearby, fumble at powerless consoles. Then a background hum begins from deep within the deckplates and cycles up. Overhead lights flicker on as power returns to the vessel.

"(*Report,*)" the black uniformed officer demands, his tone a knife's edge of impatience.

"(Sir,)" the engineering officer replies, "(warp field collapsed...Deep Space Drives shut down...presumably to prevent shear across axis of travel...)" He stalls, waiting for his console to reboot. Finally, it gives him something useful. "(Energy surge from unknown local source... *Not* an internal failure...)"

"(Damage?)"

"(Breakers tripped, resetting,)" the engineering officer says, clenched throat lifting his voice a half octave. "(Diagnostics completing.)" As the console reports more and more ship systems returning to function without damage, worry fades and he announces, "(Reactor stable, sensors coming back on-line... Whatever it was, all in formation were affected.)"

The captain steps to the side of his tactical officer and gestures toward the front of the bridge where a broad hologram used to be. "(Perhaps she would show us.)"

The tactical officer strums her console with metal-capped talons, and a wide, curving hologram projects in three dimensions at the focus of the bridge. Forty-one Eleto vessels plot in an elongated column with transponder data populating beneath their virtual projections. Vessels at the rear are dark and drifting. Vessels farther forward are already correcting for drift and returning to position.

"(All accounted for,)" the captain says as he settles into his seat. "(Orders from Command?)"

"(None, sir,)" the communications officer states. "(Comms may be dow— CONTACT DEAD ASTERN, UNKNOWN ASPECT.)"

Before the captain can respond, a white-hot slit opens on the largest vessel at center of the projection and penetrates through the far side. A blazing bead dashes from aft nacelle struts, through the mid-section flight decks, engineering, crew quarters, and straight down the tapered bow, cleaving the carrier into symmetrical halves. Decompression and secondary explosions puff each half apart as scorched machinery and crew tumble into the gap, silhouetted by flames and arcing power conduits. Wreckage of fighter craft break loose from superheated landing bays. Fuel and ordnance stores pop and flash like a convergence of meteor strikes.

"(*Such firepower...*)" the tactical officer mutters.

"(Stealth Field, active,)" the Captain barks. "(Break formation, random vector, and jump. Give us distance.)"

"(Stealth Field active,)" the tactical officer declares. Over her shoulder, she asks, "(Power to weapons?)"

"(Negative. All to propulsion, *top speed*.)"

"(Breaking formation,)" the navigator states, "(new heading, path clear, no obstructions, FTL jump...*now*.)" The vessel banks left, turns, levels off, and dashes through a tunnel of distorted brilliance, emerging into empty space far from formation.

"(Come about,)" the captain orders, "(deploy full sensing package, and report.)"

As the pilot brings the ship around, holograms at the front of the bridge re-plot.

"(Real time is catching up, stand by,)" the tactical officer states. As if by deja vu, the crew watches their distant formation as it was seconds earlier. All appears normal until a burst of energy at the rear of the formation ruptures the field surrounding the taskforce, dropping them out of warped space and spreading the tight formation into a long, thin column. At epicenter of the blast is a needle shape, more than twice the length of the Commander's flagship, with counter-rotating rings orbiting its length. D-E rails bristle from it like quills, converge upon the commodore's ship, and fire, slicing the carrier cleanly down its axis. A cloud of flaming, sparking debris belches from the carrier around its entire profile like an aura.

"(Magnify foreign object,)" the captain demands.

The holoprojection zooms in on the javelin. The entire structure seems to swell with flame and smoke, becoming ill-defined and difficult to image. The captain squints, wondering if the whole javelin is falling apart, until hundreds of brilliant pinpoints streak out from the smoke, turn on individual headings, and zip through the formation in a cascade of nuclear detonations.

Vessels at the head of the task force swing about like a school of fish. Unable to directly target through atomic glare, they launch a torpedo swarm of their own at the strange ringed needle. The needle ripples then dissolves into hundreds of individual pieces. Each segment takes a random leap away to space, converges behind the assault force, re-assembles, and spits more lances of over-penetrating energy. In the time it takes the torpedo swarm to come about, the task force is decimated.

Through gritted teeth, the captain orders, "(Comms, transmit data on new enemy combatant. Tactical, arm torpedoes, prime D-E Rails, load mass cannons and stand by. Nav, plot jump within a half light second then execute on my order.)"

A chorus of simultaneous affirmations sound from the bridge officers. The Comm officer transmits raw sensor logs to central command with warnings of new enemy tactics. The weapons officer heats up the gunship's considerable arsenal until every gauge on her console glows at maximum capacitance. The pilot plots a return path, mindful of debris and possible positions of the new threat. And the engineering officer steers reactor power flow, ensuring every system is fed the energy it needs at the instant required.

The captain clutches the edges of his seat in iron grip. "(Nav, jump, NOW.)"

The vessel plunges through space and emerges at the fringe of an expanding debris field. Friendly ships that were intact moments earlier are smoldering hulks of glowing metal, gored and pummeled by overwhelming firepower.

The captain leans forward in his seat, searching his holoprojection as it re-plots the battlefield, when he catches a glimmer of the needle much closer than anticipated. With pride at his crew's expertise, he bellows, "(*Full spread, FIRE!*)"

The weapons officer rakes her console and unleashes a hell storm of beams, slugs, and missiles along the needle's midsection. Her shots slam home, punching clear through the target and blasting violent plumes through the far side. D-E rails bristle along the needle's axis and swing en masse.

"(EVASIVE,)" the captain bellows, and the vessel dives, zipping off to the void in a perfectly executed hit and run.

The gunship emerges in clear space, comes about as before, and waits for the last few seconds of combat to arrive at the delinquent speed of light. In holoprojection, the bridge crew watches their vessel jump in near the battlefield, weapons hot. Their gunship unleashes a storm of destruction that obliterates a section of the needle four times the gunship's length, completely severing front section from rear; and the bridge crew cheers in exultation. Even the sullen captain clenches a fist in front of himself as if snatching a fly and squashing it.

"(*Got you!*)"

Their gunship dives away from the savaged needle, taking glancing shots from still functional fore and rear segments, then vanishes with a flash of DSDs. But the crew's elation ends when they watch the needle jettison the devastated modules then reconnect into a slightly shorter version of itself. Before their eyes, the last of the task force is shot apart by its withering beams. Then the needle threads its way clear of debris, orients toward the third planet, and leaps away with a flare of DSDs.

"(Comm officer, broadcast on all channels,)" the captain begins, "(Taskforce destroyed by vessel of unknown origin. Modular design and overwhelming firepower. Recommend *against* direct engagement, if possible.)"

The Comm Officer transmits as ordered then advises, "(Sir, that thing is faster than light. It will arrive well before our message does.)"

"(This one is aware,)" the Captain states. "(More a warning for any of our brethren entering this cursed system.)" He takes a deep breath. "(We're not about to abandon this fight, not while arches still beat in our chests. Resume heading, maximum speed. We will cut it down a piece at a time, if we must.)"

The crew synchronizes in a hundred practiced movements, and the gunship slides through warped space toward a blue-green planet more trouble than it has ever been worth.

THE TRUTH OF THINGS

Maiella eyes the holoscreen, watching Maddox's ship slide closer.

"Out of time," she mutters and her goggles flare with code. Course is solved, engine settings are configured, and non-essential subsystems are ordered to standby, leaving full power available to DSDs. Control macros never make it past her HDI, however. Time and time again Maiella executes but the console refuses to recognize connection.

"What the...?"

She reaches out to the console and types in coordinates by hand. The console sits inert, defiant. Every button is functionless, mere decoration on the rugged metallic plating, and the Geek slams her fists against them in frustration.

"It's a C2 lockout," Ralla offers from the floor.

"FUCK!" Maiella jumps from her seat, rips open the access panel on the console's side, and studies the photonic pathways. A plain truth is evident in simple circuits, which Ralla vocalizes an instant later.

"These are dumb terminals," Ralla states. "Once locked out, mainframe won't recognize any local commands, no matter how good you are. Control is external now."

Maiella grips the console's edges, still staring at its innards. "There's a way... *Always* is."

"Sure. You could pull all hardlines to the mainframe, standup consoles at each of the peripheral nodes, network them together, and patch an OS together from your catalog. A talented Geek like you could probably do it in twenty hours or so."

Maiella strides to the back of the bridge toward a bank of protected switches.

"You're going for the breakers?" Ralla guesses.

"That's right. Hard restart with me as the boot drive and central computer. Pulled it off once before. Can do it again."

"You *could* cut power to the computer, but there are redundant nodes in all subsystems. Unless you clear all those caches, they'll resume their last state and you still won't have control."

Maiella counters, "Then I'll shut the whole ship down."

"Cut power while the reactor's still hot? That's risky, Geek. Hard restart takes a full five minutes. Plenty of time for an unshielded, uncooled reaction vessel to breach. And if you're able to scram the reactor somehow, you're looking at a fifteen minute restart, *minimum*."

Maiella's hand rests on the main power panel, fingers hovering over the breakers.

"Even if we don't melt," Ralla continues, "Maddox and Halgrim will be here before you can finish. If you won't take orders, would you at least listen to reason? Unlock me and step aside. I'll order Maddox to stand down."

"So you can resume the fight?"

"Of course."

Maiella slumps. With a deep breath, she slaps off a row of breakers to peripheral systems, weapons, life support, DSDs and thrusters, navigation, inertial dampers, hydraulics, everything except the central computer and functions supporting the main reactor. The bridge goes dark, rushing of air through ventilator grilles abates, and only the background thrum of the ship's heart is audible. Her fingers perch on the last set of breakers, when, in silence, she remembers there is a radio aboard that has not been commandeered. Maiella collects her helmet, dons it, blinks at the radio icon in her goggles, and selects her intended recipient.

"Beckert, you out there? Respond, over."

The connection is live, but the radio is silent on the far end.

"C'mon, Beckert, I know you can hear me."

Silence.

"Okay, if you won't talk, just listen. The Cadre is killing itself out there. We have a chance to stop hiding, to stop the Rotations, forever. Look at it, Beckert, *it's right there*... a whole world we could live on. You've *been* there with Argo and Thompson. You've *seen* it; you've *breathed* it. You *know* what we're losing, and—"

"*You mutinied.*"

Maiella perks up, pleased for a reply no matter how hostile. "I *had* to, Beckert, O'Kai was going to kill us all—"

"*How can you betray your commanding officers? How could you turn your back on the Cadre—?"*

"NO, Beckert, I could *never* turn my back on the Cadre! We found a failure of leadership and acted accordingly."

"What failure? We're going to win here!"

"Maybe *today*. Then we *lose* the war tomorrow. We can't wipe out the Eleto, we just don't have anywhere near the numbers."

"Even if we lose, the enemy will think they won, and Humanity's extinct. The Europa *gets away with our MedTechs. It's a good plan."*

"It's a *shit* plan, Beckert, because where will they go? Keller used up his whole life searching for another world. Never found anything even close. Then he took his chances with Cadre One and Two. Cadre One's gone, and Cadre Two's fucking insane. Someday, the *Europa* will give out. Or, she'll be discovered. And after this sneak attack the Eleto will show no mercy. *None.*"

"We're teaching them fear. They'll keep their distance."

Maiella sighs. "Fear is why they'll hunt us, Beckert. Fear is why they'll finish the genocide and sleep soundly, after."

"You underestimate what we can do."

"Just the opposite. I think the Cadre's tougher than ever. But *we have to be more than fighters.* We have to see past war and think about what comes after. I mean, weird as the Colonists are, that's how we used to be...the way we're *supposed* to be... We don't have to be soft or petty like they are, but we can have things that make life worth living. It starts right here, with that planet below us. If you let this fight go on, we lose it all, forever." Her teeth grind. "And it'll be YOUR fault."

"Wait, what? Why are you laying this on me?"

"Because I *know* you, Beckert. Other Operators think in binary. Things are useful or not, things are a threat or not. You? You try to understand why things are what they are. You see more than utility in living things...you see the beauty..." Maiella smiles in fond recollection. "...even if they try to eat you. 'Hunger is universal,' you said."

"How did you know about—?"

"Thompson tells me everything."

"Thompson nearly bucked me from the Corps for that. Argo, too."

"I know. And Thompson admitted he was wrong for it; said you were the one who had all the good insights during the *Forestall* rotation. No one else bothers to see more than what they're told to see. But you see to the *truth* of things, Beckert. That's why I need *your* help. And that's why it's *your* fault if we all die here."

Beckert snorts. *"If I wasn't lashed to my console with stumps for legs, I'd be in there right now, locking you up and restoring Ralla to command."*

"Lucky me, then." Maiella casts an uneasy glance at the holoscreens, counting seconds until Maddox's arrival.

"*Isn't my decision,*" Beckert states, finally.

Maiella grimaces. "I don't have time, so I'll be blunt: A general's duty is to protect and preserve the Cadre, to rightly guide us through upheavals and hard times, right? Well, Cadre One is *LOST*. That's on O'Kai's watch. Now he's thrown everyone and everything we have left into an all or nothing showdown where victory is impossible. You with me so far?"

Silence on Beckert's end.

"He's dooming us all," Maiella continues, "Operators, Colonists, *and* MedTechs. The Eleto have eighty worlds. *Eighty*! We can't kill them all. We *cannot* defeat this enemy. All-out battle doesn't play to our strength. It's not survival. It's hatred. IT'S *MADNESS*, Beckert! How do we follow orders that we *know* are wrong?"

The channel is quiet and Maiella takes a breath for another round, but Beckert finally replies, "*I had trouble with that, as well, but... I can't betray the Cadre...*"

"I'd never ask you to! Stopping this attack *saves* the Cadre, Beckert. Stopping the attack serves life, on all sides. And if you still have doubts, think: Is Colonel Munro easily corrupted? No way. He was the biggest skeptic of the whole idea. He had some good points, too, which helped shape our approach. Took him a while to be come around, but he believed in what we were doing."

"*What can I do? I'm half a Geek in a Virus Ship.*"

"You got the C2 prefix codes, don't you?"

"*The new ones, you mean?*"

"Yep."

"*Sorry, I can't. Not if it means letting you harm anyone.*"

Maiella mutes her line, bellowing a long string of exasperated curses, until the holowindow chimes a proximity warning. Her eyes flick toward the screen. At center is a spot of nothingness that blots out cosmic background, growing larger. Lobes of sensing beams reach out from it, gauging, detecting, tracking, and the spot elongates as it turns into parallel heading.

Changing tack, the Geek unmutes her line and transmits, "This is all on you, Beckert. *You* brought O'Kai here. *You* brought him into a situation he didn't understand. He thought we were setting up a diversion. A *DIVERSION*! Sharon bought the Eleto's attention *with her life*. They were LISTENING...until YOU brought O'Kai here, and HE RUINED *EVERYTHING*. Now, you're gonna hide behind corrupt orders and pretend this isn't your fault? That's weakness *unbefitting the Cadre Grays*—"

"*I have ALWAYS acted to protect the Cadre!*" Beckert thunders. "*I KNOW what service means and I would give my life a THOUSAND TIMES if we could live free...*" Beckert trails off, suddenly conflicted.

"Here's your chance to prove it. YOU need to make this right. *YOU* need to fix this."

Tense seconds pass. As much as Maiella wants to shout and berate Beckert for being obstinate and blind, she knows the difficulty of his dilemma.

Thompson and I had years to figure out why Collection Rotations stopped working.... Breaking free of the Cadre rattled everything... All the assumptions, everything I was taught. Hell, I nearly self-terminated. It's too much, expecting Beckert to make the leap so suddenly...

Maiella glances at the holowindow as Maddox's ship slows in final approach. Without a thrust plume, only the sensing beams frame its unreflective outline. She faces the breaker panel.

I can shut the ship down, at least. Keep it from being a platform for genocide, maybe take out Maddox, too. I can do that much. She reaches for the last row of breakers.

"*I can't give you control of the fleet,*" Beckert radios, "*other Geeks won't allow it. So I'm giving you keys to your ship and only your ship. You and Thompson go to Cadre Two or anywhere but here. Make a life for yourselves.*"

"Beckert, there's no need for any of us to die here!"

"*DON'T PUSH ME,*" Beckert roars. "*Take your codes, and GO!*"

Maiella's HDI receives a data parcel and her goggles stream with hexidecimal strings.

"Thank you, Beckert! Maiella, out." The Geek races through the rows of breakers, switching them all back on, then rushes to the console, sending C2 codes straight from her HDI via wireless. She half expects another digital torrent of feedback to stab through her contact terminals. Instead, amber console bars turn green.

Maiella plops down sideways in her seat, too rushed to straighten the swivel, and plugs her HDI lanyard into the console port. Goggles pulse a successful interface then flash with available ship systems in all green icons save one. The weapons system icon flashes gray and remains locked out.

Damn it, Beckert, you fucking disarmed me?

Maiella glances at the holoscreen and finds it uniformly black, telling her Maddox is drawing alongside.

Time's up.

She recalls her command macro and sends it to the console. The vessel thrums with accelerated annihilations, builds to a tumult, and dives through a tunnel of warped space.

4179 TOUTATIS

In a blink, Maiella arrives in low Earth orbit at the terminator between day and night. Mountain ranges dominate her bank of holoscreens, crowded by thick cloud banks, casting long shadows across lowlands. Leeward slopes are arid brown while lush green expanses run down windward slopes. Rivers thread through highlands like veins, converging into a mighty stream that could never run dry. And then her eyes trace the river's outflow through sprawling delta to a vast basin of blue water. In a single glimpse the stories and images from the *Forestall* rotation become real in a way that feels like terror, if not for the longing and wonder that accompany it. Grandeur, natural splendor, such expanse and rarity—that a place like this could exist at all makes her heart nearly bang through her chest. Maiella swipes a tear from under her visor and reluctantly steers the ship toward the planet's night side.

Ahead, Eleto vessels rise en masse from a thick band around the equator. Unlike orderly queues she saw earlier, these are running flat out, racing each other for the safety of deep space. Spooked by the shock flash of her arrival, nearest vessels steer away chaotically, some colliding, or crossing the path of a trailing ship and scorching it with full-thrust plumes.

Watching vessels blunder into one another simply because she appeared in a Cadre warship gives the Geek a guilty twinge. But as much as Maiella wants to transmit a calming message that there is no danger, she knows Maddox would trace it. And if Maddox follows, any message of safety would be instantly untrue.

Hidden from sun's rays, her blacked-out vessel disappears against infinite sky, and Maiella steers carefully around panicked refugees.

Can't rest here... Where to?

As navigational charts update and sensors flow with new information, an obvious destination appears, bold and luminous, just over the planet's horizon. Half dark, half blazing bright, Luna calls to her, assuring a moment's peace to catch her thoughts and breathe. The Geek picks a point in Lunar Umbra, solves the jump, and executes.

Still warm from the previous jump, her DSDs plunge the vessel through warped space and she arrives a few kilometers above a landscape cratered over every meter of its silver-gray surface. The view is stark and monochrome compared to the lush view of moments ago, yet is familiar like Cadre One. Thudding in her chest echoes bittersweet memories of a past that is, even now, painful to release.

Nav charts update and plot her relative position in a three-dimensional holoprojection. Cadre and Eleto vessels still tear each other apart on Earth's day side, but Maiella watches the planet's night side for a sign of her pursuer. A shock of dispersed energy pops where she was only an instant before, and the Geek sits stone-like, waiting, with a wary glance at the temperature of her recently fired DSDs.

Maddox's Cadre-black warship slips into planetary shade and disappears against cosmic background. Maiella peers at the holoprojection, leaning close for a hint of thruster plume or some stray transmission that might leak from a battle-damaged hull. Instead, it lights up a full spectrum of active sensing apparatus, pinging away across multiple bands, and launches a swarm of drones. To her horror, it also extends D-E rails and takes opportunistic shots at fleeing Eleto ships. Distant gems of thrust pop in silent flashes that glitter with shiny fragments. Columns of vapor rising from the surface terminate in catastrophic orange fireballs.

"*Exile,*" Maddox transmits, "*surrender at once and restore Major Ralla to command. You will not receive another warning.*"

The Geek lets out a held breath. *If you could see me you'd've come for me, no warning. But you'll come looking soon enough... So what to do next?*

Maiella glances over her shoulder. Thompson's chest rises then falls, and his mask fogs in regular cadence. She deliberately avoids looking at the blood-soaked deck plates where Argo and O'Kai lie still. Likewise, she ignores the armor-bound major on the floor beside her.

"I've gotta talk to them, somehow..." Maiella mutters. "They have to know this wasn't what we wanted... That it's all a huge mistake... One man's insanity..."

She searches the holoprojection of regional space for ideas. All she finds is a planet and bright moon, tragically beautiful, with two miniscule enemies between plying their total efforts in eradicating the other.

Anxious, worried, and needing fresh air, Maiella lifts the faceplate of her helmet, surprised to hear Ralla mid-sentence.

"—did you do that? A C2 lockout *can't* be broken..."

"Do what now?" Maiella looks down at the major and finds her utterly perplexed.

"The only way to defeat a C2 lockout is with proper codes." Ralla blinks, intrigued. "*How did you hack that?*"

Maiella flips a hand, nonchalant. "Was the best Geek in the Corps, remember?"

She resumes her study of the holoscreens while Ralla continues her fascinated stare.

"My greatest error is underestimating you," Ralla states.

Maiella sits upright and shakes her head. "Okay, now I'm hallucinating. Sounded like you just offered a complement."

"Shao-Lo said something similar," Ralla continues, "after returning from Cadre Two. I should have listened then, because she was right. It's exceedingly difficult keeping you contained. If you were working *with* us, Maiella, just *imagine* what we could accomplish..."

Maiella slumps. "You *still* think I'm your enemy?" She squares her shoulders. "I AM FUCKING SICK of proving my loyalty and dedication. I *AM* working on the Cadre's behalf, Major. *And* the Colonists. *And* the Eleto. With all your intellect and processing power, you still don't get it: to secure *our* lives, we have to guarantee *theirs*." The Geek grips her chin and scrutinizes the holoprojection, trying to rebuild her situational awareness. "Just have to figure this out... What to do... What to do..."

"I watched your interactions with the Blueskins," Ralla volunteers. "Couldn't understand what they were saying, but—"

"Eleto," Maiella corrects.

"Pardon?"

"They're called *Eleto*. Not *Blueskins*."

Ralla scowls. "Fine, *Eleto*. I watched them beat you on arrival. They killed Captain Jones. Showed her off like a prize. No honors afforded for one who came in peace. Restraint was not my instinct, yet I waited."

Maiella glances down at Ralla, surprised at how raw Sharon's loss remains. Her jaw clenches, and the Geek looks back into the three-dimensional battlefield.

"There was the attempt on your life," Ralla continues, "which Colonel Munro decisively ended. Maybe Munro would be targeted next, in retribution. That could *not* be allowed, because the pattern was all too clear: they were killing you off, one at a time.

"You say you're saving *our* lives. From where O'Kai and I sit, we're saving *your* lives from a belligerent enemy. Will you consider that?"

Maiella scrunches her face. "If I did?"

"You'd see our goal is the same, from different perspectives."

"Not at all the same, Major. Not even close."

"Because you're right and I'm wrong, is that it?" Ralla struggles in her armor, scooting a few centimeters to a more comfortable viewing angle. "You claim to have better information and are singly able to make a unilateral decision for us, without discussion or consensus, yes? Even O'Kai, who—unlike you—*has authority to make unilateral decisions,* is not so closed-minded."

Maiella guffaws. "*I'm* closed minded? That's a good one, Major."

"You sit there, telling me O'Kai, Chusan, and I have all come to the wrong conclusion. You offer no proof or explanation, besides a visual log of your mistreatment at the hands of the Bl... *Eleto.* Yet you'd have us interpret it as evidence of collaboration and progress toward a non-aggression pact with a genocidal foe. In the Cadre's entire history, nothing was *ever* given to us. We take by whatever means we can. Today is no different. Regardless, when this battle is over, the enemy will fully comprehend our capability. *Then*, they'll negotiate in good faith to prevent what we do here from befalling one of their home worlds."

Maiella catches a chill from the major's cold logic. "Every life you take proves we are the monsters they claim us to be. Every life we take *increases* their hatred and desire to be rid of us once and for all."

"Because *you* say so."

"Because I've *talked* to them, Major. You think *we* were divided between Cadre and Colonist? They've been torn apart ever since they tried to wipe us out. You didn't know that, did you? They know the genocide was wrong...a terrible overreaction. Almost half of the Eleto have been looking for ways to make amends. How many of our Collection Rotations might have been a chance to reconcile? Instead, we kill all aboard like hyper-aggressive animals. The *Forestall* rotation only reinforced that opinion."

"They drove us to extinction before, but they would never do it again, is that your assumption?"

"Major, we have been the aggressors in every interaction since the beginning. It's up to us to prove to *them* we're more than killers."

"So you sit with them, and you talk with them. Do you know what they're doing on other worlds? Can you say *for certain* what they intend? Can you say without *any* doubt that they are not studying you, appeasing your requests while they manufacture more weapons and warships? Is your intel so complete you know what is going on in the minds of every...*Eleto*?

What contingency plans exist if they should change their minds *after* we agree to peace?'"

The major looks around the bridge as far as her locked armor allows.

"Jumping into a pact of non-aggression without the *slightest notion* of how you'd enforce it... Where does your *imagined* superiority of reason come from?"

Maiella laughs without mirth. "We risked only ourselves, Major. Every one of us in that delegation understood we might not live to see an end to hostility. Even Munro. Meanwhile, the Cadre could have reserved its strength in secret. *THERE'S* YOUR MEANS OF KEEPING A PEACE. But, no. You were so blinded by O'Kai's infallibility you'd burn us all up in a no-win scenario. The only sane option is to stop fighting. We do this *now* or we never have a chance again."

"Your capabilities are admirable," Ralla begins. "Just when I think there's a kernel of sense in you, I'm disappointed. But then, I've never murdered my own kind... We should have reconstituted you and been done with it."

Maiella freezes. Without a word, she rises from her seat, strides over to Argo's MedKit, and retrieves a small tube with applicator tool. On the way back, she jams the tube into the applicator gun like a cartridge and primes it. The Geek stands over Ralla a moment then descends astride her, knees pressing against the major's temples to immobilize her head. Clutching Ralla's lips in one hand, the Geek zips a bead of flesh weld across them, squeezes them together, and climbs back into her chair. She holds the applicator gun sideways and lets it drop to the deck.

Ralla thrashes in her locked armor, shouting through her nostrils in unintelligible syllables, her silver contact terminals banging against the metallic floor.

"You're *smarter* than this," Maiella says, studying the holowindows again. "There's a difference between doing what you *have to* for survival and trying to *utterly annihilate* an enemy. One can be forgiven. The other cannot."

Maiella glances down at Ralla and catches the major's cold stare. She sniffs once and adds, "You might as well know: O'Kai is dead. He tried to shoot Thompson, but caught the bullet instead. Argo's dead, too. Same reason, I guess. Wish they weren't." Her eyes defocus as she stares through a distant point. "Munro was never an Operator so he can't be general of the Cadre. Shao-Lo's off at Cadre Two, probably getting taken apart by Honniker. And since I haven't heard a word about Chusan making it to rendezvous, that would have made you ranking officer."

Maiella looks at Ralla again, and the cool stare is replaced by round-eyed surprise.

"You might have led us to a new future, Major. But it's clear you'd take us down the same dead end as O'Kai. I can't let you do that. Hate me now, hate me after, you'll be alive...if I can pull this off."

A *blip* from the console draws Maiella's attention, and she locks her eyes on a highlighted object beyond lunar orbit. It shimmers in and out of view, approaching on a heading so near the moon, it nearly skims the surface.

As much as she wants to deploy a sensing package, Maddox is on the hunt, so she studies what little she can see for hints or clues. The longer she stares, the more the shimmering reminds her of something.

Maiella clears all other holowindows and opens one large screen with the anomaly dead center. Using maximum enhancement, she peers at a distortion of space, roughly four kilometers across and two kilometers thick. Part of it shimmers in and out of view, offering a suggestion of reddish orange color. A faint halo of vaporized metal reflects like a translucent mirror, punctuated by an occasional spark. In a rush, she realizes what she sees.

Geek Korvus...overtaxing his freighter's reactor...eroding his injectors, leaving a trail of metal ions across light minutes... Stealth field was phasing in and out...

Maiella's eyes widen.

Cadre Operators welded extra struts on the freighter bows, prior to leaving Cadre One...

And Ralla's matter of fact words echo in her mind,

"You don't know all the pieces in play..."

"The freighters...they're de-orbiting an asteroid..." Maiella utters. Haunted, she pulls up a comprehensive chart for the Solar System and limits search to near-Earth objects. Multiple asteroids highlight in a three-dimensional holoprojection. All slide harmlessly by, however, one passes within a few lunar orbits. The Geek selects the oblong space rock named, *4179 Toutatis*. Overlaying the asteroid's regular orbit in her real time projection shows its path has deviated.

Well within the thrust potential of two unladen high-mass haulers given weeks or months to work...

Maiella's goggles flare as she extrapolates its path forward, and the projection plots a line that curves low through the Lunar gravity well and directly intersects the planet.

The Geek drags the holowindow where Ralla can see it plainly. "Is THIS what you were talking about, Major?"

Ralla looks at the holoscreen. She blinks once and nods.

CALLED SHOT

"Fuck radio silence."

Maiella boosts comms to full output and broadcasts in broken Eleto, "(To the People, see danger, urgent *most*. Stone from moon. Hitting will, world of green and blue. Said again, big stone from moon... Hitting will, world of green and blue.)"

Cursing her feeble grasp of Eleto, Maiella disables comms and thrusts into pursuit of the massive rock. Dusty debris hangs in a cloud around the asteroid, elongated into a tail, pointing where the rock would otherwise go if not being shoved from orbit.

With a clear approach behind, the Geek pulls up close, diverts to one side, and flies parallel. On the sunlit face, a freighter-sized object shimmers in and out of view. Maiella dials up magnification in her screens, and freezes the image mid flicker. There, in clear detail, is the ancient mass hauler she intercepted en route to Earth.

Korvus...

Maiella lets the video run again and watches the enormous vessel vanish in patches as if phasing in and out of existence a few hull plates at a time. The freighter's bow is planted deep in the asteroid's regolith, heavy gauge struts distributing the hauler's full force in a wide tripod. Stressed engines strain against the colossal rock, spitting a haze of sparks and ionized metal into the tail of dusty debris.

Maiella squints, noting the freighter's placement is well outside center of mass, yet the huge rock decelerates uniformly.

Other freighter must be here, as well, rooted to the opposite lobe, hidden.

"Cadre Freighters," she transmits, "alter asteroid heading immediately. Assault on Earth is aborted. Repeat, assault on Earth is aborted, respond."

432

"*On whose authority?*" Korvus radios.

"Mine, First Lieutenant Geek Maiella."

"*Authority not recognized. Clear channel, and do not interfere. Out.*"

Maiella leans forward in her seat. "O'Kai is dead, Chusan's missing, and Ralla's command ineffective. Munro deferred authority to me."

"*Major Keiko is next in chain of command.*"

"Until *Major Keiko* can manage quantum encryption over a meshed fleet network in real time, I'm all you got, Geek. *Now divert that rock, IMMEDIATELY.*"

The channel goes dead, and Maiella blinks in annoyance. "So it's like that, huh?" She glances at a grayed-out weapon icon in her goggles.

A single shot could lance both of the freighter's main drives. Strained as they are, the failure would be catastrophic.... If Beckert hadn't locked me out of fire control...

Maiella keys her radio once more. "Korvus, *acknowledge*, over."

The channel remains closed; no acknowledgement is given.

"All right, you *shit*," she growls, "let's see if Eleto gunships change your mind."

Maiella fires up comms, spotlights, running lights, active sensing apparatus, range-finders, and transponder, then feeds them as much power as they can handle. The vessel blazes like a new star against the cosmic background, broad spectrum, impossible to ignore. Within the glare, she encodes a message in Eleto, and the whole vessel pulses her broadcast in radio, microwave, infrared, and visible wavelengths.

"(This one is called Maiella of the Cadre. She begs all to see DANGER that comes to the People. BRING STRENGTH HERE, *NOW*)."

Maiella turns to her nav screen, hoping for any of its infinitesimal specks to disengage from combat and turn her way. She keys her mic and takes a breath to plead again when a trio of Eleto gunships arrives in a shock of dispersed energy. D-E rails shine with capacitance, swing toward the flickering freighter, and open fire. The freighter's high mass drives shatter into white-hot shards, erupting jagged slivers in all directions. Torpedoes streak from the corvettes, plunge through the freighter's compromised skin like paper, and detonate inside the vast cargo bay. Stunned, Maiella watches the freighter rip and billow apart in perplexing slowness. Then its reactor—every safety disabled and jammed in overdrive—breaches containment. The decrepit vessel's remains hurtle away in a pulse that sweeps a three hundred meter wide crater down to gray stone.

The great space rock turns ever so slightly then cracks at the joint of its two lobes, launching plumes of silicate dust. As the massive asteroid breaks in two, its joint grinding and pulverizing in low gravity, Maiella gapes in horrible realization.

I called in those shots... I killed Korvus...

The familiar sickness rises in her gut, fills her heart, and floods her mind with memory of violently torn and burned colonist bodies... Delicate parts, meant to be covered by skin and bone, laid open for all to see... Shock and pain of death on their faces... Undeniable red flecks and spatters on her hands that condemn her as the perpetrator.

"I *am* a murderer..."

Maiella's heart wrings inside her chest, telling her to vanish, to hide where no one can find her or the terrible thing she has done, if not for its reek of cowardice.

If I run now, millions die.

The Geek smacks her chest and sniffs hard, focusing on the present.

Do what must be done, now. After, let judgment come. Face it with clear eyes.

In her holoscreens, Eleto gunships probe the dusty haze with pink scanning beams, sweeping repeatedly where the detonated freighter once was. Then the beams reach out over the rest of the shifting rubble pile and sweep across a distorted hole in space on the opposite lobe. Like sharks to blood, they dart at it, D-E rails swinging toward the distortion.

Behind them, a blacked out gunship leaps in with a shock of dispersing energy. Torpedoes streak from it on brilliant blue jets, punching two Eleto vessels inside out, while D-E rails ventilate the third its full length. Torpedoed ships peel and bloom with secondary internal detonations. The third falls dark, drifting along its final heading, as the Cadre gunship turns and thrusts with casual ease toward Maiella. Her screen alerts in red block letters that its torpedo tubes are re-loading and its D-E rails are charging.

Maiella shuts down the blazing broadcasts, diverts power to DSDs, and steers for clear space. Her goggles strobe with code, her solution plots, and nav screen announces, COURSE CLEAR. DSDs flare with channeled energy and a tunnel of distorted space lugs her ship away many times faster than light.

Dead Heart

Shao-Lo rounds the limb of the planet and her new eyes spy hundreds of craft rising from below. Some gleam with fresh graphics. Others are aged, pitted from micrometeors, and scorched from countless atmospheric reentries. She finds towering heavy-lift barges, sleek pleasure craft, tiny single engine shuttles, orbital taxis, all riding intense exhaust plumes, burning massive amounts of fuel, jockeying for the imagined safety of infinite sky. Beyond a curved horizon, Cadre forces engage an Eleto fleet in brutally effective shoot-and-scoot runs. Half a million clicks farther, a heap of cosmic regolith slings through Lunar gravity on collision course with Earth.

"*This is wrong*," Saskia states with solemn conviction. "*Amplification of atrocity. Word of this will spread faster than light. No rest, no peace... humankind will be hunted to the last.*"

"They already tried," Shao-Lo replies, focusing on the sullen machine hunched on the nose of her craft. "Today, we return their attempt."

"*Bullshit! Mikato and Honniker gave you enough firepower to show the Cadre isn't just a gang of half-starved raiders... That could be a deterrent. But, no, you're using it and proving the Cadre's a mortal threat. If it doesn't happen today, the Eleto or a more distant life form will finish you off, which is EXACTLY what Honniker and Mikato want. How do you not see that?*"

Unmoved, Shao-Lo thinks commands into her console. "We've shared minds. I find no ulterior motive. This enemy brought us to the brink of extinction. If they're unprepared for a reckoning, they deserve their fate."

"*It just goes on forever! Someone has to end it.*"

"If the enemy wishes to surrender, they may do so at any time."

Shao-Lo's armada separates into component vessels, all but a small cluster orienting toward a new heading beyond the horizon. As their DSDs glimmer in build up to jump, Saskia straightens its articulated spine.

"DAMN YOUR DEAD HEART, SHAO-LO!"

Shao-Lo keeps a close watch of the machine on her bow, gauging the marginal increase of tension in its synthetic sinews, then transmits over Cadre channels, "This is Colonel Shao-Lo, arriving with reinforcements from Cadre Two. IFF Transponders active, recognize, Cadre Standard. C2 codes available to ranking Geek, code select TANGO MIKE, repeat, TANGO MIKE.

"DO NOT APPROACH THIS POSITION, repeat, DO NOT APPROACH. Hemisphere-scale weapon deploying. All Cadre assets, stay clear.

"Good hunting, Operators. Shao-Lo, out."

The armada streaks off toward distant battle, blasting an opportunistic path through lifeboats rising from the planet, and Saskia stares down the tunnel of destruction in silence.

Shao-lo's thirteen remaining ships thrust into new formation. The thickest of them opens cargo bay doors, birthing a compact gray object with twelve flat sides. The other twelve vessels take position around the periphery of the object and swing anvil-shaped bows toward it.

Saskia rotates at the waist, gawking at the moral horror taking shape only a few hundred meters away.

"Colonel, you can't," the machine pleads. *"We'll never recover from this. There are more cultures than the Eleto out there... An action like this can't be hidden, can't be cleansed...can't be forgiven. You'll mark us all too violent to live. Someone has to break the escalation, someone has to take us back from the brink...someone..."*

Shao-Lo sits calmly in her seat, weapon clusters at the ends of her arms primed. "Are *you* that someone, Geek?"

"How could I? I'm unarmed and you've got the drop on me. I wouldn't last a sec—" The machine whips itself straight at Shao-Lo, just slipping between the Colonel's rising weapon arms. Saskia slams into Shao-Lo, clamps her arms below the elbow, and stomps the Colonel with legs like jackhammers. Shao-Lo stands from her seat, rotates her arms backward at the shoulders, bashing Saskia headfirst through canopy glass behind her, rotates her arms forward with all her might and smashes Saskia into the bow hard enough to buckle armored plating. Saskia scrambles, keeping control of Shao-Lo's lethal arms, wraps a leg around one, scissors it behind a knee, and traps it. Shao-Lo detaches her hand and trapped weapon pod, withdraws the main spar of her forearm, and stabs it through Saskia's polymer-muscled

shoulder. Saskia kicks the loose weapon cluster out to space, removing it from the colonel's reach, but Shao-Lo stabs again and again, tearing through thick shoulder polymer a few cords at a time.

Saskia twists, deflecting Shao-Lo's jabs, and clamps a segmented hand around Shao-Lo's bare metal forearm; but its weakened shoulder cannot match Shao-Lo's undiminished strength. With the slow, relentless certainty of a hydraulic press, Shao-Lo drives her metal spar through Saskia's shoulder again, centimeter by centimeter. Polymer cords snap with harsh *twangs* that resonate throughout the machine's chassis.

"You've already lost, Saskia," Shao-Lo states. "Desist and resume your post."

"*Never.*"

Saskia swings its legs around Shao-Lo's waist, locks ankles, and scrabbles at Shao-Lo's shiny black photoreceptors. Shao-Lo weaves away from the awkward attack then cranks her forearm sideways, ripping through the last strands of Saskia's front shoulder muscle.

Saskia's damaged arm falls back, unable to flex forward, as Shao-Lo winds up another stab. In desperation, the machine releases its legs around Shao-Lo's waist, kicks off the edge of the cockpit toward deep space and flings its entire weight around Shao-Lo's weapon arm. Shao-Lo lurches in her stance, lifts off her feet, but her toes snag the edge of her console, just halting her launch to the void.

As Shao-Lo falters off balance, Saskia swings around to Shao-Lo's back and clamps legs around her frame. The machine rotates at the waist and rains savage blows with the backside of its double-jointed arm. A photoreceptor on Shao-Lo's crown shatters into obsidian shards.

Shao-Lo finds her footing, sets a wide, anchoring stance in her cockpit, and goes straight for Saskia's weakened arm. She stabs through more polymer shoulder cords and twists underlying framework until it cracks. All the while, Saskia keeps hold of the remaining weapon pod with its undamaged arm, hanging onto it for life.

"You only delay the inevitable," Shao-Lo growls as she wrenches through control conduits wiring Saskia's arm. "*Fall in line!*"

"*Delay is all I've got,*" Saskia retorts, "*to hold off the greatest crime ever committed.*"

"There are no humans on this planet, Geek. *There is. No. Crime!*"

Saskia unlocks its legs from Shao-Lo's waist. Still keeping death-grip of Shao-Lo's weapon arm, the machine spins itself around the colonel and lands punishing kicks. Every strike hits like a maul, bashing parallel scratches into active ceramics. Saskia soaks up telegraphed vibrations through Shao-

Lo's weapon arm, hoping to sense some ringing defect of structure or metal fatigue in the lattice underneath. There is none.

Shao-Lo counterstrikes with perfect timing, deflecting then breaking Saskia's assault. She rips the last cords of Saskia's damaged shoulder apart then starts on the other. Saskia flips and flails, striking randomly, seeking a gap in the colonel's defense. With three limbs to Shao-Lo's four, the machine goes berserk in desperate, ferocious attacks. Shao-Lo is patient, blocking, dodging, counterstriking, whittling her opponent down, watching for an opening, and is rewarded. Saskia commits to a brutal kick. Shao-Lo rotates with Saskia's momentum, stuffs the machine against the cockpit console, and pins it. Her arm draws back, forearm spar aimed at Saskia's opposite shoulder.

Saskia rocks with Shao-Lo's jackhammer stabs. In moments, its shoulder is shredded and Saskia's grasping hand falls slack.

Shao-Lo pulls her weapon arm free, takes Saskia's limp arm by the wrist, plants an articulated foot on the machine's armored torso, and rips the arm from its socket. She glances momentarily at it, tosses the avulsed limb to the void, and sets to work on the other.

Reinforced cables and alloy support structures stretch taut and snap like roots of a stubborn weed. Shao-Lo glances again at the severed limb and as she turns to toss it away, Saskia positions feet beneath itself, crouches below Shao-Lo's center of mass and explodes up from the cockpit with all its remaining might. Shao-Lo leans back, takes a hard glancing shot, catches a toe at the lipped edge, but flops against the side of her craft and bounces to space. By reflex, she extends her weapon arm and fires a stream of slugs, reversing her drift and thrusting back toward the craft. The shattered canopy frame is the closest handhold, and Shao-Lo seizes it. Its deformed frame stretches and pulls sharply against its hinges. One snaps free. The other holds with a tense wobble, leaving Shao-Lo dangling like a flag on a rope.

Saskia hangs weightless above the cockpit, dancing an armless jig. No matter how it tries the machine cannot alter its drift, falling away in slow motion.

Shao-Lo reels herself back to the cockpit like a spider climbing its silk, resets her stance, and telescopes a segmented arm, catching Saskia by an ankle. She slams the machine against the wrinkled nose plates, rolls the machine on its side, and impales Saskia through its torn apart shoulder socket. The old Gun leans in hard, burying her forearm strut up to the elbow. Centimeters apart, the two stare at one another with shiny black eyes as Shao-Lo fires up a cutting torch on her weapon arm. The colonel sets her grip carefully and methodically melts a gash down the seam of Saskia's torso plating. No matter how Saskia kicks, it cannot stop Shao-Lo's carving through one subframe spar after another. When the last spar slices Shao-Lo jabs segmented fingers into the gap and pries the chest plate wide open, laying Saskia's machine vitals bare. She goes straight for the power supply and grips it firmly.

"You *knew* you couldn't win, Saskia," Shao-Lo berates. "This was *pointless*. You accomplished nothing, and ruined yourself. *Why did you test me?*"

Saskia gazes up at the colonel. *"If I'd done nothing to stop you, I couldn't live with myself."*

Shao-Lo's arm tenses. "Last chance, Saskia. Fall in, or die."

The machine offers a weak laugh. *"May you live a thousand years, Colonel, to contemplate the monster you've become. I'll spend my last watt fighting y—"*

Shao-Lo yanks with a spray of coolant, electrolyte, and sparks. She chucks Saskia's mechanical heart over her shoulder and shoves the machine out to the void.

Saskia tumbles in a slow cartwheel above the brilliant blue and white planet below. With the last traces of power remaining in its draining capacitors, Saskia broadcasts in the clear, *"To all who can hear, Shao-Lo has a manufactured singularity called, Plasma Rain. IT IS A PLANET KILLER AND MUST BE STOPPED. Home in on this sig—"*

A fusillade of mixed munitions tears through Saskia's dying frame, piercing, melting, and shattering its last functional circuits.

The colonel lowers a soot-streaked weapon arm, smoke wisping from barrels in micro gravity. Saskia's exploded fragments scatter against the celestial background then fade from sight.

Shao-Lo yanks the remnants of the canopy from its last hinge and casts it off. Settling back into the cockpit's open bucket, she parks her one weapon pod and scans the heavens for any indication Saskia's warning was heard.

Meshed sensors from her armada report all known Eleto vessels are engaged, either in combat or in breaking down twenty-five billion tons of space rubble streaking in from the moon. The only vessels in her region are hundreds of civilian craft rising for the safety of deep space.

Free of threats, Shao-Lo thinks to her console, *Assemble and execute,* Plasma Rain. *Authority, Shao-Lo, Colonel, Zulu Bravo X-Ray.*

MORE THAN ANYTHING

Maiella's ship bursts through a shock ring of energy and swings about. All sensors converge on the spot she departed and stream data to her HDI. A holoprojection above the console refreshes with relative position amid the chaos, and her goggles augment local objects with tactical overlays.

Light seconds away, the moon gleams huge and bright. A cloud of metallic fragments rounds its limb, glittering with reflected sunlight. Immediately after follows a ruddy asteroid, its two disjointed lobes careening just above the surface at twenty-five kilometers per second. Tidal forces torque the cosmic rubble pile as it passes and the halves grind against each other, yielding, crumbling, collapsing into each other like stiff fluid. Silicate dust and rocky fragments erupt into space around it, feeding an already long tail as the mass slingshots earthward.

A dark speck shows in silhouette against the asteroid's sunlit halo. Maiella magnifies it with a double blink, and there, in three-dimensional holoprojection, is the outline of a Cadre Black warship.

Maddox...

Eyes wide, the Geek solves another random panic jump. An instant before she executes, the black speck pivots toward Earth and zips off with a flash.

Maiella blinks at her holoscreen, perplexed. *Why'd he break off pursuit? Did I lose him?*

Ship sensors stream with copious data on battling ships, debris fields, explosions, and frenzied transmissions. Wincing at the mad noise of it all, she peers through the carnage for a place to intervene when a single radioed plea calls her attention.

"To all who can hear, Shao-Lo has a manufactured singularity called,

Plasma Rain. *IT IS A PLANET KILLER AND MUST BE STOPPED. Home in on this sig—"*

The signal ends with a harsh *brap.*

Maiella's skin crawls from the eerily familiar voice. She sweeps frequencies for another broadcast to no avail, hearing only frantic cries of Eleto civilians and coded buzz of military transmissions. Curious why that one transmission caught her attention, the Geek plays it again and her eyes widen. "That's *my* voice... How the...?"

Revelation dawns.

"Saskia!"

Maiella aims the full sensing array toward the cry for help, opens a channel over tight beam, and keys her radio, "Saskia! Is that you? This is Maiella; respond, over."

Waiting for reply, the Geek finds a new curiosity magnified in her holoscreen. A plain gray dodecahedron hangs in low Earth orbit. Its electromagnetic profile, however, shimmers with interwoven and overlapping containment fields. Thermal energy bounces from it like a mirror, making it flash strongly in infrared. Magnetic lines of force curve into interlocking loops, reinforced by concentric shells of warped spacetime. At first glance, the apparatus reminds her of a powerful Deep Space Drive, minus all the external cladding, where the reaction chamber collapses space inside the reaction vessel and matter compresses into exotic states for an instant. Resultant decay yields a phenomenal burst of channeled energy, warping space in the intended direction of travel. The reaction lasts nanoseconds and consumes nearly all of a vessel's reactor output for several seconds prior to jump. Yet here, before her eyes, is a pocket of intensely compressed spacetime at equilibrium.

Nothing her vessel possesses can peer through that shimmering gray shroud, offering no glimpse of what it might contain. Field strength, however, suggests compression on par with a stellar core of one and a half solar masses. She does a double take at the figure.

That can't be right.

Maiella runs figures again then boggles at the repeated result, wondering if she could be parked a few light seconds away from a fragment of neutron star.

The Geek plays Saskia's warning once more and blinks at the unsettling *brap.*

Manufactured singularity? Impossible. You'd have to build a pocket universe to contain it, much less transport it...

The Geek runs a diagnostic on ship sensors then runs another sweep.

Result is the same, and the more she considers where this device came from, the more plausible it seems that Mikato, given unlimited time and energy, might have discovered a way to compress, store, and transport degenerate neutron gas.

Matter, compressed to nuclear density, Maiella thinks in disbelief.

The Geek runs back through her recollections of Cadre Two.

Never saw anything like this in his labs... But no way would Mikato keep it close by. Risk of accident could wipe him and Honniker out in an instant... And the amount of material he'd have to feed it...

Couldn't have collapsed all that mass at once...shockwave would devastate everything in the vicinity... It'd have to be a slow accumulation, maybe even a few kilos at a time...

Her mind races, thinking about all the inert debris hurtling around the same dusty orbit as Cadre Two.

Maybe he built a containment device at Cadre Two, then planted it on a distant asteroid or core fragment...and it just eats the thing over time...breaks it down into smaller chunks, feeds it into a compression field kilo by kilo... then, injects to containment until capacity is reached...

Energy input would be absurd! But with centuries to work, and a big star like Procyon blazing away...

She eyes the containment field readings again.

There could be billions of tonnes in there... Drop containment...neutrons decay to proton, electron, antineutrino...

Point zero eight percent mass to energy gives us a yield of...

The Geek applies a simple equation for conversion and gapes at the figure in her goggles.

10^{27} Joules

She glances at the small yellow sun blazing away at the heart of the solar system, imagining its total output shrunk to a diameter of thirty meters, loitering in low Earth orbit for a couple of seconds. Oceans boil, atmosphere leaps away to space, an entire hemisphere is scorched and blasted to cinders, sterilized. Her stomach turns with the thought.

And I thought Honniker was the madman...

Maiella looks at the wavering dodecahedron, chilled.

Could Mikato have more than one? Operating in secrecy for over a thousand years, perfecting the process, undisturbed... Likely.

But even if this is neutronium, this isn't a singularity, not by a long shot... What am I missing?

442

The Geek leans toward her console, taking in the scene as a whole. Twelve identical vessels surround the central hub, anvil-shaped bows pointing at its twelve sides, and the malevolent purpose becomes plain.

The twelve activate DSDs and leap into the hub as mass multipliers... neutronium compresses within the Schwarzschild radius...a singularity forms for an instant then evaporates...

Her jaw drops at the thought of a focused burst like the firing of a super massive DSD, punching a hole completely through the planet and sending its core hurtling down a tunnel of warped spacetime. Then, relieved of confining pressure, the singularity explodes with the intensity of a supernova. Gravitational distortions wrack the planet's charred, cored remains, flipping the crust in supersonic tidal waves of magma. Her jaw drops.

Where do I even start? Can I knock out one of the twelve and interrupt the process?

Maiella swings the ship toward the dodecahedron and her goggles flare, when a screeching rasp echoes from the corridor behind her. She whirls in her seat, staring down the hallway at the telltale whine of Cadre laser drills.

"NO NO NO NO NO NO!"

The Geek digs through her previous jump calculations, pulls her ship's mass, and compares against earlier jumps. In plain numerals, her vessel's mass has increased by an amount equivalent to a Cadre Virus Ship with Operator team. Pupils dilating, she glances at Thompson who lies helpless on the floor. She looks at Ralla with her glued shut mouth and dagger-spitting glare. She looks back at the corridor and pulls the pistol from her back, painfully aware it has no chance whatsoever of stopping a Gun and Brick in full kit.

Out of time...

Maiella parks the pistol on her console, solves the path to *Plasma Rain*, and executes.

Her ship arrives with a flash above a curved horizon of blue, green, and white serenity. Wrenching herself away from Earth's colossal beauty, she hauls at the controls and thrusts toward a cluster of twelve identical ships. At focus of the twelve is a gently rotating dodecahedron, its twelve flat sides pulled inward to concave sockets for the anvils aimed toward them.

Her goggles scroll with malicious script, and she broadcasts it at the formation, but locked out gateways refuse every attempt. Coded LiDAR pulses pass between ships, presumably confirming range and alignment, and minute puffs of thrusters fine-tune relative position.

Can I disrupt those LiDAR pulses, maybe blind them to each other? If they can't confirm alignment, maybe that'll delay detonation...

Whining screeches in the corridor behind her rise in pitch. She tries her best to ignore them and floods the formation with millions of false LiDAR pulses. There is no effect, and she mocks herself for thinking Mikato's creation could be so easily defeated.

Can I knock the hub out of position? Might prevent the singularity...but an impact could breach containment... Then neutron decay, and the planet scorches...

Pressed between the imminent death of a biosphere and the carving drills of an Operator Team, Maiella blanks her mind. Eyes closed, withdrawn in zen-like focus, an idea crystallizes.

Mid-jump mass transfer...

Make a hard J-turn around the hub and throw an offset warp field with unipolar discharge... My DSDs open a warp corridor, but the hub falls down it instead...

Her goggles strobe with calculation.

Might work...

A three-dimensional holoprojection plots of her vessel, the twelve ships, and hub. In the model, a line extends from her vessel, nearly brushing one side of the hub, then makes a hard turn right behind it. Simultaneously, a lopsided DSD field expands from her vessel, centered on the hub. Her ship's DSDs discharge in a single direction, keeping her vessel planted while opening a warp tunnel directly in front of the hub. The draw of curved spacetime pulls the glimmering jewel into the tunnel and the hub streaks away to deep space. A moment later all twelve ships leap into one another, annihilating themselves and everything else within a fifty-kilometer radius. Her ship vaporizes in the collision, the tunnel collapses, and the hub returns to its previous position seconds later, undetonated.

Still a threat but stable, and the twelve-ship trigger mechanism is destroyed...

Maiella runs the simulation again, this time bleeding off enough momentum and energy that her vessel can escape. The hub moves, but not enough, and when all twelve vessels collide the hub is caught in the blast. Containment fails, and the device erupts in planet scorching radiance.

"Gotta be a way, *c'mon!*"

Her goggles blaze with alternate models. Each solution plots in the holoprojection in quick procession. Every permutation that bleeds enough energy away for escape ends in cataclysm. Only by parking beside the hub and dedicating her ship's full output does the hub move far enough away to avoid the blast. Worse, she has to shut down her DSDs the instant before collision so that radiant energy is not channeled down the spacetime tunnel like a beam at the hub. Likewise, if she tries to run, radiant energy chases her ship down the corridor, obliterating it. Any act of self-preservation she can see returns the hub too early, its containment breaches, and the planet burns.

The only way to pull this off is to sit right in the middle of it. Figures.

She looks over her shoulder.

Could I get out in the Virus Ship?

The Geek looks at Ralla, then Thompson.

Cramped enough with a team... Even tighter with a passenger... Won't be room for all of us...

Screeches from the corridor crescendo, peak, then abate, followed by a heavy *clang* of a hull chunk dropping out of the ceiling. Boots thud to the deck and fast footfalls sprint toward the bridge. With detached acceptance, Maiella sets her final heading, locks it into navigation, and starts the count. She stands facing the bridge entryway, hands raised, fingers spread, HDI still connected by lanyard to the console.

Maddox enters so fast it is like he teleported, rifle aimed at Maiella's bare face. His finger drops inside the trigger guard.

"RALLA LIVES," Maiella shouts, "but only if you *listen*. This ship is gonna jump into that hub in thirty seconds, and *nothing* will stop it. Kill me, we launch immediately. So get Ralla AND Thompson to your virus ship, then *clear off*. Otherwise, I TAKE YOU ALL WITH ME."

Maddox scans the bridge, pausing on the bloody wreckage of Argo and O'Kai. He sees Thompson, unconscious, fogging a clear mask in ragged breaths. And he spots Ralla on the deck beside Maiella, without helmet, mouth glued shut. With cold calculation, and a colder stare at Maiella, the Gun slings his rifle and snatches Ralla up in his arms. Halgrim slings his cannon, stoops, grabs Thompson one-handed, and throws him over a shoulder. Without a word, they rush from the bridge.

Maiella turns back toward the console, feeling every second tick away. Duty and sacrifice. Confrontation of death. The life she will not have with Thompson.

But he'll survive. Maybe the planet, too. That's something.

She drops her faceplate and closes the helmet latch, knowing the bridge will depressurize once Maddox's Virus Ship breaks seal.

Trying to fit all of her final thoughts into a few words, Maiella looks into her lap, keys her radio, and speaks in broken Eleto over open channel.

"(To all who would hear, this one is called Maiella. This attack is NOT the will of our people. We are *all* betrayed by ONE who could not learn.)

"(The one who betrayed sleeps forever. Know that he and his Angry ones are *few*. With this one's last breath, she opposes them and begs the People: do not judge all by evil of few.)

"(Words no longer hold water, so this one will prove with action.)

"(Believe in our future, together. This one will not live to see it. That does not mean she failed. Maiella, out.)"

Maiella unplugs her HDI from console, shuffles over to Argo, and sits beside him. With effort, she hauls the big man up into her lap, reclines against a console, wraps arms around him, and rests her head against his.

Klanks telegraph through the floor plates as the Virus Ship detaches. A rush of escaping air jolts her then quickly settles to calm.

Maiella opens an unencrypted channel.

"Someone...please tell Thompson I love him, more than anything."

The jump timer counts to zero. She closes her eyes.

Her ship leaps at the hub, makes a hard turn around it, extends an offset warp field and fires DSDs. A corridor of warped spacetime yawns, drawing the hub downstream as if it was feather-light. Maiella looks up at the holoprojection with watered eyes, watching the hub vanish to the safety of deep space. She smiles.

Hope, after all.

Her main drives shut down and twelve anvils crash together in annihilating intensity. A luminous indigo sphere pulses then swells, trailing filaments of vaporized alloys and ceramics.

When the glare fades, all trace of ships is swept clear. At center of the fading glow is an undamaged dodecahedron, shimmering in earth orbit, as if it had never moved at all.

CADRE ONE

PART ELEVEN

OCEANIC ABYSS

Complete, absolute darkness. Not shaded from light, the total lack of it—as if the last star has collapsed and faded.

Cold that bites to marrow with teeth of dry ice. A burning, desiccating freeze that mummifies flesh to brittle fibers.

Absence of dimension. No up, no down, no *location*. Only pressure. Submerged in oceanic abyss, trapped at the bottom. Impossibility of breath... Not drowning, *smothering* in gravitational intensity.

A pinpoint of white far above. An anomaly, out of place, a thing that cannot be in such uniformity of oppression. Dim and distant, yet dazzling to light starved eyes.

Sudden buoyancy, sensation of rising from inky depths. Panic of asphyxia. Overwhelming urge to gasp. The pinpoint brightens.

Speeding faster from depth toward beckoning light... Propelled, or pulled? No landmarks to gauge, no resistance of passing matter, only awareness of acceleration that should liquefy flesh...

Glimmer steadies, no longer a pinpoint. Expanding, lengthening, widening...*opening*?

Not a star. Not an object. A hole in the darkness. Speed beyond any comprehensible velocity, crossing intergalactic spans with scant passage of time.

The hole swells as if detonated, borders streaking away from each other like the birth of a universe. Annihilating, obliterating brilliance beyond... Hurtling through...

Alive!

Thompson sucks in a great gust of air, noting first a bitter plastic taste in dry mouth. He feels a pliable tube between his teeth that dives down his parched throat. Sleep-glued eyelids tear apart like tissue paper, then clamp shut against overwhelming glare.

Overlapping conversations in vaguely familiar languages occur around him, and echoes hint at spaciousness between walls and ceiling.

Delicate, cool fabric slides over him, and its airy lightness is immediately intolerable. His first thought is to fling it away but his limbs are leaden, weak to the edge of paralysis. Thompson takes a deeper breath and seared nerve endings in his lungs smolder like embers, threatening to blaze if not so starved of oxygen.

He lies back, contemplating these mysteries of sensation, and catalogs the clues. Muscles hang slack, devoid of tone. Skull feels hollow as if his brain has been scooped. His chest feels stuffed with synthetic wadding, cushioning jagged edges of traumatized flesh. Worst of all is the overarching apathy, persuading him this is no cause for alarm and everything is just fine.

Damn it. I'm drugged.

The Gun retreats to a psychological refuge, leaving his slothful body behind. There he concentrates, pushing through the pharmaceutical cobwebs slowing his mind. In time, his wandering eyes clear and he squints at his surroundings. Mechanical arms with heavy gauge power cables are retracted against a ceiling twenty-meters high. On distant walls stand racks of bulky attachments that match the limbs' open sockets. Sealed hatches beside each rack are marked in high-contrast alien script.

Okay, so not a Human place. Too big. Eleto manufacturing, maybe? Vehicle assembly? Repair bay?

The Gun turns his head to the side, cheek sinking into a soft pillow. Whatever lines of industry once hummed along the floor have been cleared and replaced with thousands of cots like his. Small tables stand beside each bunk with tall metal hooks, hanging transparent intravenous bags. White-coated Eleto move among the rows, checking vitals, gripping long chins in thought, scrutinizing diagnostic images on handheld slates.

Burned and bandaged Eleto occupy most of the bunks. To his amazement, Cadre Operators are among them. Heavy straps lash the scarred soldiers in place with metal cuffs at ankles and wrists. Stripped to bare skin and allowed minimum modesty, Guns, Bricks, and Geeks glare with wild eyes at physicians and nurses, baring teeth like wolves with a trapped leg.

Thompson peers at one bunk that strains under the bulk of a Brick lashed to it. Eleto physicians cluster nearby, keeping a wary distance despite the more than adequate restraints. One points to an adjacent bunk, excusing himself from the group; and when the physician moves aside Thompson spies a smaller figure among them, dark hair pulled back into a ponytail. He props himself up on elbows.

That's Doctor Taggart. If she's here, that means the Europa *is, too. Okay, so where the hell am I?*

"Welcome back," says a deep voice over his shoulder.

Thompson blinks and cranes his neck toward the voice. Wicked twinges shoot through his chest, and he coughs harshly.

"Easy, man," the voice cautions, "you'll pop your stitches."

Thompson clenches his diaphragm until the spasm stops, and he takes controlled, shallow breaths. Finally, the Gun can open his watered eyes again and he looks up at a broad-shouldered man in Colonist Flight Officer uniform, eagles on the collar. Drawn cheeks are covered in at least a month's beard. The lean face is lined and pale. Dark circles around the eyes speak of sleepless nights, long shifts, and the burden of command. In those cave-like orbits, however, the man's eyes are bright.

Into a communicator at his throat, the man says, "Hey, Sahara, Thom's awake. Got a bad cough. Could you come check him out, *please.*"

Noting the man's request sounded far more like an order than a request, Thompson pushes up from his bunk then flinches at a sharp pain in his wrist. He looks down in confusion at a bandaged stump where his right hand should be.

The Gun slumps, staring at his bandaged wrist, and his eyes defocus with memory.

Argo lobbing a grenade at Maiella...

Diving for it, snatching it... Twisting the detonator out... And the detonator exploding in his hand...

Hot, electric throes of splintered bone...

"Argo... We were *fighting*? I think... I think I—"

"Easy, Thom, just lie back."

Familiar inflection in the man's voice fills in gaps of recollection. "Gregor? That you?"

"Yeah. It's me." The Russian's mouth swishes to one side. He eyes an unoccupied spot on Thompson's bunk and parks himself on it. His lips part to speak then press together. Gregor looks at his knees and offers instead, "Glad to see you coming 'round. You've been out for a month."

"A *month*? Nothing takes a month to heal." The Gun shrugs his way up to elbows again.

Gregor holds up a hand to press him back down but stops short at sight of fresh pink thoracotomy scars.

"We used up all the good meds. Takes a while to synthesize a fresh supply, so we're having to let Nature do the mending, for now."

Thompson clears his throat, tries to focus through narcotic blur, and asks, "What is this place, and...*what happened?*"

Gregor frowns and his eyebrows lift. "Where do I start?" He looks across the bunk and his expression softens. "Ah, Sahara. He's having some trouble breath—"

"*On it*," Sahara interrupts, taking a small disc from her coat pocket. Slipping two fingers through the loops on its backside, she presses the metal disc to Thompson's chest and pushes a small headphone into her ear. "All right, Thompson, take a slow, deep breath for me, in and out."

Thompson opens his mouth to protest her doting, but her fearsome glare preempts any rebellion. Rather than risk that glare again, he complies.

Sahara closes her eyes and concentrates on the ticks and pops in the Gun's airway. Her concerned frown straightens. "I don't hear any leaks, just products of inflammation. Gonna up your dose a few grains and calm things down in there. How's the pain?"

"Pain, I can handle."

"Yeah, tough guy? Well if it triggers a coughing fit, you could tear that lung loose—"

"*No more meds*! I can barely see straight."

Sahara's forehead wrinkles, lips parted for a scathing diatribe on who is doctor and who is patient. But looking the man over, she melts. "All right, trooper, we'll wean you off the skag." She shakes her head. "It's gonna be like Chinese New Year in there when your dose wears off. You tell me if it gets too bad. I can roll the edge off, okay?"

"Roger that."

Sahara nods. "Good. In the meantime, I'll not have ye undoing my good work. *Calm, slow breaths*. Hear me, boyo?"

"Clarion, doctor."

454

She lays a gentle hand on his forehead, feels for temperature. "I'm close by. If you need me *for any reason*, you call me. Got it?"

"Aye, *sir*," Thompson says with a smirk.

Sahara winks at him. "Sounds like we have a proper understanding." She looks up at Gregor and with stern insistence repeats, "For *any* reason."

Gregor nods, jaw tight. "You got it."

An Eleto howls in agony, and Sahara startles. "If you'll pardon me," she says, glancing over her spectacles in the direction of the cry, "got some other patients." The doctor turns with a swish of ponytail and hustles off.

Gregor watches her go. When he looks down at Thompson again, the Gun is staring at him expectantly.

"You were going to tell me what I missed," Thompson reminds.

"Ah, right." The Russian surveys the bay and the thousand individual tragedies occupying each bunk. "What's the last thing you remember?"

A flurry of moments runs through Thompson's mind:

> *Blissful reunion with Argo... Bizarre praise from a battered General... Then a brutal sneak attack that wrecked everything...*

> *Wrestling for a pistol in O'Kai's grip, turning the barrel away...*
> *BR-R-R-AK...*
> *Bullets plunging through soft tissues under O'Kai's jaw and blasting through his crown... O'Kai wilting as red mist fell over them both...collapsing away from the weapon, leaving Thompson clutching it by the barrel...*

> *Argo's eyes locked on the smoking pistol... Disbelief at the killing instrument in his brother's hand... Face twisting in conflict... Fraternal bonds snapping... Gaze narrowing, brow lowering, nostrils flaring with flow of combat stims... grim commitment to violence... And the desperate contest that followed...*

The Gun's body jerks as if shot.

"I was fighting Argo," the Gun answers, at last. "He thought I was his enemy... Said I wasn't human... Couldn't make him understand... Where is he, did he...?"

Gregor's mouth compresses to a straight line across his face and he shakes his head.

Thompson's cheek twitches and his head drops to his chest.

"This may not be much consolation," Gregor offers, "but taking down Ralla and O'Kai... That blunted the assault. Gave the Lizards time to act. If you hadn't, Ralla would have wiped out everything in orbit, the asteroid would have hit, and *Plasma Rain* would have wasted us all. Earth'd be a cinder and we'd all be dead."

The Gun rolls onto his side. "*Plasma Rain*? Asteroid?"

"Remember those two freighters, the ones that launched first from Cadre One? They de-orbited an asteroid, slung it around the moon straight at Earth. Could have been an extinction event, all by itself.

"*Plasma Rain* was some sinister fucking megabomb outta Cadre Two. If it'd gone off, I don't even know...like being ringside for a supernova. We might have been a cloud of ash from Venus to Mars."

Thompson frowns. "So, how...?"

Gregor nods. "Okay, go with me for a sec. Shao-Lo shows up from Cadre Two with an armada and *Plasma Rain*. Parks the bomb in orbit and hands off the armada to the ranking Geek. Probably figured that'd be Ralla. Turns out, you'd already taken Ralla out of action and Beckert, who was backing her up, got all the C2 keys. So there he is, in the middle of all out war, with a fresh armada at his disposal. He's thinking about what you told him after he snatched you out of the peace conference. And he's looking at all this crazy shit going on. Started doing the math on it, how every confrontation was escalating exponentially. Cadre One was already lost. The Cadre fleet's grinding itself down ship by ship. And here's an entire planet in the cross hairs. Not just any planet...this is *Earth*. He's been there, seen it, *lived* it. Was a line he couldn't cross. He decided you were right, the Eleto would hunt humanity to extinction. The *Europa* would eventually be found. Our only future was in ending hostilities.

"Only now he's got a bunch of Cadre Operators stimmed psycho and armed to the teeth. He's got an Eleto fleet doing its damndest to shoot them all out of the sky. There's an asteroid streaking in from the moon, and there's a planet-killing bomb in low orbit. He's gotta deal with all that.

"Thing is, Beckert can't kill his own, he just can't. So instead, he used the extra processing power of his armada and *brute forced all the other Geeks to submission*."

"Seriously? He hacked his own team, and *succeeded*?"

Gregor nods soberly. "Beckert unified the Cadre fleet under his control and turned it on that asteroid coming in. Man, those ships from Cadre Two pack a fucking *wallop*. Ground the rock down to chunks. Rained hell on the planet. Some bad impacts and a lot of fires but... not a lot of casualties. Earth's alive."

Thompson's brow scrunches. "Why start there? Sounds like *Plasma Rain* was the bigger threat. Why not deal with that first?"

Gregor frowns, turning his chin square. "Maiella took care of that."

"Good, good," Thompson says, smiling at yet another proof of her unending resourcefulness. He lifts his head and cranes it about. "Where is she? She okay?"

Gregor's silence plants an ill feeling, and Thompson looks for an answer in the Russian's averted face.

"Gregor. *Where is she?*"

Gregor grits his teeth then lets out a held breath. "She's gone, Thom."

Thompson petrifies, eyes locked.

"*Fuck*, I didn't want to be the one to tell you, but...someone had to," Gregor says. "*She's* the one who saved us. Put a message out to the Lizards. Said words weren't enough, she had to prove her commitment. She did. She really did."

Thompson slumps back and stares through the ceiling.

"It's the worst news in the world, I know," the Russian says. "Nothing makes it better. *Nothing*. But last thing she said, she wanted you to know... she loved you more than anything."

Gregor looks down at the scuffed gold band on his finger and works it off. Turning it over between thumb and forefinger, he contemplates it, sighs, then presses it into Thompson's palm and closes the Gun's fingers around it. Thompson's hand is stiff like wax.

"I know what this feels like. Don't think you have to go through it alone." Gregor lays a compassionate hand on Thompson's shoulder, but the Gun does not register.

"Thom?"

The scarred man is so still Gregor leans close to listen for breath. Though faint, there is movement of air, and the bedside display confirms the man's heartbeat with slow beeps.

"Take your time, brother."

Not knowing what else to say, Gregor parks his elbows on his knees and rests his face in his hands.

FLUID

Munro kneels beside Thompson's medical bunk, fretting. He peels back the Gun's eyelid and flashes a penlight at the pupil. "How long has he been like this?"

"About thirty-six hours," Sahara answers, her brow wrinkled. "He woke from coma on his own but slipped back. Tried everything I know. Hoping you've got an idea."

"Mind if I ask some basic questions? They aren't meant to challenge your medical expertise, it's just to elimina—"

"*C'mon*, Munro! We're past all that shite. *Ask*."

"Neurological damage from hypoxia?"

"With his burnt lung, that was my first thought. Imaged his frontal cortex, basal ganglia, and thalamus in detail. Thought I might see a loss of inhibitory cells in the striatum, but the pathways are clear, good signal."

"Metabolic function of the prefrontal cortex?"

"Low, but not abnormally so. Not enough to explain this."

"Vagus nerve stimulation?"

"No effect."

"Tried exciting the frontal cortex with Dopamine?"

"Aye. And acetylcholine, norepinephrine...and *others*..."

"Others, like?"

Sahara admits with reluctance, "Amphetamine."

Munro looks across his patient at Sahara. "That's extreme, given he's only been down thirty-six hours."

Sahara crosses her arms, discomfort evident in the down-turned corners of her face. "*Aye*, it bloody well *is*."

"What's the rush?"

She glances over at Gregor, who stands at the foot of the bunk.

"Colonel," Gregor explains, "more warships are flying in daily, and they've all got a firing solution on the *Europa*. Not exactly a stable situation. The Lizards are willing to talk now, but who knows for how long? Every second we sit here is another they might decide we just aren't worth the effort."

"What does that have to do with Thompson?" Munro asks.

"We need him to stand for the Cadre, to be their *Voice*."

Munro stands upright, indignant. "*I* can represent the Cadre. Why wasn't I asked?"

Gregor holds up a hand. "Eh, with respect, Colonel, they want someone who took a stand *against* O'Kai... They don't want someone who went along for the ride." Gregor looks down at the catatonic Gun. "They were content to wait while it looked like Thompson was healing...but now? If we can't rouse him, they've demanded we grease the Operator Corps as a pre-condition to talks."

"*Grease?*"

"Liquidate. *Execute*," Sahara translates.

Munro's eyes stretch wide. "Our Operators laid down their weapons! The enemy would exterminate them after we made clear shows of non-aggression?"

Gregor rolls his eyes. "The *audacity*..." The *Europa*'s captain takes an extended view of the improvised medical bay. "They went in, weapons hot, to a *fucking peace conference*. Your boys and girls weren't *playing around*, here, Colonel. Thompson and Maiella are the only ones they'd consider, and Maiella's, well..." The Russian looks away to a dark place, shakes himself out of it. "So Thompson's it, or your Operators get put down."

Munro turns his wide shoulders square to Gregor. "And how is it possible you know this, when I'm hearing of it for the first time?"

Gregor snorts in disbelief. "Honestly, Munro, you *might* want to take an interest in current events."

"*Current events*? Captain, we MedTechs have *quite a lot* on our hands! I'm sure it made a compelling *statement* piloting the *Europa* between Cadre and Eleto forces, but she is completely unarmored and you drove her into a *combat zone*. Never mind the hull damage, we'll be chasing down duct and pipe leaks for *months*. Add to that, there are more than enough casualties on both sides. And the *plague*, need I remind you, *did not* cure itself. As always, *we* MedTechs do the heavy labor when the Colonists are content to feed their laziness with ALL of our surplus calories—"

Sahara stomps on Munro's foot, and when the big MedTech glares down at her, she growls, "They are *watching!*"

Gregor and Munro stiffen in self-awareness. When they look about, Eleto nurses and physicians break off nervous stares and bury themselves in their work.

Munro presses his lips together. "You're correct, Doctor. We mustn't be seen in discord. And forgive my outburst. I've not had rest or a proper interval in some time."

"Forget it, Munro, I was out of bounds." Gregor extends a hand. "Hell, I don't know where we'd be without you, to be honest."

Munro takes Gregor's hand in his huge mitt, grasping firmly. "Glad to serve. But all I ask, Captain, is that we refuse any solution which does not include *all of us.*"

"Agreed. No one left out."

Sahara sighs in relief, and lays her hands on their wrists. "Thank you *both.* Well, Munro, now you know why we're trying so hard to wake this fella. Thompson was *introduced.* He sat at the table with them, spent time with them. And he bled for them. If he's General, the Eleto'll give him some room to heel his Operators. Best chance of keeping everyone breathing. Only chance, maybe."

"What about Beckert?" Munro posits. "He turned the assault, I'm told. That should count for something, right?"

"True," Gregor begins, "but the Lizards are suspicious of brain implants. They consider it barbarous. Unnatural. Plus, after what Beckert's been through, he's all stilts and prosthetics. No matter how noble they try to be, the Lizards're freaked out by—"

"Captain?" Sahara interjects.

"Yes?"

"Can we call them something *other* than Lizards?"

The Russian thinks about it and acquiesces. "Good point. Sorry, force of habit."

Munro's face scrunches. "It's difficult to accept that a general could succeed his predecessor by *homocide*...and that the Cadre would tolerate this..."

Sahara frets. "What choice do we have? O'Kai'd've been the death of us, everyone knows that. And it's not like he was the sort to roll over. Think he'd'd've handed over command willingly?"

Munro frets and shakes his head. "Not without a unified resolution from the Leadership Council. At the time, I'd have voted against one."

"I know it's hard to hear," Gregor says. "Doesn't sound like Thom had any other choice."

Munro's brow furrows. "Such *strange* times..." The big MedTech looks down at the unconscious Gun and takes a deep, lung-cleansing breath. "We must adapt."

"So what do you think?" Sahara nudges Munro with an elbow. "What's wrong with him?"

Munro kneels beside the bunk and takes a careful, sweeping look at his patient. "You said he was lucid last you saw him, Captain?"

"That's right," Gregor answers. "Was running a desk nearby. When he woke, I was there. He asked what he missed. I filled him in."

"Including Maiella's—?"

Gregor nods. "Yeah. He deserved a straight answer on that."

"How did he respond?"

"He just went...blank. Like someone flipped his switch."

"Operators do not have *switches*," Munro grumbles. He takes hold of the diagnostic cart by Thompson's bedside and thumbs through the last day and a half of metrics. Finding nothing of note there, he looks at Thompson's expressionless face and turns the Gun's head by the chin. "Could this be a *psy-cho-logical* issue?"

Sahara shrugs. "Maybe. Possibly. I don't know."

"You called the Counselor?" Gregor asks.

"Only about a hundred times," she answers. "Buried in closed door meetings, they say. No interruptions. Even got 'im boxed in a metal room so wireless can't reach."

"I'll make it an official order, then," the Russian states. Tapping the communicator at his collar, he says, "Alexei, this is Gregor. We need the Counselor here in the new hospital, *top priority*. That's an order. Copy?"

Alexei's voice buzzes back, "*Roger that, Skipper. Counselor needed in new Med facility A-S-A-F-P. But not sure how we get that message to him when the Eleto're guarding the doors. We don't speak their language.*"

"Draw them a picture if you have to. Be polite, but *make it happen*. Can you do that?"

"*Wilco, boss. We'll get the point across. Out.*"

Sahara and Munro delve into a deeper discussion of methods attempted, and methods they might try. Left behind by their medical vocabulary, Gregor studies the catatonic soldier in front of him, recalling a time he imagined this man was invulnerable, and how he yearned for that strength in himself. Submitting to Thompson's authority during training was a heap of pride to swallow and required he tame his ego lest it drive him mad. He took the hits, endured the reinforcements. When he finally graduated Gregor knew he was stronger, more confident, less fearful, and that Thompson had instilled all of that.

Seeing the Gun so utterly broken rankles as if that image of strength was a sham.

"*Bastard*," the Russian mutters under his breath. "We *need you* and you're taking a GODDAMNED *NAP*?"

Sahara and Munro break off their conversation. In genuine concern, Sahara asks, "Somethin' on yer mind, Captain?"

Gregor shakes his head in tight little jerks. Annoyed with himself for letting temper slip, he chews a thumbnail already gnawed halfway to its root. His other hand fidgets, feeling for the scuffed ring that is no longer there.

"Haven't slept...I'm frustrated. Worried. *Pissed* at this motherfucker."

Munro and Sahara look at one another in perplexed silence.

Gregor fills the void, explaining, "When Iskra died... Thom told me he '*would understand my loss.*' Didn't believe him, of course. Figured he and Maiella and Argo were just kill-crazy gorillas. But, *damn*... You can see he does."

"Aye. Breaks my heart just to look at him," Sahara adds. "He loved her to death."

Skepticism deepening every line of his expression, Munro asks, "Is such a thing possible?"

Sahara's mouth bunches on one side. "Aye. 'Tis."

The big MedTech looks back at Thompson as if a curious new layer has been peeled back, and he peers into the Gun's half-lidded eyes. With a grimace, he admits, "If this is a 'wound of the mind,' there's little I can do."

Perverse satisfaction bubbles up in Gregor from a loathsome place down deep. He knows this is a tragic scene, that Thompson gave his all for a greater cause and lost the one he cherished most. Yet there is still a feeling that balance is restored, a debt has been paid. Ashamed that such a petty thought could linger after all this time, he looks away toward the vast production floor. Among the evenly spaced rows he spies a group of Colonists huddled around a bunk, hands joined and heads bowed. Ortega is at the head of the bunk, eyes closed, lips moving inaudibly. The Russian grimaces at their embarrassing show of ancient superstition. But when the group breaks their prayer circle and approaches, his teeth grind.

"Captain," Ortega greets in as neutral a tone as he can muster. He holds a black leather-wrapped book in front of himself with both hands. His long, gray hair is combed straight back and hangs to his shoulders. A loose fitting white shirt drapes to mid thigh, overlapping his matching white pants, and his feet are strapped into sandals.

Gregor looks him up and down. "Really getting into the shepherd thing, huh?"

"Just clothes," Ortega replies. The Spaniard looks down at Thompson, instantly pitying him. "We owe our lives to this man. Come," he says to his group, "let us tend to his needs."

"*Thank you*," Gregor growls, "he's already getting the best help he can."

Ortega regards both Munro and Sahara with deferential nods. "True, the very best practitioners are here to care for his *body*. But clearly this man's *spirit* is broken. It's right there in his face, Captain." To his flock, Ortega says, "Friends, please circle about. Let's join hands and remind this man he is not alone."

Munro and Sahara step back to give them room but are invited to join with outstretched hands. Suspicious at first, then deciding not to argue, the two physicians stand awkwardly, clasping hands among the circle. When Gregor is offered a spot in the circle, however, he rebuffs with folded arms, saying, "He needs more than *well-wishes and prayers*. We don't have time for this."

Ortega replies without looking, "Respectfully, Captain, we are not aboard the *Europa*, and we are not on duty." With a brief glance at Gregor, he adds, "We offer Thompson community, belonging, and acceptance. To someone who has wrestled with isolation for so long, this may be exactly what he needs. It's clear you've done all that you can to reach this man. Please, will you let us try?"

"I'm okay with it," Sahara volunteers. Betrayed, Gregor shoots her a severe glance but relents.

"Fine. Cast your spells, Ortega, but do it *quickly*."

"Thank you, Captain," Ortega offers. He clasps hands with the colonists to either side of him, bows his head, and prays, "Heavenly Father, Master of All Life, we beg you to look upon this man, Thompson, and see him in all of his imperfections. Though he does not know You he has chosen a righteous path, entirely in service of others. Never has he sought to enrich himself while others starve. Rather, he has always given what he can, foregoing all comfort so that others may live to see another day. Forgive him his years spent in war, and see instead how well he has learned the lesson of peace.

"Almighty, we beg You to pity this man and hasten his recovery. Unburden his conscience of the terrible things he *had* to do. Remind him how urgently we need his strength and guidance so we may at last find safe harbor in the paradise of Your Holy Creation. Remind him how much he is loved and cherished by those he gave all to protect.

"In the Name of the Father, the Son, and the Holy Ghost, we pray. *Amen*."

"*Amen,*" the circle intones, and they release hands.

Gregor sighs impatiently, believing it to be over. But the gathering stays as Ortega kneels by Thompson's side and lays a hand on the Gun's shoulder.

"We're here for you, Thompson. No one was ever meant to carry the burdens you've shouldered. We are grateful beyond measure. Now it's time to let us help you carry this load. Come back to us. Unpack your heart, and speak plainly about your troubles so that you are no longer crushed beneath them. Deep down we are *all* brothers and sisters. Your pain is ours. Only together can we mend. Only *together* will we have the purpose and meaning to go on. *Do this for us*, Thompson. Come back to us and let us help you."

Ortega peels open the clenched fingers of Thompson's hand to take hold of it. A scuffed gold ring drops out, rolls off the white sheets, and bounces on the deck with a faint *ting*. Ortega picks it up, squints at it, then looks at Gregor's left hand.

"Still? After all he does for us..." Oretga accuses. "When he is mourning for Maiella, *you remind him he killed Iskra*?"

Gregor's jaw clenches and he growls through his teeth, "That's *not* how it happened."

"No wonder Thompson lies there! You perch on his headboard like a crow, pecking this hatefulness into his skull. Is our Captain *really* this cruel?"

Gregor's face and ears flush red. With eerie calm and closing fists, the Russian suggests, "Perhaps you'd like to discuss this somewhere more private?"

Ortega stands without fear, spreading his arms wide. "If you need to displace your guilt on others, then do as you will. My faith will survive your brutality."

"Gregor! Javier!" Sahara barks, inserting herself into the narrowing gap between both men. "I'll have ye bounced ta fook if ye donnae quit! Javier, Gregor's the captain now. *Get over it*. And Gregor, just 'cause you don't believe in God doesnae mean He ain't there. Now let's *fooking* settle this. *Clear*?"

A wave of murmurs ripples through the rows of evenly spaced bunks. Sahara, Munro, Gregor, Javier, and his flock all turn, expecting themselves to be the cause. But through the main entry doors marches a side by side formation of Cadre and Eleto soldiers in full combat kit. Leading the columns are two figures who, without bulky armor, seem like scale versions of the brutes marching after them.

On the left is a tall, thin Eleto who walks with a limp. An intricate sash is worn loosely over her shoulder, embroidered with velvety red fields and golden thread. A gown of translucent layers wraps her feminine form, bulging at shoulder and hip from bandages beneath. Her arm is missing below the elbow, capped with surgical steel, and her leg on the same side is a stilt-like prosthetic that clicks with each step. Following behind her is a half dozen orange-eyed Eleto bodyguards in full battle dress, stubby fat-barreled weapons suspended from lanyards around their necks.

The other column is led by a Colonist with dark hair that juts like a heap of feathers. A collared shirt, which may once have been white, covers his torso. New gray slacks clothe his lower half. Over all he wears an intricately embroidered sash of velvety red and gold threads. Behind him marches a line of six Cadre Operators in combat kit. Five carry long rifles across their chests; the last clutches a massive anvil-like cannon. Visors raised, their faces are impassive masks of overlapping scars.

The formation marches briskly up the main lane between sections, both columns in lock step as if part of the same platoon. The leaders divert down the row toward Thompson's bunk and the columns turn sharply after them.

Munro and the circle of Colonists crane their necks to see who is leading this obnoxious parade. Sahara climbs up onto Thompson's bunk for a better view and squints past her specs. Her eyes shine and a broad smile crosses her face.

"Shondre! Counselor!"

Sahara hops down and hurries toward them. Orange-eyed soldiers grip their stubby weapons. Cadre Operators tense in response, thumbing off safeties with a wary eye at their Eleto counterparts. Hearing the sudden whine of priming capacitors, Eleto soldiers flip off their own safeties, and the atmosphere charges with imminent violence.

"WHOA," the Counselor says, whirling about, hands up. "*Easy*, Maddock, *please*! There's no threat!"

Shondre hisses at the soldiers behind her. With that one syllable they reset safeties, take taloned hands from weapon grips, and snap to attention. Maddock, seeing his counterparts de-escalate, orders his team, "Stand down and sling weapons."

Shondre clears her lungs with a deep breath, faces Sahara, and her stern expression melts. Sahara embraces her friend carefully, doing her best not to squeeze where extra padding suggests injury, then she pulls back to look Shondre over and asks,

"You all right, love?"

Shondre nods and blinks with one good eye. The other is clouded, surrounded by sage green patches of grafted skin. "They ficks this hwonn oh-kay. Hurrt, ssstill. Sssoon get bett-turr arrm annnd legk. Forr na-ow, much hwoork." Shondre stands straighter, gazing past Sahara's head at Thompson.

She turns to the Counselor and asks a question in her own tongue. The Counselor nods, answers her with solemnity, and steps over to Thompson's bedside.

Gregor joins him, and with an uncomfortable glance at the soldiers, asks, "I get that you and Shondre should have escorts. But do they need to be armed?"

The Counselor nods and grimaces. "I know. Seems like asking for trouble. But this is the Eleto's idea. They believe that, unarmed, we're too tempting a target for revenge. I think they're right. But if one side is armed, so's the other..."

"They're on edge. Thought they were gonna shoot it out right here."

The Counselor nods again and snorts. "You don't know the half of it. There's a mob outside this facility right now, getting larger by the hour. Heard there were Cadre Operators being treated here and they just aren't having it. Shondre's people are trying to manage the crowd and talk them down, but...if they really want to get in here, they *could*."

"Holy shit."

"Yeah. Situation is...*fluid*." Putting his attention on Thompson, Counselor asks, "Any change in his condition?"

"None," Sahara answers. "Called in Munro to see if he might have some ideas. So far, we're both stumped."

The Counselor makes a point of looking her and Munro in the eyes. "Between the two of you, if there was something physically wrong with him you'd have found it by now. I'm afraid this is altogether different. Doctor, I'd like you to stay. Colonel Munro, you as well if you can."

"I can stay," Munro advises.

"Thank you, Colonel." To the group, the Counselor adds, "Everyone else, would you give us the space, please?"

"Of course," Ortega says. "If we can assist, please call." With arms raised, he gathers his fold and ushers them toward the exit. Gregor takes a last glance at Thompson, turns about, and strides off.

"Javier, Gregor," the Counselor calls, "a moment?"

Ortega waves to his flock, urging they go ahead without him, and he stands beside Gregor. "How can I help?"

The android steps close enough to them so only they can hear, "I don't know what was said between the two of you, but it doesn't take a genius to guess. You both need to know that *nothing you have done* could have caused this. I was concerned how vulnerable Thompson would be without Maiella, so this isn't a surprise. You also need to know how important you are. The leadership and stability you *both* provide, while radically different, supplements the other. We need *both* of you, and we need you working *together*."

The two men bow heads. Ortega looks up first and extends a hand to Gregor. "I'm sorry for what I said. It hurts to see you succeed where I failed. Sahara's right. I need to get over that."

"Yeah, me too," Gregor says, and he takes Ortega's offered hand. "I keep thinking you started your prayer group as a way to undermine me."

"No, no, never. I do not want your job, even if offered. Believe me, I'm a happier man."

Gregor grins. "I actually envy you for that."

Ortega grins as well. He pats the Russian's thick shoulder, adding with a smile, "Good thing we're friends again so you don't put me in the brig for insubordination."

"*What*? Nah. I was just gonna punch you in the dick."

Ortega laughs as the two men walk out of earshot.

Munro asks, "Our future depends on those two?"

The Counselor nods.

Sahara lifts her gaze to the ceiling. "*Jaysus.*" Then, taking the Counselor's sash between a thumb and forefinger, she studies the rich fabric. "Well, lookit you, Mr. Fancy."

"This? Just means I'm authorized to negotiate on behalf of my kind."

Sahara grins. "Aren't you coming up in the universe?"

The Counselor smiles back, deflecting, "Doctor, don't presume because I hold a position of elevated responsibility that I'm in *any* danger of enjoying it."

"Ha!" She lays a hand on his arm. "Ach, it's good to see you, Counselor. Missed ye."

The Counselor lays a hand over hers. "You, as well. Now then," he states, rubbing his hands together, "time's short. We've got an armada on hair trigger and a mob at the gate. Right now, the Eleto will talk, but Thompson is the only one they'll seriously consider talking to. Anyone else, and... Did Gregor tell you?"

Munro nods gravely. "They demand the Operator Corps be retired. That's unacceptable."

"I agree, completely. We need amnesty for all, if we're going to get through this. That said, the Eleto deserve a reasonable expectation of safety. What was done here at this planet will be remembered *long* after we're gone."

"This *planet*?" Sahara echoes. "*Earth*, you mean."

The Counselor grimaces. "Careful, doctor. That's a human name. It is *not* a human world anymore."

Sahara rocks back in genuine astonishment. "You're joking, hey? This is our rightful *home*, and its name is *EARTH*!"

"True... Regardless who was here first, the *Eleto* are in possession, and *they* decide if we live here or not. Insisting it be called Earth carries claim of ownership, which implies Eleto here are squatters, not legal residents... Just a *hint* of talk like that, our opponents could use as a fear tactic to make certain we aren't allowed to settle."

"Just because we call Earth by its proper name?"

"Slippery, isn't it? Like I said, *fluid*. Between you and me, they can call this planet anything they like. I only care that we be allowed to live here in peace, without fences or wardens."

Sahara grips her temples, "Glad you're doing the talking, then. How did you even see that?"

"Professor Herzfeld has good insights. His assistance has been incalculable."

"Fine," Munro says, losing patience. "The Blu...the *Eleto* will only talk with Thompson. How do we rouse him?"

The Counselor steps around the bed to Thompson's diagnostic cart and thumbs through the last thirty-six hours of metrics. "Well he's not in a coma."

Sahara steps to the cart and peers through her specs. "How can you tell?"

"See these spikes of activity, here, here, and here?" The Counselor asks, stepping aside and showing a graph on the main screen.

"Aye... Those are recent, just now. You see these, Munro?"

Munro steps around the bunk to see for himself.

"Those regions of the brain are associated with hearing and cognition," Munro explains. The Counselor looks from Sahara to Munro. "Did anyone say her name?"

"Who?" Munro asks.

"*Her*," the Counselor stresses.

"Mai—" Sahara begins, but the Counselor immediately raises a finger to his lips. He lowers his finger and nods.

Sahara looks nervously at Munro. "Gregor mentioned her a couple times, yeah?"

Munro scowls. "Yes. As did I when I asked Gregor if he informed Thompson of her—"

"It's okay," the Counselor says, "you didn't do anything wrong. Proves he's still in there, at least. But I was concerned this might happen. It *looks* like a dissociative state, I've just never seen one this advanced. We're talking grief on top of trauma. I think he's let himself slip away because he's at the end of his rope."

Munro's face scrunches. "Because he allowed himself to be so... *singularly* attached...to one person?"

"That's right."

Munro frowns. "That is *precisely* why we forbid it! I should have *enforced* their separation, not let them indulge these pointless encounters! The fault is mine." The big MedTech turns his back, shaking his head.

The Counselor takes a moment then says, "There's no fault, Colonel. It's called 'love,' and without it, we'd all be dead now."

The android peers down at Thompson.

"All right, he's in there... We have to draw him out."

Sahara throws up her hands. "I'm out of ideas."

Munro tilts his head. "Do we mention...*her* again?"

The Counselor shakes his head. "No. He responds, sure, but any mention may be pushing him farther away. We need someone he was close to. Someone he trusts. Someone he bonded with."

"I stitched his hide plenty," Sahara offers, "but cannae say he ever warmed up to me."

"Nor I," Munro states.

"How 'bout you, Counselor? You had plenty face time with him."

"I did. But I don't think he ever saw past the fact I'm artificial." The Counselor frets. "Maybe one day, I can help him see that flesh and blood are *not* prerequisites for being alive."

Sahara studies the Counselor's seamed face. Beneath the patched synthetic skin, beneath the facial actuators, bone-like scaffolds and framework, there is more, something she herself had never looked for in all of her waking years in his company. Something that evolved so gradually she never noticed it. Now that she sees it, she blinks as if witnessing the birth of a star.

"My God," she whispers, "you really *are*."

"Regardless," the Counselor states, "there *is* someone he's close to. Someone who understands what it's like to be ostracized from the ones you love, while still bound in service to them. Someone who has loved and lost just as deeply. Someone who carries scars from the same conflicts, both internal and external. Someone who thought if she could reach one hardened Operator, she might reach them all."

The Counselor turns his gaze toward Shondre, and the others look to her as well. Shondre, seeing her cue, excuses herself from her escorts and steps to Thompson's side. The Counselor offers his arm, and she takes it with her one hand to steady herself. Then the tall Eleto squats with difficulty, not yet accustomed to her rigid prosthetic leg. Clearing her throat, she lays her head and neck across Thompson's sheet-covered chest, hugs him, and hums a sad, sweet melody that resonates in the cavern of his lungs.

COLLAPSING UNIVERSE

Absence. Unbearable absence.

A better future held in the palm of his hand, and it slipped away. Incompetence, negligence, ineptitude. Monumental failure to be mocked for all time. Argo and Maiella. His team. His companions. His reasons. Gone.

A body, mere hardware now, lies idle. Involuntary process continues with irritating persistence. If only he could stop his machine-like heart it would finally be over. Can it be done?

Slow...
Slower...
Slooooowwwwerrrrr...

Seconds lengthen into swaying blocks of eternity. Ego desiccates, crumbles, and flies like ash in a breeze.

I am nothing.

Dimensions evaporate, and with them disappear all ties to location. Incorporeal and adrift in a blackened underworld of regret.

I am nowhere.

Awareness collapses and turns inward. His final thoughts are yearning for entropic totality, the complete unmaking of self, dissolving and radiating out to the universe like solar wind.

Wait... What was that?

A whisper from a trillion kilometers away...a mysterious suggestion of voice, just not a mystery worth solving. So close to the end, he concentrates on oblivion. But again that friendly whisper charms his attention. The harder he tries to ignore it, the more self-defeating his efforts.

That voice... I've heard it before...

Anger flares inside at being thwarted from what was so nearly done. He listens, tracking the sound like an insect to swat. Focusing on the sound makes it inaudible, and the more he seeks it, the less sure he is he ever heard it.

Am I hallucinating? Or is it background noise...?

No! There it is again!

Familiar undertones quench his anger as suddenly as it sparked. The voice is clearer, though muted as if traveling through meters of stone...then it resolves into a melodic hum.

"*Tommmmm-Ssuuuuuuunnnnn,*" the humming voice calls.

That name... I knew it once...

"*Tommmmm-Ssuuuuuunnnnnnn...*"

Lyrical and longing, the voice comes from everywhere in dimensionless abyss...

"*Arrrrr hyooooo therrrrrrre?*"

Eddies of inflection swirl around his insubstantial self, pitching him end over end like a leaf in a stream. Flashes of remembrance form a name in his stirring mind.

Shondre?

"Hyessss," the distant voice says, excited. *"Hyessss, deeeer frennnnd*!"

Where are you?

A pinpoint of light appears on the far side of existence. It flickers, so faint he is unsure if he is really seeing it. He wills it closer, and by imperceptible degrees it brightens.

"Komm bakk. Hweee missss hyoo, Tommm-Ssuunnnnn."

Swifter than any beam or particle, he speeds toward it. No longer a pinpoint, the light takes shape, more wide than tall. As the shape swells, he notices its light is uneven, blotched. There is a faint boundary around the periphery, suggesting exit from this self-imposed oblivion.

Faster he speeds without sensation of movement, and he comprehends that neither he nor the window are moving. His universe is collapsing.

Blurred shapes move in the expanding window ahead. Misty outlines coalesce into more solid forms. The blurry edges yawn wide, encompassing his entire field of view. He rockets through and is immediately yanked backwards, crashing into a half-numb body with a violent jerk.

He gasps and crushes his eyelids shut against severe glare. Rapid beeps hammer against his eardrums. Caustic stench of antiseptic stings his sinuses. And his tongue bulges in a dry mouth of chalk and plastic.

He blinks hard, shading his eyes with a hand. Dark shapes lean in over him, crowding. Faces are hazy, yet one is quite different from the others, having a long jaw line and azure skin with sage green patches on one side. Delayed faculties reconnect, at last.

"Shondre..."

Shondre purrs in delight, "Hyesss, Tom-Sun. Ssshondre iss heer."

She hugs him with her one arm, leaning the unscarred side of her face against his. Her breath hitches in involuntary stutters, and she hugs him tighter. Thompson reaches up with weak tingling arms and hugs her back.

Shondre sniffs and sits upright so she can look at him. Her eyes trace the lines of his thoracotomy scars and she touches the sage patches on her face.

"Morr, theezz," she says, melancholic. "Too mann-nee."

Shondre looks away to the expanse of surrounding bunks and chews her lower lip. The corners of her mouth draw into a frown and her eyes glisten. "Hwee looz ssssooo mann-nee. Hwee looz *hurr*, Tom-Sssun." Her expression slumps like a landslide. She tucks her chin to her chest, tears rolling down her face.

Thompson sits up, ignoring the hot bite in his chest, and he pulls her in close, shielding her, comforting. Then it dawns on him for whom she cries, and he freezes in terrible recollection.

Shondre sniffs hard and sits up, looking Thompson in the face. Colored eyeliner around her upper and lower eyelids runs down her cheek in translucent curtains, but her gaze is grave.

"Hyoo doo not go! Hyoo *ssstay*! Thisss hwon ahl-redd-dee looz too man-nee. Ssshee *nott* looz ann-nee morr. Ssshee nott looz *hyoo*, Tom-Sun!"

Shondre pulls Thompson to her and drapes her head over his shoulder.

"Mai-ell-uh loff hyoo morr than ahll. Ssshee dy ssso hyoo liff. Iff hyoo not liff, ssshee not sssuk-ssseed. Un-terr-ssstan-d?"

Shondre releases her grip so she can look Thompson in the eye again. His head droops, face contorting with an enormity of grief.

"I don't know what to do," he says, shaking. "I don't know how to live without her." The Gun inhales sharply, eyes glassy, pupils wide.

"Tom-Sssun, hwee uh-lyf bee-koss of hurr. *That* hurr gifft too usss. To giff bak, hwee do hurr good hwerk." Shondre gestures with half an arm at the expansive facility and all of the injured people in it. "Hwee help *themm*. *That* hwatt hwee do na-ow. Hwee liff to ssserff themm." She draws a line in the air connecting them. "And hwee help eech uth-urr. Bee-koss thisss hwon loff hyoo, too." Shondre's mouth bunches up on one side of her face and a tear falls down her cheek.

Thompson exhales in a gust and he pulls Shondre in tight. She hugs him back with all her might and they hold each other a long time, letting everything they held back come pouring out.

Caught in the mood, Sahara reaches into her collar and pulls out a pendant around her neck. Its opal stone flashes as she turns it in the bright overhead lights. She swipes tears from her own eyes and pushes her way under Munro's arm, wrapping herself as far around his waist as she can reach.

Munro looks down at her as if some strange animal has attacked him. But rather than peel her away, he sighs and lays his big arm over her, protectively.

Thompson takes a deep breath in and out. "Is it over, Shondre?"

Shondre blinks hard to push the last tears out, and she sits back. "Kood bee. Hwee gett thiss farr, hwith Mai-ell-uh-sss help. Hwee finn-nish hwatt ssshee ssstart. Much too doo. Nott much ty-mm lefft."

"What am I doing?" The Gun straightens his back. "Can't believe I'm sitting around; there's work to be done. Have to pull my weight." He reaches up to the unscarred side of her face. "Thank you, Shondre," the Gun pauses mid-sentence, struggling, "for *everything.*"

She nods hurriedly, then asks, concerned, "Hyoo redd-dee, ssoo ssoon?"

"Yeah." He looks at the floor, gauging whether or not his half numb legs will support him, then swings his feet over the side of the bunk.

Sahara and Munro break apart and rush to assist. He waves them off at first, tries to stand, then plunks back onto the bunk. Reluctantly, he reaches out to Munro, and lets the big MedTech haul him up. He takes a tentative step, does not fall, and regains his balance.

"Thanks, Colonel, I've got it from here," he says.

"Aye, sir," Munro answers.

Thompson does a double-take at Munro and squints in confusion.

"Here," Sahara says, passing over an off-white robe. "Cannae have you walkin' out of here starkers. I mean, you really shouldn't be walking *at all,* but..."

Thompson takes it, contemplating the Soshiba Varicorp logo over the left breast. Like everything else aboard the *Europa*, it is made for a Colonist's physique, and the Gun looks at Sahara in doubt.

"We added some length. Go on, it'll fit ye."

Dubious, Thompson unfurls the folded garment and finds extra canvas sewn onto the hem and cuffs. He slips his arms through the sleeves, pulls the lapels together. The belt is a struggle to cinch one-handed, so Sahara does it for him while he frowns at his bandaged stump.

Shondre takes his elbow. "Hwee ko na-ow?"

"Yeah, yeah, let's get going."

Together, Thompson and Shondre amble out of the facility, using each other for support. Tense columns of Eleto and Cadre soldiers fall obediently in line behind them.

Sahara glances at Munro, clears her throat, takes a half step aside, and stiffens into a more professional posture. Leaning toward the Counselor, she asks, "How in the bloody hells did you do that?"

"Pardon?" the android replies.

"I could nae do a thing for him. But you... How'd you *do* that?"

"Not so different from what you do, Doctor. I study my patient and try to figure out what they need. In this case, Thompson was lost. He needed a trusted friend to find him, lead him out, and give him something important to do."

"Could nae be as simple as all that, but...'e just hopped outta bed, like. Good as new!"

The Counselor turns toward her, his face grave. "I wish it were so. He'll be broken for the rest for the rest of his life, I fear. But as long as there are others who need help, and the work is hard enough to make Hercules groan, Thompson'll hold himself together for them."

Sahara frowns. "What does that say about us, then, that he couldn't trust his own kin? Had to be Shondre, instead."

The Counselor watches the columns of soldiers disappear through the main entrance. "No cause for shame, Doctor. Shondre and Thompson suffered together...*bled* together. That's a deep bond...one that really matters to a Cadre Operator."

Sahara nods. "By the way, been meanin' to ask... We saw ye go with Shondre and them during the attack, and she got burned awful... How are you not?"

The Counselor pops his eyebrows and crosses his arms. "I insisted they take me as hostage. Prell-Shah-Stoh refused. Said it was a military matter and it was his call. I followed as close as they'd let me then dove into their limousine last second as they were evacuating. Thought that would do it, since there was no way they'd turn around and drop me off on a station that was disintegrating behind them. And I was right... But once we were safely away, Prell-Shah-Stoh put me out of the air lock."

Sahara gasps. "He *spaced* you? The bastard!"

The Counselor looks away, staring beyond the walls of the facility.

"Limousine was hit right after. I watched fire roll down the portholes along the passenger cabin. Thought we'd lost them all. Can't even remotely explain how relieved I am we *didn't*."

Sahara's jaw drops. "Yeah, but he fookin' spaced you!"

The Counselor grunts, bemused. "Probably *saved* me."

"Well, who...how'd anyone find you in that mess?"

The android reaches into his pocket and retrieves his tablet, "The screen is reflective and the sun is plenty bright. Used it to flash a message, so I'd stand out from the rest of the debris. Beckert spotted me, reeled me in. Got a little baked in the sun, but...here I am."

"Huh. Thought your hair was wilder than usual."

The Counselor laughs and replaces the tablet in his pocket. "I'm going to join Thompson in his quarters and get him up to speed. There's...*quite a lot* to catch up on. Call if you need me."

"Right-o. And Counselor..."

"Yes?"

"Yer gonna call me Sahara at some point."

The Counselor grins. "Call if you need me, *Sahara*."

476

"*Much* better."

The Counselor turns with a flourish of his brightly colored robe and departs.

Sahara and Munro watch the Counselor as he goes. Sahara shakes her head. "Bleedin' lucky we are to have 'im. Oh, and uh..." She looks up sheepishly at Munro. "Sorry about the, uh, you know..." She makes a hoop with her arms as if hugging a huge tree.

"No harm done," the big MedTech replies.

Sahara clucks her tongue, squints, and points a finger. "And not a word of this. Cannae have anyone think I'm goin' soft."

Munro grins across his whole face. "None will hear of it."

"Better not." She winks at him for emphasis, then turns and surveys the facility. "All right, biggie. Let's go fix some people, yeah?"

The MedTech nods once and holds out an arm. "Lead the way."

CONUNDRUM

The Counselor walks beside Shondre through unpainted metal corridors. Her uneven gait makes the pace slower than the Counselor would like, current circumstances what they are, but he makes no effort to rush. Instead he busies himself studying walls, ceiling, and floor plates.

That this facility was built for manufacturing is no secret, so it makes sense there would be years of abuse marking the surfaces. Ironic wall graphics, calling out for caution, are dented and scuffed from impacts. Each intersection has padded corners where the bumpers are worn and torn by countless collisions. The occasional wall sconce is broken off at the root, left to dangle by power cords. Floors tell a tale of haste in hundreds of overlapping tire skids.

Shondre notices him studying each dent and scrape. In her own tongue, she says, "(It seems the People offer utmost modesty in accommodations. Perhaps we may soon provide something more dignified.)"

With a smile to himself, the Counselor replies, "(Madame Shondre, these walls tell the same story as ones that sheltered us every day of our lives. This one was remarking at the similarity, and at how the People could not have made us more at home if they tried.)"

Shondre swivels her head to look directly at him with her good eye. "(Konn-Zill-Urr, if our ocean liners were as buoyant as your spirit *they could never sink*.)"

The Counselor lets out a surprised laugh, then explains, "(This one is happiest in service to others.)"

"(It is known,)" she states, pulling closer to rub shoulders. "(It is one of many reasons he is so well liked.)"

The pair round a corner and see an ordinary sliding security door straight ahead, flanked by two Guns in full kit. Despite the plainness of the venue, effort has been made to dress up the entrance with hand-painted vines around the frame and Eleto script above, which the Counselor reads aloud.

"('*Embassy and Sovereign Territory of the Human Nation*.' Talks have yet to start, and already we have a land grant. Things are looking up.)"

Shondre laughs and squeezes the Counselor's arm before letting go of it. "(This is where we must part. Be with your fellows and plan well. We look forward to seeing our friends at the table once more.)"

"(This one shares your warm sentiment. May talented healers mend my friend's wounds and ease her pain.)"

Shondre lays her hand on his shoulder. "(They will.)" She is about to turn away then stops abruptly. The rigid carriage of diplomacy falls away and she asks plainly, "(Who takes care of *you*, Konn-Zill-Urr?)"

Off guard, the Counselor looks sideways at her, unsure how to reply.

Shondre holds up her hand, releasing him from an answer, and says, "(My friend needs no flesh to deserve warmth of kinship. A kind soul shines brightly no matter the body that carries it. Konn-Zill-Urr must know this one will *always* be his friend, because she loves him as her own.)"

His mouth falls open. Actuators around one eye flutter in a tug of war between expressions until he clears it with exaggerated double blinks. Before he can utter a response, she pats his shoulder, kisses his cheek, turns, and limps back the way she came. The Counselor watches her go, military entourage in tow. Then he straightens his clothes, smoothes down his hair, and faces the door into a newly established embassy.

Gun Branka and Gun Dagmar stamp to attention at his approach. Branka opens the door. The Counselor takes a step then pauses. He looks over the Operators' armor, contemplating large repaired patches that lack the light-absorbent doping. Dagmar's and Branka's cheeks are swollen. Orbits around their eyes are dark, exaggerating bright red blotches in the sclera. Whatever other abuse they endured is hidden beneath cerametallic layers and articulated joints, but if the contusions over their bodies are as severe as the ones on their faces, it could be a misery just standing there.

"Thank you, Branka, Dagmar," the Counselor says, "for your service in *very* strange times."

Gazes fixed down the short corridor, the two Guns nod once in acknowledgement but stand a little straighter than before.

Passing through the open doorway, the Counselor finds a spacious storeroom. Haloes of grime stain walls and floor where machinery or cabinets once stood. Comfortable Eleto furnishings and ornate works of art, provided as a goodwill gesture to soften the Spartan interior, have all been shoved into a pile in one corner. At center is a semicircular metal table, edges sharp from recent manufacture. Its patina is identical to the wall plating, and, when the Counselor looks up at a ceiling of exposed conduits and cables, he discovers where the materials were sourced.

Around the table's curved edge stand Ralla, Beckert, and Keiko. Gregor Petrova sits on the flat edge, one knee resting on the surface, arms crossed. Jonah Herzfeld stands beside him, talking to Cadre Officers as vehemently with his hands as with his mouth.

At the Counselor's entrance, Herzfeld looks over his shoulder then turns back and finishes, "...which is why you guys need a Chief Executive *right now*."

Ralla levels a stone-hard glare at Herzfeld, then she waves the Counselor over to the table.

"Thank you for coming, Counselor," Ralla states. "We'd welcome your impartial witness. Any matters of life and death before we begin?"

A muted chorus around the table mutters in the negative.

"Very well," Ralla states, and she places a small holo projector at the table's center. "We've received no transmissions from Colonel Chusan, or from his crew, since he departed Cadre One. And this archived video from an Eleto task force, provided via request through Madame Shondre, corroborates the report that Colonel Chusan's vessel was intercepted en route and destroyed with all hands."

Ralla touches the holoprojector and a dim three-dimensional model of space opens at table's center. Within the spherical projection, a Cadre warship drops stealth fields and launches a blistering volley at a target beyond the perimeter of the projected globe. An instant later return fire streaks through the Cadre ship, ventilating its length. Drive nacelles at the stern buckle and fail in a blazing detonation that vaporizes the ship completely. Ralla touches the projector again, and the image collapses.

"We presume Colonel Chusan is KIA, along with his crew. Therefore, we must backfill his seat on the Council."

Gregor eyes Ralla with disbelief. The Russian stands and leans on the table with his fingertips, "Is that really *all* you have to say abou—"

"Major," the Counselor says to Ralla, while laying a hand on Gregor's shoulder to preempt his rant, "Colonel Chusan provided life-saving stability aboard the *Europa* after Keller's death. We owe him gratitude for that and many other things. May we have a minute of silence to reflect upon his service?"

Gregor shuts his mouth and nods.

Ralla's eyebrows pop up and her lower lip juts. "Of course. Beckert, could you count off sixty seconds for us, silently?"

"Affirmative, Major," the Geek replies. "Begin...*now*."

Ralla, Beckert, and Keiko stand with feet shoulder width apart, hands clasped behind their backs. Gregor and Herzfeld glance at one another briefly then bow their heads and indulge their own recollections.

At the end of the minute, Beckert states, "Aaaaand *time*."

Without missing a beat, Ralla resumes, "On the issue of backfilling Colonel Chusan's vacancy, I accept the recommendation of ranking Council member, Colonel Munro, that I be promoted to full Colonel and assume Chusan's duties and responsibilities, effective immediately. Major Keiko, as the only other surviving Council member, do you object?"

"I have no objection," Keiko responds.

"Whoa, whoa, *whoa!*" Herzfeld interjects, hands raised. "No offense, Major, but you were the one directing the assault on the Eleto here. I don't think a *promotion* sets proper tone at the negotiating table."

Ralla's eyebrows knit and she asks, perplexed, "I was under orders, and I followed those orders on the authority of my general. There was no dereliction of duty, so it's correct that I fill the void left by my predecessor."

The Counselor grunts, corners of his mouth drawing back into his second awkward expression of the day. "Major, what you say is correct... However, promotion is seen by the Eleto as a *reward* for exemplary service. In other words, it would tell the Eleto that the Cadre believes this attack was... *correct*...and you're being decorated for it. To give you a promotion after being so effective at killing the very people we wish to negotiate with...puts us in a very difficult bargaining position."

"*Thank you*," Herzfeld blurts.

Ralla scowls. "Loyalty and obedience are central to our existence, Counselor. And it is highly suspect that you should attempt to influence our internal affairs."

"I agree completely," the Counselor says, showing open palms. "We have *no* say in your internal affairs, that is entirely your domain. But we must advise you on all factors, because we want what gives us our best chance to end this war in stable, lasting peace."

Ralla squints at Herzfeld then at Gregor. Returning her shrewd gaze to the Counselor, Ralla asks. "You believe that by assuming Chusan's post I would harm our chances?"

"*Absolutely*, you would," Herzfeld states. Gregor nods in agreement.

Ralla frets and lets a breath out through her nose. "*What*, then? The post is too important to leave vacant."

The Counselor grips his chin in thought. "Can you assume the responsibilities without taking the rank?"

Ralla mulls the question. "Every decision would have to be passed up for approval, and Munro's workload is already pushing the limit of—"

"You," Herzfeld says, pointing.

The Counselor follows Herzfeld's pointing finger to Beckert. The young Geek frowns at the idea and glances at Ralla before replying, "You're not suggesting I surpass a superior officer with *years* more experie—?"

"You bet your ass, I am," Herzfeld interrupts. "You're the one who stopped the madness, pulled us all back from the brink...the man who risked everything to save Human AND Eleto lives... THAT'S who they'll want to see promoted."

Ralla's jaw flexes with restraint. "Shall I speak plainly?"

"Of course, please," the Counselor says.

"We believe the Colonists would be better served by your example and leadership, Counselor. Shall we insist *you* replace Captain Petrova?"

Gregor stands. "*Wait a damn second*, Ralla, there isn't a vacuum of power here so you can *fuck right off*—"

"PLEASE, *PLEASE, EVERYONE*," the Counselor shouts, hands raised until he can be heard again. "Major, you make a valid point. In this case, however, it isn't Cadre opinion or Colonist opinion that matters. *Eleto* perception will shape our future. We offend them at our peril." The Counselor levels a stern gaze at Gregor, adding, "Neither of us will dictate to the other in *any* matter. Let me underscore this, Major: We have *no* interest in telling you how to do your job. Our *only* intent is to share vital information so we can all make our best decisions that lead us *together* to our best outcome."

The hard-set features of Ralla's face soften by degrees, and she uncrosses her arms. "Very well, Counselor. Make your recommendation."

"Take whatever duties you must, Major, just don't wear the *label* of rank. And I understand this probably makes no sense to you. Once we've safely made it through the talks, and we have a binding agreement, re-organize any way you choose...we just ask you not take a promotion in rank until then."

Ralla peers from Gregor to Herzfeld to the Counselor. Despite Gregor's red face and ears, and Herzfeld biting his tongue behind pursed lips, the Major is unruffled. "In your honest estimation, my assuming the rank of Colonel prior to conclusion of talks will jeopardize the outcome?"

"*Yes*, Major," the Counselor answers, "without a doubt."

She nods once. "Be it so ordered. I will assume the duties and responsibilities of Colonel Chusan, but I will retain rank of Major until such time as negotiations with the Eleto conclude. It is *irregular in the extreme* to hold the duties and responsibilities of a Colonel without the authority, yet it is a contortion we will endure for the good of all. Beckert, note the date and time."

"Done, Major, and...*congratulations*?"

"Thank you. On the question of who will back fill my duties and responsibilities, I nominate Captain Beckert. Colonel Munro has already voiced his approval on the record. Major Keiko, do you concur?"

"I concur."

"Be it so ordered. Captain Beckert is inducted to the Leadership Council, on the basis of having demonstrated keen intuition, decision making, and action that spared our Operators and fleet from total annihilation."

"Very glad to hear you say that, Major," Herzfeld offers.

"There will be time for comments after, Professor. Now then, Major Beckert shall wear the *title* of Colonel until negotiations conclude, at which point we will once again re-align authority with job responsibility. Colonel Beckert, do you understand that I will need you to approve *all* of my requests without discussion or delay for the normal performance of my duties?"

"Yes, Major, I do."

"Good. In the meantime I shall have to get used to calling you, 'sir.' Now then, our final order of business is to complete our Council. We must have a General, and not because Professor Herzfeld tells us so. Recommendations?"

Gregor sits back on the edge of the table. "I think we all know, who—"

"*Captain*," the Counselor calls a little louder than necessary. "With respect, we're here to witness and advise, not participate in their process."

Gregor's mouth swishes to one side and he sucks his teeth. Ralla lifts an eyebrow then nods respectfully to the android.

"By seniority and experience, it would be you, Major," Keiko begins, "but that holds the same problem as you becoming Colonel. The Eleto won't talk with someone who sided with O'Kai."

"Agreed," Ralla says.

"Colonel Munro has the seniority, but as a MedTech, he's ineligible... unless we bend the rules again."

Ralla considers it then shakes her head. "That'd be a poor fit for his talents. And he has specifically asked to not be considered."

"Major," the Counselor asks, "have you heard from Colonel Shao-Lo?"

Beckert and Keiko stiffen with an involuntary inhale.

Ralla looks down at the table. When she looks up her expression is grave. "What came back from Cadre Two...was *not* Shao-Lo. It might have had her memories, but it was so heavily augmented, it was unrecognizable. Worse, there was influence of other...*personalities*...as well. After cessation of hostilities, all agreed that Cadre Two would be a better place for it. Shao-Lo, as we knew her, is no more."

"I'm sorry to hear that," the Counselor states. "Considering the kind of firepower she has at her disposal, and how easily that could destabilize everything...I hope we kept a line of communication open."

"There was little interest in dialogue on either side. In time, perhaps." Ralla shifts her stance and takes a deep breath. "Back to the matter at hand. We have a candidate. One who has served longer than any of us. Once a Major in the Operator Corps, a heartbeat away from being on the Council. But this individual is tainted by killing his own kind. On the *Europa*, it was accident. More recently, it was *not*. Gun Thompson terminated General O'Kai and also Brick Argo, his teammate. Just speaking these words leaves a taste in my mouth I find difficult to describe. Yet if *he had not*, we would not be alive today.

"A soldier must obey, must follow orders. But a General must *lead*...must have clarity of vision and must find the path to our best future. If that vision falters and the path is lost, another must take the place. O'Kai put us on a path to annihilation, and while the method Thompson used was detestable, I must concede there was no time for debate. Thompson stopped O'Kai...and Maiella stopped *me*...from ruining all. This is the conundrum we face.

"As Madame Shondre and the Counselor have previously stated, what matters most to the Eleto are actions taken to save lives on both sides. Maiella's actions ranked highest in this regard, in halting the neutronium implosion device, *Plasma Rain*. But Maiella is dead. She can't lead us. Thompson can. As odd as this sounds, and in spite of his crimes, Thompson has demonstrated the proper vision to guide us. He has made the hardest of all choices...in his place, I could not have done what needed to be done. Therefore, I nominate Gun Thompson to succeed O'Kai as General of the Cadre."

"Seconded," Beckert chimes without hesitation.

"Any other candidates?"

Beckert and Keiko shake their heads.

Ralla pinches the communicator at her collar. "Colonel Munro, respond, over."

"This is Munro, Major, go ahead."

"Any other candidates you wish to endorse before we decide?"

"None. You know my mind. As far as I'm concerned, Thompson already has the post."

"Understood. Ralla out." She pinches the communicator again. "We have our candidate. We must decide without reservation, and we must serve loyally and obediently."

Keiko crosses her real and artificial arms. "And if he leads us *off* the path?"

"A General has always needed the input of the Council," Ralla answers. "If the rest of the Council is in agreement, we can override a General's decision and steer ourselves back on course."

"Does he even want the post?" Keiko shifts her weight to one foot. "What he's gone through might have broken him. What I'm really asking, here... Can he handle it?"

"Excellent questions," Ralla replies. "Let's bring him in and ask him."

FOR YOUR CRIMES

Thompson tugs at the sleeves of a borrowed dress gray uniform as he strides through metal hallways. Two Eleto escorts keep a wary rear guard, saying nothing. Yet something innate to soldiering crosses cultures, and all three fall into step.

When Thompson arrives at a security door wreathed by green-leafed vines, his escorts halt, bow curtly to the Operators guarding the doorway, and march off the way they came.

"(This one thanks you,)" Thompson says to their backs. Then he faces Branka and Dagmar. The Guns snap crisp salutes, which Thompson returns in kind.

"Thompson to see the Leadership Council," he announces.

"You're expected, Major," Dagmar replies. Branka taps the door panel and the thick door slides aside.

Thompson steps through into the makeshift embassy and smiles to find a semicircular table at center.

Wouldn't matter if we were standing on the surface of the moon. If that table is there, that's Council Chambers.

Around the curved edge sit Ralla, Keiko, Munro, Beckert, and the Counselor. Lounging off to the side in comfortable looking armchairs are Gregor and Herzfeld. A small wooden table stands at elbow height between them with a tray and dark bottle atop it. Both men hold fluted glasses with a honey-colored liquor inside. Their faces are flushed and both seem unusually pleased with themselves.

The Counselor peels himself away from the Cadre Officers and smiles at his guest.

"Thompson, welcome! Come right in, and, ah... Is something funny?"

"Yeah," Thompson says with a sly glance at the seated men. "That's the happiest and quietest I've ever seen those two. Did you write 'em a scrip to the pharmacy?"

The Counselor laughs deeply. "Not exactly. All I can say is the Eleto state of brewing is *advanced*. Please, won't you join us?"

The Counselor guides Thompson to the table and the Gun glances at familiar, if adversarial, faces. His eyes stop on silver eagles at Beckert's collar, and he straightens. "Colonel Beckert, congratulations, sir."

The Geek grimaces and looks to Ralla on his right.

"Colonel Beckert's promotion is in title only," Ralla announces. "I hold senior executive authority, despite maintaining the rank of Major."

Thompson squints. "That's...*unusual*."

"To say the least. We've felt the intrusion of *politics* in our organization, and I assure you it will be for the last time. Now, then, to the matter at hand. Gun Thompson, do you know why you've been summoned?"

"To serve in any way that I may."

Ralla nods. "Indeed. Though I doubt you suspect what level of service is required." She does a silent survey of the other Council members and they all nod once.

"Major Thompson, I nominate you to succeed O'Kai as General of the Cadre."

Thompson's eyes stretch wide. His mouth parts, though words are delinquent. "Sir, that is the greatest honor an Operator could ever achieve... but I cut a *poor* example—"

Ralla holds up a hand. "Stop. There is no longer any recognizable 'normalcy' in operations. We've never known such upheavals. To put it plainly, the Cadre was led astray by leaders who could not see the path. I include myself in that assessment. Getting us back on track was costly and painful, yet necessary."

"Sir, what I've done—"

"Was what *HAD* to be done," Ralla barks. "*I* could not have done it. You and Maiella saw the true path. Whether your isolation gave you better perspective, or if you possess superior cognition, is irrelevant. If not for the two of you, none of us would be here today. That is a *fact*. Do you dispute it?"

Thompson blinks, stymied for an answer.

"I'll take your silence as tacit agreement. And returning to the matter at hand, the Cadre cannot function without a General. We require a supreme authority that will best represent us to the Eleto. As I was their principal antagonist, it cannot be me."

"Major Ralla, I never served on the Leadership Council. To surpass all other Council members is—"

"*Irrelevant*. You led the Operator Corps, once. More importantly you had the confidence and will to oppose O'Kai when he took us in the wrong direction."

"It was more than opposition, sir. And Argo...my *brother*..."

"If I wasn't locked in my armor, Thompson, I'd have done *anything* to bring you down. You'd've had to kill me, as well. And I'll tell you straight, Major, you'd've been right to do so. On this we all agree."

Beckert, Keiko, and Munro nod their heads and grunt their assent.

Thompson grinds his teeth. "With respect, what I deserve is a *sentence* for my crimes."

"Then here it is: *for your crimes*, you are sentenced to spend your remaining days in highest service to the Cadre until retirement. *For your crimes*, you shall bear the burden of guiding the Cadre, of guaranteeing our future, of making our hardest choices. You must manufacture our purpose anew, mold us, and shape us into what we must be. This adaptation will be the most difficult we've ever had to make. Because you've already made that transition, you are singularly qualified to lead us through it.

"You're the first choice of the Colonists. You're the first choice of the Eleto. More importantly, you are the *only* choice of this Council. What say you?"

Thompson looks into the eyes of every council officer and finds a certainty he wishes he had in himself. The Counselor's head tilts, silently inquiring. When Thompson remains mute, the android steps over beside him and whispers, "The future Maiella dreamt of... *You'd have the authority to build it*."

Thompson's eyes crush shut and his breath leaves in a rush. When he looks up at Ralla, his eyes are bright.

"I accept."

Ralla steps from around the table and outstretches a hand. In her palm is a shiny gold star. Thompson looks down at the tiny thing, knowing it will be the heaviest object he has ever carried.

No half measures, he thinks, taking the insignia from Ralla's hand. Head high, he drives the pin through his collar.

Council officers rise, stamp to attention, swing flat hands to brows, and shout, "GENERAL THOMPSON, *HOORAH, HOORAH, HOORAH*!"

Gregor and Herzfeld startle in their seats, drinks sloshing in delicate glasses, and they perk up with red-rimmed eyes.

"Did we miss it?" Herzfeld asks.

Gregor leans forward and squints. "Hey, he accepted!"

"Thasss fucking *brilliant*," Jonah slurs. He and Gregor clink glasses, down the dregs, and sink back into the cushions.

Council officers crowd around Thompson, congratulating him and shaking his hand.

"Orders, General?" Munro asks.

Thompson thinks a moment. "There's much I've missed. Get me up to speed."

MANTLE OF THE FIRST

The makeshift embassy buzzes with Eleto couriers, liaisons, dignitaries, plaintiffs, petitioners, secretaries, attorneys, officers, escorts, and advocates. Thompson is in the thick of it behind the semicircular table, on his feet, Counselor at one side, translating, and Herzfeld on the other, advising responses to demands.

Ralla and Beckert lie in metal recliners transplanted from idle Virus Ships. HDIs ride on their shaved crowns, goggles flashing with commands and data feeds to the fleet in orbit.

Keiko and Munro occupy standup workstations on the opposite side of the room. Holowindows hover before them with Cadre and Colonist faces that enter frame and depart as swiftly as the two can issue instructions.

Overlapping conversations bounce off metal walls, floor, and ceiling, amplifying the buzz. For all its outward appearance of chaos, however, every word is harmonized with Thompson's directives, made action through limbs of authority downstream.

Halgrim, Maddock, Branka, and Dagmar assure tight security from the corridor outside, checking every visitor and parcel before it crosses the threshold. Those who attempt to see the new general without an appointment are flatly denied access; but there is one exception granted day or night admittance any time she wishes.

"General Thompson," Branka calls via communicator. "Madame Shondre is here to see you."

Thompson's eyes lift from his tablet to focus on the doorway. "Send her in."

Excusing himself from Herzfeld and the Counselor, he rounds the table, hurrying to meet Shondre as the doorway opens. The Gun smiles and spreads his arms.

"Shondre, so good to see you!"

"Jenn-hu-rahl Tom-Sun," she greets, stepping into his warm embrace. The two wrap arms around each other, resting chins on each other's shoulder before peeling apart.

Taking a step back, Thompson beckons, "Please, come in."

Shondre blinks once and nods. Before she obliges, she looks over her shoulder and crooks her finger at an Eleto porter behind her.

"Sssum-thing forr hyoo," she says with an arched brow and mysterious grin.

"Parcel cleared, sir," Branka advises from outside the doorway. "No threats."

Thompson waits for the porter to approach, noting his drab brown uniform is devoid of artistry, so plain as to intentionally render the wearer unnoticed and unremembered. Beneath the fabric, however, are muscular shoulders carried in the upright posture of one accustomed to command, and in the placement of booted feet, Thompson recognizes a fighter who will not be caught flat-footed. And one side of the porter's face is so thoroughly reconstructed he looks like a combination of two different individuals.

A twinge of recognition lifts the hairs of Thompson's nape.

Maiella battling for her life on the summit floor... Leer of an Eleto veteran astride her, blade at her throat... Her cry for help, a spurt of red... Then Munro's swing that shattered the veteran's face and ended the contest...

Tall enough to stand level with Thompson, the porter averts his orange-tinted eyes and presents a shiny black case with white-gloved hands, latch facing outward.

Shondre opens the case, revealing neatly folded black fabric with gold accents.

"Na-ow Tom-Sun *isss* Hwill of hisss Pee-pull."

She cranes her head around Thompson's wide shoulders, catching the Counselor's attention, and invites him with an upward tilt of her head.

The Counselor hurries over. Unsummoned, Herzfeld follows.

The Counselor hails Shondre with flowery words in her tongue. Shondre smirks, offers a good-natured scolding, then kisses his cheek.

"I only caught part of that," Thompson states.

"She asked that I translate to assure meaning is preserved," the Counselor replies. "She also reminded me that friends need not be so formal."

Shondre reaches into the case and lifts out a long bolt of cloth. As she turns, the hem spills from the case and drapes just above the floor in front of her. Thick black fabric hangs from a reinforced collar embroidered in gold thread. Woven near the collar's clasp are the Cadre Hawk and a single star. As the cloth sways in Shondre's grip, Thompson takes hold of the edges, spreads them for a better view in the overhead light, and finds the entire garment is embroidered with charcoal gray thread. As Thompson turns the fabric, he sees subtle images of Cadre Operators and MedTechs among constellations of stars.

"This," the Counselor translates for Shondre, "is the Mantle of The First, which denotes its wearer as *Will of the People*. Whoever wears this is recognized as a supreme authority, bringing order and direction to his kind. It is not to be confused with a *Voice of the People*, who is a representative empowered to negotiate on the People's behalf."

Thompson, still captivated by the embroidery, looks up and asks, "There's incredible detail here, but why hide it in similar shades?"

Shondre nods and answers in Eleto. The Counselor interprets her reply.

"This is to signify that the *Will of the People* is complex and motives are not always apparent at first glance," the Counselor translates. "Yet anyone who would make the effort to understand will approach close enough to see. You and I, for example... We seemed plain to one another when on opposite sides of a war. But now, we stand together, and we see the subtle details that make us worth knowing."

Thompson nods. "Absolutely."

Shondre blinks slowly, speaks, then grins.

"It is also your favorite color, which is fortunate," the Counselor translates.

"Ha! True enough." Thompson looks down at the carefully sewn images, sensing the suggestion of story in their arrangement.

"A *Voice of the People* wears a bright robe because, as a representative, motivations must be readily apparent," the Counselor explains. "There is no place for hidden agendas when one speaks for others. Do you understand the difference?"

"I do," Thompson answers, looking up at her.

Shondre looks Thompson in the eye, pointing politely at his chest, and continuing.

"It is not your uniform, perhaps not at all your custom to wear something like this," the Counselor translates. "But Madame Shondre made effort to ensure the Cadre is well-served in its design. Selflessness. Determination.

Fitness of mind and body. And commitment to providing future generations a better life. We hope this garment honors these noble qualities, and that you will wear it in pride."

"I will," the general says, "as proudly as the Cadre's highest decoration. I only regret I have nothing to offer in return."

Shondre shakes her head and speaks plainly with serious expression.

"This mantle is not a gift," the Counselor translates, "it is recognition and confirmation of what already is. The gift we have given each other is hope, which must always be renewed and never taken for granted."

Shondre steps around him and drapes the robe over his shoulders, smoothing the fabric and describing it before fastening the clasp.

"The People will honor and safeguard the one who wears this," the Counselor translates. "Wearing it any time you are outside of personal quarters is recommended for your protection and for those who travel with you."

Thompson looks up from the intricate embroidery. "Travel? Are we going somewhere?"

Shondre nods.

"A time and place has been set for the talks to resume," Herzfeld guesses.

"Hyess," Shondre states, defaulting to Human words now that formalities are concluded. "Pee-puhl ee-gurr to starrt. Hyoo redd-dee?"

Thompson glances at the Counselor and Herzfeld, who both nod emphatically. To his officers, the general announces, "*Leadership Council*, delegate tasks and pack up. We're moving."

Ralla and Beckert issue final commands then shut down their uplink feeds. Ralla springs up from her recliner and assists Beckert onto his prosthetic legs. Munro and Keiko likewise issue abrupt orders to MedTechs and Operators on screen and shut down their terminals. All four converge around Thompson, and Beckert declares, "Sir, Leadership Council assembled and ready for departure."

Maddock's voice buzzes through Thompson's collar communicator, "Security detail ready for departure. Standing by, General."

Herzfeld and the Counselor share a glance then take places alongside the Cadre Officers.

Thompson turns to Shondre and states, "Let's not keep them waiting."

Shondre gawks, open-mouthed, at the swiftness of mobilization. In another blink she collects her wits and shrugs. "Oh-kay, then. Hwee go na-ow."

EMBERS OF SUSPICION

A silver needle slips through the sky, hypersonic. Ahead of it a faint glow clears a column of air just wide enough for the craft to pass through and gently closes behind. Inside the airless tunnel, there is no buffeting for the passengers inside, no booming shockwave ripping the landscape below, just the electric sizzle of a dipole field in optimal calibration.

Gregor and Jonah perch in their amply padded seats like kids, heads swooping back and forth in cabin windows for better view of landscapes streaking past.

Munro takes up both seats in his row, and his large round head fills the porthole like an eclipse. He, too, gazes out in rapt fascination at forms and formations of a living, breathing planet. His brow gathers as if in pain, and he whispers subconsciously, "I had no concept...*none*..."

Keiko leans over Maddock in the seat beside her, both Operators pinned to the same window, gawking at a lush green world beyond.

Beckert points out at free-flowing streams, lakes, bird colonies, and grazing herds, breathlessly telling Ralla about them and other creatures he saw on rotation years ago. Ralla does her best to remain demure, but every so often she glances through the porthole and her rigid expression cracks with a furtive smile.

"Even more beautiful than I imagined," Gregor says. "I mean, the archive photos, they just don't... They're nothing compared to *seeing* it."

"Oh, right... You're a natural born citizen of the *Europa*," Herzfeld recalls. "But if you like this, you should see Tasmania, mate," Herzfeld adds. "Cradle Mountain... Freycinet...Wineglass Bay would blow your mind...if it's still there."

"Where are we, by the way?"

The Counselor looks over the back of his seat. "We're heading down a peninsula we called, Florida, then we'll continue south to an island we called, Cuba."

"Koo-Bah," Gregor mimics.

The Counselor nods. "Fascinating place, but it wasn't heavily developed in our time."

"So it didn't get bombed out like other places," Herzfeld surmises. "It's intact?"

"*Mostly*, yes. Larger cities, like Havana, Santiago, and Guantánamo were leveled. The rest of the island was relatively untouched. Climate is ideal for the Eleto, so they excavated the irradiated soil and encapsulated it at the bottom of the Atlantic. Dredged up fill from the Gulf to replace it. Possibly the largest earthworks project ever undertaken. The island's extensively settled now. You could consider it their capitol on this world, in fact."

Thompson leans his shoulder against the side of the craft, hands in lap, staring through the transparent metal porthole. Shondre steals a glance at him from the opposite row. His dour expression is stark contrast to the rest of the passengers, so she scoots over to the aisle seat and leans on the armrest.

"Tom-Sun," she says across the aisle, but the Gun continues his distant gaze. She stands, sidesteps across the gap and wedges herself into the narrow space beside him.

Thompson breaks his stare, offers Shondre a wan smile, then resumes his far off gaze.

Shondre peeks out the window to see what has Thompson so captivated, but as the southern tip of Florida slides by, all she sees is calm ocean and blue sky.

"Hyoo sssad ssshee nott heer hwith uss," Shondre guesses.

Thompson lifts an eyebrow then nods once. "And Argo. And Sharon. And *others…*"

"Mmm. This hwonn sad, ahl-ssso. Hwee kann-nott sayf ahll. But, hwee uh-lyf. Ow-wurr Pee-pull uh-lyf. That meen-sss hwee doo it *ry-tt*."

Thompson grunts. His expression wrinkles. "That's something Maiella would say."

Shondre smiles, slow blinks, and nods. "Mai-Ell-Uh *sssmart*." She lays her cheek on Thompson's shoulder, rests her hand on his arm, and sighs. "Hwee miss-ing oth-urr ssself. Hwee neffer fill hohl they leef. Ssso hwee giff loff to ow-wurr Pee-pull na-ow. Hwee loff *them* lyk hwee loff oth-urr ssself. Lyk *fam*-lee. Mayk uss good lee-durrs."

Thompson frets then lays a hand over Shondre's. "That's a solid plan." He leans back in his seat, the weight in his chest a few kilos lighter.

PLASMA RAIN

An announcement from the flight deck precedes a gradual deceleration and an end to the omnipresent electric sizzle. Faint blue glow beyond the window dissipates and wind sways the craft as it approaches a spacious gray-white landing field. Painted grid lines mark each landing zone in alternating black and white stripes. Bright lights embedded in the grid highlight boundaries and shift color as vessels land or lift off.

Sequestered from the rest of the field by high, rugged blast deflectors, gargantuan cargo haulers squat on the eastern side, mass drives aimed directly at the deck, idling. Loaders scurry up and down ramps, toting cargo to and from flat-roofed warehouses along the pad's far side. A sprawling hub of high-speed mag-lev rail terminates at the complex of warehouses and tracks fan out into the landscape, extending beyond the horizon.

On the western side of the pad, airliners disgorge passengers through rear exits while embarking travelers shuffle through entrances at front. Despite great diversity in size and capacity, all liners conform to a standard shape of long cylinder with tapered nose and tail.

Overlooking the bustle is a broad, circular platform atop an hourglass shaped tripod at the northwest corner. A long spike points skyward from its roof, hung with transmitters and receivers for every band in the broadcast spectrum. Aerials jut at forty-five degree angles around the platform's upper edge, repositioning periodically like the feelers of some giant insect.

To look upon the hectic comings and goings suggests impossibility of landing without collision. Yet during the transport's approach, its flight path clears as if by magic, and it descends toward a pad occupied by an idling liner. Just as it seems a crash is imminent, the liner lifts off and ascends through another tunnel in the traffic, clearing the pad. Grid border lights shift from departing red to welcoming blue, and the delegation's vessel touches down onto a warm pad with muted *klunks* of articulated landing struts. Main drives cycle down to a drone, and a *ding* tones through the cabin.

Shondre climbs up from her seat, excited, and steps to the front of the cabin. A doorway to her left opens with a subtle hiss, bringing whiffs of propellant, ionized air, vaporized metal, and sea salt. She inhales deeply with closed eyes, grins, then faces the passenger rows, urging all to follow her down the ramp.

Gregor and Jonah step out behind Shondre, dumbfounded at the hugeness of sky above. Gregor is more tentative, the lack of confined space around him inspiring instant vertigo. Struggling to comprehend the absence of walls or ceiling, the Russian widens his stance, focuses on the ramp, and places each step with care to avoid falling and making himself an instant joke.

Beckert eases down the ramp on prosthetic legs then stands beside Gregor. The Geek pans his head, surveying the bustling scene with unblinking ocular implants. "It was hard to take, the first time. Living inside walls my whole life, I looked at the sky and thought I was gonna fall right up into it."

Gregor takes a deep breath, feet shoulder width apart, still wrestling with magnificent enormity around him. He risks a glance at colossal white towers of cloud lazing by then lowers his gaze to the pad. "Yep, pretty much nails it."

Approaching his other side, Ralla asks, "Need a hand?"

"No, no, I got it..." the Russian says. "Just takes getting used to, is all."

Keiko and Maddock step out into bright sunlight and squint against the glare. Instinctively, they part to each side of the group and stand vigilant watch, sweeping the bustle for any sign of a threat.

Munro emerges through the hatch, having to turn sideways to fit. He tromps down the ramp, making the whole craft sway on its struts, then slows as unfiltered scents fill his sinuses. Like Gregor, he blinks at incomprehensible vastness.

The Counselor waits for Thompson at the top of the ramp, and the two stride down together. A gust of engines from a nearby departure flings their robes to one side, nearly blowing the Counselor off the ramp, but the Gun catches the android by an arm.

"Whoa, thank you! I'll have to be more..." The Counselor mutes himself when he sees Thompson staring off at the horizon. He looks down at the large hand still gripping his arm, then asks, "Uh, General, are you all right?"

Thompson shakes himself and he releases his grip, offering an abrupt, "Sorry," before resuming his path down the ramp. The Counselor hustles to keep up.

"See something?" the android probes.

Thompson frowns with one side of his face then replies, "I remembered being on an old bridge over a river valley... Gust of wind nearly blew me over the side..."

"Yes?"

Thompson glances at the Counselor, eyes narrow and guarded. "Back then, our lives depending on not being seen... Yet here we are, out in the open, unarmed and unarmored, a thousand eyes and cameras on us... It's different."

"I should hope so," the Counselor chimes.

The Gun looks around the pad, finding no obvious way across. "Where do we—?"

In answer, a square section rises in the pad's corner with an open metal door beneath it. Shondre heads toward the open door, then turns about and walks backwards, arm raised, beckoning all to follow.

The delegation files into the elevator behind Shondre. Thompson enters last, taking a last look at the transport and its sleek lines.

Glad I no longer have to destroy such beautiful things.

Elevator doors slide shut, providing welcome confinement to those craving it. Thompson, however, already misses the wide-open sunlit space, and he crosses his thick arms in thought.

After a swift, smooth descent the elevator opens, revealing a cavern of multi-tiered platforms and walkways. Thousands of Eleto travelers shuffle down orderly lanes with cases, bags, and trolleys in tow, emerging from or disappearing through archways. A few glance in the delegation's direction, do double takes, then stop and point.

Tall, rugged barricades marked in blaze orange keep an open path for the delegation, manned every few meters by Eleto in riot gear. They nod respectfully to Shondre as she passes then level stern gazes at overly curious Eleto beyond the barricades. As more and more travelers notice the strange visitors, they crowd together for a glimpse of these bizarre aliens who terrorized them for centuries. Most clutch a recording device in outstretched hands, some climb onto shoulders and railings or jump for a peek. Others shout at the top of their lungs for attention, gesturing aggressively. Minor scuffles and squabbles break out, ended by harsh shouts from the guards and occasionally by stun stick for the most agitated.

Gregor and Jonah hunch at the commotion around them, unsure what might come hurtling out of it. Thompson, having previously walked through a hall filled with Eleto who wanted him dead, sees a difference that puts him at ease. While the air is charged with emotion, there is little of the naked loathing or revulsion from before. This time there is more interest, more excitement, in shining saffron eyes.

Barricaded paths lead to a levitating train car with open doors and well-armed Eleto sentries. Keiko and Maddock insist all wait while they search the car, poring over every surface, rummaging every cabinet and pocket. After tossing the interior, and thoroughly irritating the car's driver, the Guns give an all clear hand signal and invite the rest inside.

Once interior components are returned to proper places and all are comfortably seated, doors close and the car slips into a round tunnel. Through the car's windows, fixed images placed along the tunnel walls seem to animate as they pass in rapid succession. At full speed the images move in real time, showing Eleto applying creams, salves, ingesting beverages, inhaling vapors, always with the same look of luxurious ecstasy followed by high contrast captions.

"I have no idea what any of that stuff was," Gregor says to Jonah, thumping the car window, "but it looks *amazing*."

The car rushes on a magnetic cushion, banks through sweeping curves, dips down a long decline, levels off, then slows to a gentle halt at another underground station. Unlike the bright limestone of the main hub, this terminal is hewn from dark gray, coarse-grained bedrock. Flanking the main gate, huge slabs of tan sandstone hang on vertical walls. Angled spotlights in the ceiling shine down across the slabs, enhancing shadowed impressions of spiral shells, enormous animal skeletons, and rope-like plants many meters in length.

The opening itself could accommodate dozens of Eleto side by side, yet no other travelers are present, and an empty lane of square tiles leads up to a thick gate cut from the same dark stone as the walls.

Shondre leads the way, waving to guards inside booths recessed into each side of the gate. They nod, and the thick door sinks into the floor with a lengthy groan of hydraulics. From the far side, uniformed Eleto escorts step through, bow modestly, and urge all to follow. Most in the delegation peer into the dark corridor with hesitancy, but when Shondre and Thompson do not break stride they promptly catch up.

The wide lane narrows, corralling the delegation between rails and steering them one by one under scanning beams. Afterward, the pace is swift, and the journey ends at a circular room with no windows. Portraits of elder Eleto adorn the walls, depicted in media ranging from dabbed-on pigments to high-resolution photographs, each with an engraved platinum plate directly beneath. Of the many likenesses adorning the hall, one stands out with a familiar gaze. Thompson stares at that likeness, transfixed by uncanny depth and realism imbued by the artist, fully expecting the painting might come alive and speak.

The room's only furnishings are a roundtable of polished mineral at center and high-backed swivel chairs surrounding it. A chandelier of recording devices and idle holoprojectors dangles near the ceiling, lenses arrayed so that every centimeter of the table—and its attendees—can be imaged in triple redundancy.

A section of wall recedes unexpectedly between portraits then slides aside. Eleto delegates file through the hidden door, dressed in multiple overlapping folds of cloth cinched by broad sashes at the waist. Behind the delegates, a taller Eleto strides in, wearing the black mantle of supreme authority. The tall Eleto turns his attention toward Thompson as he crosses in front of his own portrait, and, for an instant, Thompson falls under simultaneous gazes of living subject and his two-dimensional doppelganger.

Eleto delegates fill out the far side of the table, standing beside their chairs and conversing in serious tones. Some glance across the table, apprehension pulling the lines of their faces taut as they see Cadre and Colonists filling out the opposite side. Once all are in their places, Shondre steps around the table to greet the Great Eleto and his entourage. They turn as one to address her with respectful bows, hand over chest.

The Counselor steps up beside Thompson, watching Shondre and the Eleto delegates interact.

"Protocol, mostly," the Counselor advises. "Acknowledgements of titles and authority... Polite complements... Tedious necessities of procedure... You can tell, they're all eager to get past it, even Madame Shondre."

"That one in black, *Dekkto*... He isn't saying anything."

"He doesn't have to. We all know why we're here. Oh! I'm being summoned, would you excuse me, General?"

"Of course."

The Counselor moves quickly around the table, stands before the Great Eleto, and bows to his waist, humbly. When the android straightens, he moves down the line of Eleto delegates by order of rank, greeting them with progressively shallower bows.

The instant the Counselor finishes greeting the last delegate, Dekkto gruffly speaks, looks Thompson, then Gregor, in the eye, and extends a hand toward the chairs opposite his.

"General, Captain," the Counselor says, making his way back around the table, "noble Dekkto Mayah Tayaloh welcomes you and your fellows as respected guests. He asks you to honor him by sitting at his table."

"Which I am pleased to do," Thompson replies.

"As am I," Gregor adds.

Thompson, Gregor, and Dekkto take their seats in precisely measured movements, and the rest follow. The Great Eleto takes a deep breath, tension drawing his shoulders higher than usual. With rigid jaw he speaks deliberately, slowly. There is a simmering edge of restraint in his voice and his eyes narrow beneath angled brow.

"Let us rejoice that our guests are unharmed," the Counselor translates. "And we trust they found their accommodations satisfactory—"

Thompson holds up a hand to the Counselor, stopping him mid-sentence. "We are grateful for the comforts, noble Dekkto has provided us. But we all know why we're here. Encourage them to speak their minds, plainly, without fear of insult. They may ask us *anything*. We will listen and answer, because we owe them explanation."

The Counselor relays Thompson's words. Hard edges in Dekkto's expression soften slightly, and he reclines in his high-backed chair.

Gregor leans over to the Counselor and asks, "You ready for this?"

The android glances at his captain with an anxious smirk. "As much as anyone can be." He faces Dekkto and says in Eleto, "(Greatness, how may we unburden the Eleto mind?)"

Dekkto's eyes narrow and he extends a hand toward the brightly-robed delegate on his right, Fell-Marr-Ghen.

"(The People demand satisfaction for a *cowardly* attack brought under a banner of *truce*,)" Fell-Mar-Ghen snarls. "(Those recently killed shame us from afterlife, that we sit and treat with the very ones who slew them. To rest, their souls must have *justice*!)"

A murmur of agreement passes along the Eleto side of the table.

"(All who are wronged deserve justice, this is known,)" the Counselor responds. "(We all crave compensation for losses too great to count. We may list the many *many* crimes wrought against one another, and, in tally, we see we *all* have cause to pray for justice. If we grant what is deserved, where will the prosecutions end?)"

"(It matters not!)" Fell-Marr-Ghen counters. "(Who could ask us to leave our fallen as they lie? Our comrades, our Other Selves, our *children*? We cannot tolerate a future where such acts go unanswered. Before there can be discussion of any future, we must cleanse the present through sacred trials.)"

The Counselor considers the question, then asks, "(An intriguing proposal. Shall we weigh the heaps of dead to find our reckoning? To do so, we would put our entire civilizations on trial. And for the perpetrators who have long since escaped into death's embrace, what justice can be pulled from their bones?)"

"(By definition, the dead are beyond prosecution,)" Fell-Marr-Ghen posits. "(They have no way to atone and cannot be held to account.)"

"(Neither can they shape our future. Only the living can,)" Counselor says. "(It is in the *living* we must seek restitution. Yet who can decide where guilt lies? None of us are clean. Either by act or association we ALL have blood on our hands.)"

Fell-Marr-Ghen's eyes gleam. "(We choose the most egregious offenders, and make examples of *them*.)"

"(And if trial deems ones at this table most egregious, who among you will accept the verdict and sentence?)"

"(For the People, this one would pay *any* price,)" Fell-Marr-Ghen answers. "(There is no sting of conscience in this one's chest, for his actions have always been to advance his cherished People. Put this one before the bench. If by life or by death, he can serve the People best, then *he will*.)"

("We do not doubt his sincerity. And such love is to be celebrated,") the Counselor answers. "(The ones across from you have the same love for their kin. They too would pay the ultimate price if it served their people best. Yet for those who love them, and hold them righteous, their deaths at Eleto hands generate new cause for hatred. No matter what guise it takes, or how it might be justified, killing only *perpetuates* a cycle we yearn to end. What is more, death is too light a sentence, for there is nothing learned, nothing gained. How does one kill their way to atonement? The *real* work of atonement is accomplished through labor and action.)"

"(If we spare the knife,)" Fell-Marr-Ghen asks, "(how do we ease the groaning shades to rest? There *must* be a solemn price paid. Otherwise, we give no assurance to the living these atrocities will not happen again.)"

The Counselor nods shrewdly. "(My colleague raises valid points. Our great nations have paid dearly, already. We have done so much harm that it is difficult to see beyond it. But there is a way. We ALL must accept blame. We ALL must own these horrors truthfully, honestly. We must comprehend this machine of death was engineered by our fear and mistrust, and we *willingly*, *knowingly* fed this ravenous beast our beloved. Let our first act of atonement be to dismantle this machine and scatter its parts, forever. If we can do that, then we move to our second act, which will be much harder... Let us humble ourselves, accept responsibility for the past, and beg one another for forgiveness.)"

The delegate sitting to the left of Dekkto tilts his head."(Is Kon-Zill-Urr suggesting...an *amnesty*?)"

"(Yes, honorable El-Gaard. A full accounting of atrocities must be made. We require diligence in this account, so that *all* crimes are revealed. We must look at them nakedly and face our shame together. We will study how two learned cultures, blessed with the faculty of forethought, could have spent so many years tearing at each other in fruitless anger. Only by understanding our failures *completely* can we assure the living we are not doomed to repeat them.)"

"(Impossible,)" the delegate beside Fell-Marr-Ghen says with a dismissive wave of his hand. "(*Unpunished guilt* is no foundation for a lasting peace. There must be a reckoning in blood so the People know the rule of law still thrives.)"

Shondre leans forward in her seat. "(Then tell us, Prell-Shah-Stoh, whom shall we punish for the Decree of Lak-Vass-Etto? Billions of human lives ended... Shall the children of our ancient leaders bleed for the sins of their elders?)"

"(Madame Shondre, we need not exhume the graves of our forebears when we have fresh crimes at hand and living criminals in our midst! Moreover, in light of their fiendish attack, this one is not convinced the Decree was in error.)"

"(Gracious Fell-Marr-Ghen,)" the Counselor cushions, "(this one must apologize. For in acting as translator, he has certainly failed to make his point clear. While we are advocating for amnesty and reconciliation, *we do not come to this table empty-handed.* Should our great nations choose reconciliation, General Thompson swears his first efforts will be to rebuild what the Cadre has damaged. Physical structures, ships in space, even the trust abused by his errant predecessor, he will work tirelessly to restore them, however long it takes.)"

Prell-Shah-Stoh's mouth bunches as if to spit. "(He *swears*, does he? And what water is carried by his *oath*, hmm? Shall we take him at his word, Kon-Zill-Urr? This creature who sat at our table and sued for peace while his slayers maneuvered to *stab our backs!*)"

"(Tom-Sun and Mai-Ell-Uh—who also sat at this table—*broke* that attack, shrewd Prell-Shah-Stoh,)" Shonde reminds. "(They defied their masters and refused to let atrocity continue. Mai-Ell-Uh gave her life to ensure the People did not perish with this planet. Tom-Sun nearly joined her, his wounds were so deep. *They* are the reasons we are here, breathing this air today. They risked all, *for us,* and paid an ultimate price. In the arches of her chest, this one *knows* the courage of their convictions. Tom-Sun and Mai-Ell-Uh have proved their souls are pure. And Tom-Sun wishes to *continue* proving it for as long as he draws breath.)"

Dekkto takes a deep breath and frowns, asking, "(Konn-Zill-Urr, why would the Will of the Kad-Ra do this? Why would he favor the People before his own?)"

"(Mighty Dekkto,)" the Counselor replies, "(General Tom-Sun has learned one life is no greater than the other. He also believes the future of Humankind depends on a secure future with Eleto. For his nation to prosper, he must *guarantee* the safety and security of the People with equal fervor. Timing on this is crucial. Our cultures must not disentangle, lest we tempt ourselves to further animosity in separation. In time, when General Thompson's good works have helped heal the rift between us, we can concentrate once more on being the people we *want* to be...the people we were always *meant* to be.)"

Dekkto's mouth draws thin. He tents his hands and looks at them in contemplation.

Long seconds pass uninterrupted, and Prell-Shah-Stoh grumbles, "(Excellency, would we truly suffer this violent species to live? How could we permit such a threat in our—)"

The Great Eleto silences Prell-Shah-Stoh by showing the palm of his hand. "(Blood cannot cleanse blood. It merely deepens the stain.)

"(What this one hears is willingness to serve the People. Most intriguing is recognition that *mutual* security is the only path to ending generational hatred. On this point, in particular, *we agree*.)" Dekkto takes an extended breath and lets it out slowly. "(We will not speak of trust yet, for, as Konn-Zill-Urr knows, it is too much abused. We may speak of non-aggression and the long process by which we witness intentions made real. We will measure these first bridges Kad-Ra would build between our cultures. If straight and true, then reciprocity shall fortify them. And if minds remain aligned in genuine desire for peace, we will continue to meet at this table. However, before the day wanes and shadows grow long, we must know if this destination can be reached. There is no point to further discussion if Kad-Ra and Koll-Oh-Nisst would demand the impossible. Therefore, we will hear what Kon-Zill-Urr expects of the People.)"

The Counselor spreads his arms. "(Noble Dekkto, we expect nothing. Yet we would ask for a place on this planet to deploy our colony. Somewhere temperate, beyond the edge of Eleto settlement where we can be near without crowding. An island, perhaps, if that gives the People comfort. With sufficient growing season, the machinery we possess is more than adequate to sustain us.)"

"(Then why did Koll-Oh-Nissts not deploy it elsewhere, away from here?)"

"(Noble Dekkto, we never found a place safe from discovery. Anywhere we went, we believed the People would find us to complete the Decree of Lak-Vass-Etto. Moreover, our machines must be fed ores, organics, water, and air to produce what we need. We never found a place that had such materials in the amounts required...at least not a place unsettled by the People. Lastly, Great Eleto, we ask for space here, because this is the land of our birth. And we wish to come home.)"

Prell-Shah-Stoh grunts. "(A factory for weapons, no doubt! Deployed here? Never!)"

"(Worthy Prell-Shah-Stoh,)" Counselor advises, "(the Colonists have neither talent nor interest for war. We would invite your scientists and engineers to inspect the apparatus to satisfy we are no threat. Add to this, our needs are so small it is unlikely our communities would touch, even after fifty generations. But, if we are wise, we will *want* to raise our young together.)"

The Great Eleto knits his brow. "(Explain.)"

"(Noble Dekkto, for those of us who carry the scars of conflict, those of us whose memory is filled with recent terrors, it may be too much to ask that we live side by side in blended communities. But our *young*, whom we are eager to meet, are innocent of these terrors. They need never witness how brutally their parents fought. Rather, Human and Eleto deserve to be raised alongside one another so they can see the beauty of both and never seem strange to one another. They can mature with untroubled minds, richer with the combined wisdom of *two* cultures.)

"(If we allow them to be raised in segregation, external differences will inevitably reinforce themselves. Embers of suspicion and doubt will smolder. Those embers could ignite once more into outright conflict. Integration, alone, can prevent this.)"

The Counselor looks across the table at his opponents. From their downturned faces, he guesses many of them are still mourning lost children of their own.

"(This one speaks too eagerly of children, perhaps. Before we can serve children, we must serve *each other* to ensure there is bedrock upon which to build. For those of us who have lived through these hard times, perhaps respectful distance is what many will require. That is fully the right of any to *not* associate if they so wish. But if we desire a lasting peace, we will make effort to remain in contact. We can watch *over* one another without *watching* each other. We should pass freely through the gates of any community as citizens of the same world. Most important, we *must* combine our futures. And when we speak of our future, we are, of course, speaking of our children.)

"(For them, we must not be enemies. From their earliest days, their eyes should be unclouded, so they can see for themselves how elegant Eleto and Human can be. Forgive this one for indulging an emotional appeal, but he is much pleased at the thought of our young ones exploring this magnificent world together, as beautiful equals. As they play together, work together, celebrate together…the idea of racial hatred will become pointless, puerile... archaic.)

"(If we do this right... Our children will have better lives than any of us have ever known. If we do this *right*, our children will never feed their talents to machines of death, as we have. But to *do* this right... Our days will be full. We will make the first efforts, and we commit this offer in good faith: Before our shelters are built, we will rebuild yours, because we are determined to prove ourselves good neighbors. Let us show you that we *are*

505

more than warriors. We are *builders*. We are *engineers*, and *scientists*, and *artists...mathematicians* and *explorers*. Most of all, we are loving parents, just like you.)

"(The best gift we can give our children is the world they deserve. Noble Dekkto, let us commit to this hard work and make sure they have it.)"

Eleto delegates look at each other, uncertain, wary. They turn to the Great Eleto with questioning faces.

"(The destination is far, indeed,)" Dekkto intones, "(too far for some to reach in this lifetime. That is not desirable.)"

Sighs of relief from Fell-Mar-Ghen and Prell-Shah-Stoh. Shondre and the Counselor both open their mouths in protest. Before any can utter another word, Dekkto adds,

"(So we will build a road that *all* can travel, and for those who cannot make the journey themselves, we will carry them at a pace they can accept.)"

Shondre and the Counselor bow graciously. Fell-Mar-Ghen, El-Gaard, and Prell-Shah-Stoh also bow, disappointed yet subservient. Dekkto regards all at the table gravely, places both hands on the polished table, and leans forward on his elbows.

"(Jenn-Hu-Rahl Tom-Sun, we have much to do. Let us begin.)"

INNOCENCE IN DISCOVERY

Shondre slouches through the doorway of her apartment and slumps against the threshold. Bleary-eyed, exhausted, she rubs her face and forces herself across the last few meters to her favorite chair. Her thinned frame flops into molded cushions and she melts as they undulate, gently working stiffness from legs, hips, back, neck, and shoulders.

"(It is a relief to have Madame Shondre home once more,)" a voice says from a hidden intercom. "(May we provide her refreshment? Perhaps a hot bath?)"

"(A kind offer, faithful friend. This one is so tired, if she bathed she might drown.)"

"(Then Madame's bed is made and warmed. We have taken liberty of setting analgesics on her night stand. Should she wish *anything* else, we will provide on the instant.)"

Shondre smiles fondly. "(This one is blessed to have such loving care for old bones.)" She sits up a bit straighter. "(How grows the family?)"

"(They thrive, Madame. And...the work you do for them...we could not love you more for it, even if you were one of our own.)"

Shondre's breath catches in her throat. "(That... *That* is why she does it.)"

"(May the Spirit bless you and keep you, Madame.)"

"(Elders protect you and yours.)"

With a contented sigh, Shondre taps a device on the side table and a holowindow projects on the wall in front of her.

"(Let us see what we missed in the last several weeks.)"

An assortment of live video windows fills the view with excited newscasters rushing to recap stories, commenting, analyzing, interpreting, questioning. She drags a talon across the device, scrolling through hundreds of options, and halts on a video preview of a dark haired human in brilliantly colored robe. With a tap, she selects the feed.

"(To the Will of the People, Noble Dekkto Mayah Tayaloh,)" the Counselor begins, "(to Prell-Shah-Stoh, High Commander of the People's Defense, to El-Gaard Brek-Takar, Prime Defender of the eightieth region, to Fell-Marr-Ghen, Opposition leader of the Eighty Regions, and to Madame Shondre, our tireless advocate and Voice-elect of the Eightieth Region, we are honored and grateful to be heard once more. Great are those who grant mercy in difficult times. For the People's gifts of patience and restraint, we pledge our promises into actions.)"

"(Sixty-five times, the Sun has dawned since we began our talks. At last, we conclude our discussions the way we always intended. Let civility and candor be the standard for every interaction that follows. And through total transparency we will never have cause to mistrust again. Should the People ever wish to speak with us, we are available, day or night.)"

The pre-recorded feed shifts to live broadcast of a male Eleto in tasteful gray garb, recapping key points from the peace summit, what implications arise, and next steps in the process. The facts of the newscaster's report are accurate and unassailable, yet in its omissions Shondre notes a particular slant pushing toward a perspective she does not share. She snorts in annoyance, scrolls through more options, and taps her device.

A colossal ship—possibly white beneath all the dents and grime—fills her screen. The view dials in to a mural on its side, depicting a nude human female with long red hair on the back of a horned white beast, while the narrator spins a tale of deathless occupants inside who have been travelling for lifetimes...

She taps.

Blacked-out warships hang motionless, silhouetted against a bright lunar disk. Angular hulls bristle with D-E rails and are pocked with torpedo launch tubes. Eleto battleships, cruisers, carriers, and frigates surround them at a safe distance, weapons locked.

"(Though unrecognizable to us now, these deathly-black vessels were once the People's own ships, captured long ago,)" the narrator relates. "(The People's Defense maintains vigilant guard over these re-captured vessels, ensuring they no longer carry out the malevolent intent of their captors. Yet it is most intriguing how extensively these vessels have been stripped and

508

remade into gunships of cunning efficiency. With our own tools, Da-oma Kachi-in waged war on the People from shadow, instilling terror beyond our wildest nightmares. That any of us might have been savagely attacked at any time, from out of nowhere, disappearing forever...was *devastating* to trade and travel between the Eighty Regions. Costs of military escort have long carved a hole in fiscal budgets and delayed our more lofty ambitions. Yet the real costs in lost productivity, exploration of natural resources, risk of new ventures, are incalculable. Conservative estimates suggest full economic recovery will be a generation away or longer.)

"(How strange, then, to learn how few Da-oma Kachi-in number. To an individual transport, the odds of an attack were infinitesimally low, and yet the *fear* of attack was so great, it cast a pall across our entire space-faring enterprise. We all breathe easier now that this threat is neutralized by our heroic soldiers and the mighty People's Fleet—)"

Tap.

Shondre sees herself on a talk show, wearing the same outfit, her eyes far brighter than they are now. The synthetic humanoid, Konn-Zill-Urr, shares one side of a round table with her. An Eleto interviewer sits across from them, leaning on elbows with keen interest.

Shondre smiles at that ordinary face the android wears, loving the person behind it, synthetic or not.

His moral compass always points true, she admits. *In worst of times, this one fell prey to anger and frustration. Yet you never tire, Konn-Zill-Urr, never lose sight of the ultimate goal. Your people are fortunate to have you.*

We are fortunate, as well.

On screen, the interviewer turns to the audience and invites questions. Konn-Zill-Urr slides to the edge of his seat and lays hands on his knees.

Some questions are softballs of general curiosity, others are hard hitting, seeking, demanding, accusing. He handles them all with grace. And as she watches herself participate in discussions of difficult topics, she is relieved to see herself less flustered than she remembers.

Tap.

An interior view of grungy, off-white hallways, showing frequent signs of repair. Some wall panels bear a diffuse haze of fluorescent paint, leaving only a faint halo of words or images scoured away... Symmetrical humans in colored coveralls and their larger asymmetrical Kad-Ra cousins are introduced via on-board camera broadcasts. Communication is a challenge for all, yet captions at the bottom of the screen convey basic meanings. Shondre scrunches her brow, unsure what she is watching, until it gradually becomes clear this is a day-in-the-life-of sort of show from inside the Koll-Oh-Nisst ship, *Hyoo-Roh-Pah*.

A petite woman with long straight hair and spectacles guides the camera team through a pristine medical facility. The view pans across medical equipment that conveys a curious blend of technological refinement and extreme durability: delicate, twinkling lights in face plates of rugged rack-mounted chassis, high-precision optics mounted to solid metal frames, interconnected with heavy gauge cables, Lab kits with ultra-high resolution screens and reinforced cases that look like they could shrug off bullets. Every horizontal surface gleams in polished stainless steel.

Shondre shivers in recollection of her time on those cold surfaces, yet the woman on camera proved herself a warm caregiver—far more so than the gruff, mountain-like Mun-Ro. She is glad the harsh colonel is not present to remind her of their time together.

Otherwise, the tour is mundane, almost boring, as the camera crew records hallways and berths she has personally visited dozens of times. Despite the banality of Koll-Oh-Nisst life, view count listed at bottom of the screen soars, and the scrolling feed of comments echo a common refrain: These odd-looking aliens seem like average, every day people...not that different...certainly not what they feared...

Tap.

The screen shows a distant view down a sandy beach toward a gray-white landing pad. An archway at its seaward side serves a tunnel leading down into the surf and beneath the waves. The camera view zooms in to Kad-Ra Opp-Purr-Ray-Torrs in armor moving about the pad, and Shondre flinches. So stoic, so taciturn...motives inscrutable behind cold eyes...the mere sight of them inspires instant fear, mistrust, revulsion. Video crews keep their distance, vigilant of every movement, and narrate in hushed, wary tone as if spying on malevolent super-crocodiles that could attack on sight.

When the camera pans, Shondre sees heaps of building materials and large-wheeled trucks delivering more. Kad-Ra soldiers coordinate seamlessly, guiding materials to proper stacks, organizing staging areas, hauling out beams, off-loading huge wire spools.

The teamwork among them, the strength, efficiency, and incredible endurance—not to mention the black carapace they wear—bring to mind hives of ground dwelling insects.

Vast caverns tunneled underground... How they toil endlessly, incapable of despair, every one knowing its place and purpose in the collective... Could there be happiness in such a life?

The camera dials in on a huge, barrel-chested individual toting a metal brace that four or five stout Eleto might carry. Then the camera tilts up to armored men and women, working without fear on high spans, swinging and leaping casually between them... Using two-handed tools single-handed, never fumbling, never missing the seam, bolt, or rivet...

Tap.

An underwater scene of hazy blue water, looking down at a forest of seaweed that undulates with passing waves overhead... Diving down between those gently swaying stalks... The view tilts up and reveals a geodesic dome in the distance. The camera zooms in on its base, where Opp-Purr-Ray-Torrs in dark armor gather around a ragged hole in the structure. One Kad-Ra soldier in armor looks the same as another, and Shondre wonders if she has met the persons shown. Then her eyes widen when one is captioned, *Jenn-Hu-Rahl Tom-Sun*. His voice channels through her living room speakers as he directs the project, assisting his team heft, place, and secure parts a crane barge should be lifting.

Shondre drags a talon, fast-forwarding through hours of video, watching black specks swarm around the hole, welding, mending, sealing. Once the hole is closed, air pumps into the restored dome, driving the ocean out, and a high-water line falls from the apex to its base.

The view switches to an angle inside the dome. Again she fast-forwards through days of video. Waterlogged, slouching structures are imploded, rubble hauled off... Sodden, corroded materials are peeled from intact structures, recycled, and reinstalled...

New building frames are erected, floored, framed, and skinned by a flurry of dark specks. New data nodes are installed, new power service lines are run, inlet and outlet pipes are placed, tested, and certified... Lights switch on, and restored buildings are ready for occupancy...

The screen returns to the beach of bright, sunlit sand and a spacious gray-white pad. Shondre lets the video roll at normal speed and sees hunched, lop-sided men and women reverse engineering what resembles ventilation machinery. Physical impediments slow their movements and limit their carrying ability, yet they demonstrate the same skill and precision as their more able-bodied brethren. Mun-Ro directs the operation from a standup drafting desk, upon which he has arrayed a labset and schematics. In his complete absorption there is visible joy of being useful, of being needed again...

Tap.

A close-up of Tom-Sun, announcing the restored community is ready for occupancy. He turns it over to local Eleto officials for inspection...

Tap.

Another view from inside the dome... Buildings stand as they once did, all seems to be as it was, and Shondre wonders if this is a 'before/after' kind of story. Then as the camera team tours newly reconstructed interiors they find rooms finished in bare metal plating. Not a lick of paint, not a single decoration or piece of trim, anywhere...

Eleto foremen fret and do their best to explain that this is not how it was supposed to be... Beaming with pride, Mun-Ro replies in broken Eleto, "(Yes. Is *better*.)"

Tap.

Another close-up of Tom-Sun, wearing the Mantle of the First. With a fair grasp of the People's speech, he states, "(Now, with build finished on underwater community, this one keeps Kad-Ra busy in wild areas around the globe. Where the People live in warm, sunny places, Kad-Ra keeps to cool places. Places his people once named, Tierra del Fuego, British Columbia, Alaska and the Aleutian Islands, Scandinavia, Iceland, and Kamchatka...)"

Always, Eleto escorts monitor activities from a safe distance, dutifully documenting how the hardened soldiers leap from hovering transports on narrow cords, detach the instant they hit the ground and deploy at full sprint across the landscape. Every action is done at top speed, as if time were the greatest enemy of all, but every once in a while the camera catches an Operator pausing to look, just *look*. A mountain vista, a waterfall refracting morning sunlight, a valley carved by glaciers, a polar bear plodding across frozen tundra, rays of sun bursting through clouds after a drenching rain... In each moment of candid amazement is another possibility that these terrifying killers could someday become more than soulless automatons of death.

Leaving weapons behind, these once-killers brave harshest landscapes and return with racks stuffed full of collected samples. In a way, watching these fearless explorers reminds Shondre of innocence in discovery... Every new thing is studied, compared, catalogued...

Before long, Operators start lifting their faceplates in the field, letting unfiltered air pass through their sinuses, some giddy from richness of sensation... Always, discipline kicks in and abbreviates the indulgence, yet ever so gradually even hardened Kad-Ra veterans give in to their senses. They smell things, taste things occasionally, remove gauntlets and run bare hands over stone or bark.

In ways too numerous to count, Nature introduces herself to these curious strangers, reminding them that *this* is where they are from, *this* is where they belong. One narrator describes it like watching a hostage, upon liberation, learning to let down her guard. Another describes it more artfully as watching children, abducted at birth and raised as orphans, being welcomed home by a loving mother who desperately missed them and longed for their return.

Shondre thinks about that a long time.

Tap.

A white marble facade of an institutional building with columns propping up a colossal overhang above... Broad stairways descend on three sides like a stepped pyramid, all sides leading away from a shaded entrance between the central columns. Atop the stairs stand a Kad-Ra phalanx on the left and a matching phalanx of Eleto soldiers on the right. From dark recesses between them strides Tom-Sun, wearing his onyx mantle, leading the Kad-Ra Leadership Council. At Tom-Sun's side is Gregor, not as large or nearly as scarred, yet similarly proportioned and likewise draped in onyx cloak. Behind him follow the Counselor, Jonah Herzfeld, Javier Ortega, Sahara Taggart. Opposite Tom-Sun strides Dekkto-Mayah-Tayaloh, wearing his mantle of supreme authority. Behind the Great Eleto files Fell-Marr-Ghen, Prell-Shah-Stoh, and El-Gaard Brek-Takaar.

Shondre leans toward her screen, brow knitting at how she might have missed an assembly of so many important players. The camera view pulls back, runs down the steps, and pans across a vast crowd of cheering Eleto, many holding handmade signs and banners. When the camera swings back upon the delegation atop the stairs, Dekkto steps to the front where hundreds of tripod-mounted microphones are clustered, and he speaks into them.

"(This one is proud beyond words to announce conclusion of negotiations. Please welcome the Will of the Kad-Ra, Jenn-Hu-Rahl Tom-Sun, and the Will of the Koll-Oh-Nissts, Kapp-Tan Peh-Troh-Vah. Hear their thoughts, as Konn-Zill-Urr will faithfully translate, and come to know them better, as we have.)"

Tom-Sun nods in deference to Dekkto, looks briefly at Gregor who urges him to go ahead, then approaches the rows of microphones with Konn-Zill-Urr at his shoulder.

Shondre huffs in irritation, perplexed how it could be possible she missed this event, until the words *Live Broadcast* crawl across the bottom of the screen.

Shondre sits up in a panic. Without a word, she jumps out of her seat and races out of her apartment.

No More, Forever

Standing atop a tall stairway, Thompson blinks at the brilliant setting sun. Long sessions in a windowless room have put dark circles under his eyes. Lines of his face have deepened, and there is little color left in his graying hair and beard. Nevertheless, his spine is straight, shoulders square. Taking a deep breath through his nose, he surveys a multitude gathered below that extends into streets, green spaces, and intersections beyond.

My neighbors...no longer my enemies.

Eleto guards in thick riot gear maintain security barriers at the base of the stairway, watching behind darkened visors and radioing status to patrol cars hovering in the distance. No one in the crowd pays the guards or hover patrols any mind, however, as eyes are riveted to the tall gray-haired human atop the steps and the delegations fanned out behind him.

Thompson leans toward the array of microphones, and the crowd quiets. In the lull, a birdsong carries from the boughs of a nearby tree. He looks toward it, noting in fractal randomness of branches how exposure is maximized for thousands of thin green solar collectors. A tiny creature sings from its wind-swayed branches, knowing nothing of the saga that has played out. An infinitesimal component of a magnificent living system. Innocent, delicate, and unique. Alive. *Important.*

Reeling himself back from distraction, he takes another breath of richly scented air. Voice raspy from overuse, the general leans forward and speaks into the microphones, Counselor translating.

"At last we stand here before you, stripped of all pre-conception. We see each other as we *are*, for the first time ever. And we have found we are not so different.

"It is difficult to know what to feel today. Pains inflicted are still fresh, and aching wounds will remind us for ages to come. Yet we can be glad reason has finally prevailed. Because of that, what this one feels most today is *relief*.

"*Relief* that we can stand together in the same place, under the same sky, and be safe in each other's presence... *Relief* that we no longer waste our efforts in protracted war... *Relief* that this one may holster his weapons and pour all of his energy into a better, shared future."

The Counselor's amplified translation booms through public address speakers, and the crowd cheers with arms raised, hands clapping.

Thompson looks down at the microphones, not yet able to indulge the mood. And once the crowd settles he looks out across a sea of faces.

"Never before have we had so much to look forward to. We embrace this new future, and the Cadre's new goal, *our singular mission*, is to establish trust. If we want this hard won truce to last, we must ensure you, the People, feel safe and secure around us. We have seen how easily one man upset this delicate process, and we all feel the burning betrayal of it." He points at his chest. "It falls upon *this one*, General Thompson, to prove the Cadre is no longer an enemy to be feared. And this vital endeavor is the first of many in which we demonstrate new purpose: to build a future where *all* children thrive, together."

The crowd cheers with thunderous stomps that shake the ground. Riot guards perk up in alert and brace their barricades, helmeted heads swiveling for threats or signs of a surge. While the crowd settles, Thompson fishes in his pocket and retrieves a scuffed gold ring. He looks at it, turns it over, then closes his hand around it.

"There was a time this one had no concept of love. Duty, devotion, sacrifice, yes...but not love. Drugs suppressed natural feeling to make this one a more effective soldier. By leaving those drugs behind, crucial, natural instincts have returned... This one understands what it means to join with another, to combine so completely there is no longer any boundary... how uplifting and empowering...and, in loss, how devastating. Maiella... my Other Self...gave her life so that we could survive. This one knows why she did what she did. Her sacrifice allows us to stand here today, under this magnificent dome, called 'Sky'... Yet in every moment, this one feels her absence. He longs to see her again to such distraction he could lose hours to staring at walls, if there was not so much work to do...

"This one's loss is no greater than any other's. This one asks only that we remember them fondly and do not let our grief tempt us to despair or revenge. We must not lose sight of those who are *right here in front of us*. For them, and the ones who come after, we are obligated to do our best. Our solemn duty is to build the world they deserve. Doing less is theft of their rightful inheritance.

"We have this chance *right now* to abandon hatred. Let us serve one another as neighbors, as partners...and, if we remain on this path, then someday...as friends.

"We have earned this reprieve with blood and sweat. We *deserve* it, because we have paid so dearly for it. And because, as a very wise person once told me, 'Life is its own reason for being.' Until his last day, this one will keep that message and he will defend the People as fervently as he defends his own.

"This one has little art with words. So, in summation, he borrows from an ancient leader of men, Chief Joseph of the Nez Perce: '*From where the sun now stands, I will fight no more forever.*'

"That is all this one has to say."

Thompson dips his head and steps back from the microphones as the Counselor completes his translation.

Individual hoots spring out and spread in chain reaction. Whistles, yells, and shouts merge with clapping hands in jubilation, rippling throughout the crowd. Horns resound through the loudspeakers, blasting triumphant conclusion to centuries of conflict.

Operators stare in anxious awe at the agitated masses around them, but Gregor and Herzfeld grin at one another, knowing what comes next.

The Great Eleto steps toward the microphones and the masses hush so he can be heard. His voice carries across the crowds and intersections, bold and clear.

The Counselor is about to translate for the others when Thompson does it for him.

"He said, 'Let us celebrate with our new neighbors and welcome them home, as equals.'"

There is a tap at his shoulder again, and Thompson turns about to see Shondre standing breathless behind him.

"Shondre!" Thompson sweeps her into an embrace, lifting her off her feet, and she hugs him back with all her might.

"Nott miss thisss," she says into his ear.

Thompson sets her down, takes her hand, and leads her over to the microphones. Leaning toward them, he speaks and the Counselor translates for him.

"Sometimes, one person makes all the difference. Madame Shondre changed this one's mind with her compassion and her unbreakable spirit. She made this day possible."

Thompson squats, gets a shoulder under her backside and stands, lifting her high for all to admire. She sways unsteadily, eyes wide, as Thompson shouts her name to the crowd. The crowd chants back, "*SHON-DRE! SHON-DRE! SHON-DRE!*"

Giddy, Shondre sneaks a glance at Dekkto. The Great Eleto smiles at her, unconcerned by the breach of formality, and nods in approval.

Behind the delegations a smartly-dressed Eleto emerges from the building, pushing a trolley with a bottle almost as large as himself. Following him, uniformed servants carry a table with embroidered black cloth draped over it and a wide tray of goblets.

The trolley driver parks the bottle in front of Dekkto, who glances once at the label and gestures to proceed. When the driver wheels his cargo over to Thompson, the general sets Shondre back onto her feet, looks at the enormous green bottle, and relieves the trolley driver of his burden. Hefting the massive bottle high overhead for the crowd to see—alarming the servants to near frenzy—he marches it over to the table then sets it onto its broad base. Eleto servants wilt to see the bottle unshattered, recover their dignity, and set goblets evenly around the table.

Unaware of the stir he caused, the new general looks for his companions and finds them standing back. He waves them over, and they gather, passing uncertain expressions back and forth as the trolley-driver produces a tap from an inside coat pocket. He plugs it into a port near the bottle's base, ratcheting it into place with fastidious ritual, then takes the first pull into a taster glass. He swirls the glass, holds it up to the setting sun, and scrutinizes its color. He brings it down to his face, and, eyes closed, inhales deeply from its fluted rim. Finally, he sips, searching with his tongue for any hint of adulterant, then savors balance, character, and flavor. Satisfied, he steps back and directs a subordinate to serve equal draughts.

Servants ferry goblets to Human and Eleto leaders atop the stairs, ending with Gregor, Thompson, and Dekkto. Once all are served, public address speakers blare a celebratory hymn. After a few bars, pockets of the crowd sway in joyful chorus.

Thompson glances to his right and sees Gregor looking up at him.

"We made it, brother," Gregor says.

Thompson grits his teeth, sensing multiple meanings: journey's end for the *Europa* and her crew, an end to the fear, an end to killing, and, most of all, an end to hatred between them.

"Yeah, we did," Thompson echoes.

"They'd be real proud of us," Gregor finishes.

Thompson nods. He looks at the ring he holds then presses it into the

Russian's hand. "They would, Gregor. They really would." Thompson throws his arms around Gregor and Gregor claps Thompson heartily on the back.

The Great Eleto cradles the bulb of his goblet, allowing the stem to hang between his fingers. He sways the glass, coating the inside with dark red liquid, and inhales from it deeply, eyes closed in satisfaction. When he opens his eyes, he approaches the microphones and speaks to his people, voice reverberating through towering speakers on each side of the staircase, goblet aloft in tribute. When finished, he turns to the cluster of humans, sighting Thompson directly. His stone-like face has lost none of its intensity, yet there is a roundness to his angular features.

"*To hyoo,* Tom-Sun."

"And to you, Dekkto Mayah Tayaloh." Thompson raises his chalice in an equal gesture.

Dekkto bellows, "TOM-SUN," and the crowd roars back, "*TOM-SUN!*"

The ancient Eleto puts goblet to his lips. Thompson mimics the motions then his eyes flick open. A delicate aroma, far more complex than at first whiff, is by itself intoxicating. He sips from the bulb-shaped crystal, letting its contents wash over his tongue. In a rush of amazement, he turns to Gregor. The Russian's flared cheeks empty with a great gulp, and he smacks his chops.

"What?"

Thompson gives in, laughing from his gut. Without warning, he turns to the Great Eleto, the assembled leaders, servants, and the crowd around him.

"*TO US ALL!*" Thompson takes a deep draught, already feeling lightness in his head and heart.

Shondre steps up beside him, chalice hoisted. "*Too uss ahl!*"

The speakers blare again with a brassy, percussive piece, amplifying the crowd's cheers.

Thompson tilts his head back for a deeper draught and spies a glowing orange disk in the sky. He lowers his chalice, but keeps his view skyward. With his prosthetic hand, he points at it, yelling above the din.

"That's the colony, right, Gregor?"

"Roger, that," Gregor answers.

"Where's it heading?"

"Herzfeld sold me on Tasmania. Unspoiled. Pretty to look at, and all. Eleto liked the idea, too, being an island with natural boundaries. It's a cooler climate than they care for, so none of 'em settled there. They don't have to move anyone." Servants refill Gregor's goblet, and he hefts it for another gulp. "Glad I don't have to drive tonight."

Thompson stares at the distant disk re-entering Earth's atmosphere, marveling how all of that machinery, so carefully designed, built, and packaged for flight left this world more than a thousand years earlier—how the *Europa* crossed light years to colonize another world but is colonizing Earth, instead.

He recalls how he, Argo, and Maiella crawled through almost every part of it to restore faltering, decrepit systems. With that enormous orange disk comes phenomenal work and responsibility. Farms. Ore harvesting and processing in full gravity. Management of environmental factors, like rain and snow, oxidation, corrosion. So many new processes to learn, so much to adapt. Not to mention the cultural gaps between Cadre and Colonist, nearly as challenging as those between Eleto and Human. And longing for combat bred into the DNA of every Operator will require constant re-direction, lest his razors find something else to cut.

In sundown twilight, the first stars shine through purple sky. Thompson locks on to the brightest of them and reminds himself, *Cadre Two is still out there... Maybe Shao-Lo has a lid on it. Maybe not. Gotta keep that on radar.*

On top of everything, he thinks about Argo and Maiella, the ones who made every impossible order happen, the ones who found a way through ingenuity and sheer toughness.

Wish you were both here to see this.

He lowers his gaze to the crowd of Eleto celebrating joyously, openly. The Great Eleto confers with his attendants yet he catches Thompson's glance, smiles, and hoists his goblet in friendly show. Thompson responds in kind then looks behind himself at his own people. The Counselor stands at Shondre's side, arm around her as she sobs with joy. Gregor's arm drapes over Herzfeld's shoulder as he swirls a refilled goblet and taunts the stiff Operators to finish their drinks. Beckert accepts the Russian's challenge, downs his glass, and orders the rest to do likewise. Maddock and Keiko drain their chalices, doing their best to avoid any appearance of enjoyment. Ralla squints at Beckert and the borrowed eagles on his collar, clucks her tongue once, then complies.

Thompson looks out to the dimming horizon, imagining the future ahead and still wishing Argo and Maiella could have been part of it.

It's gonna be tough without you two, the general thinks to himself.

Then Thompson turns and looks at the people standing beside him. Tinges of rosy color show through thickly scarred faces, and involuntary smiles have chiseled through more typical Cadre austerity. Shondre and the Counselor prop each other up, as happy and exhausted as new parents at delivery. And Munro looms over them all, hoisting a goblet in each mitt and draining them in succession while Gregor and Jonah cheer him on.

That same involuntary smile breaks through Thompson's somber features.

We're gonna make it.

EPILOGUE

Uninterested in affairs of state, Munro dutifully plans, engineers, fixes, heals, innovates, and administrates as needed. Cantankerous colony machinery, having been stored on the *Europa* for centuries and recently deployed, absorbs as much time as he is willing to give it. The old MedTech welcomes the challenge, happiest in being useful and needed.

His real passion project, however, is recreating his MedLab from Cadre One. Once the embryos from *Europa*'s cold storage are successfully incubated and the first herds decanted, he initiates a new project with the close assistance of Sahara Taggart. All other Colonists and MedTechs are kept at bay. And any attempt to spy is met with a stern redirection by a Cadre Operator both able and willing to remove those who do not voluntarily vacate.

Beckert quietly returns his borrowed rank of Colonel to Ralla and settles into his new role regulating colony mainframes. Gifted with more natural looking prosthetic arm, legs, and eyes, the former Geek is also a tireless farmer, taking shifts alongside Colonist agricultural details, as he says, "...to get out in the sun and fresh air and see things grow."

Of all Cadre Operators he adapts easiest to life without combat, delighting in the variety this new land offers, breathing deeply, taking time to appreciate Nature the way he wished he could have during the Forestall Rotation.

Having earned the People's respect and adoration all over again, Aeolia Shondrekar Bakkar enjoys long tenure as *Voice of the Eightieth Region*. And because she was instrumental in orchestrating the new peace, redeeming her

People from the bloody Decree of Lak-Vass-Etto, she is elevated to *Guiding Voice of the Eighty Regions*, a position of authority and influence second only to *Will of the People*.

There is wide speculation she should succeed as Great Eleto when Dekkto decides to relinquish his mantle. Always modest, Shondre answers, "(We are blessed to already have a Will who is both wise and strong. This one has no ambition other than to serve where she is needed, and her days are filled with vital work for the People and for their new neighbors.)"

When Shondre's supporters unveil a plan to carve her likeness in a stone cliff face, she politely, yet resolutely, insists no monuments be erected, stating, "(Seeing our two nations thrive, free from threat, is the greatest monument of all. She needs and wants nothing more.)" This only galvanizes the efforts of those who wish to immortalize her, and her kind face appears on buildings in countless cities and villages renamed for her across the Eighty Regions.

Prell-Shah-Stoh, derided for his adamant opposition to peace, retires early from the People's Defense, with El-Gaard Brek-Takkar replacing him as High Commander. Despite voluntarily stepping down from his post, he publically maintains that, "(Anyone charged with defense of the People must have the most skeptical mind and must prepare for *any* contingency with a hostile adversary. This one's actions, *in those circumstances*, were correct and proper in every way.)"

He quickly finds his diminished life stultifying, and he yearns to retake reins of power. Friends suggest he is already well known among the People, and many in the opposition still believe his views were the correct ones. Political office is surely within his grasp, they counsel, should he reach for it.

When Shondre learns of his intention she crushes the notion immediately, informing him there is no place in leadership for one so lacking in grace and compassion—and never will be—as long as she draws breath. Instead, Shondre recommends he enter service in the Eleto War College, imparting practical knowledge and experience to fresh cadets who will someday defend the People from threats internal and external. With few other options, and none that would offer as much respect for his talents, he follows the path opened for him.

To his surprise, young minds eagerly soak up his battle-tested tactics, valuing him as both a veteran and master strategist. Reluctantly, he admits Shondre has provided a role that suits him well, and he keeps that post until the end of his days.

PLASMA RAIN

Fell-Marr-Ghen, Regent in Shondre's absence and usurper of her title, is shunned to the sidelines of Eleto politics. His public persecution of Shondre, attempts to silence her, denounce her as mentally compromised, and his conversion of her estate to a cemetery are lasting strikes against his character. No longer viable for leadership, he puts his long years of political experience to use as an archivist and historian.

The quality of his work, balanced with newfound humility, earns him second success as the foremost expert on government and public policy. Frequently, he appears behind the scenes as legal consultant on major Eleto initiatives. Over time, collaborations with Shondre and his truly excellent attention to detail bridge the animosity between them. She finds in him a new purpose, one that has learned from prior mistakes, and when Fell-Marr-Ghen finally asks her forgiveness, she gives it without hesitation.

Dekkto-Mayah-Tayaloh, *Will of the People*, departs for the Eleto homeworld to attend his awesome duties. Despite the demands of his schedule, he returns to check on his new neighbors, taking special interest in the bourgeoning human community, personally touring their cultivated rows and pastures. The botanical varieties Colonists have cultivated—carried to the stars and brought back centuries later—now exist nowhere else, and Dekkto delights in the unique sights, smells, and flavors.

The Great Eleto is even more impressed at the communities Kad-Ra soldiers have constructed for Eleto families. These communities are high-efficiency, extremely durable, impervious to storms, and produced entirely for the cost of materials. The only ones who disapprove are companies of Eleto builders. Unable to compete, they nearly give up their trade entirely.

Pleased that his new neighbors have made good on their promise to rebuild what they have damaged, yet concerned an entire industry is being marginalized, Dekkto asks Shondre what she would do about it. Shondre smiles, thanks him for asking, and describes a new project of enormous scope for the Eightieth region. Lost habitations of man should be excavated so that human culture may be rediscovered, that buried art may be recovered, and that the soul of humanity may be restored. Areas still scarred by ancient war should be scoured of radiation so the last wounds of hateful conflict can finally be healed, and all can enjoy a world made whole. She hands Dekkto a tablet.

The Great Eleto skims the overview then frets at her cost estimates at the bottom. He glances at Shondre, shakes his head, and approves the entire proposal as written.

The Counselor remains an essential liaison between Human and Eleto. Being the only one adept in both languages is unsustainable, however, and he knows if something happened to him, a breakdown of communication could be destabilizing, dangerous. There must be others who can replace him, and the sooner the better.

The Counselor also knows there are cultural insights that can only be gained through learning another's language, and these insights are crucial to long-term integration. So he teaches classes in Eleto and Human language studies, letting his brightest students assist with the work load.

His chief duty, of course, remains as counselor. Enormous change proves a hardship for both Cadre and Colonist, especially those recently decanted from cryosleep. No matter that the threat of annihilation no longer looms, physical labor of raising crops, building shelters, battling storms and pests, uncertainty that peace will last, plus inevitable strains in relationships still vex the human condition. So the Counselor always blocks off space on his calendar for private appointments.

In time, routines settle and a new normalcy descends. Fewer counseling appointments mean more time spent with Thompson and Shondre, which is always welcome. Seeing Thompson often means seeing Ralla, as well, where the young Colonel is attached to her General in day to day duties. Regardless her ferocity and ruthless efficiency, the Counselor is glad Thompson has someone close by watching over him, keeping him busy, and not allowing him to indulge grief over Argo and Maiella.

Where Ralla was so willing to utterly annihilate the Eleto it would be easy for the android to dismiss her as irretrievably cold, brutal, heartless. Yet two moments stand out in the Counselor's recollection.

First, the difficulty Ralla had at a Lieutenant Colonel's retirement, the way her jaw clenched when Anders begged her to let him go, how bitterly she choked back attachment so she could be the pragmatist Anders needed her to be. It was the one time he ever saw her mask slip, revealing a warmer person within. He makes it a mission to coax that person out more often.

Second, his introduction to Ralla when the *Europa* was newly arrived at Cadre One. She questioned how it could be that his only appellation was, *Counselor*. His answer then was that by not carrying a familiar name, it made him impartial in disputes and gave him a professional distance that made his job easier. Ralla raised an eyebrow and said, "We don't keep secrets about ourselves, and there are no disputes. Everything is planned. You could have a name here."

Every time he sees her, that moment comes to mind, proving how much perception and sensitivity lives behind those brilliant, shrewd eyes. And still, after everything they have been through together, she surprises him by asking point blank,

"So, Counselor. Ready for a name yet?"

The Counselor thinks about it and grins. "You know? I believe I am. How do I choose?"

"Colonist names mean something, right?"

"They don't have to, but they can."

Ralla lowers her goggles and they flash momentarily. She lifts them and asks, "How about Manfred?"

The Counselor considers her suggestion, knowing its root derivation: Germanic, *Man of Peace*.

Ralla adds, "It's not flashy, or anything—"

"It's *perfect*." The android reaches his arms around Ralla and hugs her. She grimaces, brow bunched at the bizarre physical contact, then she pats his back.

"Okay, okay, as you were."

The Counselor releases her and steps back, trying the name out.

"*Manfred*. I love it."

Ralla nods. "I'll update our database and send out notification. The Cadre will address you properly from here on. Now then, if you'll excuse me."

"Of course. And thank you!"

Ralla offers a dismissive flick of her head and strides off to her next obligation, oblivious that she has given the Counselor—Manfred—the most profound and meaningful gift anyone ever could.

General Thompson, never able to rest more than four hours a night, keeps his days filled with physical activity and administrative duties. Most of his time is spent making good on his promise to rebuild Eleto settlements, though his chief concern is integrating his Cadre with the Colonists. MedTechs are off to a good start, having lived aboard the *Europa* after evacuation of Cadre One and working closely with Colonists ever since. His Operators prove a more challenging lot to keep focused, however. No matter how strenuous the work of building, it does nothing to sate their hard-wired need for *action*.

Seeking an outlet for his Operators' more aggressive tendencies, and simultaneously wishing to avoid the appearance of military exercises, the general looks to a landmass directly to the north, formerly known as "Australia." Incomprehensibly vast to those accustomed to living on an asteroid, the continent's Eastern Highlands, Western Plateaus, Central

Lowlands, Temperate and Tropical forests, arid deserts, fresh water basins, and offshore reefs offer endless mission potential. From fangs of venomous snakes to trailing tentacles of box jellies and crushing maws of Saltwater Crocodiles, the general finds plenty of danger to keep his Operator Teams fit and alert.

Despite his brimming schedule, memories of Maiella and Argo remain stones in his heart. Between every thought, he grapples with their loss. Maiella's sacrifice was the ultimate expression of her love for him and others...he knows this. To have lived so deeply with her, to have shared her passion, to be awakened and alive like never before... Stale gray existence without her is unbearable contrast. And to have taken Argo's life, his most stalwart friend, teammate, comrade in arms...his *brother*...

Anhedonia leeches taste from meals, steals pride from accomplishments. No matter how much good he does, he cannot keep any of it for himself. In quiet moments alone he sometimes catches himself staring at his unloaded rifle on the wall, daydreaming about the razor touch of its bayonet. And then he startles himself with how much work there is to do, and how it would crash down onto others...how difficult it would be for them when *he* is the rightful one to carry it, to bear the burden of his sins, the one who *deserves* to live this way until the work is finished and he can, at last, reward himself with retirement.

The Counselor checks in regularly, reminding Thompson that the grief he feels is perfectly normal. He shouldn't wish it away, because loss is natural. But he shouldn't cling to it, either. He should allow the feelings to run their course until they gradually fade. Then, he can focus on good memories of Maiella and Argo, not just their absence. The general glumly tolerates the Counselor's unwanted sympathy, nodding and acknowledging the astute diagnosis without believing any of it whatsoever.

To battle through, and be the general his Cadre needs, Thompson concentrates on what it was about Maiella that made her such an excellent teammate and Operator. For the most part, her gut instinct is what guided them home from the abyssal Black. Somehow, she always knew the right thing to do, even if she couldn't explain how or why. Maybe because her emotions were so strong, maybe it was her sensitivity to the environment and to others that pointed the way. When facing any difficult choice he asks himself what she would do, letting the answer inform his most crucial decisions. In that way, he feels, a part of her is still with him, looking over his shoulder, giving him the strength to get through one more day.

Time passes, and as the frenzy of construction yields to easier schedules of maintenance, Operators and MedTechs ask that the Cadre Memorial be rebuilt. Thompson agrees, understanding the need for a visual lineage, giving the Cadre roots in history and continuity toward the future. A monument is erected in the new settlement, emblazoned with images of those who gave their all in Honorable Service, so mankind did not perish.

At center, space is dedicated to one Operator who risked more, dared more, than all who came before—one whose final act saved two nations and a world from annihilation. Her clarity of vision saw past blind obedience and found a higher duty, redefining the standard for all Cadre Operators. The central portrait on that new wall is confident, grinning, with golden contact terminals on her head, and questions of her service are forever resolved: Maiella is—and always was—the finest Operator the Cadre has ever known.

Colonists want to go further and name the new community after her. Most suggestions, while attempting to honor her, come off ridiculous like Maiellaburg, or Ellaville. And then Gregor suggests it doesn't have to be her name, but something she *was*, something she *embodied*, something she was *known for*. With that, the community unanimously decides the new town will be named, *Spirit*.

Despite the trials of leadership, many honest mistakes, and efforts to lose subsequent elections, Gregor is voted back to office by landside. The title of Captain seems an ill fit, where his crew no longer resides aboard the *Europa*, but the matter is so far down a list of priorities that the title sticks.

Despite vast improvement in living conditions, some things never change, and Gregor has his hands full managing petty squabbles. Frequently, he has to break up arguments between his duty crew and those recently decanted. The content always surrounds a sense that those who were in cryofreeze had it lucky and were spared the suffering, so deserve the most menial tasks. Clan-like tendencies are so strong the captain has to routinely intervene in the most fundamental work assignments, mixing details to ensure the *us vs. them* mentality cannot flourish.

Often, he yearns for the efficiency of Cadre authority and seeks advice from Thompson. When he gets it, he remembers immediately why democracy is better, no matter its frustrations.

Never at risk of falling in love with the job, Gregor works his hardest at it. And when things go right, there is an abiding sense of pride in a tough job done well. His favorite example is a secret project he approved for Sahara and Munro. Nine months later, that project yields a bounty of healthy babies; and the day Munro places them into nursery, Colonists turn out *en masse*, begging to adopt.

Gregor sits back and watches Munro hand over cooing, *robust* infants to overjoyed new parents. Colonists laugh and cry; they hug each other and kiss. Optimism brightens watery, sparkling eyes...drudgery of so many years melting away, replaced by new loves... real hope for the future and gratitude just pouring out... The day is so moving, so special, Gregor declares it an annual holiday forever after.

There is one child in the nursery, not available for adoption. She is smaller than the rest though not for any reason of defect or malnutrition. This child is a pairing of Gregor and his lost love Iskra, unmodified by Cadre MedTechs, complete with all of his and Iskra's imperfections. When Munro places the babe into Gregor's arms, and Gregor looks into the eyes of a daughter he thought he would never meet, the rugged man collapses into a blubbering, adoring mess.

Javier Ortega fashions a house of worship on the outskirts of town far enough to not annoy the atheists, but close enough to call for help if some slavering wild thing crawls from the bush. Always he makes room in the pulpit for members of his congregation to tell their own stories and find God in their own way, occasionally guiding the conversation with passages from his leather bound book.

Javier realizes at last why he was never comfortable with command, preferring to let the free will of others steer their conscience. While he is a leader in this new church, he claims no authority at all, and wants none, either. In this way, his gatherings are less sermons as they are intriguing discussions, explorations, and investigations of life's great mysteries. Even those skeptical of religion find themselves drawn in by the debates, welcomed as vital counterpoints on a road to greater understanding.

Because of its accepting nature, the church avoids becoming the divisive feature Gregor feared it could be. Rather, it is a stimulating meeting of minds, stirring passionate debates at times, calm contemplation at others. Tolerance of *any* viewpoint, while provoking strong disagreement on occasion, never calcifies into opposing camps, and anyone who wishes to wring out their spiritual anxieties can do so, free from judgment. Because of this, Ortega's house becomes a preferred venue for town hall meetings, where all who enter know they will be respected and heard, equally. Ironically, this brings a sense of community between the duty crew and those newly decanted that Gregor could not enforce on his own.

Jonah Herzfeld reinvents himself as keeper of codes and ordinances, assisting Colonists with new property claims, contractual agreements, adjudication of disputes, and matters of law. His expertise in legal language helps avoid gray areas and ensures clarity in matters that could otherwise devolve into feuds. This role suits him right down to the ground as he never had much interest in any kind of manual labor, and, with no building skill at all, he arranges for himself a larger living structure, higher on the hillside, with a better view than any of his neighbors.

In addition to their regular duties as Gregor's aides, Alexei, Ulrikka, Azhar, Vinh, and Birgitte open a dojo near the community center. There, they keep Thompson's teachings and train anyone interested. Few opt for the more strenuous combat training (and none go for the reinforcements), choosing instead the more therapeutic stretches and meditative techniques.

Enclosed by sliding glass walls, the dojo allows the beauty of nature to permeate in all seasons, with classes meeting at sunrise and sunset, daily.

Her mission accomplished at long last, the *Europa* is parked in stable Earth orbit. Ancient propulsion systems that thrust the great ship out to the stars and back are shut down for the first time in centuries. Without the colony apparatus she is like the shell of an egg, cracked open and hollowed. Her reactor is taken off-line, her decks are pressurized with inert gasses to maintain seal integrity, and she enters well-earned slumber.

To the Eleto, the *Europa* represents the possibility of Human expansion, the chance (however small) that mankind could escape to the Black and become a threat once more. They push for scrapping the antediluvian vessel, yet no Colonist can agree to it. Not a soul would trade their new dwelling on Earth for one of the *Europa*'s tight cabins, and there's no desire to take another extended, sensory-deprived flight out to uncertain destinations ever again. Yet her great white bulk soaring high above is reassurance the Colonists are not trapped, and should they need her again she is there for them in the worst possible scenario. Maybe she'll be repurposed as an orbital hub someday, possibly a mass hauler in the unlikely event they can't source what they need on the ground. But under no circumstances will she be taken apart, that much is sure.

And so, her dented, pitted, flight-stained hull slings around the globe, catching dawn and setting sunlight, shining down like a wandering star over the brood she carried, sheltered, and nurtured over a thousand years.

Stung by her rejection from the Cadre, ashamed how blind she was in allowing herself to be so drastically altered, Shao-Lo finds no place for herself among the Cadre or Colonists. She retreats to Cadre Two, the one place in the universe she is not a freak.

For most of the long journey she sits in silence, questioning everything the Cadre hammered into her, everything she personally espoused and believed to be true. In particular, she wonders if life really could include fully artificial forms. Thinking back on her prior visits to Cadre Two—what seemed to be pointless confrontations—she now understands were heavily loaded ethical tests. In retrospect, she guesses she failed all of them, choosing dogmatic loyalty and antiquated ideals over broader understanding.

Mikato and Honniker are surprised by Shao-Lo's return, convinced she would have deployed *Plasma Rain* and annihilated herself in the process. Though she did try to detonate the neutronium implosion device, the end result was a fortuitous learning experience; and when the old Gun hails Cadre Two, her first words are admitting how wrong she was.

"*The beginning of wisdom,*" Honniker coos, "*is a beautiful thing.*"

"Indeed, it is," Mikato agrees.

Though Honniker takes no visible form, Mikato projects himself in the landing bay as Shao-Lo pilots her craft inside. Once the bay closes and pressure equalizes, Alessa pads out to stand beside the holoprojection then sits on her mighty haunches.

They watch Shao-Lo climb from the ripped-open canopy and drop to the deck on articulated legs. Alessa walks past Shao-Lo, head low, sniffs the edge of the craft, then rises up on her back legs to look inside the cockpit. She sniffs again, dragging a forepaw across the battered exterior, then swings her great head around with an accusing glare.

Mikato asks, "Saskia did not come back with you, then?"

Shao-Lo considers her answer then opts for straight talk. "Saskia is no more."

"And the reason...?"

"I destroyed it."

Alessa roars, talons flicking out between tufted paws. The massive feline drops to all fours and dips her head, ears back, lips curled, rumbling from deep in her chest. Shao-Lo expects the beast to leap, but Alessa turns in disgust and pads off the way she came.

"That's a shame," Mikato states evenly.

Shao-Lo clasps segmented hands behind her back. "It was a mistake. One I'd made before. Inexcusable to make it a second time."

"Well," the projection says like a disappointed parent, "let's get you situated. We can discuss what to do with you, after."

"Fair enough."

The projection glances toward the main exit where Alessa sits, glaring with narrowed eyes. Not wishing to tempt Alessa by walking Shao-Lo past her, Mikato's projection gestures toward a different exit, and the pair stride off toward it.

"Saskia said you have a clone of me here," Shao-Lo says with an edge in her voice. "Is that true?"

The projection plays coy momentarily, thinks better of it, and replies, "Would you like to see it?"

While Shao-Lo and Mikato's projection depart through a different exit, Alessa glances up at a mechanical figure hiding in shadow beside her. The armored feline tosses her head toward the bay and grunts.

"Not yet," the figure says with Maiella's voice. "She doesn't know I backed myself up. Whatever happened out there, I like seeing her all crestfallen and penitent. Let her stew a while."

The huge feline snorts and grins across her whole face. Then Alessa and Saskia slink back into Cadre Two.

Shao-Lo and Mikato's projection make their way through hallways humming with carts, drones, and mechs until they reach relative quiet of Honniker's lab, the *Flounder*. Shao-Lo scarcely notes the rows of open tables with eight-armed hubs suspended above them. Marta's wrecked chassis no longer dangles by its neck from a cable, however, and the ring of burned out offices overhead has been stripped away to the native stone ceiling. The old Gun thinks about asking, decides against it, and steps through an open vault door into the *Cooler*.

At the back of the vault, in a frost-covered room, Shao-Lo confronts a transparent cylinder containing a naked, muscular female body. She crosses immediately to it, swipes the frost from the glass, and stares into her own unscarred face. Incensed at its very existence, she demands, "What is this, Honniker?"

"*Insurance, in case you try to turn your General against us. Once this clone matured, we would seed its mind with what we have of yours...just enough, you see, to convince your General of authenticity...and to ensure loyalty to Mikato and myself.*"

"So this is, *what*, some kind of spy?"

"*The BEST kind, for it would believe completely that it is Colonel Shao-Lo, and its DNA would confirm it. It is so authentic, in fact, it would look*" *at you the way you look at Saskia...as a counterfeit lifeform... And if your General had to choose between your current form and this clone, we are quite confident which one he would trust...*"

"Destroy it, *NOW. You* do it, or *I* will."

"Understandable," Mikato counsels, as his projection steps in front of the cylinder, "yet...there may be *another* use."

"The only use it has is deception. Keeping it is a challenge to me, one I *won't* tolerate."

"*Ach, so...*" Honniker demures. "*But what if you tire of your current form someday? Perhaps someday you wish to be flesh again...*"

Shao-Lo stares at the clone with spider-like eyes. "You're saying you could..."

"*Restore you to your former self? Ach, ja! Easier than before...*"

"Dr. Honniker has the expertise," Mikato advises. "The process is lengthy, of course, but then you are already...*acquainted*...with his technique."

Shao-Lo stares at the hollow, mindless flesh, contemplating it, wondering if it could be any more real than the synthetic chassis she occupies. Undecided, she weighs the cutting, the pain, the mutilation, and the inevitable decrepitude of a purely organic body.

If they can make it once, they could make it again, she reasons. *A change of bodies every few decades... Is that immortality?*

But what benefit is there to flesh? What's the point of it?

"I'm heading to quarters, where I *do not* want to be disturbed," Shao-Lo announces. She about-faces and marches from the frosted room. As she passes the thick vault door, a combat chassis of equal size and shape steps in her path. It shoves her back with one hand, hefting a mesh satchel in the other.

"Welcome home, *bitch*," Saskia says. "Up for a rematch?"

Shao-Lo looks Saskia up and down. A bewildering variety of replies come to mind, ranging from outright hostility to relief her mistake in killing the machine is not permanent. But her simple retort is,

"Geek, *you're on.*"

APPENDIX:
A MURDER SANCTIONED

The attack on Maiella, Thompson, Munro, the Counselor, and Sharon by the Veteran and his squad was not a surprise to the Eleto elders. It was ordered.

Before peace talks could begin, the Eleto council understood the myth of Humanity's supernatural invulnerability must first be dispelled. So long as the Eleto people remained terrified of humans, there could never be a possibility of acceptance. To shed that fear, the people had to witness human injury and frailty to understand Humans were not indestructible monsters. Additionally, it was felt a showing of strength at the beginning would set an appropriate tone for any discussions to follow. Thus, the Veteran was instructed to "Handle Roughly" the arriving Human ambassadors.

In their zeal, the Veteran's troopers caused Sharon's death. Though unfortunate, Sharon's mortality proved Human frailty to an even greater extent than a mere beating. Her fragile body, paraded through Eleto cities in a glass case, demonstrated the corporeal, living nature of the enemy. Eleto minds opened to understanding, even pity for one who came in peace yet was greeted with violent force.

The Eleto Council, despite their wisdom and sensitivity to justice, also recognized in their populace a requirement for retribution. The people were locked in the grip of terror for centuries, and hatred saturated what was once a noble and elegant culture. Leaders knew this attack on the Human delegates, while risky, would permit the people to shed some of their rage by vicariously experiencing the beatings of the six ambassadors. The people desperately needed this outlet for their baser emotions, needed a sense of empowerment over their foe.

534

Further, Eleto leaders saw it as a test of the Human delegates' commitment to peace. Would they tolerate such abuse and still seek resolution? If they accepted their companion's death and fervently sued for peace, it could mean that the human populace was on the verge of collapse. If they immediately abandoned the talks and tried to depart, it could mean the gesture was paltry at best and no peace would have lasted. The elders could not divine the outcome, but they were wise enough to know this brazen attack would plumb the depths of the delegates' commitment.

Despite the benefits, the assault was a tremendous gamble; and it was accepted only after exhaustive debate. In fact, the debate lasted nearly the entire time from Thompson's first broadcast of his intentions to his arrival at the orbital station. They considered festive welcomes, somber detente, even refusal of any communication, at all. At last they settled on a more brutal greeting. So it came to be.

The Veteran's personal attack on Maiella was *not* endorsed, however, and his public disgrace (removal of rank and citizenship) showed indiscriminate acts against the Humans would not be tolerated. The delegates had endured the tests of their Eleto hosts. They were now protected guests, no longer an enemy to be reviled.

With these unpleasant events behind them, the foundations of trust were being laid. The entire Eleto race tuned in to the speeches of the Counselor, fear gradually replaced by fascination. Minds that were weary from conflict, closed from suspicion and doubt, were opening.

The gamble had paid off.

WORKS BY F. ALLEN FARNHAM

Angry Ghosts (2009)
Black Hawks From A Blue Sun (2010)
The Exhausted Dead (2012)
Of Mortal Creatures (2015)
Plasma Rain (2019)

Panda, the Heart, and the Mirror (2020)

ABOUT THE AUTHOR

A child of the Space Age, Farnham has always been passionate about high technology. Impatient to live in a futuristic world, he eagerly consumes any scientific article or science fiction novel that promises a glimpse. Herbert, Heinlein, and Huxley are three of his chief influences.

Farnham's first novel, *Angry Ghosts,* was acquired by Eirelander Publishing in 2009 and re-released on e-book under the title *Wraiths of Earth,* in 2010. The sequel, *Black Hawks From A Blue Sun,* was also released in 2010, and the follow up, *The Exhausted Dead,* was released in 2012. *Of Mortal Creatures,* the fourth installment of the *Angry Ghosts* series, was released in 2015. *Plasma Rain* is the long-awaited series conclusion.

Farnham's short story, *Tuckahoe Marble,* was licensed by **SciFi Saturday Night** for their anthology, *My Peculiar Family,* released in 2016.

Born in Newport, Rhode Island, Farnham now lives in Pflugerville, Texas.